The French Art of War

ALEXIS JENNI is a French novelist and biology teacher. His debut novel, *The French Art of War*, won the 2011 Prix Goncourt. He lives in Lyon.

The
French
Art of War

—ALEXIS JENNI—

*Translated from the French
by Frank Wynne*

Atlantic Books
LONDON

First published as *L'art français de la guerre* in France in 2011 by Éditions Gallimard.

First published in trade paperback in Great Britain in 2017 by Atlantic Books, an imprint of Atlantic Books Ltd.

Copyright © Éditions Gallimard, 2011
Translation copyright © Frank Wynne, 2017

10 9 8 7 6 5 4 3 2 1

A CIP catalogue record for this book is available from the British Library.

Trade Paperback ISBN: 978 0 85789 753 4
E-book ISBN: 978 0 85789 755 8

Printed in Great Britain by Bell & Bain Ltd, Glasgow

Atlantic Books
An Imprint of Atlantic Books Ltd
Ormond House
26–27 Boswell Street
London
WC1N 3JZ

www.atlantic-books.co.uk

Contents

What is a hero? Neither the living man nor the dead,
but one [...] who infiltrates the other world and returns.

PASCAL QUIGNARD

It was so stupid. We frittered people away.

BRIGITTE FRIANG

The best order of things, as I see it, is the one that includes me;
to hell with the best of all possible worlds if I am not part of it.

DENIS DIDEROT

Commentaries I

The departure for the Gulf of the Spahis of Valence

T HE FIRST DAYS OF 1991 were marked by preparations for the Gulf War and the mounting escalation of my utter irresponsibility. Snow blanketed everything, blocking the trains, muffling every sound. In the Gulf, mercifully, temperatures had dropped; the soldiers no longer sweltered as they had in summer when, stripped to the waist, they would splash each other with water, never taking off their sunglasses. Oh, those handsome summer soldiers, of whom barely one had died! They emptied whole canteens over their heads and the water evaporated before reaching the ground, running in rivulets over their skin and immediately evaporating to create a misty mandorla shot through with rainbows about their lithe, toned bodies. Sixteen litres they had to drink every day, the summer soldiers; sixteen litres, because they sweated so much under the weight of their equipment in a part of the world where there are no shadows. Sixteen litres! The television peddled numbers and those numbers became fixed as numbers always do: precisely. Rumour peddled figures that everyone bandied about before the attack. Because it was about to be launched, this attack upon the fourth largest army in the world; the Invincible Western Army would soon begin their advance, while, on the other side, the Iraqis dug in behind twisted hanks of barbed wire, behind S-mines and rusty nails, behind trenches filled with oil, which they would set ablaze at the last moment, because they had lots of oil, so much oil they did not know what to do with it. Television reeled off details, invariably precise, delving at random through old footage. Television dug up images from before, neutral images that offered no information; we knew nothing about the Iraqi army, nothing about its forces, its positions, we knew only that it was the fourth largest army in the world; this we knew because it was endlessly repeated. Numbers imprint themselves on the memory, because they are unambiguous, we remember them and therefore believe them. On and on it went. There seemed to be no end to the preparations.

In the early days of 1991 I was barely working. I went into the office only when I ran out of ideas to justify my absence. I visited doctors who were prepared, without even listening to my symptoms, to sign me off sick for implausible periods of time, which I made every effort to further extend by slowly honing my skills as a forger. At night, in the lamplight, I would retrace the figures as I listened to music on my headphones; my whole universe reduced to the pool of light, reduced to the space between my ears, reduced to the tip of the blue ballpoint that gradually afforded me even more free time. I would practise on a scrap of paper and then, with a sure hand, transform the symbols made by the doctors. In doing so, I doubled, I tripled the number of days I could spend in the warm, far from my work. I never discovered whether changing these symbols, falsifying numbers with a ballpoint pen, was enough to change reality, I never wondered whether there was some record other than the doctor's certificate, but it didn't matter; the office where I worked was so badly organized that sometimes when I didn't go in, no one noticed. When I showed up the following day, no one paid any more attention than they did when I wasn't there, as though absence were nothing. I was absent and my absence went unnoticed. So I stayed in bed.

On Monday early in 1991 I heard on the radio that Lyon was cut off by snow. The snowfall had brought down telephone cables, most trains were marooned in the stations, and those caught unawares outside a station were covered with eiderdowns of snow. The people inside tried not to panic.

Here on the Scheldt river a few scant snowflakes fell, but further south everything had ground to a halt except for the huge snow-ploughs moving at a snail's pace, each trailed by a line of cars, and the helicopters bringing aid to isolated villages. I was delighted that this had happened on a Monday, since no one knew here what the snow was like, so they would make a mountain out of it, a mysterious catastrophe, mindlessly trusting the pictures they saw on television. I phoned the office 300 metres away and claimed to be 800 kilometres away amid the white hills being shown on the news. Everyone at work knew I was from the Rhône, the Alps; I would sometimes go home for the weekend, they knew that; and since they had no real conception of mountains, of snow, everything tallied, there was no reason for me not to be snowed in like everyone else.

Then I went to my girlfriend's house opposite the train station.

She was not surprised; she had been expecting me. She, too, had seen the snow outside her window and the flurries across the rest of France on the TV. She had called in sick, in that feeble tone she could adopt on the phone: she said she was suffering from the acute flu devastating France that had been all over the news; she could not come in to work today. She was still in her pyjamas when she let me in, so I got undressed and we lay on the bed, sheltering from the snowstorm and the sickness that were ravaging France and from which there was no reason, no reason at all, that we should be spared. We were victims, like everybody else. We made love undisturbed, while outside a light snow went on falling, floating, landing, flake after flake, in no hurry to arrive.

My girlfriend lived in a studio flat consisting of a single room with an alcove, and the bed in the alcove took up the whole space. I felt at peace next to her, wrapped in the duvet, our desires sated; we were happy in the quiet heat of a timeless day when no one knew where we were. I was happy in the warmth of my adoptive sanctuary with this woman who had eyes of every colour, eyes I wanted to draw in green and blue crayons on brown paper. I wanted to, but I had no talent for drawing; and yet only art could have done justice to her eyes and the miraculous light in them. Words are not enough; they needed to be depicted. The transcendent colour of her eyes defied description in words and left no clues. I needed to show them. But showing is something that can be improvised, as idiotic TV sets demonstrated every day of the winter of 1991. The TV was turned towards the bed, so we could see the screen by plumping up the pillows to raise our heads. Sperm tugged at the hairs on my thighs as it dried, but I had no desire to shower; it was cold in the tiny bathroom and I was happy lying next to her, and so we watched television as we waited for desire to return.

The big news on TV was Operation Desert Storm, a codename straight out of *Star Wars*, cooked up by the scriptwriters of a special Cabinet. Gambolling alongside came Daguet, the French operation with its limited resources. 'Daguet' is French for a young stag, a fawn, a barely pubescent Bambi just starting to sprout antlers that frisks and frolics, never far from his parents. Where do these army types come up with these names? Who uses a word like 'Daguet'? It had probably been suggested by a senior officer, the sort of guy who goes deer-hunting in the grounds of the family estate. Desert Storm is a name anyone on Earth can understand, it bursts from the mouth, explodes in the heart, it's a video-game title. Daguet is elegant, it elicits a knowing smile from those who get the reference. The army has its own language, which is not the common tongue, and that is rather worrying. Military types in France do not speak, or do so only among themselves. We laugh about it. We think them so profoundly stupid they have no need of words. What have they ever done to us that we should treat them with such contempt? What have we ever done that the military should want to keep themselves to themselves?

The French army is a thorny subject. We don't know what to think of these guys, we certainly don't know what to do with them. They clutter up the place with their berets, the regimental traditions about which we know little and care nothing, and their ruinously expensive equipment that makes such a dent in our taxes. The army in France is silent, ostensibly it answers to the Head of the Armed Forces, an elected civilian who knows nothing, takes care of everything and allows it do as it pleases. In France we have no idea what to think about 'the troops', we don't even dare use the possessive, which might allow us to think of them as *ours*: we ignore them, fear them, mock them. We wonder why they do it, this tainted job steeped in blood and death; we assume conspiracies, unwholesome impulses, serious intellectual limitations. We prefer our soldiers out of sight, holed up in their secure bases in the south of France or travelling the world defending the last crumbs of Empire, gadding about overseas as they used to, in white uniforms with gold piping, on gleaming boats that shimmer in the sun. We prefer them to be far away, to be invisible, to leave us in peace. We prefer them to unleash their violence elsewhere, in far-off countries inhabited by people so unlike us that they hardly qualify as people.

This is the sum total of what I thought about the army – which is to say, nothing; but what I thought was no different from everyone, from everyone I knew; until that morning in 1991 when I allowed only my nose to emerge from beneath the duvet, and my eyes. With my girlfriend curled up next to me, gently stroking my stomach, together we watched the beginnings of World War Three on the TV at the end of the bed.

We gazed at streets filled with people, idly leaning out of this Hertzian window on to the world, contented in that blissful calm that follows orgasm, which makes it possible to see all without thinking ill, without thinking anything, which makes it possible to watch television with a smile that lingers for as long as the programmes keep coming. What to do after an orgy? Watch TV. Watch the news, watch this hypnotic device that manufactures insubstantial time, a thing of polystyrene, with no essence, no quality, a synthetic time that perfectly fills the time remaining.

During the preparations for the Gulf War, and afterwards, while it was being waged, I witnessed strange things; the whole world witnessed strange things. I saw a lot, since I scarcely left our cocoon of Hollofil – that marvellous hollow polyester fibre invented by DuPont to fill duvets, which keeps its shape, which insulates better than feathers, better than blankets, a revolutionary material which at last makes it possible – this is technological progress – to stay in bed and never go outside; because it was winter, because I was going through my phase of professional irresponsibility, I simply lay next to my girlfriend, watching television, while we waited for desire to return. We changed the duvet cover when it became sticky with our sweat, when the stains from the come I ejaculated copiously – and indiscriminately – dried and made the fabric crusty.

Leaning out of this electronic window, I watched Israelis attending a concert wearing gas masks – only the violinist was not wearing one, and he went on playing; I watched the ballet of bombs over Baghdad, those fantastical fireworks with their greenish trails, and in doing so learned that modern warfare is conducted in the glow of computer screens; I saw the faint, grey outlines of buildings shudder into focus only to explode, destroyed from within with everyone inside; I watched the huge B-52s with their albatross wings that had been taken out of mothballs in the deserts of Arizona to fly once more; they carried heavy bombs, bombs with highly specialized functions; I watched missiles skim the desert sands of Mesopotamia seeking out their targets, heard the protracted yowl of engines distorted by the Doppler Effect. I watched all this and I felt nothing, it was just something on TV, like in a second-rate movie. But the image that most shocked me in those early weeks of 1991 was a simple one – I doubt anyone remembers it – but it made that year, 1991, the last year of the twentieth century. On the news I witnessed the Spahi regiments from Valence leaving for the Gulf.

These young men were no older than thirty, their young wives standing next to them. They kissed their husbands for the cameras, cradling children, most of whom were too young to talk. Tenderly, they embraced, these muscular young men and these pretty young women, and then the Spahis of Valence clambered into their sand-coloured trucks, their APCs, their Panhards. No one knew then how many would come back, no one knew then that no Western soldiers would be killed in this war – or almost none – no one knew then that the burden of death – like pollution, like the encroaching desert, like debt repayment – would be borne by countless others, the nameless others who inhabit hot countries; and so the voiceover could offer a melancholy commentary and we were united in grief as we watched our young boys leave for a far-off war. I was shell-shocked.

Such images are banal, they appear all the time on American and British television, but 1991 was the first time that we in France watched soldiers hug their wives and children and set off to war; the first time since 1914 that French soldiers were portrayed as people whose suffering we might share, people we might miss.

The world had shifted slightly on its axis. I flinched.

I sat up and more than my nose appeared from beneath the duvet. My mouth, my shoulders, my torso emerged. I had to sit up, I had to watch, because what I was witnessing – something beyond all understanding, yet in full view of everyone – was a public reconciliation on national television. I drew up my legs, wrapped my arms around them and, resting my chin on my knees, I carried on watching this primal scene: the Spahis of Valence leaving for the Gulf; some wiped away a tear as they climbed aboard trucks painted the colour of sand.

In those first days of 1991 nothing happened: preparations were being made for the Gulf War. Forced to go on talking while knowing nothing, the television networks prattled on. They spat out a torrent of meaningless images. They interviewed experts who made up statistics on the spot. They broadcast archive footage, what there was of it, what had not been censored by one service or another, ending with wide-angle shots of the desert over which a disembodied voice reeled off figures. They fabricated. They fictionalized. They repeated the same details, searching for new ways to say the same things without it becoming tedious. They drivelled.

I watched it all. I witnessed the deluge of images, let it flow through me; I followed its meanders; it flowed aimlessly, but always following the line of least resistance; in those first days of 1991 I was engrossed by everything, I had taken a break from life, I had nothing to do but watch and feel. I spent my time lounging in bed, to the regular rhythm of desire blossoming and being spent. Perhaps no one still remembers the Spahis of Valence leaving for the Gulf, apart from those who left and I who watched everything, because during the winter of 1991 nothing happened. People commented on this nothingness, filled this nothingness with empty air, they waited; nothing happened except this: the army was welcomed back into society.

One might wonder where on Earth it had been all this time.

My girlfriend was surprised by my sudden fascination with a war that never started. Usually, I affected a vague air of boredom, an ironic detachment, a taste for the intellectual flurries that I found more reliable, more restful and certainly much more entertaining than the crushing weight of reality. She asked me what I was watching so intently.

'I'd love to drive one of those big trucks,' I said. 'The sand-coloured ones with the caterpillar treads.'

'That sort of thing is for little boys and you're not a little boy any more. Not remotely,' she added, laying her hand on me, right on that magnificent organ which has a life of its own, which has its own heart and consequently its own feeling, thoughts and impulses.

I didn't answer, I wasn't sure, so I lay down next to her again. Officially, we were ill and snowed in, and, sheltered here, we had the whole day to ourselves, and the night, and the following day; until we were breathless and our desire exhausted.

That year, I dedicated myself to obsessive absenteeism. Day and night I thought only of ways to malinger, to shirk, to skive, to hide out in some dark corner while others marched in step. In a few short months I destroyed everything I had ever had in terms of social ambition, professionalism, my sense of belonging. Beginning in the autumn I had taken advantage of the cold and damp, natural and thus incontrovertible phenomena: a sore throat was enough for me to take time off. I skipped work, I neglected my duties, and not always to go to see my girlfriend.

What did I do? I wandered the streets, skulked in cafés, sat in libraries reading books about science and history, I did all the things a single man can do in a city when he has no desire to go home. More often than not I did nothing.

I have no memory of that winter, nothing specific, nothing to relate, but when I hear the jingle for the France Info news bulletin, it plunges me into such a state of gloom that I realize that this was how I spent my time: listening to the radio, waiting for the world news bulletin, which came every fifteen minutes like the ticking of some great clock, the clock of my heart which was beating so slowly back then, the clock of the world inexorably ticking towards midnight.

There was a management reshuffle at the company where I worked. My line manager had wanted only one thing: to leave, and he succeeded. He found another job and the vacant post was filled by someone else, someone who planned to stay, and he restored order.

My former manager's questionable competence and desperate need to leave had protected me; his replacement's ambition and IT skills scuppered me. Though he had never said a word to me, the two-faced bastard who had left had made a note of all my absences. He kept files recording attendance, lateness, efficiency; everything that could be measured he had itemized. It had kept him busy while he planned his escape, but he had never breathed a word about it. The obsessive-compulsive left behind this dossier; his ambitious successor was trained to cut costs. Any available information was useful; he inherited the dossier and immediately suspended me.

The Evaluaxe software presented my contribution to the company as a series of curves on a graph. Most of these languished at the base of the x-axis. One – a red curve – had been rising in jagged peaks ever since preparations began for the Gulf War, and still hovered in the upper strata. Far below, a dotted line in the same colour indicated the norm.

He tapped the screen with the rubber of a meticulously sharpened pencil he never used for writing, only for pointing at the screen, tapping to emphasize key points. Against such technology, such meticulous records, against software capable of producing such unassailable graphs, the ballpoint I had used to fake doctor's notes was ineffective. I was, visibly, a weak link.

'Look at the screen. I should fire you for professional misconduct.'

He went on tapping at the curves with his rubber, seemingly lost in thought; it sounded like a rubber ball trapped in a bowl.

'But there might be a solution.'

I held my breath. My mood shifted from depression to hope; even when you don't care, no one likes being given the boot.

'As a result of the war, the economic situation has deteriorated. We have to lay off several members of staff. Everything will be done according to standard procedures. You'll be among the redundancies.'

I nodded. What could I say? I stared at the figures on the screen. The numbers formed a graph that showed exactly what it was intended to show. I could clearly see my economic inefficiency, it was unarguable. Numbers pass through language without even acknowledging its presence; numbers leave you speechless, open-mouthed, panting for breath in the rarefied air of the mathematical sphere. I assented with a monosyllable. I was happy that he was laying me off according to standard procedures rather than firing me for gross misconduct. He smiled and spread his hands as if to say, 'Don't mention it... I'm not sure why I'm doing this. Now get out quick, before I change my mind.'

I backed out of his office, I left the building. I later learned that he pulled the same stunt on everyone he was letting go. He proposed overlooking their failings if they would agree to redundancy. Rather than protesting, everyone had thanked him. Never had a redundancy scheme gone more smoothly: a third of the staff stood up, thanked him and left; that was that.

They laid the blame for these cuts on the war, because wars have unfortunate consequences. There is nothing to be done, it's war. Reality cannot be stopped.

That night I packed up all my belongings in boxes I got from the mini-mart and decided to go back to where I came from. My life was shit, so it hardly mattered where I lived. I'd love to have a different life, but I'm the narrator. The narrator can't simply do what he likes: for a start, he has to narrate. If I had to live as well as narrating, I don't think I would be up to it. Why do so many writers write about their childhoods? It's because they have no other life: they spend the rest of it writing. Childhood is the only time when they could live without thinking about anything else. Ever since, they have been writing, it takes up all their time, because writing uses up time the way embroidery uses thread. And we have only one thread.

My life is a pain in the arse and I am telling it; I'd prefer to show; and for that, to draw. That's what I would like: to just wave my hand so everyone could see. But drawing requires skill, an apprenticeship, a knack, whereas telling stories is a part of being human: you only have to open your mouth and let out your breath. I have to breathe, and talking amounts to the same thing. And so I tell stories, even if reality always escapes. A prison made of breath is not very secure.

A while back I had marvelled at the beautiful eyes of my girlfriend, this woman I was so close to, and I tried to depict them. 'Depict' is a word appropriate to narration, and also to my lack of ability as an artist: I depicted her and managed only a scrawl. I asked her to pose with her eyes open and to look at me, while my vivid, coloured pencils moved across the paper, but she looked away. Her beautiful eyes misted over and she cried. She was not worthy for me to look at her, she said, much less paint her or draw her or depict her; she talked to me about her sister, who was much more beautiful, who had magnificent eyes, gorgeous breasts, like the ones you see on the figureheads of old-fashioned sailing ships, whereas she... I had to set down my pencils, take her in my arms and gently stroke her breasts while I reassured her, wiped away her tears and told her over and over how I felt when she touched me, when I was with her, when I saw her. The pencils on my unfinished sketch fell still, and I told and told when what I really wanted was to show; I sank deeper into the tangle of storytelling, when all I wanted was to show how it was, and I was condemned again and again to narration to make everything right. I never did draw her eyes. But I remember the desire to do so, a desire on paper.

My boring life could easily be relocated. Having no ties, I was governed by the force of habit, which acts like gravity. In the end the river Rhône, which I knew, suited me better than the Escaut, which I didn't know; in the end, meaning at the end, meaning for the end. I went back to Lyon to put an end to things.

Desert Storm got me fired. I was collateral damage from an explosion that no one ever saw, but which could be felt in the empty images on television. I was so tenuously connected to life that it took only a distant sigh for me to become unmoored. The butterflies of the US Air Force flapped their wings of steel, setting off a tornado in my soul on the other side of the world; it triggered something in me and I went back to where I came from. This war was the last event in my former life; this war was the end of the twentieth century in which I had grown up. The Gulf War reshaped reality and reality suddenly collapsed.

War took place, but what difference did it make? For all we know it could have been made up. We were watching it on screens. But it altered reality in some of its little-known areas; it changed the economy; it triggered my redundancy and was the reason I went back to what I had been running from; and, people said, the soldiers when they returned from those sweltering countries never truly recovered their souls: they fell mysteriously ill, insomniac, grief-stricken, and died from an internal collapse of the liver, the lungs, of the skin.

It was worth being interested in this war.

War took place, we knew little about it. It was for the best. Such details as we had, those we managed to glean, offered a glimpse of a reality better kept hidden. Desert Storm happened. Daguet, our little Bambi, frolicked alongside. The Iraqis were pounded by a quantity of bombs difficult to imagine, more than had ever been dropped. There was one for every Iraqi citizen. Some of the bombs pierced walls and exploded inside, others flattened floor after floor before exploding in the cellar among those hiding there; 'blackout bombs' emitted clouds of graphite particles that caused short-circuits and destroyed electrical installations; thermobaric bombs sucked up all the oxygen within a vast radius; still others sniffed out their targets like dogs following a scent, nose to the ground, pouncing on their prey and exploding on contact. Later, crowds of Iraqis were machine-gunned as they stumbled from their shelters; perhaps they were attacking, perhaps they were surrendering; we never knew because they died, there was no one left. They had been given weapons only the day before, because the wary Ba'ath Party, having eliminated every competent officer, did not issue their troops with weapons for fear they might rebel. These scruffy soldiers might as well have been issued with wooden rifles. Those who did not manage to get out in time were buried in their shelters by bulldozers that moved forwards in a line, shovelling up the earth before them, sealing the trenches and burying everything and everyone inside. It lasts only a few days, this curious war that looked more like a demolition site. The Iraqis, equipped with Soviet tanks, tried to launch a vast battle on level ground like the Battle of Kursk, only to be ripped to shreds by a single pass of propeller planes. These lumbering planes, designed for ground strikes, bombarded the tanks using rounds of depleted uranium, a newly discovered metal as green as the colour of war, more dense than lead and therefore capable of piercing steel. The corpses were left to rot; no one came to peer inside the smoking tanks after the black birds which killed them had flown past. What did they look like? Like tins of ravioli torn open and tossed into a fire? There are no pictures and the bodies stayed in the desert, hundreds of kilometres from anywhere.

The Iraqi army collapsed. The fourth largest army in the world fled; a disorderly retreat along the motorway north of Kuwait City, a ragtag column of several thousand vehicles, trucks, cars and buses, bumper-to-bumper, loaded with plunder and moving at walking speed. The whole convoy was set ablaze by helicopters, I think, or maybe ground-hugging planes, that flew in from the south and unleashed sticks of smart bombs that carried out their tasks with a marked lack of discrimination. Everything was torched: tanks, civilian cars, men, and the treasures which they had plundered from the oil-rich city. Everything congealed into a river of molten rubber, metal, flesh and plastic. After that the war ended. The sand-coloured tanks of the Gulf War Coalition stopped in mid-desert, turned off their engines and there was silence. The sky was black and dripping with the greasy soot from the burning oil wells, and the foul stench of burning rubber and human flesh hung in the air.

The Gulf War did not take place, people wrote, to explain the failure of this war to register in our minds. It would be better had it not taken place, for all the dead whose number and names we will never know. During this war the Iraqis were stamped out like irritating ants, the kind that sting you in the back while you're taking a nap. There were few Western fatalities; we know their names and we know exactly how they died – mostly accidentally or from friendly fire. We will never know the number of Iraqis fatalities, nor how each of them died. How could we? It is a poor country; they cannot afford one death each; they were killed en masse. They burned together and died, melted into blocks like some Mafia gangland killing, buried beneath the sand of their trenches, crushed into the concrete rubble of their shelters, charred amid the molten metal of burnt-out vehicles. They died in bulk, not a trace of them was found. Their names were not recorded. In this war, it dies the way it rains; 'it' is a state of affairs, an act of Nature about which there is nothing to be done; and 'it' kills, too, since none of the players in this mass slaughter saw who was killed nor how they were killed. The bodies were distant, at the far end of the missiles' trajectory, far below the wings of the planes that had already disappeared. It was a clean war that left no marks on the hands of the killers. There were no real atrocities, just the great calamity of war, refined by research and industry.

We could choose to see nothing, to understand nothing; we could let words wash over us: it wars like it rains, it is fate. Narration is powerless, there is no way to recount this war; the fictions that are usually so vivid are, in this case, allusive, awkward, clumsily pieced together. What happened in 1991, what filled our television screens for months, is insubstantial. And yet something happened. It cannot be related using traditional storytelling, but it can be identified by number and by name. This was something I later understood through a film. Because I love film.

I have always watched war movies. I enjoy sitting in the dark, watching films with helicopters, to a soundtrack of cannon and the rattle of machine-gun fire. It's Futurism, as beautiful as a Marinetti, it is thrilling to the little boy that I have always remained, little, a boy, *pow!* and *pow! kapow!* It's as beautiful as primitive art, as beautiful as the kinetic art of the 1920s, but with the addition of a thunderous soundtrack that pounds, that heightens the images, that thrills the viewer, plastering him to his seat like a gale-force wind. I have always loved war movies, but this one, the one I saw years later, sent cold shivers down my spine, because of the names and the numbers.

Oh, how well movies show things! Look, just look at how much more can be shown in two hours of cinema than in whole days of television. Image after image: framed images spew forth a torrent of images. The fixed frame projected on to the wall, as unblinking as the eye of an insomniac in the darkness of the room, makes it possible for reality to finally appear, by virtue of its slowness, its intensity, its pitiless permanence. Look! I turn towards the wall and I see them, my queens, he would say, this man who stopped writing, this man who still has the sexual habits of a teenager. He would have loved the cinema.

We sit on cushioned seats that cradle us like shells, the house lights dim, the seat backs hide our actions, hide our thoughts and gestures. Through the window that opens up before you – and even now, sometimes, a curtain is raised before the images are projected – through this window you see the world. And slowly in the darkness I gently slide my hand into the cleft of the girl with me, and on the screen I see; I finally understand.

I no longer know the name of the girl who was with me then. It is strange to know so little about the people you sleep with. But I have no head for names and we mostly made love with our eyes closed. At least I did; and I don't remember her name. I regret that. I could force myself to, or I could make one up. No one would be any the wiser. I would pick a commonplace name to make it seem real or maybe an unusual name to be cute. I hesitate. But inventing a name would change nothing; it would not change the fundamental horror of the mental blank and the fact we are unaware of that mental blank. Because this is the most terrifying, the most destructive cataclysm of all, this blank one does not notice.

In this film I saw, this film that terrified me, this movie by a famous director which was shown in cinemas, released on DVD, this film the whole world saw, the action takes place in Somalia – nowhere, in other words. An American Special Ops unit has to cross Mogadishu, capture some guy and make it home. But the Somalis fight back. The Americans are fired on, and they fire back. There were dead, many of them American. Every American's death is shown before, during and after the event; they die slowly. They die one by one; each has a moment to himself as he dies. The Somalis, on the other hand, die as in a trap shoot, en masse; no one troubles to count them. When the Americans retreat, they find one of their number is missing; he has been taken prisoner, and a helicopter flies over Mogadishu, blasting his name over a loudhailer cranked up to maximum volume to let him know he is not forgotten. The closing credits give the number and names of the nineteen Americans who died, and mentions that at least a thousand Somalis were killed. No one is shocked by this film. No one is shocked by this disproportion. By this imbalance. Of course not; we are used to it. In unequal wars – the only wars in which the West takes part – the ratio is always the same: at least ten to one. The film is based on a true story – unsurprisingly, that is the way these things go. We know this. In colonial wars we do not count the fatalities on the other side, because they are not dead, nor are they enemies: they are natural obstacles that must be overcome, like rocks or mangrove roots or mosquitoes. We do not count them, because they do not count.

After the destruction of the fourth biggest army in the world – a fatuous piece of journalese that was repeated like a mantra – we were so relieved to see almost everyone come home that we forgot those deaths, as if the war really had not taken place. The Western fatalities died by accident, their names are known, they will be remembered; the others do not count. It took a movie to teach me this: as bodies are massacred by machine, their souls, unnoticed, are erased. When no traces of a murder exist, the murder itself disappears; still the ghosts pile up, we simply cannot see them.

Here, right here, I would like to raise a statue. Bronze, maybe, because bronze statues are solid and you can make out the facial features. It would be set on a small pedestal, not too high, so that it is still accessible, and surrounded by lawns where anyone is allowed to sit. It would be erected in the middle of a busy square, a place where people pass, meeting, then head off in all directions.

It would be a statue of a little man with no physical charm, wearing an unfashionable suit and a pair of huge glasses that distort his features; he would be depicted with a pen and paper, holding the pen out so that someone could sign the piece of paper like a pollster in the street or an activist trying to persuade you to sign a petition.

He is not much to look at, his pose is humble, but I would like to erect a statue to Paul Teitgen.

There is nothing physically impressive about him. He was weedy and short-sighted. When he came to take up his pose at the *préfecture* in Algeria, when he arrived with others to take control of the *départements* of North Africa that had been abandoned, indiscriminately, to personal and racial violence, when he arrived, he shuddered in the doorway of the plane from the heat. In an instant, he was bathed in sweat, despite the safari suit bought from the shop for colonial ambassadors on the Boulevard Saint-Germain. He took out a handkerchief and mopped his brow, removed his glasses – which had fogged – in order to wipe them, and in that moment he could see nothing: only the harsh glare of the runway, the shadows, the dark suits of the welcoming committee. He considered turning around and going straight home, then he put his glasses back on and went down the gangway. His suit was plastered to his back and, scarcely able to see a thing, he stepped on to the tarmac, into the shimmering heat haze.

He took up his post and fulfilled his duties above and beyond what he could have imagined.

In 1957 the paras had all the power. Bombs were going off in Algiers, several a day. The paratroopers had been ordered to make the bombings stop. They were given no rules of engagement. They had just come back from Indo-China, so they knew how to run in the woods, to hide, to fight, to kill in every way possible. They were asked to make the bombings stop. They were paraded through the streets of Algiers cheered on by crowds of Europeans.

They began arresting people, almost all of them Arabs. Those arrested were asked whether they made bombs or whether they knew anyone who made bombs, or, failing that, anyone who knew anyone, and so on. If you ask enough people, use enough force, you eventually find what you are looking for. If you forcibly interrogate everyone, you eventually find the person making the bombs.

To fulfil the order they had been given, they built a death machine, a slaughterhouse through which they dragged the Arabs of Algiers. They drew numbers on the houses, wrote up a file for every man, which they pinned to the wall; they pieced together the 'hidden tree' of the kasbah. They cross-referenced information. Whatever was left of the man afterwards, a crumpled, bloodstained husk, they made disappear. You don't leave such things lying around.

Paul Teitgen was the Sécretaire Général de la Police, working at the *préfecture* for the *département* of Algiers. He was the civilian assistant to the general commanding the paratroopers. He was a silent shadow, all that was asked of him was that he agree. Not even agree: nothing was asked of him.

But he, on the other hand, did ask.

Paul Teitgen succeeded – and for this he deserves a statue – in getting the paratroopers to sign an arrest warrant for each of the men they detained. He must have used up a lot of pens! He signed all the warrants given to him by the paratroopers, a thick sheaf of them each day; he signed every one of them, and every one represented someone imprisoned, someone interrogated, someone helping the army with their enquiries, always the same enquiries, asked with too much force for all these men to survive.

He signed the warrants, he kept copies, each one carried a name. A colonel would come to do an audit. When he had tallied the number of those released, those incarcerated and those who had escaped, Paul Teitgen would point out the discrepancy between his figures and the list of names he used to cross-reference. 'What about them?' he would ask, and give a warrant number and a name; and every day the colonel, who didn't like this, answered with a shrug: 'Them? They disappeared. That's all there is to it.' And ended the meeting.

Behind the scenes, Paul Teitgen kept a tally of the dead.

In the end he knew how many. Out of all of those brutally snatched from their homes, stopped in the street, tossed into a jeep that suddenly appeared and immediately disappeared, or into a covered truck, destination unknown – though everyone knew the destination all too well – out of these men, who numbered 20,000 of the 150,000 Arabs of Algiers, of the 70,000 residents of the kasbah, 3,024 'disappeared'. It was claimed that they had fled to join their comrades in the mountains. Some were found on the beaches, thrown up by the tide, their bodies bloated and ravaged by the salt, bearing wounds that could be blamed on fish, on crabs, on prawns.

For each of these men Paul Teitgen had a file with a name that he had personally signed. What does it matter? you might argue. What does it matter to those men who disappeared? What does it matter, this scrap of paper with their name, since they did not survive? What does it matter that below their name you can read the signature of the civilian assistant to the general of the paratroop regiment? What does it matter when it does not change their fate? Kaddish does not change the fate of the dead, either: they will not be coming back. But it is a prayer of such power that it confers honour on those who say it, and that honour goes with the departed, and the wound it leaves among the living will heal over, it will hurt less, for a shorter time.

Paul Teitgen counted the dead. He signed brief, bureaucratic prayers so that the slaughter would not be indiscriminate, so that the number of the dead would be known, and their names.

For this he deserves our thanks. Helpless, horrified, he survived a reign of terror by counting and naming the dead. During a reign of terror, when a man could disappear in a jet of flame, when a man's fate was etched on his face, when he might never come back from a ride in a jeep, when trucks transported mangled, still-breathing bodies to be killed, when whimpering bodies on a street corner in Zéralda were finished off with a knife, when men were tossed into the sea like so much garbage, he did the only thing he could do, having decided not to leave on that first day. In this maelstrom of fire, of jagged splinters, of stabbings, blows, water torture, electric shocks, he did the only human thing: one by one, he made a census of the dead, he safeguarded their names. He registered their absence and, when the colonel made his daily audit, he asked questions. And the colonel, embarrassed, annoyed, replied that they had disappeared. OK, fine, they've disappeared, Teitgen would say, noting down the warrant number and their name.

What we are clinging to is all too slight, but inside the death machine that was the Battle of Algiers, those men who believed that people were people, that they had a number and a name, those men saved their owns souls, the souls of those who understood, and the souls of those over whose fate they agonized. Long after their mangled, broken bodies had disappeared, their souls remained, they did not become ghosts.

Now I understand the importance of that act, although I didn't back when I was watching TV footage of Desert Storm. I understand now because I learned it from a film; and also because I met Victorien Salagnon. From this man, who was my teacher, I learned that the dead who are named and counted are not lost.

Victorien Salagnon lit the path for me, meeting him at a point when I had hit rock bottom guided me. It was he who forced me to see that symbol that runs like a thread through history, that obscure yet obvious mathematical symbol that pervades all things, it is a ratio, a fraction, and it can be expressed as 10:1. This ratio is the clandestine symbol of colonial massacre.

On my return to Lyon I settled into humble digs. I filled the furnished room with the meagre contents of my boxes. I was alone and that did not bother me. I was not thinking of meeting someone, as single people often are: I was not looking for a soulmate. I didn't care, since my soul has no mate, no sisters, no brothers; it has always been an only child, and no relationship will ever coax it from its isolation. Besides, I liked the single women of my age who lived alone in cramped flats and who, when I came round, would light candles and curl up on the sofa, hugging their knees. They were hoping for an escape, they were waiting for me to disentangle their arms, so that they could hug something other than their knees, but living with them would have destroyed the quivering magic of flickering flame that illuminated these single women, the magic of those folded arms opening to me; and so, once their arms were opened, I was disinclined to stay.

Thankfully, I wanted for nothing. The tortuous workings of the Human Resources department in my former company, coupled with the first-rate social welfare in this country – no matter what people may say, no matter what they may have become – afforded me a year of peace and quiet. I had a year. A year in which to do so many things. I did one thing. I prevaricated.

When my income began to dwindle I became a distributor of free newspapers. I would set out in the morning with a cap on my head to push freesheets through letterboxes. I wore woollen mittens that looked a little shabby but were perfectly suited to the task of ringing doorbells and grabbing paper. I dragged along a shopping trolley laden with the newspapers I had to give out; it was very heavy because paper is heavy, and I had to force myself to push just one copy through each letterbox. After a hundred metres, the temptation would take hold to dump the whole lot in one batch rather than distribute them. I was tempted to fill the rubbish bins, stuff discarded boxes, to accidentally-on-purpose shove two, five, ten through a letterbox rather than one in each; but there would have been complaints, a supervisor followed my route, and I would have lost a job that earned one centime for every paper, 40 centimes per kilogram of paper lugged, this job that kept me busy in the mornings. From daybreak I roamed the city, preceded by the white mist of my breath, hauling an obscenely heavy old lady's trolley. I tramped the streets, humbly greeting the upstanding citizens I passed, well-dressed and groomed, on their way to work, careful not to stare. With a keen eye versed in class warfare they sized me up – my anorak, my cap, my gloves – decided to say nothing, walked past and let me go on my way; moving quickly, shoulders hunched, almost invisible, I stuffed one copy into each letterbox and moved on. I covered my area systematically, painstakingly blanketing it in a pollution of publicity that would end up in the bin the next day; and at the end of my route I always stopped at the café on the boulevard separating Lyon from Voracieux-les-Bredins, where I would drink a small glass of white wine around noon. At one o'clock I headed off to load up again. The papers for the following day were delivered at fixed times. I had to be there, I couldn't hang about.

I worked mornings, because after that everything closed. No one comes to lock up: the doors themselves decide when to open and close. The keypads have timers that tick off the time required for the postman, the cleaners, the delivery men, and at noon they close; after that, only someone with a key or an entry code can get in.

So I spent the mornings plying my parasitical trade, cap on my head, lugging a trolley weighed down with paper, inveigling myself into people's nests to lay my promotional egg before the doors closed. It's creepy, when you think about it, that objects can decide something as important as when to open and close; but no one thinks about it, we prefer to assign difficult tasks to machines, whether their difficulty is physical or moral. Advertising is a form of parasite; I wormed my way into people's nests, deposited my sheaves of garishly coloured, unmissable offers as quickly as possible, then went next door to deposit some more. All the while the doors silently counted off the minutes. At noon the mechanism was activated. I was locked out. There was nothing I could do. So I went to celebrate the end of my day, my short, irregular working day, with a few glasses of white wine at the nearest bar.

On Saturdays I walked faster. By distributing my papers at a jogging pace and dumping the remainder into the recycling bins, I gained a good hour, which I spent at the same bistro at the end of my route. Some of the other customers there, like me, worked insecure jobs or lived off their pensions. We gathered in this bistro at the frontier between Lyon and Voracieux-les-Bredins, all of us finished or nearing the finish line, and on Saturdays there were three times as many of us as on other days. I drank with the regulars and on Saturday I could stay a bit longer. Soon I was part of the furniture. I was younger than they were. I couldn't hold my drink, and that made them laugh.

I first saw Victorien Salagnon in that bistro, one Saturday, saw him through the thick yellow coke-bottle glasses of my midday wine, which made reality more fuzzy but much closer, more fluid and impossible to grasp, which in those days suited me well.

He was sitting on his own at the sort of sticky old wooden table you seldom see in Lyon now. He was drinking alone, a half-bottle of white that he made last, and reading the local paper which he spread over the table. The local paper was a broadsheet; unfolded, it took up four places, so no one came to sit with him. Towards noon, in the packed café, he casually presided over the only free table in the bistro, while others stood huddled at the bar, but no one bothered him, they were used to him, and he went on reading the trivial titbits of local news without raising his head.

Someone told me something that helped explain this one day. The man standing next to me at the bar leaned over, pointed to Salagnon, and whispered in a voice loud enough for everyone to hear: 'See the guy with the paper taking up all the space? A veteran of the Indo-China War, he is. And I tell you, the stuff he got up to over there...'

He gave a knowing wink to indicate he knew much more and that it explained a lot. He straightened himself and drained his glass of wine.

Indo-China! There was a word you never heard any more, except as a term of abuse for veterans, l'Indochine as a region no longer exists; the name has been mothballed, put in a glass case, even to utter it is bad luck. In the vocabulary I had learned from my left-wing parents, on the rare occasions the word was spoken it was uttered with the same hint of disgust or contempt used for anything colonial. It was unsurprising for it to pop up in a crumbling bar, among men in whom liver failure and cancer were running a race; I had to come here, to the arse-end of the world, down in its basement, among the dregs, to hear the word spoken again as it must once have sounded.

This was said in a stage whisper; I had to reply in the same tone. 'Oh, Indo-China!' I said. 'A bit like Vietnam, wasn't it? Well, a French-style Vietnam, meaning cobbled together with no equipment! Since we had no helicopters, the soldiers jumped out of planes and, assuming their parachutes actually opened, they carried on on foot.'

The man at the table heard me. He looked up and made an attempt to smile. He stared at me with icy-blue eyes whose expression I couldn't make out, but maybe he was just staring at me. 'I suppose you've got a point. Well, about the lack of resources, anyway,' then he went back to reading his outspread newspaper, turning the huge pages, never missing one, until he came to the end. The conversation moved on to something else; standing at the bar is no place for serious conversation. That's the whole point of the aperitif: the rapidity, the lack of gravity, the lack of inertia, the fact that everyone assumes physical characteristics that do not belong to the real world, the one that burdens us, bogs us down. Through wine-tinted spectacles the world we saw was smaller and better suited to our half-hearted ambitions. When the time came I headed off with my empty trolley and went back to my room for a nap to sleep off what I had drunk that morning. This job was threatening to give me cirrhosis and, as I drifted off, I kept promising myself I would find something else soon, but I always fell asleep before I worked out what.

The old man's stare lingered with me. The colour of a glacier, with no emotion, no depth. Yet it radiated a calm, an attentiveness that took in everything around him. His gaze fostered a sort of intimacy, there seemed to be no barriers that prevented you from being seen or distorted how you were seen. Maybe I was just imagining things, deceived by the curious colour of his eyes, that emptiness like an ice floe on black water; but this look that I had seen for a fleeting second stayed with me, and for the whole week I dreamed of Indo-China, and the dream I woke from each morning haunted me all day. I had never thought about it before, about Indo-China, now I dreamed about it in images that were precise but totally imaginary.

I dreamed of a vast house. We were inside; we did not know how big it was or what was outside; I did not even know who 'we' were. We climbed a large, creaking wooden staircase that rose in a languid spiral to each landing, from which corridors lined with doors branched off. We moved in single file, marching slowly, lugging heavy backpacks. I don't remember any weapons, only the old-fashioned khaki canvas backpacks with their metal frames and straps padded with felt. We were in uniform, climbing this endless staircase, moving in silence, single file, down long corridors. The lighting was dim, the panelling absorbed all the light; there were no windows or the inside shutters were closed.

Behind half-open doors we saw people sitting, eating in silence or asleep, sprawled on huge beds, flanked by thick cushions, lying on chequered bedspreads. We climbed for a long time and, reaching a landing, we piled our rucksacks in a heap. The officer in charge showed us where to take up our positions. We slumped, exhausted, behind the rucksacks, he alone stayed standing. Scrawny, legs apart, arms akimbo, he kept his sleeves rolled up, and his cool demeanour ensured our safety. We barricaded the staircases, made a barrier with our rucksacks, but the enemy was in the walls. I knew this because on several occasions I found myself looking through their eyes, staring down at us from above, through cracks in the ceiling. I never named this enemy, because I never saw it. I simply saw through its eyes. I knew from the start that this close combat was the Indochine War. We were attacked, we were constantly under attack. The enemy ripped the wallpaper, surged from the walls, fell from the ceiling. I don't remember any guns, any explosions, just that ripping sound, that surging, that danger that streamed from the walls and the ceilings that enclosed us. We were outnumbered, we were heroic, we retreated to a narrow strip of landing behind our rucksacks, while our officer, fists on his hips, stood, implacable, jerking his chin to let us know where we should be positioned during the various phases of the attack.

I thrashed about during this dream and woke bathed in a sweat that stank of wine. All the next day I could not shake off the overpowering image of that house, the walls closing in, and the self-assured swagger of that scrawny officer standing over us, reassuring us.

After the violence of the dream had dissolved, all that remained was the 'we'. A nebulous 'we' ran through this dream, ran through my account of it, one that, for want of a better one, described the non-specific viewpoint through which I lived this dream. Because we live our dreams. The point of view through which I lived it had been undefined. I was one or other of the marching soldiers shouldering a rucksack. I was one of the soldiers huddled behind a rucksack, trying to defend himself, forced to retreat again, but I was also a part of the surreptitious gaze that watched them from the walls. I was part of the collective breath that made it possible to tell this story. The only person I was not, the only one who was not part of this 'we' and who kept his 'he', was the skinny officer, unarmed and standing to attention, whose keen eye saw everything and whose self-control saved us. Saved us.

'We' is performative; simply to utter the word creates a group; 'we' denotes a group of people that includes the speaker, and the person speaking can speak in their name; their ties between them are so strong that the one may speak for all. How was it possible, in the spontaneity of a dream, that I had used this impulsive 'we'? How can I have experienced something I had never experienced and I do not even know? How can I morally say 'we' when I know all too well that terrible acts were committed? And yet 'we' acted, 'we' knew; there was no other way to say it.

Whenever I awoke from these alcohol-induced naps, I read books, I watched films. In the attic room where I lived I was free until the evening. I wanted to find out everything I could about this lost country of which only a name remains, a single, capitalized word filled with sweet, unhealthy vibrations, preserved deep within the language. I learned all there was to learn about this war of which there are no images, since few photographs were taken, many were destroyed, and those that survive are difficult to understand, eclipsed as they are by the photographs, so numerous and so easily understandable, of the American war.

What to call these men who tramped in single file through the forest, shouldering old-fashioned, khaki canvas rucksacks like the one I carried as a boy, when my father gave me the one he had carried as a child? Should these men be called 'the French'? And if so, what would that make me? Should they be called 'we'? Is it enough to be French to be implicated in what other Frenchmen do? The question seems futile, semantic, a matter of knowing which pronoun to use to denote those who marched through the forest, with rucksacks whose metal frame I felt digging into my back when I was a child. I want to know who I'm living with. I shared a common language with these men, and it is good to share things with those you love. I shared a sense of place with them; we walked the same streets, went to the same schools, listened to the same stories; we ate particular foods that other people do not eat and we enjoyed them. We spoke together in the only language that counts, the one you understand unthinkingly. We are all organs of the body united by the caresses of a common tongue. Who knows how far that great body extends? Who knows what the left hand is doing while the right is busy fondling? What is the rest of the body doing when your attention is diverted by the caresses of that tongue? I wondered as I fondled the cleft of the girl lying next to me. I've forgotten her name; it's strange to know so little about the people you sleep with. It is strange but, most of the time, when we are lying next to each other, we have our eyes closed, and when we open them by accident we are too close to make out the person's face. It is impossible to know who 'we' is, impossible to resolve semantic questions, so what cannot be said is passed over in silence. And we will talk no more about those men tramping through the forest than we do about the name of the woman lying so close, that we will soon forget.

We know so little about those close to us. It is terrifying. It is important to try to know.

I saw him several times, the man with the unfolded newspaper. I did not know his name, but that was not important in this out-of-the-way café. Here, the regulars were just hoary clichés; each existed as a single detail, mentioned over and over; this detail, endlessly repeated, unchanging, meant people knew who you were; it meant others could laugh, and everyone could drink. Alcohol is the perfect fuel for such machines. It explodes, the tank is quickly emptied. The sudden emptiness is brutal; you have no choice; you refuel. He was the war vet who spread out his newspaper at a busy time so as not to be disturbed; I was the young man on a slippery slope who never went anywhere without a little old lady's shopping trolley, and at one o'clock every afternoon went to get topped up: no one tired of making jokes about that.

This could have carried on for a long time. It could have carried on until he dropped. It could have carried on until he withered and died, because he was older than me. It could have carried on until my final humiliation, until I had no money, no energy, or words left to hold my own, no strength left to sit with these men at the bar where we were all lined up, waiting for the end. It could have carried on for a long time, because that kind of life is designed not to change. Alcohol pickles the living in the last pose they struck. You see it in museums, where the bodies of those once living are preserved in jars.

But Sunday saved us.

Some people find Sundays tedious and avoid them, but that blank day is essential to change; it is the space reserved where change can come to pass. On Sunday I discovered his name and my life took a different turn.

The Sunday I learned his name I was strolling through the Artists' Market along the Saône. The name makes me laugh. It precisely sums up what it is: a flea market for art lovers.

What was I doing there? I had seen better days. I'll tell you about it sometime. I once had education, and taste. I loved the arts and knew a little about them. I may be disillusioned with them, but I'm not bitter, and I completely understand Duchamp's maxim: 'Even the fart of an artist is art.' That, to me, seems conclusive; it may sound like a joke, but it perfectly describes what inspires painters and those who come to see them.

There is nothing particularly expensive at the Artists' Market, but there is nothing particularly beautiful. You stroll in the shade of the plane trees, idly studying the works of the artists, who size up those browsing behind their tables with increasing contempt as they swan past without buying anything.

I prefer this to the closed world of art galleries, because what is on display here is clearly art: oil on canvas, painted in a traditional style. The subjects are familiar, recognizable, easily expressed, and from behind these irrefutable canvases glower the feverish eyes of the artists. Those who choose to exhibit their work also put themselves on show; they come to save their souls by virtue of their status as artists, not onlookers; as for the onlookers, they save their souls by coming to see the artists. He who paints can save his soul as long as someone buys, and buying his paintings is like buying indulgences, a few hours of paradise snatched from everyday damnation.

I would go and be amused to confirm, yet again, that artists look like their work. People lazily assume the contrary, like some bargain-basement maxim by Sainte-Beuve: the artist expresses himself, gives form to his work, hence that work must reflect his personality. Bullshit! A stroll beneath the plane trees at the Artists' Market reveals everything. The artist is not expressing himself – after all, what does he have to express? He is constructing himself. And what he is exhibiting is himself. Behind his stall, he exposes himself to the gaze of passers-by whom he envies and despises; they return his feelings, but differently, inversely, and thus everyone is happy. The artist creates his work and in return his work gives life to him.

Consider this tall, skinny guy who paints terrible portraits in bold strokes of acrylic: every portrait is him from a different angle. Put them together and they show what he would like to be. Hence what he would like to be, is.

Consider the guy who methodically paints watercolours that are too brash, too clear-cut, the colours are garish, the forms too solid. He is deaf and can barely hear the remarks of the curious onlookers; he paints the world as he hears it.

Consider the beautiful woman who paints only portraits of beautiful women. Each one looks like her, and as the years pass she takes more care in how she dresses, she withers, and the beauty of her painted ladies seems more and more disproportionate. Predictably, she signs herself 'Doriane'.

Consider the shy Chinese man exhibiting paintings of brutal violence, faces in close-up distorted by thick impasto strokes. Never knowing where to put his huge hands, he apologizes with a charming smile.

Consider the man who paints miniatures on waxed wooden panels. He sports a pudding-bowl haircut the likes of which are seldom seen outside the margins of an illuminated manuscript; he has a waxy pallor and his repertoire of gestures is gradually diminishing until he is no more than a medieval statue.

Consider the fat lady with the dyed black hair, she has seen better years, she is fading now, but she stands straight and has a twinkle in her eye. In lissom lines of Indian ink she sketches tangled bodies, assertively erotic yet innocuous, restrained.

Consider the Chinese woman sitting amid decorative canvases. Her hair enfolds her shoulders in a curtain of black silk, framing her dazzlingly red lips. Her gaudy paintings are of little interest, but when she sits among the canvases they become the perfect background for the deep crimson of her lips.

I went, and I recognized him, recognized his stiffness, his gangling frame, his lean, handsome head held aloft as though planted on a pikestaff. From a distance I recognized the clean lines of his profile, the close-cropped white hair, the straight nose pointing the way ahead. His nose was so thrusting it seemed to leave his pale, hesitant eyes behind. His bone structure was active, but his eyes pensive.

We nodded a curt greeting, not quite knowing how informal we could be in word, in deed, outside the familiar confines of the bistro. In a sense, we were in civvies: hands in pockets, we stood, speaking cautiously, without having had a drink, without a glass in front of us, without the usual ritual. He stared at me. In his clear eyes I saw only clarity; he seemed to see right into my heart. I did not know what to say. I flicked through the watercolours in front of him.

'You don't look much like a painter,' I said unthinkingly.

'That's because I don't have the beard. But I do have the brushes.'

'Very beautiful, very beautiful,' I said politely as I leafed through the pictures, and then realized that what I had said was true. Finally, I looked. What I had thought were watercolours were actually painted in ink wash. Technically these were *grisailles*, built up using various dilutions of Indian ink. From the deep black of the unadulterated ink he drew such a variety of shades, greys so varied, so transparent, so luminous, that they conjured everything, even colour, although there was none. From black he brought forth light, and from that light all else followed. I looked up, wordlessly commending him on his achievement.

As I approached his stall, I had been expecting to find the sort of work turned out by those who take up art late in life, almost as a hobby. I was expecting landscapes and careful, meticulous portraits, flowers, animals, all those things that people consider 'picturesque' and hordes of amateurs stubbornly churn out, with great precision and little interest. And then I touched the outsized sheets washed with ink, held them, one by one, between my fingers, fingers that were more and more sensitive and sure, I felt the weight, the grain, I gazed at them and my gaze was a caress. Scarcely daring to breathe, I leafed through this explosion of grey, the translucent wreaths of smoke, the sweeping shores of untouched white, the solid slabs of pure black whose shadows brooded over the whole.

He was offering them by the boxful, badly organized, badly sealed, at ridiculous prices. The dates stretched back half a century. He had used every conceivable kind of paper, watercolour paper, drawing paper, wrapping paper in every shade of brown and white, old yellow pages and crisp new ones bought from an art supply shop.

He painted from life. The subjects were merely a pretext for working with ink, but he painted what he had seen. There were rugged mountains, tropical trees, strange fruits, stooped women bent in paddy fields, men in floating *djellebas*, mountain villages; palls of mist over jagged hills, rivers lined with forest. And, everywhere, there were men in uniform, heroic and thin, some stretched out, visibly dead.

'Have you been painting long?'

'About sixty years.'

'Are you selling the lot?'

'It's all just clutter. So I cleared out the attic and I'm taking the Sunday air. At my age, those are two important tasks. In the process I come across drawings I've forgotten and try to remember when they dated from, and I talk to passers-by about art. But most of them talk shit. So for now, don't say a word.'

I continued to browse, silent, following his advice. I would have liked to have talked to him, but I didn't know about what.

'Were you really over there, in Indochine?'

'See for yourself. I can't make thing up. Which is a pity, otherwise I could have painted more.'

'Were you there at the time?'

'If "at the time" means "with the army", then yes. With the French Far East Expeditionary Corps.'

'Were you a war artist?'

'God, no. Paratroop officer. Must have been the only para who ever drew. The men used to take the piss out of me a bit. But not too much.

33

Because if the colonial army didn't have this kind of refinement, it had all sorts. And, besides, I would draw portraits of the lads who took the piss. They're better than photos. They loved that. They asked me for more. I always took along paper and ink; wherever I went, I would draw.'

I turned the pages feverishly, as though I had discovered a lost treasure. I moved from box to box, opening them, taking out the drawings, feeling his brushstrokes within myself, following their flow, their feeling in my fingertips, my arm, my shoulder and my belly. Each sheet appeared before me like a landscape glimpsed suddenly at a bend in the road, my hand fluttered over them, tracing whorls in the air, and in every limb I could feel a weary weight, as though I had travelled every step of the journey. Some were small sketches, others large, detailed compositions, but all were bathed in a raking light that transfixed the subjects, and gave them the presence on paper that they had had in that moment in life. In the bottom right corner, he clearly signed his name, Victorien Salagnon. Next to the signature had been added dates in pencil, sometime the exact date, sometimes the time, others were more vague, mentioning only the year.

'I go through them. Try to remember. I have boxes of them, suit-cases, trunks full.'

'You painted a lot?'

'Yes. I work quickly. When I had the time I'd turn out several a day. But a lot of them were lost, mislaid, abandoned. In my time in the army I often had to beat a retreat, and at times like that you don't load yourself down, you don't take everything. You abandon things.'

I marvelled at his inkwork. He stood facing me, a little stiff. He had not moved an inch; being taller, he looked down on me, his gaze frank, a little sardonic. He looked at me with that raw-boned face, those transparent eyes in which the lack of barriers seemed like gentleness. My droll theory about art and life no longer seemed of any interest. So I put down the drawing I still held and looked up at him.

'Mister Salagnon, would you teach me to paint?'

*   *   *

34

Towards nightfall it started to snow; big flakes floating down and hesitating before they settled. At first they were invisible against the grey air, but as night drew in, rubbing the sky with charcoal, their whiteness stood out. In the end it was all you could see, snowflakes shimmering in the air beneath an ink-black sky, and whiteness on the ground covering everything with a damp blanket. The little house was cloaked with the snow, in the violet glow of a December night.

I was happy sitting there, but Salagnon was gazing out. Standing by the window, hands behind his back, watching as snow fell on his suburban house and garden in Voracieux-les-Bredins, on the eastern edge of the town where the rolling meadows of the Isère break like waves.

'The snow enfolds everything in its white coat. Isn't that what they used to say? That's how we talked about snow at school. Its white shroud unfurled. There was a time when I never saw snow, or shrouds, for that matter – all we had were tarps at best, and if we didn't have them, we covered everything with dirt and put a cross on top. Sometimes we left them where they fell, but not often. We tried not to give up on our dead, we tried to bring them back with us, to count them, remember them.

'I love snow. We don't get much of it these days, so I stand at the window and watch each snowfall like it's a major event. I lived out the worst moments of my life in sweltering heat and noise. So for me, snow is silence, it's peace, and a bracing cold that makes me forget that sweat even exists. I can't abide sweat, but for twenty years I was constantly bathed in it, never able to dry off. So to me, snow is human warmth, a dry body, safe and sheltered. I doubt the soldiers who fought on the Russian front with threadbare uniforms, terrified of freezing to death, shared my love for snow. The old German veterans can't bear it; they head south at the first sign of winter. Me, it's the opposite. I can't stand the sight of palm trees. In all the twenty years I spent fighting, I never once saw snow; and now, what with global warming, there won't be any. So I make the most of it. I'll go when it goes. I spent twenty years in hot countries; in the tropics, I suppose you'd call them. To me, snow is

France: toboggans, Christmas decorations, thick, patterned jumpers, ski-pants and après-ski drinks; all the stupid, boring things I fled, the very things I returned to in spite of myself. By the time the war was over, everything had changed; the only pleasure I have now is the snow.'

'What war are you talking about?'

'You didn't notice it, the twenty-year war? A never-ending war that started badly, ended badly; a faltering war that even now might still be going on. A constant war that permeated our every action, although nobody realized it. The start date is a little vague – 1940, maybe 1942, it's hard to say. But the end is clear-cut: 1962, not a year more. And as soon as it was over, everyone behaved as though nothing had happened. You didn't notice?'

'I wasn't born until after.'

'The silence after war is still war. You can't forget what you're struggling so hard to forget. It's like being told not to think about an elephant. Even if you were born afterwards, you grew up surrounded by the symptoms. For example, I'm sure you hated the army, even though you knew nothing about it. That's one of the symptoms I'm talking about: a mysterious loathing that spreads from person to person without anyone knowing where it comes from.'

'It's a matter of principle. A political choice.'

'A choice? Just when it had ceased to matter? When it made absolutely no difference? Choices that have no consequences are just signs. The army itself was a symptom. Didn't you think it was disproportionate? Didn't you ever wonder why we kept such a large army, on a war footing, pawing the ground, jittery, when it served no purpose? Keeping it completely cut off from the world, never speaking, never spoken to? What enemy could justify a war machine in which every man – that's right, every single man in this country – had to spend a year of their lives, sometimes more? What enemy?'

'The Russians?'

'Bullshit. Why would the Russians have destroyed the only part of the world that just about worked, one that was providing them with all the things they didn't have? Come on! We had no enemies. The reason we maintained a powerful army after 1962 was simply to mark time. The war was over, but the warriors were still around. So we waited for them to disappear, to grow old and die. Time heals everything, because in time the problem dies. We kept then penned in to stop them escaping, to stop them recklessly using the skills they had been taught. The Americans made a weird film about it. There is this man, a trained soldier, who gets lost in the woods. He has only a sleeping bag, a dagger and a working knowledge of all the ways to kill burned into his soul, into his nerves. I can't remember what it was called.'

'*Rambo?*'

'That's it, *Rambo*. They made a couple of stupid sequels, but I'm just talking about that first film: there was a man I could understand. He wanted peace, he wanted silence, but no one would give him space. He laid waste a small town, because he didn't know any other way. That's what you learn from war and it's something you can't unlearn. People think of this man as far away, off in America somewhere, but I've known hundreds like him here in France, and if you add the ones I don't know, it must run into thousands. We kept the army to give them somewhere to cool their heels, so they wouldn't lash out. No one realizes it, because no one talks about it. All the ills in Europe concern society as a whole. We nurse them in silence. Health is life lived in the silence of the organs, to quote an old army doctor.'

This elderly gentleman spoke without looking at me. He stared out of the window, watching the snow fall gently, and spoke with the same gentleness, his back to me. I didn't understand what he was saying, but I sensed he was talking about a history I didn't know, that he *was* that history, and I happened to be here with him, in this godforsaken place, in the arse-end of nowhere, in a house out in the suburbs where the town sinks into the marshy fields of the Isère; and he was ready to talk to me. My heart began to beat faster. Here in the town where I used to live, the town to which I had returned to end things, I had stumbled on a secret space, a dark room I hadn't noticed the first time around; I had pushed open the door and discovered a vast, dim attic, long since boarded up, with not a single footprint in the thick dust that covered the floor. And in that attic I had found a chest; and in that chest – who knew what? It had not been opened since it was first put there.

'What was your part in this story?'

'Me? Everything. The Free French Forces, the war in Indochine, the *djebels* of Algeria. A few years banged up, and since then, nothing.'

'Banged up?'

'Not for long. You know, the whole thing ended badly: in slaughter, resignation and despair. Given your age, when your parents conceived you, the whole country was sitting on top of a volcano. The volcano was shuddering, threatening to erupt, to annihilate the state. Your parents had to be blind or hopeless optimists or idiots. But people back then preferred not to see what was going on, not to listen, it was easier to live heedlessly than in the fear that the volcano might erupt. And in the end, it didn't, it became dormant again. Silence, bitterness and time prevailed over the explosive forces. That's why everything these days smells of sulphur. It's the magma, still smouldering beneath the surface, escaping through the cracks. It surges slowly beneath volcanoes that don't erupt.'

'Do you regret it?'

'What? My life? The silence that surrounds it? I've no idea. It's my life: I cling to it no matter what it's been. It's the only one I have. This life killed those who stayed silent, and I have no intention of dying.'

'He's been saying that ever since I've known him,' said a loud voice behind me, a sweet, feminine voice that filled the whole room. 'I keep telling him he's wrong, but I have to admit that, so far, he's been right.'

I flinched and got to my feet. Before I even set eyes on her, I liked the way she spoke, her exotic accent, the sadness in her voice. A woman was walking towards us, moving sure-footedly, her skin covered with a tracery of fine wrinkles like rumpled silk. She was Salagnon's age and she came over to me, extending her hand. I stood, mute and transfixed, staring and open-mouthed. As she had held out her hand to me, we shook hands and her touch – gentle, forthright, charming – was a pleasurable surprise, unusual in women, who often don't know how to shake hands. She radiated strength, you could feel it in her palm; she radiated a genuine strength, one that was not borrowed from the opposite sex, but entirely feminine.

'This is my wife Eurydice Kaloyannis, a Greek Jew from Bab El Oued, the last of her kind. She goes by my name these days, but I still use the name by which I first knew her. It's a name I wrote so many times, on so many envelopes, with so many sighs, that I can't think of her any other way. My desire for her bears that name. Besides, I don't like the idea of women losing their names, especially since there is no one to carry on her name; and besides, I had a lot of respect for her father, in spite of our differences, but most of all, Eurydice Salagnon sounds a bit ugly, don't you think? Sounds like a list of vegetables. It doesn't do justice to her beauty.'

Yes, her beauty. It was that, precisely that. Eurydice was beautiful. I realized it instantly without having to formulate the thought, my hand in hers, my eyes staring into hers, standing frozen, foolish and lost for words. The age gap can cloud your perceptions. You think of yourself as not being the same age, as being very distant, when in fact we are so close. Our being is the same. Time flows, we can never step twice into the same stream, our bodies move through time like boats drifting with the current. The water is not the same, is never the same, and the boats, so distant from each other, forget they are just the same; they are simply displaced. Age difference makes it difficult to gauge beauty, because beauty feels calculated: a woman is beautiful if I feel the desire to kiss her. Eurydice was the same age as Salagnon. Her skin was the same age, her hair was the same age, her eyes, her lips, her hands made no pretence to the contrary. There is nothing more odious than the phrase 'well-preserved', and that nervous laugh, the false modesty that accompanies the observation that someone 'doesn't look' their age. Eurydice looked her age and she was life itself. The intense life she had lived was present in her every gesture, a whole life in the way she carried herself, a whole life in every tone of her voice, she was filled with a life that brimmed over, dazzling, infectious.

'My Eurydice is strong, so strong that when I brought her from hell, I didn't have to look back to know that she was following. I knew she was there. She's not a woman you can forget. You can feel her presence even when she's behind you.'

He put an arm around her shoulder, bent and kissed her. He had said precisely what I was thinking. I smiled at them, my mind was clear again and I could take back my hand, and my gaze stopped trembling.

Victorien Salagnon taught me how to paint. He gave me a Chinese calligraphy brush, a wolf's-hair brush with a lively touch, which glances off paper without losing its impetus. 'You can't find these in the shops,' he said. 'Only goat's-hair brushes, which are fine for calligraphy or for filling in backgrounds, but they're useless for line drawing.'

He taught me to cradle the brush in the hollow of my hand, the way you might an egg, gripping it so lightly that a breath can jog it. 'So you need to control your breathing.' He taught me to judge inks, to distinguish between shades of black, to assess their sheen, their depth, before using them. He taught me to appreciate the blank page, a perfect expanse as precious as a moment of clarity. He taught me to value space over solidity, since what is solid can no longer move, but he taught me, too, that solidity is existence, so we must reconcile ourselves to disrupt the emptiness.

He drew nothing in my presence. He simply talked to me and watched me draw. He taught me how to use the tools. How I handled them later was my responsibility. And what I chose to paint was my responsibility. It was up to me to paint, and to show him if I wished. If not, he was happy simply to watch how I held the brush as it made contact with the paper, or how I traced a line with a single stroke. For him, that was enough to see me on the road to becoming a painter.

I visited often. I learned through practise, while he watched. He no longer painted. He made the most of the free time. He told me he had a series of notebooks and had started to write his memoirs.

We were well met indeed. Men of war often pride themselves on their ability to write. They strive to be efficient in everything. Being men of action, they think they can tell a story better than anyone. And, conversely, lovers of literature think they know about strategy, about tactics and siege warfare, all those things that in real life are often deployed to disastrous effect, with consequences one cannot but regret, and yet more powerfully than they are in books.

He talked to me about his memoirs several times, almost in passing, and then one day, unable to contain himself, he went to fetch his notebook. He wrote on a blue, ruled exercise paper in neat, schoolboy handwriting. He took a deep breath and started to read aloud. It began like this: 'I was born in Lyon in 1926 to a family of shopkeepers. I was an only child.'

He stopped reading, set down the notebook and looked at me.

'Can you hear the boredom? Even the very first sentence is boring. I read it and I'm desperate to get to the end; and I stop there, I never carry on. There are a few more pages, but I stop here.'

'Take out the first sentence. Start with the second or somewhere else.'

'But this is the start. I have to start from the beginning, otherwise it makes no sense. This is a memoir, not a novel.'

'What do you actually remember? What's the first thing?'

'I remember fog, a damp cold. I remember how much I hated sweat.'

'Then start with that.'

'But I have to be born first.'

'Memory has no beginning.'

'Do you really think so?'

'I know so. Memory comes in a jumble, in a torrent, it has no beginning, except in obituaries. And you have no intention of dying.'

'I just want to be clear. My birth makes a good start.'

'You weren't there, so it's meaningless. Memory is full of beginnings. Choose whichever one suits you. You can be born whenever you like. In a book, people are born at all sorts of ages.'

Puzzled, he reopened the exercise book. Silently, he read the first page, then the rest. The paper was already yellowing. He had set down the details, the circumstances and the events he had experienced, those he felt should not be forgotten. It was methodical. But it did not say what he wanted it to say. He closed the book and held it out.

'I don't know how to do these things. You start it.'

I was annoyed that he had taken my advice literally. But I'm the storyteller. I have no choice but to tell stories. Even if it's not what I want, even if it's not what I aspire to, since I would much rather show than tell. This is why I'm here in Victorien Salagnon's house, so that he can teach me to wield a brush better than I do a pen, so that at last I can show. But maybe my hand is better adapted to the pen. And besides, I have to find some way to pay him back, I have to take the trouble to make up for the trouble he has taken for me. Paying him would be easier, but I have no money, and besides, he wouldn't take it. So I took the notebook and started reading.

I read the whole thing. He was right, it was tedious; it was no better than those self-published books of war memoirs. Reading those books with large type and short paragraphs, you realize that, when told like this, not much happens in a single life. Whereas a single moment in life contains more than can be described in a shelf full of books. There is something about an event that is not resolved in the telling. Events pose a boundless question, which telling cannot answer.

I don't know what talent he thinks I have. I don't know what he thought he saw when he looked me up and down with those pale eyes, those eyes in which I can discern no emotion, only a translucence that gives me an impression of closeness. But I am the storyteller, and so I tell stories.

Novel I

The life of rats

FROM THE BEGINNING, Victorien Salagnon trusted in his shoulders. His birth had endowed him with muscles, with breath, with powerful fists, with those pale eyes that glittered like ice. And so he divided the world's problems into two categories: those he could resolve by force – and there he ploughed ahead – and those about which he could do nothing. The latter he treated with contempt, pretending not to notice them as he passed; or else he fled.

Victorien Salagnon had everything he needed to succeed: physical intelligence, moral simplicity and the ability to take decisions. He knew his strengths, and to know one's strengths is the greatest treasure one can have at the age of seventeen. But during the winter of 1943 his natural gifts were of no use. Seen from France that year, the whole universe seemed utterly, intrinsically wretched.

This was no time for faint hearts or for childish games: it was a time when strength was sorely needed. But in 1943 the young forces of France, the youthful muscles, the adolescent brains, the churning balls, could find no work other than cleaning hotel rooms, working abroad, straw men in the pay of the victors they were not, provincial sportsmen, but nothing more, or great awkward lumps parading around in shorts, brandishing shovels like rifles. Though everyone knew that the world was full of real weapons. All over the world people were waging war and Victorien Salagnon was going to school.

When he reached the edge he leaned over; far below La Grande Institution he could see the city of Lyon hovering in the air. From the terrace he saw what the fog allowed him to see: the rooftops of the city, the abyss of the Saône, and, beyond that, nothing. The rooftops floated; no two were alike in size, in height, nor in how they were aligned. The colour of weathered wood, they jostled each other gently, beached, higgledy-piggledy, on this oxbow of the Saône, washed up like flotsam that the current was too weak to shift. Seen from above, the city of Lyon looked utterly chaotic. It was impossible to see the fog-bound streets, and the arrangement of roofs offered no logic by which to intuit the layout: nothing indicated where the thoroughfares might be. This ancient city is not so much constructed as laid down, like rubble from a rockslide. The hill to which it clings has never afforded it a stable base. At times the waterlogged moraines could hold no longer and collapsed. But not today: the chaos Victorien Solagnon was looking down on was merely an illusion. The old town where he lived had not been built straight, but the uncertain, floating look it had on that morning in the winter of 1943 was entirely the result of the weather, surely.

To convince himself, he tried to draw it, since sketches can perceive order that the eyes cannot. He had seen the fog from home. Through the window everything was reduced to blurred shapes, like lines of charcoal on sugar paper. He had taken a pad of rough paper and a thick pencil, slipped them into his belt and tied up his schoolbooks with a strip of cloth. He did not have a pocket big enough for his sketchpad, but he did not like to mix it up with his schoolbooks or to flaunt his talent by carrying it in his hand. And he was not unhappy with the subterfuge, since it reminded him that he was going not where people might assume, but somewhere else entirely.

He did not draw anything much. The graphic nature of the fog that had been obvious when framed and given perspective by the window faded when he stepped outside into the street. All that remained was a hazy presence, pervasive and piercing and impossible to record. You cannot create a picture while remaining within it. He did not take out his sketchpad. He re-buttoned his school cape to stop the damp air from penetrating and walked on to the school.

He arrived at La Grande Institution having drawn nothing. On the parapet of the terrace he tried to give a sense of the labyrinthine rooftops. He started a line, but the sheet of paper, damp from the humidity, ripped; it did not look like anything, just dirty paper. He closed his drawing pad, tucked it back into his belt and, like the other pupils, went and stood beneath the clock in the courtyard, stamping his feet while he waited for the school bell.

Winters in Lyon are harsh. It is not so much the cold as the revelation, crystallized by winter: the essential constituent of the city is mud. Lyon is a city of sediment – sediment compacted into houses, rooted into the sediment of the rivers that run through it; and sediment is just a polite word for encrusted mud. In winter everything in Lyon turns to mud: the ground gives way, the snow refuses to lie, the walls ooze; the very air itself, viscous, dank and cold, soaks into clothes, leaving transparent stains of mud. Everything feels heavy, bodies sink; there is no way to safeguard against it. Except to hole up in the bedroom with a stove burning, day and night, curl up in sheets reheated several times a day by a warming pan filled with glowing embers. And in the winter of 1943 who could afford the luxury of a bedroom, of coal, of embers?

But in 1943, precisely, it seems rude to complain; the cold is far worse elsewhere. In Russia, for example, where *our troops* are fighting – or *their troops*, or *the troops*; no one knows what to call them any more – in Russia cold is like a natural disaster, a lingering explosion that lays waste to everything before it. They say that the corpses are like lumps of glass that shatter if handled incorrectly; that losing a single glove means death, because the blood freezes into needles that tear the hand apart; that the soldiers who die on their feet stay standing, rooted like trees all winter, only to melt and dissolve with the spring;

that many die when they drop their trousers, their arseholes frozen in an instant. Rumours of the cold are recounted like monstrous horror stories, although actually they are like the tall tales of travellers, embroidered by distance. Barefaced lies circulate, mingled with a dash of truth, no doubt, but who, in France, still has the least interest, the least desire, the least vestige of intellectual and moral scruple to tell one from the other?

The fog hangs its icy laundry in the streets, in corridors, on staircases, even in bedrooms. The damp sheets cling to passers-by, brush against their cheeks, insinuate, licking at the neck like tears of icy rage, like the drip of numbed furies, like the tender kisses of the dying who long for us to join them. In order not to feel, one must not move.

Beneath the clock tower of La Grande Institution the schoolboys survive by remaining as still as possible: shifting just a little to ward off the cold, but no more, lest the fog seep in. They stamp their feet, protect their hands, hunch their shoulders, lower their faces to the ground. They tug down their berets, pull their capes tight, while they wait for the bell to summon them. It would make a fine ink drawing, all those identical boys, round-shouldered, swaddled in black capes, standing in random groups against the classical architecture of the courtyard. But Salagnon had no ink, his hands were tucked away, and the frustration of waiting was beginning to get to him. Like the others, he was waiting for the bell. With a slight pleasure, he felt the stiff sketchbook digging into him.

The bell sounded and they raced to class. Shoving and sniggering, pretending to be quiet while making as much noise as possible, elbows flying, pulling faces, stifling giggles, they rushed past the two prefects standing guard at the door, who feigned an utterly impassive air, a military rigidity much in fashion that year. What do we call them, these pupils of La Grande Institution? They range in age between fifteen and eighteen, but in France in 1943 age is irrelevant. Boys? The word makes too much of what they are living through. Young men?

That makes too much of what they have yet to live through. What can you call someone who hides a smirk as he passes a prefect, but a kid? Kids sheltered from the storm, living inside the compact box of icy stone, jostling like puppies. They wait as life passes by, yapping while pretending not to yap, doing things while pretending not to do them. They are safe.

The bell sounded and the kids assembled. The Lyon air is so damp, the air of 1943 of such poor quality that, rather than take flight, the clanging bronze notes did not ascend but dropped with the sound of wet cardboard, slithered down into the courtyard and mingled with the tattered leaves, with the remnants of snow, with the dirty water and the mud gradually submerging Lyon.

In serried ranks the boys headed to their classrooms down a vast stone corridor as cold as bone. The muffled thud of boots echoing against the bare walls was drowned out by the rustle of capes and the incessant jabber of kids desperate to be quiet, but unable to be silent. To Salagnon it created unspeakable cacophony. He hated it and strode through the hubbub stiffly, as he might have held his nose when passing through a foul-smelling room. The cold does not bother Salagnon; he rather enjoys the chill air of the institution; he can even bring himself to endure the school's preposterous regulations. He could rise above his unfortunate circumstances if only everything could be done in silence. He finds the clamour in the corridors embarrassing. He tries to ignore it, to mentally stop his ears, to retreat into his own silent world, but his whole body is alert to the pandemonium. He is keenly aware of where he is. He cannot forget it: in a classroom full of boys, of kids, whose every action is accompanied by infantile noises that reverberate back as echoes, a commotion that envelops them like sweat. Victorien Salagnon has a horror of sweat; it is sludge secreted by a nervous, overdressed man when he exercises. A man who is free in his movements does not sweat. He runs naked, his perspiration evaporating as he moves; he is bathed in his own filth, he keeps his body dry. The slave sweats, hunkered in the mineshaft. The infant sweats, all but drowning, swaddled in layers of wool by his mother. Salagnon had a phobia about sweat; he dreams of having a body carved from stone that does not drip.

Father Fobourdon was standing in front of the blackboard, waiting for them. The boys fell silent and each stood behind his desk waiting until the silence was total. The slightest rustle of fabric, a creaking floorboard, would prolong the moment. They would have to stand until the silence was absolute. Eventually, Fobourdon gestured for them to sit, and the resultant scrape of chairs was brief and stopped almost immediately. Then he turned and, in elegant cursive hand, wrote on the blackboard: 'Commentarii de Bello Gallico: unseen translation.' They set to work. That was Father Fobourdon's method: not a word more than was absolutely necessary, no verbal confirmation of what he had written. Actions alone. By example, he taught internal discipline, which is a practical art that exists only through actions. He saw himself as a Roman, a block of rough stone, hewn and engraved. Sometimes he would launch into a brief commentary that drew some moral from the minor incidents that punctuated school life. It was a life that he despised, although he was proud of his vocation as a teacher. He considered the teacher's rostrum superior to the pulpit, since the latter is used to censure and chastise, the former to guide, to lead, to act, thereby revealing the only worthwhile aspect of life, the moral aspect, which has none of the foolishness of the tangible world. And language is a worthy tool with which to reveal this facet.

They were to translate the account of a battle in which the enemy was skilfully surrounded and then slashed to pieces. Language allows for beautiful brushstrokes, thought Salagnon, wonderful touches that scarcely mark the page, delicate watercolour effects that enhance a story. But the Gallic wars themselves had been fought in the dirtiest way, without recourse to words, to metaphors. Using sharp, double-edged swords, you hacked the enemy to bloody pieces which you stepped over in order to slash another limb, until your enemy was dead or you fell on the battlefield.

Caesar the adventurer had marched into Gaul and put it to the sword. Caesar willed it and his will was strong. He wanted to crush nations, to found an empire, to reign; he wanted to be, to grasp the known world in his fist; he coveted. He wanted to be great and he wanted it now.

Of his victories, conquests, his mass murders, he wrote a spirited account, which he despatched to Rome to win over the Senate. He described battles as though they were sex scenes in which *Vir Romanus* – Roman virtue – triumphed, in which the flashing sword was like a glorious phallus. His skilled storytelling made it possible for those at home to experience the vicarious thrill of battle. He repaid their trust, gave them their money's worth, he paid them in stories. And the senators sent men, more funds and tributes, which came back to them in the form of chariots laden with gold, and unforgettable anecdotes, such as the severed hands of enemies heaped into huge piles.

Through language, Caesar fashioned a fictional Gaul, one he created and conquered in a single sentence, a single gesture. Caesar lied as historians lie, describing only the reality that suits them. And hence the novel, the hero who lies, shapes reality more effectively than deeds, a great lie lays the foundation; indeed, it is at once the hidden foundations and the sheltering roof for those deeds. Together, word and deed carve up the world and give it shape. The military hero must be a novelist, a great liar, an inventive wordsmith.

Power is bought with imagery, it feeds on images. Caesar, a genius in all things, treated warfare, politics and literature equally. He attended to each aspect of a single act: leading his men, conquering Gaul, and writing the account of it, each reinforcing the other in an infinite spiral that would lead him to glory, to those lofty heights where only eagles fly.

Where reality evokes images, an image gives substance to reality: every political genius is a literary genius. At such a task, the Maréchal fails miserably: the 'great novel' he offers a humiliated France is no novel at all; it scarcely qualifies as a primary school reader, *Le Tour de la France par deux enfants* purged of anything controversial, a book to be coloured by children, tongues poking out in their concentration. The Maréchal's voice quavers, he talks like an old man, he can hardly seem to stay alert. No one believes in the puerile goals of the *Révolution Nationale*. People nod distractedly, but their minds are on other things: sleeping, going about their business, slaughtering each other in the shadows.

Salagnon translated well, but slowly. The pithy Latin sentences inspired daydreams. He filled them out with the details they lacked, restoring them to life. In the margin of the page he sketched a plan. The battlefield, the oblique edge of the forest enclosing it, the slope that would provide momentum, the Roman legions in serried ranks, each knowing the man next to him, never changing places; facing them, the hapless, half-naked hordes of Celts, our ancestors, the brave, moronic Gauls, always ready to fight for the thrill of battle, for the thrill itself, without caring about the outcome. Salagnon put a drop of violet ink on his finger, diluted it with spit and added translucent shadows to the sketch. As he gently rubbed, solid lines dissolved, space widened, light appeared. Drawing is an astonishing skill.

'Are you sure of their positions?' asked Fobourdon.

Salagnon started, blushed, instinctively covered up his work with his elbow, then regretted it. Fobourdon made to tug his ear, but gave up; his pupils were seventeen years old. After a momentary awkwardness, they both straightened up.

'I would prefer you made some progress with your translation, rather than wallowing in marginalia.'

Salagnon showed him the lines he had already completed; Fobourdon could not fault them.

'Your translation is excellent and the battle plan is accurate. But I would prefer it if you added your doodles to a Latin text that represents the summit of human thought. You will require all your faculties if you are to reach the lofty heights of the Ancients. So kindly stop fooling around. Develop your mind, it is the only thing you truly possess. It is time to put away childish things and to render unto Caesar the things that are Caesar's.'

Satisfied, he wandered off, trailing a gust of whispered voices in his wake. Arriving back at the rostrum, he turned. The silence was immediate.

'Carry on.'

And the pupils carried on mangling the Gallic wars in schoolboy Latin.

'That was a close call.' Chassagneaux spoke without moving his lips, a vital classroom skill. Salagnon shrugged. 'Fobourdon can be strict. But at least we get a bit of peace and quiet here. Don't you think?'

Salagnon grinned broadly. Under the desk he pinched the boy's fat thigh and twisted.

'I'm not one for peace and quiet,' he whispered.

Chassagneaux whimpered and let out a stifled cry. Still smiling, still writing, Salagnon went on pinching. It must have hurt: Chassagneaux uttered a strangulated word, which sent out ripples of laughter, a stone tossed into the silence of the classroom. Fobourdon hushed them with a glare.

'What's going on? Chassagneaux, stand up, boy. Was that you?'

'Yes, sir.'

'May one ask why?'

'Cramp, sir.'

'Cretinous boy. In Lacedaemon young men endured being disembowelled rather than break the silence. You will clean the brushes and the blackboard for a week. You will focus on the moral of these tasks. Silence is the clarity of the mind. Let us hope your mind can learn to recapture the clarity of a blank blackboard.'

There was laughter, which he ended with a curt 'Enough!' The boys got back to work. Chassagneaux, lips quivering, gingerly felt his thigh.

Chubby-cheeked, with his hair neatly parted, he looked like a little boy about to cry. Salagnon slipped him a note folded over several times: *Well done. You kept quiet. You keep my friendship*. The boy read the note and shot him a look of maudlin gratitude that made Salagnon feel nauseous: his whole body stiffened, he shuddered, he felt he might vomit. So he dipped his pen in the inkwell and started to recopy what he had already translated. He concentrated entirely on the act of writing, focused on the pen nib, on the ink flowing across the steel. His body became calmer. Given life by his breath, the letters looped out in violet arabesques, living curves, the steady rhythm soothing him until he finished his lines with a spirited thrust, as precise as a fencer's riposte. Classical calligraphy provides the calm necessary to violent and troubled people.

You can see the warrior through his calligraphy, the Chinese say; so people say. The gestures of the pen are those of the whole body in microcosm, perhaps of life itself. The posture and the decisiveness remain the same, regardless of scale. It was a maxim he agreed with, though he no longer remembered where he could have read it. Salagnon knew little about China, no more than chance details and rumours, but he knew enough for his imagination to conjure a Chinese scene, distant, a little hazy, perhaps, but utterly present. He filled it with fat, laughing Buddhas, carved stones, blue vases that were somewhat graceless, with the dragons used to decorate bottles of *encre de Chine* – ink the English falsely claim hails from India. His fascination with China stemmed from *Chine*: a word, a single word on a bottle of ink. He so loved the black ink that he felt it could give birth to a whole nation. Dreamers and fools oftentimes have powerful insights into the nature of reality.

Almost everything that Salagnon knew about China came from a lecture given by an elderly man during a Philosophy class. The man had spoken slowly, he remembers, he had repeated himself, favouring long-winded generalizations that stultified the attention of his audience.

Father Fobourdon had invited the elderly Jesuit, who had spent his life in China, to speak to the class. The man had lived through the Boxer Rebellion, witnessed the sacking of the Old Summer Palace, survived the uncertain period when warlords struggled for power. He had loved the empire, even in its dying days, had adapted to the republic, made his peace with the Kuomintang, only for them to be ousted by the Japanese. By then, China had descended into a terrible chaos that seemed likely to endure for some time; given his advancing years, he had little hope of seeing the end. He had returned to Europe.

The old man walked with a stoop, breathing heavily, leaning on anything within reach; the pupils stood while it took him an eternity to cross the classroom and slump into the chair that Father Fobourdon never used. For an hour – precisely one hour marked by the school bell – he droned on, reeling off the sort of banal clichés that might have appeared in the newspapers – the ones before the war, the usual newspapers. But in this same wheezing voice, this colourless voice which brought nothing to life, he also read from strange texts that you couldn't have found anywhere else.

He read the precepts of Lao-Tzu, through which the world seemed at once clear, concrete and utterly unknowable; he read excerpts from the I-Ching, whose meaning seemed as manifold as a hand of cards; finally he read from Sun Tzu on the art of war. He demonstrated that it is possible to drill and discipline anyone for battle. He demonstrated that obedience to military order is a human characteristic and diso- bedience is an anthropological exception; or an error.

'Give me a horde of unschooled peasants and I will have them drilled and disciplined as precisely as your guard,' Sun Tzu once said to the emperor. 'Following the principles of the art of war I can drill and discipline the whole world, as in a war.'

'Even my concubines?' asked the emperor. 'That flock of featherbrains?'

'Even them.'

'I do not believe you.'

'Allow me complete freedom and I will have them drilled as precisely as your finest soldiers.'

Amused, the emperor accepted, and Sun Tzu began to instruct the courtesans. The girls played along; they giggled, they tripped over themselves, nothing good came of it. The emperor smiled. 'I expected no better of them.'

'If words of command are not clear and distinct, if orders are not thoroughly understood, the general is to blame,' said Sun Tzu.

He explained again, more clearly this time. The drill began again, they went on laughing, they broke ranks and hid their faces behind their silken sleeves.

'But if his orders are clear and the soldiers nevertheless disobey,' said Sun Tzu, 'then it is the fault of their officers,' and he ordered that the emperor's favourite be decapitated, since she had started the laughing. The emperor protested, but his strategist respectfully insisted; he had been granted complete freedom. If His Majesty wished to see his plan accomplished, he had to allow the man he had entrusted with this mission to do as he saw fit. The emperor agreed, a little reluctantly, and the young woman was beheaded. A heavy sadness hung over the terrace where they played at war, the birds themselves fell silent, the flowers breathed no perfume, the butterflies ceased to flutter. The beautiful courtesans marched in silence, as disciplined as the finest soldiers. They moved as one, in serried ranks, united by the bonds of survivors, by that exhilaration triggered by the smell of fear.

But fear is merely a pretext given for obeying; for the most part, people prefer to follow orders. They will do anything to be together, to bathe in the stench of terror, to drink in that comforting thrill that dispels the terrible unease of loneliness.

Ants communicate through scent: they have scents for war, for flight, for attraction. They obey them invariably. As human beings, we are subject to unpredictable psychological humours that act like scents, and we like nothing better than to share them. When we are together, united, we think of nothing but running, slaughtering, fighting, one man against a hundred. We are no longer ourselves; we are as close to being who we truly are.

On a palace terrace, in the oblique evening rays that tinted the stone lions yellow, the courtesans marched in tiny steps before the heavy-hearted emperor. Night was drawing in, the light began to take on the dull hue of military uniforms, and still, to Sun Tzu's terse orders, the courtesans continued to march in rank, to the rhythmic clack of clogs, the rustle of dazzling silk tunics, whose colours no one thought to marvel at. Each individual body had vanished, all that remained was the movement determined by the strategist's orders.

The shop is loathsome. It had always been foul, now it is hateful, too. The thought occurs to Salagnon coming home after school on one of those winter days when afternoon is night.

Coming home from school is not Salagnon's favourite moment of the day. In the darkness a viscous cold rises from the ground; it feels like wading through water. Coming home on winter afternoons is like walking into a lake, heading home to a sleep like drowning, to numb unconsciousness. Coming home is like denying you have ever left, it means giving up on a day that might have been the start of a new life. Coming home is like crumpling up the day and tossing it aside like a botched drawing.

To come home in the afternoon is to throw away the day, thinks Salagnon, as he tramps the streets of the old town, where the huge wet paving stones glow more brightly than the street lamps that are too far apart. In the ancient streets of Lyon it is impossible to believe in the constancy of light.

Moreover he hates this house, though it is his home; he hates this shop with its wooden frontage, its storeroom at the back where his father piles his wares, the loft space above where the family live, his mother, his father and himself. He loathes it because the shop is hateful; and because he comes back here every afternoon as though it were his house, his home, his personal fount of human warmth, whereas it is no more than the place where he can take off his shoes. But he comes back here every afternoon. The shop is hateful. He says it over and over, and he goes inside.

The bell tinkles, instantly the tension mounts. His mother calls out before he has time to close the door.

'You took your time! Run and give your father a hand. He's snowed under.'

The bell tinkled again, a customer came in bringing a blast of cold air. With astonishing reflexes his mother turned and smiled. She has the same reflex as a gentleman passing a young woman with interesting curves: a reflex which precedes thought, a swivel of the neck triggered by the bell. Her forced smile is perfectly convincing. 'Monsieur?' She is an attractive woman with an elegant bearing who looks customers up and down with an air that everyone finds charming. They *want* to buy something from her.

Victorien ran to the storeroom, where his father was perched on a stepladder, struggling with boxes and sighing.

'Ah, there you are!'

From the top of the stepladder, glasses perched on the tip of his nose, he handed down a bundle of forms and invoices. Most were crumpled because 1943 paper cannot withstand Monsieur Salagnon's impatience, his sudden rages when his calculations go awry, the clamminess of his hands when he gets frustrated.

'It doesn't add up, the invoices don't tally. I can't make head or tail of it. Here, you're good with figures, you look over the accounts.'

Victorien took the sheaf of pages and sat on the bottom rung of the stepladder. Dust hovered, suspended in the air. The low voltage lamps are not up to the task, they shine like tiny suns through dense fog. He could not see properly, but it did not matter. If it was just figures he had only to read and add them up, but what his father is asking is not simple bookkeeping. The Maison Salagnon keeps various sets of books and they change from day to day. Wartime requires negotiating a bureaucratic labyrinth without getting lost or injured; it entails making a careful distinction between items of various categories: those whose sale is permitted, those tolerated, those restricted, those that are prohibited but incur minor penalties, those prohibited and punishable by death, and those that have escaped legislation. The Maison Salagnon dabbles in all aspects of the wartime economy. The entries in its ledgers are a jumble of the real, the hidden, the invented, the plausible-just-in-case, the unverifiable that dare not speak its name; there are even a few accurate entries. Needless to say, the boundaries of the various categories are vague, agreed in secret, known only to father and son.

'I'll never be able to sort it out.'

'Victorien, there's about to be an inspection, so I've no time for your moods. The stock has to tally with the accounts and with the regulations, otherwise we're dead. You and me both. Someone informed on me. Bastard! And he did it so subtly I don't know who struck the blow.'

'Usually you come to some arrangement.'

'I did come to an arrangement: that's why I'm not banged up. They're just coming to take a look. Given the circumstances, that amounts to favouritism. It's all change at the *préfecture*: they want everything shipshape. I don't know who to deal with any more. In the meantime, there can be no errors in that stack of papers.'

'How do you expect me to sort it out? It's all fake, except what is true. I don't know any more.'

His father fell silent and stared at him intently. Being higher up the stepladder, he looked down on him. When he finally spoke, he articulated every word.

'Tell me, Victorien: what's the point of you studying instead of working? What is the point if you're not capable of keeping books that look real?'

He has a point: what is the point of studying if not to understand the intangible and the abstract, to learn how to disassemble, reassemble and repair the mechanism that regulates the world? Victorien hesitated and sighed, and that is what he felt bad about. He stood up with the crumped bundles and took from the shelf a large notebook tied with cloth.

'I'll see what I can do,' he says, his voice barely audible.

'Be quick about it.'

Taken aback, he stops at the door, weighed down with documents.

'Be quick about it,' his father says again. 'They could come and inspect the place tonight, tomorrow, any day. And the Germans will be with them. They can't stand seeing their loot being diverted. They suspect the French of doing deals behind their backs.'

'They're not wrong. But that's the rules of the game, isn't it? Taking back the stuff they take from us.'

'They've got all the power, so there are no rules in this game. The only way to survive is to be clever but careful. We have to live like rats: never seen but ever present, weak but cunning, nibbling at our masters' food right under their noses at night, while they're asleep.'

Clearly pleased with his simile, he gives a wink. Victorien curls his upper lip. 'Like this?' He bares his incisors, rolls his eyes in a shifty, worried way, giving little squeaks. His father's smile disappears: the rat, so well imitated, disgusts him. He regrets his simile. Victorien relaxes his features; he is the one smiling now. 'If we have to bare our teeth, better a lion's than a rat's. Or a wolf's. It's easier and just as effective. I'd like to bare my teeth like a wolf's fangs.'

'Of course you would, son. So would I. But we don't get to choose our nature. We have to follow the instincts we are born with, and from now on we'll be born rats. It's not the end of the world, being a rat. They thrive as well as humans, and at our expense; they live better than wolves, even if it is away from the light.'

Away from the light, that's how we live, thought Victorien. The city is dark enough already, with its narrow alleyways, its black walls, the fog that hides it from itself; and now they impose a blackout, paint the windows blue, keep the curtains drawn day and night.

In fact, there is no daylight. Only shadows where we can scurry like rats. We live like Eskimos in endless polar night, like Arctic rats moving from inky darkness to murky twilight. Maybe I'll move there, he thought, to Greenland, whoever wins this war. It might be dark and cold, but outside everything will be brilliant white. Here, everything is yellow, a sickly yellow. The dim streetlights, the roughcast mud walls, the packing crates, the dust from the shops, everything is yellow, even the ashen faces utterly drained of blood. I dream of seeing blood. Here it is so well protected it no longer flows. Not from wounds, not through our veins, we no longer know where blood is. I want to see crimson trails in the snow, just for the dazzling contrast, to prove there is still life. But everything here is yellow, murky; there is a war on and I can hardly see to put one foot in front of the other.

He almost tripped. He caught the sheaf of papers just in time and trudged off, muttering, dragging his heels, in that sullen way that teenagers have at home, two steps forward, one step back, then suddenly stopping altogether. Though he has boundless energy when outside, at home with his parents he scarcely moves; it does not suit him, but he doesn't know how to overcome it: within these walls he plods, he feels a yellowish fever, a hepatic malaise the colour of a piss-poor painting lit by a faint glow.

It is past closing time and Mme Salagnon has retreated to the back of the shop, where they live. Victorien looks at her from behind, the curve of her shoulders, the arch of her back and the thick, protruding knot of her apron. She is bent over the sink – women spend a lot of time making things wet. 'This is no place and no position for a boy,' she would often sigh; and that sigh changes, sometimes weary, sometimes outraged, but always strangely curiously satisfied.

'I want you downstairs early,' she says without turning. 'Your uncle is coming round to dinner tonight.'

'I have to work,' he says, waving his exercise book at his mother's back.

This is how they communicate, through gestures, never looking at each other. He goes up to the loft with a spring in his step; he likes his uncle.

His room was exactly his size; his head brushed the ceiling when he stood up, a bed and table were enough to fill the space. 'We had planned to use it as a cupboard,' his father would say, half joking, 'and when you're gone, it'll be a junk room.' A carbide lamp cast a bright glow on the table just big enough for an exercise book. It was enough. The rest of the room needed no light. He lit the lamp, sat down and hoped something would happen to stop him finishing his work. The hiss of acetylene sounded like the constant chirrup of crickets, making the night deeper still. He sat alone in front of this circle of light. He looked at his motionless hands in front of him. From birth, Victorien Salagnon had had large hands attached to sturdy forearms. He could clench them into heavy fists and pound the table, hard; and he could strike true, because he had a keen eye.

In other circumstances such a trait would have made him a powerful man. But in the France of 1943 there was no outlet for such strength. You could be touchy, short-tempered, give the impression of being reckless, you could talk about action, but it was all a diversion. Everyone bent with the times, made themselves as small as possible so as to give no purchase to the winds of history. The France of 1943 was closed up like a country house in winter, the door bolted, the storm shutters secured. The wind of history could seep in only through the cracks, cold draughts that would not fill a sail; just enough to catch pneumonia and die alone in your room.

Victorien Salagnon had a gift he had not wished for. In other circumstances he might not have noticed it, but having to spend so much time holed up in his room meant staring at his hands. His hand could see, as an eye can see; and his eye could touch like a hand. Whatever he saw, he could trace in ink, in brush, in pencil, and it reappeared in black on a white sheet of paper. His hand followed his eye as though joined by a nerve, as though some cord had been laid by accident at the moment he was conceived. He was able to draw anything he saw, and anyone who saw his drawings recognized what they felt when they looked at a landscape, at a face, but were unable to understand.

Victorien Salagnon would have preferred not to tie himself up in subtle shades of meaning, he wanted to attack, but he had a gift. He did not know where it came from and it was both gratifying and frustrating. This talent manifested itself as a physical sensation: some people hear a ringing in their ears, see spots in front of their eyes, have pins and needles in their legs; Victorien Salagnon felt the heft of a brush between his fingers, the viscosity of ink, the grain of the paper. Superstitiously, he attributed these feelings to the properties of the ink, which was black enough to contain a host of dark designs.

He had an enormous inkwell carved from a block of glass, which contained a reservoir of this miraculous liquid. It sat in the middle of the table; it was never moved. It was so heavy it was probably bomb-proof; even after a direct hit it would have been found unscathed amid the human remains, its contents unspilled, ready to capture the deeds and actions of another victim in its gleaming pitch.

The sensation of ink was like a pang of emotion. Forced by circumstance in 1943 to spend long hours shut away, he nurtured this gift that he might otherwise have ignored. He allowed his hand to move restlessly, bounded by the edges of a page. The restlessness served as an outlet for the inactivity in the rest of his body. He vaguely thought of moulding his talent into art, but it was a notion that stayed within his room, never leaving the circle of light, wide as an open book, cast by the carbide lamp.

The sensation of the ink eluded him; he did not know how to follow it. The perfect moment was always the desire that came just before he picked up the brush.

He opened the lid. The dark mass in the hefty glass inkwell did not stir. The Indian ink gives off neither movement nor light; its perfect blackness has characteristics of a vacuum. Unlike other opaque liquids, like wine or muddy water, ink is impervious to light, lets none pass through. Ink is a chasm whose true size is difficult to know: it could be a single drop the brush will suck up or an abyss into which it will disappear. Ink confounds light.

Victorien thumbed through the invoices, opened his exercise book. From a pile, he dug out a rough draft of a Latin translation. On the back of it he sketched a face. A gaping mouth. He had no desire to deal with the dubious accounts. He knew exactly what he needed to change to make it look convincing. He drew a pair of round eyes and closed each with a blot of ink. All he had to do was to try to remember which entries were fake. Not all of them. He was the one who had made up the invoices in the first place. Behind the head he painted a shadow that extended to one side of the face. There was a sense of mass. He excelled at doing two things at once. It's like tensing antagonistic muscles simultaneously: it is as tiring as working; it gives you pause to think.

Suddenly a siren erupted; others joined the wailing chorus, ripping the night like a crumpled tissue. The building was in uproar. Doors slammed, loud cries in the stairwell, the shrill, grating voice of his mother already fading: 'We have to tell Victorien.' 'He will have heard,' came his father's voice, barely audible; then, nothing.

Victorien wiped his nib on a piece of cloth. Otherwise the ink cakes; the liquid glue that gives it its sheen dries to a thick crust. Ink is actually a solid. Then he extinguished the lamp and walked up the main staircase. He groped his way, but he encountered no one else, heard nothing but the brassy chorus of sirens. As he reached the top, they fell silent. He opened the little window overlooking the roof. Outside, the world was still. He struggled through the opening, which was scarcely wider than his shoulders, and cautiously crept along the roof, crouching, testing the tiles with his feet as he moved. When he reached the edge he sat down, letting his legs dangle over the side. He felt nothing but his own weight resting on his buttocks and the icy damp of the terracotta through his trousers. A six-storey abyss yawned in front of him, though he could not see it. Fog enveloped him; faintly luminescent, it was not bright enough to see, but cast enough light that he knew his eyes were not closed. He was sitting in an emptiness. A space that had neither shape nor form. He was suspended; below him the notion of the void, above him, the incoming planes laden with bombs. But for the cold, he would not have believed he was there at all.

A faraway rumble came from far up in the sky; there was no source, merely the generalized resonance of the heavens rubbed with a finger. Suddenly, shards of light appeared, groups of them, long wavering reeds, feeling their way through empty space. Orange blots blossomed as they reached their peak, dotted lines trailing behind; a moment later he heard muffled explosions and crackling. He could now see the roofline and the dark gulf beneath his feet; anti-aircraft guns were firing at the planes laden with bombs he could not yet see.

He felt a hand on his shoulder; he flinched, slipped, felt a firm fist pull him back.

'What are you playing at?' his uncle breathed in his ear. 'Everyone is down in the shelter.'

'Given the choice, I'd prefer not to die in a hole. Can you imagine a direct hit? The whole building collapses and we all die in the cellar. It would be impossible to tell my remains from my mother's or my father's or the tins of pâté he's got stockpiled. Everything would be buried.'

His uncle did not answer, nor did he take his hand from Salagnon's shoulder; he often held his tongue and waited for the person speaking to run out of steam.

'Anyway, I love fireworks.'

'Idiot.'

The sound of the planes dwindled, headed towards the south, then there was silence. The spears of light suddenly guttered out.

The all-clear sounded. He felt his uncle's hand relax.

'Come on, let's get you down. Careful not to slip. All you did was risk falling off the roof. You'd have been picked up and tossed into a mass grave of those who died of unknown causes. No one would have known anything about your bid for independence. Come on.'

In the stairwell, the lights had been turned on again and they encountered pyjamaed families. Neighbours called out to each other, carrying their unfinished dinners back up in baskets. The children were still playing, whining about having to go inside again, and required a clip round the ear to send them back to bed.

Victorien followed his uncle. His presence, even if he did not speak, changed things. When he returned their son, his parents said nothing, but took their places at the table. His mother was wearing a pretty dress and had put on lipstick. Her lips quivered and she smiled when she spoke. Her father read the label on a bottle of red wine aloud, stressing the vintage with a wink at the uncle.

'You can't get it any more,' he said. 'No one in France can lay hands on it. The English used to drink it before the war. These days the Germans confiscate it. I managed to palm them off with a few bottles of something else; they know nothing about wine. And I kept back a few bottles, including this one.'

He poured a generous glass for the uncle, one for himself, and a more modest measure for Victorien and his mother. His uncle, a man of few words, ate thoughtlessly while his parents bustled around his uncompromising bulk. They babbled, keeping the conversation alive with feigned enthusiasm, taking turns recounting jokes and stories that elicited a wan smile from his uncle. They gradually came adrift, balloons propelled aimlessly around the room by the hot air escaping from their mouths. His uncle's sheer size inevitably shifted the centre of gravity. It was impossible to know what he was thinking or even whether he was thinking; he was content merely to be present and his presence distorted space. Being around him you felt the Earth list; it was impossible to stay upright; you stumbled, flailing your arms ridiculously so as not to fall. Victorien was fascinated by his uncle. He longed to understand the mystery of his presence. How to explain the atmospheric disturbance caused by his uncle to anyone who had not met him? More than once he had made the attempt: his uncle, he had said, was physically impressive; but since he was neither large, nor fat, nor strong, nor anything in particular, such a description inevitably trailed off. He did not know what else to say, so he said nothing. He would have had to sketch, not his uncle, but everything around him. Art has that power; it is a shortcut that shows, to the great relief of the written word.

Tirelessly, his father held forth on the intricacies of wartime commerce, unthinkingly punctuating the high points where the interlopers were swindled by the occupied with an elbow jab, a wink. The fact that the Boche did not notice anything amiss triggered his loudest laughs. Victorien joined in the conversation; since he could not mention his rooftop adventure, he recounted the Gallic wars in minute detail. He became impassioned, inventing little details, the clash of swords, the charge of the cavalry, the chink of steel on steel; he expounded on the discipline of the Romans, the strength of the Gauls, the parity of arms and disparity of spirit, the role of authority and the efficacy of terror. His uncle listened with a fond smile. At length he placed a hand on his nephew's arm. This shut him up.

'That was all two thousand years ago, Victorien.'

'It's full of timeless lessons.'

'In 1943 we don't tell war stories.'

Victorien blushed and his hands, which had added verve to his tale, fell on to the table.

'You're brave, Victorien, and you're full of spirit. But oil and water inevitably separate. When your courage has separated from childish things, and if it is courage that rises to the surface, then you can come and find me and we'll talk.'

'Find you where? To talk about what?'

'When the time comes, you'll know. But remember: wait until oil and water have separated.'

His mother nodded; she glanced from one to the other as though counselling her son to pay attention and do as his uncle said. His father gave a hoarse laugh and topped up the glasses.

A knock at the door; everyone started. His father froze, the bottle aslant over his glass, no wine flowed. The knock came again. 'Well, go on! Open it!' Still his father hesitated, not knowing what to do with his bottle, his napkin, his chair, uncertain which to deal with first and so rooted to the spot. The knocking grew louder, swift raps that were clearly an order, an intimation of mistrust. He opened the door a crack and in slipped the local police officer with a little pointed face. His flickering eyes took in the room and he smiled, baring teeth too big for his mouth.

'Took your time, didn't you? I've just been down in the shelter. Came by to make sure everything's all right after the alert. Doing my rounds. All present and accounted for. Lucky we didn't take a hit tonight, because some didn't make it to the shelter.'

While he talked he greeted Madame with a nod, lingered on Victorien with his toothy smile, and when he had finished he turned to the uncle. He had noticed him immediately, but he had bided his time. He stared at him, letting a faint unease creep in.

'And you are, monsieur?'

'My brother,' said Victorien's mother with guilty haste. 'My brother, he's just passing through.'

'Is he sleeping here?'

'Yes. We've made up a bed with a couple of armchairs.'

He hushed her with a wave: he recognized the self-justification in her voice. A pleading tone that gave him his power. He wanted something more: he wanted this man he did not know to look away, to babble breathlessly when addressing him.

'Are you registered?'

'No.'

The cadence of the phrase indicated that he had finished. The word dropped, a steel ball in the sand, and rolled no further. The officer, accustomed to the garrulous torrents usually unleashed by a single glare, all but lost his balance. His eyes flickered restlessly; he did not know what to do next. In this game where he was master, everyone had to play their roles. The uncle was refusing to play.

Eventually, Monsieur Salagnon broke the awkward silence with a jovial laugh. He grabbed a glass, filled it and proffered it to the officer. Victorien's mother pushed a chair behind him, knocking against his knees, forcing him to sit. This allowed him to lower his eyes, to save face, to smile broadly. He sipped the wine with a thoughtful expression; they could talk of other things now. He declared the wine excellent. Victorien's father smiled modestly and once again read the label aloud.

'Of course. Is there anything left of the vintage?'

'Two – including this one. The other is for you, since you're clearly a connoisseur. You've done a lot for the people in this building, you deserve a little reward.'

He took out an identical bottle and pressed it into the officer's hands. The man feigned embarrassment.

'Come, come, I want you to have it. You can drink a toast to us. It'll be a little reminder that Salagnon sells only the best.'

The officer savoured the wine, rolling his tongue noisily, being careful not to look in the direction of the uncle.

'And what is your role, exactly?' the uncle asked innocently.

The officer made an effort to turn to face him, but his eyes were unsteady and he had trouble focusing.

'I uphold law and order, make sure that everyone's home, that everything's going as it should. The regular police have too much on their plates. They'd never be able to cope. It's the duty of responsible citizens to help.'

'It's a noble task, and a thankless one. Order is important, isn't it? The Germans realized it before we did, but we'll get there in the end. In fact, it was a lack of order that did for us. People were not prepared to obey orders, to know their place, do their duty. It was the pursuit of pleasure that ruined this country; especially among the working classes, egged on by permissive, moronic legislation. They preferred the fantasy of an easy life to the hard truth of impending death. Luckily we have men like you to bring us back to reality. I salute you, monsieur.'

He raised his glass and drank, and the officer felt obliged to clink glasses, though he could not help but feel this convoluted speech contained a trap. But the uncle adopted a demure expression that Victorien had never seen in him. 'You're not serious?' he whispered. The uncle's affably naive smile cast an awkward pall over the table. The officer got up, hugging the bottle to him.

'I have to finish my rounds. You, you'll be gone by tomorrow. And I won't have seen a thing.'

'Don't you worry. I won't cause you any trouble.'

The tone, simply the tone, sent the officer scurrying. Victorien's father closed the door, pressed his ear to it, mimed listening to the retreating footsteps, then crept back to the table in pantomime fashion.

'Such a shame,' he laughed. 'We had two bottles, but thanks to the disasters of war we have only one now.'

'That's precisely the problem.'

The uncle could make people uneasy with a few words. He said nothing more. Victorien knew that one day he would follow this man or men like him, wherever they went; as far as they would go. He would follow these men who, through the melodic precision of their words could cause doors to open, winds to cease, mountains to move. He would entrust all his purposeless strength to such men.

'No one forced you to give it to him,' said his mother. 'He'd have left anyway.'

'It's safer like this. This way he'll feel a little in our debt. You have to know how to compromise.'

The mother said nothing more. She simply gave a half-mocking, half-defeated smile, her lips, beautifully red that evening, curling slightly. In war, she knew her place, since it had not changed; to her, the enemy remained her husband.

* * *

A walled park thick with trees stretched behind La Grande Institution. It was so vast that from the centre it was impossible to see the boundaries, and it seemed as though the paths that disappeared into the thick foliage extended all the way to the blue peaks that floated above the treetops. Crossing the park by following the paths was a long meander between crudely trimmed shrubs, beneath low-hanging branches, through dense thickets of ferns that closed up as you passed, along rutted paths; walking further, you passed dried-up ponds, moss-covered fountains, cabins whose doors were chained shut but their windows gaped wide, before finally reaching the far wall you had quite forgotten in the struggle to dodge branches and avoid sinking into the thick bed of leaves. The wall stretched away, soaring, endless, a number of small locked gates, half-buried, offering the only way out, though the locks, thick with rust, no longer opened. No one ever came this far.

La Grande Institution allowed the local scout troop to use the grounds. It was like a forest, but safer, and no one could care less what they got up to within this enclave of nature and virtuous athleticism, as long as they stayed within its boundaries.

The scout troop met in the gatekeeper's lodge, which had been furnished with pews from the church. There was no longer a gatekeeper. The house was ramshackle; year upon year it stored up the cold. The little scouts shivered in their shorts, breathing clouds of mist. They rubbed their hands on their knees, waiting for the signal that started the big game, so that they could finally run around and warm up. But they had to wait and listen to the preamble by a young priest with a sparse beard, the sort who hiked up his cassock in the playground and played football with the pupils.

He always spoke beforehand and his speeches were too long. He gave them a lecture on the virtues of the gymnasial arts. To the little, bare-kneed scouts this clearly meant 'gymnastics', which was a posh word for 'sports', and they shivered patiently, knowing exercise would warm them up and eager to get on with it. Only Salagnon remarked on the young priest's insistence on using the term 'gymnasial', a word he was clearly taken with. Every time he uttered it, his voice would hover, suspended, Salagnon would nod, and the young priest's eyes flashed a brief metallic glint, the way a window being opened shimmers as it catches the sun for a brief instant; it goes unseen, too fleeting to be observed, but you sense the dazzle without knowing whence it comes.

The bored scouts waited for the end of the speech. In their threadbare uniforms they were as cold as if they had been naked. On this winter afternoon nothing could have kept them warm, nothing except moving, running, physical activity of some sort. Only movement could protect them from the all-pervading cold, and they were forbidden to move.

As the young priest finished his speech the scouts stood up, as though paying close attention. They listened for the end, for the unmistakable falling cadence that marks the last full stop. Accustomed to the rhythms of these speeches, the scouts, as one, would get to their feet. The young priest was moved by their energy, the purity of that delicate age as childhood passes, one that, alas, like flowers, does not last. He announced a big game of Touch-or-See.

The rules of the game were simple: two teams were sent into the woods, each to capture the other. One team captured by touch, the other by seeing. For one team being seen is fatal, for the other, being touched.

The young priest called the teams Minoses and Medusas, being a man of letters, but the scouts called them Touchers and Seers; theirs was a more straightforward language and they had other preoccupations.

Salagnon was King Minos, leader of the Touchers. He and his group disappeared into the dense thickets. As soon as they entered the woods he had them march in step. He told them to take short strides, to stay in rank; and they obeyed, because at first we always obey. As soon as they reached a clearing, he organized them, splitting them into groups of three, whose members must always stay together. 'They only have to see us and we lose; but we've got to get within arm's reach. Their weapon has much greater range than ours. But luckily we've got the forest. And we're disciplined. They're too cocky because they think they'll win, but it's their confidence that makes them vulnerable. Our weakness forces us to be cunning. This is your weapon: discipline and obedience. You have to think as one, you have to act as one, very precisely, as soon as you sense a moment of opportunity. You can't afford to hesitate; those moments will not come again.'

He had them march in step around the clearing. Then had them all perform the same action: at his signal, they were to silently throw themselves to the ground, then at his signal jump up and all run in the same direction. Then throw themselves on the ground again. At first, the drill amused them, later they protested. Salagnon had been expecting this. One of the taller boys, whose handsome face had a dusting of downy hair and whose hair was slicked back and neatly parted, led the protest.

'What, again?' he said, as Salagnon whistled for them to throw themselves to the ground.

'Yes. Again.'

The boy remained standing. The other scouts lying on the ground now raised their heads. Their bare knees against the damp leaves were starting to feel the cold.

'Until when?'

'Perfection.'

'I'm not doing this any more. It's got nothing to do with the game.'

Salagnon betrayed no emotion. He stared at the boy, who forced himself to hold his gaze. The scouts on their bellies hesitated. Salagnon nodded to two of the taller lads, almost as tall as the boy defying him.

'Vuillermoz and Gilet, grab him.'

They scrabbled to their feet and grabbed his arms, tentatively at first, then, when he started to struggle, more firmly. As he resisted, they held him solidly with triumphant smiles.

Some brambles were growing in a hollow. Salagnon strode over to the prisoner, undid his belt and tugged down his shorts.

'Toss him in there!'

'You've got no right!'

The boy tried to run, but was thrown, trouserless, into the brambles. The thorny tendrils held him fast, beads of blood appeared on his skin. He burst into tears. No one came to his rescue. One of the scouts picked up his shorts and threw them into the brambles, and the more he struggled the more entangled they became. There were giggles.

'If we want to win, our team has to be a machine. You have to perform like cogs in a machine. And if you want go round saying you're not machines, that you've got feelings, that's too bad. You lose. And we have to win.'

He organized each group to act as a single soldier: one was designated the 'head', he listened for his orders and, using finger signals, passed them on; the other two were the 'legs', they followed, they ran; when necessary they became 'arms', in order to catch. These sets of three he divided into two groups under the command of the two boys who had become his henchmen, prepared to follow his every command. 'And you,' he said to his victim, who had emerged from the brambles and was pulling on his shorts, sniffling, 'get back in rank and don't let me hear another peep from you.'

The drilling continued and cohesion was achieved. The 'heads' vied with each other in their zeal. When everyone was ready, Salagnon put them into position. He hid them in the bushes and behind the big trees that lined the path that led from the gatekeeper's lodge deep into the woods. They waited.

In silence they waited, blending in with the leaves, crouching under ferns, eyes fixed on the clearing where the other team would appear. They waited. The damp from the ground seeped into their clothes to their skin, which drew in the cold as a lamp's wick draws in paraffin. Dry branches pierced their bivouacs, prodding them in the stomach, the thigh; at first they shifted noiselessly to avoid them, then learned to endure the prodding. Their faces were screened by ferns with velvet fronds, their tightly curled crosiers ready to burst open at the first sign of spring. They could smell the intense, green perfume that cut through the whitish odour of damp mushrooms. Their breathing became so calm that they could now hear what resonated inside them; their thick arteries boomed, each channelling the pounding drum of their heart. Trees gently collided, creaking restlessly; raindrops fell here and there with a noise of rustling paper; some fell on them and they had to steel themselves and make a slow, silent gesture to wipe them away.

The others were coming.

There came the booming thwack of wood, clear and sharp, of branch against tree trunk: the Seers were passing the first group. They had struck the trunk of a hollow tree.

The Seers baulked, but continued on their way. There are forest noises that can be ignored and others one should listen for, but who is to know which is which? There were four of them, moving shoulder to shoulder with measured steps, each watching the edge of the path. The Touchers could not get close without being seen. Step by step, they moved forwards, nostrils flaring; it is not of much use, but when your senses are heightened all the organs are stirred. They passed Salagnon, who did not flinch. No one moved; the four boys passed. Then Salagnon shouted: 'Two!' and the nearest second group bounded to their feet and dashed towards the Seers, who turned towards the noise of snapping twigs and triumphantly cried: 'Seen! Seen!' Obedient to the rules, the Touchers froze and raised their hands. The Seers, forgetting all caution, went over to seize their prisoners. They were laughing at this easy victory, but their weapon was so much the stronger. They were about to name the prisoners, as the rules required, but they were laughing too hard to be able to speak. They missed a beat. 'Three!' roared Salagnon, and Group Three leapt up from the ferns and, in a single bound, crossed the few paces separating them from the Seers and grabbed them from behind before they could turn. All but one, who took off without a word, running as fast as his legs could carry him down the first path he found. 'Four!' shouted Salagnon, cupping his hands into a loud-hailer. The runner, breathless, stopped at the first sheltered spot on the path and leaned against a tree to marshal his wits, only to be seized by the group hiding behind the very tree where he had sought refuge.

Shouts rang out from the direction of the lodge. Group One arrived, holding the last Seers by the shoulders, bewildered, ambushed from behind as they were rushing towards the commotion. They had run heedlessly, confident that they could make multiple captures with a single blink, keeping out of reach, their eyes their only weapon. But no. Every one was captured.

'And there you have it,' said Salagnon.

'But we saw you first,' they protested.

'You didn't say their names. No name, no game. Losers have no rights, they shut their traps. Let's head back.'

The young priest had made himself comfortable in the scouts' hut, near the stove lit with twigs and kindling. They marched in, making him jump; he got to his feet quickly, dropping the book of which he had just read a single page. He picked it up again and held it back to front so the boys could not see the title.

'We won, Father.'

'Already? But the game was supposed to last at least two hours.'

The Touchers roughly pushed the dejected Seers, each flanked by two boys, into the hut. The boy who had been tossed into the brambles was no less eager than his teammates, shoving his prisoners just a little harder than was necessary to guide them; and they allowed themselves to be pushed.

'Well, congratulations, Salagnon. You are a fine leader.'

'This is all foolishness, Father. These are children's games.'

'Games are a way of preparing for adulthood.'

'There's no such thing as adulthood in France now, Father, not for men, anyway. The whole country is peopled by women and children, and one old man.'

Embarrassed, the priest did not know what to say. The subject was a sensitive one, Salagnon's tone perhaps provocative. His cold blue eyes tried to pierce his. The scouts huddled around the stove, where the fire of twigs gave scant warmth.

'Good. Well then, if the game is over, let's stay here for a while. Send out the prisoners to collect firewood, that'll teach them. Stoke the fire, gather round. We'll tell some stories. I propose that we recount Captain Salagnon's gallant feats in the appropriate manner. With an epic poem and an ode to his glory. We'll publish it in the patrol journal and he can provide the illustrations of the battle himself, with his lively brushstrokes. Because a hero is not only the one who wins, but the one who knows how to proclaim his victory.'

'As you wish, Father,' said Salagnon in a tone that was ironic or perhaps bitter, he was not sure himself; and he assigned the tasks, divided up the groups and supervised the activity. Before long the fire was roaring.

The day was already drawing in. The darkness became impenetrable, and this happened more quickly in the park than it did in the city. The stove crackled; through its open door they could see the embers flicker and throb with light like the surface of a star. Sitting huddled on the floor, scouts listened to tales invented by the others. Shoulder pressed against shoulder, thigh against thigh, they made the most of the accumulated body heat. They gave themselves up to simple dreams based on simple perceptions related to the group, to rest, to heat. Salagnon was bored, but he liked these little scouts. The flickering fire cast shadows on their faces, throwing their wide eyes, their plump cheeks, their fleshy, childlike lips into sharp relief. Although scouting was an admirable institution, he thought to himself, it was curious to be playing such games at seventeen. His director of studies understood this. He in turn might become a priest, a scout leader, look after children, devote himself to a future generation that might escape the fate of this one. He might become like this man sitting among them who smiled at the angels, wedged in by the shoulders of the two biggest boys, arms cradling his cassock-covered knees. But the light he sometimes saw in the priest's eyes deterred him. He did not want to take this man's place. But what place could he take in the France of 1943?

He did as he was told: he drew sketches for the patrol newspaper. He took pleasure in this, people praised his talent. Because this, too, is art: creating a space in which to enjoy oneself, setting its boundaries, inhabiting it with one's whole being, and getting praise for it to boot. But he was not sure that the life of a man could be bounded by a sheet of drawing paper.

The inspection came about. They arrived at night, four of them, like guests; a bored officer led the way, because his gait was longer than the others'; trailing behind came a civil servant from the *préfecture*, swaddled in coat and scarf, hat pushed down over his eyes, clutching a leather briefcase; two soldiers with rifles at their shoulders followed in step behind.

The officer saluted with a click of his heels, though he did not remove his cap. He was on duty, for which he apologized. The civil servant shook Salagnon *père* by the hand for a little too long, and made himself comfortable. He put down his coat, keeping his scarf on, set his briefcase on the table and opened it. They brought him the ledgers. One soldier stayed by the door, rifle at his shoulder, while the other disappeared into the storeroom to inspect the shelves.

Teetering on the stepladder, he was soon covered in a film of brown dust. He read the labels and barked figures in German. The civil servant ran a pen down the columns and asked detailed questions, which the officer translated into his brutish tongue; from the depths of the storeroom the soldier called back the answers, which the officer translated into a mellifluous French for the benefit of the official sitting behind him, not looking at him. One hand in his pocket, which rucked the tails of his jacket, the tall, slim officer perched a single buttock on the table like a bird about to take wing. His shoulders were straight, his cap tilted at a rakish angle, the neatly pressed trousers tucked into his moulded boots. He was not yet thirty, though it was impossible to be more precise, since in his face youth warred with hard-won experience. A purple scar traced a line across his temple, along his cheek and down his neck, disappearing into the collar of his black jacket. He was an SS officer, his cap emblazoned with a *Totenkopf*, but no one could remember his rank. Thus suspended, an elegant bird of prey, a nonchalant athlete, he resembled one of those extraordinarily beautiful posters which proclaimed that, throughout Europe, the SS dispassionately settled matters of life and death.

Sitting behind him, facing the official going over the accounts, Salagnon was working on his Latin composition; in the margin of his notebook he sketched the scene: the motionless soldier, the official bent over his task, the officer who waited with obvious indifference for these day-to-day problems to be resolved; and his own father smiling, candid, open, amenable to all requests, biddable without being obsequious, friendly without being cloying, with the aloofness that might be expected of the vanquished; a magnificent performance.

At last the official closed the ledger, pushed back his chair, sighed.

'Monsieur Salagnon, your books are entirely in order. You have respected the laws of wartime economy. Do not think that we doubted it for a minute, but these are terrible times and we are obliged to verify.'

He concluded his remarks with an exaggerated wink behind the back of the German. Salagnon *père* returned the wink then turned to the officer.

'I have to say I'm relieved. Everything is so complicated these days...' His lips quivered with a suppressed smile. 'It's so easy to make a mistake whose consequences in wartime could be incalculable. May I offer you a glass of my finest cognac?'

'We shall take our leave. There will be no drinks. We did not come here for an aperitif, Monsieur, we came to investigate your dealings.'

The official snapped shut his briefcase and pulled on his coat, helped by an anxious Salagnon, who dared not insist. The German declining to accept his offer unsettled him.

Emerging from the storeroom, the soldier dusted himself off and carefully buckled the chinstrap of his helmet. Hands behind his back, the officer paced distractedly while waiting for the others to finish dressing. He paused behind Victorien, leaned over the boy's shoulder and ran a gloved finger under a line of text.

'That verb should take the accusative rather than the dative, young man. You need to pay attention to your cases. You French people often get it wrong. You don't know how to decline a verb, you're not accustomed to it as we are.'

He tapped the page to drum in his advice, dislodging the page on which Victorien had been writing. He noticed the sketch in the margin: the soldier standing stiffly to attention as though carved in stone, the officer, seen from behind, like a crestfallen bird, the official bent over the ledger, peering over the glasses perched on the bridge of his nose, and Salagnon *père*, smiling, tipping him the wink. Victorien blushed, but made no move to cover the drawing, it was too late. The officer placed his hand on his shoulder and squeezed.

'Be careful in your translations, young man. These are difficult times. Devote your energies to your studies.'

His hand took wing, the officer stood up straight, barked an order in German and the men trooped out together; the officer leading the way, the two privates bringing up the rear. On the threshold he turned back to Victorien. Without smiling, he gave him a wink, then disappeared into the darkness. Salagnon *père* closed the door, waited in silence for a few moments, then stamped his feet with joy.

'We got them! They didn't suspect a thing. You have a great gift, Victorien, your work is perfect!'

'Do men know why they survive the battle? Seldom through bravery, more often through indifference: the indifference of an enemy who, on a whim, chose to strike another; the indifference of Fate, which chose to forget us this time.'

'What's that you're saying?'

'It's the text I'm translating.'

'Foolishness, your Latin verses. The cunning survive, that's all there is to it. A little luck, a little silver-tongued eloquence and you're home free. Leave your Romans in their graves and go and do something useful. A little bookkeeping, for example.'

Victorien carried on with his homework, not daring to look up at his father. The officer's wink would for ever remain his worst memory of that war.

The uncle reappeared, had his dinner, slept and was off again in the morning. No one dared tell him about the inspection. They sensed that telling him that everything had gone well would not have made him happy; on the contrary, it would have piqued his contempt, even his anger. The uncle was a brute, the times willed it so; these were no times for the soft-hearted. Over the past fifteen years the whole world had seen a gradual increase in seriousness. In the 1940s this brute force reached an intensity that was difficult for a human frame to endure. The soft-hearted suffered most. They withered, became limp. They dissolved into a viscous liquid. They ended up as compost, an ideal nutrient that allowed others to grow more swiftly, more aggressively, and thereby win the race for sunlight.

The uncle had fought in this war for the two months of France's involvement. He had been issued a rifle, one that he cleaned, checked and oiled every night, but he had never fired a shot, except in the practice grounds behind the Maginot Line. He spent three-quarters of the year in a blockhouse, his rifle by his side, guarding fortifications so well designed that they were never captured. France was captured, but not these ramparts worthy of Vauban, which were abandoned without so much as a crack in their handsome, camouflaged concrete.

It was cosy inside. Everything was provided. The previous war had been marked by crude, makeshift work. The French trenches had been hellish quagmires, so utterly disorganized, so shoddy compared to the others; they had so admired the captured enemy trenches – so clean, so sturdy, so well drained – that they had decided to make up for lost time. All the problems thrown up by the previous war were painstakingly resolved. By 1939 France was in excellent shape to fight the battles of 1915. As a result, the uncle had spent several months underground in a barrack room that was clean, not infested by rats and considerably less damp than the muddy dugouts in which his father had once rotted – literally rotted, with fungus sprouting between his toes. They alternated between air raid warnings, target practice and sunbathing in an underground room fitted with UV lights that they entered wearing sunglasses. Army medics reckoned that, given the heavy fortifications of the garrisons, rickets would be more lethal than enemy fire.

Early in May they were moved to a forested area that was less well fortified. The weather was conducive to working in the woods, the earth beneath their spades remained dry and smelled wholesome. They dug in around the gunners, who had hidden their barrels in holes camouflaged with logs. By mid-May, having heard no sound but their comrades' jokes, the song of the birds and the rustle of the wind in the leaves, they discovered that they had been outflanked. The Germans were advancing steadily in a roar of engines and bombs, something they remained blissfully unaware of as they lay down on the soft moss beneath the trees for their afternoon nap. Their officers discreetly suggested that they leave, and within the space of two days, in flakes and fragments, the whole regiment disappeared.

They walked the country roads in groups that grew ever smaller, ever more distant, until eventually they were only a handful, all friends together, heading more or less south-east without encountering a soul. Only the odd car that had run out of petrol by the roadside or an abandoned farm whose inhabitants had fled days earlier, leaving their livestock milling around the dirt farmyards.

France was silent. Under a summer sky, with no breath of wind, no cars and no sounds but their footsteps on the gravel, they walked along tree-lined roads, between hedges, weighed down by their rifles and their uniforms. May 1940 was gloriously hot. They felt stifled in their regulation greatcoats; their puttees clung to their legs; their coarse cloth caps produced sweat without absorbing it; their long rifles jolted and clanked and proved useless as walking sticks. Slowly but surely they tossed everything into the ditches and walked on in trousers and shirtsleeves, bare-headed. They even threw away their rifles. After all, what use were they? An encounter with an enemy unit would have left them dead. Some were keen to take pot-shots at lone soldiers, but, given the enemy's organization, such small pleasures would have cost them dear; besides, even the braggarts knew that it was just talk, a way not to lose face; at least verbally, since in every other sense they had already lost face. So they tossed away their rifles, having deactivated them just to be safe, to comply with regulations, and they walked on unencumbered. Passing a deserted house they rummaged through the wardrobes and helped themselves to civilian clothes. Gradually, they ceased to be soldiers, their fervour melting like hoarfrost at sunrise, until they were no more than a group of tired young men heading home. Some cut themselves walking sticks, others slung their jackets over their arm, and it was a pleasant stroll under the bright May sun on the deserted country roads of the Lorraine.

It lasted only until they encountered the Germans. A column of grey tanks parked under the trees along a trunk road. The bare-chested tank crews lay sunning themselves on their machines, smoking, eating and laughing, their bronzed, handsome bodies utterly unscarred. A line of French prisoners marched up in the opposite direction, led by veteran reservists clutching their rifles like fishing rods. The tank crew sat, dangling their legs, calling out to each other, joking and taking photos. The prisoners seemed older, gaunter, more unkempt; they trudged through the dust, shamefaced adults walking along with heads bowed through the barrage of jeers from these handsome young athletes in bathing suits. With a snap of the fingers, the uncle and his group were captured. Literally. A potbellied guard snapped his fingers, shot them a look like a schoolteacher and gestured to the column of men. Without so much as a question, without taking the trouble to count them, they were added to the daily growing procession marching north-east.

This was too much; the uncle ran away. Many ran away; it was not without risk, but it was not difficult. It simply meant taking advantage of the scarcity of guards, a momentary lack of attention, a bend in the road, a thicket of bushes; at every turn a few prisoners slipped away. Some were caught and dragged back, summarily shot and dumped in a ditch. But some managed to escape. 'What I find astonishing, what I always found astonishing,' the uncle used to say, 'was how few people ran. Everyone blindly obeyed.' The predisposition to obey is over-whelming, it is one of the commonest human traits; blind obedience can always be relied on. The greatest army in the world voluntarily disbanded and willingly went to the prison camps. Meek obedience achieved what bombs could never have done. It takes only a click of the fingers: we're used to it. When people don't know what to do, they do as they are told. He looked as though he knew what to do, this man who clicked his fingers. Obedience is so deep-rooted in our slightest gestures we no longer notice it. We follow. The uncle never forgave himself for submitting to that order. Never.

Victorien did not understand what his uncle meant. He did not see himself as obedient. He did his translations, he learned Latin through reading old books, but that was education, not obedience. And he drew; something no one had ever asked of him. So he listened to his uncle and thought of his stories as fascinating tales. One day he would leave, but for now he would carry on with his life at school.

He and a group of classmates sometimes went out. Going out in Lyon meant pacing up and down the main street. It is something that happens in gangs, girls on one side, boys on the other, with lots of giggling, winking and muffled laughter, punctuated by the fleeting heroism of a flattering remark that is quickly drowned out by the awkward restlessness of young men. A restless energy they exhausted by walking the length of the rue de la République, first one way and then the other; it is what everyone in Lyon does before stopping for a drink at one of the cafés with a canvas awning overlooking the square, the vast empty square that is the centre of the city. It would not occur to a seventeen year old from Lyon to do otherwise.

One of his friends from the streets and in the cafés – although 'friend' is an exaggeration – suggested he come to the life-drawing class. 'Come and study the nude, you're the one with the talent,' he sniggered, raising his glass, while Victorien blushed and buried his nose in his own glass, not knowing what to say. The other boy was older, unkempt, artistic; he talked in hints and allusions, mocked rather than making jokes, and insisted that it was not possible to just walk into the life-drawing class.

'My friend here has got real talent,' he had told the teacher, slipping him a couple of bottles which Victorien had liberated from his father's wine cellar. With a bottle wedged under each elbow, the bearded gentleman had his hands full, and by the time he had set them down to make full use of his limbs, Victorien was already sitting next to his friend – an overstatement – staring at a sheet of white paper pinned to an easel. Fair enough. The drawing teacher shrugged and affected not to notice the sardonic smiles this incident had provoked. Pencils in hand, with studied seriousness, Victorien began to study a lone young girl among these boys, the young naked girl who struck poses, poses he did not know were possible.

A large crowd had gathered so they might finally see a naked girl. His friend – an overstatement – had snickered as he described the scene and the intimate anatomy of young women, the boys with their eyes on stalks, the apoplectic expression of the teacher, whose beard quivered every time the young girl, her charms exposed, shifted her position. 'For that,' he added, 'you have to pay. It's obvious! What did you expect?'

But that was not it. A crowd had gathered to see a young girl nude, but that was not what captivated Victorien. The breasts, for example, the breasts of a naked, living woman are utterly unlike those of a statue or in the engravings he sometimes studied: real breasts are visibly heavier than one might think; they are less symmetrical; they have mass, they droop; they have a particular shape which follows no geometry; they confound the eye, crying out for hands so they might be better sensed. And hips, too, have creases and furrows that statues do not have. And skin is flecked with details, fine hairs, birthmarks, that statues do not have. Unsurprisingly, since statues have no skin. The skin of this young woman bristled with goosebumps and was tremulous with shivers, because the studio was cold.

Victorien had expected some sort of erotic spectacle. He had imagined going wild, cringing, drooling, at the very least trembling, but there was none of that: faced with this girl, with this flawed statue, he did not know what to feel, where to look. His pencil gave him composure. He sketched, followed the lines, smudged the shadows, and gradually drawing taught him the real weight of hips and breasts, of lips and thighs; and gradually the expected emotion stole up on him, but in a very different form. He wanted to take the girl in his arms, to search every inch of her body for warmth, for shivers, to lift her up and carry her away from this. His line became more and more fluid, and by the end of the session he had made some fine sketches, which he rolled up tightly and hid in his bedroom.

His consorting with art students did not last. One evening his uncle caught his friend – an overstatement – outside the café where they were lurking. He waited on the pavement, arms folded, one shoulder pressed to the wall. When the little gang emerged, laughing, he strode over to the lanky artist and slapped him hard, twice. The young man crumpled to the ground, as much from surprise and from the blows as from the alcohol he had drunk. The other boys scattered and disappeared into the alleys, all except Victorien, shocked by this sudden violence. His friend – an overstatement – lay sprawled on the ground, unable to pick himself up, sobbing at the feet of the uncle, who stood stock-still, looking down at him, his hands in his pockets. But even more than the downfall of a young man who but a quarter of an hour ago had seemed so invincible, so charismatic and so clever, what terrified Victorien in that moment was how much the uncle resembled his sister, his face utterly impassive as he towered over the young man at his feet, who had crumpled because he had slapped him. It terrified him, because he could not comprehend what they could possibly have in common, and yet the resemblance was undeniable.

The uncle led him back towards the shop without a word. He held open the door and waved the boy into the darkness beyond. Victorien shot him a quizzical glance. 'Draw. Draw as much as you like. But have nothing more to do with that world, those people. Forget those boys, those mediocrities who call themselves artists, but can be cured of their vocation with a slap or two. He should have got back on his feet and knocked me out. He could at least have tried. Or hurled abuse at me, one solitary curse at least. But he did nothing. He blubbed. So forget about him.'

He pushed Victorien into the shop and closed the door behind them. It was dark inside. Victorien groped his way to his bedroom. He slept badly. In the darkness of his room, which was twice as deep when he closed his eyes, it seemed to him that sleeping was weakness. Exhaustion dragged him down towards the submission of sleep, but nervous energy soared, lifting him up, up to where he bumped against the low ceiling. These twin forces waged a civil war inside his body, tearing him apart. In the morning he woke up shattered, breathless and bitter.

Victorien Salagnon lived a foolish life, one that made him feel ashamed. He did not know what he might do when he had finished translating the antiquated texts that currently occupied his days. He could study accountancy, take over his father's business, but the shop is hateful. The shop had always been horrid and now, in wartime, it seemed utterly vile. He could study, pass his exams and end up working for a French government that was actively collaborating with the Germans, for a company that was contributing to the German war effort. The Europe of 1943 *was* German. It was *völkisch*, every citizen was corralled within the *Völk* as into a prison camp. Victorien Salagnon would for ever be a second-class citizen, a loser who had had no opportunity to fight, for he was born that way. In German Europe, those bearing a French name – and his name was something he could not hide – were born to provide fine wines and elegant women to those with German names. In Nazi Europe he would never be more than a bondsman; this was written in his name and would endure for ever.

It was not that he resented the Germans, but if things carried on as they were his birth would determine his whole life, something he would never go beyond. The time had come to do something, to resist, instead of bowing his head and grumbling. He talked about this to Chassagneaux and they decided – or rather Chassagneaux enthusiastically accepted Victorien's suggestion – that they should paint radical slogans on the walls.

It was just a start, and it had the advantage of being something they could do quickly and unaided. Such an act would show the French that resistance festered, even in those cities where occupying forces were most deeply entrenched. France is defeated, it is bloodied but unbowed: this is what their graffiti would proclaim, loud and clear.

They found paint and two large brushes. The Maison Salagnon had so many suppliers that it was not difficult to procure a large tin of gloss paint – good and thick, it covers well and it's water-resistant, said the man giving it to Victorien, thinking he was doing a favour for the father. It was deep crimson, not white, but simply getting hold of paint in 1943 was an achievement; they could not be picky about the colour. It would do the job. They decided on the night, they practised writing slogans on scraps of paper which they later swallowed, and spent several Sundays searching for the perfect wall. It had to be long enough to fit a whole slogan, smooth enough so it was easy to read. The location could not be too secluded, the slogan had to be seen in the morning, but it could not be a busy intersection or they might be interrupted by a patrol. In addition, the surface had to be white enough for the red paint to be legible. That ruled out adobe, cinderblock and drystone walls. This left only the factories to the east of the city, the long white warehouse walls that factory workers walked past every morning on their way to work. At night, these streets were deserted.

On the appointed night, they set off. By the light of the moon they crossed the Rhône and walked due east. Their footsteps echoing, the cold biting deeper, they picked their way using the street names they had learned by heart before setting out. The brushes hidden in their sleeves were cumbersome; the huge paint tin strained their arms; they frequently had to change hands and swiftly stuff the other hand into a pocket. By the time they came to the wall they had chosen, the moon had traced an arc across the sky. At every street corner they crouched, listening for the pounding footsteps of a patrol or the rumble of an army truck. They encountered no one and found themselves standing in front of the wall. It streamed in the moonlight like a roll of white paper. In the morning, workers would read the message. Salagnon had no real idea what the working classes were like, except that they were tough, bull-headed and Communist. But their common heritage would make up for any class difference: they, like him, were French and vanquished. The words they would read in the morning would kindle that spirit that had no place within a German Europe. The vanquished must rise up, because if they are subjugated by their race, they will never achieve anything. All this, needless to say, they had to convey in simple words.

Opening the paint tin took some time. The lid was stuck fast and they had forgotten to bring a screwdriver. They tried to prise it with the brush handles, but they were too thick and skittered off; they bashed their knuckles, the blood pounding through their veins made their fingers tremble, they sweated as they stared at this paint tin they could not open. They slid a flat stone into the groove and wrestled with it, muttering curses, and finally they prised it open, spilling it over the ground, all over their hands and the brush handles. They were bathed in sweat. 'Phew!' they whispered softly. The pungent smell of turpentine wafted from the open can; in the silence, Salagnon could hear his heart. He could hear it as though it were not his. All at once he felt a powerful need to piss.

He crossed the street, which was particularly wide at this spot, ducked behind the corner of the wall. Here, hidden from the moon, he pissed against the base of a concrete post. He felt a wave of relief, almost of exhilaration, he would be able to write; he was looking at the stars in the cold sky when he heard a '*Halt!*' that made him jump. He had to grip himself with both hands to control the stream of piss. '*Halt!*' That word whistles through the air like a bullet: the word itself is an action understood by every living soul in Europe: the 'h' propels it like a rocket engine, the clipped 't' hits the target: '*Halt!*'

Salagnon, who had not finished pissing, turned warily. Five Germans running. The moon glittered on the metal of their helmets, their guns. The paint can sat, still open, next to the wall, under a large daubed 'N', whose solvent stench reached even his patch of shadows. Chassagneaux was running, his footsteps echoing against the walls, becoming more high-pitched as he got farther away. A German shoul-dered his rifle and fired, making a sharp crack, and the footsteps stopped. Two soldiers dragged the body back by its feet. Salagnon did not know what to do – carry on pissing, run for it, put his hands up? He knew you were supposed to raise your hands when captured, but perhaps what he was doing exempted him. He did not even know whether he had been spotted; he was cloaked only by shadows. He did not move. The Germans laid the body under the 'N', put the lid back on the tin, exchanged a few words, gruff syllables that would for ever be engraved on Salagnon's mind, liquefied by fear and shame. They saw nothing. They left the corpse underneath the letter and marched off in an orderly file, taking with them the paint tin and the brushes.

Salagnon was trembling. He felt naked in his corner. There was nothing to hide behind. The soldiers had not seen him. The shadows had concealed him. Absence is a better defence than walls. When he buttoned himself up, his flies were all sticky. He was trembling so hard that he had smeared paint all over his dick. He walked over and looked at Chassagneaux: the bullet had hit him right in the head. Red pooled beneath him and spread over the pavement. Salagnon headed back, moving west along the streets that would lead him home, taking no precautions. A rising mist meant he could not see or be seen. Had he encountered a patrol, he would not have run, he would have been arrested; streaked with paint, he would have wound up in jail. But he encountered no one, and in the early hours, having cleaned his prick using industrial cleaner, he slipped into bed and slept for a while.

A vehicle was sent to collect the body, but no one removed the daubed letter and the pool of blood was left on the pavement. The *Propagandastaffel* guys decided that leaving behind the symbol of resistance would demonstrate how quickly it had been crushed. Or perhaps no one thought to send someone to scour the wall and wash away the blood.

The body of Robert Chassagneaux was put on display in the place Bellecour; the corpse was splayed out on its back, guarded by two French police officers. The blood had blackened; his head lolled against his shoulder; his eyes were closed, his mouth open. A printed sign stated that Robert Chassagneaux, seventeen, had breached curfew and had been gunned down while trying to escape a patrol that had caught him painting hostile slogans on the walls of a factory of strategic importance. Regulations regarding curfew were reprinted below.

People filed past the body in the square. The officers guarding it kept their heads down, avoided looking at anyone; their guard duty weighed heavily on them; they could not bring themselves to look anyone in the eye. On this too large, too quiet square, roiling all winter with fears and mists, no one lingers. People pass with heads bowed, hands thrust deep into pockets, quickly retreating to the shelter of the streets. But around the young dead man, small groups began to cluster, housewives with shopping baskets, and old men. Silently they read the printed sign and stared down at the face, the mouth agape, the hair plastered with blood. The old men drifted away again, muttering to themselves; some of the women shouted at the police guards, trying to shame them. The officers did not respond; they kept their heads down, mumbling 'Move along! Move along!' in a barely audible tone, like an exasperated click of the tongue.

When the corpse began to stink it was returned to the parents. It was buried as quickly as possible. That day, all the pupils in his class arrived wearing black armbands on which Fobourdon refrained from commenting. When the last bell sounded, they did not get up; they remained seated, staring at Fobourdon. For two or three minutes, no one moved. 'Gentlemen,' Fobourdon said finally, 'tomorrow is another day.' And so they got to their feet, without scraping their chairs, and filed out.

Like everyone, Salagnon asked about the circumstances of the death. Rumours were rife, exaggerated stories that many felt had the ring of truth. Each time, Salagnon nodded in agreement, and he repeated the stories, adding details of his own.

The death of Chassagneaux needed to be seen as an example. Salagnon produced a letter purportedly written by the boy on the night he died. A letter of apology to his parents, of farewell to his friends, and of tragic determination. He had carefully forged his friend's hand-writing and crumpled the paper slightly to make it seem more authen-tic. He showed this letter around, gave it to Chassagneaux's parents. They invited him in, asked endless questions and wept profusely. He answered as best he could, inventing what he did not know, casting everything in a favourable light, and this simply made them all the more ready to believe him. They thanked him, walked him to the door with numerous courtesies, dabbing at their red-rimmed eyes, and said their goodbyes. Out on the street he set off at a run, his cheeks flushed, his hands slick with sweat.

For several weeks he did nothing but draw. He honed his technique, copying the Old Masters, standing in front of paintings in the Musée des Beaux-Arts or sitting in the library surrounded by piles of open books. He drew the human body in various poses, first ancient nudes, until he tired of them; he reproduced dozens of naked Christs, every one he could find, and then invented new ones. He strove to reveal his nakedness, his suffering, his surrender. When some artifice hid the private parts behind the folds of a shroud or a spray of leaves he drew nothing. He left a blank space, because he did not know how to draw testicles.

One night he stole the little mirror his mother used for her make-up. He waited until everyone was asleep and got undressed. He set the mirror between his legs and, tensing his thighs, he drew that organ the statues lacked. Now he could finish his drawings. To his drawings of women's bodies he had copied, he added nothing, simply closing the line, and that seemed to be that.

This went on for much of the night. Drawing kept him from sleep.

How did other people live? Elsewhere, boys of the same age, the same height, the same build, boys who had the same preoccupations when left to their own devices, were crouching in the snow, hoping they would not fall asleep and praying that their machine guns did not ice over; or in the desert, filling sandbags to shore up foxholes, beneath a blazing sun one cannot imagine unless one has experienced it; or crawling on their bellies through the foul mire of the tropics that moves of its own accord, clutching their rifles, which jammed all too easily, above their heads, but careful not to raise their heads, so as not to present a target. Some died with their hands in the air, stumbling from burning blockhouses only to be mown down in serried ranks like nettles being scythed; others vanished without trace, in a flash of light, in the hammer blow that follows the whistle of shells that are fired together, slashed the air and fell together; others died from a simple knife wound, a slash across the throat that slices through the artery, leaving the blood to spurt until there is no more. Still others waited for an explosion to tear through the steel walls protecting them from being crushed in the depths of the ocean; some lay on their bellies, peering through bombsights, waiting for the moment to unload their deadly cargo on the houses flashing past; some waited for death in wooden huts ringed by barbed wire that they would never leave. Elsewhere life and death were intimately entwined, while they were sheltered by La Grande Institution.

Granted, it was not warm. All fuel having been diverted to the war effort, to the ships, the tanks, the planes, it was impossible to heat the classrooms, but still here they were, sitting on their chairs, at their desks, behind thick walls that allowed them to remain in this sitting position. Not safe and warm, that would be an overstatement, but safe.

La Grande Institution survived, it remained assiduously neutral. The word 'war' was never uttered. Their greatest worry was the exam.

Father Fobourdon was interested only in the moral aspect of his job. He communicated in curt commands, and in a few scholarly digressions that hinted at more than was said. But one had to search for this hidden meaning, and if anyone had remarked on the fact he would have feigned surprise; before working himself up into a rage, which would have closed down the debate.

Every winter he watched the snow fall, these weightless, fluttering flakes that melted as they settled on the paving stones. Then, abruptly, in a brusque voice that made everyone jump, he would bark: 'Work, boys! Work! It's all you have left.' Then he would slowly pace the classroom, moving between the rows of schoolboys poring over Latin texts. They would smile without raising their heads, their secret smiles like lapping water, an echo of the terse phrases hurled into the cold air of the class, and then the eternal stillness of study would once more resume: the rustle of paper, the scratch of nibs, hushed sniffles, and sometimes a quickly suppressed cough.

Or else he would say: 'To know that you exist is all you will ever attain.' Or else: 'When this is over, in this brutish Europe, you will be like emancipated slaves, mutely performing your master's tasks.'

He never elaborated, never returned to a subject, never repeated a phrase. Everyone was familiar with Fobourdon's maxims, his teacher's quirks. His pupils would repeat them, although they did not understand them, collect them for a laugh, remember them out of respect for this man.

They learned that in ancient Rome work counted for nothing; that skill and craftsmanship were left to slaves and emancipated slaves, while free citizens busied themselves with power and warfare. Even when he became a freedman, a slave could never distance himself from his humble origins, his craft betrayed him; he worked, and he was knowledgeable.

They learned that in the depths of the Dark Ages, when everything was obliterated by war, the art of writing was preserved by monasteries, like islands; it was here, isolated from the world, that a memory of it was kept alive through the great meditative silence of work. They learned.

And so, when in spring a man in a black uniform visited their class to talk of the future, it felt like a surprising intrusion. He wore a curious black uniform that belonged to no pre-existing army. He introduced himself as a member of one of the new organizations governing the country. He wore boots that were more elegant than those worn by the Germans, which looked as though they would be more at home on a building site; he wore the high, glossy black boots of the French cavalry, which placed him without question in the tradition of national elegance.

'The border to Europe is the Volga,' he began, sharply. He spoke with his hands clasped behind his back and his shoulders thrown back, as if about to take wing. Father Fobourdon scratched his neck and took a step to one side to stand in front of the map on the wall. He hid it with his broad shoulders.

'On this border it is constantly snowing. It is minus thirty degrees. The ground is flecked with ice and so hard that the dead cannot be buried before summer. On this border our men are waging war against the Red Ogre. I say *our* men. We must say so, because they are ours, these European troops, these young men from ten nations fighting together as brothers to save our culture from the Bolshevik invasion. The Bolshevik is the modern incarnation of the Oriental, gentlemen, and the Oriental has long considered Europe to be its natural prey. Now this has ended, because we are defending ourselves. Now it is Germany, the most advanced of the New Order, who leads the uprising of nations. Old Europe must trust her, and follow her. France has been ailing, but she is being purged, she is returning to her former glory. France is engaged in a national revolution and will once again take her position in the new Europe. It is a position that can be won only through war. If we want a role in the Europe of the victors, we must fight alongside the victors. Gentlemen, you have a duty to join the troops fighting on all fronts. You will soon receive a call-up to the Chantiers de Jeunesse, where you will receive the necessary training, and from there you will take your place in the new army that will ensure our place in the world. We will be reborn through blood.'

The dumbfounded class listened in silence. Then one pupil, open-mouthed, without thinking of asking permission to speak, murmured plaintively:

'But what about our studies?'

'Those who return will be able to take them up again. If they are still deemed necessary. You will come to understand that the new Europe needs soldiers, strong men, not lily-livered intellectuals.'

Standing in front of the map, Father Fobourdon shifted from one foot to the other. No one dared to speak, but a buzz of unrest swelled into a commotion that upset him. He surveyed the class. He pointed at one boy whose head rose above the others.

'You, Salagnon. You seem to have something to say. Speak. But keep it brief.'

'So we will not be able to pass our *baccalauréat*?'

'No. You will be permitted to sit the examination later. This has been agreed with the Institution.'

'It's the first we've heard of it.'

The officer spread his arms wide to demonstrate that he was powerless to help, which triggered a further commotion; this widened his knowing smile and added still further to the uproar.

'This has always been the way of things!' yelled Father Fobourdon. 'Now shut up, the lot of you!'

The boys immediately fell silent and stared at Father Fobourdon, who seemed about to explain by means of some scholarly example. He looked down, hiding his trembling hands behind his back.

'This has always been the way of things,' he muttered. 'If it is the first you've heard of it, then you have not been paying attention.'

They all shivered. The cold felt more piercing than usual. They felt naked. Hopelessly naked.

The spring of 1944 broke out a few days later. March exploded in yellow flares along the river banks, in rosaries of bright flame dropped from the sky, in sunbursts of flowers in the gardens along the Seine. In March the forsythias all lit up together like tracer fire, a line of yellow explosions rising silently northwards.

The uncle came knocking one evening and stood in the doorway before coming in. He was dressed in new clothes, a short-sleeved shirt, baggy shorts with a wide belt, knee socks and thick hiking boots. He smiled awkwardly. The uncle, awkward! He knew all eyes would be on his outfit. His uniform might offer little protection against the chill that evening, but it heralded summer, exercise drills, the great outdoors; it advertised it with a naive flamboyance. Behind his back he crumpled a beret, one of those flat military berets emblazoned with a badge, to be worn at an angle over the ear.

'Well, come in then!' Salagnon Senior said at last. 'Show us how fine you look. Where does it come from, your uniform?'

'The Chantiers de Jeunesse,' muttered the uncle. 'I am an officer with the Chantiers de Jeunesse.'

'You? A pig-headed person like you? What the bloody hell do you plan to do in the Chantiers?'

'My duty, Salagnon, nothing more than my duty.'

The uncle stared straight ahead, he did not move, did not say anything more. The father thought about saying something, but decided against it; you never knew where you were with insinuations. Sometimes it was better not to know. Best to look sleepy, innocuous.

'Come on, come in. Let's have a drink to celebrate.'

The father bustled about, rooting out a bottle of champagne, very slowly, very carefully removing the wire cap, then popping the cork. A series of simple gestures to hide his embarrassment. The world was in turmoil, and much of this confusion was beyond him. It was a thunderstorm. No one could be trusted. But still he had to carry on, to skipper his boat without letting it founder. Carry on: that was enough. He filled the glasses and took a moment to admire them.

'Take a sip. In the Chantiers you'll get a quarter litre of piss-weak plonk in a canteen if you're lucky. Enjoy it while you can.'

The uncle drank as a thirsty man drinks water. He raised his glass and set it down in the same motion.

'True enough,' he said vaguely. 'I see business is good.'

'Not too bad; you have to work at it.'

'Is Rosenthal still closed? I see his shutters are still closed. Did he go bust?'

'They left one morning, as though they were going on holiday. They took one suitcase each. I don't know where they went. I never had more than a nodding acquaintance with Rosenthal. We'd see each other in the morning at opening time, and at night when closing up. He talked to me about Poland once, but with an accent like his, you couldn't have much of a conversation. They probably went back to Poland.'

'Do you really think anyone is going on holiday in Poland right now?'

'I've no idea. I've got work to do. All the more so since they closed down. One morning, *poof*, they were gone, and I have no idea where they went. I'm hardly going to move heaven and earth to track the Rosenthals when I don't know them from Adam.'

The saying made him laugh.

'What about you, Victorien, did you know the Rosenthal boy?'

'He was younger. In a different class.'

The uncle sighed.

'Don't tell me you're feeling sorry for some guy you know only from a name on a sign above a closed shutter. Go on, drink up.'

'No one looks out for anyone, Salagnon. France is vanishing because it has been reduced to a series of individual problems. We're dying because we refuse to stand together. That's what we need: to proudly stand together.'

'France! France is a fine thing! But it doesn't put food on the table. And besides, the Rosenthals weren't French.'

'They spoke French just like you or me, their children were born here, they went to the same school as yours. So...'

'He's not French, I'm telling you. Not according to his papers, anyway.'

'His papers? Don't make me laugh. Your papers were faked by your own son. More real than the real thing.'

Father and son blushed at the same time.

'Come on, let's not argue. Drink up. At any rate, I don't give a shit about the Rosenthals. I've got a job to do. And if everyone worked as hard as I do, we wouldn't have these problems; we wouldn't have the time to worry about them.'

'You're right. You're working. And I'm about to leave. So let's have a drink. It might be our last.'

That night Victorien walked his inebriated uncle home to spare him an unpleasant encounter with a patrol, one he could not easily have avoided and might even have provoked, it was the sort of thing he might do when he was drunk. He had knocked back the wine, little caring how much he drank, he had asked for more, then insisted on heading back to the barracks he was sharing with the others leaving for the Chantiers de Jeunesse the next day. 'Go with him, Victorien,' his mother had said. And Victorien took his uncle's elbow to stop him tripping over a corner of the paving stones.

They parted on the Saône, a black trench cut through with an icy wind. The uncle had sobered up and stood straight; he could walk the rest of the way on his own. He shook his nephew's hand solemnly, and when he had started to cross the bridge, Victorien called out, ran over to him, and told him about La Grande Institution's plan. The uncle heard him out, even though his shirt and shorts offered no protection from the wind. When Victorien had finished, he shivered; they were silent.

'I'll send you travel documents for my camp,' he said at last.

'Can you do that?'

'A forgery, Victorien, a forgery. You're used to that, aren't you? There are more fake documents produced in this country than real ones. It's a business in itself; and if the fake ones look a lot like the real ones, it's because they are made by the same people, who produce one lot by day and the other by night. So don't worry, the papers I'll give you will hold up. I'm going to get going. I wouldn't like to die of pneumonia. In the times we live in, that would be too idiotic. I'd never get over dying of pneumonia. I'd never get over it,' he repeated, with a drunken laugh.

He gave Victorien a hard, clumsy hug and left. All the lights in the town were out, and it was so dark that halfway across the bridge he had disappeared.

Victorien headed home, hands thrust deep in his pockets, collar turned up, but he did not shiver. He was not afraid of the cold.

Commentaries II

I have known better days and left them behind

I LIVE NOW IN A TINY HUTCH perched on a rooftop. I once saw an antique engraving that showed how common rooftop cabins were in Lyon once upon a time, half-timbered, built of brick and roughcast, the roof all of a piece, the east-facing wall a huge mullioned window. There is no need of any other windows: the old town is built at the foot of a hill, almost a cliff, which screens the afternoon sun. Through my crudely leaded windows the streaming sun blinds me every morning. I can see nothing in front of me, nothing around, nothing behind. I float above the rooftops in a light that falls straight from the heavens. I used to dream of living in one of these cabins; now I do. Ordinarily, people make progress, they long for and they buy a bigger, more comfortable house, with more people inside. They make more connections. The place I live now is barely habitable, no one comes to visit, I am alone and happy to be so. Filled with the joy of being nothing.

Because I've seen better days; I owned a house. I had a wife, too. Now I live in a garret. Where I live is strange, a simple swelling on the confusion of rooftops, in this piecemeal city where nothing is ever demolished, nothing ever changes, where things accumulate, they pile up. I live in a crate, in a trunk perched atop the buildings that, over the course of centuries, have accumulated along the banks of the Saône, just as the silt from that river accumulates, hardens and becomes dry land.

I like living in a box above the rooftops. I always dreamed of it. I used to look up at these spare rooms fashioned in the air, the shoots of a city that is not built, but grows. My head in the clouds, I longed to live in them, but I did not know how to get there. I half suspected that there was no staircase leading there; or only a narrow passageway that closed up as soon as one had passed. I dreamed of standing in front of a window in front of nothingness, and I was well aware that in this hectic city there are places that cannot be reached, that are no more than wisps of a dream. That is where I live.

Life is simple here. Wherever I choose to sit, I can see everything I own. As far as heating is concerned, I deal with the sky: in winter, heat evaporates and you freeze; in summer, the sun beats down so hard you suffocate. I always suspected as much, now I know it, now I live in one of these cabins I always dreamed of, and I never tire of the pleasure. I live in a single cramped room that serves as a home. From my window I see the roof tiles and the internal balconies stretching out endlessly, the pillared galleries and the winding staircases that form a low, jumbled horizon; the rest is sky. When I sit staring out at the sky, there is nothing behind me: a bed, a wardrobe, a table no bigger than an open book, a sink that serves all purposes, and especially the wall.

It thrills me to have reached the sky. It thrills me to have reached this shack that people usually shun, that they would do anything to escape as soon as they get on in life. I don't get on. That thrills me.

I had a job, a house and a wife, three facets of a single reality, three aspects of a single victory: the spoils of the class war. We are still Scythian horsemen. Work is war, a profession is an act of violence, a house is a fortress, and a woman is plunder, thrown over the back of a horse and carried off.

This will surprise only those who believe that they live according to choices. Our life is statistical. Statistics offer a more accurate description of life than any story. We are Scythian horsemen and life is a military campaign: I am not proposing a world view, I am stating a statistical fact. When everything crumbles, look at the order in which it crumbles. When a man loses his job and cannot find another, they take his house, and his wife leaves him. Look at the way life crumbles. A wife is plunder and sees herself as such; the wife of an unemployed executive will abandon the vanquished man, since he no longer has the power to possess her. She can no longer live with him, he disgusts her, hanging around at home during working hours; she cannot bear this worm who rarely shaves now, dresses badly, spends the day watching television and moves more and more listlessly; the vanquished man disgusts as he tries and fails to drag himself from the quicksand, tries again and again, struggles, founders and sinks inexorably into an absurdity that saps his eyes, his muscles, his virility. Women forsake Scythians who have fallen to the ground, the horsemen thrown from their horses and spattered with mud: this is a statistical reality that no story can change. All stories are true, but they are no match for statistics.

I had started out well. In the era of the First Republic of the Left we were governed by a gentle Leviathan, embarrassed by his size and his age, too busy dying of solidification to think of devouring his own children. The village Leviathan offered everyone a role in the First Republic of the Left. It took care of everything; it took care of everyone. I worked in a state institution. I had a good job. I lived in a beautiful flat, with a beautiful wife who had been christened Océane. I loved this name that meant nothing, since it is devoid of all memory; such names are given out of superstition, like a gift from a fairy godmother, so that the child will have good fortune from the start. I had my foot on the social ladder. It led ever upwards. There was no question of it leading down, that would be a contradiction in terms. What language cannot say, cannot be conceived.

What glorious times they were, the early days of the First Republic of the Left! We had waited for so long. How long did it last? Fourteen years? Three months of summer? No longer than the Sunday evening it came to power? The next day, as early as the next day, it began to dissolve, like snow which begins to melt when the last flake has fallen. The rungs of the social ladder suddenly led downwards; and what's more, I jumped. A fall is a kind of sensual pleasure. We have all experienced it in dreams: when you fall, your stomach gently lurches and floats like a helium balloon in the abdominal heavens. This floating is like that feeling of sensual excitement we experience before we realize our genitals can be aroused. Falling is a very antiquated form of sexual pleasure; so I enjoyed falling.

I have almost reached rock bottom. I am living in a part of the old town which no one ever renovates because they cannot find the stairs to reach it. I am above the roofline; all I see of buildings are anonymous slates and tiles, and the roofs themselves are so haphazard that it is impossible to make out the streets below. The cabling dates back to the invention of electricity, with light switches that rotate and wires insulated with cotton. The rendering in the corridors is never painted and is home to a thriving colony of algae that live off electric light. The floor is covered with terracotta tiles that crack, break, disintegrate, giving off the clayey smell of potsherds in an archaeological trench.

When I step outside, I see him. He is lying at the foot of a 'No Parking' sign, zipped up in a sleeping bag from which only a filthy hank of hair emerges. Outside my front door, the local tramp lets nothing show. In sleep, he offers only the vestige of a human form, the very form that body bags seek to mask when transporting casualties of war.

The pavements are narrow. I have to step over him to get past. He is curled around the 'No Parking' sign. He looks like prey trapped in a spider's web. He is kept alive, suspended in a cocoon, waiting for the spider to devour him. He has reached rock bottom, but even after the fall is over it takes a long time to die.

I can see how people might be surprised by my attraction to falling. I could have made things simple: jumped out of the window. Or got a sleeping bag and taken to the streets. But what would I do in the streets? I might as well be dead; and that is not what I want. I want to fall, and not to have fallen. I would like to fall slowly, such that the length of my fall describes the heights I had reached. Is that not offensive, in the same way that the disgust of rich people is offensive? Offensive to those who are really falling without wanting to? Surely true suffering entails silence? Yes: silence.

Those who suffer never ask for the right to be silent. Those who do not suffer, on the other hand, turn suffering to their advantage. It is a gambit in the power game, a veiled threat, an inducement to shut us up. Go and live on the streets if you want to! If you're not happy, get out! If you don't like it, there's the door! There are plenty of people waiting who would be more than happy to take your job. In fact, they would be happier with a lowlier position. We'll offer them a lowlier position and they'll keep their mouths shut. Glad to get anything. We will negotiate positions downwards, hack a few rungs off the social ladder. We will arrange it so that the rungs go down. People need to keep busy, keep quiet. To limit their expectations. Demand less. Keep their mouths shut. Tramps are like the skulls on spikes at the entrance to a warlord's territory: they intimidate, they enforce silence.

I am gradually uninstalling myself. I now live in a single room that serves for everything I do; I do very little. All my worldly possessions can be contained in two suitcases; I can carry both at once, one in each hand. But even that is too much. I do not have a free hand. I must fall further. I would like to reduce myself to my earthly body, to be clear in my own heart. Clear about what? I don't know; but when it comes, I will know.

Be still, my heart: the great fall will come soon. And then I shall know.

I have known better days, and I left them behind.

With my wife, everything went wrong without a word, without a flare-up. The creaking noises we heard we blamed on the failure of communication between the sexes, something so well established that books are written about it; or on compassion fatigue, which is so well attested that ever more books are written on that subject; or else to the vagaries of life, which as everyone knows, is never easy. But our ears were deceiving us: the creaking noises were whirring noises; what we could hear was the sound of a mineshaft being drilled below our feet. The mine exploded in due course, one Saturday. Weekends are ideal for a break-up. You see more of each other, and however much you try to reschedule things, you will invariably end up with some free time. There will always come a point during those two days when you are not working. In the end it was complete carnage!

It began, as always, with a very precise timetable. Do not delude yourself into thinking that free time is genuinely free; it is simply organized differently. For example, Saturday morning: shopping; Saturday afternoon, *shopping*. Though the words are the same, the concepts are different, since one refers to groceries, the other to anything and nothing. The first is a necessity, the second is a pleasure; the first is a practical constraint, the other a hobby actively pursued.

Saturday evening: friends come round to our place. Other couples we invite for dinner. Sunday morning, a lie-in, on principle. Perhaps a sensual frolic, a little exercise, casual clothes, a spot of brunch, then in the afternoon something I cannot remember. Because we never got as far as the afternoon. That Sunday we did nothing. She cried the whole time. She did nothing but sob in front of me as I said nothing. And then I left.

As a couple, we spent much of our time buying things. Buying is the basis of any couple; as is sex, but sex defines us only personally, whereas buying defines us as a social unit, skilled economic forces who spend what time is not already filled with work or sex spending money on furniture. Together we would talk about buying things and we would buy things; with friends, we would talk about things we had bought and things that we hoped to buy. Houses, clothes, cars, accessories and subscriptions, music, holidays, gadgets. It takes time. Like-minded people can talk about an object of desire indefinitely. It is something that can be bought, since it is an object. Something that can be expressed, and it is reassuring that language can describe it; and it brings with it a boundless despair that cannot be expressed.

On the Saturday everything exploded we went to the supermarket. We pushed our shopping trolley through a crowd of other smartly dressed couples. They came together, like us, some with small children in the trolley's baby seat. Some even brought infants in carrycots. Sprawled on its back, eyes wide, the baby would stare at the false ceilings hung with garish images, aware of a bustle, a commotion he could not understand, blinded by a light only he could see, since he was lying on his back with his eyes wide open. Before long, the baby would burst into tears, howl and be unable to stop. Before long, the parents would start bickering. The man would invariably be impatient: it was taking too long, the woman wanted to look at everything; she hesitated, determined to make sure she was making the right choice, something that took a while; then she would take offence, while he dragged his feet as though he were bored of being there with his family; he grabbed whatever came to hand, bought recklessly. He adopted a weary air, pretended to be looking elsewhere. An argument would flare; the same words, the same phrases that were formed before they opened their mouths. A quarrel between a couple is as codified as the Indian classical dance: the same postures, the same movement, the same words with their symbolic meanings. It is simply a matter of performance: everything is said without needing to be said. This is how it played out; we were no exception. Except that in our case a quarrel never exploded, it oozed like sweat, because we had no child to flush it out.

That Saturday when the mine beneath our feet exploded, we were pushing a shopping trolley through the supermarket. I went to the chilled meat cabinet and stood, stunned, staring at the trays that seemed to glow from within. I leaned over and stood, frozen, and I must have looked a terrifying sight, the light from below casting inverted shadows on my face, my jaw hanging open, my eyes staring. My breath came out as plumes of white mist. I grabbed a vacuum-packed tray of diced meat in one hand and slowly moved it to the other, then put it down, took another, then another, shuffling trays of meat in slow motion like a conveyor belt, a circular movement that had no beginning and no end, cramping from the cold. The cycle continued almost without my involvement. I needed to choose something, but I did not know what. It was impossible not to waver when faced with such overstocked shelves. I could have simply reached my hand into this cornucopia, closed it at random and thereby solved the problem of the menu for that evening; but today it was not simply about eating. Hovering over the chill cabinet, I was acting out a cycle I was powerless to interrupt. I passed trays of stewing steak from hand to hand, picking them up and putting them down in the same movement, I moved the meat around, unable to stop, unable to break the cycle, illustrating against my will – oh no! against my will! – a parody of time frozen. I did not know what to do.

I must have looked terrifying, lit from below, wreathed by the mist streaming from my mouth, standing motionless over the cabinet, with only my hands moving, performing the same action over and over, hesitating as I handled this meat that had been diced dispassionately, sensibly, in the most technical manner possible, such that it was no longer flesh but meat. Everyone who noticed me gave me a wide berth.

I did not know what to do, because I felt nothing; I could not choose, because what I saw did not appeal to me. The meat remained mute, talking through labels; it was just vivid pink shapes, cubes sealed in plastic, nothing but pure form; and to decide between forms requires discursive reasoning; and discursive reasoning does not help to decide anything.

The meat formed piles in front of me, in the chill cabinet so perfectly designed to preserve flesh, beneath fluorescent lights that cast no shadows and gave everything the same colour; I did not know what to do. I could no longer tell which way time was headed. And so I performed the same action over and over, picking up, looking, replacing. I might have carried on until I died of hypothermia and toppled, frozen stiff, into the chill cabinet, to lie among the trays of the meat, a rough-hewn shape, too organic, too crude, laid on top of the neat piles of prepared cuts.

It was Océane's voice that saved me from dying of cold or being carted off by security guards. Her voice always woke me, always a little too loud, a little too forceful, driven by a glut of decisiveness.

'Look,' she was saying. 'What do you think?'

She waved a black tray full of red cubes under my nose, as though for me to smell, but I could smell nothing. I could not really see either, because my eyes were glazed, having ceased to distinguish between near and distant.

'A good beef bourguignon,' she said, 'with carrots. And a little salad as a starter. I've got two packs and a nice cheese platter. I'll handle this. Will you decide on the wine?'

She continued to wave the meat in front of me in a mechanical gesture, under my nose, in front of my eyes, waiting for approval, for some sign of enthusiasm, anything that might indicate that I understood, that I agreed, that it was a good idea; but I was admiring the geometry of the meat. The smooth, perfectly orthogonal cubes that contrasted perfectly with the black plastic tray. A little serviette at the bottom absorbed the blood; taut plastic film sealed everything from the air and from prying fingers. The cut was perfect, the blood invisible.

'These are cuboid. There are no cuboid animals.'

'What animal?'

'The one they killed to cut up the meat.'

'Stop it, you're being gruesome. So, are you OK with tonight's menu?'

I took charge of the trolley again, which passed as a sign of masculine approval, an appalling gesture, but one that everyone understands. Rolling her eyes, she tossed the tray into the trolley. It fell on to the bags of chopped, washed and prepared salad leaves, next to a pack of frozen carrots covered with hoarfrost.

Pushing the trolley past the open chill cabinets, we came to a vast window that looked on to the in-house butcher's counter. Diffused light reflected on the tiled walls, casting no shadows, accentuating every detail of the butcher's art. Carcasses hung from meat hooks in the ceiling, some in the middle of the room, others waiting behind plastic curtains. These were large mammals, I could tell from the outlines, from the arrangement of bones and limbs, identical to our own. Men in masks came and went, carrying butcher knives. They wore plastic overboots smeared with crimson; they wore baggy white overalls on top of their work clothes; their hair was covered by plastic caps, the kind you might wear in the shower. Paper masks hid their noses and mouths; it was impossible to tell them apart, only to see whether they wore glasses. Some had a mesh glove on their left hand and wielded the knife with the other; with their gloved hand they controlled the hanging carcasses, turning them into the light, while the knife glittered in their other hand. Various ghostly apparitions pushed trolleys full of buckets, and in the buckets floated blood-red offcuts marbled with white. Younger figures hosed down the floors, the corners, the areas beneath the cutting tables, then rubbed them down with rubber squeegees. Everything gleamed spotlessly, everything glittered hollowly, everything was translucent. They wielded dangerous tools like razors, as jets of water continually hosed the floors. It was impossible to recognize anyone.

Why can we no longer deal with flesh? What have we done? What have we done, without realizing, so that we can no longer stomach it? What have we forgotten about the processing of flesh?

They rolled a bisected cow, hung from a hook through the legs. I assumed it was a cow by the size, but I could not be sure since the skin, the head, in fact every identifying feature had been removed. All that remained were the bones upholstered in red, the white tendons at each end of the muscles, the blue joints of the limbs, the muscles gorged with blood, covered by a white film of fat. Armed with a power saw, a man in a mask attacked the fleshy body. The carcass quivered under the blade, a vast hunk came loose, quavered, teetered, then suddenly toppled. He caught it as it fell and tossed it on to the metal table where other men with masks and mesh gloves got to work with knives.

I could not hear the sounds. Not the wail of the saw or the grinding of bones, not the thud of falling meat or the soft snick of the knives, not the faint clack of the gloves or the jets of water constantly pounding the floor, preventing pools of blood from collecting under the table. I saw only the image. An image that was too detailed, too perfect; too bright and too clear. I felt as though I were watching some S&M movie, because of the lack of sound, of smell, of touch, the supple feel of the flesh as it gave itself up to the knife, the flavourless scent of death, the limp thud as it falls on to a hard surface, the fragile suppleness of a body flayed of skin. There was nothing to assure me I was really here. There was nothing but a brutal thought, assiduously cutting meat into cubes. I felt myself retch. Not from the sight of it, but from the sight disconnected from my other senses. The image alone hovered before me and prickled unpleasantly deep in my throat.

I looked down, turned away from the window intended to high-light the hygienic nature of the slaughter, and continued past the chilled cabinets where the meat was organized by type. OFFAL, BEEF, LAMB, PETS, PORK, CHILDREN, VEAL.

'PETS', I could understand. It's a truncated phrase: what they mean is 'pet food'. But 'CHILDREN'. Sandwiched between 'PORK' and 'VEAL'. I studied the plastic trays from a distance, reluctant to pick one up for fear of reproach. Beneath the taut plastic film the flesh was small and pink. It corresponded to the name. Meat: children. I showed the label to Océane, a faint smile trembling on my lips, ready to burst into a loud laugh if she gave me the sign, but she always understood everything. She dismissed this infantile gesture with a shrug, with a weary shake of her head, and we set off again down the long aisles. We continued with our purchases; she read her list aloud, while I pushed the trolley, vainly ruminating on the nature and the uses of meat.

We were driving home when we got stuck in a traffic jam along the Saône. Trucks were double-parked next to the market, narrowing the lanes. The traffic lights spent too long on red. We had to wait much longer than we would have liked. The cars, bumper-to-bumper along the embankment, inched forwards in fits and starts, spluttering clouds of noxious fumes that were fortunately dispersed by the light breeze from the river. I tapped my fingers on the steering wheel, looked everywhere and nowhere, while Océane put the finishing touches to her menu.

'What can we come up with for dessert that's original? What would you like?'

What would I like? I regained control of my eyes and looked at her intently. What would I like? My stare must have been unsettling, I did not answer the question. She looked uncomfortable. What would I like? I opened the car door and got out. The engine purred. We were waiting in line for the light to turn green.

'I'll see what I can find,' I said, gesturing towards the market.

I slammed the door and slipped between the stationary vehicles. The light turned green, they started up again. I was in the way. I leapt over to the kerb, acknowledging those who had hooted their horns and revved their engines with a grateful gesture. I assumed that Océane had taken the wheel, preferring not to block the road, rather than follow me and abandon the shopping. Slipping on a pile of discarded vegetables, regaining my balance on a piece of damp cardboard, crushing an orange crate with a terrific crash, I stumbled into the market.

I slipped though the crowd of basket-carriers slowly circulating among the stalls. I was looking for the Chinese. I tracked them by smell. I followed the strange smell of Chinese food, that utterly distinctive scent that is unfamiliar at first, but once smelt is never forgotten, because it is instantly recognizable, always the same, due to the use of certain ingredients and certain practices about which I know nothing, but whose effects I can locate from a distance because of the smell.

Given that they eat this way all the time, do the Chinese smell the way they do? What I mean is, does the smell cling to them, to their skin, their mouths, their sweat, their armpits, their groin? To find out, you would need to slowly make love to a beautiful Chinese woman – or a not so beautiful one, it hardly matters – and lick her all over in order to make sure. To know whether the difference between human races boils down to a difference of diet, a difference in eating habits that, over time, permeates one's skin, one's whole being, including language and finally thought, would require a meticulous study of the flesh.

Following this scent I quickly found a Chinese butcher. Glossy *tripaillons* hung beneath a canvas awning. I do not know the word for this cut of offal. I am not sure that it has a name in French or in any European language: it consists of the viscera, intact with nothing left out, crimson entrails, hung by the trachea from a meat hook. Since I know a little anatomy, I can vaguely tell which organs are which, without being able to precisely identify the animal: I suspect it is a bird or some sort of feathered creature.

I do not know what the Chinese do with *tripaillons*. The Chinese cookbooks you can buy in France make no mention of it. They mention only prime cuts, to be carved with a knife in accordance with carefully delineated rules of butchery, following the natural curves of the animal. They never show revolting entrails, despite the fact they can be eaten. Those hanging beneath the awning are lifelike enough to make you shudder, and I shudder even more to think how they must be harvested. There is no way that I know of to dissolve the skin, the flesh, the bones, leaving only the entrails intact, still in their natural arrangement. Consequently, it would require sticking a hand down the animal's throat, perhaps while it is still alive, grasping the aortic bulb or some other purchase point, twisting to rip it loose, then yanking it free: it yields, and the whole of the insides come out in your hand, still steaming and breathing. You swiftly plunge them into red caramel sauce to preserve them in their original forms, to display them without embellishment or invention; but how could you invent such organs? How could you invent tripe? Could you invent the inside of the body, its deepest flesh, quivering, dying, hung? How can you invent what is real? It is enough to seize it and to show it.

And so I stopped beneath the Chinese butcher's awning, admiring the red-glazed entrails. Oh, Chinese wisdom! Applied to gestures and to the flesh! I have no idea how to eat these lacquered viscera, no idea how to cook them. I cannot even begin to imagine; but every time I pass here I see them hanging, so real, so crimson, and I stop and dream, and it makes my mouth water, though I do not dare to swallow. I finally decide to buy a knot of entrails. The white-smocked butcher's French is difficult to understand. He speaks Chinese with most of his customers. I decide not to ask questions, since any explanation will doubtless be tedious and probably disappointing; besides, my imagination will direct me. Confidently and with a knowing air, I gesture to the viscera and he wraps them in sealed plastic.

I set off again through the crowd, pushing through the throng, the shopkeepers' cries, the endless chatter, the scents of all manner of food; I feel unaccountably happy carrying my heavy plastic package.

But it would not be enough to feed our guests. My nostrils quivering, I sought out something else. A heady vapour stopped me. Oily and fruity, alarmingly rich, it wafted from a pot-bellied cauldron hanging from a trivet over a gas flame. A fat man girdled with an apron that trailed on the ground was stirring the contents. The crockpot came up to his waist and the handle of his wooden spoon was like a truncheon; I would have had trouble using it with one hand, but he did so as effortlessly as if stirring coffee with a teaspoon. What he was stirring was a deep red, almost black, that bubbled in the centre, while herbs and slivers of onion eddied on the surface. '*Boudin!*' he shouted. 'Genuine *boudin noir!*' He emphasized the 'genuine'. 'Not for the faint hearted this: genuine blood sausage!'

It smelled incredibly good, it shivered deliciously, making a little noise as it simmered like the gleeful snicker you make when doing something horrifying but alluring. A young lad with jug ears and a few stray hairs on his chin brought over some buckets, staggering under the weight. The buckets were filled with blood: crimson, completely opaque, flecked at the edges with foam. The young helper proffered the cargo with difficulty and the *maître charcutier* seized a bucket in one huge, hairy, purple hand and, in a single motion, tipped the blood of a whole slaughtered pig into the pot, and the bubbling began again. He was stirring a cauldron of blood using a ladle with a handle like a truncheon and spooned the contents into lengths of intestines until they were full to bursting. He worked in a cloud of heavy, fragrant steam. I bought several metres of *boudin noir*. When I asked him not to cut it up but to leave it intact, he seemed surprised, but coiled the *boudin* up carefully without asking questions. He double-bagged it, so that the plastic would not give way, and handed it to me with a wink. This second package counterbalanced the first, and increased my satisfaction tenfold.

What I had was good, but it would not be enough; entrails are not everything. I needed to find other parts if my banquet was to be a triumph.

I found inspiration in an African man. He was hawking loudly in a deep bass voice, shouting at men, calling them 'boss', laughing all the while, greeting the women with a wink and a compliment tailored to each one, and they smiled as they passed. He was selling ripe mangoes and little bananas, jagged heaps of spices, garishly coloured fruit and prepared poultry: carcasses plucked, wings clipped, claws intact. From him I bought bright red cockscombs that seemed pumped with hydrogen, about to burst into flame or float away. As he wrapped them, he talked meaningfully about their beneficial effects. He held them out with a smile that filled me with joy.

I've lost my head, I thought. And besides, two heads are better than one, as they say. I found it with a Berber. Dressed in a grey smock, the sleeves pushed up to reveal forearms with muscles and tendons like cables, the old butcher was deboning a sheep with a cleaver. Behind him, other carcasses looked on. Rows of heads were grilling in a rotisserie. You could watch them whirl through a slightly grubby pane of glass; they turned in fits and starts, aligned in a row, browning over a low heat. Their eyes had rolled back in their heads, their tongues lolled from the corners of their mouths; neatly aligned, cut off at the larynx, the sheep's heads had been revolving for hours in the rotisserie, golden brown and sizzling, mouth-watering, each individual recognizable. I bought three. He wrapped them in newspaper, put them in a carrier bag and, with a nod that spoke volumes, he held them out to me. This is a delicacy enjoyed usually only by elderly Arab gourmands, those content to wait for death. That made me even happier.

Weighed down with fragrant parcels, I headed home. I tossed them on the table and they made a squelching noise. I opened the bags and the aromas escaped. Smells are volatile particles, they break free from corporeal forms and fashion an image in the air you sense in the depths of your soul. Some of the foodstuffs I had brought home gave off a physical scent: I could see a bluish vapour rising from the bags, a heavy gas which crept to the ground, clung to the walls, pervaded the room.

Océane saw it too, her eyes were wide and staring, I could not tell whether she was about to scream or throw up; she did not seem to know either. And so she said nothing. Before her, the bags slumped on the table, they moved of their own accord. I unpacked the meat and as I finished she gave a gulp of distaste, but recovered herself.

'You found all that at the market? Out in the open air? It's disgusting!'

'What is? The open air?'

'Of course not: that is! Isn't it against health and safety regulations?'

'I have no idea. But look at the colours. Red, gold. The brilliant lustre, the bronze, all the colours of the flesh. Just leave it to me.'

I tied on a large apron, put my hands on her shoulders and steered her out of the kitchen.

'I'll take care of everything,' I reassured her. 'Take some "me" time, make yourself pretty, you're good at that.'

My private enthusiasm was not the kind of feeling I could discuss: I closed the door behind her. I poured myself a glass of white wine. The light streaming through the liquid was the colour of pristine bronze; the bouquet was that of a pickaxe in the hot sun striking a limestone boulder. I took out my tools: the handles of the knives fitted neatly in my palm; I felt a flash of inspiration. I arranged the cuts of meat on the table. Each was recognizably a piece of a slaughtered animal. My heart raced to see them so recognizable, and I was grateful to them for appearing just as they were. After a moment's pause, the hesitancy one feels before a blank page, I took the knife to them.

In an orange haze of alcohol and blood, I performed culinary alchemy; I transmuted the breath of life that swelled these cuts into symbolic colours, appetizing textures, scents that were recognizably those of food.

When I opened the kitchen door again, my fingers were tentative, everything I touched slipped from my fingers, which left a reddish trail. And everything I saw, when it moved, left a luminous wake, a vectorial aura that took some time to fade.

Océane appeared before me and I could not fault her. She was sheathed in a white dress, her every contour glittering with silvery light. Her body thus displayed on the plinth of her stilettos filled out her curves: her buttocks, her thighs, her breasts, her delicious belly, her shoulders, everything shimmered as the silk caught new reflections as she moved. Her hands with their painted nails fluttered with gentle, birdlike movements, stroking the air, touching objects, unconsciously arranging everything more perfectly. She moved slowly around the table as she laid the place settings and her slowness troubled me. Her intricate hairdo gleamed like polished oak, revealing the nape of her neck, the curve of her ears studded with diamonds. Her powdered lashes flickered like the wings of a languid butterfly, each flicker setting the perfumed space around her aquiver. She laid settings at the four cardinal points, arranging the plates at perfect intervals, the cutlery forming tangents, the glasses in perfect triads. At the centre of the table, on a white embroidered table runner, the candles cast shadows and soft reflections on the silver, the glass, the china. The small tongues of flame painted her dress with fleeting, iridescent touches as delicate as caresses.

When I entered, wearing my bloodstained apron, my hands crimson even under the fingernails, with curious stains at the corners of my lips, the little flames flickered and threw ghastly shadows on my face. Her eyes widened, her mouth gaped, she started back and just then the doorbell rang. Her recoil became a move towards the door.

'I'll finish off,' I told her. 'Have everyone come in and sit down.'

I rushed back into the kitchen and closed the door. She will be perfect, irreproachable, the ideal hostess to our friends – whose names escape me just now – expertly steering the conversation, radiating calm, making tactful excuses for my absence until I appear. She will be faultless. It is something she can force herself to do. She always succeeds. Which, when you think about it, is a frightening miracle.

The scents from my cooking crept past the door, straining at the hinges, cleaving the soft-wood panels, stealing through the gap at the bottom, and dispersed. But when I came out and shouted 'Grub's up!' a little too loudly, it seemed as though they did not suspect a thing. Sitting on our sofas, they were sipping champagne and chatting carelessly, their relaxed poses exhibiting a cool indifference.

Excitement coursed through my veins, fuelled by the white wine – I had drained the bottle. My loud, hoarse voice fractured the carefully calibrated background noise of soft chatter and music crafted by Océane. I had not taken off my apron or wiped my lips. When I burst into the soft halo of the living room, the atmosphere became so heavy, so stilted, that I found it hard to speak; but that may have been the drink or a failure of my excitement. I found it difficult to move under their watchful eyes, difficult to fill my lungs with this rarefied air, so that I could say a few words they might understand.

'Come,' I said, a little more quietly. 'Come, sit down. Dinner is ready.'

Océane, smilingly, ushered them to their seats; I carried in huge platters. I set before them a horrifying mass of pungent smells and bloody forms.

I had arranged the Chinese entrails to represent the mythic cabbage under whose leaves we are all found, that fecund vegetable that does not grow in any garden. I created a nest of green cabbage leaves and piled the crimson entrails at its centre, the trachea exposed, arranged as they would be inside the bird itself. I had made no attempt to slice it, since preserving the entrails intact was what gave the dish its piquancy.

I had lightly sautéed the cock crests, reflating them to accentuate the vivid red. I served them, piping hot and swollen, on a black platter that offered a striking contrast, a smooth plate on which they glided, quivered and shifted.

'You pick them up with chopsticks – I almost said tweezers – and you can dip them in this yellow sauce. But be careful, the yellow sauce is laden with chilli, packed with pepper, tinted with turmeric. If you prefer, you might try this one. It is a soft green, but just as powerful. It is a mixture of onion, garlic and daikon radish. The first will scorch your mouth, the second will scorch your nose. The choice is up to you; but as soon as you try one, it will be too late.'

The fried cockscombs – I had forgotten to drain off the oil – were wildly sliding around the black plate. A brusque movement as I set down the platter sent one of them skittering and then arcing into the air as if from a trampoline, where it hit the hand of one of our guests. He flinched and jerked his hand away, but said nothing. I kept going.

I had chosen not to slice the black pudding, and had cooked it only gently. I had coiled it into a spiral on a large hemispherical platter; a light dusting of curry powder and ginger gave off a piquant aroma.

Finally, in the centre of the table, I placed the three severed heads, the sheep's heads arranged on a raised platter, nestled on a bed of shredded salad leaves, each gazing in a different direction, eyes rolled back, tongues protruding, like a parody of the three monkeys who see no evil, hear no evil, speak no evil. Stupid fuckers.

'There we go,' I said.

There was a silence. The pungent scents filled the room. Were it not for the fact that our guests were caught up in this moment of unreality, they might have felt awkward.

'This is disgusting!' one man said in a shrill falsetto. I don't know who, because I never saw any of them again. I forgot them and even moved to live elsewhere, so that I would never again encounter them in the street. But the precise musicality of the word he used to express his unease often springs to mind: the 'd' like a hiccup, the long 'u', the final 'ng' dragged out like the snarl of an aeroplane making a belly landing. I remember the cadence of the word better than his face, because he had said the word 'disgusting' like an actor in a 1950s film, when it was the crudest word that could be uttered in public. In our beautiful living room, in the presence of the irreproachable Océane, this was all he could think of to say. They did what they could to express their disapproval of me, but, steeled by booze and bravura, oblivious to everyone but myself, I heard nothing. They should have spoken to me plainly, but unable to find the words – because in our social circle, language is so degraded as to be useless – they tried to communicate their disapproval with their eyes, tried to give me the withering glare that is usually effective. But they could not hold my gaze, they gave up trying. I am not sure why; but something in my eyes made them turn away, so that they would not be sucked in, wounded, consumed.

'Let me serve you,' I said with a politeness they would happily have foregone.

I used my hands to serve, since there is no fitting tool but a hand – and a bare hand at that. Using my fingers I prised open the generative cabbage, grabbed fistfuls of the glistening entrails and proceeded to break up the hearts, the spleens, to split the livers; with a crimson thumb I ruptured the tracheae, the larynges, the colons, to reassure my guests as to the degree of doneness: for such meats only the gentlest heat is appropriate, the flame should be a caress, a rosy touch: inside the flesh should still bleed. The cook's flame should not be that of the potter, which goes to the heart of a thing and transmogrifies its very substance; the cook's flame serves only to set the form, to fix the colours in their natural delicacy, it should not spoil the taste, the tang of animal functions, the flavour of animation now suspended, the taste of life, which, beneath its apparent stillness, must always be fluid, evanescent. Beneath the delicate, flushed surface, the blood remained. Taste it. This taste – the taste for blood – is one we never lose. Dogs that have tasted blood, they say, have to be put down before they become murderous monsters. But Man is different. He has a taste for blood, but he controls it; we each keep it to ourselves, nurture it on an inner fire and never show it. No more than the dog, when Man tastes blood, he does not forget; but the dog is an emasculated wolf and if he should change his nature, he must be killed, whereas Man, once he has tasted blood, is finally whole.

I served offal to everyone, a little more to the men than to the women, with a certain smile to explain the disparity. The heads I served only to the men, with an exaggerated wink they did not understand, but which made sure they did not refuse. As I placed each head on a plate, I turned it so the eyes stared at the women, and from each head, with its milky, sightless eyes, the tongue lolled out in a ludicrous expression that was excruciatingly funny. I burst out laughing, but no one joined me. I redoubled the nudges and the winks, the meaningful smiles, but it did nothing to dispel their terror. They did not understand. They may have suspected, but they understood nothing.

When I attacked the blood sausage, I was a little heavy handed with the steel and, with a sigh, a jet of black blood gushed out, splattering not only the serving dish but the tablecloth and the plates, two drops landed in a glass and immediately, imperceptibly mingled with the wine, a single drop landed on Océane's dress, just below the curve of her left breast. She collapsed as though she had been stabbed through the heart with a fine stiletto. The others silently got to their feet, taking the time to fold their napkins, then walked over to the coat rack. They helped each other into coats and jackets without a word, their polite assents communicated only with their eyes. Lying limply on her back, Océane was breathing evenly. The table was still illuminated only by candlelight. The small shivering flames sent shadows scurrying over the dress that enveloped her magnificent body like a breath; it shimmered like an expanse of water moved by a soft swell, an evening breeze, by a zephyr at sunset, the whole surface of her body quivered;

the one fixed point, the black bloodstain beneath the curve of her breast just above her heart.

With a nod, the guests said their goodbyes and left us. I picked up Océane and laid her on our bed. She immediately opened her eyes and began to cry; she gurgled, caught her breath, howled, sobbed, choking back phlegm and tears, unable to utter a word. Black tears coursed down her cheeks, ruining her dress. She wept without stopping, face buried in the pillow. The vast white pillowcase was smudged by her sobs, streaked with red, with browns, with faint metallic grey, with brackish water and this square of fabric became a painting. I stayed by her, wearing, I think, an idiotic grin. I did not try to console her or even to talk. I finally felt close to her, closer than I had ever felt. I hoped that it might last. I knew that all this would evaporate with the drying of her tears.

When she finally fell silent and dried her eyes I knew that everything was over between us. Everything that had gone before and everything that might have happened later. We fell asleep, lying side by side, not touching; she: washed, hair brushed, under the sheets; me: fully dressed, on top.

On Sunday morning she cried when she woke up, then hardened like concrete as it sets. On Sunday afternoon I left.

By Monday morning I was living a different life.

I never saw her again, or any of the friends we had in common. I moved to the other end of the country, to the dreary, northern coast where I had a modest apartment, more modest than the house I left when I abandoned my wife.

I was uninstalling myself the way you uninstall a computer pro-gramme; one by one I shut down the thoughts that sustained me, trying not to act, so that I would not be acted upon. I hoped that my last task would be the one that precedes death: to wait.

Victorien Salagnon was the person for whom, without knowing, I had planned this wait.

Novel II

Going up to the maquis in April

W HAT PLEASURE IT WAS, going up to the *maquis* in April! When the fighting is not bitter, when the enemy is busy elsewhere, when you are not being chased by dogs, when you have not yet fired a shot, going up to the *maquis* is just as it is in a dream, but more vivid.

April buds, April blooms, April takes wing; April strains towards the light, leaves jostling each other to reach the sky. What pleasure to go up to the maquis in April! You always say 'go up', because the only way to reach the *maquis* is to climb. This secret forest where they hid is at the top of the slopes; the *maquis* is the other half of the country, the part above the clouds.

The column of young men scrabbled through the dense scrubland. Leaves quivered as the sap rose, the little corks stoppered by winter burst in the heart of the wood. With a little effort it was possible to hear the sap, to feel the palpitation by laying a hand on a trunk.

The column of young men scrabbled through undergrowth so dense that each could see only the three comrades walking in front and, if they turned, the three behind; each could believe that there were only seven of them plunging into the forest. The slope was steep and the leader marched above the eye level of those following behind. Their military air was of its times, the gaudy uniforms of 1940 had been repurposed for the members of the Chantiers de Jeunesse. To this was added a wide beret, worn at a rakish angle, to symbolize the French spirit. Armies can be distinguished by their hats; they allow for a touch of the whimsical, adding a flash of patriotic brilliance to drab, utilitarian clothes.

They climbed on. The trees shuddered. Their feet ached in thick clodhopping boots that would never fit. Military leather does not soften, so feet are forced to mould themselves to boots, as laces close like the jaws of a trap.

Their heavy kitbags cut into their shoulders. The metal frames chafed; the weight dragged them backwards; they struggled on, as sweat trickled into their eyes, made their armpits and necks sticky; they struggled to climb in spite of their youth and all the weeks spent in the open air at the Chantiers de Jeunesse.

They had been on marches, in the time they spent at the school for unarmed soldiers. Since they could not shoot, they marched, they hauled rocks, they learned to crawl, learned to hide in foxholes, to hide behind bushes, and most of all they learned to wait. They learned to wait because, first and foremost, the art of war is to wait without moving.

Salagnon excelled at these games, he threw himself into them wholeheartedly, but he was waiting for what was to come, for the moment when blood, rather than flowing round and round these cramped bodies, would finally spill forth.

'Sweat saves blood,' he was told. The motto of the Chantiers de Jeunesse was painted on a banner at the entrance to the forest camp. Salagnon understood the elegant logic of the maxim, but he loathed sweat more than he did blood. He had always looked after his blood, it coursed tirelessly through his veins, and spilling blood was only a figure of speech; whereas he was all too familiar with the stickiness of sweat, the disgusting glue that soaked his boxer shorts, his shirt, his sheets when summer came, and this stickiness was something he could not escape, it followed him everywhere, choking and disgusting him like the spittle of an unwanted kiss. All he could do was wait for the temperature to drop, for time to pass, doing nothing, and that frustrated him. This choked him even more. The motto was not appropriate, nor was the uniform of a defeated army, the lack of weapons or the duplicity cloaked by every action, every word, every silence.

When he reached the Chantiers with a forged travel warrant, they were surprised by his lateness, but he presented his excuses duly written out and stamped. No one read them, they simply skimmed from the letterhead to the indecipherable signatures half-hidden by official stamps; because the reasons did not matter – everyone has reasons, all of them excellent – what matters is whether they are officially sanctioned. They filed his paperwork and allocated him a camp bed in a huge blue tent. That first night he had trouble sleeping. The others, exhausted from the fresh air, slept fitfully and restlessly. He watched for the insects grazing the canvas. The darkness made it seem colder, the smell of damp earth and grass grew stronger until he felt a pang of sadness, but most of all this first adventure made him anxious. It was not passing himself off as someone else that bothered him, but the fact that they had accepted his false papers and asked no questions. On the whole, of course, the ruse had been a success; but it was a hollow victory. The plan was working, but there was nothing to be proud of, and he needed to feel proud. His mind fixated on these details, followed them to illogical conclusions, retraced the path, looked for some other way out and, finding none, he fell asleep.

The following day he was put to work in the forest. Under the trees, the bare-chested young men swung axes, hacking at tall, sturdy beeches. With each swing they let out a muffled grunt, echoing the shock of the axe-handle throbbing in their hands, and each swing produced great hunks of pale, pristine wood, as crisp as the pages of a new exercise book. Sap gushed from the notches, spattering them; they could imagine they were felling some creature engorged with blood. After a while the tree would quiver and fall in a booming crack of timber and a rustle of twigs and leaves.

Leaning on the axe-handles, they mopped their brows and peered up at the gaping hole in the foliage. They could see the bright blue sky, and the birds once more began to sing. Using crosscut saws, as lithe and dangerous as snakes, they worked in pairs to cut the trees into logs, synchronizing their movements, singing sawyers' songs learned from a twenty-five-year-old they called 'boss', who, to them, seemed to possess the wisdom of a sage – though a sage in the modern sense, meaning he had a broad smile, wore shorts and was not one to waste words.

They piled the logs into neat steres along the wide dirt track. Trucks would later come to collect the timber. Salagnon was issued with a long, straight graduated rod, which served as a ruler when cutting the logs. Before he started, the boss touched his shoulder: 'Come and have a look.' He led him over to the steres. 'See that?' 'What?' He gripped one of the logs and slid it out a dozen centimetres, leaving a round hole in the cube of neatly stacked wood. 'Put your hand in there.' Inside, the stack was hollow. The chief slid the fake log back into place as though replacing a cork.

'You see? This is all about volume, not weight. This way we can exceed our quotas without having to work so hard. You need to cut the logs carefully to make sure the steres are hollow. Check that rod of yours, it's been marked already.'

Salagnon looked from the ruler to the boss, then looked at the stacks.

'But when the unit comes to collect them, won't they realize the stacks are hollow?'

'You don't need to worry about that. We work to volume and we make our quotas. The truckers work according to weight, but they load up their trucks with stones – usually the same ones – that way, they make their quotas, too. And the guys who make the charcoal, well, they just say that half of it has gone up in smoke. Because all this is to make charcoal for the gas generators to keep the trucks rolling. It's all about the war effort; but not all the effort needs to be ours.' He gave a wink that Salagnon ignored. 'The most important thing is to say nothing to anybody.'

Salagnon shrugged and did as he was told.

He went to fetch some logs. The foremen had all disappeared from the clearing, the lads had set down their saws and several were lying asleep on the ground. Two of them were sitting at the foot of a tree, singing the sawyer's song as they tugged at tufts of fragrant grass. Another lad had pursed his lips and was imitating the buzz of a saw as he lay on his back, arms folded behind his head. Still holding a log in each hand, Salagnon stared at them, bewildered.

'The foremen have fucked off,' muttered one of the lads, who looked like he was asleep. 'You can drop the logs. We're just setting back the war effort a little,' he said, and opened one of his eyes, gave a wink, and closed it again.

They carried on mimicking the sounds of work. Salagnon stood awkwardly, feeling himself blush. When they suddenly burst out laughing, he was startled, only to realize that they were laughing at their little trick.

At the Chantiers de Jeunesse Salagnon did exactly as he was told. Nothing more. He did not dare ask who, in the chain of command, knew that the forestry unit was producing hollow stacks of timber. He had no idea how far the secret extended. He watched the leaders. Some only seemed to be interested in whether the workers' boots were polished, constantly looking for signs of dust and dirt and severely punishing such infractions. They were wary of such leaders, since sticklers for detail are dangerous; they do not care which side they are on, they care only about order. Other leaders were conscientious in organizing physical activities: marches, hiking with packs, press-ups. They inspired trust, since they seemed to be preparing the young men for something they were not allowed to talk about; no one dared to ask, since it could as easily be the *maquis* as the Eastern Front. Then there were the officers they did not think about, those interested only in military procedures – the perfect salute, the correct form of address; they enforced regulations just to pass the time.

The young men in the Chantiers de Jeunesse referred to themselves as 'we', an ambiguous pronoun that offered no information about the group, its size or it aims. It was 'we' who waited, who went unnoticed, and meanwhile, 'we' supported France; a France that was young and beautiful, but utterly naked, since 'we' did not know how to dress her. In the meantime 'we' tried not to mention that France was naked; pretended that it did not matter, that no one cared. It was April.

The uncle arrived with a new column of recruits. He did not come to say hello to his nephew. The two men pretended not to know each other, although each always knew where the other was. Salagnon found his presence reassuring; it signalled that his time in the Chantiers was only temporary, and the rumours of a National Revolution was just talk; it had to be. How could anyone know? The flag offered no information. Every morning the tricolour was hoisted and the recruits lined up to salute, each man seeing in its folds the face he expected to see, each one different. But, being unsure, no one dared not speak of it, just as no one talks about an inkling or a private dream for fear of being mocked. Though in this case, it was for fear of being killed.

They ate badly. With hunks of bread, they sopped up the revolting stew of vegetables and beans that had spent too long bubbling in a cast-iron pot. The mess tins were washed in a stone trough with cold water from a diverted spring. One night Salagnon and Hennequin were assigned to washing-up duty. The thick gloop that did not stick to the stomach stuck fast to the aluminium tins. Hennequin, a tall, heavy-set activist, scrubbed with steel wool, scouring away metal with the traces of food to create a hideous green-grey sludge from the green spinach and the grey aluminium, which he rinsed away with clear water.

'It's not so much washing-up as sanding down,' Hennequin chuckled. 'Six months of this and I'll go right through the bottom.'

And he started to whistle as he scrubbed for all he was worth, fore-arms red-raw from the cold water, shoulders heaving from the effort. He whistled some well-known songs, a few obscure ones, some smutty ditties, and lastly 'God Save the King', loudly and repeatedly. Though Salagnon did not recognize the tune, he accompanied his friend with a series of deep bass *bum-bums* that inspired Hennequin to whistle more loudly, more clearly, and even to sing to himself, but just the notes, not the words, because he did not know the English apart from the title. They scrubbed harder, to the rhythm of the tune, the encrusted food disappearing before their eyes, the anthem rising loud and clear above the scrape of metal, the bubbling of the spring, the splashing of the trough. An officer – one of those obsessed with trivial regulations, like parents or teachers – raced over to them.

'We don't sing that sort of thing around here!' He seemed livid.

'Lully? We're not allowed to sing Lully? I didn't know that, boss.'

'What Lully? I'm talking about what you're singing.'

'But it's by Lully. He's not seditious, he's dead.'

'Are you taking the piss?'

'No, boss.'

Hennequin began to whistle again. With grace notes, it sounded very seventeenth century.

'Is that what you were humming? I thought it was something else.'

'What's that, boss?'

The officer muttered something and turned on his heel. As soon as he was out of earshot, Hennequin sniggered.

'You've got a hell of a nerve,' said Salagnon. 'Is it true, that story of yours?'

'Musically speaking, perfectly true. I could have argued my case note by note, and that boot-licker wouldn't have been able to prove I was whistling anything illicit.'

'We don't need to prove anything to kill you.'

Salagnon and Hennequin flinched and spun around, scrubbing brush in one hand, a huge mess tin in the other: the uncle was standing there, looking as though he was just wandering around, strolling with his hands behind his back.

'In certain situations, a bullet in the head is as good an argument as any.'

'But it *was* Lully...'

'Don't play dumb with me. In other circumstances, a flicker of hesitation, a hint of a defiance, anything other than a brisk "Yes, sir" – the slightest gesture beyond lowering your eyes – could get you shot. Put down like a wayward animal. Faced with such idiocy, any officer would be within his rights to flick the clasp on his holster, casually take out his pistol and, without even taking you aside, put a bullet in your head and leave your corpse for someone else to ship back to wherever they want, he doesn't give a shit.'

'You can't just kill people just like that.'

'In the times we live in, you can.'

'It would be impossible to kill everyone. There'd be too many bodies! How would they get rid of them all?'

'Bodies are insubstantial. They only seem solid while they're alive. They take up space because they're bloated with air, because they're blowing hot air. Once they're dead they can be stacked into piles. You wouldn't believe how many bodies can be packed into a trench after they've stopped breathing. They dissolve, they liquefy. You can churn them into the mud, you can burn them and leave no trace behind.'

'Why are you talking like that? You're making this up.'

The uncle held out his wrists. They were encircled by neat scars, as though his skin had been gnawed at by rats trying to chew off his hands.

'I've seen it. I've been a prisoner of war. I escaped. The things I've seen, you couldn't begin to imagine.'

Hennequin flushed red and shifted from one foot to the other.

'Get back to your washing-up,' said the uncle. 'Don't let spinach dry out or it'll stick. Scout's honour.'

The two young men silently went back to work, their heads bowed, too embarrassed to look at each other. By the time they raised their heads again, the uncle had disappeared.

It all happened early one morning. The officers were racing around, suddenly anxious, packing their belongings ready for the off. Some disappeared. A convoy of trucks arrived to evacuate the camp. The tents had been struck and were loaded into the trucks. They had to clamber aboard and drive down to the Val de Saône train. They were being sent to help the war effort.

The lads witnessed a strange argument between their leaders. The topic was the details of loading the trucks and their position in the convoy. It seemed important to them whether they were to lead or bring up the rear, and the spirited argument led to abruptly raised voices and angry gesticulations; but all remained ambiguous as to their reasons for wanting to be in one position rather than another. They were adamant, yet they provided no rationale. Lined up along the roadside, the boys waited, their kitbags at their feet, laughing to hear such pettifogging, such hierarchical importance being applied to the ramshackle trucks parked along the dirt track.

The uncle tensely insisted on riding in the last truck with a hand-picked group he had taken aside. Others grumbled, one in particular, an officer of the same rank with whom he did not get on. He, too, wanted to be in the last truck, to be the 'file closer', as he put it. He repeated this phrase several times with particular emphasis; to him it seemed argument enough, a sufficiently important and military phrase, to carry the decision, and he designated the lead truck as the uncle's.

Salagnon was standing, waiting, as the uncle passed, close enough to brush against him, and as he passed he mumbled: 'Stay with me and only get aboard if I say so.'

The argument continued and the other officer conceded. Furiously, he took the leading truck and with exaggerated gestures gave the signal to set off. 'Maintain visual contact!' he yelled from the head of the convoy, half hanging out of the door, standing stiff as a tank commander. Salagnon climbed aboard and, at the last moment, Hennequin came to join him. He squeezed in next to him and sat down, laughing.

'They're fucking crazy. It's like the army of San Theodoros in the Tintin comics: three hundred generals and five corporals. Give them an officer's stripe and straight away they start putting on airs, preening and pouting like a couple of old biddies outside a door, waving each other in, because they're too polite to go first.'

When the uncle climbed into the cab and spotted Hennequin, he was about to say something; he half opened his mouth, but the convoy was already under way. The trucks set off with a clatter of suspension springs and the roar of powerful engines. As they juddered along, the recruits clung to the slatted sides of the truck; they drove through the forest, heading for the road to Mâcon.

The rutted track, strewn with rocks and branches, made for heavy going. Spaces opened up between the trucks, the convoy leader was soon out of sight and, before they emerged from the forest, the three vehicles bringing up the rear turned on to a narrow track that rose steeply towards the very ridges they were supposedly heading away from.

Hanging on to the truck, they jolted along. Hennequin seemed concerned. His wide eyes flickered from face to face and saw not a glimmer of surprise. He struggled to his feet, banged on the glass partition. The driver continued while the uncle turned and glanced at him coldly. Hennequin began to panic, tried to jump out and had to be restrained. They grabbed him by his arms, his neck, his shoulders, and forcibly sat him down again. Salagnon had no idea what was going on, but it all seemed so straightforward that he just behaved like everyone else. He helped hold down Hennequin, who was thrashing about and yelling. No one could make out what he was saying as he was drooling.

The uncle tapped on the window and signalled for them to blindfold him, which they did using a scout's scarf. 'Not my eyes, not my eyes!' Hennequin spluttered painfully. 'I promise I won't say anything. Let me go, I got in the wrong truck, that's all. It's not a crime, taking the wrong truck. I won't say anything, but don't blindfold me, I can't stand it! Let me see! I won't say a word, ever.'

He sweated and sobbed, he stank. The other lads held him at arm's length, reluctant to get too close. His thrashing subsided, his cries became whimpers. The truck pulled to a halt and the uncle climbed into the back.

'Let me go,' said Hennequin softly. 'Take off the blindfold. I can't bear it.'

'You weren't supposed to be here.'

'I swear I won't say anything. Just take off the blindfold.'

'Knowing will only put you at risk. The German police break men's bodies the same way you would break a nut, to get at the secrets inside. It's much better for you if you don't see.'

At that moment, Hennequin pissed himself, and did worse. The stench was too much, they left him by the roadside, trussed just tightly enough to make sure it would take some time to wriggle free. The truck moved off again, the other lads carefully avoiding the wet patch left by the boy they had thrown out.

The trucks dropped them off at a spot where the track became a dirt trail that wound through the trees, and headed back empty, safeguarded by bureaucratic tricks too complicated to explain here, but which served well enough at the time.

They cut through the forest, moving in a straight line, heading for the *maquis*. They had been climbing for a long time when a glimpse of sky finally appeared between the trunks, the slope became less steep, the walk less strenuous, until eventually they reached level ground. They emerged into a sprawling, upland meadow ringed with beech trees. The sparse ground rang with their footsteps; the rock beneath the grass rose up in huge mossy crags to which clung strong, squat beeches, deformed by the mountain climate.

They stopped, pouring with sweat, set down their kitbags and slumped on to the grass with exaggerated groans and loud sighs.

Waiting for them in the middle of the meadow, a thin, wiry young man stood leaning on a walking stick. He wore a colonial *chèche* around his neck, and the pale blue kepi of the French Camel Corps pushed back on his head; he wore his revolver in a leather holster strapped to his chest, making it look not regulation-issue, but once again a weapon for killing. He was known as 'mon Colonel'. For most of the young men, this was the first French army officer they had seen who did not look like a rural policeman, a quartermaster or a scout leader; he looked more like the officers who manned road blocks, the impeccably dressed *Kommandanturs*, or the terrifying officers scouring the country roads in caterpillar trucks. He was like a German, a modern warrior, with just a touch of French flair that put fire in their bellies. Even standing alone, he filled the mountain pasture; the breathless boys, full of silent admiration, smiled, and one by one they stood to attention as he approached them.

He moved towards them with an easy gait, saluted the officers, addressing them as 'Lieutenant' or 'Capitaine', according to their age. He sized up the lads and gave each a curt nod. He gave a welcome speech, and although no one could remember the details, the overall message was: 'You are here. This is the moment. You are in exactly the right place at precisely the right time.' He reassured them and gave them space to dream; he was both tradition and an adventure, they knew that with him things would be dangerous, but they would never be bored.

They set up camp. A derelict grain store served as their headquarters. They restored a crumbling ruin, repairing the roof of thin stone slates, made bivouacs using green tarpaulins and saplings cut from the forest. The weather was sunny and cool, the work invigorating and pleasurable. They set up stores, a camp kitchen, a water supply, everything they would need to live for some time, far from everything, cut off from everyone.

Amid the scattering of rocks and the sturdy trees, the grass seemed to grow before their very eyes, pale stalks rippling in the breeze. A multitude of yellow flowers glistered in the sun; from certain angles they looked like a vast, golden platter reflecting its rays. On the first night they lit campfires, stayed up late, laughed heartily and fell asleep where they lay.

The following day it rained. The sun rose grudgingly and was so well hidden behind the bank of cloud it was impossible to say just where it was. Youthful enthusiasm, like cardboard, becomes limp when wet. Exhausted, chilled to the bone, poorly sheltered by their makeshift camp, the young men found themselves plagued by doubts. Silently, they watched raindrops trickle from their tents. Wisps of fog stole across the meadow, gradually engulfing it.

The Colonel did the rounds of the camp, carrying his gnarled box-wood cane, a coiled spring of hard wood whose power he controlled. The rain did not seem to make him wet, it streamed over him like light. He shone even more brightly. His features closely mirrored his bone structure, rivulets of water followed the folds of his skin, tracing a map that exposed its rocky contours. He was, in everything, the quintessence. He wore his Saharan *chèche* carelessly knotted around his throat, his pale blue kepi tilted at a rakish angle, his regulation-issue pistol hung over his chest, and he moved from one bivouac to the next, knocking his cane against the saplings, bringing downpours in his wake that left him unscathed. During the rains his effortless fortitude was a blessing. He gathered the boys inside the big ruin with the patched-up roof. The floor was covered with straw. A large man known as 'Cook' handed out loaves of bread to be divided into eight, tins of sardines to be shared between two (this was the first of countless tins of sardines Salagnon was to open) and, for each of them, a steaming carafe of real coffee. They drank it with relish and some surprise, since it was neither dishwater nor coffee substitute, but real coffee from Africa, aromatic and scalding hot. This, however, would be the only time they got to drink real coffee in the *maquis* – to celebrate their arrival, or to ward off the effects of the rain.

*   *   *

They were trained, with the sole purpose of waging war. An infantry officer who had escaped from Germany taught them to use firearms. His uniform permanently buttoned, his face clean-shaven, his hair cropped to within a millimetre of his skull, nothing about his appearance betrayed the fact that he had spent two years hiding in the woods, except for the way he moved, stepping without ever cracking a branch, rustling a leaf, without touching the ground.

When he gave lessons, the lads sat in a circle on the grass, their eyes shining. He brought out a few wooden crates painted military green and placed them in the centre of the circle, opened them slowly and took out the weapons.

The first object he unveiled was disappointing; something about the shape made it seem innocuous. 'The FM 24/29,' he said. 'The *fusil mitrailleur* – the standard light machine gun of the French Army.' Their eyes glazed over. They disliked the term 'gun', even more so the word 'light', while the adjective 'French' made them sceptical. The gun seemed fragile, the magazine looked as though it had been accidentally inserted back to front. It did not have the stark, austere gravity of the German machine guns they had seen on every street corner, with their perforated muzzles ready to growl, their inexhaustible cartridge belts, the ergonomic metal grips that looked nothing like the preposterous wooden butts that made these guns seem childish. The small box magazine could not possibly contain many bullets. Surely the purpose of a machine gun was the ability to fire continuously?

'Don't be fooled,' the officer smiled. Nothing had been said, but he could read their thoughts. 'This weapon is the weapon of the war that we are going to wage. It can be carried. It can be shoulder-mounted. It takes only two men to operate: one to scan for targets and load the magazine, one to fire. See this little forked rest under the barrel? You can place it on a flat surface to take aim, making it possible to accurately fire high-calibre bullets from considerable distance. The clip holds twenty-five rounds, which can be fired one by one or in bursts. You think the magazine is too small? That you'll empty it in ten seconds flat? Ten seconds is a long time when you are shooting; in ten seconds you can gun down a whole platoon and get away. The trick is never to stay in the same position; it gives the enemy time to think, the opportunity to counter-attack. You wipe out a platoon in a few seconds, then get the fuck out. The FM 24/29 is the ideal weapon if you need to get in and out quickly, the perfect weapon for an infantry on the move, an infantry that is tactical but deadly. The strongest in the group carries it on his shoulder; the magazines are shared out among the rest of the unit. When it comes to weapons, size isn't everything, lads. Besides, the Germans have the big guns. We have only men, so we'll wage an infantry war. They dominate the terrain? We'll be the rain and the rivers they cannot control. We'll be the tide that eats away, the waves that break against a cliff; the cliff can do nothing since it cannot move, and eventually it crumbles.'

He raised an open palm and they all stared; he opened and closed it several times.

'You will form close-knit units as swift and deft as hands. Each man is a finger, independent but inseparable. Hands can surreptitiously slip into unseen places, they close into a fist to strike, then open again to become nimble hands that flutter and vanish. We will fight with our fists.'

He gestured as he said the word, his powerful hands clenching to become hammers then opening again, harmless, munificent. The young men watched enthralled. He could hold them spellbound, could teach without seeming like a ridiculous old fogey on a parade ground. Two years in the *maquis* had made him lean, honed his every movement, and he communicated through physical images that one wanted to experience.

He demonstrated the Garand semi-automatic rifles, several cases of which they had just received with plenty of ammunition. And the grenades, which were dangerous to use, since the shrapnel travelled further than it was possible to throw them if they were thrown like stones; the young men had to unlearn the simple throwing action they had learned as boys, and learn to stretch their arms behind them before throwing. He showed them plastic explosives, as soft as modelling clay to the touch, but explosive if handled roughly. They learned to field-strip and reassemble the Sten gun, constructed from tubes and rods and capable of withstanding any amount of abuse and continuing to fire. They practised shooting in a small valley ringed with bushes that deadened the noise, firing at straw targets already riddled with bullets.

Salagnon discovered that he was an excellent marksman. Lying on his belly on a bed of dead leaves, the rifle pressed to his cheek, the far-off target in his sights, he had only to picture the line extending to the target in order to hit it. It never failed: a slight contraction of his abdominal muscles, an image of the straight line, and he hit his target; all in an instant. He was thrilled to find he was a naturally good shot and beamed as he handed back the rifle. 'Accuracy is good,' the instructor said, 'but it's no way to wage a war.' And he handed the rifle to the next man, without paying him any further heed. It took Salagnon a moment to understand. In combat there is no time to lie down, to aim, to fire; more importantly, in battle the target hides, aims and returns fire. You have to shoot as best you can. Sheer luck and blind fear are the determining factors. At this thought, he felt the urge to sketch. Whenever Salagnon was restless, his fingers prickled with the urge to draw. The atmosphere in the *maquis*, as they dreamed of war in the springtime, made his fingers twitch constantly. He groped around him, found some paper. That night they had received a consignment of crates containing ammunition and explosives. Planes flew overhead; they had set a line of small fires in the darkness; as the roar of the engines faded, white parachutes blossomed against the inky sky. They had been forced to search for the supplies tangled in the branches, unravel and fold the parachutes, stow the crates in the rebuilt ruin and extinguish the fires; only then could they breathe a sigh of relief as they heard the crickets in the tall grass begin to chirrup.

While opening one of the ammunition crates, Salagnon froze when he saw a slip of brown paper. His fingers trembled and he felt his mouth water. The magazines were stored in grey cardboard boxes, and the boxes were packed in a fibrous paper, as soft as suede. He unwrapped the packages, careful not to tear anything, opening out each sheet, smoothing it, cutting along the folds, until he had a wad of sheets two hand-spans wide, the perfect size. Roseval and Brioude, who were on packing duty with him, watched his obsessive care. They had hastily unpacked the boxes of bullets, ripping the paper and setting it aside as kindling.

'What the fuck are you doing?' Brioude asked finally.

'Making a sketchbook. For drawing.'

They laughed.

'This is hardly the time or the place to be drawing. Me, I left my pencils and copybooks back at school. I don't even want to think about that shit any more. It's over. What are you planning to draw?'

'You.'

'Us?' They laughed even harder. Then stopped. 'Us?'

Salagnon got started. In a metal box he had a stash of Conté pencils of varying hardness. Now, finally, he took them out and sharpened them with a penknife. He shaved only as much graphite as was necessary to produce a point. Roseval and Brioude struck a heroic stance: standing in three-quarter profile, one fist on his hip, Brioude rested his elbow on the shoulder of Roseval, who adopted a classic pose, one foot forward, his weight resting on the other leg. Salagnon sketched them quickly, working happily. The pencils left soft lines on the thick wrapping paper. When he was done, he showed them the drawing and their jaws dropped. From the soft clay of the paper burst out two granite statues. They were instantly recognizable and the comic gallantry of their pose had been stripped away to reveal two heroes, brothers in arms, neither mocking nor mocked, striding forwards, building a future.

'Do another,' Brioude said. 'One each.'

They unpacked the remaining crates without damaging the paper. Salagnon stitched some of the sheets into a sketchbook with covers made of stiff cardboard he took from a box of food rations sent from America; the rest of the paper he left loose, to give away.

In late May the meadows and the woods reached their full beauty. The vegetation, gorged with light, finally filled every inch of space. The myriad greens would become uniform, the infinite variety of tones would fade and merge into a rather sombre, tarnished emerald. The brash greens of April and May gradually gave way to the soft, deep-water shades which had the force of constancy.

Combat units had been formed, whose members knew each other well. Every man knew who he could count on, who took the lead, who carried the ammunition, who gave the orders to hit the deck or to retreat. They had learned how to march in single file, letting no one fall behind; they had learned how to vanish at a signal, disappearing into foxholes, behind rocks and tree trunks, they knew how to fire in unison and how to cease firing, they knew how to work as a team. The Colonel was responsible for everything, from military training to camp maintenance. With a single glare he persuaded them that a well-run camp was, in itself, a weapon against the Germans. They felt themselves growing taller and more lithe, becoming stronger.

Salagnon carried on with his drawing; he became known for it; people would ask for portraits. The Colonel decided that this could be one of his duties. During the afternoon siesta, men would come and pose for him. He made sketches in his notebook, which he later copied on to loose sheets. He fashioned heroic portraits of boys brandishing their weapons, berets tilted at a rakish angle, shirts unbuttoned; young boys who were self-confident and smiling, proud of their uniforms, of their hair a little too long, and the rippling young muscles they liked to show off.

No one now tore the packing paper. They treated it with respect and brought it to Salagnon, wads of carefully smoothed sheets, as large as the folds in the wrapping allowed.

He also drew scenes of the camp: young men sleeping, gathering firewood, washing pots, doing weapons drill and sitting around the fire in the evening. The Colonel pinned a number of drawings to the wall of the barn that served as their command post. He often studied them in silence, sitting at his makeshift desk of parachuted crates or standing dreamily, leaning on his gnarled walking stick. The sight of these young heroes reduced to simple lines made his heart swell with pride. He considered Salagnon invaluable. Pencil and paper put fire in their bellies.

He gave Salagnon a complete set of Faber-Castell pencils, a flat metal tin containing forty-eight different colours. It came from a German officer's briefcase which had been stolen from the *préfecture* for the documents it contained. A number of suspects were arrested and tortured on the flimsiest evidence. The man responsible for the theft was betrayed and executed. Information from the documents dispatched to London had been used to bomb a number of railway junctions while valuable cargo was being transported. The pencils were used by Salagnon, who never knew that they had been paid for in blood. He added depth to the shadows and made good use of the colours. He drew landscapes, sketching the tall trees and the great moss-covered boulders at their base.

Since he had no ink, he was forced to improvise with rifle grease and lampblack. Applied with a wooden spatula, this rudimentary, glistening black ink brought a dramatic chiaroscuro to certain scenes and faces. The young men in the camp saw each other in a new light; Salagnon helped them to adapt to life as a team.

For a very long time one early June night the sky remained a deep blue. The stars did not appear. They struggled to catch fire, while the soft, diffuse glow made lanterns redundant. A blue balminess made it difficult for the young men to sleep. Lying in the shadows or leaning against boulders, they quaffed the red wine they had stolen that afternoon. The Colonel had authorized the mission on condition that they did not get caught, that they abide by the rules he had drummed into them, and that they leave no man behind.

Armed with buckets, hand drills and wooden dowels, they had headed down the hill to the train station on the banks of the Saône. They slipped between the carriages in the shunting yard. When they had come to the tank-wagons stencilled with German writing, they assumed they had reached their goal. The spigots were sealed, but the tanks themselves were made of wood; so they drilled holes in the sides and wine spurted into their bucket with a splashing sound that made them giggle. They plugged the holes using the wooden dowels and headed back up the hill, careful not to be seen, sweltering under the blazing sun, spilling a little wine, and, as they moved further from the station, their laughter grew louder. They left no one behind and arrived back as a unit, so the Colonel could not complain. He had left the buckets of wine in the cool spring waters to chill and suggested they wait a while before drinking it.

Through the night that never quite drew in, they drank at a leisurely pace, and every now and then they would laugh at some joke or at their accounts of the day's adventure, which they told over and over, embellishing and embroidering it as they did so. The stars did not come out, time stood still. It had stopped, just as the pendulum of a clock stops when it comes to the top of its arc: stops for a moment and then starts up again.

A paraffin lamp glowed in the barn that they used as their head-quarters, and the yellow light trickled through cracks in the door. The Colonel had summoned the perfect team of officers to lead the units – those young men the boys looked up to like big brothers, like young schoolteachers – and, behind closed doors, they talked for many hours.

A little tipsy, Salagnon was lying on his back next to the bucket. He scrabbled at the grass beneath him, the grass damp with dew and sap, his fingers sinking between the roots, and he felt the cold breath rising from the earth. In his fingertips he could feel the night swelling beneath him. It is foolish to say that night falls when, in fact, it rises from the ground, gradually suffusing the sky, which, to the very last moment, remains the only source of light. He stared at a lone star suspended above his head and fathomed the depths of the sky; he felt against his back the curve of the Earth, a vast sphere on which he lay as it whirled in space, for ever falling through the dark blue immensity that encompasses all things, at the same pace as the motionless stars above him. Together they fell, pressed against the vast sphere to which they clung, fingers buried among the roots of the grass. That presence of the Earth beneath him coursed through him with a profound happiness. He tilted his head back: the trees were black shadows against the pale night, each an immeasurable weight, the unmoving rocks gleamed softly at the base of the trees, the Earth buckling under their weight, while the vast expanse of space was a sheet stretched taut by the weighty presences of the boys lying on the grass, the squat trees, the mossy boulders, and this thought filled him with the same deep, enduring joy.

He felt an endless, boundless goodwill towards all those stretched out on the grass like him, those drinking from the same bucket of wine; and he felt the same goodwill tinged with hope towards the officers gathered in the barn, towards the Colonel with his sempiternal, sky-blue Camel Corps kepi. They had been talking for hours now behind closed doors, huddled around the only lamp, whose light spilled through the cracks in the door, a yellow light against the outside world that was blue or black.

The paraffin lamp was extinguished. The unit leaders came out to join them, drank with them until finally the night grew dark and the grass was wet with crisp dew.

The next day, standing before the serried ranks of men, before the flag fluttering atop a pole, the Colonel solemnly declared that the battle for France had begun. It was time to go down and to fight.

Commentaries III

A prescription for painkillers from the all-night pharmacy

THIS HAPPENED ON A NIGHT when I went out, a summer night when I was out walking, when I was sick, when I could not even swallow my own saliva, could not swallow at all because of the damage to my throat caused by a viral raiding party. If I was not to drown in my own spittle, I had to prattle on and on, letting the saliva evaporate. Mouth open, I meandered through this summer night and glimpsed a reality I had never seen before. It had been hidden from me. I had walked through it yet never noticed it. But that night I was ill, my throat was red-raw from the marauding virus and, unable to swallow, I was forced to walk the streets with my mouth wide open to allow my saliva to evaporate. I talked to myself as I prowled the streets of Lyon, heading for the late-night pharmacy in search of painkillers.

We enjoy a riot; we relish the thrill. We dream of civil war, just for fun. And if our little game results in a few deaths, that only serves to make it more interesting. Since time immemorial, *douce France*, the land of my youth, has been laid waste by violence, just as my throat has been ravaged by this virus that causes me so much pain that I can't swallow. So I walk the streets, my mouth agape, and I talk.

How dare I speak for my whole country?

I speak only of my throat. A country is nothing more than a tongue, a dialect with an army. France is the sum of spaces in which French is spoken; my aching throat merely the most obvious, the most real, the most palpable instance, and so that night I was wandering the streets in order to heal it, looking to get painkillers from the all-night pharmacy.

It was a balmy June night, there was no reason for me to have a cold. I had probably been infected on the protest march, from all the tear gas and the shouting.

In France we know how to hold a first-rate protest march. No country in the world can rival us in staging a demonstration, because to us they are one of the pleasures of our civic duty. We fantasize about street theatre, of civil war, with slogans like nursery rhymes and people thronging the streets; we dream of hails of tiles, of paving stones and catapult bolts, of mysterious barricades that appear in the night and of daring escapes in the morning. People take to the streets, people are angry, and *wham!* we all pile outside to perform the ultimate gesture of French democracy. In other languages 'democracy' translates as 'the power of the people', but in French, by virtue of the tongue that throbs in my mouth, it becomes an imperative: 'Power to the people!' and it is played out on the streets, with brute force, the timeless force of street theatre.

It is axiomatic that the French state does engage in discussion. It issues orders, directives, pokes its nose into everything. It does not debate. Nor do the People want a debate. The State is violent; the State is generous; everyone may benefit from its largesse, but it does not debate. Nor do the People. The People's interests are defended by the barricade, and our militarized police are trained to breach that barricade. No one wants to listen; we all want to fight. To accede would be to surrender. To understand the other would be tantamount to accepting his words in our mouths, to have our mouths filled with the power of the other, to fall silent when he speaks. It would be humiliating; we find the very idea offensive. We must make the other shut up, force him to capitulate, overpower him, leave him speechless, we must slit his talking throat, ship him to a penal colony in the sweltering forests of some island where only the birds and the dormice will hear him scream. All that is noble is the struggle, the overthrow of the adversary, and his eventual silence.

The State does not debate. The People hold their tongue; and when they are dissatisfied, they riot. A society devoid of language is sapped by silence, it mumbles and whimpers, but it does not speak; it agonizes, tears itself apart, it communicates its pain through violence, it explodes, smashes windows and crockery, then lapses back into fretful silence.

Whoever has been duly elected tells us how gratified he is to have been granted such power. Now, finally, he will be able to govern, he tells us, to govern without wasting time on debate. Our immediate response is to call a general strike, bring the country to a standstill and the people into the streets. Finally. The people, who have had enough of tedium, of aggravation and of work, join forces in order to take action. We are off to the theatre.

When we see protest marches in Britain, we can't help but smile. People march past, one by one, with their cardboard signs, with individual placards mounted on sticks, each with a hand-written message that needs to be read to be understood. They march past, the British, waving their carefully crafted, slyly humorous placards for the television cameras. They are flanked by lines of relaxed policemen in standard-issue uniforms. It is as though their police forces do not have the riot shields, the pads, the nightsticks or the water cannon to clear the streets. Their demonstrations give off an aura of politeness and boredom. In France we stage the most glorious protests in the world, they are outpourings of excess and joy.

We pile into the street. People taking to the streets is an everyday reality; taking to the streets is the dream that unites us, the French dream of solidarity with the common man. I went down into the street wearing running shoes and a tight T-shirt that would allow no purchase for anyone attempting to grab hold of me. I didn't know anyone. I joined the swelling ranks, took up a position behind the banner and added my voice to the crowd shouting slogans. It took several people to carry our huge banners with short slogans written in big letters, and large vents to stop them being whisked away by the wind. A number of people are needed to carry these words that stretch for several metres, and they flutter, they are difficult to read; it hardly matters since no one needs to read them, they simply need to be large and red, and the words emblazoned on them are those we chant in unison. When you are part of a demonstration, you shout and you run. Oh, the delights of civil war! Heavily armed police cordon off the streets, massed behind riots shields, shin guards, helmets with lowered visors that make them indistinguishable; with long truncheons they pound on their shields, beating out a constant drumroll. Inevitably, things turned ugly. That was the purpose of our presence.

A hail of stones was answered by a volley of grenades, a cloud rose and spilled across the street. 'Fine, then we'll fight them in the shadows!' laughed those among us who had come with helmets, with balaclavas, with iron bars and slingshots, and began smashing shop windows. Our throats were already burning from the tear gas and the shouting. A shower of steel bolts fired from catapults shattered shop windows into glittering splinters like crystal waterfalls.

Riot police moved along the street, tooled up with old-fashioned weaponry, moving with the precision of a legion, stones clattering against the polycarbonate riot shields; the muffled explosions of grenades filled the air with tear gas; groups of plain-clothed officers plunged into the crowd, grabbed a few of the rioters and dragged them behind the wall of shields that continued to advance with its implacable drumroll of truncheons. The racket! Our banner fell. I picked it up and, with the help of someone else, hoisted it above my head; we were now leading the march, then we tossed it aside and ran. Oh, the joys of civil war! The joys of street theatre! We raced past show windows that splintered as we ran, past gutted shops where young men masked with scarves helped themselves, as though from their own cellars, then they too turned and fled, pursued by determined, square-jawed young men. This last group ran faster; they wore orange armbands and when they managed to pin a masked youth to the ground they took out their handcuffs. I was running. This was why I had come: a demonstration without a frantic chase is a waste of time. I was zigzagging through the side streets.

The sky began to flush pink. Night was drawing in. A bitter wind whipped away the acrid gas. Sweat trickled down my back and my throat was beginning to hurt. In the surrounding street, squad cars moved slowly, each carrying four square-jawed officers, scanning the scene through a different window as the car wheels crunched over the shards of glass. There was a smell of burning. The streets were littered with abandoned clothes, shoes, a motorcycle helmet, pools of blood.

Me, I was in pain, in agony.

The government, having gone too far, retreated; it reversed its hastily adopted measures with counter-measures born of panic. As always, stability was restored: the unspoken compromise was ineffective and unwieldy. France engineers its laws as it creates its cities: the imposing avenues of the Napoleonic Code are at the centre, while all around is a confusion of ramshackle, temporary buildings connected by a warren of roundabouts and inextricable contraflows. We improvise. The balance of power matters more than the law, chaos proliferates through the accumulation of individual cases. Each of these laws stands, because, while it would be inflammatory to enforce them, it would be embarrassing to repeal them. So they remain on the books.

Oh, I am in terrible pain!

It was June, yet here I was suffering from a cold, my throat was sore, my throat was inflamed, the throat which is the mouthpiece and the target. With a prescription in my pocket I tramped through the streets of Lyon to buy medicine from the all-night pharmacy. I crossed the city in the dead of night, my mouth hanging open so my saliva could evaporate. I couldn't swallow anything, not even the natural secretions of my own mouth, its natural functions thwarted by pain, and so I wandered, open-mouthed, constantly talking to myself so that my saliva could evaporate, so I would not drown with drool I could not swallow.

I moved along the night-time pavements of shifting shadows, stepping aside to avoid the flotsam of cuddling couples, lone wanderers, excitable groups. I moved without seeing them, preoccupied by my pain. I passed white cars emblazoned with blue-and-red stripes that moved in slow motion, as their occupants scanned the street. The word POLICE was stencilled in large letters on the cars, and on the similarly decorated vans parked along the street, from which these same young men studied the shifting shadows.

Ô douce France! Mon cher pays de fraîcheur et d'enfance! O sweet France! The dear country of my youth, so serene, so heavily policed... Another car passes in slow motion carrying muscular young men... It swims silently through the night aquarium, draws level with me, studies me and moves off again. The summer nights are muggy and dangerous, and the streets of the city centre are under close police control; all night they circulate: the highly public police presence makes pacification possible. Yes, *pacification*! We practise *pacification* in the very heart of our cities, in the very heart of power, for the enemy is all around. We have no adversaries, only an enemy; we have no truck with any adversary that would lead to endless debates, but an enemy that we can counter with brute force. With the enemy, there is no debate. We fight him; we kill him, he kills us. We don't want to talk, we want to fight. In a country famed for its gentle way of life, for the fine art of conversation, we no longer want to live together.

But I don't give a shit. I'm in pain. I walk and talk. I am walking to rid myself of what would drown me. If I am thinking about my country it is only to give me something to talk about, because I must keep talking on my odyssey through the streets of Lyon, otherwise I'll be forced to drool to keep from drowning.

I am thinking about France; but can anyone say they are 'thinking about France' without laughing, without making others laugh? Anyone except for grand old men, and then only in their memoirs. Who but de Gaulle could say he is 'thinking about France' with a straight face? Me, I am simply in pain and I have to go on talking as I traipse to the all-night pharmacy that will save my life. So I talk about France the way de Gaulle used to talk about it, confusing characters, muddling tenses, mangling grammar to cloud the issue. De Gaulle is the greatest liar of all time, but he was a liar in the way all novelists are liars. By the sheer power of his words he gradually fashioned everything we needed to live in the twentieth century. He could give us reasons to live together, reasons to be proud of ourselves, because he invented them. And we now live in the ruins of what he built, among the tattered pages of this novel he wrote, the novel we mistook for an encyclopaedia, for a clear-cut image of reality when it was pure fabrication; a pleasant fabrication it was tempting to believe.

Home is a common language. France is the cult of the written word. We lived between the pages of the Général's memoirs, on a stage-set fashioned from the words he wrote.

I was walking the streets at night, my throat red-raw, and the mute violence that walks beside us now walked beside me. It took a subterranean path, scuttling beneath my feet, under the pavement: the cannibal mole of French violence crawled, unseen, beneath me. From time to time it came up for air to snatch at its prey, but it is always there, even when we cannot see it. We hear it scrabbling. The ground is unstable; it could give way at any moment, the mole could surface.

Enough! Enough of all this! But still I cannot swallow. My spittle drains away, dissipates as I babble. I trade my pain for a torrent of words, and the torrent that pours out of me saves me from drowning in my own spit. I am imbued with the spirit of France. I find verbal solutions to my pain, and in speaking I survive the winter ills I catch in summer months.

Finally, I arrived at the all-night pharmacy. I would do better to shut up. In public, while I queued, I choked back my pain.

* * *

The restless queue formed a parabola inside a cramped pharmacy scarcely big enough to contain us. We did out best not to make eye contact; we kept our thoughts to ourselves. Because we all had our suspicions. After all, who goes to an all-night pharmacy other than nutjobs who don't know day from night and addicts looking for drugs they understand better than any medical student? Other than people too sick to wait until morning, emergency cases whose great, purulent bodies infect everything they touch? Time drags on. It drags on for far too long, because in an all-night pharmacy people move at a snail's pace, their every gesture slows until there is barely any movement, until there is no movement, and the impatience swells until it fills this cramped space with its locked doors where so many of us are huddled in the queue.

An assistant pharmacist with an African name dealt with the patients, never raising his voice or quickening his pace. His round face, black and utterly smooth, offered no purchase to anxious eyes. We did not look at each other for fear of contamination; instead we looked at the man doling out the medication, and he was not moving quickly enough. He carefully read the prescriptions, meticulously checked them several times, tilted his head without saying a word, but with a suspicious air, framed his questions as sighs, weighed up each customer; then he would disappear into the shelved back room and bring back whatever urgent medication the patient was waiting for, shifting his weight, silently fuming with unutterable rage, sick.

Outside the reinforced glass door that closed at 10.30 p.m., gangs of athletic young men came and went, hurling insults, shouting into mobile phones, laughing and high-fiving. They came out at night and pretended to stroll along the street, loitering on the pavement, jostling and shoving, sneering at passers-by; they gathered outside the all-night pharmacy at night, in the square of light cast by the reinforced glass door that was closed and locked at 10.30 p.m. They came like moths, fluttering outside the door that was closed to them, since they had no prescriptions. They never tired. Every time they walked past, they peered inside; they shouted, high-fived and laughed. They were excited by the flow of victims, the flow of money, the flow of drugs, they mocked passers-by, and though they never said a word, everyone understood. The fear on the faces of the sick people who had to elbow their way through the crowd made them laugh; the patients who passed, head down, clutching their prescriptions, pretending not to notice anything, but who had had to push their way through the gang to ring the doorbell and wait, cap in hand, looking as though they were simply waiting for the pharmacy to open.

A lady inside, a lady in the queue, said: 'I don't know what's got into them, but they seem very jittery these days.' A wave of approval ran through the queue. Without exchanging a glance, without looking up, without any explanation, they all understood. But no one wanted to talk about it, because this is not something that is talked about: it is something to be stated, believed.

Tensions rose early in the summer; tensions rose in the short, sweltering nights. Athletic boys prowled the streets stripped to the waist. The assistant pharmacist with the African name carefully checked prescriptions, asked for proofs of identity, guarantees of payment. Out of the corner of his eye he kept watch on the quadrangle of light cast on the pavement as gangs of young men swaggered to and fro.

When he had finished serving a customer, he would unlock the bulletproof glass door with a big bunch of keys, open it a fraction to let them out, then lock it again in a clatter of keys and the whisper of the rubber seal sealing out the air itself. The customer would find himself locked out, alone on the pavement, clutching a white paper bag printed with a green cross, and this would trigger a restless commotion among the young men strutting back and forth, a sardonic commotion like the flitting of mosquitoes that come and go, never landing, never seen, with a high whine that is a laugh; meanwhile, alone in the darkness, the customer would have to negotiate a path through the gang of muscular young men, clasping the paper bag of boxes filled with the precious active ingredients intended to cure him;

he had to steer a course through the gang, duck out of their path, avoid their eyes, but nothing ever happened; it was just fear.

The assistant pharmacist admitted only those he felt he could trust, those who rang the bell and showed their prescriptions. He agreed to open the door or he did not. He said nothing else. He scanned the prescriptions, checked the labels on the little boxes, processed the payments. Nothing more. He performed tasks related to his business. He was no more present than a machine. He doled out boxes of active ingredients. In the all-night pharmacy full of the seriously ill people, who were queuing while trying not to make eye contact, tensions rose. The round, black face of the assistant, his eyes fixed on the display of the cash register, afforded no purchase.

A small, thin woman stepped forwards, thinking it was her turn. A tall, handsome man stepped in front of her; his eyes were penetrating, a lush fringe of hair fell over his forehead, his nose was arrogant. His tone, as befitted his height and his elegance, was curt: 'Did you not see that I was ahead of you?' She mumbled something, but she did not blush – her dry skin made blushing impossible. She was trembling. Muttering inaudible excuses, she let him pass. He was intelligent, well-heeled, dressed in elegantly crumpled linen; she was small and gaunt; her whole body seemed worn out; and I cannot recall what she was wearing. The man was savage, ready to hit her, and she was terrified.

Waves of liquid darkness crashed against the hull of the all-night pharmacy. All around, the capricious carnival carried on, stray shadows that seemed like people but were simply shadows that moved through the streets; these shadows appeared in the rectangle of light, appeared for an instant before the locked door, teeth flashing for a moment, eyes shining in their dark faces, while we huddled in the all-night pharmacy, waiting our turn, angry that it was taking so long; terrified that it might never come. We were given painkillers.

The arrogant man slapped down his prescription on the counter, unfolded the paper, muttering that this was intolerable, absolutely intolerable, that it was always the same. He pointed to a single item, tapping the page several times with his forefinger.

'I just want that one.'

'What about the other items? The doctor prescribed them all together.'

'Look, the doctor is a friend of mine. He knows what I need. He only prescribed the rest so I can claim it back on the insurance. But I know what I'm doing. I know what I take. Just give me the one I asked for.'

He broke the sentences into fragments, enunciating each syllable, speaking with the air of a man who knows what he is talking about, who knows just as much as the doctor, and certainly more than an assistant pharmacist working the graveyard shift. He seemed to be spoiling for a fight. The haggard little woman took several steps back and adopted a submissive air to avoid being hit, while the arrogant man shot her furious looks that weighed on her delicate shoulders of bone and cardboard. We all waited silently in the queue at the all-night pharmacy; we did not want to speak to each other for fear we might be mad or depraved or ill; we did not want to know, because to know would require communication and communication is dangerous, it aggravates, it contaminates, it lacerates. We wanted medication to soothe our pain.

Without thinking, the scrawny little woman shuffled forwards a little, perhaps anxious not to give any more ground than she had already, so she stepped into the no-man's-land around this overwrought man, who bristled like the spikes on a floating mine. She encroached on his personal space; she was close enough to read the prescription and so he slapped his hand over it, annihilated her with a single glare; she beat a hasty retreat.

'This is ridiculous!' he roared. 'It's always the same! People don't know their place! They're always trying to jump the queue! You need eyes in the back of your head!'

He slapped his prescription several times, pushed his fringe back with an elegant gesture, the folds of his linen suit following his movements.

'I want this one,' he said, growling as menacingly as he could.

The assistant remained impassive. His plump face was immobile. His dark skin gave no clue as to what he was thinking, and the furious man brushed back his fringe again. His eyes glittered, his face flushed red, the hand resting on the counter quivered; he wanted to lash out again, to smack the counter, smack the prescription, smack anything to get this stone-faced man to listen.

'So are you going to give it to me or what?' he roared. The assistant did not flinch.

The fat guy standing in front of me, a tall man with a moustache and a pot belly straining at his shirt buttons, started to breathe harder. Through the thick glass we could see the idle young men swaggering past the door, and each time they passed they shot a look at those of us trapped inside, a look designed to provoke. Things were taking a nasty turn. But I said nothing. I was in pain.

The handsome, arrogant man in the linen suit was quivering with rage at being put into the same category as the plebs at the all-night pharmacy, while behind him – as far behind as she could get now – the haggard little woman was trembling as she probably always trembled. He might whirl around and slap her, the way you might slap a child who is being irritating, just to vent your anger and to show who is boss. And, after the slap, she might let out a high-pitched wail and roll on the floor, her limbs twitching; or, for once, she might raise her head and hurl herself at him, fists flailing, battering him with the ineffectual punches that weeping women throw; then again, she might just as easily say nothing and just endure the blow, a sharp crack in her back, leaving her even more stooped, racked by silent sobs, more hunched, more worn out.

And the guy in front of me, the one with the moustache and the pot belly, how might he react to seeing a little woman crumple to the floor, or a little woman lash out with shrill sobs, or a little woman shrinking down to erase herself a little more from the surface of the Earth? How would he react? He might snort loudly, his breath rumbling like a vacuum cleaner on full power; he might step forward, shifting his fat frame to punch the arrogant shit. The elegant man would crumple, his nose streaming blood, screeching in protest, dragging shelves of diet pills on top of himself, while the fat man with the moustache would stand, massaging his fist, gasping for breath like a moped on a hill about to stall, his pot belly straining against his shirt buttons, one of which is threatening to fly off. Meanwhile, scrabbling on all fours, the other man would hurl abuse and threats of legal action, but make no attempt to get to his feet; then the African assistant – unruffled, because he has seen it all before – would try to calm the situation. 'Come on now, messieurs. Calm down,' he would say. Then the little woman would rush over as if to help the arrogant shit bleeding on all fours, shooting a reproachful look at the man with the moustache, who by now would be obviously struggling for breath, and at serious risk of congestive heart failure, a pulmonary embolism, the cessation of all blood flow through arteries that are too constricted, too narrow, too clogged to contain the violence within him.

The assistant pharmacist would carry on dealing with prescriptions, tapping gently on the touchscreen of his till, while continuing to appeal for calm in measured tones – 'Messieurs, that's enough now! Come on, madame!' – all the while thinking about the tear-gas canister in the drawer under the counter that he would happily whip out to spray the lot of them. But that would mean having to air the room, and the only door is the one on to the street, which he could not open, since the people prowling around outside would need to be kept out. And so he would appeal for calm, while dreaming of gunning them all down, just to make it all stop.

And me? How would I have reacted to this flare-up of French violence? I was in pain. The virus had ravaged my throat. I needed painkillers. I needed something that would transform my pain into a muted nothingness I could no longer feel. And so I said nothing. I waited my turn. I waited for my hand-out.

It goes without saying that nothing actually happened. What do you expect in an enclosed space with double-locked doors fitted with bulletproof glass? Nothing, except maybe suffocation...

Business as usual. The assistant heaved a sigh and gave the man what he had asked for. He washed his hands of the whole thing. Once he had what he had come for, the man grunted 'Honestly!' and turned on his heel, looking daggers at everyone in the queue. The assistant opened the door, then resumed his position behind the counter. 'Who's next?' For him, it was an uneventful night. The line inched forwards. The little woman handed over a crumpled prescription, which had clearly been used many times before, pointed to a line with a trembling finger, and the assistant shrugged. He dispensed psychotropic drugs, he dispensed somatotropins. To those who knew their doctors well, he gave whatever they asked; to the others, he gave precisely what was written on the prescription; to some, he gave a little extra. The rules varied. He was swayed by violence, and dispensing favours forestalled any conflict.

Eventually, I emerged with my medicine. The door was opened and closed for me. I cut a path through the gang on the pavement and nothing happened.

Shadows flitted in the darkness; people talk to themselves at night, but these days it is impossible to tell whether they are insane or whether they have bluetooth phones. The heat of the day radiated from the stones; the air throbbed with an oppressive tension. Two police cars full of young men passed each other in slow motion, discreetly signalled with their headlights, and glided on without a ripple. They were searching for the source of violence, and when they found it, they would be ready to pounce.

Everything is shit! I can't swallow a thing. I can't help but wonder what this sickness is that forces me to talk endlessly to evaporate spittle that would otherwise drown me. What disease? A marauding, viral raiding party from the great desert outside? And since the attack, my immune system has been ravaging my throat; my internal defences have been purging, pacifying, rooting out and liquidating my cells in search of sedition. Viruses are nothing more than language, a packet of information transported by sweat, saliva or sperm, and that information insinuates itself into my cells and merges with my own language, leaving my body to speak the language of the virus. Forcing my immune system to slaughter my own cells, one by one, to purge them of the alien language whispering inside me.

The streets are brightly lit, yet still they seem frightening. They are so dazzling you could read under the street lamps, but no one reads because no one lingers. It is not the done thing to loiter in the streets. Everywhere is brightly lit. The air itself seems to shimmer, but it is an illusion: the street lamps cast more shadows than light. This is the problem with lamps: they accentuate the shadows that they do not dispel. As on the desolate plains of the moon, the slightest bulge, the slightest ridge casts a shadow so dark it cannot be distinguished from a crater. And so, in the high contrast of night, we sidestep shadows, lest they be chasms.

We are loathe to stay outside. We rush along while squad cars, in slow motion, glide past at walking pace, scanning the pedestrians; a multiplicity of eyes peers through tinted windows, studying us, then they glide on down the street, searching for the root cause of the violence.

Society is sick. Bed-ridden and shivering. It doesn't want to listen. Curtains drawn, it keeps to its bed. It is no longer interested in itself as the totality. I realize that an organic metaphor of the State is a fascist construct; but the problems of our society can be described in fascist terms. We have issues involving order, blood, land; problems involving violence; problems involving force and the use of force. These words spring to mind, regardless of their connotations.

I wandered through the night like a crazed shadow, a talking phantasm, a walking logorrhoea. Eventually, I arrived home to find a gang of youths skulking beneath a lamp post in my street. They were huddled around a moped parked on the pavement; its owner stripped to the waist but for a motorcycle helmet, the chin-straps dangle over his shoulders.

In the desolate street every window was dark. I could hear their raised voices, although I could not make out the words, but their clipped phrasing told me all I needed to know: where they were from. From a distance, from the rhythms of their speech, I could tell from which hereditary strata of society they came. Apart from the boy with the helmet sitting astride the moped, not one of them was sitting. They were leaning against the wall, prowling the pavement, their arms sweeping the air like basketball players; they were scouring the street in search of adventure, however slight. They were passing around a huge bottle of something fizzy, throwing their heads back and drinking in long draughts.

I made my way through the gang. They stepped aside. They flashed mocking smiles and danced around me, but I kept walking. I was not afraid. I did not give off the slightest whiff of fear. I was too preoccupied by my pain, too busy not drowning in my own saliva. I passed through, muttering as I had been all night, mumbling to myself, vaporous words that no one could understand; this made them laugh. 'Hey, mate, you'll use up all your fixed tariff minutes talking to yourself all night.'

I was in pain. I was suffering from a national sore throat, from a French flu that squeezes the windpipe, leaves the throat red-raw and swollen, infects the precious organ of speech and triggers this torrent of words, these words that are the true lifeblood of the French nation. Language is our blood and it was flowing from me.

I walked away from the gang without bothering to reply. I was too preoccupied, and besides I had not understood the reference to technology. The rhythms of their language were not quite the same as mine. They fidgeted without moving, these boys, like saucepans left on the stove, the surface bubbling and seething within. I walked away, heading for my front door. I did not care about the outside world. (I knew only that I was in pain, and I clutched the little paper bag of medicines that became more and more crumpled as I walked. Inside the bag, in the little cardboard boxes, was something that would heal me.)

A police car decked out with blue-and-red stripes glided along the street through the sheet of rain. It drew level with the gang. Four uniformed young men leapt from the car as one, flexing their muscles; one hitched up his belt in a clatter of weaponry. They were young, they were fit, there were four of them with limbs like coiled springs; there was no older, experienced officer to keep them in line. No one older or slower; no one with that detachment born of experience; no one who would not react recklessly; no one to defer this firepower. They were all of an age, these four warriors with sharpened steel jaws; they were very young and there was no one to keep a tight rein on them. Older officers are reluctant to pound the beat on muggy June nights; and so unpinned grenades are let loose, jittery young men searching in the darkness, playing hide-and-seek with other jittery young men.

The young men in sober blue approached the young men in baggy, garish gear, one of whom was bare-chested. With only a perfunctory greeting, they demanded to see the boys' papers and the papers for the moped. They studied the laminated cards, scanning the surrounding area, their movements gradually slowing. Without bending down, they gestured at a cigarette butt on the ground and had it picked up to be examined. Their movements became slower and more meticulous. Each of the boys was forced to empty his pockets and was frisked by one of the boys in blue, while another officer stood, his hand on his weapons belt, watching their every movement. It dragged on. They were searching; and if you search for long enough, eventually you will find something. The sluggish movements had slowed almost to immobility. It could not last. Stasis does not last long. The body is a coiled spring; it abhors stillness. There was a sudden jolt, shouts, the moped fell. The boys dissolved into the darkness, leaving only one, the shirtless lad, lying on the ground, his helmet having rolled away, pinned by two of the athletic men in blue. He was dragged to the squad car in handcuffs. In the silence of the dark street I could clearly hear them talking into their radios. Lights flickered on in some of the windows, faces appeared at the crack in the curtains. I heard the charges being read: 'Refusal to submit to an identity check. Resisting an officer. Fleeing the scene.' I heard the words clearly. I was still standing in the street, but no one asked me anything. Preoccupied with my own physiology, I had nothing to fear; shut away inside myself I had no interest in anything but obliterating my pain. One by one the lights in the windows flickered out; the squad car drove away with one additional passenger; the moped was left lying on the pavement, the helmet in the gutter.

People can be arrested for resisting arrest: it is magnificently circular logic. The legal reasoning is impeccable, but circular. The reasoning seems rational once it has appeared; but how does it appear?

Obviously, nothing had happened on my street that night. But the situation is so tense that the slightest judder triggers a spasm, a brutal convulsion of the whole body politic, as though fighting off a genuine disease; except that there are no enemies, excepting a part of ourselves.

Society is racked by a raging fever. The bilious body politic cannot sleep; it fears for its sanity and its integrity; the fever makes it restless; the bed is too hot for it to get comfortable. Every sudden sound is interpreted as an act of aggression. The sick cannot bear loud voices; they find them as painful as physical blows. In the sweltering heat of their rooms, the sick confuse signifier and signified, fear and effect, words and blows. I closed the door behind me. I did not flick the switch, the light streaming in from outside was enough. I went to the sink and poured a glass of water. I swallowed the medicine I had been prescribed, then I fell asleep.

The mind hangs on by a thread. The mind teeming with thoughts is a helium-filled balloon in the hands of a child. The child loves his balloon, he clutches the string, terrified of letting go. The psychosomatotropics dispensed in pharmacies alleviate anxiety; the medications open the hand. The balloon drifts away. The psychosomatotropins dispensed in pharmacies promote a sleep that is disconnected from the physical world, where insubstantial ideas seem real.

How can anyone tell them apart in the darkness?

Real-life grammar is not a theoretical grammar. According to the rules of grammar I have read in books, when I use a pronoun it is an empty box; nothing, absolutely nothing, indicates who is meant. The pronoun is a box; its contents are unknown; the content is provided by the context. Everyone knows this. The pronoun is a closed box, and without opening it, everyone knows what is inside. People understand me.

How do they manage to distinguish? Tension heightens the senses. And the situation in France is very tense. One discarded ticket and a whole train station can be ransacked, committed to the flames. You think this is an exaggeration? Actually, it's an understatement. I could reel off many worse horrors, all of them true. The situation in France is tense. A metro ticket tossed on the floor of a station prompted a militarized public order operation.

A single spark and everything burns. When a forest burns, it is because it is arid and overgrown. Forces are despatched to track down the spark, to arrest the guilty party. Everyone wants whoever created the spark to be caught, to be named and shamed and hanged. But sparks are constantly being struck. And the forest is as dry as tinder.

One day an inspector asked to see a young man's ticket. He had just tossed it away. He said he would go back and find it. The inspector was determined to take him aside and record the offence. The young man protested. The inspector ruthlessly insisted; he could not bend the rules. There followed a commotion that cannot be fully explained by all the witness statements. Witnesses are always inconsistent about how violence erupts. Actions appear as quantum leaps; events are entirely unknowable in nature, their outcome depends solely on probability. The event might not have taken place, but it did take place; it is therefore inexplicable. It can simply be recounted.

Events unfold with the logic of an avalanche: everything gave way because everything was unstable, everything was ready. The ticket inspector tried to take the offender aside; the young man protested. Other young men gathered round. The police arrived. The young men shouted wildly. Riot police showed up to clear the metro station. The young men ran and began to throw small things, then larger objects that it took several of them to dislodge. The police adopted the regulation configuration. Officers in riot gear lined up behind their shields. They lobbed tear-gas grenades, they charged, they barked orders. The station began to fill with gas. More young men spilled from the metro. They did not need the situation to be clarified: they chose sides without the need for explanations. Everything is so volatile: confrontation is always possible.

The metro station was littered with broken glass, filled with gas, devastated. People emerged, sobbing, bent double, clinging to each other for support. Blue vans with bars on the windows were parked everywhere. Traffic came to a standstill; metal barriers cordoned off the streets; access was vetted by uniformed officers and by lines of muscular young men in plain clothes clutching crackling radios.

A plume of smoke as thick as tar shattered a window and rose into the sky. The station was ablaze. A column of firemen was despatched, flanked by men protecting them with shields. A hail of small objects rained down on the plastic shields and the station forecourt; the firefighters sprayed the building with dry ice.

This might seem absurd: the two things are incommensurable, a metro ticket and a train station. But this is not anarchy: the rival forces to the clash knew their roles in advance. Nothing was premeditated, but everything was ready; the ticket started the riot the same way that a key starts a truck. It is enough for the truck to be there, it will start when you turn the key. No one takes issue at the disparity between the key and the truck, because it is the design of the truck that allows it to start. The key does nothing; or very little.

We like to think that a magnificent train station in the centre of a city represents order, and a riot represents disorder; this is reassuring, but false. We do not take the time to look at stations, we are merely passing through. But take the time to study them, sit for a while as others bustle about, and it becomes clear that nowhere is more chaotic than this intermodal passenger complex where trains, metros, buses, taxis and pedestrians all converge, each obeying their own private logic, attempting to go on their way without obstructing the others, each following a broken line, like ants on a huge anthill made of pine needles. It takes only a minor jolt, a slight stumble, an impurity in this fluid system, and the order masked by stillness immediately reappears. The spate of impatient people filling the station solidifies, arranges itself into lines, takes shape. People pair up, groups form; eyes which cast all around now focus on a few particular spots; empty spaces appear which were previously crowded; perfectly straight, blue lines form where previously there was a motley mass; objects fly along particular trajectories.

The forces of law and order do not maintain order, they *create* it; they create it, because there is nothing more orderly than war. During a battle everyone knows their place; there is no need for explanations: all that is required is an organizing principle. Everyone knows, and acts; in war everyone knows his role, everyone is in his place. Those who do not know leave the battlefield in tears. Those who do not know their place pretend they understand nothing; they think the world has gone mad and they complain; they watch the train station behind them burn. They cannot comprehend this absurdity; they believe that order has broken down. They live or die at random.

The moment the ticket was discarded, the station was ablaze. There were bodies clashing and others fleeing. People got organized. The organizing principle was race.

The young man who was stopped for discarding his ticket was black. The station burned.

Race does not exist. It exists just enough for a station to burn, for hundreds of people with nothing in common to group themselves according to colour. Black, brown, white, blue. After the incident in the station, the groups of colours were uniform.

After the troubles the police passed through the carriages of the terrorized trains. Thumbs hooked into their weapons belts, they moved
slowly down the aisles, studying the faces of the passengers. They
were equipped like shock troops; they were lithe and determined in
their militarized uniforms. They no longer wore the old *gendarme*
uniform with straight-fit trousers, flat shoes, cloak and kepi; instead
they wore trousers cinched at the ankles for jumping, high-top shoes
for running, baggy jackets and helmets jammed tight on their heads.
From their belts hung the implements of beating and restraint. Their
redesigned uniform was based on the paratroopers.

They stroll through multi-coloured, multi-cultural trains at a leisurely
pace, checking identity papers. They do not check at random, that would
be inept. They use a colour-coded system everyone understands. This
is common knowledge. It is part of our human capacity to perceive
similarities. When the trains stop at stations, there is a nasal crackling
of loudspeakers, the primal sound that marks the divisions of urban
areas. 'People loyal to France, the police are safeguarding your security.
The police are hunting outlaws. Comply with inspections, be on the
alert, follow instructions. Populations loyal to France, the police are
watching over you. Help them to help you. This is about your security.'

Security. That is something we know a thing or two about.

Having surrendered my body to psychosomatotropins, I was not
sleeping.

From the outside, there was nothing to distinguish this sleep from
death; my body is immobile; it is wrapped in a sheet that could serve
as a winding sheet or a shroud, which could help carry me through
the darkness or across the River Styx. Freed from the body, the mind
becomes a gas lighter than air. It becomes helium, a balloon; it is
important not to let it go. In neurochemical sleep, the mind is a helium
balloon no longer tethered by a thread.

The constant roar of thoughts carries on, language continues to spill
out. The flow is Man. Man is a talking puppet, a marionette worked

by strings. Gorged with medications to quell the pain, unmoored from my thin-skinned body, I allow the helium balloon to drift. Language flows of itself, it rationalizes what it thinks, and it thinks only of its flowing. Only a thin thread keeps the balloon bloated with fears anchored to the ground.

To whom can I talk? From whom do I descend? To whom can I say that I belong?

I need race.

Race has the simplicity of the great follies, those that are easily shared since they are the noise made by our cogs when there is nothing to direct them. Left to its own devices, thought fabricates race; because thought automatically classifies. Race knows how to speak to me of who I am. Resemblance is the simplest notion I possess. I search for it in others' faces. I feel for it in my own. Race is a method of classifying people.

Who will I talk to? Who will talk to me? Who will love me? Who will take the time to listen to what I say?

Who will welcome me without asking anything of me?

Race answers me.

Race speaks of human beings in an irrational, disordered fashion, but it speaks.

Race responds to the serious questions that weigh on my heart. Race is capable of simplifying complex questions with outrageous answers. I wish to live among my own. But how can I recognize them if not by their appearance? If not by faces that resemble my own? Resemblance tells me where the people around me are from, what they think of me, what they want. Resemblance does not need to be measured, it is apparent.

When the mind is idling, it classifies; when the brain is thinking, even about nothing, it classifies. Race is classification based on resemblance. Everyone understands resemblance. We understand it; it understands us. We look a lot like some people, less like others. We read similarities in every face, the eye seeks it out, the brain finds it, even before we think to look, even before we think we have found it. Resemblance helps us to live.

Race survives all refutation, because it is the product of a habit of thinking that precedes reason. Race does not exist, yet reality never disproves it. Our minds constantly evoke it; it is an idea that recurs time and again. Ideas are the most enduring characteristic of human beings, much more so than the flesh that shrivels and decays. Ideas can be passed on, unchanged, encoded in the structure of language.

The brain goes its own way. It seeks out differences and finds them. It creates forms. The brain devises classifications useful to its survival. It classifies instinctively, trying to predict events, it wants to know in advance how those around it will act. Race is idiotic and eternal. No need to know what is being classified, it is enough to classify. The concept of race does not necessitate contempt or hatred, it functions with the feverish meticulousness of the psychotic who carefully places a fly's wings, its legs, its body in different, carefully labelled boxes.

Where am I from? I wonder.

The helium balloon floated away on the wind, no longer anchored by the thread of language. What race, I wonder, do people see in me?

I have an ancestry, of course, though it does not amount to much. If I trace back the source of the blood that courses through me, I can go no further than my grandfather. He is the mountain from which all springs flow, the ridge that blocks my view. I cannot see beyond; close as he is, he is the horizon. He, too, wondered about his ancestry, but he found no answer. He talked tirelessly about procreation. He talked about many things, he talked endlessly, and he had fixed ideas on every subject, but he was at his most voluble and his most clear-cut on the subject of procreation. The merest mention of the subject would set him off. 'Watch,' he would say, raise his hand and, with his right forefinger, point to the joints on his left hand, the middle finger extended. He would count off the phalanges, the wrist, the elbow. Each joint represented a degree of kinship. 'Among the Celts,' he would explain, 'the prohibition on marriage alliances extended all the way to here.' He would indicate his elbow. 'The Germanic peoples permitted marriage as far as the wrist. These days, we are here,' he said, indicating the joints of his extended middle finger. 'It is a gradual decline,' he would say, running his index finger from elbow to finger with disgust, showing the inexorable progress of promiscuity. On his own body, he would locate the precise point of the taboo according to the epoch and the people. He spoke with such certainty he left me speechless. On the subject of bloodlines, he had an extensive knowledge. He knew all there was to know about the passing on of material goods, of bodies, of names. He would speak in a tone that frightened me a little, that slightly nasal, histrionic drawl formerly used for speaking French, and now heard only in old movies or on crackly recordings of radio programmes where everyone tried to speak properly. His voice had the metallic ring of the past. I would be crouching in front of him, squatting on my stool, and I found the whole thing a little frightening.

My grandfather would speak beneath the blade. He would sit in his blue velvet armchair in the corner. On the wall above him hung a knife in its sheath. From time to time, it swayed in the breeze without making a sound. I had seen him take it down, seen the knife removed from the battered leather scabbard. The crusted red flakes on the blade might have been rust or blood. I was deliberately left in doubt; everyone laughed at me. Once, someone mentioned 'the blood of a gazelle' and everyone laughed harder. On the other wall hung a large framed drawing of a city that I have never been able to identify. The houses were lopsided, the people were veiled, the streets half hidden by canvas awnings: it was difficult to make out the shapes. I remember this drawing the way you remember a smell, without ever knowing which continent it might have come from.

It was here that my grandfather would sit and talk, in the big blue velvet armchair that only he used. He would hike up his trousers before he sat down, to stop them creasing at the knees. The rounded chair back traced an arc over his shoulders, encircling his head with a halo of studded timber. He would sit bolt upright, arms resting on the armrests, never crossing his legs. When he had settled himself comfortably, he would address us. 'It is important to know the origins of our name. Our family lives on the border, but I have found instances of our name in central France. It is an ancient name that means working the land, taking root. Names spring up from places, like plants that later spread their seeds. Names contain their own origin.'

Sitting on my little stool, I would listen. My grandfather had an enormous wealth of knowledge on the subject of bloodlines. He could read the past through the way that names were spelled. He could trace the phonological shifts that led to a place name being transferred to the name of a clan.

Later, much later, when I had found my voice, I never discovered a single detail of what he had told us in any book, nor in any of the conversations I had. I think he made it up. He drew on hearsay, he embellished, pushed the slightest link to its logical conclusion. He took his need to explain very seriously, but the realities he described to us existed only at the foot of his blue velvet armchair for long as his story lasted. What he said existed only as words, but it was spellbinding, since it made it possible to hear the nasal sound of the past. On the subject of bloodlines, his desire for rules was inextinguishable and his thirst for knowledge inconsolable. No encyclopaedia could ever fill his boundless appetite, so he invented those things he wished existed.

Towards the end of his life he became obsessed with genetics. He learned the fundamentals through popular science magazines. Genetics finally gave him the clear-cut answer he had longed to hear. He had his blood 'read'. It took twenty years and a lot of study for me to understand how blood could be 'read'. My grandfather contacted a laboratory that classified the mitochondria that bind to white blood cells. Mitochondria never die, they are handed down, like words. Mitochondria are the words and we are the sentences. By counting the frequency of words in speech, we can know the secret thoughts in the hearts of others.

He had a laboratory analyze all the blood groups he carried. He explained to us what he was looking for. I would get mixed up and call them 'bloody groups'. This made everyone laugh, but kindled a spark of curiosity in my grandfather's eyes. 'Blood,' he said, 'is the most important ingredient. We inherit it, we share it, and we see it from outside. The blood you carry gives you colour and form, because it is the broth in which you were simmered. The human eye can distinguish between different blood types.'

My grandfather had a sample of his blood taken, and one from his wife. The sealed vials were labelled with their names. He then sent them to the laboratory and from these few drops of blood he learned the mysteries of the bloodlines. Look around at the turmoil in the world. You'll be able to discern something that will give it order. That thing is resemblance; and it can be spoken of as 'race'.

The results arrived in the sort of thick envelope used for government documents; he opened it, his heart hammering. Beneath the state-of-the-art logo of the laboratory were the results of the tests he had requested. My grandfather was a Celt and my grandmother Hungarian. This, he announced to us on a winter day when we had all gathered for dinner. He was a Celt, she was Hungarian. I wonder how he persuaded my grandmother to hand over some of her blood. The laboratory had 'read' it, using a process whose details he did not trouble to explain. He had little interest in details. The results had arrived in an envelope and only one thing mattered: she was Hungarian, he was a Celt.

His knowledge of the life sciences was superficial, the sort of information not found in academic textbooks, but frequently reprinted in the popular magazines, which are the only ones anyone actually reads. He had no interest in abstractions; he wanted concrete answers, answers he called facts. Of the wealth of twentieth-century science, he remembered only this one ghostly idea, which would haunt him all his life. The idea which was repeatedly dismissed, refuted by academic papers, yet still he would come back to it, through half-truths and rumours, through his longing to finally understand; if you want something badly enough, if you are prepared to read between the lines, molecular analysis makes it possible to recuperate the concept of the bloodline. Tacitly, the study of molecules and how they are passed on seems to corroborate the idea of race. This is not something we believe, it is something we long for only to dismiss. Yet such is our desire to impose order on the confusing mysteries of resemblance that the idea constantly reappears.

So my grandmother was Hungarian and my grandfather a Celt. She was a monstrous horsewoman with slitty eyes; he a naked colossus smeared with woad. She galloping across the steppes in a cloud of dust raised by her horses' hooves, seeking out villages to plunder, children to abduct and devour, buildings to raze, leaving the land grassy and barren; he drunk and holed up in a circular, stinking hut, practising insalubrious music-related rites from which the body cannot emerge unscathed.

How did it come about, their coupling? Their coupling. Because they must have coupled, they are my grandparents. How did they manage? She a Hungarian, he a Celt, savage peoples of an ancient Europe, how did they even manage to meet? To meet. How did they come to be in the same place, to be settled for long enough, since they did not travel through Europe at the same pace? Were they forced by threats? By the threat of spears with jagged heads, bronze swords, quivering arrows threaded on the strings of double bows? How did they manage to remain still next to each other without one of them being drained of their lifeblood?

Did they protect themselves? Did they protect themselves from the cold, the bitter chill of an ancient Europe roamed by primeval tribes? Did they protect themselves against the blades they lunged towards each other the moment they came within striking distance? They wore leather clothes which smelled of rot, thick furs ripped from animals, and breastplates of boiled hide studded with nails, shields emblazoned with bulls' heads ringed by red symbols, nostrils streaming with blood. Could they protect themselves?

And yet they must have managed to couple, because I am here, but where could it have happened? Where could they have found a place to lie when they had no common ground beyond the battlefield? When one tribe spent their days astride sweating horses, while the other congregated in huge enclosures scattered with bones and defended by palisades of sharpened stakes.

Where could it have happened but on a patch of trampled grass, amid smoking ruins strewn with broken weapons? How could such a thing have happened between two mismatched peoples except in the aftermath of war, in the flickering shadows of great pennants planted in the ground at the close of some conjuration; how but on the mossy ground in a forest of tall trees, or on the flagstone floor of some colossal castle? How?

I know nothing about their coupling. I know only two words: 'Celt' and 'Hungarian'. I do not know what he means by informing me and the rest of the family about the results of his blood test. He floats the words on the warm air of a wintry living room, 'Celt', 'Hungarian', and, having uttered them, he marks a silence. The words swell. He had had his blood analyzed and I have no idea what he was trying to find out, why he was telling us, those of us gathered around him, me sitting on my little stool, on a winter's day when we were all together. 'Celt,' he said, 'and Hungarian.' He let loose these two words as one might take the muzzles from two huge hounds and let them prowl around us. He was demonstrating how much could be read from a drop of blood. He was telling those of us gathered around him: we are bound by blood. Why did he say this, and to me, a child? Why did he want to silently conjure the coupling that was the source of that blood?

He suggested that each of us have a drop of our blood read, so that all of us gathered in this winter room could know what peoples we are descended from. Because each of us was descended from some ancient tribe. In so doing, we would discover who we were, and the mystery of the fraught tensions we felt when we were together would finally be solved. The table around which we gathered would be transformed into the icy continent roamed by ancient peoples, each with weapons and pennants that looked alien to the others' eyes.

His proposal fell on deaf ears. It terrified me. I was sitting lower than the others on my little stool, and from below I could see their awkwardness. No one responded. No one said yes or no. They let him speak; left him unanswered; left 'Celt' and 'Hungarian', the two huge hounds he had unleashed, to lick the floor, to slobber over us, to threaten to bite us.

Why, on this winter day, did he want to recreate a primeval Europe peopled by barbarians and clans? We were gathered around him, a single family sitting around the blue velvet armchair where he sat, ringed by a halo of brass upholstery nails, beneath the knife that hung on the wall, swaying silently. He wanted us to read a drop of our blood and in that blood to find the story of warring peoples, the history of insurmountable differences written in our bodies. Why did he want to divide us, we who were gathered around him? Why did he want to see us as unrelated? When we were, as much as possible, of one blood.

I have no interest in knowing what can be read into a drop of my blood. I feel queasy enough thinking about their blood. Enough is enough. I don't want to say any more about it. I don't want to hear about the blood that flows between us. I don't want to hear about the blood that flows over us, but still he keeps talking about the race that can be read in us and which confounds reason.

He went on talking. He claimed to know how to read the stream that represents lineage. He wanted us to follow his example, to become intoxicated by this reading, to bathe together in this stream that constitutes human history. He was inviting us to bathe with him in the stream of blood; this would be our bond.

My grandfather was thoroughly enjoying himself. In veiled terms, he embellished the laboratory report in which nothing was said but everything was implied. The narrative of race is never far from madness. No one dared say anything; we all looked the other way. I watched from below, silently squatting on my little stool. In the crystalline air of the wintry room he eagerly performed his theatre of the races, staring at us, one by one, looking through us, looking past us, to the never-ending clash of ancient peoples.

I do not know what people I am descended from. But it doesn't matter, does it?

Because there is no such thing as race. Is there?

These warring peoples do not exist.

Our life now is much more peaceable. Isn't it?

We are all the same. Aren't we?

Don't we all live together as one?

Don't we?

Answer me.

In the area where I live the police never venture; or rarely; and when they do venture here it is in small groups who chat lazily, who stroll along, hands behind their backs, staring into shop windows. They park their blue cars on the kerb and, arms folded, they watch the young girls go by like everyone else. They are athletic, armed, but they behave like gendarmes from the sticks. I like to believe my neighbourhood is quiet. The police never notice me; I barely notice them. That said, I have witnessed an identity check.

I'm talking about it as though it were a big deal, but in my area ID checks are rare. We live in the city centre; we are protected from such checks by the distance between the city and the suburbs. We never venture into the suburbs, and when we do, we go by car to supermarkets in shopping malls, and even then we keep our windows closed and ensure our doors are locked.

In the street, no one has ever asked me to prove my identity. Why would they ask? Don't I know who I am? If someone asks my name, I tell them. What more could they want? Like most people who live in the centre, I never carry the little card with my name on it. I am sufficiently certain of my name not to need an aide-memoire. When politely asked for my name, I give it, the way I would give directions to someone who is lost. No one in the street has ever asked me to produce my card, the little card the colour of France that bears my name, my photograph, my address and the signature of the *préfet*. Why would I need to carry it on me? I know all the information by heart.

This, of course, is not the issue: the *carte nationale d'identité* is not intended as a reminder. It could just as easily be blank, the colour of France, blue with the scribbled signature of the prefect of police. It is the act itself that counts. This is something every child understands. When little girls play at being shopkeepers, it is the act of handing over imaginary money that forms the basis of the game. An officer carrying out an ID check does not give a damn about the contents of the card, he doesn't bother to decipher the writing, to read the names; an ID check is an unvarying sequence of actions. It begins with a brusque request, there is no greeting, just a simple, resolute demand; the subject fumbles for the card, proffers it; those who know they may have to produce it always keep it within easy reach; the card is scrutinized, first one side, then the other, for much longer than it takes to read the printed words; it is handed back reluctantly, almost regretfully, and may be followed by the subject being searched. Time stands still. This can take a while. The subject of the inspection must be patient and silent. Both parties know their roles; all that matters is the sequence of actions. I am never subjected to an ID check, my face is self-evident. Those who are asked to produce the card I never carry are identified by something in their faces, something unquantifiable but instantly recognizable. ID checks follow a circular logic: officers check the identities of those whose identities are checked, and in doing so confirm that those whose identity they are checking belong to the group whose identities are checked. The check is a gesture, a hand on the shoulder, a physical call to order. Tugging on the leash reminds the dog he is wearing a collar. No one checks me, my face inspires confidence.

So, I witnessed an identity check at first-hand. No one asked me for anything, no one checked my ID. I know my name by heart. I never carry the little France-blue card that corroborates it. I was carrying an umbrella. It was because of the storm that I witnessed the ID check. The lowering clouds burst and the downpour came just as I was crossing the bridge. The bronze expanse of the Saône was hammered by the raindrops, overlaid by thousands of intersecting circles. There is no shelter on the bridge, nothing before you reach the far bank, but I had my umbrella, so I crossed it at a leisurely pace. People scurried through the torrent, shielding their heads with jackets, with a briefcase or a newspaper that quickly became sodden, even a hand – anything that offered a token display of protection. They were warding off the rain; everyone was running, while proving they were trying to shelter, while I sauntered across the bridge, savouring the fact that I did not need to run. I clutched the canvas sail sheltering me from the raindrops that beat like a drum roll, splashing all around me. A sodden young man grabbed my arm, laughing, and huddled against me, and we walked together. 'Lend me your umbrella till we get to the end of the bridge?' Chuckling and dripping wet, he nestled against me, he was supremely cocky and smelled nice; his impudence made me want to laugh. Arm in arm, we walked in step to the far side of the bridge. I now had only half an umbrella and one side of me was getting soaked, he cursed the rain and chattered to me incessantly. We made fun of the people running and making protective signs above their heads. I smiled at his audacity, his brazen cheek made me laugh, the guy was a livewire.

As we came to the far side of the bridge, the storm began to abate. Most of the rain had fallen and was now coursing through the streets, only a light drizzle now hung in the freshly washed air. He thanked me with the same zeal he invested in everything; he gave me a pat on the shoulder and set off at a run through the last of the raindrops. He dashed too quickly in front of the blue car parked next to the bridge.

The handsome athletes scanned the street, arms folded, standing like statues beneath a shop awning. He was running too quickly; he noticed them and this modified his path; one of them stepped forward, gave a curt salute and said something; he looked confused, he was running too fast; he did not hear straight away. They all leapt out and chased after him. He did not stop, instinctively, observing the laws of momentum. They took him down.

I continued walking at the same pace, my black umbrella over my head. I drew level with them, hunkered on the pavement. The young men in blue uniforms were pinning the young man with whom I had crossed the bridge. I made to slow, not intending to stop, just to slow down, perhaps say something. I did not know exactly what.

'Please move along, monsieur.'

'Has this young man done something wrong?'

'We know what we are doing, monsieur. Move along, please.'

Lying on his belly, one arm twisted behind his back, his face pressed into the ground by a knee. His eyes rolled back, looked up at me. He gave me a look that was unfathomable, in which I saw disillusionment. That is what I thought I saw. I moved along. They hauled him to his feet in handcuffs.

They had asked nothing of me; of him, with a gruff gesture, they demanded that he produce a card to prove his identity. Should I have said something? I don't like to argue with the musclemen of law and order; they're as tense as coiled springs, and armed. They never talk. They are all about action, control, power. They implement. I heard them on the radio behind me, giving the reasons for the arrest: 'Refusal to comply. Resisting arrest. Failure to produce an ID card.' Glancing behind me surreptitiously, I saw him sitting in the squad car, hands behind his back. Silently, he watched as his fate was played out. I did not know him, this young man. Justice was taking its course. Our paths diverged. Maybe they knew what they were doing, the men in blue, these plumbers of the social order; maybe they knew something I did not. I felt as though this was their business, nothing to do with me.

This was what nagged at me for the rest of the day. Not the injustice, not my cowardice, not the display of violence right in front of me; what nagged at me until I felt sick to my stomach were the two words that had spontaneously occurred to me: 'their business.' The most terrible thing about this story is imprinted in the very fabric of the language. The words had come to me unbidden, and the most repulsive thing was how natural they sounded: '*their* business.' As always; as in the past. Here, just as over there.

Through the unrest, through the tension, through the violence, wanders a ghost we cannot quite define. Ever present, ever near at hand, its great achievement is to create the illusion that everything can be explained. Race in France has substance, but no definition, it is visible, yet it cannot be described. Everyone understands it. Race is an actual identity that unleashes real actions, but we do not know what name to give to those whose presence would explain everything. None of the names we give them are apposite, and from each name we can immediately identify who gave it to them and what they want.

Race does not exist, but it is an actual identity. In a classless society, in a molecular society given to turbulence, everyone against everyone, race is the visible idea which makes identity checks possible. Resemblance, mistaken for identity, makes it possible to maintain order. Here, just as over there. Over there, we honed the perfect identity check. I can say 'we', because it was a product of French engineering. Elsewhere in the peaceful world, people developed the abstract concepts of Mister von Neumann to create machines. IBM invented actual thought using a system of punch cards. IBM, which was destined for great things, devised cards with holes, and simulated logical operations by manipulating these punch cards with long, pointed, metallic spikes jokingly nicknamed 'knitting needles'. Meanwhile, in the city of Algiers, we were applying this same logic to human beings.

Here, we need to pay tribute to the brilliance of the French. The collective intelligence of my people knows how to develop both the most abstract and the most extensive concepts, and simultaneously how to apply them to human beings. The brilliance of the French made it possible to take control of a North African city by applying the principles of information theory in the most concrete fashion. Elsewhere, people made calculating machines; over there, we applied the theory to people.

We daubed a number on every house in the city of Algiers. We created an index card for every man. Over the entire city of Algiers we traced a web of coordinates. Each person was an input value; we proceeded to calculate. No one could make a move without disturbing the web. Every disturbance of the norm constituted one byte of suspicion. Every quiver of identity was transmitted along the strands of the web to the villa up the hill, where we kept sleepless watch. At the slightest suspicious movement, four men would leap into a jeep, careening through the streets, riding on the running board, one hand gripping the bodywork, the other clutching a sub-machine gun. They would screech to a halt outside a building, leap out, run up the stairs, sputtering with an electric energy. They would arrest the suspect in his bed, on the stairs, in the street, bundle him into the jeep in his pyjamas, and drive back up the hill without so much as slowing down. They always found their man, because there was a file on every man, a mark on every house. It was military triumph by index card. They always brought back someone, the four armed warriors who sped around in jeeps without ever slowing down.

The very knitting needles that were used to fish for punch cards elsewhere, were used to fish for men in Algiers. Having punched a hole in one man with a long needle, you could hook another man. We applied the knitting needle to human beings, while IBM was applying it merely to cards. We pushed needles into men, punched holes in them, and one man was bait to catch others. Using the holes punched in one card, we could use long needles to hook other cards. It was a great success. Everything that moved was arrested. Everything ceased to move. Once used, these punch cards were unusable. Cards in such a state could never be reused, and so they were thrown away. Some into the sea, some into ditches that were be filled in, but there is no telling where many of them ended up. People disappeared as though tossed into a rubbish bin.

If the enemy is like a fish in water, then drain away the water! And for good measure barb the ground with electrified spikes. The fish died, the battle was won, and our victory was a mound of rubble. We triumphed, thanks to the methodical use of information theory; but everything else was lost. We were masters of a ruined city, purged of men to whom we could speak, haunted by electrocuted spectres; a city where nothing remained but hatred, suffering and a generalized fear. The solution we found demonstrated a particular aspect of the French genius. Generals Salan and Massu implemented the magnificent folly espoused by Bouvard and Pécuchet to the letter: draw up lists, apply logic to all things, provoke disasters.

We were bound to have trouble living together after that.

Oh shit, it's happening all over again!

It's happening again! He said it, I heard him use those very same words, heard him use the same terms, the same tone. It's starting again! We are infected by colonial corruption. It eats away at us. It constantly reappears. It has always been there, coursing under our feet, flowing unseen, just as sewers run beneath the streets, ever hidden, ever present, and when a heatwave comes we wonder where the stench comes from.

He said it, I heard him say it, the self-same words.

I was buying a newspaper. The newsagent was a nasty piece of work. I give nothing away, but I could instantly tell from the information provided by my senses. He reeked of fine cigars and aftershave. I'd rather deal with someone who is tubby and bald, with a cigarillo dangling from his lips and a nightstick under the counter. But this particular newsagent concealed his baldness by cropping his hair close. He was smoking a fat cigar that was clearly top quality. He proudly claimed to have a cellar with a hygrometer. He was obviously a connoisseur. He knew about cigars and how best to appreciate them. I almost envied him his shirt, it looked good on him. He was about my age, not quite fat, carrying just enough weight to have his feet planted firmly on the ground. He was attractively plump, with a good complexion and a quiet self-confidence. His wife, who manned the other till, exuded a commercial but nonetheless charming eroticism. Cigar clenched firmly between his teeth, he held forth.

'They make me laugh.'

The newspaper lay open in front of him and he was commenting on the headlines; it was a quality paper, not a tabloid rag. These days we cannot depend on stereotypes to protect ourselves. Thirty years of media editorials mean that everyone now puts their best foot forward, ensuring that their private thoughts are not so readily apparent. The only way to know who you are dealing with is to look for subtle signals; or to listen. Everything is communicated through music. Everything is expressed in the structure of language.

'Makes me laugh, this idea they've had about anonymous CVs.'

People had recently had the idea of no longer giving their names when submitting job applications. It was proposed that no name should be included on a CV. It was suggested that candidates be discussed sight unseen, with no mention of a name. The goal being to create a level playing field in terms of access to jobs, since the resonant colour of a surname might prove troubling. And a troubled mind makes decisions that reason cannot justify. Those elements of language which carried too much meaning would be passed over in silence. People hoped that, through silence, violence would go unspoken. Gradually, it was hoped, people would stop speaking, would use words that were numbers; or speak English – a language that tells us nothing of importance.

'Anonymous CVs! They're having a laugh! More smoke and mirrors. As if that was the problem.'

I was about to agree, because it is always easier to absent-mindedly agree with a newsagent who has a nightstick under their counter.

You never have to see them again, you will never come back, there is no obligation. I was about to agree, and I *did* agree that this was not the problem.

'This is something we should have sorted out long ago.'

I remained noncommittal. I picked up my change, my paper, I sensed a trap. Because surely a beaming smile around a firmly planted cigar always conceals a trap. He studied me with a look of amusement; he knew my type.

'If we had hit the agitators hard ten years ago, when there was still time, we might have a bit of peace and quiet now.'

It took me several attempts to pick up the change, the coins kept rolling away from me. Objects always resist you when you want to be rid of them. He kept me there. He was a past master.

'Ten years ago, at least they knew their place. There was only a handful of troublemakers: that's when we needed to come down hard. Really hard. Whack anyone who stuck their head above the parapet.'

I made to leave, backing away slowly, but he was an old hand. He looked me in the eye, he spoke to me directly and had a good laugh while he waited for me to agree. He knew my type.

'This is what you get for all their bullshit. Look where it's got us. They're in charge now. They're not afraid of anyone. They act like this is their home. We don't control anything any more, except when it comes to business. This bullshit about anonymous CVs is just another way of making it easier for them to access the one place where we still had some control over them. So, obviously, they're laughing: we're opening the doors for them. They get to infiltrate the last bastion of privilege with no one any the wiser.'

I tried to leave. I held the door ajar with one hand, my paper with the other, but still he would not let me go. He was an expert. Staring hard into my eyes, never pausing for a moment, his cigar planted with smug satisfaction, he held me mesmerized by the power of human relationships. In order to leave, I would have had to interrupt him. I would have had to turn my back in mid-sentence, an affront I was keen to avoid. We are programmed to listen to someone who is talking to us and looking us in the eye; it's an anthropological reflex. I did not want to get involved in a sordid discussion. I wanted it to be over, without some horrendous scene. And he just laughed, he knew my type.

He said nothing specific, but I knew what he meant, and the very fact that I understood amounted to tacit approval. He knew that. We are bound by language, and here he was bandying pronouns about without ever being specific. He knew I would say nothing, since it would mean getting into an argument with him and he was ready for me. If we got into an argument it would prove that I understood, which would mean confessing that we shared a language: that we thought in the same terms. He made his pronouncement, I pretended not to comprehend: those who accept what is can lay claim to a stronger grasp on reality; he already had the advantage.

I hovered in the doorway, not daring to tear myself away and leave. He kept me open-mouthed, force-fed me, an innocent goose, until my liver exploded. His wife, in her prime of life, radiated blonde perfection. She casually stacked the magazines into neat piles in a graceful ballet of red fingernails, accompanied by the tinkling music of her jewellery. He knew my type and he was using it to his advantage. He had recognized in me a child of the Mitterrand generation, of the First Republic of the Left, who refuses to speak and refuses to see. He had recognized me as someone who glories in anonymity, someone who avoids certain words for fear of violence, someone who no longer speaks for fear of being sullied, and thereby leaves himself defenceless. I could not contradict him, without acknowledging that I understood what he was saying. And, thereby, with my first words, admit that I thought in the same terms. He laughed at his trap as he gracefully pulled on his fat cigar. He let me come to him.

'If we'd done something back then, we wouldn't have to deal with what we're dealing with today. If we'd put our foot down when there were only a handful of agitators. If we'd come down hard, really hard, on the ones who stuck their head above the parapet, we wouldn't have the problems we have now. We would have had peace for ten years.'

It's starting again! Colonial corruption has resurfaced and the words have not changed. 'Peace for ten years.' He said it to my face. Here, just as over there. And that word, 'they'! The French all collude in using the word 'they'. It is a tacit collusion between the French who understand, without having to specify who 'they' refers to. We do not need to specify. Simply understanding admits us to the group of those who understand. Understanding what is meant by 'they' makes us complicit. Some pretend not to say it and even not to understand it. But it is futile; we cannot help but understand language. We are immersed in language and all of us understand. Language understands us; and it is language that determines who we are.

Where did we come by the idea that firmness calms? Where did we come by the idea that a couple of slaps can bring peace? Where did we come by these notions, so simple they appear self-evident, if not from over there? And we do not need to explain what we mean by 'over there': every Frenchman knows precisely where it is.

Slaps restore peace; the idea is so simple that families use it. We wallop children to calm them down, we raise our voices, we glower, and it seems to have a little effect. So we carry on. In the closed world of the family this has little consequence, since more often than not the shouting, the empty threats, the arm-waving, are simply play-acting; but transposed to the free world of adults, it results in terrible violence. Where do we come by the notion that slaps bring about the peace we crave if not from 'over there', from colonial illegalism, from colonial infantilism?

Where does it come from, this belief in the virtue of violence? Where does it come from, this notion that 'they are restless'? That we 'need to show them who's boss' in order to calm them down. Where, if not from 'over there'? From the siege mentality that haunted the nights of the *pieds noirs*. From their American dreams of pioneers conquering virgin territory overrun by savages. They dreamed of having power. To them, power seemed the simplest solution. Power invariably seems the simplest solution, it is something that everyone can imagine, since everyone was once a child. Looming grown-ups commanded our respect through their unimaginable power. They raised a hand and we cowered in fear. We bowed our heads believing that order stemmed from power. This sunken world lives on; the flotsam drifts through the very structure of our language, certain word associations we did not realize we knew occur to us unbidden.

Finally, I managed to turn away. I stepped across the threshold and fled. I fled this nasty piece of work who smelled of cigar smoke, fled the mocking smile, the squarely planted cigar, this man who would stop at nothing to keep everyone in their place. I ran without offering a response; he had posed no questions. I cannot see what I could have argued. In France we do not argue. We assert our group identity with all the force required by our insecurity. France is splintering; the pieces are drifting further and further apart; very different groups no longer want to live together.

I ran out into the street, my eyes unfocused so as not to have to look at anyone; my shoulders hunched the better to move through the air, striding briskly to avoid a chance encounter. I fled as far as I could from the bastard who had forced me to agree to terrible things, without saying anything specific, without me objecting. I raced along the street, trailing the stench that rises from the sewers of language, briefly ajar.

I remember the origin of those words. I remember when they were first spoken, and by whom. 'I will give you peace for ten years,' Général Duval said in 1945. The Muslim villages along the coast were bombed by the navy; those inland were shelled by fighter planes. During the riots, 102 Europeans – this is the precise figure – were gutted in the town of Sétif. This is not a figure of speech, they were literally eviscerated: their abdomens slashed open with a variety of sharp tools and their still pulsating intestines spilled out and spread over the ground as they screamed. Guns were handed out to anyone who asked for them. Police officers, soldiers and armed militias – meaning just about anyone – roamed the countryside. They randomly massacred everyone they came across. Thousands of Muslims were slaughtered simply because they had the misfortune to encounter them. We need to show them we had the power. The streets, the villages and plains of Algeria were drenched in blood. People were butchered if they looked the type. 'We will have peace for ten years.'

It was extraordinary, the massacre we executed in May 1945. Hands smeared with blood, we could once again rejoin the ranks of the victors. We had power. At the last minute, we took part in an indiscriminate slaughter that was entirely French in its virtuosity. Our participation was passionate, unbridled, a little sloppy, and above all open to all comers. The massacre was haphazard, probably fuelled by alcohol, marked by *furia francese*. Even as the dead of the great world war were being counted, we participated in the sort of indiscriminate massacre that offers nations a place in history. We relied on French ingenuity, which was utterly unlike that of Germans, who understood how to plan mass murders and tally the corpses, whole or in pieces. Nor was it like the British, distanced by technology, entrusting the responsibility of killing to huge bombs dropped from the night skies, who did not see the corpses vaporized in the phosphorus flash. We were not like Russians, who counted on the bitter cold of sweeping plains to ensure mass fatalities; nor the Serbs, with their wholesome village mentality, who slit the throats of their neighbours as they might a pig that they had fed and cared for; nor even the Japanese, their bayonets skewering the enemy with the precision of fencing masters as they uttered theatrical screams. This was *our* massacre, and at the last minute we rejoined the ranks of the victors by smearing our hands with blood. We had power. 'Peace for ten years,' said Général Duval. And the general was not mistaken. We had ten years of peace, give or take six months. After that, everything was lost. Everything. Them and us. Over there. And here.

I am still talking of France as I tramp the streets. This would be laughable were it not for the fact that France is a manner of speaking. France is the French language. Language is the landscape in which we are raised; it is the blood that we pass on, the blood that nourishes us. We swim in this language that someone has taken a shit in. We dare not open our mouths for fear of swallowing one of these linguistic faeces. We hold our tongue. We cease to live. Language, like blood, is pure movement. Language, like blood, coagulates when it ceases to flow. It forms small black clots that stick in our throats. Suffocating us. We hold our tongue, we cease to live. We dream of speaking English, a language that does not affect us.

We are dying of thrombosis. We are dying of an embolism. We are dying of the deafening silence filled with gurgling and rumblings and suppressed rage. This viscous blood has ceased to flow. This is France, this way of death.

Novel III

The Zouave regiments arrive in the nick of time

T HE ZOUAVE REGIMENTS arrived from North Africa just in time. It was as well they came when they did. The machine-gunners had realized their limitations: the bullets from the French guns ricocheted like hazelnuts off the sides of the German Tiger tanks. The 11cm-thick armour plating was impervious to anything a single gunner could fire. What they needed was cunning: dig trenches like elephant traps across the road with iron spikes planted in the bottom; or spend days burning the convoys that brought them petrol and wait for their engines to croak their last.

Lying on the terracotta tiles of a rubble-strewn kitchen next to a hole in the wall, looking out on to the meadows, Victorien Salagnon dreamed up fantastical schemes. The square turrets of the Tiger tanks slipped between the hedges, easily flattening them. The long barrel, capped with a bulge whose purpose he did not understand, turned like the muzzle of a hound scenting its prey, and fired. The explosion made him duck as he heard a wall and a roof collapse, the timbers splintering as one of the houses rumbled to dust, and he did not know whether one of the young men he knew was sheltered there.

It was time for this to end. The Zouaves arrived in the nick of time.

The crumbling houses sent up thick clouds of dust that took time to settle; the diesel engines of the advancing tanks belched thick black smoke. Salagnon huddled closer to the thick door jamb, the sturdiest piece of stone in the ruined wall, shards of which already littered the floor or teetered, ready to fall. Mechanically, he cleared the patch of ground around him. Cleaning up the tiles. He gathered up shards of broken crockery fallen from the sideboard. He could piece them together using the blue flower pattern. A direct hit had devastated the kitchen. He glanced around, looking for pieces to fit together. He kept himself busy, so as not to have to look behind him at the figures buried under white rubble. The bodies were sprawled amid the remains of the table and the upended chairs. An old man had lost his cap; a woman was half hidden beneath a torn and charred tablecloth; two girls lay side by side; they were about the same height; two little girls whose age he did not dare to guess. How long does it last, a direct hit? A flash as it arrives, a fraction of a second as everything crumbles, although it seems to happen in slow motion; no more.

He clung to his Sten gun, he had counted the remaining bullets over and over. He watched the turrets of the Tiger tanks moving through the fields towards the village. They could not hold out much longer.

Sprawled in the rubble, a gaping wound in his belly, Roseval was struggling to breathe. Each breath produced a gurgling sound like a canteen being emptied. Salagnon did his best not to look at him; he knew from the sound that he was still alive; he toyed with the shards of crockery, clutched the metal stock of his weapon as it gradually grew warmer, watching the advancing column of grey tanks, as though sheer vigilance might save him.

And it came to pass as he had hoped it would. The tanks moved away. He continued to watch as the tanks wheeled around and dis-appeared into the fields marked out with hedgerows. He scarcely dared believe it. It was then that he saw the tanks of the Zouave regiments, dozens of small, green, rounded tanks with short, squat barrels – Sherman tanks, he later learned – and his first glimpse of them that day was an immense relief. At last, he could close his eyes, at last he could breathe deeply, without fear of being spotted and killed.

Lying a few feet away, Roseval did not even notice. He was conscious only of his pain now; his whimpered in short, halting bursts, his death dragged on.

It had all started out well; but the Bataillons de Zouaves Portés arrived just in time. When their tanks came to a halt beneath the trees, among the bushes, among the half-ruined houses of the village, they could read French words on the green gun turrets. They had got there in time.

It had all started out so well. The June weather brought them back to life. They had had several weeks of armed freedom, which consoled them for the long grey winters. The Maréchal himself had given them that courage based on contempt that they so freely dispensed. On 7 June he made a speech which was distributed and pasted up all over France. The Colonel had read it aloud, as the *maquisards* lined up, dressed in their scout shorts. Their shoes were spit-polished, they pulled up their socks and tugged their berets over their ears in a gesture of French superiority.

> Frenchmen,
>
> Do not aggravate our misfortunes by acts which risk bringing tragic reprisals upon you. It will be innocent French citizens who suffer the consequences. France will be saved only by adhering to the most rigorous discipline. Therefore, obey the orders of the Government. That each may stand firm beside his duty. The circumstances of battle may lead the German army to take special measures in the combat zones. Accept this necessity.

An insolent whoop of joy greeted the closing words of the speech. With one hand, they each held the guns by their side; with the other they tossed their berets in the air. 'Hurrah!' they yelled, 'let's go!' And the speech ended in joyful chaos as each boy hunted, found and donned his beret, keeping a tight grip on the rifle by his side as it clattered against the others. 'You hear what he said, the mummified maréchal? There he is signalling from behind the glass, like a fish in a tank. But we can't hear him, because he's pickled in formaldehyde!'

The grass glittered in the June sun; a breeze rustled the beech trees. They laughed and vied with each other as they boasted and bragged. 'What is he saying? That we should lie down and play dead? Even though we're not? Are we dead? What's he saying, the pickled old prick? To act like nothing's happened? Let foreigners fight it out in *our* country, to keep our heads down, to dodge the bullets, to say "*Jawohl!*" to the Germans? He's asking us to play at being Swiss, while there's a war on in our own backyards! No way! There's time enough to play dead later. When we're all dead.'

It felt good.

In crocodile formation, they tramped along forest paths, new-minted adults, as yet untainted by violence, but seething with an urge to fight that twitched in their limbs like steam under pressure. It rained that afternoon, a fine summer shower of fat raindrops. It refreshed but did not drench them, and was quickly absorbed by the trees, the ferns, the grass. This gentle rain released the musky scent of the earth, of resin and wood like a visible halo, as though wreathing them with incense, as though urging them to war.

Salagnon wore his machine gun slung between his shoulders, while behind him Roseval carried a rucksack full of cartridge clips. Brioude led the march and twenty of them followed behind, breathing deeply. As they emerged from the woods, the clouds parted to reveal the blue depths of the world. They lay down behind a tall thicket of ferns overlooking the road. Droplets of rain beaded on the fronds, dripped on to their necks and rolled down their backs, but the dry straw beneath their bellies kept them warm.

They opened fire the moment the grey Kübelwagen rounded the bend, followed by two army trucks. Salagnon kept his forefinger pressed on the trigger, emptied the first clip and replaced it, something that took only a few seconds, then went on firing, barely varying his aim. The munitions man lying next to him kept one hand on his shoulder and with the other passed him a full magazine. Salagnon fired; it made a glorious racket, and this thing pressed tightly against his body grew hot and jolted, while in the distance something in the crosshairs of his sights disintegrated, toppled beneath the rain of invisible blows, crumpled as though deflated from within. Salagnon took an intense pleasure in firing; his willpower was emitted through his eyes and, with no contact, the car and the trucks were hacked to pieces like logs with an axe. The vehicles crumpled, the bodywork buckled, the windows shattered into glittering clouds, flames began to appear; all this he could do with a simple impulse in his belly, focused by his eyes.

When the firing stopped, there was not a sound to be heard. The ruined car teetered over the hard shoulder, one truck lay in the middle of the road, its tyres blown; the other was ablaze, smashed into a tree. The *maquisards* crept from brush to bush, then stepped out on to the road. Nothing was moving now except the flames and a slowly rising column of smoke. The drivers, lacerated by bullets, lay dead, hunched uncomfortably over their steering wheels; one of them was burning, the stench was appalling. Beneath the tarpaulins of the trucks were sacks of mail, crates of rations and huge bales of grey toilet paper. They left everything. In the car there were two uniformed officers, a man of about fifty and another of about twenty, their bodies thrown back, heads lolling against the seat, mouths open, eyes closed. They could have been a father and son parked in a lay-by and taking a nap. 'They don't send their crack troops around these parts,' muttered Brioude, bending over them. 'Just the old men and the kids.' Salagnon mumbled his agreement, trying to keep his composure as he studied the bodies, pretending to check under their feet for something or other – something important. The younger man had taken only a single bullet in the side, which had left a small red hole, and he seemed to be asleep. This was surprising, because the chest of the man behind the wheel was slashed to ribbons; his jacket looked as though it had been ripped open by sharp fangs, exposing the brutally masticated crimson flesh from which rows of white bones protruded at impossible angles. Salagnon tried to remember whether he had fired at the left side of the vehicle. He could not recall, and it did not matter. Grimly, he traipsed back into the forest.

An airdrop of weapons arrived that night; invisible planes roared overhead. The boys lit petrol fires around the vast meadow and suddenly a series of white flowers bloomed in the ink-black sky. The fires were extinguished, the rumble of the planes faded and they had to fetch the metal tubes that had fallen on the grass. They carefully folded the parachutes, the silk already wet with dew. Inside the containers they found crates of equipment and munitions, machine guns and cartridges, a British machine gun, hand grenades and a field radio.

And from the wilted silk flowers they saw men scrabble to their feet and calmly unhook their harnesses. When they moved forwards to get a closer look, they were greeted in broken French. They led the men to the large barn that served as an HQ. In the flickering glow of the paraffin lamps, the six commandos sent by the British looked very young, blond and rosy-cheeked. The French boys clustered around them, eyes shining, laughing easily, calling to each other loudly, gauging the effect of their movements and their raucous cries. Unflustered, the young Englishmen explained to the Colonel the purpose of their mission. Their faded uniforms fit them perfectly, the threadbare fabric following their movements; they had lived in them so long they were a second skin. The eyes in their young faces barely flickered, maintaining a strange, fixed stare. They had already survived something very different. They had come to train the French in radically new killing techniques developed outside France in the months while they had been hiding in the woods, while others had been fighting elsewhere. All this they were easily able to explain. Their rudimentary French hesitated over words, but flowed slowly enough for them to understand and even to gradually comprehend what it really meant.

Sitting in a circle, they listened to the Englishman's lesson. The young man whose wispy hair floated in the slightest breeze demonstrated the 'break-neck' knife, of which a crateload had been sent. It looked like a standard Swiss army knife. It could be used for picnics; there was a blade, a can opener, a nail file, a tiny saw. But also, concealed in the handle, was a metal punch as long as a finger. This awl is designed for 'break-necking', which, the young blond man explained in slow, halting words, entails creeping up on the enemy, clapping the left hand over the mouth to stop him screaming and, with the right hand, plunging the awl into the depression at the base of the skull between the muscle walls; this hollow, which you can feel at the base of your skull with your finger, seems designed to be punctured, like an opening placed there deliberately. Death is instantaneous; breath rushes out as air rushes in; the enemy goes limp and crumples silently.

Salagnon was troubled by this simple weapon. It fitted the hand like a penknife and its flawless design was a tribute to industrial practicality. An engineer had sketched a design, calculated how long the awl needed to be to fit its purpose; he might work with a skull on his desk, so he could check the details. He took measurements using a calliper rule he allowed no one else to touch. When his pencils were blunted by his sketching, he sharpened them meticulously. Later, using his plans and calculations, a machine tool had been set up in Yorkshire or Pennsylvania so that the 'break-neck' knife could be mass-produced in the same way as a tin cup. With this in his pocket, Salagnon considered the people around him differently: he pictured the small door at the base of their skull, which, although closed, could be opened, could let out their breath and let in the cold air. Every one of them could be killed in an instant, by his hand.

Another commando, red-haired and ruddy-faced like a caricature of an Englishman, explained the commando knife. If thrown, the weapon always landed point-first. It was sharp enough to stab deeply and could also be used to slash. To use it, it was important not to grip it in the fist like Tarzan fighting crocodiles, but with the thumb aligned with the blade, the way one might hold a steak knife. After all, in both cases the purpose is to carve meat. So the approach is similar.

The slowness of the explanations, the halting French, their determination to ensure they were understood, left more than enough time for everyone to realize what they were really talking about: the atmosphere was pervaded by a vague unease. None of the young men was larking or boasting now: they handled these simple objects with a slight awkwardness. They were careful not to touch the blades. They greeted the discussion on explosives with relief. The plastic explosive, like children's plasticine, had a comforting feel unconnected to its purpose. And the wiring used to detonate it was an abstraction. Thankfully, it is impossible to think about everything all of the time. Technical details are a welcome distraction.

The attack on the convoy of trucks crossing the Saône Valley was more serious. It felt more like a battle. The thirty trucks filled with German footsoldiers were caught in a hail of bullets from the machine guns hidden in the undergrowth of the valley's steep slopes. Leaping from their trucks and diving into ditches, the seasoned troops returned fire, attempted a counter-attack, only to be driven back. Bodies lay slumped on the grass and on the road between the burnt-out trucks. When their clips were empty, the attack stopped. The convoy beat a somewhat ignominious retreat. The *maquisards* let them go; they surveyed the extent of the damage through binoculars and then they, too, retreated. A few minutes later two planes arrived and raked the valley slopes with machine-gun fire. Their hefty bullets laid waste the shrubs, dug up the ground, branches as thick as forearms were sliced away and fell. A large splinter buried itself in Courtillot's thigh, as long as a man's arm and as sharp as a blade, it was still dripping with sap. The planes made several passes above the smoking debris, before finally departing. The *maquisards* headed back into the forest, carrying their first wounded casualty.

*   *   *

Sencey was captured. It was easy. They simply marched forwards, keeping their heads low to avoid being hit. The machine guns were trained on the main road but the bullets whistled uselessly overhead, hindered by the steep incline. In the dazzling glare it was just possible to make out the gun emplacement, the perforated muzzle of the German machine gun, the curve of helmets peeping above the sandbags, just out of range. Their bullets zipped through the warm air with a long, shrill whine that ended in a dull thud as they hit stone. They kept their heads low as the white walls towering over them crackled, sending out small clouds of chalky dust and a smell of limestone being broken in the blazing sun.

Sencey was taken because it had to be taken. The Colonel insisted, so he could mark the advance on his map. Seizing a town is the greatest military action, even if it is a sleepy little village in Mâcon during the afternoon siesta. They advanced, heads down, evading the bullets the machine gun fired too high. They took cover in doorways. They crawled along the walls, crouched behind boundary stones, making themselves so small they completely disappeared, but when they came to the main road, they could go no farther.

Brioude moved forwards in little bounds, his legs bent, his back horizontal, the fingers of his left hand resting on the ground, his right hand gripping his Sten gun; his knuckles were white from squeezing this gun that had, as yet, seen little action. Behind him, Roseval was also stooped; then came Salagnon and the others, spread out along the walls, sheltering in corners, behind stone benches, in doorways. The streets of Sencey were gravel paths, the walls were pale stone; every surface reflected the glare. The heat was visible, a rippling haze, and they were on the move, squinting against the light, sweat trickling down their backs, down their faces, down their arms; even their hands were slick with sweat, but they wiped them on their shorts, so as not to lose their grip on their guns.

Every door and shutter in the village was closed. They did not see a living soul. They would deal with the Germans without a single inhabitant getting involved. But sometimes as they passed a doorway, this procession of men in white shirts moving in little bounds, the door would open and a hand – they only ever saw the hand – would set a full bottle on the doorstep, then the door would close with a ridiculous sound, the clack of a latch amid the crackle of bullets. They drank and passed it along, it was chilled wine or water, and the last in the line would set the bottle on a window ledge. They continued to advance along the main street. They needed to cross the road. The stones gave off a white heat, searing their eyes and their hands. The German machine gun at the far end fired at random, at the slightest movement. On the far side of the street, shady alleyways offered shelter. They could be there in two bounds.

Brioude gestured to the street. He spun his wrist twice to signify the two bounds and pointed to the alley on the other side. Crouching, silent, the others nodded. Brioude bounded, dived and rolled to safety. A hail of bullets followed, but came too late and too high. He was already on the other side; he waved to them. Roseval and Salagnon set off together, running quickly. Salagnon thought he felt a rush of air from the approaching bullets. He was not sure whether bullets could create a rush of air; perhaps it was just a sound or simply the effect of his running; he sat down heavily against the shady wall, his chest about to explode, panting for breath after two quick bounds. The sun was splitting the stones, the glare from the street was painful; on the far side the crouching men hesitated. In this sweltering silence every gesture became stultified and slow; Brioude was beckoning insistently, soundlessly, as though at the bottom of a swimming pool. Mercier and Bourdet made the leap, the hail of bullets caught Mercier in full flight, hit him in mid-air like a racquet striking a ball and he landed on his belly. A pool of blood unfurled beneath him. Bourdet could not stop shaking. Brioude signalled for them to stop; the others on the far side froze, hunkered in the sunlight, while those who had managed to cross followed him down the alley.

Mercier's body still lay in the street. The machine gun fired again, aiming lower this time, and the gravel around him danced, several bullets hit the body with a sound of hammer on flesh, the corpse juddered with spurts of blood and torn fabric.

In the backstreets, among stone houses, in the shadows and the silence, they took no precautions, they simply ran. They happened on two Germans stretched out behind a well, their gun trained on the main street. Pointed in the wrong direction. Alerted by the sound of running footsteps behind them, they turned, but too late. Brioude, leading the charge, fired instinctively, holding his Sten gun at arm's length, as though protecting himself from something, as though he were stumbling in the dark, afraid he might bump into something; he was thin-lipped, his eyes reduced to narrow slits. The two Germans crumpled, slowly bleeding to death, their helmets askew, but the *maquisards* did not slow, they bounded over the corpses, racing towards the hidden machine gun.

They managed to get close, they could see helmets above the sandbags and the moving, perforated barrel. Roseval quickly lobbed a grenade and threw himself on the ground. His toss fell short. The grenade rolled to the sandbags and exploded, raising a cloud of dirt and gravel that hovered over their heads; shards of metal fell with a dull clang. When the dust had settled, the four men looked again. The helmets and the gun had disappeared. Checking, they crept slowly forwards, circled the gun post until they could be sure there was nothing there. Only then did they stand up straight. Sencey had been captured.

From the doorway of the church they looked at the patchwork of fields and hedges. The meadows gently rolled down towards Porquigny. They could just make out the train station and beyond it the tree-lined banks of the Saône, and the valley, bleached by the sunlight, almost dissolved in the dazzling air. Three trucks were jolting away along the road to Porquigny. Sun flashed intermittently from the windscreens as they encountered hills and bends. Twin columns of smoke rose above the asphalt from what must have been trains.

In front of the entrance to the church, on the outermost edge of the village from where one had a vista of the surrounding country-side, Salagnon had to sit down; his muscles were twitching; his legs no longer had the strength to carry him; he was sweating profusely. Water poured out of him as though his skin were made of gauze; he was streaming with sweat. It reeked, it was sticky. Sitting down, both hands holding his gun tightly so that at least it did not tremble, he thought about Mercier, abandoned in the streets, killed randomly, almost by accident. But it was inevitable that one among them should die, it was the age-old rule, and he felt the extraordinary joy, the extraordinary absurdity, of having survived.

Capturing Porquigny was easy. They had only to follow the paths downhill, hide among the bushes. At Porquigny they would reach the train tracks, the trunk road, the Saône; and there they would meet the new French army and the Americans marching north as quickly as their heavy kitbags would allow.

They crept through the meadows, came to the outlying houses. Sheltering behind corners, they listened. Pestered by fat, sluggish blowflies, they shooed them away with little waves. The only sound was the buzzing of the flies. The air around them rippled, but air that shimmers in the heat makes no sound: it is visible; it warps lines and shapes, making it difficult to see; you find yourself blinking rapidly to unstick tangled eyelashes, then wiping your eyes with a sweaty hand. The stifling air makes no sound; it is the flies. In the little village of Porquigny flies gathered in listless swarms and buzzed continu-ally. Only broad gestures could shoo them and even then they barely reacted, flying off only to land again on the same spot. They had no fear of threats, nothing could keep them away; they stuck to faces, arms, hands, to every surface slick with sweat. In the village the air quivered with a muggy heat and with flies.

The first body they saw was a woman lying on her back; her pretty dress lay spread around her, as though she had held it wide before lying down. She was about thirty years old and looked as if she came from the city. She might have come here on holiday or was perhaps the village schoolmistress. In death her eyes were wide and she retained an air of serene independence, assurance and sophistication. The wound to her belly was not bleeding, but the red scab slashed across her dress quivered with a thick velvet of flies.

They found the others in the church square, lined up along the walls, crumpled in half-open doors; several piled on to a cart hitched to a horse that stood motionless but for its blinking eyes, its twitching ears. The flies moved from corpse to corpse, forming chance eddies, their buzzing filling the village.

The *maquisards* moved forwards warily, remaining in strict formation, mindful as never before of the distance between them. The pulsing air left no place for sound, so much so that they forgot they were gifted with the power of speech. Instinctively, they covered their noses and mouths to ward off the smell and the flies; and also to demonstrate to their comrades that the sight had left them speechless, unable to say a word. By their count, they found twenty-eight bodies in the streets of Porquigny. The only male was a boy of sixteen in a white, open-neck shirt, his forehead slashed by a fringe of blond hair, his hands tied behind his back. The back of his head had been shattered by a bullet fired at close range; it had spared his face. Flies teemed only on the back of his skull.

They left Porquigny, heading for the train station built further down the hill, beyond meadows pitted with dense thickets, behind a line of poplar trees. They heard a shriek across the sky and the ground in front of them was pockmarked by a perfect line of small explosions. The earth shuddered and they stumbled. Then they heard the dull crack of shots fired. There was a second salvo; explosions echoed all around them, showering them with dirt and damp splinters. They took shelter behind the trees, some dashed back towards the village, others lay on the ground. 'The armoured train!' yelled Brioude, but no one heard in the thunderous bombardment; his voice did not carry and it was every man for himself. The ground shook, thick smoke mingled with earth settled slowly, small shards of debris rained like hail around them, over them; they were deafened, blinded, panicked, and they raced towards the village, thinking of nothing but getting away.

When they reached the houses again, some of them were missing. The salvoes stopped. They heard the roar of the engine. Through the curtain of poplars came three Tiger tanks, moving up the hill towards Porquigny, leaving deep ruts of churned earth; behind them came men in grey, protected by huge panels whose ceaseless metallic grating they could hear.

The first shell punctured a window and exploded inside a house, bringing the roof down. The beams gave way, the roof tiles tumbled in a jangling of terracotta and a plume of reddish dust rose above the ruins and rolled through the streets.

The *maquisards* sought refuge in the houses. Behind the tanks, the grey-uniformed soldiers marched, heads low so as not to make easy targets. They marched in step; they did not fire, did not leave themselves open to attack; they allowed the tanks to clear the way. The young French boys in white shirts so eager to fight were about to be crushed like shells by the huge steel jaws of a nutcracker. Not so much by the machines themselves as by the discipline.

Once within range, the bullets from their machine guns bounded off the thick armour with even denting. The Tiger tanks lumbered forwards, flattening the grass. When they fired, their whole bulk reared up with a sigh and in front of them a wall disintegrated.

Roseval and Salagnon had taken shelter in a house, having kicked open the front door. A family with no husband, no sons, was huddled in the kitchen. Roseval went to reassure them, while Salagnon stood by the door, studying the elegant lines of the gun turret as it slowly advanced, slowly turned, training its great dark eye on everything. A direct hit obliterated the kitchen. Salagnon was covered with dust; the only thing that remained standing was the door jamb – the door had been ripped from its hinges. Protected by a thick wall of stone,

Salagnon was unscathed. He watched as the tank advanced, followed by battle-hardened soldiers; though he could see their weapons, he still could not see faces, but they were moving towards him. Covered in dust, cowering behind a wall of teetering stones, he watched vigilantly as if vigilance could save him.

The three planes came from the south, a white star painted on their fuselage. They were not flying very high and the roar as they passed was the sound of a sky being ripped asunder. They made the sound one expects when the sky is ripped asunder, for only a sky ripped through every layer can produce this sound that makes you cower, convinced there is nothing more powerful; and yet there is. They passed a second time, firing heavy shells at the Tiger tanks, explosive shells that sent up showers of earth and gravel and ricocheted off their armour with a loud clang. They banked with the deafening roar of huge circular saws and headed south. The tanks turned around, the battle-hardened soldiers still sheltering behind them. The *maquisards* stayed in their makeshift shelters, which had miraculously remained standing, listening intently, waiting for the sound of the engines to fade. The silence was filled by the continual drone of the flies they had forgotten.

When the first Zouaves arrived in the village, the *maquisards* emerged, blinking, into the light. They hugged their guns, warm and sticky with sweat, staggered as though after a heroic effort, an overwhelming exhaustion, as though they had spent the night drinking and now it was morning. They waved wildly to the green soldiers marching between the Sherman tanks, weighed down by their kitbags, their rifles slung over their shoulders, their heavy helmets hiding their eyes.

The boys hugged the soldiers of the Armée Africaine, who returned their effusive greetings with kindness and patience, having become accustomed in recent weeks to the joy triggered by their arrival. They spoke French, but with a cadence unfamiliar to the boys, in a tone they had never heard before. He had to strain to understand and it made Salagnon laugh, since he had never imagined anyone might talk this way. 'It's funny, the way they talk,' he said to the Colonel. 'You'll see,

Salagnon. The African French are sometimes difficult to understand. You'll often be surprised, and not always in a good way,' he muttered, pulling his Saharan scarf tighter and adjusting his sky-blue kepi to the precise angle required by sky-blue.

Salagnon, exhausted, lay down on the grass; above him floated perfectly delineated clouds. They hung suspended in the air with the majesty of mountains, with the aloofness of a snow-capped peak. How can so much water hover in the air? he wondered. Lying on his back, alert to the ebb and flow coursing through his limbs, he could think of no better question to ask. He realized now that he had felt fear; but a fear so great that he would never again feel fear. The part of him that made it possible to feel afraid had been snapped in two and swept away.

The Zouaves set up camp around Porquigny. They had an extravagant quantity of equipment, which arrived in trucks and was unloaded in the meadows. They set up their tents in regimented lines, stacked up piles of green crates stencilled in white with English words. Tanks were parked in rows as effortlessly as automobiles.

Salagnon, exhausted, sitting on the grass, watched as the camp took shape, as vehicles arrived, as hundreds of men went about the business of setting things up. Rolling past came tanks with rounded, toad-like bodies; all-terrain vehicles with no sharp corners; sullen trucks with bovine musculature; soldiers wearing pith helmets and loose-fitting uniforms, their baggy trousers flaring over laced-up boots. Everything was a murky frog green, a little muddy as though it had just emerged from a pond. American equipment uses organic lines, he thought, it is designed like skin over muscle, with forms well adapted to the human body. The Germans, on the other hand, think in grey, bulky forms, better designed, more striking, as inhuman as sheer will, as angular as irrefutable arguments.

His mind empty, Salagnon began to see shapes. In his idle brain his talent resurfaced. At first he pictured lines, tracing them with the mute, delicate concentration of a hand. Army life fosters such mental blanks, or imposes them on the unwilling.

The Colonel, a man who was unfailingly thoughtful, rallied his men. He ordered a search for the bodies left in the meadows, ploughed up by shells, and beneath the ruined houses. The wounded were carried to the field hospital tent. Salomon Kaloyannis dealt with everything. The surgeon-major welcomed, triaged, operated. This affable little man seemed to heal with the simple laying on of hands that were gentle, articulate. With his preposterous accent – this was the word that occurred to Salagnon – and too many words, he had the seriously wounded settled in the tent, while the others were lined up on canvas chairs set out on the grass. He constantly barked orders to a tall, moustached man he called Ahmed, who invariably answered in a soft voice, 'Yes, Doctor,' before repeating the orders in a language that could only be understood by the brawny, dark-skinned men, the stretcher-bearers and nurses, who dealt with the wounded with sure, swift movements made easier by habit. Ahmed, whose moustache and thick bushy eyebrows made him fearsome, ministered to the patients with extraordinary gentleness. A young *maquisard* with an injured arm, who had spent hours without uttering a word, cradling his bloody limb, sustained by sheer rage, broke down in tears as soon as Ahmed, with delicate strokes, began to clean the wound with a cotton swab.

A nurse in a white smock brought bandages and bottles of antiseptic to the tent. She talked to the wounded men in a sing-song voice and used a firm tone to relay instructions from the busy surgeon-major to the male nurses; they assented in their thick accents and smiled as she passed. She was very young and attractively curved. Salagnon, who thought in shapes, followed her with his eyes at first, dreamily, giving free rein to his talent. She strove to remain impersonal, but did not quite succeed. A curl spilled out of her scraped-back hair; her curves spilled out of her tightly buttoned smock; her sensuous lips spilled out of the serious air she tried to adopt. Her womanliness spilled out of her, radiated from her every gesture, emanated from her every breath; but she did her utmost to play the role of a nurse.

All the men in the Zouave regiment knew her by name. Like them, she was doing her best in this summer war, which they were constantly winning; she had earned her place among them; she was Eurydice, the daughter of Dr Kaloyannis, and no one failed to greet her when she passed. Victorien Salagnon would never know whether falling in love with Eurydice in that moment depended on circumstances or on the woman herself. But perhaps individuals are simply the circumstances in which they appear. Would he have noticed her in the streets of Lyon that he moved through, unseeing, among the thousand passing women? Or did he notice her because she was the only woman among a thousand exhausted men? It hardly matters; people are their environment. And so, one day in 1944, as Salagnon dreamed only of lines, as a weary Victorien Salagnon thought only in shapes, as his prodigious talent returned and his hands were finally free, he saw Eurydice Kaloyannis walk past; he never took his eyes off her again.

The Colonel introduced himself to the other colonel, Naegelin, of the Zouave regiment, a pale Frenchman from Oran, who welcomed him politely, as he had all the soldiers of freedom who had swelled his ranks since Toulon, if a little sceptical about his rank, his name, his service record. The Colonel had his men line up; he had them salute; he stepped forward and presented himself, throwing out his chest and booming in an affected tone that his men did not recognize. But they cut a fine figure as they lined up in the sunshine, equipped with mismatched British weapons, uniforms that were a little worn, a little dirty, a little rough and ready as they stood to attention, but trembling with excitement and jutting their chins with a zeal one no longer sees in soldiers, not in those made soft by a long peace nor those disillusioned by a long war.

Naegelin saluted, shook his hand and immediately turned away and busied himself with other tasks. They were integrated as a reserve company under their usual command. That night in the tent, the Colonel gave them fictitious ranks. Pointing at each of them in turn, he appointed four captains and eight lieutenants. 'Capitaine? Isn't this a bit much?' one of them asked, confused, winding between his fingers the length of gold ribbon he had just been given.

'Are you saying you don't know how to sew? Put those stripes on your sleeve right now. If you've got no stripe, you keep your trap shut; when you've got stripes, then you can open your mouth. Things are moving fast. Woe betide those who lag behind.'

Salagnon was among them, because he was there, because men were needed. 'I like you, Salagnon. You've got a good head on your shoulders. Now, get sewing.'

No sooner said than done. Decisions were made quickly in 1944. If, since 1940, no one had made a decision unless it was to keep shtum, they were making up for it now. Everything was possible. Everything. In every sense.

All night, tanks took the road heading north. Each illuminated the tank in front with their lowered headlights, each pushing before them a stretch of lighted road. By day, the planes flew in low and fast in orderly groups of four. According to the wind, they heard rumblings or explosions, the sound of a forge that seemed to come from the ground itself, the dull roar of shells being fired. By night, haloes of flame flickered on the horizon.

They were left to their own devices. The Colonel accepted all missions, but decided nothing. In the evening he would walk through the lanes and with gruff swings of his cane decapitate thistles, nettles and any weed that poked its head above the long grass.

The wounded arrived by the truckload, battered and bruised, crudely bandaged, covered in blood, the most serious hidden under blankets. They were taken to the hospital tent, where the Kaloyannis, with equal gentleness, helped them to survive or to die. The Colonel's reserve company helped with the transport, they carried stretchers, lined up corpses in the sunshine as they were carried, one by one, from the green tent marked with a red cross. Or else they spent long hours doing nothing, since army life is divided into periods of feverish, back-breaking activity and lulls to be filled with marches and fatigue duties. But here in the countryside, with nothing, many dozed, cleaned their weapons until they knew every little scratch or foraged so there would be more to eat.

For Salagnon this free time was given over to drawing; when time stood still he felt a tingling in his eyes and in his fingers. On the scraps of American wrapping paper he could find he sketched engineers, stripped to the waist, tinkering with the tank engines or patching truck tyres in the shade of the poplar trees, and others beneath the shifting foliage siphoning petrol using thick hosepipes which they wound around their waists; he sketched the *maquisards* scattered on the grass, lying among the flowers, giving shape to the clouds scudding across the sky. He drew Eurydice as she passed. He drew her several times. And as he was drawing her for the umpteenth time, unthinking, utterly focused on his pencil and the line it traced, a hand alighted on his shoulder, but so gently that he did not start. Kaloyannis stood, silently admiring the sketch of his daughter on the paper. Salagnon froze, not knowing what to do, whether to show the man the drawing or apologize and try to hide it.

'You draw my daughter very well,' he said at length. 'Perhaps you would like to come to the hospital more often? So you could draw her portrait and give it to me.'

Salagnon assented with a sigh of relief.

Salagnon often came to sit by Roseval's bed. When the patient closed his eyes, Victorien would sketch him. He gave him a very pure face on which there was no trace of sweat, no sign of his wheezing breath, the tenseness in his lips or the shivers that moved in waves over his bandaged belly until he trembled all over. He did not depict the sallow, greenish pallor or any of the unintelligible words he muttered without opening his eyes. He sketched the portrait of a man half-asleep, lying on his back.

Before closing his eyes, Roseval had clutched his hand, had squeezed it hard and spoken in a low, clear voice.

'You know Salagnon, there's only one thing I regret. Not dying, nothing to be done about that. The thing I regret is dying a virgin. I'd like to have... Can you do it for me? When the time comes, can you think of me?'

'Of course. I promise.'

Roseval let go of his hand, closed his eyes and Salagnon sketched his portrait in pencil on the coarse, brown paper used to wrap American munitions.

'You draw him as though he were asleep,' said Eurydice, leaning over his shoulder. 'But he's in pain.'

'He looks more like himself when he's not in pain. I want to preserve him the way he was.'

'What did you promise him? As I came in I heard you promise him something before he let go of your hand.'

He blushed a little, added a few shadows to the drawing, making the features more pronounced, like a sleeper dreaming, a sleeper who is still alive inside, although he no longer moves.

'To live for him. To live for those who die and will not get to see the end.'

'Will you get to see it, the end?'

'Maybe. Or maybe not; but in that case someone else will see it for me.'

He considered adding something to the drawing, and decided against for fear of spoiling it. He turned to Eurydice, looked up at her. She was studying him carefully.

'Would you live for me if I should die before the end?'

In the drawing, Roseval was asleep. A tranquil, handsome young man lying in a field of flowers, waiting, awaited.

'Yes,' he murmured, blushing as though he had just kissed her. Salagnon felt his hand quiver. Together they walked out of the hospital tent and, after a simple nod, they went their separate ways. They walked without turning back and each felt swaddled, something like a veil, a cloak, a sheet, the attentiveness of the other enveloping them completely, following their every movement.

In the afternoon they went in a truck to fetch the dead. Brioude knew how to drive, so he took the wheel, the others huddled together on the seat: Salagnon, Rochette, Moreau and Ben Tobbal, which was the surname of Ahmed. Brioude had asked him before they all clambered into the truck. 'I can't call you by your first name. I'd feel like I was talking to a child. And with that thick moustache of yours...' Ahmed had told him: Ben Tobbal, smiling under his moustache. Thereafter, Brioude always referred to him by his surname, though he was the only one. It was simply a result of his mania for order, his rather gruff egalitarianism, something he did unthinkingly. The summer air whipping through the windows smelled of warm grass; they drove through the meadows bordering the Saône, jolting along the rocky path, clinging to whatever they could find, bouncing in theirs seats, thrown against each other, trying not to knock Brioude's hand off the gearstick, their hair dishevelled by the war air whirling through the cab.

Brioude hummed as he drove. They were going to collect the bodies, to bring back the dead. This was one of the tasks Naegelin assigned to the Colonel's irregulars, and whenever he mentioned the Colonel's rank, he did so in quotation marks, with a little pause before and a sort of wink after.

They crossed the Flemish landscape of the Saône Valley, where fields of lush green are carved out by the slightly darker threads of hedges. Across the blue sky floated flat-bottomed clouds, dazzlingly white, while below, the Saône, which sprawls rather than flows, was a bronze mirror that glides, mingling reflections of sky and clay.

On the banks of the river a number of tanks were burning. The vast meadow had lost nothing of its beauty or its sweeping proportions; someone had simply placed disturbing things in the pristine landscape.

Tanks burned on the grass, like hulking ruminants slaughtered where they grazed. On a promontory that overlooked the meadow, a lopsided Tiger tank was visible above the hedge, its turret hatch blackened and gaping.

Bumping across the rutted field, they circled the green tanks. Each had sustained a direct hit at the base of the turret; and each time the hollow-charge had caused the lightly armoured Sherman tank to splutter and explode from within. The abandoned hulks were still smouldering. Around them floated an oily smell that caught in the throat, a thick smoke that reeked of rubber, petrol, scorched metal, explosives and something else. The smell caught in the nose like soot.

In coming to fetch the dead, they had hoped to find bodies laid out as though asleep, marked by shrapnel wounds, with perhaps some part of the body neatly severed, some limb missing. What they collected looked more like animals that had fallen into a fire. They were shrunken in size and though their stiff limbs made them easy to carry, it made them difficult to stack. All the delicate parts of the body had disappeared, the clothes were unrecognizable. They collected them like logs. When one of these objects moved, emitting a feeble groan – they could not tell from where, since there was no mouth left to speak – they dropped it in alarm. They stood around, their faces pale, their hands trembling. Ben Tobbal stepped forward, knelt down beside the body, holding up a syringe. He injected something into the chest on which fragments of an officer's stripes were still visible on the charred fabric. The movement and the sound ceased. 'You can put him in the truck,' said Ben Tobbal softly.

They walked as far as the Tiger tank, climbed up on the hull and peered inside. Aside from the soot on the hatch, it seemed undamaged, simply teetering over the ledge with one caterpillar tread in the air. They were curious to find out what these invincible Panzers were like inside. The stench was worse than that of the burned-out tanks. It did not spread but pooled inside, liquid, heavy, it corroded the soul. The walls were spattered with a revolting, viscous slime that coated the controls and covered the seats; a liquefied mass from which bones protruded quivered deep within the hull. They recognized the remains of a uniform, an undamaged collar, a sleeve with an arm still inside, half a gunner's helmet caked with a viscid liquid. The stench filled the cockpit. On the side of the turret they saw four neat holes, the edges crisp and clean, the marks of bullets fired by the planes.

Brioude vomited. Ben Tobbal patted him on the back as though to help him get it all out. 'You only react the first time, you know. After this, you won't care.'

When he got back to the camp Salagnon sketched the tanks in the field. He made them small, set on the horizon, scattered throughout the field, while a great cloud of smoke filled the page.

After this they were assigned to work in the hospital tent under the genial command of the surgeon-major. The Colonel angrily protested, but Naegelin pretended not to remember his name or notice his presence. And so they looked after the wounded, who lay on campbeds in the shadows of the tent. They waited to be transferred to hospitals in towns that had been liberated; they waited to get better; they were waiting in the muggy shadows of the hospital tent; they shooed the flies that buzzed around the sheets; they spent hours staring at the canvas roof, those who could still see, their limbs bandaged and stained crimson.

Salagnon would sit with them and draw their faces, their bare chests half covered by a sheet, their mangled limbs bandaged in white. Posing was comforting; it gave purpose to their stillness and drawing kept him occupied. Afterwards he would give them the drawing, which they carefully packed away in their kitbags. Kaloyannis encouraged him to come often and had the Supply Corps sent him fine-grained paper, pencils, nib pens, ink and even some of the small brushes usually used to oil the parts of telescopic sights. 'My patients heal faster when they're watched,' he explained to the quartermaster sergeant, who was worried about handing over paper usually used for official orders and mentions in dispatches, uneasy about providing Salagnon with materials for drawing, a pointless activity that strangely seemed to interest everyone.

In the hospital tent Kaloyannis operated, bandaged, healed; he left to the Muslim nurses the task of giving injections, which, if performed tactfully, is a prayer for the dead. He had set aside a corner of the tent where he rested during the hottest hours of the day, chatting with a few officers, mostly French soldiers from France. He had Ahmed serve tea fragrant with mint. The sitting area, screened by a curtain, consisted of little more than a rug, some cushions on which to sit and a copper tray set on a munitions crate, but the first time the Colonel stepped inside he exclaimed joyfully, 'You've brought a little piece of Africa home!' He pushed back his sky-blue kepi at a rakish angle that made Kaloyannis smile.

The Colonel often visited the doctor's 'Moorish café' with *maqui-sards* who were at a loose end, and especially with Salagnon. They reclined on the cushions, sipping tea and listening to the chattering of Kaloyannis, who loved to talk. He lived in Algiers, rarely set foot outside Bab El Oued and had never seen the Sahara; this seemed to reassure the Colonel, who said little of his life outside the army beyond brief anecdotes.

Salagnon carried on drawing Eurydice and she never tired of his gaze. The kindly Kaloyannis would look at his daughter with an air of tender admiration, while the taciturn colonel observed the situation with a keen eye. Outside, during the hottest hours, the landscape was bleached white by the sun's glare; the open flaps of the tent let in a light breeze that soothed the skin, blowing gently on the sweat. 'This is the principle of Bedouin tents,' said the Colonel and launched into an explanation of the ethnography and the physics of the black tents in the desert, which, it went without saying, he had visited personally; without saying. Kaloyannis teased him, pretending to know nothing about Bedouins or even whether there were any in Algeria. Having only ever encountered Arabs in the street – excepting Ahmed and his nurses – the only exotic stories he could tell were of shoe-shine boys. And he told them. And by dint of his joviality and his passion, his listeners were transported.

Salagnon recounted what he had seen in the fields. He remembered the smell as though it were a physical ache, his nose and his throat bore the scars.

'What I saw in the German tank was appalling. I don't know how to describe it.'

'A single German Panzer can wipe out several of our tanks,' said the Colonel. 'They have to be destroyed.'

'It was barely scratched and inside there was nothing; nothing but this thing.'

'We're lucky that we have machines,' said Kaloyannis. 'Can you imagine having to do it by hand? Having to liquefy four people in a car by pushing a blowtorch through the door? You'd have to get close enough to see them through the windscreen, push the nozzle through the keyhole and light it. It would take a long time for the car to fill with flames and all the while you'd see everything through the windows while you held the blowtorch steady; you'd be forced to watch through the window as people burned, making sure to keep the nozzle firmly pressed against the lock until everything inside had melted and, when you were done, there would hardly be a blister on the paintwork. Can you imagine standing that close? You'd be able to hear everything, and for the person holding the blowtorch the sight would be unbearable. No one would do it.'

'Most of the American pilots are decent guys with a strict sense of morality, because of their bizarre religion. They wouldn't be able to bring themselves to kill anyone if they didn't have machines. The pilot who did it didn't see a thing; he lined up the tank in his sights, pressed a little red button on the joystick; he never saw the impact, he was long gone by then. It's thanks to machines that we can burn men alive. Without technology we wouldn't be able to kill so many; we wouldn't have the stomach for it.'

'You've got a weird sense of humour, Kaloyannis.'

'I've never seen you laugh, Colonel. It's no indication of strength. Or of health. You're stiff as a board. If someone knocked you down, you'd splinter. And what would the pieces look like? A jigsaw puzzle?'

'It's impossible to be angry with you, Kaloyannis.'

'That's the best thing about prattling in patois. If you lay it on thick, people find it easier to swallow.'

'But that thing you said about machines is gruesome.'

'I'm just articulating the philosophical truth of this war, Colonel. I cannot help it if the truth rankles.'

'It's a paradoxical philosophy.'

'You see that, Colonel? Comedy, medicine, philosophy: I'm everywhere. We are everywhere; isn't that what you were trying to say?'

'I wouldn't have put it that way, but now that you've said it...'

'Well, there you go, the great paradox has been uttered: I am one, yet I am everywhere. Glory be to the Lord, who compensates for my limited number with the gift of ubiquity. It allows me to tease men driven by sad passions. Maybe one day I'll manage to get them to laugh at themselves.'

Ahmed was there, staying in the background, crouching beside the stove, silently brewing the mint tea, smiling from time to time at the doctor's gibes. He filled the tea glasses, pouring from a great height, a technique the Colonel did not emulate, though he insisted he was familiar with it. When they had drunk the scalding tea, the flaps of the tent fluttered, a little sweat evaporated and they heaved a contented sigh.

'At this time of day, I'd rather an anisette,' said Kaloyannis. 'But the eccentricities of Islam mean that Ahmed won't touch it and I would feel uncomfortable drinking without him. And so, gentlemen, it shall be tea for everyone, the whole war long, as a mark of respect for the hare-brained ideas of all and sundry.'

'Tell me something, Kaloyannis,' the Colonel said after a moment, 'are you a Jew?'

'I could tell that was eating you up. Indeed I am, Colonel. My first name is Salomon. Though obviously, these days, you don't saddle yourself with a name like that without solid family reasons.'

The Colonel twirled his glass, making a little eddy of the tea; the flecks of mint leaf pooled in its navel and as he whirled faster it threatened to overspill. He drained the glass and reframed the question.

'But Kaloyannis is a Greek name, isn't it?'

Salomon Kaloyannis let out a joyous laugh that made the Colonel blush. Then he leaned forwards, jabbing his forefinger as though chiding.

'I can see what's troubling you, Colonel. It's the old problem of the clandestine Jew, isn't it?'

The Colonel, as embarrassed as a child caught threatening an adult with a wooden sword, gave no clear answer.

'The fear of the hidden Jew is just a question of classification,' said Kaloyannis. 'I have a rabbi friend, he lives in Bab El Oued like me. I've never been one for religion, but he's still my friend, because, as boys, we played truant together. Bunking off school with someone creates more of a bond than going to class with them. We know each other so well that we know the shortcomings of our respective vocations – nothing to be proud of – and that spares us endless arguments. When he's sober, he can explain to me with impeccable logic why certain animals are impure and certain practices are abomination. Kashrut has the precision of a book of natural science, and that is something I can understand. What is classified is pure, what defies classification is impure; for the Lord created an orderly world – it's the least one could expect of Him – and those who do not fit into his categories do not deserve a place there, they are monsters.

'Now, of course, after a few drinks, the boundaries are not quite so clear. They seem porous. The shelves of the divine cabinet are no longer level. The compartments no longer fit together, some are missing dividers. After an early afternoon anisette, the world looks less like a library and more a tray of cocktail snacks, where everyone helps themselves to a little of everything in no particular order, just for the pleasure.

'A few more glasses and we have overcome our outrage, our indignation, our terror of monsters. We adopt the only sane reaction to the bedlam of the world: we laugh. An uncontrollable laugh that elicits knowing looks from those around us. They know that this is what always happens when the doctor and the rabbi start discussing the Torah and the sciences on the Place des Trois-Horloges.

'The next morning I wake up with a headache and my friend feels a little guilty. We avoid each other for a few days and go about our jobs with great care and proficiency.

'But let me answer your question, Colonel. My name is Kaloyannis because my father was Greek: his surname was Kaloyannis and we inherit our names from our fathers. He married a Gattégno from Salonika, and since Jewishness is passed down through mothers, they called me Salomon. When Salonika as a Jewish city disappeared, they washed up in Constantine, like the survivors of a shipwreck who climb aboard a new vessel when theirs sinks. Oh yes, we deserted a sinking ship; a metaphor you've doubtless heard before in a different, more zoological, form. But when a ship sinks, you either jump or drown. In Constantine I was French and I married a woman named Bensoussan, because I loved her and also because I did not want to interrupt a thousand-year-old tradition. After I qualified as a doctor, I settled in Bab El Oued, which is a glorious melting pot, and though I love my community I find life in the community frustrating. There you are, Colonel, now you know the secret of the Greek name that masks the hidden Jew.'

'You're cosmopolitan.'

'Absolutely. I was born an Ottoman, something that no longer exists, and now I am a Frenchman, because France has always been a refuge welcoming the non-existent, and we speak French, the language of the Empire of Ideas. Empires have much to recommend them, Colonel, they leave you in peace, and you can always belong.

There are no conditions to being an imperial subject – you need only agree to be one. And you get to keep your ancestral roots, however contradictory, without being martyred for them. Empire allows a man to breathe easily, to be similar and different at the same time. To be a citizen of a nation, on the other hand, is something one earns, by birth, by nature, by a painstaking investigation of one's origins. This is the drawback of nations: you belong or you do not belong, and there is constantly suspicion. The Ottoman Empire left us in peace. Once the tiny Greek nation got its hands on Salonika, people were forced to state their religion in their identity papers. This is why I love the République Française – the capital 'R' makes all the difference. The République does not have to be French; this glorious concept can take a new adjective without losing its nature. Talking as I am to you, in this language, allows me to be a citizen of the world.

'But I have to confess that I was disappointed when confronted with France itself. I was a citizen of *la France universelle*, far removed from the Île-de-France, and then suddenly metropolitan France was picking a fight with me. The Maréchal, ever the rural policeman, inherited a city and he wants to turn it into a village.'

The Colonel made an irritated gesture, as though this were an issue only to be discussed among one's own.

'And yet you came to fight for France.'

'Not at all. I came to take back something that was stolen from me.'

'Assets?'

'Of course not, Colonel. I am a little Jew with no capital and no assets. I'm a doctor in Bab El Oued; it's a far cry from Wall Street. I was living a peaceful little life, a French citizen basking in the sun, when murky events took place in the far north of my *quartier*. The result was I was robbed of my status as a French citizen. I had been a Frenchman, now I was merely a Jew. I was forbidden from practising my profession, from studying, from voting. Education, medicine, the Republic, everything I believed in was taken from me. And so I got on the boat with various other people and came to take it back. When I go home I will distribute what I have recovered to my Arab neighbours. The Elastic Republic that is our language can encompass an infinite number of speakers.'

'You think the Arabs are capable?'

'As capable as you or I, Colonel. With education, I'm sure I could transform a Pygmy into a nuclear physicist. Look at Ahmed. He has been trained, he works with me, his nursing care is impeccable. Put him in a French hospital and no one would notice. Apart from his moustache, of course; the men in metropolitan France have rather small moustaches. We were surprised by that, weren't we, Ahmed?'

'Yes, Doctor Kaloyannis. Very surprised.'

And he poured the tea, brought over a glass. Salomon thanked him gently. Doctor Kaloyannis got along very well with Ahmed.

Commentaries IV

Here and there

T HE MORNING AFTER my night of pain, I felt better. Thank you. This pain was mine, it ravaged my throat; not seriously, but it was my throat. I could not get rid of it. My pain stayed with me like a mouse accidentally trapped in my spacesuit. I was the cosmonaut; we had been launched in a rocket ship that was to orbit the Earth several times before returning. All the cosmonaut can do is wait; and he feels the mouse scurry here and there over his body; it is trapped with him; he flies through space, it flies with him. He can do nothing. The mouse will land with him at the appointed hour, and until then he can only wait.

In the morning I no longer felt my pain. I had taken analgesics, anti-inflammatories, vasomodifiers, and they had dispelled it. The mouse in my spacesuit had disappeared, dissolved. Analgesics are the greatest achievement of medicine. Together with anti-inflammatories, antibiotics and tranquillizers. Unable to actually cure the agonies of living, science gives us the means to feel no pain. Day after day, pharmacists dole out the means of inaction by the crateload. Doctors and pharmacists urge the patient to have more patience, always more patience. The priority of the sciences as applied to the body is not to cure, but to soothe. Someone who complains is given help to endure their reactions. He is advised to be patient and rest; in the meantime he is given a calmative. The pain will be dealt with, but later. Meanwhile he needs to calm down, not get himself in such a state, sleep a little, so he can carry on living in this devastating condition.

I wolfed down the remedies and the following morning I felt better. Thanks.

Thanks to analgesics, I felt like nothing was wrong. But everything's going wrong.

Everything's going wrong.

I visited Salagnon once a week. I went to a painting class in Voracieux-les-Bredins. The mere mention of the name would make a native of Lyon shudder. It is a name that makes people flinch, or makes them smile.

This town of towers and suburban houses is at the terminus of all lines of transport. The buses go no further, the city ends. The metro dropped me in front of the bus station. The platforms are arranged under a plastic awning stained by rain and sunlight. Large orange numbers on a black background indicate the destinations. Buses departing for Voracieux-les-Bredins leave rarely. I sat on a sun-bleached plastic seat with its scuffed back, leaning against a glass windbreak crazed with cracks from some impact. In the glorious analgesic haze, my feet did not quite touch the ground. The badly designed seat did not help; too deep, the front edge too high; it raised my legs, so my feet barely grazed the stained tarmac. The uncomfortableness of street furniture is not an accident: discomfort discourages loitering and encourages fluid movement. Fluidity is the necessary prerequisite of modern life, without it the city dies. But, stuffed to the gills with psychosomatotrophic drugs, I was feeling fluid inside, I barely connected with my body, while my eyes floated above my seat.

I was far from home. People like me do not go to Voracieux-les-Bredins. To the east, the last metro station is the tradesman's entrance to the city. A harried crowd of people exits, enters, and they are nothing like me. They brushed past without seeing, a rushing throng, dragging heavy luggage, clutching children, pushing strollers around the maze of platforms. They walked singly with heads bowed, or in tight little groups. They were not like me. I was reduced to my eye, my body absent, loosed as it was from my weight, disconnected from my sense of touch, floating in my skin. We are nothing like each other; we brush past each other, unseeing.

All around me I heard voices, yet I could not understand what was being said. The voices were talking too loudly, hacking sentences into short phrases, blunt exclamations enunciated with a curious emphasis; when I finally realized they were speaking French, the language was utterly transformed. All around me, as I sat perched on this seat nearly too small to hold me, I could hear a strain of my own language as though distorted by echoes. I found it difficult to follow this music, but the analgesics that soothed my throat impelled me towards indifference. What was this weird plastic cavern in which I found myself? I did not recognize anything.

I was sick, feverish, probably still contagious, and everything seemed strange. People came, they went and I could not make sense of anything. They were not like me. All these people passing were alike, but they were not like me. In the area where I live, I experience the opposite: the people I meet are like me, but they are not alike. In the centre, where the city warrants its name, where one can be most confident of being oneself, the individual takes precedence over the group; I recognize each person, each is an individual, but here in the suburbs it is the group that I see, the individuals blur together. We are primed to identify groups, it is an anthropological necessity. Inherited social class can be spotted at a distance, it is worn on the body, it is written in the face. Resemblance is a form of belonging and I do not belong here. I float in my seat-shell while I wait for the bus; my dangling feet do not touch the ground. I see only through my eyes, which float, oblivious to my body. Thought completely disconnected from body is entirely focused on resemblances.

These people recognized each other, greeted each other, but I did not recognize the greeting. The boys slapped fingers, bumped fists in complex sequences I was surprised they could remember. Older men solemnly shook hands and, with their free arms, hugged the other closer and kissed without using their lips. In less effusive greetings they brought the hand that had touched the other person to their heart, and the very sight of this triggered an intense emotion in me. Unsteady young men waited for buses, gathered in jostling groups, wavering on the edge of the circle they formed, looking outwards and then looking back, rolling their shoulders, shifting their weight to the other foot. The girls passed in gaggles, giving the boys a wide berth, rarely saying hello to anyone. And when they did, when a fifteen-year-old girl said hello to a fifteen-year-old boy, who drifted away from his unstable group, she did so in a way I found baffling as I floated above my sun-bleached seat-shell, barely touching the ground: she shook his hand, as though she were a businesswoman; her hand perfectly straight at the end of her outstretched arm, independent of her body, which remained stiffly aloof when she touched a boy's hand. In a loud voice she would inform the girls with her that he was a cousin; loud enough so that I could hear her, me and anyone else waiting for the bus to Voracieux-les-Bredins.

I don't understand these rules. At the end of the metro line people greet each other differently. How can we live together when the gestures that make contact possible are not the same?

Two black veils floated past with people inside. They walked together, floating in the wind, hiding everything. Satin gloves hid their fingers, only their eyes were visible. They walked together, passed in front of me. I could no more see them than I could a patch of darkness. Two shrouds with eyes swept through the bus station. They had to be women it was forbidden to look upon. My gaze would have sullied them with its powerful desire. Because seeing female forms would have roused me, would have reminded me of my loneliness, of my uncomfortable, creaking plastic seat-shell; it would have urged me to get up, to touch, to kiss this other I would desire as myself. Not seeing them, my body is left to its own devices, unresponsive, almost numb, utterly absorbed by abstract calculations. The rule of reason makes me a monster.

How would I be able to bear this burden that is the other if my desire for it did not cause me to forgive it everything? How could I live with those I meet if I cannot look upon them, follow them with my gaze, delight in and anticipate their passing, since the mere sight of them stirs my body? How? If love between us is not possible, what then remains?

When veiled by a black bag, the other privatizes the street to some extent. Fences off the public space to a degree. Ousts me from my space. Occupies the place where I might be; all I can do is clumsily bump into this other or avoid it with a groan, causing me to waste time. This other is in the way. With an other who reveals nothing I can have only reasonable relations, and nothing is more unreliable than reason. What is left if we cannot lust after each other, even with our eyes? Violence?

The two black veils moved calmly along the platforms without touching anybody. They checked the timetable and climbed aboard a bus. In doing so the veils were lifted slightly and I saw feet. One was wearing women's shoes with gold trimmings, the other a man's shoes. The bus started up and I'm glad I didn't catch it. I'm glad not to be shut up in a bus with two dark shrouds, one wearing women's shoes, the other wearing men's. The bus disappeared at the junction and I don't know what happened after that. Nothing, probably. I took another psychosomatotrope, because my head was starting to throb again, my throat could barely swallow. Pain racked my head and my mucous membranes. Pain racked the organ of thought and the organ of touch. Proximity becomes painful, the closeness becomes phobic; you begin to dream of having no neighbours, of eliminating everything apart from the self. Violence works on the contact surface; it is here that pain manifests itself and from here that the urge to destroy spreads at the same speed as the fear of being destroyed. The mucous membranes become inflamed.

Why hide under such a large chador? Unless it is to plot dark deeds, to announce the disappearance of bodies: through relegation; through repudiation; through mass graves.

Salagnon smiled at me. He took my hand in his hand, his gentle yet firm hand, and he smiled at me. Oh, that smile! For that smile you forgive him everything. You forget the harshness of his features, his military crop, his cold stare, his terrible past; you forget that he has so much blood on his hands. The smile that softens the lines of his mouth when he greets me wipes away everything. In the moment that he smiles Victorien Salagnon is naked. He says nothing, he simply opens a door and allows me to step into an empty room, into one of those magnificent empty rooms filled only with sunlight that exist in apartments before you move in. His gaunt features are stretched over the bones of his face. A silk curtain next to an open window, and the sun behind it playing in the folds, it flutters in the breeze that carries with it the joyous sounds of the street, the murmur of shady trees filled with birds.

When he shakes my hand I feel prepared to listen to everything he has to tell me. I will say nothing. All desire has flowed from my tongue to my hands. I have no linguistic desire other than to take the brush, dip it in the ink, lay it on the paper; my only wish is a trembling in my hands, a physical desire to pick up the brush and the first black stroke that appears on the paper will be a relief, a release for my whole being, a sigh. I want him to guide me in the path of the unique brushstroke, so that I can hold my head up and unfurl the splendour of ink between my hands.

It doesn't last, of course; such things never last. He opens the door and shakes my hand, then our hands disengage, his smile vanishes and I step inside. He walks ahead of me down the hallway; I follow behind, peering as I pass at the rubbish he hangs on the wall. He decorates the walls of his house with paintings. He also displays other objects. The wallpaper is so baroque, the lighting so dim, that the corridor ahead looks like the tunnel of a cave, the angles appear rounded, and against the background of repeated patterns it is difficult to make out the objects hanging on the walls. I do not stop in the hallway, I simply follow him; in passing, I spot a barometer with its needle permanently stuck on 'changeable'; there was a clock with roman numerals, the hands of which, I noticed after several months, no longer moved; there was even a mounted antelope head and I wondered how it came to be there, whether he had bought it – where? – whether he had inherited it – from whom? – whether he had hacked it from the body of an animal he had killed – how? I don't know which of these three possibilities I found most revolting. Apart from that there were frames, horrid, gilded baroque frames in which slumbered pseudo-Dutch landscapes so murky you had to step close to make out the subject and the mediocrity, and garish scenes of Provence full of affected joy and clashing colours.

I had imagined Salagnon's house to be very different: Asian curios and a kasbah atmosphere; or perhaps nothing, a white space and windows with no curtains. I would have expected the decor to reflect him, if only a little, if only by little touches, something that reflected his life story. But not this banality pushed to the point where it was crushing, where it was stifling. If every person's home reflects their soul, as people claim, the home of Eurydice and Victorien Salagnon had the good taste to divulge nothing.

When at last I found the courage to point out a pathetic seascape in a polished wooden frame, a storm raging on a craggy stretch of coast, where the rocks looked like pumice stone and the waves like curdled resin (to say nothing of the sky, which looked like nothing), he simply gave a disarming smile.

'It's not one of mine.'

'You like it?'

'No. It's just a wall. It's just a decoration.'

A decoration! This man, whose brush trembled, whose brush pulsed with life the moment he fed it with ink, this man surrounded himself with 'decorations'. He lived in rooms that were decorated. In his home he had recreated a furniture warehouse catalogue from twenty years ago, maybe thirty, I don't know. Time here was irrelevant, it was rebuffed, it did not pass.

'You know,' he said, 'those paintings are made in Asia. The Chinese in particular have always been particularly talented; they bend their bodies according to their will, by dint of practice. They learn how to paint in oils in vast studios and they produce Dutch, English, Provençal landscapes for the western market. Sometimes several at a time. They paint much better and much faster than the Sunday painters here; the canvasses are shipped here in cargo freighters, rolled up in containers.

'They're fascinating, these paintings: their ugliness belongs to no one, neither those who paint them nor those who look at them. It is calming for everyone. I have been much too present all my life, too much in the moment. I'm exhausted.

'The thought process of the Chinese does me good; their indifference is a balm. I have spent my whole life obsessed with their ideals, although I have never set foot in China itself. I have seen China only once, from a distance. A hill on the far bank of a river where we had just blown up a bridge. A couple of Molotova trucks were burning, and behind the curtain of smoke rising from the flames I could see the steep hills covered with pine trees exactly like the trees framed against drifting clouds in their paintings. But the clouds from the burning petrol were too black that day, an error of judgement. And I thought: so this is China; it's a stone's throw away, but I'll never go there, because I've blown up the bridge. I didn't hang around; we had to get out of there fast. We ran all the way back, we ran for days. One of the guys with me died of exhaustion just after we got back. I mean actually died; he was buried with full military honours.'

'You never show your paintings?'

'I'm not going to hang something I've done on a wall. It's finished. What remains of those times is a burden.'

'You never thought about exhibiting, selling, becoming an artist?'

'I sketched what I saw, so that Eurydice could see it. Once she had seen it, the drawing was complete.'

When we stepped into the living room, there were two guys waiting for us; and when I saw them slumped on the sofa, I felt another rush of disgust at the preposterous decor. How could he and Eurydice live in this fake setting? How could they live in this TV set that looked as if it were made from hunks of cut out, painted polystyrene? Unless they no longer wanted to know, no longer wanted to speak, not ever.

But this strategy of mediocrity was no match for the physical violence that these two guys gave off. They sprawled on the sofa like regular visitors, making themselves at home. Against the mawkish backdrop of fake furniture, against the idiotic background of the wallpaper, they looked like adults in a kindergarten. They did not know where to put their legs, their very weight threatened to demolish the sofa.

The older man looked like Salagnon, but stockier, and his features had begun to sag, despite the energy he put into every gesture. I could not really see his eyes, because he was wearing tinted glasses, huge lenses with a gold wire frame. Behind the greenish glass, his eyes darted like fish in an aquarium and I could not make out the expression behind the reflections. Everything he was wearing seemed strange: the baggy, checked jacket, the shirt open to reveal his chest gaped too wide, the gold medallion, the flared trousers, the shiny loafers. He looked like what passed for flashy style thirty years ago, wearing colours that no longer existed. He was like a ghost. Only the dent in the sofa beneath the weight of his buttocks made it clear he really existed.

The other guy was thirty at most. He was wearing a leather jacket from which jutted a little pot belly, hair close cropped on his round head; the head set on a fat neck with folds of flesh, folds at the front when he leaned forwards and folds at the back when he sat up.

Salagnon introduced us, although he remained evasive. Mariani, an old friend, and one of his lads. Me, his pupil; his student in the art of the brush. This brought a laugh from the man in the 1972 jacket.

'The art of the brush! Still plugging on with your ladylike hobbies, Salagnon. Knitting and embroidery: that's how you're spending your long retirement, instead of joining us?'

He laughs loudly, as though he finds this really funny, and his kid laughs too, but more maliciously. Salagnon brought in four beers and glasses and, as he passed, Mariani slapped his buttocks.

'You make a fine servant! You know back when we were marching, he'd get up before everyone else and make us coffee? He hasn't changed.'

Mariani's kid sniggered again, grabbed a beer and, pointedly ignoring the glass, drank from the bottle. He looked me straight in the eye and was about to let out a macho belch when the older men glared at him and he stopped himself, swallowed it down and mumbled an apology. In a silence I found embarrassing, Salagnon poured the beers with the polite aloofness of a host.

'Don't worry,' Marini said to me after a moment, 'I've been teasing him for half a century. They're private jokes between us that he wouldn't put up with from anyone else. He's good enough not to get riled when I lapse into my natural stupidity. He indulges me, the way you do survivors.'

'And besides, I'm light years ahead of him when it comes to being offensive,' said Salagnon. 'He carried me through the jungle on a stretcher. Being carried was so painful that I spent the whole time I wasn't unconscious screaming abuse at him.'

'Capitaine Salagnon has genuine talent. I don't know much about these things. He drew a portrait of me one night when we were standing guard in a different time, a different place, and this portrait that he tossed off in a few seconds, tore out of his notebook and handed to me is the only picture of me that is true. I don't know how he does it, but he does. He probably doesn't know himself. If I tease him about his genteel hobbies, it's only to get back at him for the abuse I got when I was carrying him, which was pretty vile. His talent as a painter was an oddity back in the places, in the times we served together, where nobody much had anything to do with the arts. It was like having blond, flowing locks when everyone around you has a military buzz cut. It's not his fault, and it says nothing about his strength of character.'

Salagnon sat, sipping from his glass, saying nothing. His face was once again that bony mask that could inspire fear, which divulged no more than might a crumpled piece of paper: the lack of signs, the same blank whiteness. But though it was scarcely visible unless you knew what to look for, I could just make out the flicker of a smile playing on thin lips, like the shadow of a cloud gliding over the earth without disturbing a thing; I watched as it passed over his skin like a shadow, this indulgent smile of a man content to listen. I could see it, I knew his every gesture. I had pored over every drawing he was prepared to show me until my vision blurred. I knew his every gesture, because ink-wash painting, more even than the ink itself, is composed of inner impulses expressed as gestures. And I could see them in his face.

'We all had the greatest respect for Salagnon over there.'

Mariani's kid squirmed in his seat, toying with the bottle. The older men turned towards him as one, the same smile playing on their weathered lips. They gave him the same tender look they might a puppy stirring in its sleep, its dreams of hunting revealed by faint shudders and slight twitches of its paws.

'That's right, my lad! Over there!' Mariani said, slapping the boy's thigh. 'Over there is something you never had to go through. Nor did you,' he said, nodding at me.

'So much the better,' said Salagnon, 'because men died over there, died in the most idiotic or the most appalling way. And even those who came home did not come back in one piece. Over there we lost limbs, we lost chunks of flesh, we lost whole sections of our minds. So much the better for your physical integrity.

'But it's a pity in a way, because you've had no forge in which to form your character. You're unmarked as the day you were delivered into this world, the original wrapping paper is still intact. Packaging protects, but a life lived wrapped up is no life at all.'

The boy squirmed, looked sullen, but his manner was still respectful. When the two old men paused, grinned broadly at each other and winked, he finally managed to get a word in edgeways.

'Life on the streets is just as brutal as your colonies.' He leaned back against the cushions to make himself seem bigger. 'The wrapping paper is ripped off pretty quickly, let me tell you. You learn stuff there they don't teach you in school.'

This was directed at me, but I had no desire to get involved in this sort of conversation.

'You're not wrong,' said Mariani, amused to see the pup bare his fangs. 'The streets are getting to be like over there. The forge is getting closer, lad, soon everyone will be able to prove their worth at home. Then we'll know the strong from the weak, and those who act tough but crumple as soon as someone throws a punch. Just like over there.'

The boy sat fuming, his fists clenched. The gentle mockery of the two old men had him spluttering with rage. They were trying to exclude him, but who could he take out his fury on? On these men who represented everything to him? On me, who represented nothing, except perhaps a class enemy? On himself, given that, having never been tested, he didn't yet know what he was made of?

'We're ready,' he grunted.

'I hope you're not shocked by me saying such things,' Mariani said to me with a hint of malice. 'But life in the outer zones is changing in very different ways from anything you have experienced. And that's where we are, in the outer zone. The law is different here, life is different. But the people in the cities are changing too; these days even the city centres are stalked by armed gangs; infiltrated, day and night. You can't tell that they're armed, but they are, every last one of them.

If they were frisked, if the laws of our gutless Republic authorized stop and search, we'd find every one of them has a flick knife, a Stanley knife, some even carry guns. When the police set us loose, when they turn tail and leave the zones to go to hell, just like we did over there, you'll be all alone, alone and surrounded, just like the people we went to defend over there. We have been colonized, lad.'

Comfortably slouched against the cushions, his son nodded, not daring to say anything, since he was suppressing a burp, but empha-sizing each key idea with a large swig of beer.

'We're colonized. We need to use that word. We have to have the courage to use that word, because it fits. No one dares to use it, but it accurately describes our situation: we are in a colonial situation and we are the colonized people. We have retreated so much it was bound to happen. You remember, Salagnon, when we were running through the jungle with the Viets up our arse? We had to abandon our position or we would have died there, so we abandoned it. Back then, an orderly retreat with few casualties seemed like a victory; you could get a medal for it. But let's call a spade a spade: we ran away. We ran away with the Viets hot on our tail and we're still running. We're almost at the core now, at the core of ourselves, and we're still retreating. City centres have become the blockhouses of our fortified camp. But when I stroll around a city centre, when I walk around the heart of who we are, clapping my hands over my eyes like everyone else so as not to have to see, when I walk around the city, I hear. I hear because my ears are still open, because I don't have hands enough to block out everything. Do I hear French? The French I should hear as I wander through the heart of who we are? No, I hear something else. I hear the sound of "over there" arrogantly blaring out. I hear the French that is who I am, but it is mangled, degraded, barely intelligible. This is why we need to use the right words, because we judge by ear. And when you listen, it's obvious that we are already somewhere that is not home. Just listen. France is retreating, it is falling apart; our ears tell us as much, only our ears, because we choose to close our eyes.

'But I'll leave it there. Time is ticking away and your bourgeois friends will be here soon. I don't want any trouble and I don't want to cause you any. We'll leave you to your knitting.'

He got to his feet with a little effort and smoothed his jacket. Behind the green glass of his lenses his eyes looked tired. His kid jumped up and stood next to him, waiting respectfully.

'Do you remember everything, Salagnon?'

'You know I do. When I finally die, they'll bury me with my memories. Every one present and correct.'

'We need you. When you eventually decide to give up your ladylike hobbies and do something worthy of you, come and join us. We need strong men who remember everything to train our young people. So that nothing is forgotten.'

Salagnon assented with a flicker of his eyelids, a gentle, vague gesture. He shook the man's hand. He was showing that he would always be there; to what end, he did not indicate. The boy touched his hand, scarcely looking at him.

When they had left I could breathe more easily. I leaned back in the plush armchair and finished my beer; I let my eyes wander over this furniture that was soulless and deliberately ugly. The velvet cushions were rough, the armchairs offered no comfort; that was not their purpose.

'The paranoid and his puppy,' I said, spitting the words.

'Don't say that.'

'One rants, the other barks. And the little one is just begging to go walkies. Friends of yours, are they?'

'Just Marini.'

'Strange friend who can come out with shit like that.'

'Mariani is a strange friend. He's the only one of my friends who isn't dead. The others died off, one by one, but not him. I owe it to them to be loyal to him. When he comes round I feed him, I give him something to drink, something to eat to shut him up. I prefer him to be eating rather than eructating. Luckily, we have only one orifice for both functions. But since you were here, he went off on one. He's a sensitive soul, Mariani. He immediately detected your roots.'

'My roots?'

'Educated middle classes, consciously blind to differences.'

'I don't understand this whole thing about differences.'

'That's what I say. But with you here, he laid it on thick. Mostly he's an intelligent guy, quite capable of being profound.'

'That's not the impression he gives.'

'I know, it's sad. He only ever killed people who fired at him first. But he surrounded himself with dogs that waded through blood and could see in his eye when he wanted someone's throat ripped out. He's not quite right in the head, Mariani. Out in Asia he had a breakdown, ripped his insides out, something inside him snapped. If he'd stayed here, he would have been a lovely man. But he went over there, and over there he couldn't stand the way the races were separated. He was shipped out, raring to fight, but something broke, and for him it had the same effect as taking amphetamines. He never came down, it left a rip in his soul, a tear that has been widening ever since, these days he can see only through that hole, through the rip of the difference between the races. What we went through over there could have cut the sails of the strongest man.'

'But not you?'

'I had my drawing. It allowed me to re-sew the tears caused by events. At least that's what I think now. There was always a part of me that wasn't quite there; a part that was wilfully absent, I owe my life to that. Mariani didn't come back in one piece. I owe a loyalty to those who didn't come home, because I was with them.'

'I don't understand.'

He stopped talking; he got to his feet and started to pace up and down his ridiculous living room. He kept his hands behind his back and his jaws moved as though he were muttering, causing his jowls and his wrinkled neck to quiver. He suddenly stopped in front of me and stared into my eyes with eyes so pale their only colour was translucence.

'It takes only a single act, you know. A precise moment, one that will never come again and can be the basis for an undying friendship. Mariani carried me through the jungle. I was wounded, I couldn't walk, so he carried me through the Tonkin forest. The jungles around there are hellishly steep, and he marched through them with me on his back and the Viets on his tail. He carried me as far as the river and the two of us managed to get to safety. You can't know what that means. Get up.'

I stood up. He stepped towards me.

'Carry me.'

I must have looked stupid. Though tall, he was so scrawny that he could not weigh much, but I had never carried an adult, never carried a man, never carried someone I didn't know well... But I'm getting muddled: the simple fact is I had never done what he was asking of me.

'Carry me.'

So I picked him up and carried him. I held him across my chest; he slung one arm around my shoulder, his legs dangled. His head lolled against my chest. He was not very heavy, but I felt completely overcome.

'Take me out to the garden.'

I did as he dictated. His feet hung loose. I crossed the living room, walked down the hallway, using my elbow to open the doors; he did not help. He was heavy. He was a burden.

'Over there, we carried our dead,' he said, his mouth close to my ear. 'The dead are heavy, useless, but we tried to bring them back. And we never left a wounded man. Nor did they.'

The front door was not easy to open. I almost tripped on the steps. I could feel the bones poking through his skin, against my arm, against my chest. I could feel his papery old skin against my fingers, smell his exhausted old man's smell. His head weighed nothing.

'To carry, to be carried, is not easy,' he said, his voice close.

On the path through his garden I looked foolish, cradling him in my arms, his head against my chest. Finally, he was beginning to feel heavy.

'Imagine you had to take me back to your place, on foot; imagine it going on for hours, in a jungle with no trails or paths. And if you should fail, the guys following you will kill you; and they will kill me, too.'

The gate creaked and Eurydice stepped into the garden. The gates squeak, because it's rare for anyone to take the trouble to oil them. She was carrying a shopping basket with a baguette sticking out; she walked in long strides, her head held high, and stopped in front of us.

'What the hell are you two doing?'

'I'm explaining Mariani.'

'That arsehole? Has he been round again?'

'He was careful to leave before you got back.'

'Just as well. It was because of men like him that I lost everything. I lost my childhood, my father, my street, my history, all in the name of their obsession with race. So when I see them re-emerging here in France, I'm fucking incensed.'

'She's a Kaloyannis from Bab El Oued,' said Salagnon. 'She grew up listening to torrents of abuse being shrieked from one window to the next. She knows insults you could not imagine. And when she's angry, she makes up new ones.'

'Mariani is very wise not to cross me. Let him go finish his wars somewhere else.'

Taking her basket of vegetables and holding her head high, she strode into the house and shut the door with enough force that it did not quite slam, but almost. Salagnon tapped me on the shoulder.

'Relax. It's fine. You managed to carry me into the garden without dropping me and you escaped the tigress of Bab El Oued. A very rewarding day and you came through it alive.'

'Mariani I can understand at a push, but what is he doing hanging around with guys like that?'

'The kid who was belching? He's a member of GAFFES – the Guild of Autonomous Freeborn French Elders. Mariani heads up the local branch. And just like he did over there, he keeps his dogs around him.'

'Freeborn Frenchman? Mariani, with an "i"?' I said with the withering sarcasm one uses in such circumstances.

'The physiology of what constitutes pure stock is complicated.'

'We're not trees.'

'Maybe, but "pure stock" is a broad concept. It's instinctive, felt. Deciding what is pure is a matter of delicate judgement that can't be explained to someone who doesn't feel it.'

'If it can't be explained, it's bullshit.'

'What is truly important does not need to be explained. You simply feel it. You surround yourself with those who feel as you do. Pure stock is something you can hear.'

'So I've got a tin ear?'

'No. It's your way of life. You're so completely surrounded by people like you that you're blind to differences. Like Mariani was before he went away. But what would you do if you lived here? Or if you'd been shipped over there? Do you really know for certain? It's impossible to know what we will become when we are truly uprooted.'

'Roots, stock, it's all lunacy. Family trees are nothing more than a metaphor.'

'Probably. But that's how Mariani is. There is a touch of madness in him, and there is something in him that carried me through the jungle. Defining people by a single trait is something I can do only with a brush. But it's something I found easy in wartime; it was simple, straightforward: them and us. And if there was any doubt, you made the call. Now that we're in peacetime, things can't be so simple without being unfair, without risking destroying that peace. That's why some people would rather go back to war. Why don't we go and do some painting?'

He took me by the arm and we went indoors.

That day he taught me how to choose the thickness of my brush. He taught me to choose the weight of the line I would lay down on the paper. It is instinctive, an action easily confused with that of reaching for a brush, but the brush you choose defines the rhythm of your work. He taught me to choose the heft of my strokes; taught me to decide on the scale of my gestures on the paper.

He explained it in simple terms. He had me practise and I realized that painting with ink is a musical act, a dance performed not just by the hand, but the whole body, the expression of a rhythm that is deeper than myself.

To paint with ink, you use ink, and ink is simply darkness, a brutal obliteration of light that follows the line of the brush. The brush traces the blackness and in doing so the white appears. White and black appear at one and the same time. The brush, loaded with ink, trails a dark mass in its wake, and in doing so it traces the white, allowing it to appear. The rhythm that binds the two depends on the thickness of the brush. The density of the bristles and the amount of ink define the thickness of the stroke. This weighs down the paper in a sense, and it is the thickness of the brush that determines the balance between the conscious black and the untouched white, between the mark that I make and the echo that, although I do not make it, exists nonetheless.

He taught me that virgin, as yet untouched, is not white: it is as black as it is white; it is nothing, it is everything, it is the world as yet untouched by the self. Choosing the size of the brush means choosing the rhythm one will follow, the force one plans to adopt, the breath of the trail that will follow our breath. We can leave behind the impersonal now, move from 'one' to 'we', and very soon I will say 'I'.

He taught me that the Chinese use a single, tapering brush, deciding at every moment how much pressure to exert on it. The logic is the same, since pressure is the same as force. Through the tension of their wrist they regulate, moment by moment, the forcefulness of their presence, the scale of their action.

'I met one of those demiurgical painters in Hanoi during the war,' he told me. 'He used a single brush and a single drop of ink in a soapstone dish. From these simple tools he could draw the power and range of a symphony orchestra. He claimed to worship his brush, which is cleansed in pure water after use, before laying it in a silk-lined box. He talked to the brush; he claimed he had no dearer friend. For a while I believed him, but he was making fun of me. In time I came to understand that his only tool was himself, and more especially the presence he allowed himself in each moment. He had a precise sense of his presence, and the self-assured variations created the drawing.'

We would paint until we could not carry on. We painted as one; he teaching me what to do, by which I mean that I painted with brush and ink and he by eye, by voice. He would appraise my strokes and I would start over; there was no reason for it to end. By the time I realized how utterly exhausted I was, it was already the middle of the night. My brush as I applied the ink now blotted the paper; I could no longer give it form. By then, he was saying only 'yes' or 'no', and by the end simply 'no'. I decided to go home; my body no longer responded to my wishes; it longed to lie down, to sleep, despite the thirst for ink that would have had me carry on and on and on.

When I left he gave me a smile and those smiles were enough to last me a lifetime. As I left he gave me a smile, as he had when I arrived, and it was enough for me. He opened those eyes so pale that their only colour was translucence; he let me come to him; he let me see inside him; and I went, without wondering where it might lead; I came back empty-handed, having seen nothing, but fulfilled simply by the access he granted me. The smiles he gave me when I arrived and when I left threw open the door to an empty room. Light streamed into the room, unhindered. I had a place there, and that made my world larger. I needed only to see this yawning door before me; that was enough.

I stepped out into the streets of Voracieux-les-Bredins. My mind teemed with inchoate thoughts I could not quite grasp; I let them slip away. As I walked, I thought about Percival, the foolish knight, who did whatever he was bid, since he blindly believed everything he was told.

Why did I think of him? Because of that vacant room filled with light to which Victorien Salagnon's smile held the key. I stood on the threshold and, though I understood nothing, I was happy. 'The Story of the Grail' focuses entirely on this moment: Percival prepares for it, he anticipates it, but when the moment comes it eludes him; he regrets it and seeks it out again. What has happened? Quite by chance, Percival encounters the crippled Fisher King. The king fishes in a river that cannot be crossed, using a line baited with a glittering fish no larger than a minnow – it is his one remaining pleasure in life. He fishes from a small boat moored by the bank of the river that cannot be crossed; he can no longer step outside. To return home, four sturdy servants must take the corners of the blanket on which he sits and carry him. He cannot walk, having been crippled by a javelin that speared him through both thighs. The king could do nothing now but fish, and he invited Percival to the castle that cannot be seen from afar.

Percival the Fool became a knight, although he knew nothing of the world. His mother taught him nothing for fear that he would leave her. His father and his brothers had been wounded and killed. He became a knight, although he knew nothing. He reached the castle that cannot be seen and there saw the Grail, although he did not know it. While he talked to the Fisher King, while they ate together, squires and maidens passed through the room in silence, carrying objects of great beauty. One of these was the bleeding lance on which pearled a drop of blood that never dried; another was a silver carving platter fit for all who might use it, being so wide and deep, and piled with choice meats in their juices. The maidens moved slowly, soundlessly, through the room and Percival watched, but did not understand, he did not ask whom they served, whom it was he could not see. He had been warned against talking too much. It was a decisive moment. Percival would never see the Holy Grail close up, although he did not know this, since he did not ask.

Wandering the streets of Voracieux-les-Bredins, I thought about Percival the Fool, the gormless knight who is never at home anywhere, since he understands nothing. To anyone else the world is cluttered with objects, but to him it is meaningless, because he does not understand these objects. All he knows of the world is what he has been told by his mother, and she has told him nothing for fear of losing him. He is simply filled with joy. Nothing troubles him, nothing encumbers him, nothing hinders his progress. I thought of him, because Victorien Salagnon had opened himself to me, I had seen without seeing, it had filled me with joy and asked nothing of me in return. Perhaps that was enough, I thought, as I walked along.

I headed for the bus shelter on the avenue, to wait for the first bus of the morning, which would arrive soon. I sat on the plastic bench, leaned back against the glass wall of the shelter. I dozed in the chill air of the slowly fading night.

I longed to wield a huge brush over a tiny sheet of paper. A brush with a handle fashioned from a tree trunk, with bristles made of tightly packed hanks of horsehair. It would be taller than me and, loaded with a whole bucket of ink, would be too heavy for me to lift. I would need ropes and pulleys bolted to the ceiling to move it. Wielding this huge brush, with a single stroke I could completely cover the little sheet of paper, and it would scarcely be possible to make out a trace of motion within the blackness. What is happening in the painting would be this scarcely perceptible motion. Power would pervade everything.

I reopened my eyes suddenly, feeling as though I was falling. In front of me an armoured convoy passed by in silence. As I got to my feet I could have reached out and stroked their metal flanks, the fat, bulletproof tyres as tall as me.

They towered over me, these armoured vehicles. They passed with no other sound than the crunch of gravel and the muffled purr of powerful engines running in slow motion. They moved in strict formation down the broad avenue in Voracieux-les-Bredins, one of those too-wide streets they have there, empty at this hour. The steel-blue trucks, their windscreens protected by wire mesh, were followed by police vans, each towing a cart that probably contained the heavy equipment necessary for enforcing law and order. As it came to a block of flats, the column divided; some of the trucks stopped, while the others rolled on. A number of vehicles parked next to the bus shelter, where I was waiting for the night to melt away. Militarized police jumped down; they were equipped with helmets, conspicuous weapons and riot shields. Their silhouettes, distorted by shin guards and shoulder pads, made them seem like warriors in the metallic, early morning half-light. On his shoulder one officer was carrying a fat, black cylinder fitted with handles used for breaking down doors. They waited outside a block of flats. A number of cars arrived and hastily parked, disgorging men in civilian clothes with cameras and camcorders. They went and stood next to the policemen. Camera flashes ripped through the orange glow of the streetlights. A light flickered on over one of the television cameras, only to be extinguished after a curt order. They waited.

By the time the first bus finally arrived to pick me up it was already crammed with ordinary people, half-asleep, on their way to work. I found a seat and dozed, my face pressed against the window; twenty minutes later the bus dropped me off in front of the metro station. I headed home.

I found out the rest in the newspapers. At a precisely appointed hour, a large contingent of police had carried out a dawn raid on a problem neighbourhood. Individuals known to the police, mostly young men living with their parents, had been dragged from their beds. Riot squads had stormed through family living rooms and burst into their bedrooms, smashing down doors. No one had a chance to flee. The operation was swiftly brought to a successful conclusion in spite of minor domestic scuffles, heartfelt insults, a few slaps to calm things down, some broken crockery and girlish, high-pitched screams, mostly from mothers and grandmothers, though a number of young women joined the chorus. Volleys of abuse were hurled in stairwells and from windows. The handcuffed suspects were whisked away, some voluntarily, others forcibly. Stones began to rain down from nowhere. In a clatter of rigid polycarbonate, the officers raised their riot shields as one. The projectiles bounced off. Crowds gathered at a distance, dressed in pyjamas or in underwear. Tear-gas canisters were fired into apartments, which had to be evacuated. The officers involved retreated in good order. They hauled away young men wearing babouches, slippers, trainers with the laces undone. They bundled them into police vans, pushing their heads down. A washing machine tossed from a window fell with a dull thud as the counterweight buried itself in the ground; the shriek of metal caused everyone to flinch, but no one was injured; soapy water still belched from the plastic pipe snaking along the ground. Slowly everyone backed away, the line of officers careful to stay behind their riot shields, the locals half hidden in the shadows did not dare move forwards, but lashed out at the armoured trucks as they drove past at a walking pace. The apprehended suspects were dragged before the courts. The media – who had somehow been alerted – brought back footage and gave an account of the events. The stories focused on the media presence. All editorial comment was about the presence of the media. People were shocked at the way the suspects had been publicly paraded. They were hostile or they accepted it, but about the incident itself they had nothing to say. All the suspects were released the following day; nothing had been found.

No one commented on the militarization of the public order. No one seemed to notice that convoys of armoured trucks could roll into troublesome neighbourhoods at dawn. No one seemed surprised by the use of an armoured column in France. They could have mentioned it. It could have been discussed from a moral standpoint: is it right for police to break down doors and burst into apartments to arrest a bunch of little brats? Is it fair to brutalize everybody, to arrest many, only to release everyone, since it could not be proved they had done anything much wrong? I say 'right' and 'fair', because the discussion needs to be had at the most fundamental level.

It could be discussed from a practical standpoint: we are all familiar with the armoured column; that explains why no one notices it. This is how we waged the wars fought over there, and we lost those wars by using armoured columns. Armour makes us feel protected. We brutalized everybody; we killed many; and we lost the wars. All of them. We.

The police officers are young, very young. We dispatch young men in armoured columns to retake control of no-go areas. They wreak havoc and leave again. Just as they did over there. The art of war does not change.

Novel IV

The first times, and what came after

V ICTORIEN AND EURYDICE walked between the lines of tanks. Night had drawn in, but a darkling summer night, the sky bright with stars and moon, filled with the chirrup of insects and the noise of the camp. Salagnon, being sensitive to shapes, marvelled at the beauty of the tanks. They squatted there, five obstinate tons of steel, sleeping cattle, they radiated mass; for simply to see them, to walk in their shadow, to touch their steel flanks was to sense something immovable, anchored in the depths of the earth. They were like so many caves in which nothing bad could occur.

But Salagnon knew all too well that such power saved no one. He had spent hours gathering up the mangled bodies of dead tank crews, piecing them together, placing them in caskets in which, by the end, it was impossible to tell how many bodies they contained. Armour plating, fortresses, body armour afford a sense of protection, but to believe in that protection is folly: feeling safe is the easiest way to get oneself killed. Victorien had seen how easily armour plating could be pierced, since there is ammunition that can pass right through. It is easy to place a childlike trust in the steel plate hiding you. It is very thick, extremely heavy, totally opaque; it hides you and so you believe that as long as you cannot be seen, no harm can come to you. Behind this thick steel plate, you become a target. Naked, we are nothing;

protected by a shell we become a target. Several men climb into a steel cage. They view the world through a slot no bigger than a letterbox. They see little, they move slowly, they are crammed with other men into a shuddering steel box. Unable to see, they assume they cannot be seen; it is childish. This hulking machine sitting on the grass is the only thing that is visible; it is the target. They are inside. Everyone outside is trying desperately to destroy it; they invent weapons, cannon, mines, dynamite; trenches dug in the ground, missiles fired from planes. Everything; until they destroy it. They end up mangled inside the box, mingled with twisted steel, a tin of corned beef opened with a sledgehammer and left lying on the ground.

Salagnon had seen the remains of these targets. Neither stone nor steel can offer protection. If a man remains naked, he can run among countless identical men and stray bullets may waver and miss their target; probability offers greater protection than layers of armour plating. Naked, he is forgotten; protected by a tank, he will be targeted relentlessly. Protection impresses, it creates the illusion of strength; the layers of armour become thicker, become heavier, they become slow and visible, they cry out to be destroyed.

Eurydice and Victorien slipped between the tanks lined up in neat rows, into the narrow gaps between them. They walked away from the camp along a rutted path lined with hedgerows; when they reached the darkness, they held hands. They could see the vast expanse of sky, which glittered with stars so precise they seemed freshly polished. They can make out fleeting images, crystal-clear pictures that shifted to become something else the moment they looked away. The air smelled of boiling sap, as warm as a bath; their clothes could have melted away and their skin would not have shivered. Eurydice's hand in Victorien's throbbed like a tiny heart. He sensed her not by her warmth but by a gentle quivering, by her breath, so close it seemed nestled in her palm. They walked until they could no longer hear the clamour of the camp, the engines, the clanging of metal, the voices. They wandered into a meadow and lay down. The grass that had been cut in June had grown back, so that it rose above them as they lay on their backs, surrounded by a wall of slender leaves and grass flowerets, a crown of delicate, distinct, ink-black strokes framed against a sky a shade more grey. They saw it scattered with stars and shifting images. They lay, unmoving. Around them the crickets resumed their chirruping. Victorien kissed Eurydice.

He first kissed her by pressing his lips to hers, the sort of kiss one knows one must perform, since it marks the entry to an intimate relationship. They both entered. Then he kissed her with his tongue, anxious to taste her lips. Desire kindled in him, although he had never thought about it, and Eurydice in his arms felt the same desires. Lying on the grass, they propped themselves on their elbows and their mouths opened to one another, their lips fitting together snugly, their tongues, safely sheltered, marvellously lubricated, sinuously entwining. Never had Victorien imagined such voluptuous caresses. The sky thrummed from end to end with the sound like a sheet of metal being shaken. Invisible planes flew high overhead, hundreds of planes laden with bombs moving as one across the steel surface of the sky. Victorien's heart pounded in his throat, there where the carotids swell with blood. Eurydice's belly quivered. Their beings rose to the surface like fish thrown breadcrumbs; they were deep in the lake, the water was still, then suddenly they appeared all at once, mouths pressed into the air, while the whole surface quivers. Eurydice's skin was alive and Victorien could feel that life coursing beneath his fingertips; and when he curved his hand to cup her breast, he felt he held Eurydice's whole life, full and round, in his palm. She was breathing rapidly, her eyes closed, her whole being surging through her. Victorien's penis was cramped, hindering his every movement, and when he unbuttoned his trousers he felt a great relief. This new limb, which never emerged like this, brushed Eurydice's bare thighs. It moved with a life of its own, snuffled at her skin in panting breaths, moved along her thighs in little bounds. It wanted to bury itself in her. Eurydice gave a heavy sigh and whispered:

'I want it to stop, Victorien. I don't want to be reckless.'

'It's nice, isn't it?'

'Yes, but it's so overwhelming. I want to keep my feet on the ground. But just now I don't really know where my body is. I want to find it again before I fly away.'

'I know where mine is.'

'I'll hold it close.'

With infinite tenderness, she grasped his sex – yes, that is the word, in spite of appearances, the word in its oldest sense – and with great nobility of spirit she stroked his sex until he ejaculated. Lying on his back, Victorien watched the stars moving, when they all suddenly snuffed out and re-ignited. Eurydice nestled against him and kissed his neck, behind his ear, precisely where the carotid passes, and gradually the drumming subsided. To the north, the muffled roar was like an echo in which it was impossible to make out the detail; a constant, unceasing rumble, while on the horizon reddish lights flickered in counterpoint and yellow flashes appeared and quickly faded.

This was the first time anyone had touched his penis. It troubled him so much he could think of nothing else. When Eurydice pressed herself against him, he saw time suddenly open up before him: he knew that this young woman would for ever be right here, even if it happened that they never saw each other again.

He wondered whether he had kept the promise he had made to Roseval. The thought occurred to him as he arrived back at the camp, holding Eurydice's hand. He blushed in the balmy darkness, although only he was aware of it. But still he wondered. His hand on Eurydice's shoulder, pulling her towards him, he decided that he had. Though not entirely. But he would happily have stayed this way for ever. He had escaped the bitterness of loneliness and disappointment. The business of war made it possible for him to remain in this situation which, otherwise, would not last. Every day the wounded arrived in greater numbers; they had to be scraped off the ground, farther and farther afield, and brought back in the truck; he was sent out on urgent missions that took him away from Eurydice. Each time he left he would slip her a short message, a drawing, a loving word, and when he had to leave immediately, when he had to run to the truck, he would take a scrap of wrapping paper and, with a single stroke, sketch a heart, a tree, the bend of a hip, a pair of parted lips, the curve of a shoulder; these drawings – elliptical, unfinished, not yet dry, pressed into her hand as he rushed away – she cherished most of all.

An armoured car impresses, but it is a metal tomb. An armoured train? It is as fragile as a glass bottle; when hit, it shatters. Two men wearing espadrilles ambling along a path, their backpacks stuffed with explosives the size of cakes of soap, can bring it crashing to a halt without ever seeing it. In a few short minutes they blow up the tracks. Two men are sent, so the task will be more enjoyable, so they can chat while they work; one man would be enough.

The armoured train running through the Saône Valley never made it past Chalon. The tracks were sabotaged under cover of darkness, forcing it to stop in a squeal of brakes, an agonizing shriek of grinding metal, a great horizontal spray of sparks. The buckled rails curled like the tusks of a fossilized elephant, shattered sleepers fell in splinters into the freshly gouged crater. Four American planes, in two passes, blew up the engine and the two freight wagons at the front and the rear, from where, sheltered behind sandbags, multi-barrelled autocannon attempted to track them. In a fleeting fireball, everything disappeared; the sandbags ripped, the barrels twisted, the gunners disfigured, burned, mutilated and mingled with the sand in the space of a few seconds. Those in the train carriages piled out on to the tracks, heads low, running, trying to dodge the explosions, throwing themselves to the ground to avoid the hail of bullets hitting the tracks. Up above, the pilots turned the knife in the wound, wheeling around again and again to strafe the tracks, bloodying the gravel. The survivors plunged into the thickets, where they came face to face with the French soldiers lying in wait since the night before. The first were killed in the confusion, the others were forced to lie on their bellies, hands behind their heads. The train was burning; bodies in grey uniforms lay sprawled on the railway embankment. The planes flicked their wings and flew off. A whole column of prisoners was marched back to the camp; they went willingly; they were relaxed, their jackets slung over their shoulders, their hands in their pockets, happy that it was all over and they were still alive.

The Colonel went to see Naegelin.

'These are the prisoners from Porquigny. The massacre. Old men, women, children. Twenty-eight corpses in the streets, forty-seven in the houses, gunned down in cold blood, some with their hands tied behind their backs.'

'So?'

'So, we shoot them.'

'Don't even think about it.'

'OK, then we have a trial and then we shoot them.'

'Who is going to judge them? Your men? That would be an act of revenge, just another crime. Our men? We're soldiers, it's not our job to judge. The civilian judges? Two months ago they were passing sentence on *résistants* on behalf of the Germans. I'm happy to believe that the law is impartial, but that would be taking things too far. There is no one in France to judge them right now.'

'So you're not going to do anything?'

'I will transfer them to the Americans. I'll advise them that they were involved in a civilian massacre. They'll decide. That will be all, "Colonel".'

The clearly enunciated quotation marks dismissed the colonel as definitively as a wave of the hand.

The German prisoners were put into a paddock. A square of ground was marked out with barbed wire and they were left there. Stripped of their weapons and helmets, scattered throughout the field, lacking the discipline that caused them to act as one, the prisoners looked like what they really were: exhausted men of varying ages whose faces bore the mark of many years of tension, fear and acquaintance with death. Now lying on the grass in random groups, heads resting on their folded arms or on each other's stomachs, with no belts, no helmets, the jackets unbuttoned, they closed their eyes and let the sunlight wash over their tanned faces. Other amorphous groups stood next to the rolls of barbed wire, smoking, one hand in their pockets, saying nothing, scarcely moving, staring vacantly into the distance at the French sentry guarding them, his rifle shouldered, attempting to project a rigid severity. But the sentries, having attempted their harshest glares, no longer know where to look. The Germans, vaguely amused, gazed blankly at them, calmly ruminating in their paddock, and after a time the sentries took to staring at the ground, at the feet of those they were guarding, and this seemed to them absurd.

The *maquisards*, who were issued with American uniforms, came to see these half-dressed soldiers lolling in the sun. The Germans narrowed their eyes and waited. Salagnon was struck by the haughty grace of an officer standing off to one side. He wore his casually unbuttoned uniform like a summer suit. He stood, smoking coolly as he waited for the game to end. He had lost. Too bad. Salagnon found himself drawn to this face. Mistaking it for some sort of attraction, he did not dare look him in the eye; eventually he realized it was simply recognition. He planted himself in front of the man. Hands in his pockets, the German went on smoking, looking at him without seeing, squinting against the sunlight and the smoke from the cigarette dangling from his lips. They were standing in the same field, facing one another, and the two metres that separated them was a no-man's-land of wire bristling with spikes; they were as close as if they had been sitting at the same table.

'You carried out an inspection on my father's shop. In Lyon in 1943.'

'I inspected a lot of shops. I was appointed the stupid task of inspecting shops. An attempt to stamp out the black market. I found it particularly tedious. I don't remember your father.'

'So you don't recognize me?'

'You, yes. I recognized you the moment I saw you. You've been hanging around here for an hour pretending not to notice me. You've changed, but not too much. I'm guessing you've discovered how to use your prick. Am I wrong?'

'Why did you spare my father? He was trafficking and you knew it.'

'Everyone traffics. No one follows the regulations. So I spare or I condemn. Depending. We were not planning to kill everyone. If the war had carried on, perhaps we would have. As we did in Poland. But now, it's over.'

'Were you responsible for Porquigny?'

'Me, my men, orders from above: everyone was responsible; no one in particular. The *Résistance*, as you call it, commanded support; so we terrorized to undermine that support.'

'You killed civilians.'

'If we killed only soldiers it would be a conventional war. Terror is a sophisticated weapon; it involves spreading panic and clearing the way ahead. That way, we calmly advance while our enemies lose their support. It's important to create a sense of faceless terror; it is a military strategy.'

'Did you kill?'

'Personally, I have no taste for blood. Terror is merely a technique; to employ it requires psychopaths; to coordinate it requires someone who is sane. I have a number of Turkmen I brought back from Russia, nomads for whom brutality is a game, who laugh at the slaughter of their animals before they eat them. Now they have a taste for blood; they simply need to be encouraged to abandon their flocks and apply it a little more widely. They're capable of dismembering a man with a saw. I've seen them do it. They were aboard the armoured train with me, a secret weapon for sowing terror. They are my hounds. I set them loose or I hold them back. I simply control the leash. But what would you have done in my place? In our place?'

'But I'm not. I specifically chose not to be in your place.'

'Things change, young man. I was tasked with maintaining law and order. Perhaps tomorrow it will be you. Yesterday I spared you, because you were a little sad, because you had made a mistake in your declension, and today I am your prisoner. Yesterday we were the masters, now I don't know what you plan to do with me.'

'You will be handed over to the Americans.'

'Things change. Make the most of your newly won victory. Make the most of this glorious summer. The summer of 1940 was the most wonderful of my whole life. Later, it was not so good. Things had changed.'

It was bound to happen. By relentlessly attempting to kill him with explosive projectiles, they almost succeeded. He was wounded. During sorties to recover their dead, they were met with gunfire. Germans were prowling through the countryside. Shells following the arc of the sky landed twenty kilometres away. A lone plane would appear suddenly from the clouds to strafe everything in sight and disappear again. It was possible to die by a quirk of fate.

With Brioude, Salagnon escaped the sniper hiding in the water tower. The Germans had moved on, but he had stayed behind, forgotten perhaps, perched on a slab of concrete thirty metres high. All around him the fields were littered with corpses and burned-out vehicles, the relics of a battle he must have been a part of and which everyone thought was over. When the Colonel's *maquisards* came to recover the bodies, working in pairs, carrying a stretcher, he started shooting and hit Morellet in the thigh. They dived behind a hedge and returned fire, but the German was out of range. Brioude and Salagnon found themselves exposed, standing in the middle of the broad meadow, beneath the water tower strewn with bodies and smouldering tanks. The sniper got them in his sights, taking his time, intent on killing them before they could find a place to hide. From behind the hedge, the rest of the platoon fired in bursts; their bullets pitted the concrete without reaching him. Perched high in the air, he was out of range; he would draw back only to reappear and fire at what he estimated was his enemy's position. Brioude and Salagnon plunged into the long grass as a bullet buried itself in the ground; they sheltered behind corpses and felt one of the bodies judder softly with the impact of the bullet; ducked behind a burned-out jeep as a bullet ricocheted against the metal, missing them once more. They crawled, they got up again, they jumped, they varied their speed, signalling to each other, their hearts pounding, and each time the sniper missed them. Metre by metre they gained ground, attempting to cross the field, each time gaining a few more metres of life as the sniper shifted his aim and missed again. When they burst through the hedge and rolled on the ground next to the others, they were greeted by a muffled cheer. They lay on their backs, panting for breath, sweating horribly; and they burst out laughing, happy to have won, happy to be alive.

And then the sky was ripped open like a sheet of silk, and at the base of the tear a great hammer hit the ground. The ground caved in, stones and splintered wood rained down around them. Then came the screams. Salagnon felt something pierce his thigh and then a warm, liquid sensation. It was torrential, draining: he was bleeding out; the ground was probably steaming. Someone came to help him up. He could see only a whirling that made it impossible to walk. He had to be carried. A sort of damp haze blurred his vision, but that might have been tears. He could hear screams nearby. He tried to say something to whoever was carrying him. He tugged at his collar, pulled him towards him and very slowly whispered in his ear: 'He's not doing so good, that guy.' Then he released his grip and slipped into unconsciousness.

When he came round, Salomon Kaloyannis was next to him. He found himself in a little room with a mirror on the wall and knick-knacks on a shelf. He was lying on a wooden bed, propped up on plush, monogrammed pillows. He could not flex his leg. A tight bandage ran from ankle to groin. Kaloyannis showed him a sharp, twisted sliver of metal about the size of a thumb; the edges were as fine as a shard of glass.

'Take a look, this is what it was. During explosions you only ever see the light, it's like a firework; but the aim is to spray things like this, pieces of shrapnel. To shoot razorblades from catapults at people who are stark naked. If you knew the terrible gashes I have to suture. The war has taught me a lot about cutting up men and the techniques for stitching them together again. But you're awake now and you seem all right, so I'll leave you alone. Eurydice will come and see you.'

'Am I in a hospital?'

'You're in Mâcon Hospital. We're all set up now. I found you a private room, because the whole place is crowded. There are guys lying in the hallways, even out in tents in the grounds. I put you in the guard's room, so I can keep an eye on you. I don't want them discharging you until I've got you cured. I don't know where the security guard is, so make the most of your little room and get better. I even found you a real sketchpad. Get some rest. It's very important to me that you pull through.'

He pinched Victorien's cheek and shook him vigorously. He laid a large, canvas-covered sketchpad on the bed and then left, his stethoscope swaying, his hands in the pockets of his white coat.

The afternoon sun slanted through the wooden blinds, tracing parallel lines on the walls and on the bed. He could hear the constant commotion of the hospital, the trucks, the screams, the jostling in the hallways, the bustle in the courtyard. Eurydice came to change his bandage. She brought a metal tray with crêpe, antiseptic, cotton wool and safety pins – a whole new box of them with English writing. She pinned her hair back tightly and buttoned her blouse all the way to the throat, but it took only a flicker of her lashes, a quiver of her lips, for Victorien to picture her whole, her naked body, her every curve, her tremulous skin. She set down the tray and sat on the bed. She kissed him. He pulled her to him, the injured leg he could not bend made it awkward, but he felt enough strength in his arms and in his tongue to cope. She lay down next to him, her white coat rucking up over her thighs. 'I want to be reckless,' she whispered into his ear. Her thigh pressed hard against his injured thigh, their sweat mingled; outside the constant roar grew quieter in the afternoon heat. Victorien's penis had never been so big. He could no longer feel it, no longer tell where it began and ended, his whole body felt engorged, sensitive; it fit together snugly with the body of Eurydice. When he entered her, she tensed and then sighed; tears trickled; she squeezed her eyes shut, opened them again; she was bleeding. Victorien caressed her from within. They moved in perfect balance, trying not to fall, their eyes never leaving each other. The pleasure that followed was like nothing they had ever known. The exertion, the effort, reopened Victorien's wound. He was bleeding. Their blood mingled. They lay there for a long time, pressed against each other, watching the parallel lines of light moving slowly over the wall, passing over the mirror, which shimmered but reflected nothing.

'I'll change your dressing. That's why I'm here.'

She made the new bandage a little less tight; she also cleaned his thighs. She kissed him on the lips and left. He could feel the wound in his thigh throb, but it had healed over. He exuded a musky odour that was not entirely his own, or one that he had never given off before. He opened immaculate white pages of the handsome sketchpad Salomon had given him. He made light, supple strokes. He tried to convey in ink the softness of the sheets, their infinitely sinuous folds, their smell, the parallel bands of light reflected in the mirror on the wall, the pervasive heat, the clamour and the sun outside, the clamour outside that is life itself, the sun that is its source, and himself in this dappled room, central and secret, the beating heart of a great joyous organism.

He recovered, but his progress was less swift than that of the war. The Zouaves continued on their northward march, leaving a trail of wounded in their wake. When Salagnon could finally manage to get up, he joined a different regiment and, with a new rank, they continued on their way to Germany.

*   *   *

The summer of 1944 was sunny and warm; people did not stay cooped up: everyone was out in the fresh air. Men strolled around in oversized shorts fastened at the waist with a leather belt, shirts open to the navel. There was much yelling and shouting. They joined the thronging crowds, they marched, they cheered, they followed the victory parade as it moved through the streets at a leisurely pace. Army trucks moved at walking pace as the crowds parted; in the back of the trucks sat soldiers, affecting a stiff military bearing. They were wearing clean uniforms, American helmets; they forced themselves to keep their eyes front, to grip their rifles manfully, but each sported a quivering smile that threatened to split his face. Painted cars followed behind filled with young boys in scout uniforms waving flags and ill-assorted weapons. Officers in jeeps shook the hands of hundreds who reached out to touch them; they opened the path for tanks recently baptized with French names daubed in white paint. Next came the vanquished: soldiers with hands raised high, stripped of their helmets, their belts; they were careful not to make any sudden movements, not to make eye contact with anyone. Lastly came a few women, hemmed in by the crowds closing up behind to follow the procession; the women were all alike, their bowed faces streaked with tears, their features so expressionless as to be unrecognizable. They brought up the rear of the parade, and behind them the jubilant groups lined up along the pavement poured into the street to join the procession; every-one marched; everyone thronged; the crowd marched between two watching crowds; the crowd was triumphant, revelling in its victory, a rapturous crowd jeering these women who walked on in silence. With the defeated soldiers, they alone were silent, but they were jostled, they were mocked. The armed men surrounding them brandished their rifles light-heartedly and did not intervene. An armband served as their uniform, they wore their berets at a rakish angle and their shirts undone; an officer wearing a kepi led them to a spot where they paused for a moment to expiate their shame. Then the crowd moved off again on a different footing, louder, stricter, sturdier. The carnivalesque crowd drank deeply of the summer air of 1944; everyone breathing the open air of the streets where everything takes place. France would never again be a German whore, a dancer in lurid lingerie teetering on a table, stripping her clothes off, drunk on champagne; France was manly and muscular now; France had been reborn.

Throughout the afternoon, in the empty streets far from the victory parade, in houses whose doors stood open, in empty rooms – everyone was outside, net curtains fluttered from the windows, warm breezes gusted from room to room – isolated gunshots rang out with no echo; scores being settled, funds transferred, captures and transport; unobtrusive men slipped down side streets carrying suitcases to be stashed somewhere safe.

It was a glorious French celebration. When making a casserole in a stockpot, there comes a moment when the soul of a dish is born; simmered over a high heat, the flavours mingle, the flesh falls away from the bone; it is this that produces the characteristic aroma. The summer of 1944 provided the heat that warmed the national melting pot, the moment that produced the distinctive flavour that the dish would have after long hours of simmering. Needless to say, peacetime was quick to re-establish its filters, and in the days that followed these strainers were patiently shaken and the little people slipped through the sieve and found themselves, as they had been before, inferior to the others. People were sifted according to their size. But something had happened, something that left a tang of solidarity. France needs its regular popular uprisings, its celebrations: everyone outside! and we all rush out and this creates a sense of togetherness that lasts a long time. Otherwise the streets are deserted, people do not mix; we often wonder who our neighbours are.

In Lyon the leaves of the chestnut trees were beginning to shrivel; the shop was where it had always been, of course, and still standing. A large French flag fluttered over the doorway. Three strips of cloth had been stitched together, but the colours were wrong – all except the white, which came from a bedsheet – the blue was too pale, the red too mottled, the fabric used to make it was too worn, too washed-out, but in the sunlight, when the dazzling sun of the summer of 1944 shone through it, the colours blazed with just the right intensity.

His father seemed happy to see him. He let him give his mother a long, silent hug, then he hugged him. He led him away and opened a dusty bottle of wine.

'I kept this for when you came home. Burgundy – that's where you were stationed, isn't it?'

'I disobeyed you.'

'You chose the right path all by yourself. That's why I didn't say anything; and now everything is clear. Look,' he said gesturing to the flag, the badly chosen blue was visible through the doorway.

'Were you on that path?'

'Paths fork, they don't always lead where you expect... but now our paths have met up again. Look.'

He opened a drawer, delved under a pile of paperwork and took out a gun belt with a revolver and an F.F.I. armband.

'You weren't afraid?'

'Of who? The Germans?'

'No... of the other resistants... because of what you used to do...'

'Oh, that... I've got all the secret documents I needed to prove that I was only providing supplies to the right people. Going back far enough, so that no one could doubt that I was on the right side.'

'And did you?'

'I've got the proof right here.'

'And how did you get it, this proof?'

'You're not the only one who knows how to forge documents. In fact, it's a commonplace skill.'

He gave his son a wink. The same one, which had the same effect.

'What about the guy at the *préfecture*?'

'Oh... someone informed on him and he was thrown into jail. Like a lot of people who had dealings with the Germans.'

He took the revolver from the battered leather holster and examined it quietly.

'It came in handy, you now.'

Victorien looked at his father, incredulous.

'You don't believe me?'

'I do. I'm sure it was useful. But I don't know in what way.'

'A revolver in the right hands is much more useful than all your military fireworks. Have you got any plans?'

Victorien got to his feet and walked out, without turning back. As he left, he got tangled in the flag flapping over the door. He tugged, the crude stitches gave way and suddenly it was a three-tongued flag, a tongue for each colour, waving him off.

Victorien spent the summer in the uniform of Free France. People hugged him, shook his hand, bought him drinks, offered intimacies which he sometimes refused and sometimes accepted. He was enrolled in an officers' training corps and graduated as a lieutenant in the new French army.

In the autumn he was in Alsace. In a forest of fir trees he guarded a fort made of logs, filled in with earth. The fir trees grew straight despite the steep slope, the base of their trunks twisting forcefully. Darkness drew in at about four o'clock and daylight never truly returned. It was increasingly cold. The Germans were no longer on the run; they were dug in on the other side of the knoll, on the far slope. They sent out patrols, wearing cloaks that blended with the undergrowth, accompanied by dogs trained to be silent and to point with their muzzles when they caught a scent. They threw grenades, blew up blockhouses, captured young French soldiers who had enlisted only weeks earlier; boys who, after so many years, no longer remembered what it was to sleep without gripping a loaded rifle.

When it rained the water coursed in torrents beneath the carpet of pine needles; the floors of the blockhouses became quagmires; the mud reinforcing the logs began to dissolve. The fervour of the young

French soldiers faltered faced with Germans who, though not much older, were hardened by five years of survival. Massive assaults were ordered by officers, who competed with each other, who had much to prove or much they wished to forget. They launched raids of light troops on Germans hiding in foxholes, but they were repelled. Many died in the cold, sprawled in the mud, and still the Germans did not retreat. Ranking officers took charge. They needed to be patient, methodical, disciplined. They eked out their ammunition as best they could; the men became calmer, more cautious. The war was no longer fun for anyone.

The Zouave regiments returned to Africa. Victorien forged on into the heart of Germany, a lieutenant in command of a group of young men who sheltered in abandoned farmhouses, waging bitter, brief battles against the remnants of the Wehrmacht, who no longer knew which way to turn. They captured all those prepared to surrender and liberated prisoners whose emaciation and exhaustion frightened them. But their protruding bones were less terrifying than their glassy stares; like glass, the gaze of the prisoners had only two states: vacant and clear or shattered.

The spring of 1945 arrived like a sigh of relief. Salagnon was amid the ruins of Germany, gun in hand, commanding a group of muscular young men who no longer hesitated to act. Everything he said was immediately followed by actions. People fled before them, they surrendered, spoke to them fearfully, mumbling in broken French. Then the war ended and he had to return to France.

For a few months he stayed in the army, then he was returned to civilian life. 'Returned' is the word people use, but for those who have never led a civilian life, the return came to seem like being naked, left by the roadside, sent back to what was called home, a place that, to them, did not exist. What could he do? What could he possibly do in civilian life?

He enrolled in the university, attended classes, tried to broaden his mind. Young people sitting in a lecture theatre, heads bowed, transcribing the words read to them by an old man. The place was freezing; the voice of the old man trailed off in a shrill falsetto; he stopped in order to cough; one day he dropped his notes, which scattered over the floor; in the long minutes while he gathered them, put them back in order, muttering to himself, the students sat, pens poised, waiting for him to continue. Victorien bought the books he was supposed to read; he read only the *Iliad*, but that several times. He would read lying on his bed, wearing linen trousers, shirtless and barefoot in hot weather or wrapped in a coat and huddled under a blanket as winter drew in. Again and again he read the description of the terrible fray in which bronze cleaves limbs, cuts throats, pierces skulls, plunges through the eyes to emerge at the neck, dragging warriors into the shadows of death. Open-mouthed, trembling, he read of the fury of Achilles as he avenges the death of Patroclus. Breaking every rule, he cuts the throats of Trojan prisoners, defiles their corpses and spurns the gods without every ceasing to be a hero. He acts ignobly towards men, towards the gods, towards the laws of the universe, yet he remains a hero. Throughout the *Iliad*, throughout this book which people have been reading since the Bronze Age, he learned that the hero does not have to be good. Achilles radiates vitality; he bestows death as a tree bestows fruit; in feats, in bravery, in prowess he excels: he is not good; he dies, but he does not have to be good. What did he do afterwards? Nothing. What could anyone have done afterwards? He closed the book. He did not go back to the university. He looked for work. He found a job, several jobs. He left them all; they bored him. In October that year he turned twenty. He collected all the money that he could and left for Algiers.

It rained all through the crossing; grimy clouds scudded over the dark waters; a relentless wind made being on deck painful. The choppy autumn waves slapped the sides of the ship with a harsh crack, sending muffled vibrations shuddering throughout the structure of the ship and into the very bones of passengers who could not sleep, like kicks to a man lying on the ground. When she is not smiling brilliantly, when she is not laughing with that throaty laugh of hers, the Mediterranean is vicious and spiteful.

In the morning they hove in sight of a grey stretch of coast where nothing was visible. Algiers is very different from what people say, he thought, leaning on the ship's rail. He could just make out the outline of a drab city clinging to a slope, a little town on an unprepossessing hill bereft of trees, which would be bare earth in warm weather and, just now, mud. Salagnon landed in Algiers in October and the ship from Marseilles had to pass through curtains of rain to reach it.

Fortunately, the rain stopped as the ship pulled into the quay. The sky yawned wide as he stepped on to the gangway, and as he started up the steps leading from the docks – in Algiers the port is set low – it became blue again. The white, colonnaded façades quickly dried; a bustling crowd spilled out on to the streets; children wheeled around him, making offers he did not listen to. An elderly Arab in a thread-bare, possibly official, cap offered to carry his bag. He politely refused, gripping the handle of his suitcase tighter, and asked for directions. The man muttered something that was clearly unfriendly and vaguely pointed towards an area of the city.

He set off up the steep streets; in the gutters brown water flowed towards the sea; a reddish sludge coursed down from the Arab districts through the European city, cut a path through it and disappeared into the sea. He noticed this sludge was scattered with flecks of debris; some were clots of congealed blood of a purple so dark it was almost black. The clouds had dispersed; the white walls mirrored the light, they shimmered. He navigated by the blue-tiled signs on the street corners. French plaques inscribed in French, a fact he did not notice, since it seemed so unremarkable: the words that he could read were underscored by the jagged undulations of Arabic, which he could not read, so they formed a simple ornament. He walked on, with no detours, and found the house whose address he had copied out so often, where Salomon joyously welcomed him.

'Come in, Victorien, come in! It is such a pleasure to see you!'

Salomon took his arm and led him into a grubby little kitchen with dishes piled up in the sink. He found a bottle and two glasses and set them on the oilcloth-covered table. He quickly wiped away the crumbs and the larger stains with a dubious-looking dishrag.

'Sit down, Victorien! I'm so happy you're here! Here, taste, it's an anisette. It's what we drink here.'

He filled the glasses, gestured for Victorien to sit, then sat down himself and looked his guest in the eye; but his red-rimmed eyes could not see straight.

'Stay, Victorien, stay as long as you like. This is your home here. Your home.'

But after this fulsome welcome, he began to repeat himself, his voice a little softer each time until finally he fell silent. Salomon had aged. He no longer laughed. He talked loudly, tremulously served more anisette. His hands trembled and a few drops splattered next to the glasses. His hands trembled constantly, although it was hardly noticeable since, when not holding something, he hid them, slipping them under the table or stuffing them into his pockets. They exchanged snippets of news, talked about themselves.

'Where's Ahmed?'

'Ahmed? Gone.'

Salomon sighed, drained his glass and refilled it. He did not laugh at all now; the network of laughter lines that criss-crossed his face seemed disused, while other wrinkles had appeared that made him look older.

'You know about what happened here last year? Suddenly, the whole world was turned upside down, everything that had seemed so solid was reduced to cardboard and *pfft* it was ripped apart and blown away. And all it took was a flag and a single gunshot. A single gunshot, just as people were taking their aperitif, like in some *pataouète* tragedy.

'The Arabs wanted to have a march to celebrate the victory when the Germans up there in the north decided to throw in the towel. The

Arabs wanted to show how happy they were that we had won, but no one here agrees who we mean by "we". They wanted to celebrate victory, to glory in having won, and also to say that now that we had won, nothing would be the same again. They wanted to stage an official parade, so they got out the Algerian flags; the problem is that the Algerian flag is banned. Personally, I think the Algerian flag is ridiculous; I don't know what it's supposed to be. But they got it out and the Muslim scouts were carrying it. Some guy was coming out of a café, a cop, and when he saw this group of Arabs marching with the flag, he thought he was hallucinating and he panicked. He'd been wearing his service revolver in the café, so he pulled it out and fired, and the little Muslim scout carrying the flag was killed. This dumb fucking cop goes for a drink wearing his gun and starts a riot. Things might have calmed down. I mean, it's hardly the first time an Arab has been killed for no reason, just for looking at someone the wrong way; but there was a whole troop marching, carrying the banned Algerian flag and this was 8 May, Victory Day, the day of our victory, except no one here agrees on who we mean by "we".

'At that point, the rioters fell on passers-by; people killed each other for having the wrong type of face, slaughtered each other for a look or a scowl. Dozens of Europeans were gutted with all manner of weapons. I stitched many of their wounds, they were ugly and filthy. The wounded – those who managed to avoid being ripped apart – suffered agonies because their wounds became infected; but much worse was the terror they suffered, a terror far worse than any I saw during the war, when the disciplined Germans were firing on us. These wounded souls were living through a nightmare, because these people who lived among them, whom they rubbed shoulders with in the streets every day and passed without seeing, had suddenly turned on them with sharp tools and struck them. More terrible than the pain of the injuries was their disbelief, though the wounds were savage and deep, since they had been made with tools, gardening forks and butcher's knives that sank deep into their vital organs; but their failure to understand went deeper still, it went to the very heart, to the core of these people. And because they could not understand, they died of fear: someone living alongside you has turned on you. As though, without warning, a faithful dog had turned and bitten them. Can you imagine? The faithful dog you feed and care for suddenly turns on you and mauls you.'

'The Arabs are your dogs?'

'Why do you say that, Victorien?'

'You said it, not me.'

'I didn't say anything of the sort. I made a comparison so you would understand the surprise, the horror of a betrayal of trust. And what can a man trust if not his dog? In its mouth it has the means to kill you, but it does not. So when it does turn on you with those vicious teeth it has always possessed yet never used to bite you, then all trust is destroyed; as in a nightmare where things turn against you, where animals return to a nature long since tamed. It is beyond comprehension; or perhaps it is something you always knew, but never dared to say. In the case of dogs, we call it rabies, a virus that drives them insane, a virus they contract by being bitten that causes them to bite in turn, and that explains everything. With Arabs, no one knows.'

'You're talking about people as if they are dogs.'

'Spare me the lecture on which words are acceptable. You're not from here, Victorien, you know nothing. What we have experienced is so terrifying that we are not about to mince words to spare prissy, French sensibilities. We have to face facts, Victorien. We have to tell the truth. And the truth hurts.'

'Whether it is the truth is another matter.'

'I wanted to talk about trust, so I talked about dogs. To explain the sudden rage dogs sometimes suffer, we say they have rabies; we accept that as a natural explanation and we have them put down. With the Arabs, I don't know. I've never believed in all this business about race, but now I can see no way to explain it except that it's in the blood. Violence is in the blood. Treachery is in the blood. Can you give me another explanation?'

He said nothing for a moment. He poured himself another glass, spilling a little, and forgetting to pour one for Salagnon.

'Ahmed has disappeared. When all this started, he helped me. The wounded were sent for me to treat and he worked alongside me. But when the patients saw him bending over them, with his hook nose and his moustache and his swarthy skin, they whimpered in a weak voice and asked me to stay. They begged me not to go away, not to leave them alone with him, and at night they wanted me to watch over them, not him.

'Now it occurs to me that I forgot to ask Ahmed what he thought, but I found it funny. I'd pat Ahmed on the shoulder and say: "Go on, leave me to it, they're not well, they're allergic to moustaches," like it was a joke. But it was no joke; men who have been ripped open with gardening tools don't joke.

'And then, late one night, while we were cleaning and sterilizing the instruments we had used during the day – because there was so much work, we had to do everything, but it wasn't very different to the years we had spent at war together – so, there we were, the two of us, standing in front of the sterilizer and he told me that I was his friend. At first, it made me happy. I thought that exhaustion and the late hour and everything we had been through together over the years had suddenly made him talkative. I nodded and I was about to say that I felt the same, but he carried on. He told me that soon the Arabs would murder all the French. And that since I was his friend, when that day came he would kill me himself, quickly, so I did not suffer.

'He spoke without raising his voice, without looking at me; he carried on working, a blood-spattered apron around his waist, his hands covered in soap suds in the middle of the night, when, but for a few patients who couldn't sleep, we were the only ones awake, the only ones standing, the only healthy, rational men. He reassured me that he would not let just anyone do it any old how, and he said it as he cleaned the bloodstains from the razor-sharp blades; he said it standing in front of a shelf full of scalpels, of pincers and needles that would have terrified a butcher. I had the presence of mind to laugh it off and thank him, and he smiled too. When everything had been tidied away, we went to bed. I found the key to my bedroom. It was a tiny, flimsy key that slotted into a tiny, flimsy lock, but it was all I had, and, besides, this had to be a nightmare, and I locked my door. Rituals are enough to ward off nightmares. In the morning, even I was shocked to find that I had secured the door with such a little lock. Ahmed was gone. Men from the neighbourhood armed with rifles and pistols, men dressed in short-sleeved shirts – I knew every one of them – they came to my house and asked me where he was. But I didn't know. They wanted to take him away and give him a beating. I was relieved that he had left. These armed men told me that there were murderers gathering in the mountains. Ahmed, they said, had probably gone to join them. But there were so many hunts, so many executions, so many mass burials that he may very well have disappeared; actually disappeared without a trace. No one knows how many have died. No one keeps count. All the wounded I treated were Europeans. Because during those weeks no Arabs were wounded. The Arabs were killed.

'You know what they mean by a hunt? You comb the countryside and flush out your quarry. For weeks, they hunted those responsible for the dreadful acts of 8 May. Not one could be allowed to escape. Everyone was involved: the police, obviously, but they were not up to the task, so they were joined by the army, but they failed too, and so the country folk, who know the terrain, and the people from the city, who got to know it, and even the navy, who bomb the villages along the coast, and the air force, who had been bombing the remote villages. They all took up arms and all the Arabs suspected of having some role, however small, in the tragedy, were caught and eliminated.'

'How many in all?'

'A thousand, ten thousand, a hundred thousand, how would I know? If necessary, a million; all of them. Treachery is in the blood. There is no other explanation, because otherwise why should they turn on us when we lived side by side? All of them, if need be. All of them. We'll have peace now for ten years.'

'How were they recognized?'

'Who? The Arabs? Surely you're joking, Victorien?'

'The guilty men.'

'The guilty men were Arabs. And this was no time to let one of them escape. If others got caught up in it, too bad. It was crucial to eradicate, to cauterize as quickly as possible, for that to be the end of the matter. Most Arabs are guilty of something or other. You just have to look at the way they walk, the way they look at us. They're all in this together. They have huge families, you know. Like tribes. They all know each other, they support each other. So they are all guilty men. They're not difficult to recognize.'

'You didn't talk this way in 1944. You talked about equality.'

'I don't give a shit about equality. I was young. I was in France. I was winning the war. Now I'm home and I'm scared. Can you believe that? This is my home and I'm scared shitless.'

His hands were shaking, his eyes red-rimmed, his shoulders sagged as though he were about to curl up into a ball and go to sleep. He poured himself another glass and stared at it in silence.

'Victorien, go and see Eurydice. I'm tired now. She's down at the beach with some friends. She'll be happy to see you.'

'At the beach, in October?'

'What do you think, boy, you think they dismantle the beach in August when the French go home after your holidays? The beach is still there. Go on, go. Eurydice will be glad to see you.'

On the beach in Algiers there is no need to bathe. The coast plunges steeply into the sea, the strip of sand is narrow, small waves slap against the rocks that appear out of the water with brusque impatience. The sand dries quickly beneath the blazing sun; the sky is a spotless, pale blue; a neat line of clouds floats above the horizon to the north, over Spain and France.

Young people wearing open shirts over their swimming costumes come and sit on this beach ringed with rocks. They bring a towel, a beach bag; they sit on the sand or at makeshift refreshment stalls: little more than a concrete windbreak, a bar and a few stools. Here people live outdoors, they scarcely dress; they nibble spicy snacks and sip their drinks and they talk, they talk interminably as they sit together on the sand.

On her white beach towel Eurydice sat at the centre of a group of lithe, tanned young men, who were talking and laughing. Seeing Victorien appear, she got to her feet and ran towards him a little cautiously over the uneven sand; she ran to him as fast as she could and threw her bronzed arms around his neck. Then she led him back to the group and introduced him to the others, who greeted him with unexpected enthusiasm. They bombarded him with questions, told him jokes, touched his arm or his shoulder when they spoke to him as though they had known him for ever. They laughed loudly, they talked quickly, they got worked up over nothing and then laughed again. Salagnon was left behind. He quickly proved disappointing; he lacked a quick wit; he did not measure up.

Eurydice laughed with her friends, who pretended to flirt with her. When the sun grew brighter she put on sunglasses, which blotted out her eyes so that she was simply a pair of mischievous lips. She turned from one to the other; her hair, falling over her shoulders, followed her every movement after a flicker of hesitation; every time she laughed she was the queen of a troop of monkeys. Salagnon scowled resentfully. He did not take part. He watched from a distance and thought that he would rather paint the undulating line of clouds floating over the horizon to his right. His talent was rekindled, a tingling in his hands; he sat in silence. Suddenly he despised Algiers, he who had loved the garrulous affability of Salomon Kaloyannis; despised Algiers and the French Algerians who talk too quickly in a language that is no longer his, an informal language, one that he cannot follow, cannot join in. They pranced around him, mocking, cruel, as they dug an impassable moat around Eurydice.

Eventually, they went back up to the city by a flight of concrete steps between the rocks. The young men took their leave, kissing Eurydice, shaking Victorien's hand with an enthusiasm that seemed to him different, more ironic than it had been at first. The two of them walked home together, shoulder to shoulder. From time to time they glanced at each other a little awkwardly, but mostly they stared straight ahead. They made banal small talk along the way. The walk seemed endless; the bustling crowds slowed their progress.

The evening meal with Salomon was ponderously polite. Eurydice was tired and went to bed early.

'What do you plan to do now, Victorien?'

'Go back, I think. Maybe re-enlist in the army.'

'The war is over, Victorien. Life has resumed. Why would we need musketeers now? Make a life for yourself, do something important. The last thing Eurydice needs is a sabre-rattler; their time has passed. When you've made a life for yourself, come back. The young men here are all talk, but you, you're nothing. Live a little, then come back to us.'

The following morning he took the ferry for Marseille. On the afterdeck he began a letter to Eurydice. The Algerian coast began to shrink: he sketched it. The harsh sun picked out the shadows, made the kasbah bristle with teeth. He drew the small boat of the ferry: the funnel, the gunwales, the passengers leaning against the sides, looking out to sea. He sketched in ink on small white cards. From Marseille he sent her some as postcards. He sent them often. On the back he wrote a few brief lines about what he was doing. She never replied.

He met his uncle, who was back from Indochine. He spent several weeks in a room without even unpacking his bags; he was waiting to put out again. There was nothing for him here in France, his uncle said. 'These days, I live in a trunk.' He would say it without a smile, staring into the eyes of his interlocutor, who would inevitably look away, because it made him think of a pine coffin and he did not know whether to smile or shudder. He was talking about a metal trunk painted green, not particularly large, that held all his belongings and followed him wherever he went. He had dragged it through Germany, through Africa, both North and Equatorial, and now through Indochine. The paint was flaking, the sides were dented. When he tapped it affectionately, it boomed hollowly.

'This is my real home, because it contains everything I own. We all end up in a trunk in the end, but I'm already living in one. I'm ahead of the game. They say that to study philosophy is to learn how to die. I haven't read the books that explain the idea, but it's a philosophy I understand in practice. It saves a lot of time, and that is one thing I run short of: given the life I lead, I'm likely to go before most people.'

His uncle did not laugh. Victorien knew that there was no humour in what he said: he simply said what he had to say, but he did it so bluntly that it sometimes sounded like a joke. He just told it like it was.

'Why don't you give it up?' Victorien asked all the same. 'Why don't you come back now?'

'Come back to what? From the moment I stopped being a child, I've been fighting wars. Even as a child I played at war. Then I did my military service and that led straight into the war. I've spent my whole adult life at war, although I never planned it that way. I've always lived out of a box. I never imagined things any different, and it suits me. I can hold my whole life in two hands. I can lug it around without getting tired. How else would I live? Go to work every day? I don't have the patience. Build myself a house? It would be too big for me. I wouldn't be able to pick it up and move it. All you can carry when you move is a box. And sooner or later we all end up in a box. So why make a detour? I carry my home with me and I travel the world. I do what I've always done.'

In the tiny room where he spent his furloughs, there was hardly space for a single bed and the chair on which he set his folded uniform. Victorien gingerly moved the uniform, careful not to crease it, so he could sit stiffly on the edge of the seat, not leaning back. Lying on the bed, the uncle talked to him, staring at the ceiling, his feet bare, his ankles crossed, his hands clasped behind his head.

'What book would you take with you to a desert island?' he asked.

'I've never thought about it.'

'It's a stupid question. No one goes to a desert island, and people who find themselves on one wind up there without prior notice: they don't have time to choose. It's a stupid question, because nothing is at stake. But I've played the desert island game. Because my trunk is my island. I've asked myself what book I'd take with me in my trunk. The colonial troops get letters, and they've got time to read them while they travel on ships and spend long nights lying awake in countries where it's too hot to sleep. Me, I carry the *Odyssey*, which recounts the long-drawn-out wanderings of a man who is trying to go home, but cannot find the way. And while he wanders all over the world, searching, his country is given over to sordid ambition, to greed, to pillage. When he finally arrives home, he sorts everything out through the strategies of war. He clears, he cleans house, he restores order.

'It's a book I read piecemeal, in places that Homer never knew existed. In Alsace, buried in the snow, by the glow of a cigarette lighter so as not to fall asleep, because if I'd fallen asleep in that cold I would be dead; at night in Africa, in a straw hut, this time I was trying to get to sleep, but it's so hot you'd take off your skin if you could; I read it in steerage on a cargo ship, leaning against my trunk, so I could think of something other than throwing up; in a bunk built of palm trunks that shudders every time a mortar explodes, and each time a little dirt drifts down on to the pages, and the lamp hanging from the ceiling starts to swing, making the text difficult to read. The effort I have to make to follow the sentences makes me feel better; it focuses my attention and I forget to be afraid of dying. The Greeks knew this book off by heart, apparently, learning it was their education; they could recite a few lines or a whole book any time and anywhere. So I'm learning it, too. I aim to learn the whole thing and that will be the extent of my education.'

In the tiny little room where there was scarcely any room, the very trunk they talked about sat between the end of the bed and the chair, such that Salagnon could not stretch his legs. The more they talked, the more the green metal trunk gained in significance. 'Open it.' It was half-empty. A carefully folded piece of red cloth hid the contents. 'Lift it up.' Beneath it was the book about Odysseus, a large paperback volume that was beginning to shed its pages. It rested on another piece of cloth, which served as a cushion. 'I protect it as best I can. I don't know if I'd find another copy in Upper Tonkin.' Under the book there was nothing but a few items of clothing, a pistol in a leather holster and a washbag. 'Unfold them, the two pieces of cloth.' Salagnon unfolded two flags of medium size, both of them predominantly red. The first was emblazoned with a swastika inside a white circle, now fading to blue; the second a single, gold, five-pointed star.

'I picked up the Nazi flag in Germany at the end of the war. It was flying from the aerial of an officer's car. He kept it flying to the end at the head of the armoured column we captured. He made no attempt to shield himself; he drove at the head of the convoy in an open-topped Kübelwagen, followed at a distance by a line of tanks. They carried on until their tanks were empty, then there would be no more petrol and their war was over. His peaked cap singled him out and he was wearing a jacket that, though patched and worn, was clean and immaculately pressed. He had polished his Iron Cross and was wearing it around his neck. He was the first to die, with his arrogance intact. We wiped out the tanks one by one. The last tank surrendered, only the last one. There was no one left to see, so they could afford to. My comrades wanted to burn the flag flying from the officer's car. But I kept it.'

'What about the other flag, the one with the star? I've never seen one like it.'

'It's from Indochine. The Viet Minh designed a flag for themselves, communist red with yellow symbols. I got this one when we retook Hanoi. They were expecting us; they had fortified their defences, dug trenches across the streets, foxholes in the lawns; they'd cut down trees to create barricades. They had stitched flags to let the world know who they were; some were made from cotton, others from expensive silk requisitioned from shops. They had something to prove, and, having been driven back by the Japanese, we had something to prove, too. Both sides were proud of their flags. It was all very heroic, and then they fled. This particular flag was one a young lad had used to taunt us. I prised it from his dead fingers in the street amid the rubble. I don't think I shot him, but in street battles you can never know for sure. I took it to protect my book. Now it is safe.

'Both of these guys terrified me. The arrogant Nazi officer and the fanatical young Tonkinese lad. Both were alive when I first saw them, then they were dead. I stole both flags and folded them to wrap up Odysseus. These men terrified me, because they chose to brandish a red flag rather than hide themselves and save their skin. They were little more than flagpoles, and they died. That is the horror of systems, of fascism and communism: man disappears. They talk on and on about mankind, but they don't give a shit about man. They worship dead men. And there I am, fighting wars because I never had the time to learn anything else. I try to place myself in the service of a cause that does not seem too immoral: to be a man, for my own sake. The life I lead is a way of being a man, of remaining a man. With the things you see over there, it's a full-time objective; it is something that can take a lifetime, take every ounce of strength; you can never be sure that you'll succeed.'

'What is it like, over there?'

'Indochine? It's like the planet Mars. Or Neptune. I don't know. It's a world that is nothing like this one: imagine a country where there is no dry land. The muddy sludge of the delta is the most disgusting substance I know. That's where they grow their rice, and it grows terrifyingly fast. It's hardly surprising they bake this mud to make bricks: it takes a sort of exorcism, a trial by fire, for the soil to hold together. It takes extraordinary rituals, a thousand degrees in a kiln, to overcome the despair you feel when faced with land that's constantly slipping out of sight and out of reach, earth that sinks under your feet and slips through your fingers. It is impossible to grasp that mud; it bogs you down, it is thick and sticky and it stinks.

'The mud in the rice fields sticks to your legs, sucks at your feet, gets daubed over your hands, your arms; you find it smeared over your forehead as though you had fallen; as you tramp through it, the mud slithers over you. And all around, insects drone, some chirrup, they all sting. The sun beats down. You try not to look at it, but it reflects in every puddle, throwing off dazzling sparks that follow your gaze, blinding you, even when you lower your eyes. And everything stinks. Sweat streams from under your arms, down your legs, into your eyes, but you have to keep marching. It is vital that we not lose a single piece of the heavy kit weighing on our shoulders, the rifles that must be kept clean in order to work. We have to march without slipping, without stumbling; the mud comes up to our knees. Aside from being inherently toxic, the mud has been booby-trapped by the people we are hunting. At times it explodes. At times it gives way: you fall twenty centimetres and find your feet impaled on bamboo spikes. Sometimes there's a crack of gunshot from behind a bush on the outskirts of a village or from behind a ditch and a man goes down. You rush towards the place from which the shot was fired, scrabbling through the thick sludge, making little headway, and by the time you get there, there is nothing, not a trace. We stand like fools around the wounded man, beneath a sky that is too vast for us. Now we have to carry him. He seemed to fall suddenly, for no reason, and the dry crack we heard before he fell must have been the snap of the thread keeping him upright. In the delta we move like puppets, silhouetted against the sky, our every movement seems clumsy and awkward and predictable. Our limbs are wooden; the heat, the sweat, the crushing tiredness leave us senseless and slow-witted. The peasants watch us pass without troubling to interrupt their work. They crouch on raised banks on which they build their villages, doing God knows what, or they stoop into the mud, which they cultivate with simple tools. They scarcely move. They do not speak, do not run away; they simply watch as we pass; and then they bend again and carry on with their humble work, as though their task is for all time and we are nothing, as though they are here for all eternity and we, despite our slowness, are merely passing through.

'The children are more active; they follow us, running along the dykes letting out shrill cries, their voices much more high-pitched than children here at home. But even the children come to a stand-still. They often lie on the back of their black buffalo as it plods along, grazing, drinking from streams, not even realizing it is carrying a sleeping child.

'We know they are all informers for the Viet Minh. They tell them where we are heading, what equipment we have, how many there are of us. Some of them are fighters themselves: the Viet Minh militia's uniform is not different to the black pyjamas worn by the locals. They roll up their rifle and a few bullets in a piece of tarpaulin and bury it in the paddy fields. They know where it is, we would never find it; and when we have left, they dig it out again. Others, especially the children, remotely set off booby traps, using a length of wire to trig-ger grenades tethered to a stake planted in the mud, hidden in a tuft of grass or in a bush. As we pass, they tug the wire and it explodes. So we've learned to keep the kids away, to fire so that they don't come near us. We've learned to be particularly suspicious of the ones who look like they are sleeping on the backs of black buffalos. That piece of string they're holding that dangles in the mud might be the reins or it might be a trigger. We shoot wide to scare them off and sometimes we slaughter the buffalo with a machine gun. Whenever there's a gunshot, we round up everyone, all those working in the paddy fields, we smell their fingers, bare their shoulders, and we deal harshly with anyone who smells of gunpowder or sports the tell-tale bruise made by a rifle's recoil. When we approach a village, we machine-gun the scrubland all around before we advance. When there is nothing left moving, we go in. The people have fled. They are afraid of us. And besides, the Viet Minh tell them to leave.

'The villages are like islands. Islands beached on low embankments, towns ringed by curtains of trees; from outside you can see nothing. In the villages there is solid ground, you do not sink into it. Standing in front of the huts, we are almost on dry land. Sometimes we see people and they tell us nothing. This almost always sparks us to fury. Not their silence, but the fact of being on dry ground. Of finally seeing something. Of being able to grasp a handful of earth without it trickling away. As though in villages we are free to act, and that action is a reaction to being mired, bogged down, helpless. As soon as we have the ability to act, we act harshly. We have destroyed whole villages. We have the power: in fact, it is the hallmark of our power.

'Luckily we have machines. Field radios that connect us to each other; aeroplanes that drone above out heads; they are vulnerable, solitary planes, but from up there they can see much better than we who are stuck on the ground; amphibious tanks that move through water, through mud, as easily as they do on the road, in which we are sometimes transported, packed like sardines behind the white-hot armour plating. We are saved by machines. Without them, we would be swallowed by this mud and devoured by the tendril roots of rice.

'Indochine is the planet Mars or Neptune, a place like nowhere we have ever seen, a place were it is easy to die. But sometimes it offers a sizzling spectacle. Sometimes we step on to dry land and we do not strafe anything. In the middle of the village is a pagoda, the only permanent structure. Pagodas are often used as bunkers in our battles against the Viet Minh; by us or by them. But sometimes we step quietly into the almost cool shade and, there, once our eyes have adjusted, we see only deep red, dark wood, gold leaf and dozens of tiny flames. A gilded Buddha gleams in the shadows, the flickering glow of the candles flows over him like clear water, making his skin luminous and trembling. Eyes closed, he raises one hand and that simple gesture is astonishingly calming. We breathe. Crouching monks are swathed in huge orange robes. They whisper, bang gongs, burn incense. We feel like shaving our heads, wrapping ourselves in bedsheets and staying here. When we go back into the sunlight, when we sink back into the muddy delta, at that first step, we almost feel like crying.

'The people over there never speak to us. They are shorter than us; they tend to crouch and their stiff politeness makes it impossible to look them in the face. So our eyes never meet theirs. When they do speak, it's in a shrill, piercing language we don't understand. I feel like I'm meeting Martians; and fighting men I can't tell apart from the rest. But sometimes they talk to us: village peasants, townspeople who went to school just like we did, or soldiers fighting alongside us. When they speak to us in French it makes up for the things we endure, the things we commit to every day; with a few words we come to believe we have forgotten the horrors, that they will not return. We gaze at their women, who are as beautiful as silken veils, as palm fronds, as gossamer things that flutter in the breeze. We dream of the possibility of living here. Some do. They settle in the mountains where the air is cooler, where the war is less invasive, where, in the morning light, those mountains float on a sea of iridescent mist. We can dream of eternity.

'In Indochine we live with the most abject horrors and the most spectacular beauty; the biting cold of the high peaks and the torrid heat 2,000 metres below; we endure the terrible dry heat of the limestone karsts and the overwhelming humidity of the delta marshlands; we suffer constant fear of attack by day and night, and experience a blissful serenity when faced with wonders we did not know existed on Earth; we are constantly veering between terror and exaltation. To be subjected to such conflicting forces is a brutal ordeal and I fear we will split the way timber does when forced to endure such pressures. I don't know what state we will be in afterwards, those of us who don't die, I mean, because men die quickly.'

He was staring at the ceiling, hands folded behind his head.

'It's crazy how quickly a man can die over there,' he murmured. 'Guys arrive, they come in by the boatload from France. I hardly have time to get to know them; they all die and I'm left behind. It's crazy how many men die; they slaughter us like tuna.'

279

'What about them?'

'Who, the Viet Minh? They're Martians. We slaughter them, too, but how they die we never know. Always hidden, always elsewhere, never there. And even if we did see them, we wouldn't recognize them. They all look the same, they dress the same; we don't know what we're killing. But when we're ambushed, when they're hiding in elephant grass, in the trees, they kill us methodically; they spear us like fish. I've never seen so much blood. It's plastered over the leaves, the rocks, the lush ravines, the black mud runs crimson.

'It reminds me of a passage from the *Odyssey*. This is the passage that made me think of fish.

There I sacked the city, killed the men...

Then I urged them to cut and run, set sail,
but would they listen? Not those mutinous fools...

And all the while the Cicones sought out other Cicones, called for
help from their neighbours living inland: a larger force, and stronger
soldiers too, skilled hands at fighting men from chariots, skilled,
when a crisis broke, to fight on foot. Out of the morning mist they
came against us – packed as the leaves and spears that flower forth
in spring – and Zeus presented us with disaster, me and my comrades
doomed to suffer blow on mortal blow...

Long as morning rose and the blessed day grew stronger we stood
and fought them off, massed as they were, but then, when the sun
wheeled past the hour for unyoking oxen, the Cicones broke our lines
and beat us down at last. Out of each ship, six men-at-arms were
killed; the rest of us rowed away from certain doom.

From there we sailed on, glad to escape our death, yet sick at
heart for the dear companions we had lost. But I would not let

our rolling ships set sail until the crews had raised the triple cry,
saluting each poor comrade cut down by the fierce Cicones on
that plain...

'Shit! That's not the right passage. I could have sworn there was something about spearing fish. Pass me the book.'

He sat up on the bed, grabbed the battered book from Victorien
who was holding it gingerly in case pages should fall out and feverishly
thumbed through it, taking little care.

'I could have sworn... Ah! Here it is! The Laestrygonians. I got the
Laestrygonians confused with the Cicones. Listen: *The nightfall and*
the sunrise march so close together...

> *But the king let loose a howling through the town that brought tre-*
> *mendous Laestrygonians swarming up from every side – hundreds,*
> *not like men, like Giants. Down from the cliffs they flung great rocks*
> *a man could hardly hoist and a ghastly shattering din rose up from*
> *all the ships – men in their death-cries, hulls smashed to splinters.*
> *They speared the crews like fish and whisked them home to make*
> *their grisly meal.*

'Here, listen to this...

> *There, for two nights, two days, we lay by, no let-up, eating our*
> *hearts out, bent with pain and bone-tired.*

'Homer describes us much more accurately than the newsreels. When
I watch them, those pompous little newsreels in the cinema, they make
me laugh: they show nothing; what this ancient Greek poet is describing is much closer to the Indochine I've spent months travelling the
length and breadth of. I just got two of the cantos mixed up. You see,
I don't know the book yet. When I can recite it by heart, like a Greek,
with no mistakes, I will be done. I'll take no further responsibility.'

With the book closed on his lap, his hand on the cover, his eyes closed, he recited the two cantos in a half-whisper. He smiled happily. 'Odysseus is fleeing, pursued by hoards of men who want him dead. His companions are all slaughtered, but he is left alive. And when he goes home, he sets his house in order; he kills the men who plundered his storehouses; he slaughters all those who collaborated. By the time he is finished, it is dark, hardly anyone remains, only corpses. A great peace finally descends. It is over. Life can recommence; twenty years to come back to life. Victorien, do you think it will take us twenty years to extricate ourselves from this war?' 'It seems like a long time to me.' 'Yes, it is long, too long...' Then he lay back again, placed the book on his chest and fell silent.

November is not auspicious for anything. The sky looms closer, the weather closes up, the leaves on the trees shrivel like the hands of a dying man; then fall. In Lyon a mist hangs over the rivers like the heavy smoke that rises from the piles of smouldering leaves, but in reverse. In reverse, because it is not smoke but vapour, not flame but liquid, not heat but cold, everything is the other way round. It does not rise, it creeps, it spreads. In November nothing remains of the joy of being free.

Salagnon was cold; his greatcoat did little to protect him; cold draughts pervaded his room under the eaves; the damp walls forced him outside, where he wandered aimlessly, hands in his pockets, coat buttoned tight, collar up, between floes of fog that seeped from the façades of buildings and listlessly broke away like scraps of wet paper.

Drawing was becoming difficult. He needed to stop, to wait for the forms that would appear on the paper to come to him; it requires a receptive quivering of skin that cannot be left bare in the cold and damp. Quivers and shivers merge, diverge and shrivel as one walks, aimlessly, simply to drive off restlessness.

Near Gerland he stopped, transfixed, at the foot of a dead Christ. He had walked the length of the huge slaughterhouse that killed in slow motion, past the open-air Gerland Stadium, where grass grew in unkempt tufts. He had spent the whole day walking along this avenue that leads nowhere and he stopped in front of a concrete church whose façade was dominated by a huge bas-relief of the crucified Christ. He had to look up in order to take it in: the feet touched the ground, the ankles were at head-height and the head dissolved into the greenish mist that becomes impenetrable as it unfurls. Standing so close and being forced to look up warped the perspective of the body like a spasm, the statue threatened to rip out the nails holding the wrists, to collapse and crush Salagnon.

He stepped inside the church, where the equable temperature felt comforting. The feeble November light failed to pierce the thick stained glass, getting lost inside the glass blocks, which glowed like red, blue, black embers about to snuff out. Old women moved slowly, silently, busying themselves with particular tasks they knew by rote, never looking up, as diligent as mice.

November is good for nothing, he thought, pulling tightly on the thin coat that failed to provide him with warmth. But it's just a bad patch you've got to get through. It dismayed him to think that to be young, strong and free was a bad patch to be got through. He had clearly started his life a little hastily and now felt suddenly tired. Runners who want to run long distances are advised not to start too strongly, to set off slowly, to keep a reserve of energy, to avoid running out of steam or getting a stitch that would jeopardize their finish. He did not know what to do. November, which is not auspicious for anything, which seemed to drag on indefinitely, seemed to him to be his own finish line.

The priest stepped out of the shadows and crossed the nave. His footsteps echoed so loudly beneath the vaulted ceiling that, without intending to, Salagnon watched him as he walked.

'Brioude!'

The name boomed through the church, making the old ladies start. The priest turned suddenly and squinted, peering into the darkness, then his face brightened. He came towards Salagnon with his hand outstretched, his long, hurried strides hindered by his soutane.

'Your timing is perfect,' he said by way of greeting. 'I'm seeing Montbellet tonight. He's in Lyon for forty-eight hours; after that he leaves for I don't know where. Come by at eight o'clock. Call for me at the presbytery.'

Then, just as brusquely, he turned and left Salagnon standing there, still holding out his hand.

'Brioude?'

'Yes?'

'After all this time... are you well?'

'Of course. We'll talk tonight.'

'You're not surprised by the coincidence: me here, you there?'

'I'm not surprised by life any more, Salagnon. I accept it. I let it happen and then I change it. See you tonight.'

He vanished into the shadows, and there came the resounding clicking of his shoes on the flagstones, then the clicking of a door closing, then nothing. An old lady pushed past Salagnon while clicking her tongue irritably; she tottered as far as the wrought-iron stand in front of the statue of a saint. She planted a tiny candle on one of the iron spikes, lit it and made a cursory sign of the Cross. Then she stared up at the saint with that look of exasperation one reserves for those of whom we expect great things, but who fail to do anything, or do it badly, or not as they should.

She turned and shot Salagnon the same look as he was leaving. Outside, he tried to turn up the collar of his coat, but it was too small; he hunched his shoulders, drew in his head and walked off, without looking up to see the horribly misshapen Christ. He did not know where to go between now and this evening, but the sky seemed less sickly, it no longer looked like a grimy sheet of rubber about to collapse. Soon it would be dark.

*   *   *

The presbytery where Brioude lived looked like a pied-à-terre, an abandoned hunting lodge, a shack where people take shelter but are ever ready to leave. Paint flaked from the walls to reveal older layers beneath; the large, chilly rooms were stacked like a lumber room with old furniture, piles of timber planks, warped doors leaning against the walls. They ate in a dimly lit room where the wallpaper was peeling and the dusty floorboards badly needed a coat of polish.

They ate indiscriminately, lukewarm, overcooked noodles and left-over meat in sauce that Brioude served up in a battered pot. He doled out the food perfunctorily, letting the ladle clang against the plates, and poured them glasses of thick Côtes du Rhône from a small cask in a dark corner of the room.

'Church food isn't up to much,' said Montbellet, 'but it's always had good wine.'

'That's why we forgive this venerable institution. It has grievously sinned, it has often failed, but it provides intoxication.'

'So you're a priest. I never knew you had a vocation.'

'I didn't know either. Blood showed me the way.'

'Blood?'

'The blood we were soaked in. I saw so much blood. I saw men whose boots were soaked in the blood of those they had just killed. I saw so much blood it was a baptism. I was bathed in blood, and then transformed. When the blood stopped flowing, we needed to restore those things we had broken, and everyone joined in. But we also needed to restore our souls. Have you seen the state of our souls?'

'What about our bodies? Have you seen the state of our bodies?'

They laughed at how scrawny they were. None of them weighed much. Brioude's skin was translucent, taut, Montbellet was desiccated by the sun and Salagnon was haggard, his face sallow with exhaustion.

'It has to be said, that given the way you eat...'

'...you've forgotten the meaning of good food.'

'Precisely, gentlemen. The food is bad, so I don't eat much, just enough to maintain a minimal presence in this world. Our thinness is a virtue. All around us people gorge themselves on food, trying to gain back the weight they lost during the war. For us, staying thin is a sign; we're not behaving as though nothing had happened. We came through the worst, so we are striving for a better world. We are not trying to go back.'

'Except my thinness isn't deliberate,' said Salagnon. 'For you, it's self-denial and you have the face of a saint; with Montbellet, it's a life of adventure; but for me it's poverty, so I just look like a sad case.'

'Salagnon! "There are no riches other than men." Are you familiar with that phrase? It's old, four centuries old, but it's an unchanging truth, summed up in few words. "There are no riches other than men." Think about what that phrase means in 1946. At the point when we were using the most powerful means to destroy mankind, physically and mentally, at the very moment when we realized that there are no resources, no riches, no power other than man himself. The sailors trapped aboard metal tubs that were scuttled, the soldiers buried alive by bombs, the prisoners starved to death, the men forced to conform to death-dealing systems, these men survived. In desperate situations they survived with nothing other than their courage. We made no attempt to understand their miraculous survival, we were too afraid. To come so close to annihilation is terrifying, and all the more terrifying because of this indomitable life force that comes from us at the last moment. Machines were crushing us and, in extremis, life saved us. In material terms, life is nothing; and yet it saved us from the infinite matter intent on crushing us. How can that not be seen as a miracle? Or as the sudden advent of a profound universal law? For this life to emerge, it is necessary to stare the terrifying prospect of annihilation in the face; such a prospect is unendurable. Suffering brought forth life; the greater the suffering, the greater the life. But that is too hard. We prefer to grow richer, to ally ourselves to that which would annihilate us. Life does not spring from matter or from machines or from wealth. It springs from the absence of matter, from the sheer nothingness to which we must submit. As living beings, we are an affront to overcrowded space. Abundance and excess oppose our plenitude. There must be nothingness for man to emerge again; accepting the void that, in extremis, saves us from the threat of extermination is the greatest fear imaginable; yet we must overcome it. The urgency of war gave us the courage; peace has made it more difficult.'

'Don't communists say the same thing, that there is only man?'

'They are talking about Man in general. Of Man manufactured by a factory. They no longer even talk about the people, they say "the masses". I think of each man as the sole source of life. Each man deserves to be saved, spared; no man is interchangeable, for life can burst forth in him at any moment, especially in the moment when he would be crushed, and the life that bursts forth in a single man is life itself. One might call that life... God.'

Montbellet smiled, threw his hands wide in a gesture of welcome and said: 'Why not?'

'You believe in God, Montbellet?'

'I have no need. The world is enough in itself. Beauty helps me to live.'

'Beauty, too, might be called God.'

He made the same gesture, parting his hands, and said again: 'Why not?'

The ring he wore on the ring finger of his left hand underscored his gestures. Highly ornate, in tarnished silver, there was nothing feminine about it. Salagnon had no idea such rings existed. The designs chased into the silver framed a large, deep-blue stone shot through with shafts of gold that seemed to move.

'This stone,' said Brioude, nodding towards it, 'looks like the sky in an illuminated manuscript; all this in such a tiny space; a Romanesque church hewn into rock, where the sky is represented by stone.'

'That's a bit much, it's just a stone. Lapis lazuli from Afghanistan. The idea of a chapel wouldn't have occurred to me, but you're not wrong. I often look at it and stare at it; it gives me the pleasure of meditation. My soul nestles there and contemplates the blue, which seems to me as wide as the sky.'

'The sky is so immense that it is embedded in all small things.'

'You priests are amazing. You speak so well that everyone hears you. Your words are so fluid they infiltrate everything. And with those beautiful words you tint everything in your colours, a mixture of sky blue and byzantine gold, tempered somewhat with sacristy yellow. You call life God, and beauty too; my ring, a chapel; and poverty, existence. And when you say it, I believe you. And that belief lasts for as long as you speak.

'But it's just a ring, Brioude. I travel the length and breadth of Asia for the Museum of Mankind. I send them objects, explain their uses, and they show them to a public who have never set foot outside France. I travel, I learn languages, I make strange friends, and I feel as though I am exploring the world of AD 1000. I am within a hair's breadth of eternity. But I understand what you mean: man is not the measure of things, he is simply not to scale. Man is too small on mountains that are vast, naked. How do such men manage? Their houses are built of stones found lying around, you can scarcely see them. They wear clothes the colour of dust and when they lie on the ground, rolled up in the blanket that serves as a coat, they disappear. How do they manage to exist in a world that is not intentionally hostile, but simply repudiates you?

'They walk, they trek the mountain, they possess small objects in which all human beauty converges, and when they speak, their few scant words break your heart. Rings like these are worn by men who combine the greatest refinement with the greatest savagery. They are careful to circle their eyes with kohl, to dye their beards, to always carry a weapon with them. They wear a flower behind their ears, walk hand in hand with their friends, and treat their wives more contemptuously than their mules. They savagely massacre intruders, and they bend over backwards to welcome you as though you were a distant cousin, much beloved, finally returning home. I don't understand these people, they don't understand me, but now I spend my life with them.

'The first day I put on this ring, I met a man. I met him at a mountain pass, a col in the foothills where a lone tree grew. In front of the tree, next to the road, stood a house. And when I say "road" you have to imagine a dirt track; and when I say "house" you have to imagine a flat-roofed, stone shack with a narrow door and a single window opening into a dark, smoky room. Here, at the pass, where the path wavers before plunging down the other side, there was a teahouse where travellers could rest. The job of the man I'm talking about, the man I met that day, was to greet those who climbed the mountain and serve them tea. Under the tree, he had set up a "conversation bed", I don't know if such a word exists in French. It is a raised wooden frame strung with rope. It is possible to sleep on it, but it is more common to sit cross-legged on it, alone or with other people, and to watch the world unfold beyond the bed. You float, like a boat on the ocean. You look out, as from a balcony over the roofs. Sitting on that bed, you feel a wonderful tranquillity. The man who worked at the house at the pass invited us to sit down, my guide and me. On a fire made of twigs he boiled water in an iron kettle. The tree provided shade and it also provided the kindling. He served us mountain tea, which is a thick beverage full of spices and dried fruits. We made the most of the shade of the lone tree that grew at that altitude, watched over by a lone man living in a stone shack. We surveyed the valleys between the mountains, which in that country are canyons. He asked me to describe where I was from. Not to name the place, but to describe it. I drank several cups of tea and I told him about Europe, the cities, the smallness of the landscapes, the damp and the war we had just ended. In exchange, he recited poems by Al-Ghazali. He intoned them magnificently, and the breeze that blew through the pass whipped each word into the air like a kite; he would hold them with the thread that was his voice and then let go. My guide helped me to translate the words I did not quite understand. But the simple rhythm of the verses and what little I could understand made my bones tremble; I was a lute of bone strung with marrow. This old man sitting on a rope bed plucked me; he made me sound out my own music, a music I had never heard.

'Leaving him to continue on my journey, I was overcome with gratitude. He gave me a little wave and poured himself more tea. I felt as though I was floating in the mountain air when we finally arrived at the garden deep in the valley; when I smelled the scent of the grasses, the humidity of the trees, I felt as though I was stepping into a perfect world, an Eden I wished I could commemorate in poetry; but I'm incapable. And so I have to go back there. This is the world this ring opened up to me; one I cannot be parted from.'

'I envy you,' said Salagnon. 'I'm just poor. I have no heroism, no desire. My thinness is the result of cold, of boredom, of insufficient food. My thinness is a flaw I would gladly do without; I wish I could be free of it.'

'Your thinness is a good sign, Victorien.'

'Ecclesiastical painter!' roared Montbellet. 'He shows up with a pot of blue and a brush to dip in gold! He'll repaint you, Victorien, he'll repaint you.'

'Signs are persistent, you heathens! They are even immune to irony!'

'You're going to tell him his haggard appearance is a blessing. That's the real miracle of your religion: it's just a coat of paint. The Church spends its time refurbishing life with blue paint.'

'Signs are reversible,' said Montbellet.

'That is something religion is good at.'

'That is why religion is great: it puts signs in the correct order, so that when they stumble, people can begin again. And common sense is what allows them to grow.'

He refilled the glasses, they drank.

'OK, Brioude, I'm prepared to see things your way. Carry on.'

'Your thinness is not a sign that would have become enslaved. It is a sign of a new departure, with no baggage, with a clean slate. You are ready, Victorien; you have no ties. You are alive, you are free, you lack only a little air in order to understand. You are like a stringed instrument, like Montbellet's lute, but trapped under a bell jar. Its music cannot be heard; the string quivers in vain, because there is no air to vibrate. There needs to be a crack in the glass, so air can rush in and you can finally be heard. Something around you needs to be broken, so that you can breathe again, Victorien Salagnon. Perhaps it is an eggshell. Perhaps the crack in the shell that will let in air is art. You used to draw. So draw.'

Montbellet got to his feet, brandished his glass, darkly crimson in the dim glow, as warm as blood in the cold half-light.

'Art, adventure and spirituality drink to their common gauntness.'

They drank, they laughed, drank again. With a sigh, Salagnon pushed away his plate on which the remains of the cold noodles had congealed in the gloopy sauce.

'All the same, it's a shame that the Church serves such terrible food.'

'But it has excellent wine.'

Brioude's eye gleamed.

Victorien applied himself to drawing. That is to say, he sat with a pot of ink in front of a blank page. And nothing came. The white remained white, the black of the ink remained in the well, nothing took form. But what could he have drawn, bent over this piece of paper? Drawing is a mark, the outward sign of something that lives within; but inside, he had only Eurydice. Eurydice was far away, living in a topsy-turvy world, beyond the murderous Mediterranean, in that hell of caustic sunlight, of dwindling words, of hastily buried corpses; she was far away, beyond the too-broad river that cut France in two. And outside there was nothing either, nothing he could set down on paper; nothing but greenish mist that stagnated between buildings about to dissolve in their own dampness. He wanted to weep, but that, too, was no longer possible. The page was white, there was not a single mark.

He sat for hours, motionless, his elbows propped on the desk. In the dark room the blank page was the only source of light, a faint glow that never guttered out. It went on all night. Morning came, a horrid metallic dawn in which shapes appeared that had no depth, equal parts shadow and light merging into an unvarying luminescence. It offered no contours, nothing that stood out that might allow him to capture his surroundings. Having left no trace, with no sadness, no regret, he lay down on his bed and instantly fell asleep.

When he woke, he took the necessary steps to have himself posted to Indochine.

Commentaries V

The fragile nature of snow

'**W**OULD YOU LISTEN TO THAT BULLSHIT!' roared Mariani, sitting in front of the television. 'Did you hear? Did you hear that? They're saying the guy who won is Irish.'

'The guy who won what?'

'The 5,000 metres you've been watching for the past ten minutes.'

'So? Are you saying he's not Irish?'

'But he's black!'

'You start every sentence with a "but", Mariani.'

'But that's because there is a "but", a big "but". "But" is a conjunction between two statement indicating a reservation, a paradox, a contrast. He is Irish, but black. I'm indicating a reservation, highlighting a paradox, pointing out the absurdity; but also the stupidity of failing to notice the absurdity.'

'If he's running for Ireland, then he's legally Irish.'

'I don't give a damn about legally. I don't give a shit. I've seen laws dismantled a thousand times and patched together any old how. I don't care and I've never cared. I'm talking about reality. In reality, there are no more black Irishmen than there are squared circles. Have you ever seen a black Irishman?'

'Yeah. On TV. In fact, he's just won the 5,000 metres.'

'I despair of you, Salagnon. You see things stupidly. You rely too much on appearances. You're nothing but a painter.'

I wondered what I was doing there. I was sitting in the air, on the eighteenth floor in Voracieux-les-Bredins, in the tower block where Mariani lived. Backs to the windows, we were watching television. Somewhere far from here they were holding European Championships. On screen, guys ran, they jumped, they threw things, while the voices of commentators, using a clever mixture of slow drawl and sudden interjection, attempted to make this spectacle interesting. I make the point that we were sitting with our backs to the windows, because it is an important detail: we could afford to turn our backs, since the windows were secured, barricaded with piles of sandbags. Sprawled on flabby sofas, we drank beers with the lights on. I had been seated between Salagnon and Mariani and around us, sitting on the floor, standing behind or off in some other room, were some of his 'lads'. They all looked the same, heavyset guys who inspired physical fear, monosyllabic most of the time, but capable of roaring when necessary, coming and going in this vast, empty apartment, making themselves at home. Mariani was as uninterested in furniture as Salagnon, but while Victorien filled the space with pointless objects, the way you might fill a box containing something fragile with polystyrene chips, Mariani preferred to leave a little space for the restless, potbellied giants who could hardly stand still.

Through the sandbags barricading the windows they had fashioned arrow slits that made it possible to see out. When we first arrived, Mariani had shown me around. I visited his fortifications. He talked as he patted the fat hessian sacks filled with sand.

'Amazing invention,' he told me. 'Go on, touch.'

I touched. Beneath the coarse brown fabric the sand felt hard if you tapped it, but fluid if you pressed gently; it behaved like water in slow motion.

'When it comes to protection, sand is much better than concrete, especially this kind of concrete,' he said, rapping the wall, which rang hollow. 'I'm not sure these walls are bulletproof, but the sandbags are. They can shoot pellets and shrapnel. They penetrate a little, but the momentum is absorbed and they don't go any farther. I ordered a truckload of sand. My lads brought it up by the bucketful in the lift. The lads up here shovelled the sand into sacks and arranged them in regulation fashion. There was a crowd of rubberneckers in the car park, but they kept their distance, they didn't ask any questions. They could see there was work going on; they were intrigued; they wondered what was happening. We put it around that we were re-laying the flagstones and the tiles. They all nodded. "High time, too," they said. We had a good laugh. They never imagined that up here we were filling sacks and setting them at firing angles, like we used to do over there. Practical geometry, that's the art of fortification. You keep the firing lines clear, avoid the blind spots, you take control of the space. We now control the whole area around Voracieux. We organize sentry duty. When the day comes, we'll serve as a fire support base. And I've put a thick layer of sand under my bed to serve as a flak jacket in case of an attack from below. I never did trust ceilings. This way, I sleep in peace.'

After that, thankfully, he gave me a drink and we sprawled on the overstuffed sofas and watched sport on the TV. Mariani's lads did not say much; nor did I. The commentators did all the talking.

'Irish people can't be black,' Mariani went on. 'Otherwise nothing means anything any more. Could people make camembert with camel's milk? And could you still call it camembert? Or wine out of redcurrant juice? Would anyone dare to call that wine? The whole *appellation d'origine contrôlée* idea should apply to people. A man is more important than a cheese, and just as connected to the land. An AOC would put an end to farces like black Irishmen winning races.'

'Look, I'm sure he's naturalized.'

'That's what I'm saying: he's Irish on paper. But it's blood that determines nationality, not paper.'

'Blood is blood, Mariani; it's red.'

'Always the dumb painter! I'm talking about true blood, not about the red paint that flows from the slightest scratch. Blood will out. The only kind that matters.

'Words don't mean anything any more,' he sighed. 'The dictionary is a wasteland, like a forest that's been hacked down. Great trees have been felled and replaced by shrubs, all of them the same, thorny softwoods with toxic sap. And what have we done with the great trees? What have we done with the colossi that sheltered us? What have we done with these wonders that took centuries to grow? We turned them into throwaway chopsticks and garden furniture. Beauty has crumbled into absurdity.

'There should be no more talk, Salagnon, because it's impossible to speak with ruined words. We have to get back to what's real. We have to return to reality. It has to happen. In the real world, at least every man can count on his own strength. Power, Salagnon, the power we once had and let slip through our fingers. The life force that drained from the bodies of our fallen comrades and is still leeching out of us now we've come home. That's the reason for the sandbags and the guns: to prevent that force from leaking away.'

'You've got guns here?' Salagnon's voice grew hoarse with worry.

'Of course we do! Stop being so naive. And real weapons, not the kind of popguns you use for shooting squirrels. Guns that kill, weapons of war.' He turned to me. 'Have you ever seen a weapon of war? Held it, handled it, tested it? Fired it?'

'Leave him out of this, Mariani.'

'You can't leave him out of reality, Salagnon. Teach him to paint if you like, I'll teach him about weapons.'

He got up and came back, carrying a large semi-automatic revolver.

'A pistol, to be precise. It's a Colt .45. I keep it under my bed for personal protection. It takes 11.43-calibre rounds. I don't know why we've adopted such warped measures, but they're big bullets. I feel safer with big bullets, especially when I'm asleep. There's nothing worse than being defenceless when you're asleep; nothing worse than waking up and being helpless. So, if you know that you've got a solution under your bed, if you know that in an instant you can reach for a large semi-automatic pistol, locked and loaded, then you can defend yourself, you can survive, come back to reality by force; then you can sleep soundly.'

'Is sleeping really so dangerous?'

'Someone can cut your throat in a few seconds. Over there, we slept with one eye open. We took turns keeping watch over each other. Closing both eyes meant taking a risk. Nowadays, here is "over there". That's why I occupy the high ground. I've had my lads fortify the post, I see them coming from every side.'

From under the sofa he took out an impressive weapon, a sniper rifle fitted with a telescopic sight. 'Come and look.' He led me over to the window, leaned on the sandbags, slipped the barrel through one of the arrow slits and aimed it outside. 'Hold it.' I held it. Guns are heavy objects. You can feel the weight of the compact metal in your hand; the slightest touch gives you a shock. 'Look down there. The red car.' A garish sports cars looked out of place beside the other cars. 'She's mine. No one touches her. They know I keep watch, day and night. I've got a night-vision scope, too.' The telescopic sight worked perfectly. You could see the people coming and going eighteen floors below, oblivious to anything. The sights framed the head and torso, and crosshairs made it possible to decide where the bullet would go.

'No one touches my car. It's alarmed and, day or night, I'm ready to put a bullet in someone's head. They know me. They watch their step.'

'Who are you talking about?'

'Don't you see them? I can recognize them at a glance: from the way they stand, from the smell, the sounds. I recognize them instantly. They call themselves French and defy us to prove that they're not. As proof, they wave what they call an ID card and what I call a scrap of paper. A Get Out of Jail Free card offered by an administration that's been compromised and infiltrated.'

'Infiltrated?'

'Salagnon, you need to teach your boy about more than painting. He knows nothing about the world. He thinks that reality is what it says on paper.'

'Cut it out, Mariani.'

'Look, there they are! Eighteen floors down. They're everywhere, but I can follow them with the sights. Just as well, because when the time comes, *bang! bang!* They multiply like rabbits. They're given nationality as fast as the photocopiers can duplicate a scrawl on a scrap of paper, and when that happens there's nothing we can do. They multiply under cover of that meaningless phrase that looms over us like a dead tree: "French national". No one knows what the term means any more. But I can tell who is French, I can see it in the crosshairs, just like I did over there; it's easy to spot and easy to deal with. So why talk for the sake of talking? All you need is a few determined men and we can put an end to the legal bullshit standing in our way, the pernicious prattle confusing everyone and a society of like minds can finally govern with common sense. That's my political policy: common sense, force, efficiency, give power to people who trust each other; my policy is the naked truth.'

I nodded. I nodded without thinking, nodded without understanding. He had left me holding the rifle and I looked into the gunsight so I did not have to look at him, and I followed the people eighteen floors below, followed their heads engraved with black crosshairs. I nodded. He carried on; I made him laugh, holding the rifle so seriously. 'You're getting a taste for it, am I right?' I knew I should put down the gun but I couldn't; my hands were fused to the metal, my eye to the sights, as though, for a laugh, someone had smeared the gun with superglue before handing it to me. I followed people's eyes and my eye inscribed their faces with a cross, a cross they had no idea existed, one that never left them. The metal grew warm to the touch, the gun responded to my every movement, the sights became one with my eye. The rifle is the man. 'Look, Salagnon, the lad's just had his first shooting lesson from me. To look at him, you would think he had a place in a command post. Let's leave him at the window, with him standing guard, we're safe.' Mariani's lads burst out laughing, a bellowing laugh that set their paunches quivering; they laughed at me and I blushed so hard my cheeks were scorched. Salagnon got to his feet without a word and led me away like a child.

'They're fucking crazy, aren't they?' I said, as soon as the lift doors had closed. The cabin of a lift is not very large, but it is not worrying when the doors close. The little room is well lit and furnished with mirrors and a carpet. When the doors close you don't feel claustrophobic, you feel rather reassured. The corridors in the tower block where Mariani lived, on the other hand, awaken latent fears of the dark: the lights are smashed and the corridors wind, windowless, through the building and you quickly lose your sense of direction and fumble around for doors. You don't know where you're going.

'Pretty crazy,' he said indifferently, 'but I have a soft spot for Marini.'

'Even so, guys with guns, turning an apartment into a fortified bunker...'

'They've got lots more like them, and things never get out of hand. Mariani keeps them in check. They dream of living the life Mariani lived, and since he's already lived it, he can control them. When he dies, they won't know what to dream about. They'll disperse. When the last player from the colonial caravanserai is dead, GAFFES will disband. No one will even remember it once seemed possible.'

'That sounds optimistic to me. We've got lunatics armed to the teeth in a residential tower block and you just dismiss it out of hand.'

'They've been there fifteen years. They haven't fired a single shot outside the rifle club, where they've got official membership cards with their real names and photos. Any fuck-ups have been accidents that would have happened with or without them; in fact, there would probably have been more.'

Soundlessly, with no reference points, the lift brought us back to earth. I found Salagnon's calmness exasperating.

'I find your calmness exasperating.'

'I'm calm by nature.'

'Even when dealing with bullshit like that, guys with a taste for war, a taste for death?'

'There's a lot of bullshit in this world. I've got my fair share. I'm no longer intimidated by war; and as for death, well, I don't give a shit about death. Nor does Mariani. That's why I have a soft spot for him. You don't know what you're saying. You know nothing about death, and you can't imagine what it's like for someone not to give a shit about it. I've seen men who didn't give a flying fuck about dying. I've lived with them. I'm one of them.'

'Only lunatics are not afraid to die, and even then... only a certain kind of madman.'

'I didn't say I'm not afraid, just that I don't care about my own death. I see it. I know where it is and I don't care.'

'That's just talk.'

'Actually, it's not. I've lived with that disregard. I've witnessed it in others. It is unequivocal and horrifying. Over there, I took part in a charge of legionnaires.'

'A charge? People still charge in the twentieth century?'

'It just means to advance on an enemy position that is firing at you. I've seen it, I was there, but I hid behind a rock. I kept my head down, like everyone does the first time, but they charged, by which I mean that at their officer's command, these guys stood up and advanced. They're being fired on, they know they could be shot, could die at any minute, but they advance. They don't even run: they march, shooting from the hip, firing as though this were a manoeuvre. I've done it myself. I've charged an enemy firing on me, but in that case you scream, you run; screaming means you don't have time to think, running makes you believe you're dodging bullets. But that's not what these men do: they stand up and they calmly advance. If they die, tough luck; they know that. Some men fall, others don't, and they carry on. It's a terrifying spectacle, watching men who don't care whether they die. War is based on fear and protection, so when these guys stand up and advance it is genuinely terrifying; normal rules have been suspended; this is not war. More often than not, the guys they were advancing on, the ones who were protected, they turned and ran. They were scared shitless and they ran. Sometimes they stood their ground and it ended in hand-to-hand combat, fighting with knives, rifle butts, stones. The legionnaires care as little about other men's deaths as they do about their own. They kill a man the same way they might sweep a floor. They call it scrubbing the enemy position; they talk about it like it was taking a shower. I've seen men drop dead from exhaustion so as not to slow down their comrades. I've seen them hang back to slow down the enemy pursuing them. And they all knew what they were doing. These men have stared into the sun, their retinas are burned out; they set something on the ground, their kitbag for example, and they stand there, fully aware of what will happen. I have been privileged to see such things. Afterwards, nothing had the same meaning: fear, death, man, nothing.'

I did not know what to say. The lift stopped with a little spasm and the door opened. We stepped out into the hallway where a gang of youths were hanging around.

He walked through the group without breaking his stride, not slowing, not speeding up, not bowing his head or straightening up. He walked through the crowded hallway as through an empty room, stepping over the legs of a lad sitting across the doorway with a polite apology so perfectly judged that the boy automatically apologized and pulled up his knees.

They didn't care about their deaths, he had said; I was not sure what exactly that could mean. Maybe they set something down on the ground, as he put it, and then nothing moved. The youths nodded at us and we responded, but they did not interrupt their conversation as we passed.

When we got outside, it was snowing. Hands in the pockets of our coats, we strolled through the empty streets of Voracieux; streets empty of everything, devoid of people, devoid of buildings, devoid of beauty, of life; shabby streets that are little more than the empty spaces between tower blocks; streets run down by constant use and little maintenance. The streets of Voracieux are as disorganized as a city in the East: everything is random, nothing goes with anything. Even people, in these streets, seem out of place. Even vegetation, which, as a rule, naturally finds its own balance: there were weeds where the ground should be bare, while tracks of bare earth snaked across the lawns. The snow falling that night made everything whole. It covered all things, drawing them together. A parked car became a pure mass, made of the same substance as a shrub, a low shed housing a convenience store, a bus shelter where no one waited, a kerb that ran the length of the avenue. All these things were transformed into paper-white shapes, sharp edges smoothed, textures unified, transitions obliterated; each object appeared as a simple presence, a swelling beneath the same vast blanket, they were sisters under the snow. Strangely, being hidden united them. For the first time we walked through a harmonized Voracieux, a silent Voracieux suffocated with white, all things afforded an equal life by the soothing snow. We walked in silence. Snowflakes, pressed against our coats, clung for an instant to the wool, then dissolved and disappeared.

'So what do they actually want, GAFFES?'

'Oh, they have simple wants, nothing but common sense: they want to settle things between men. As happens in small groups where there are no laws. They want the strong to be strong, the weak to be weak; they want the difference to be obvious; they want the obvious to be the guiding principle of government. They don't want to argue, because it's impossible to debate the obvious. For them, the use of force is the only worthwhile action, the only truth, because it requires no words.'

He said no more, this seemed sufficient. We wandered through Voracieux, calmed by the snow that covers all things. In the silence the 10,000 people were no more than wrinkles in a single white shape. Objects did not exist, they were merely the illusion of white, while we, in our dark coats, the only movement, were ink brushes traversing the empty space, leaving behind two streaks of dirty snow.

By the time we came to his garden the snow had begun to peter out. Snowflakes descended, less heavy now, fluttering rather than falling, and, without our noticing, the last flakes were absorbed into the purplish air. It was over.

He opened the squeaking gate and he looked ahead at the expanse of white that hugged the bushes, the flowerbeds, the patch of lawn and a few things it was impossible to identify. 'You see, just when you come to my garden gate, the snow stops and in that moment the mantle is perfect; it will never be more perfect. Do you want to stay out here with me for a bit?'

We stood in silence, looking at nothing in particular, the garden of a suburban house in Lyon covered with a thin layer of snow. The glowing street lamps glinted purple. 'I wish it would last, but it never does. You see this perfection? It's already passing. As soon as the snow stops falling, it subsides, it melts, it disappears. The miracle of presence lasts only for the instant it appears. It's terrible, but we must delight in the presence and expect nothing of it.'

We walked along the paths. The light dusting of snow sank beneath our feet, each footstep accompanied by a wonderful sound that combined the crunch of sand and the sigh of settling feathers in a huge eiderdown. 'Everything is perfect and simple. Look at the roofs, how they end in a graceful curve. Look at the flowerbeds, how they melt into the pathways. Look at the washing line, how beautifully it stands out: we can see it now.'

A tall, narrow, uninterrupted band of snow had settled on the line, strung between two posts, and balanced there perfectly. It followed the sweep of the curve with a single stroke. 'Snow unintentionally traces the sort of lines I would love to trace. It knows without knowing how to follow the line perfectly, impeccably accentuating the sweep of the curve; it describes the washing line better than it can itself. If

I had wanted to arrange snow on a line, I could not have done it as beautifully. I am unable to deliberately do what the snow achieves by its indifference. Snow can draw washing lines in the air, because it doesn't care about the line. It falls and, following the three basic laws of gravity, temperature and wind speed, and perhaps the law of humidity, it traces curves that I cannot match with all my skill as a painter. I am jealous of the snow. I would give anything to paint like that.'

The garden furniture, a circular table and two painted metal chairs were also covered by cushions so precise that it would have been difficult to cut and sew them as perfectly with a measuring tape. Beneath the snow these decrepit pieces of furniture, with spots of rust showing through the flaking paintwork, had become masterful works of harmony. 'If I could achieve that same indifference I would truly be a great painter. I would be at peace. I would paint the things around me and I would die in peace.'

He walked over to the table covered by a flawlessly proportioned eiderdown, fashioned simply by the forces of nature. 'Look how beautiful the world is when you let it be. And how fragile.'

He scooped up a handful of snow, compacted it and threw it at me. Instinctively, I ducked, more because of the gesture than to avoid the projectile, and when I stood up again, surprised, the second snowball hit me square in the forehead. It settled on my eyebrows and immediately began to melt. I wiped my eyes and he ran off, scooping up snow as he ran, which he scarcely took the time to shape into balls before throwing them; I gathered my own ammunition and set off after him. We ran through the garden, shouting; we laid waste the whole mantle of snow and threw it at each other, taking less and less time to tamp it, aiming less and less carefully, throwing less and less far, shivering and laughing in the cloud of powdery snow.

It ended when he caught me from behind and dropped a fistful of ice harvested from a branch down the back of my coat. I gave a high-pitched yell, choking with laughter, and sat down hard on the cold ground. He stood in front of me, struggling to catch his breath. 'I got you, I got you... but we have to stop. I can't keep this up. And anyway, we've already thrown all the snow.'

We had spoiled everything, trampled everything, a jumble of criss-crossing footprints with amorphous piles of dirty snow between.

'Time to go inside,' he said.

'Shame about the snow.'

I got to my feet and tried to smooth one of the piles with my foot; it no longer looked like anything.

'And there's no way to put it back.'

'You just have to wait for another snowfall. It always falls perfectly, but it's impossible to imitate.'

'Better not to touch it at all.'

'You're right, don't move, don't walk, just stare and be satisfied to contemplate its perfection. The problem is, as soon as it stops falling, it starts to disappear. Time ticks on and the magnificent bas-relief dissolves. Such beauty cannot bear for us to be alive. Let's go in.'

We went in. We shook out our shoes and hung up our coats.

'Children are the ones who love to announce that it's snowing. They run around, they shout, and it sets off a joyous frenzy of activity: parents smile and fall silent, schools close, the whole landscape becomes a playground that can be modelled. The world becomes soft and malleable; you can do anything without worrying about anything, there will be time enough to dry off later. It lasts as long as you are filled with wonder. It lasts as long as it takes to say the words. It lasts as long as it takes to say "It's snowing", then it's over. So it goes with dreams of order, young man. Now, let's go and paint.'

In brush-ink drawing the most important strokes are those the artist does not make. These leave a void and only the void can create space: the void space causes the eye, and hence the mind, to move. Drawing is a series of skilfully placed voids, it exists first and foremost as that movement of the eye. The ink, ultimately, is superfluous to the drawing, you paint with nothingness.

'I find your Chinese paradoxes irritating.'

'But any truth that is remotely interesting can be expressed only in paradoxes. Or demonstrated with actions.'

'But given what you're saying, you could just remove the lines. A blank page would do.'

'Yes.'

'Oh, very clever.'

Through the window the devastated garden gently gleamed, a glow marbled with irregular black streaks.

'Such a drawing would be perfect, but too fragile. Life leaves a lot of traces.'

I did not persist. I went back to painting. I made fewer strokes than was my habit or my intention; it was no more difficult. And the remaining strokes traced themselves around the deeper white. Life is what remains; what the ink has not obliterated.

I returned to the fray; because they worried me, the home-grown sectarians with their guns camped out high above the roofs.

'Mariani's a dangerous guy, don't you think? His lads have weapons of war and they aim them at people.'

'It's all show. They amuse themselves and they take pictures of each other. They'd like to imagine that people seeing them are physically afraid. But in the fifteen years they've been play-acting, they haven't had a single victim, if you don't include the skirmishes that would have occurred with or without them. The damage they do bears no relation to the arms they possess.'

'You don't take them seriously?'

'Of course not; but when people listen to them, they become horribly serious, and that's the worst part. What GAFFES has been saying for the past fifteen years has had more effect than their flabby muscles and their prop guns or the cosh they carry around in their car.'

'And race?'

'The stuff about race is all hot air. A curtain hung across the room as a screen for a shadow theatre. The lights go down, you take your seats, and all that's left is a lantern casting shadows. The show starts. People howl, they clap, they laugh, they boo the villains and cheer the good guys; but they're talking to shadows. They have no idea what's going on behind the screen; they believe in the shadows. Behind the screen are the real actors we cannot see, behind the screen they deal with the real problems, which are always social. When I hear a guy like you talking about race with that heroic quiver in his voice, I realize that GAFFES has won.'

'But I'm opposed to everything they stand for.'

'When you oppose, you take part. Your inflexibility is a comfort to them. Race is not something that exists in nature; it exists only if you talk about it. By dint of talking about it GAFFES has convinced people that race is the problem we are most concerned about. They spout hot air and everyone thinks there's a hurricane. A wind can be measured by its effects, so from racism we deduce that race exists. They've won; everyone thinks like them – they don't give a shit whether they're for or against: people once again believe in the division of humanity. I can understand why my Eurydice is furious and despises them with all the passion of Bab El Oued. I took her away from a life you can't imagine, one that they want to recreate here, just as they did over there.'

'But what do they want?'

'They just want to want, and for that to have an effect. They want strong men to have free rein. They want a natural order in which every-one has their place and for that place to be obvious. Up there on the eighteenth floor of Mariani's tower block they've created a commune, which, in modern France, is the dream of what life was like over there. The use of force was permitted; you could flout laws and laugh it off. You did what you had to do in the company of men you knew. Trust was earned within an instant; you could read it in their faces. Social relations were power-based and you could see it in action.

'The dream of forming a pack. They want to live like *commandos de chasse*. For them, the vanished Eden is a group of lads living in the mountains, rifles slung over their backs, commanded by a captain. Not that such things didn't exist, but you can't turn a whole country into a boy scout camp. And it's tragic to think that, in the end, we lost. Force never admits defeat: when the use of force fails, people think that if they'd used a little more force, they might have won. So they try again, harder this time, they lose again, there are a few more casualties. Force never understands and those who use force brood over their failures, they dream of trying again.

'Over there, things were simple. Our lives depended on force: people utterly unlike us were trying to kill us. And so were we. We had to defeat them or escape them; success or failure; our lives were as straightforward as a game of dice. War is simple. Do you know why war is never-ending? Because it is the simplest form of reality. Everyone wants war, it simplifies things. When it comes down to it, we like the knots entangling our lives to be cut by force. Having an enemy is the most precious of possessions, it offers us a fulcrum. In the forests of Tonkin we hunted the enemy so that we could finally do battle.

'This model for a solution to all life's problems comes from the beating we give a child, the kick we give a dog. It is a release. When people annoy us, we all dream of using force to make them see reason, like a dog, like a child. People who refuse to do what we tell them need to be put in their place by force. It's the only language they understand. Over there, we governed by common sense through beating, which is the most unambiguous social act. It is tragic to forget that in the end we lost; it is tragically stupid to think that with a little more force we would have succeeded. Mariani and his lads are the disconsolate orphans of power; it is a tragic mistake to take them seriously, because their seriousness taints us. They force us to talk about their ghosts, and in doing so we cause them to reappear, to linger.

'I understand Eurydice's anger. When she sees Mariani she wants to put a stake through his heart so that he never comes back, so that he disappears and all his ghosts with him. When he comes here, "over there" comes back to haunt us; when we spend our lives trying not to think about it. I understand Eurydice's anger, but Mariani carried me through the jungle.'

'And that's enough? It's not much.'

'Where would you find more? Friendship is the result of a single gesture. It is given in an instant and, once given, it rolls on; it will not change direction unless something major knocks it off course. The guy who patted your shoulder at a particular moment is someone you will love for ever, much more than the person you talk to every morning. Mariani carried me through the jungle, and I can still feel the jolting pain in my leg every time the dumb fucker tripped on a root. You would have to cut my leg off to make me forget it. I was wounded, and he was wounded in a place where I was left unscathed. We see each other as two crippled men who know the reason why.

'I don't like his "lads", but I can understand why he hangs around with them. The GAFFES' political views are moronic, pure and simple. But I can understand that kind of stupidity. They learned it over there, where we never managed to govern. De Gaulle used to call them braggarts, the guys over there, and in his treachery he was often right. Over there, men bragged. Power was elsewhere. They relied on that power without having it, and when things turned nasty they called in the army. They had no idea how to govern; they didn't even know what the word meant: they issued orders, and at the slightest challenge they lashed out; like slapping a child, like beating a dog; and if the dog got its hackles up, if it looked like it might bite, they called in the army. And the army meant me, Mariani and a lot of other guys, most of whom are dead: we would do our best to put the dog down. Some job! Mariani believed in it and he never got over it; me, I think painting saved me. I wasn't as good a soldier, but I saved my soul.

'Dog killer,' he muttered. 'And when the dogs died, they looked at me with the eyes of the men they had been all along. Some life. If I had children, I don't know how I could bring myself to tell them about it.

But I'm telling you. I don't know if you understand; like everyone else, you don't understand anything about France.'

'Not that again,' I groaned, 'not that again.'

I was irritated by the France with the big, emphatic 'F', the capital 'F' you can hear when De Gaulle pronounces it, a pronunciation no one dares use nowadays. That big 'F' is something no one understands any more. I'm sick and tired of the big 'F' I've been talking about ever since I met Victorien Salagnon. I'm sick and tired of the preposterous, misbegotten capital 'F' that is spoken with a hiss of menace and utterly incapable of balancing: if it leans to the right, it topples, dragged down by the weight of its asymmetric bars; 'F' can only stand upright if forcibly supported. Ever since I met Victorien Salagnon, I've been talking about that big 'F' at every opportunity. I've ended up talking about France, capital 'F', as much as de Gaulle, that barefaced liar, that brilliant novelist, who, with the stroke of a pen, with a single word, made us believe that we were victors, when we were no longer anything at all. By a literary tour de force he transformed our humiliation into heroism: who would have dared disbelieve him? We believed him: he said it so persuasively. It felt so good. We sincerely believed that we had fought. And when we took our seat at the victors' table, we brought our dog along to emphasize our wealth, and gave it a kick to demonstrate our power. The dog whimpered, we hit it again, and then it bit us.

France is pronounced with a faulty letter, as cumbersome as the Général's cross at Colombey. We find it hard to pronounce the word: the unequivocal grandeur of the upper-case 'F' makes it difficult to correctly inflect the crowd of lower-case letters following behind. The capital 'F' exhales, the rest of the word has trouble breathing, how then can we go on talking?

What is there to say?

France is a way of expiring.

Everyone here sighs. We recognize one another by our sighs, and those who are weary of sighing go elsewhere. I don't understand them, the ones who leave; they have their reasons. I know them, but I do not understand them. I do not know why so many French people go elsewhere, why they forsake this place, the 'here' I cannot imagine leaving, I do not know what makes them want to go. But they are leaving in droves; the statistics clearly show they are emigrating. There are almost a million and a half of them, 5 per cent of the electorate, 5 per cent of the working population, a sizeable group of us, running away.

I could never go elsewhere. I could never breathe without the language that is my breath. I cannot do without my breath. Others can, it seems, and I cannot understand that. So I asked an expatriate who was here for a few days' holiday before going back there, where he earned more money than I could dare dream of, I asked him: 'Don't you want to move back?' He didn't know. 'Don't you miss life here?' Because I know that elsewhere people love life here, they often say as much. 'I don't know,' he said with a faraway look. 'I don't know whether I'll move back. But I know' (here his voice became more self-assured and he looked me in the eye) 'I know that I'll be buried in France.'

I was so surprised that I didn't know how to respond, although 'respond' is not the right word: I didn't know how to carry on the conversation. We talked about other things, but it has been preying on my mind ever since.

He lives elsewhere, but he wants to be dead in France. I had assumed that a dead body, stricken by ataraxy and deafness, by anosmia, blindness and a general insensibility, is indifferent to the ground where it decays. This is what I believed, but no, even in death the body clings to the earth that nurtured it, that saw it take its first steps, heard it stammer its first words with that characteristic way of modulating the breath. Much more than a way of life, France is a way of expiring, a way of almost dying, an incoherent hiss followed by little, muted sobs.

France is a way of death. Life in France is a never-ending Sunday that ends in tears.

That never-ending Sunday intrudes early on a child's sleep. The window is briskly opened, the shutter thrown wide and light floods in.

We sit up with a start, blinking in the light, longing to curl up in the sheet rumpled by the night that no longer fits snugly with the blanket, only to be told to get up. We get up, eyes puffy, shuffling slowly. Thick *tartines* are cut from a large baguette; we dunk them and the sight is faintly disgusting. We have to drain the large bowl, cradling it in both hands, holding it before our faces for a long time.

Clean clothes are laid out on the bed, clothes we do not often wear, not enough to make them soft, to become fond of them; but we must put them on, taking care not to crease or dirty them. They are never exactly the right size, because we rarely wear them and they last too long. Having been worn only infrequently, the shoes are too tight; the stiff uppers cut into the ankle and the tendon, making holes in the socks.

We are all set. The discomfort and the awkwardness are not visible; the outfit looks perfect, we are beyond reproach. We polish the shoes, which have already begun to pinch, but so what? We will not be walking far.

We go to church. We join the congregation – 'we' is no one in particular. We go together, and it would be such a pity if we were not there. We stand, we sit, we sing like everyone else, badly, but the only escape is not to be there, and so we sing, badly. Outside the church we make polite small talk; the shoes are painful.

We buy cakes and have them packed in stiff, white cardboard boxes tied with ribbon. We hold the box delicately, one finger hooked through the loop in the ribbon. We are careful not to shake the box, since inside there are miniature castles of cream, caramel and butter. These will be the culmination of the substantial meal already simmering at home.

It is Sunday. Shoes hurt. We sit where we are told to sit. Everyone sits down in front of a plate, we each have our own; we sit down with a sigh of contentment, although it could just as easily be weariness, resignation, you never can tell with sighs. Everyone is here, although we might wish we were elsewhere; no one wants to come, but we would be mortified not to have been invited. No one wants to be here, but we dread being left out; being here is tedious, but not being here would be agony. And so we sigh, we eat. The meal is good, but too long and too heavy. We eat a lot. Much more than we would have liked, but we feel pleasure and gradually belts tighten. Food is not merely a pleasure, it is a substance, it has weight. Shoes hurt. Belts dig into bellies, making breathing difficult. Before we even leave the table we feel queasy and long for some fresh air. We are sitting with these people for all time and we wonder why. And so we eat. We ask ourselves. Just as the answer comes, we swallow. We never answer. We eat.

What do we talk about? About what we are eating. We anticipate it, we prepare it, we eat it: all the time we talk about it. What we eat occupies the mouth in more ways than one. While we eat, the mouth is busy saying nothing; we keep it busy so we cannot talk, to finally fill this bottomless tube that opens outwards, opens inwards, this mouth that, alas, we cannot plug. We busy ourselves filling it, to justify the fact that we have nothing to say.

The shoes pinch, but under the table they cannot be seen, merely felt, so it is of no importance. Belts are loosened a notch, discreetly or with a raucous belly laugh. Under the table, the shoes pinch.

Then comes the promenade. We dread it, because we do not know where to go, so we go somewhere obvious; we long to walk, because we cannot breathe in here. We will walk with hesitant steps, reluctant steps that scarcely inch forwards, a shuffle stumbling at ever step. Nothing is less interesting than a Sunday walk, all together. We get nowhere; footsteps trickle like the listless sands of time; we pretend to move forwards.

Eventually we come home, take a little nap; this we do lying on our back with the window open. Throwing ourselves on the bed, we finally kick off the shoes, the shoes that pinched, we rip them off and toss them at the foot of the bed. Shirt collars are unbuttoned, belts opened, we lie on our back, because our bellies are too swollen. Very slowly the heat outside dies down.

The heart beats a little too fast from the effort of coming upstairs to the bedroom, from too quickly unbuttoning those things that restricted the belly and the throat, that kept the toes curled tight, from having jumped too eagerly on the bed with a loud sigh. The squeaking of the mattress slows, and at last we can gaze at the silent room and the tranquil outdoors. The throat beats a little too fast, struggling to push the syrupy blood that moves sluggishly, fat-rich blood that struggles to move, that slithers rather than flows. The heart works away, exhausting itself with the effort. When standing, blood naturally flowed towards the bottom; the leisurely stroll helped it to move; while sitting, at table, it was warmed by conversation, eased by volatile alcohol; but lying down, the thick blood spreads, it pools, it clogs the heart. We die without any drama of inertia, of viscous, fatty blood, because in a horizontal position nothing circulates. It is a slow process, each organ struggles on, each dies in turn.

Dying in France is a long Sunday, a gradual congealing of blood that is no longer going anywhere; that stays where it is. The dark source no longer moves, the past is frozen, nothing stirs. We die. It is better this way.

Beyond the open window the gentle splendours of twilight unfurl. Floral scents disperse and mingle; the sky that we can see in its entirety is a huge sheet of copper that quivers as the birds drum on it with tiny sticks wrapped in felt. In the gathering purple darkness, they begin to sing. We were neatly dressed. We have no stains on our shirts. We put up a good show. We took part in the feast like all the others. We are dying now from our clotting blood, from the thickening of veins and arteries blocking our circulation, from an asphyxia that chokes the heart and makes it impossible to cry out. To call for help. But who would come? Who would come at siesta time?

France is a way of dying on a Sunday afternoon. France is a way of failing to die at the last minute. Because the door bursts open; young, bullet-headed men rush into the room; they crop their hair so short that all that remains is a shadow on their skull; their shoulders stretch their clothes so taut that they rip, their muscles bulge; they are carrying heavy objects and moving quickly. They race into the room. Behind them comes another man. He is older, thinner. He barks orders, but never panics. He reassures, because he sees everything; he directs everything with his finger, with his voice; the wolves around him curb their strength. They race into the room and we feel better; they give us oxygen and we breathe; they open out a gurney and lay on it the motionless body that is about to die, pick it up and rush out. They push the wheeled stretcher down the corridor with the suffocating body strapped to it; they put it in the ambulance, whose engine has been running all the time. The gurney is adapted to all kinds of vehicle. They drive through the city much too fast; the wailing ambulance leans into the bends, runs the red lights, scorns rights of way with an arrogant wave; they are no longer following the rules, because there is no time to follow rules.

At the hospital they race down the corridors, pushing the stretcher on which lies the suffocating body. They run. They kick open the double doors, jostle those who do not get out of the way in time. Finally they arrive in the sterile room where a masked man is waiting. It is impossible to recognize him, because his face is hidden by the surgical mask, but it is clear who he is from his posture: he is so calm, so confident that he knows that in his presence no one else knows. They fall silent. He addresses the leader of the young men by his first name. They know each other. He takes charge. Around him, masked women hand him shiny instruments. Under the glare of a spotlight that casts no shadows, he cuts the artery, he operates, he sutures the gash with minuscule stitches with the troubling gentleness of a man who excels at women's work.

We wake up in a pristine room. The young, bullet-headed men have set off again to other suffocating patients. The fortunate man who knows how to wield the scalpel and the needle has pulled his mask down to his throat. He is dreaming by the window, smoking a cigarette.

The door opens soundlessly and a beautiful woman in a white coat brings a light meal on a tray. On the thick crockery the food looks like a toy: the fat-free ham, the thin slices of bread, the little mound of mashed potato, the sliver of Gruyère, the dead water. Every day the food will be like this: transparent to the point of recovery.

With their older, thinner leader, the muscular young men have headed off to another operation; the faceless master to whom they bring bodies that are all but dead, almost lifeless, saves them with a simple gesture.

This is the nature of French life: almost dying, only to be saved by the thrust of a blade. Choked by blood, by blood that has thickened until it no longer moves, then suddenly saved by a spray of bright blood spurting from the wound.

Lost, then saved. France is a peaceful almost-death and a brutal resuscitation. Though I could not explain it, I could understand why the man I asked was hesitant to come back, the exile who lived elsewhere and had no desire to return, and why he also knew that he had to be buried here.

I knew nothing about this death, this languid, gentle death, and the brutal salvation by men who are constantly running; of salvation by the scalpel thrust of a skilful man to whom one would be eternally grateful; I was not expecting it. And yet everything I was told in France, everything I have made my own through the language that courses through me, everything I know, everything that has been said, written and recounted in the language I call my own has meant that, from the beginning, I have been prepared to be saved by the use of force.

'You understand nothing about France,' Victorien Salagnon would say to me.

'Oh, but I do. It's just that I don't know how to put it into words.'

So I got to my feet, kissed him, kissed his leathery old man's cheeks, stubbled here and there with white hairs, since he no longer shaved properly; I kissed him tenderly and thanked him, and I went home.

I walked home through the empty streets of Voracieux-les-Bredins, through snow blighted by tyre tracks and footprints. When I passed a patch of undamaged snow, lawns and footpaths as yet untrammelled, I walked around, so as not to spoil it. I understood only too well how fragile was this white harmony, which, in any case, would not survive the day.

Novel V

The war in this bloody garden

T HERE IS NO CITY in the world that Salagnon despised more than Saigon. The horrendous everyday heat and the noise. To breathe is to suffocate; the air is hot and waterlogged. Open the window you think will protect you and you cannot hear yourself speak or think or breathe: the deafening roar of the street drowns out everything, even inside your head; close it again and you cannot breathe; you feel a clammy sheet wrap around your head and tighten. In his first days in Saigon he opened and closed the window of his hotel room many times, then gave up; and he lay in his boxer shorts on the damp bed; he was trying not to die. Heat is the sickness of this country; you have to acclimatize or you die from it. Better to acclimatize and gradually it subsides. You no longer think about it, so it takes you by surprise when you are called upon to do up the buttons of your jacket, make a vigorous gesture, carry even the slightest weight, lift a kitbag, climb a flight of stairs; in such moments the heat returns like a crashing wave that soaks your back, your arms, your forehead, as dark stains spread over the pale uniform. He learned to wear light clothes, to leave everything unbuttoned, to save his energy, to make sweeping gestures so that skin never touched skin.

He did not like the teeming streets, the constant noise, the swarming anthill that was Saigon; because to him, Saigon was like an anthill

319

in which an infinite number of indistinguishable people scurried here and there, for reasons he could not fathom: soldiers, unobtrusive women, gaudy women, men in identical clothing whose expressions he could not interpret, more soldiers; people everywhere you looked pulled rickshaws, human-powered vehicles; and a bewildering array of businesses on the pavements: food stalls, hawkers, barbers, toe-nail clippers, sandal repair, and nothing: dozens of crouching men in threadbare clothes, some smoking, others not, half watching the commotion, although it was impossible to know what they were think-ing. Soldiers in striking white uniforms passed, sprawled in the back of rickshaws; others sat on the terrace of the grand cafés, sometimes with other soldiers, sometimes with women with long black hair; a few sporting golden uniforms moved through the crowds in automo-biles, opening up a path with honking horns, threats and a rumble of engines, and as soon as they had passed, the crowds merged again into a teeming throng. He loathed Saigon from the very first day, because of the noise, the heat, all the horrid invasions it endured; but once outside the city, having ventured a few kilometres into the countryside with a good-natured officer keen to show him the calmer, more serene, outlying villages, some of which had swimming pools and pleasant restaurants, when he found himself in the boundless paddy fields beneath motionless clouds, he experienced such utter silence, such emptiness, that he thought he was dead; he suggested they cut short the excursion and go back to Saigon.

He preferred Hanoi, because on his first morning there he was woken by the sound of bells. It was raining; the light was grey and the chill air made him think he was elsewhere, back home, perhaps in France, although not in Lyon, because he did not want to think of anyone waiting for him in Lyon; he thought he was in another part of France, somewhere he felt at ease, a green-grey place, an imaginary place drawn from his readings. He shook himself awake and found he did not sweat while getting dressed. He was to meet someone in the hotel bar, 'after Mass' he had been told, the Mass at the cathedral; the bar in the Tonkin Grand Hôtel, a curious mixture of provincial French and far-flung colonial. In Saigon you had to squint into the light, an overexposed yellow, dotted with patches of colour; in Hanoi the light was simply grey, sometimes ominous, sometimes a beautiful melancholy grey, and the city teemed with people who wore only black. It was just as difficult to move through the streets congested with goods, carts, convoys, but Hanoi worked with a seriousness that was quietly mocked elsewhere; Hanoi worked and was never distracted from its gold; here, even war was waged seriously. The soldiers were thinner, wiry and as tense as live cables, their eyes burned in faces haggard with exhaustion; they did not dawdle; harried, economical in their movements, there was nothing extraneous in their gestures. Dressed in ragged uniforms of indeterminate colour, there was nothing Oriental or decorative about them; they moved unaffectedly, like Boy Scouts, explorers, mountaineers. One might have encountered them in the Alps, in the middle of the Sahara, in the Arctic, crossing vast wastes of stone or ice with the same unvarying tension in their gaze, the same eager leanness, the same economy of movement, because meticulousness makes it possible to survive, mistakes do not. But these things he discovered later, by then he was already a different man; his first contact with Indochine was the revolting hot wet rag that enveloped Saigon and smothered him.

The heat, the gaping wound of the Far East, had begun in Egypt at the point when the *Pasteur*, which sailed the route to Indochine, sailed into the Suez Canal. The crowded ship slowly followed the watercourse, wending its way through the desert. The inshore wind had dropped; they were no longer at sea, and it was so hot on deck that touching metal fittings was dangerous. Below decks, filled with young men who had never seen Africa, it was impossible to breathe; soldiers melted in the heat, several of them fainted. The colonial doctor brutally brought them round, bawling at them to make them understand: 'From now on you keep your bush hat and you take your salt tablets, unless you want to pass out like an idiot. How stupid would it be to set off for war and die of sunstroke? Imagine the telegram being sent to your families. If you're going to die over there, at least die in a decent fashion.' After Suez, a veil of melancholy settled over the soldiers crowded into every space aboard the ship; only now did it dawn on them that some men would not be coming back.

At night they heard loud splashes against the hull. There were rumours of legionnaires deserting. They dived in, swam, climbed the sides of the canal and, soaking wet, set off on foot into the dark desert to a different fate, and no one would hear from them again. NCOs kept watch on deck to stop men from jumping. On the Red Sea a steady breeze returned, ensuring they would not all die overwhelmed by the sweltering sun that beats down on Egypt. But heat of a different kind was waiting for them in Saigon: a sauna, a steam bath, a pressure cooker whose lid would remain firmly screwed on for the duration of their stay.

At the Cap Saint-Jacques they disembarked from the *Pasteur* and headed up the Mekong. The noun was enchanting, as was the verb; putting verb and noun together, 'heading up the Mekong', they felt the thrill of being somewhere alien, of setting out on an adventure, a feeling that quickly faded. There was not a ripple on the glassy river; it gleamed like sheet metal covered with dark oil, while the barges carrying them left a dirty trail in their wake. The flat horizon was very low, the sky came down very low, blanching at the edges of crisp white clouds that hung motionless in the air. What Salagnon saw was so flat that he wondered how they would be able to get enough footing to stand up. In the back of the barge the young soldiers, exhausted by the crossing and the heat, were dozing on their knapsacks in the sickly sweet smell of mud rising from the river. Guys in shorts with bare, tanned chests sat in the stern, scanning the banks, with tripod-mounted machine guns. Their faces expressionless, they did not even trouble to look at these brand-new tin soldiers, this herd of pale, neat men whose transhumance they were charged with, half of whom would soon be dead. Salagnon could not know that within a few months he would have the same face. The engine of the barge boomed over the water, the armour plate clattered beneath the men and the deafening roar rolled away and died on the vast Mekong, since it met no obstacle, nothing that might reverberate. Huddled with the others, silent like the others, heart in his mouth like the others, throughout the journey to Saigon he had a feeling of hellish solitude.

He was summoned by some old fogey from Cochinchine who had fixed ideas about how war should be conducted. Colonel Ducroc held meetings in his office. Lounging on a Chinese sofa, he served champagne that remained chilled until the ice cubes melted. His magnificent white uniform, elaborately embellished with gold, was a little tight, while the ceiling fan dispersed his sweat and filled the room with a scent of cooked fat and eau de Cologne; as, outside, the tropical day advanced – a series of dazzling slashes in the venetian blinds – the stench of him grew stronger. Between pudgy fingers he held out a tiny object that all but disappeared.

'You know how they say "hello" here? They say "Have you eaten rice yet?" That's how we're going to win, by focusing all of our forces on *this*.'

He squeezed his fingers, wrinkling them, but Salagnon realized that he was holding out a grain of rice.

'In this country, young man, controlling the supply of rice is vital!' he said enthusiastically. 'Because in a famine-stricken country everything is calculated in rice: numbers of men, tracts of land, the value of inheritances and the length of journeys. This yardstick by which everything is measured grows in the mud of the Mekong; so if we control the rice getting out of the delta, we can crush the rebellion, just as we might starve a fire of oxygen. It's physics, it's mathematics, it's logic. Look at it whatever way you want: by controlling the rice, we win.'

The fat folds in his face obliterated his features, unwittingly giving him an impassive, faintly pleased air; when he squinted for any reason, his eyes were transformed into two Annamese slits, making it look as though he knew whereof he spoke. The country might be vast, the population at best indifferent, his forces meagre and his equipment falling apart, but he had very fixed ideas about how to win a war in Asia. He had been living here for so long that he believed he had melded with it. 'I'm not completely French any more,' he would say with a little laugh, 'but French enough to use the statistics of the Intelligence Service. Subtlety in Asia, precision in Europe: by combining the wisdom of both worlds, we can achieve great things.' With the point of his pencil he tapped the report lying next to the champagne bucket, and the confidence of his gesture was as good as proof. The figures explained everything about rice production: production in the delta area, capacity of junks and sampans, daily consumption by combatants, maximum weight transportable by the coolies, walking speed. If you integrate these data, you realize you only need to confiscate a certain percentage of the production from the delta to tighten the noose and strangle the Viet Minh. 'And when they are dying of hunger they'll come down from the mountains. They'll come down into the plains and then we'll crush them, because we have the numbers.'

This glorious old codger gesticulated as he explained his plan; the ceiling fan turned overhead, dispersing his muggy scent, the smell of a local river, warm and perfumed and slightly sickly; behind him on the wall, the large map of Cochinchine was criss-crossed with red lines that indicated victory as certainly as an arrow indicates its own extremity. He concluded his explanation with a complicit smile that had the ghastly effect of causing his many chins to pucker and discharge an excess of sweat. But this man had the power to distribute military equipment. With a stroke of his pen, he granted Lieutenant Salagnon four men and a junk to win the rice war.

*　　*　　*

Outside, Victorien Salagnon plunged into the molten tar of the street, into the boiling air that clung to everything, filled with potent, penetrating scents. Some were scents he had never smelled before. He did not even know that a smell existed that was so pervasive, so intense that it was also taste, texture, object, the flow of fickle, mellifluous matter within him. It mingled plant and animal; it might have been the scent of some giant flower with petals of flesh, the smell of meat that oozed sap and nectar; you long to bite into it, you feel you might pass out or throw up, you do not know how to react. The streets were pervaded by the scent of pungent herbs, the scent of honeyed meats, the scent of sour fruits, the musky scent of fish that triggered a craving not unlike hunger; the smell of Saigon awakened an instinctive desire mingled with a little instinctive repulsion and a longing to know. They had to be cooking smells, because all along the street, at makeshift stalls wreathed in steam, the Annamese were eating, sitting at stained, rickety tables, worn out through too much use and too little repair; the wisps of steam all around made his mouth water, triggered the physical symptoms of hunger, although he had never smelled any of these scents before; it had to be their local food. They ate quickly from little bowls, noisily slurping soup, spearing threads and morsels using chopsticks they wielded like paintbrushes; they brought the food quickly to their mouths, drinking, sucking, moving the food around with a porcelain spoon; they ate their fill, their eyes lowered, focused on their gestures, without speaking, without pausing, without exchanging a single word with the two people sitting shoulder to shoulder on either side; but Salagnon knew that they were aware of his presence, that even with their heads lowered they were watching him; with those eyes that seem closed they were tracking his every movement through the fragrant steam, every one knew where he was, the only European on this street where he had vaguely lost his way, having taken several arbitrary turns after leaving naval headquarters, where he had just been assigned four men and the command of a wooden junk.

He did not know how to communicate with the Annamese people sitting at tables, did not know how to interpret their expressions. They were tightly packed, their eyes fixed on their bowls; their attention confined to the short trajectory of the spoon moving between the bowls they cradled and open mouths, sucking with the gurgling sound of a pump. He could not see how he might say a word to anyone, how he might notice anyone, isolate him, talk to him and him alone in this cacophonous throng of men focused on eating and nothing else.

A stiff blond head rose above the heads of dark hair bent over their bowls. He walked towards it. A tall European was eating, keeping his back straight, a legionnaire wearing a short-sleeved shirt and no hat; on either side were two Annamese, but there was no one sitting opposite, or on the empty seat where he had placed his white kepi. He ate slowly, emptying his bowls in turn and pausing momentarily after each one to sip from a small, glazed, earthenware jar. Salagnon gave a vague salute and sat down opposite him.

'I think I need help. I'd like to eat, everything smells amazing, but I don't know what to order or how to go about it.'

The other man continued to chew, keeping his back straight; he drank from the neck of his small, earthenware jar; Salagnon politely insisted, although he did not beg, he was simply curious; he wanted to be guided and once again asked the legionnaire how to go about things; around him the Annamese went on eating without raising their heads, their backs bowed, deliberating making that slurping sound; these people were so reserved, so discreet in everything, with the exception of this noise they made when they ate. Customs are unfathomable. When one of them finished, he got to his feet without looking up and another man took his place. The legionnaire nodded to his kepi on the chair.

'Already two lunches,' he said in a thick accent.

He drained the earthenware jar. Salagnon carefully moved the kepi.

'Well then, now three lunches.'

'You have money.'

'Like a solider off the boat with his pay packet.'

The other gave a terrible roar. The Annamese, busy with their soup, did not flinch, but an elderly man appeared, dressed in black like the others. The dirty dishrag tied around his waist was clearly his cook's apron. The legionnaire reeled off a list in his booming voice, his thick accent noticeable even in Vietnamese. A few minutes later the bowls arrived, coloured morsels that the sauce made glossy as though lacquered. Unfamiliar aromas floated around them like clouds of colour.

'That's fast...'

'They cook fast... Viet cook fast.' He eructated with a huge laugh, starting on another jar. Salagnon also had one. He drank. It was strong, unpleasant, slightly foul-smelling. '*Choum!* Rice wine! Like potato alcohol, but with rice.' They ate, they drank, they got dead drunk and by the time the elderly, slightly grubby cook doused the fire beneath the large black pan that was his only utensil, Salagnon could not even stand; he was bathed in a mixture of sauces, salty, spicy, sour, sweet, that had engulfed his nostrils and glistened on his sweat-drenched skin.

When the legionnaire got up, he stood almost two metres tall and had a pot belly that could have accommodated a normal man if he curled up into a ball. He was German. He had seen all of Europe and he liked it in Indochine, where it was a little warm, hotter than in Russia, but in Russia the people were annoying. His crude French ground away the words and gave everything he said a strange concision that implied more than it actually said.

'Come play now.'

'Play?'

'Chinese play all time.'

'Chinese.'

'Cholon, Chinese town. Opium, gambling and many, many whore. But careful, stay with me. If problem, shout "À moi la legion!" Always walk, even in jungle. And if not walk, make pleasure scream.'

They went on foot and it took a long time. 'We take tuk-tuk, the engine it explode!' roared the legionnaire in the teeming streets, spangled with the dim glow of lamps and candles set on the pavements, around which the Vietnamese crouched and chatted in their unfamiliar, unpredictable language, which sounded like a radio when you turn the capacitor, looking for a station lost in the ether.

The legionnaire walked without staggering. He was so massive that his drunken lurches remained within the confines of his body. Salagnon leaned against him, as he might against a wall he was using to fumble his way along, although fearing he would be crushed if the big man toppled.

They stepped into a noisy, brightly lit room in which no one paid them any heed. Crowds of people quivered around the gaming tables, where supercilious young women shuffled cards and chips, while saying as little as possible. When the die was cast or the wheel was spun, a ball of lightning would run through the crowd; the hunched Chinese players would fall silent, their eyes narrowed to thin lines, their black hair blacker, standing on end, crowned with a halo of blue sparks; and when the card was turned over, when the ball stopped, there was a shudder, a cry, a loud sigh that was at once angry and silent, and conversations suddenly started up, just as shrill and shrieking, while men took great wads of cash from their pockets and waved them like a challenge or an appeal; and the impassive young women collected the chips with a long-handled rake, which they wielded like a fan. They played again.

The legionnaire gambled away the rest of Salagnon's money, lost, and they both laughed. They wanted to go to a different room, since, behind a red-lacquered double, door people seemed to be playing for higher stakes; richer men and prettier women went in and came out; this attracted them. Two men dressed in black blocked their path by simply raising their hands; two thin men whose every muscle was visible and who both had pistols tucked into their belts. Salagnon insisted. He stepped forwards and was pushed back. He fell on his behind, furious. 'Who gives the orders here?' he roared, his voice slurred by the *choum*. The henchmen did not budge, their arms folded in front of them, not looking at him. 'Who gives the orders?' None of the players looked round; they busied themselves at the tables with their shrill cries; the legionnaire helped him to his feet and led him outside.

'Who's in charge here? This is France, isn't it? Huh? We give the orders, don't we?'

This made the legionnaire laugh.

'Funny man. Here, French only order in restaurant. Maybe not. Viet give what he give. Viet Minh order. Chinese order. French eat what he get.'

He bundled him into a rickshaw, growled instructions to an Annamese and Salagnon was driven back to his hotel.

In the morning he woke up with a throbbing head, a dirty shirt and an empty wallet. Later, someone told him that he got off lightly, that such evenings often ended with someone floating in a river, naked, their throat cut, sometimes even castrated. He never knew whether this was true or whether it was just a story people repeated; but in Indochine no one ever knew anything that was true. Like the lacquer applied layer by layer to create a form, reality was the sum of layers of lies, which, by slow accretion, took on an appearance of truth that was perfectly satisfactory.

He was given four men and a wooden junk, but the four referred only to French soldiers. The junk came with a crew of Annamese deckhands he found it difficult to put a number to: five, six, maybe seven. They dressed identically and could spend long hours utterly motionless; they disappeared without warning only to reappear, but it was impossible to tell which of them was which. It took him some time to recognize that they did not look alike.

'The Annamese are pretty loyal to us,' he had been told. 'They don't like the Viet Minh, who are mostly Tonkinese; but be careful just the same, they sometimes belong to sects or to criminal gangs, and some of them are just crooks. They might be serving their immediate interests or some long-term goal you wouldn't understand. They might even stay loyal to you. There is no way you can ever know; the only sign that you've been betrayed is if they slit your throat, but that can be a bit late.'

Afloat on the South China Sea, Salagnon learned to live in a pair of shorts and a bush hat. He became tanned like the others, his body became harder. The large fan-shaped sail swelled in sections; the ribs of the boat creaked; he could feel the beams lurching when he leaned on the bulwark, when he lay on deck in the shade of the sail, and it made him slightly nauseous.

They were never out of sight of land. They inspected the rice barges that plied the waters along the coast serving the villages of the delta. They inspected the villages built on sand, when there was sand, and otherwise raised on stilts above the muddy banks just above the waves. Sometimes they found an old flintlock musket, which they confiscated in the way they might a dangerous toy; and if one of the rice barges did not have the necessary papers, they sank it. They took the coolies aboard and set them down on the shore or, if it was not far, they tossed them into the water and left them to swim for it, cheering them on with gruff laughs as they leaned over the gunwale.

They lived bare-chested, tying a scarf around their heads. They were never without their machetes, which hung from their belts. Standing on the bulwark, hanging on to the halyard, they leaned out over the water, shielding their eyes with their hands in a striking pose that did not offer much visibility, but amused them greatly.

The villages along the coast consisted of thatched bamboo huts set on thin piles, not one of which was straight. They rarely saw men in the villages. They were told the men were out at sea, fishing, or up in the forests fetching wood, and would be back later. On the beaches, above the narrow boats that put out at night, small fish were drying on lines; the stench they gave off was disgusting, but even so it made their mouths water; it suffused the air, the food, the rice, and even the Annamese seamen, who steered the junk without a word.

Shots were fired at them from one village. They were tacking to windward, sailing close to the shore, when a shot rang out. They returned fire using the machine gun, causing one of the huts to collapse. They came about, jumped down into the shallow water, excited and suspicious. In one of the huts they found a French rifle and a half-empty box of grenades inscribed with Chinese characters. It was a small village. They razed it to the ground. It burned quickly, like crates filled with straw. They did not feel as though they were burning houses, just shacks or hayricks that quickly exploded in vivid balls of flame that roared and crackled, then dissolved into fine ash. And besides, the villagers were not crying. They stood in a tight group on the beach: women, small children, old men – all the young men were missing. They bowed their heads, they muttered a little; only a handful of women let out a high-pitched wail. All this seemed so unlike war. What they were doing looked nothing like an abuse of power, like those historical paintings of villages being burned. They were simply destroying huts; a whole village of huts. They stood, watching the flames, their feet sinking into the sand. The huts collapsed, sending up glimmering sparks, and the smoke disappeared into the sky so vast, so blue. They had not killed anyone. They climbed aboard the junk again, leaving behind a row of charred stilts sticking out of the sand.

They used the Chinese grenades to fish in the river. They scooped the dead fish out with their hands and the Annamese cooked them in a chilli so hot that they cried just at the smell, howled as they ate, but they were determined not to leave a crumb; they rinsed between mouthfuls with warm wine and together cleaned the huge communal plate from which they were eating, the four soldiers in shorts and Lieutenant Salagnon. They fell asleep, feeling sick and drunk, and the Annamese deckhands steered the junk without a word, sailing out to sea, where they threw up, to the open sea where the wind quickly sobered them. When he awoke, Salagnon's first thought was that the deckhands had been loyal to him. He smiled at them a little foolishly and spent the rest of the day silently clearing his headache.

They encountered the Viet Minh at the bend of a creek. A line of men dressed in black were unloading a junk, wading up to their chests in water, each balancing a green crate on his head. From the bank an officer in a pale uniform shouted orders. Next to him an orderly was taking notes on a writing tablet; the men in black crossed the beach with their crate and disappeared behind the dunes like a mirage in the rippling heat haze. The five Frenchmen were thrilled. They hoisted a black flag made from a pair of Viet pyjamas, and sailed straight at the anchored junk. The officer pointed to them, shouted, soldiers in palm-leaf helmets leapt from behind the dune, jumped down on to the beach and unlimbered a machine gun. A neat line of bullets punctured the bulwark; they did not hear the gunfire until after the impact. A mortar shell erupted from the junk and exploded in the water in front of them. Another burst of gunfire ripped down the sail, shattering the wooden battens. The Annamese sailors let go of the shrouds and took shelter behind the splintered bulwark. Salagnon set down the machete hindering him and grabbed his revolver in its canvas holster. A fresh salvo of bullets embedded themselves in the mast; the whole junk juddered; the untethered sail began to luff. There was no wind in her now, they were drifting, they were about to run aground. The Annamese chattered briefly. One of them asked a question. Salagnon thought it sounded like a question, although in a tonal language it was difficult to tell. They hesitated. Salagnon cocked his revolver. He glanced at them, then he grabbed the halyard, took the rudder and beat to windward. The sail immediately swelled, the junk gave a start and they moved off. 'Nothing broken?' said Salagnon. 'All fine, Lieutenant,' said the others, getting to their feet. Through the binoculars they watched the men continue to unload crates. They did not seem in any great hurry: the orderly went on scribbling on his writing tablet; the line of men carried the last of the boxes past the dunes. 'I don't think we're scaring them,' sighed the soldier with the binoculars.

In the distance they saw the other junk slowly cast off and disappear beyond a headland; they tossed the black flag into the sea with their scarves and the century-old muskets they had confiscated, then packed the machetes away with their bush kit. The Annamese sailors manoeuvred skilfully, despite the rips in the sail. They headed back to the naval port and there was no more talk of the rice battle. They gave back the junk.

'It's not serious, this pirate lark of yours.'

'Not my idea. It came from Duroc in Saigon.'

'Duroc? Not there any more. Sent back to France. Ravaged by malaria, addled with opium, a roaring alcoholic. A bonehead of the old school. You're being sent to Hanoi. That's where the war is.'

In Hanoi Colonel Josselin de Trambassac affected an air of nobility: a gentleman with Cistercian tastes, a Knight of the Cross in his crusader castle, facing down the Saracen hordes; he worked in a spartan office, with a large map of Tonkin mounted on an easel. Coloured pins marked the location of posts, a forest of drawing pins covering the Haute-Région and the delta. When a post was under attack, he drew a red arrow pointing to it; when a post fell, he removed the pin. The pins he removed were never reused; he kept them locked in a long wooden pencil box. He knew that putting a pin in that box symbolized the burial of a young lieutenant who had come from France, and several soldiers. There were Viet back-up troops, too, but they could escape, disappear, go back to their former lives, while the lieutenant and his men would never come back, their bodies lay forgotten in the jungles of Tonkin among the smouldering rubble of their post. One last rite that could be done for them was to store this pin in a wooden box, which would quickly fill with others pins; and to take them out from time to time and count them.

Trambassac never wore the formal uniform befitting his rank; he only ever appeared in battledress, his immaculate camouflage uniform with a frayed canvas belt, the sleeves rolled up to reveal his sunburned forearms. As in a war situation, his rank was apparent only from the bars on his chest, and there were no dark sweat patches under his arms, because this wiry man did not sweat. He greeted subordinates standing with his back to the glare of the window, so that he appeared as a shadow, a shadow that talked: sitting facing him, staring into the light, the man could hide nothing.

Salagnon had relaxed his posture slightly, having been told to, and he waited. Behind him, in a wicker chair, the uncle sat, motionless.

'You know one another, I believe.'

They nodded curtly. Salagnon waited.

'I've heard of your escapade as a corsair, Salagnon. It was foolish and, more importantly, ineffective. Duroc was nothing but a reactionary old fossil, sitting behind a desk, drawing arrows on a map, and when he had coloured in the arrows, he would watch them dance, so stupefied was he by opium and by the whiskey shots between the opium pipes. But in your farcical adventure, you proved yourself resourceful and you managed to stay alive, two qualities we value extremely highly here. You're in Tonkin now. This is where the real war is. We need resourceful men who stay alive. The *capitaine* here knows you and was willing to vouch for you. I always listen to my *capitaines*, because this is their war.'

His yellow eyes gleamed in the darkness. They turned to the uncle in his wicker chair, sitting motionless in the shadows, saying nothing. He carried on.

'We're not in Kursk, nor in Tobruk, where thousands of tanks weaved across minefields, when men only mattered when they numbered a million, where thousands were killed by mistake in carpet-bombing raids. This is a war of *capitaines*, where you die by the blade, just like the Hundred Years' War, the battles led by Xaintrailles and by Rais. In Tonkin the unit of measure is the group, regardless of its size, and they are mostly small groups; and at the centre, the soul of the group, the collective soul of the men, is the *capitaine*, who spurs them on and whom they follow unquestioningly. This is a return to feudal warfare, Lieutenant Salagnon. The captain and his vassals, a few valiant knights who share his adventures, their squires and their menials. Isn't that right, Capitaine?'

'If you say so, sir.'

He always asked the uncle's opinion, seeming to mock him, but actually seeking an approval that never came; after a moment, he went on.

'What I propose, therefore, is that you form your own company and set off for war. Recruit partisans from the islands in Halong Bay. They're terrified of the Viet Minh there; they've never actually seen one. They don't know the meaning of the word "communist", so they support us. Recruit them, we'll provide you with weapons, and you head off with them to fight in the jungle.

'We're not from here, Salagnon. The climate, the sun, the terrain, we're not adapted to any of these things. That's why they're thrashing us. They know the terrain, they know how to live here, they melt into the background. Drumming up local troops means taking the war to them, beating them on their own ground with the help of people who know it as well as they do.'

In the shadows, the wicker creaked. The colonel slowly bared his teeth, which glittered in the half-light.

'Bullshit!' muttered the uncle. 'Bullshit!'

'Bluntness is the natural language of *capitaines*, and one we heartily encourage. But would you care to explain to Lieutenant Salagnon exactly what you mean?'

'Colonel, only fascists really believe in the spirit of place, in the idea that man is rooted in the land.'

'I believe it, and I can tell you that I am not a... fascist, as you put it.'

'Of course you believe in it. I'm guessing your family name dates back to the Middle Ages. There's probably some corner of France named after you. But the earth does not exude a vapour that shapes the soul and strengthens the body.'

'If you say so...'

'The Tonkinese don't know the jungles any better than we do. They're peasants from the delta. Their shack, their paddy field, that's the only terrain they know. And the Viet Minh are no more familiar with the mountains they're holed up in than we are. The reason they're thrashing us is because they outnumber us, because they're driven by rage, because they're inured to hardship and, more importantly, to unconditional obedience. When we can spend three days in a hole in the ground because a superior officer tells us to, when we can lie silently in the mud with nothing to eat but a bowl of cold rice, when we can leap out of that hole when a whistle blows to be gunned down, then we will be like them, then we'll have what you call an understanding of the terrain; that's when we will beat them.

'And even if these were people of the jungle, I maintain that a soldier who has been trained and motivated, a man who has been drilled hard, can survive better in the jungle than someone inexperienced, who has know it since childhood. The Vietnamese are not Indians, they're not hunters. They're peasant farmers hiding in the jungle. They're as lost and uncomfortable as we are, as exhausted and as ill. I know the jungle better than most of them, because I've learned to, by accepting the hunger, the silence and the obedience.'

The cat's eyes – or snake eyes – of the colonel flashed.

'Well, then, Lieutenant, you know what you have to do. Recruit, train and come back here with a company of men drilled to be obedient and to endure hunger. If hardship is what shapes a warrior then – given the means at the disposal of this task force – it is something we can give you in abundance.'

He smiled again with all his dazzling teeth and with a flick, brushed a speck of dust from his spotless battledress. The gesture was as good as a dismissal; it signalled it was time to fall out. Josselin de Trambassac had a sense of timing; he knew when decorum required him to stop, because everything that needed to be had been said. It was the business of the other to know everything else. To spell things out was vulgar.

Salagnon left, followed by the uncle, who gave a limp salute and slammed the door. They walked down the long hallway, hands clasped behind their backs, staring at the tiled floor. They met orderlies weighed down with files, tanned officers to whom they gave a faint salute, Annamese servant boys in white jackets who stepped aside as they passed, prisoners in black pyjamas who spent their days mopping the floors. Down the hallway lined with identical numbered doors, there came the echo of footsteps, the scrape of furniture being moved, the constant murmur of voices, the clatter of typewriters, the rustle of paper, angry outbursts, barked orders and the clack of shoes on concrete steps as orderlies and officers went up and down, taking them three at a time; outside, engines roared into life, making the walls shake, then drove away. A hive, thought Salagnon, a hive, the humming hub of war, where everyone did their damnedest to be modern, swift, straightforward. Efficient.

The uncle laid a reassuring hand on his shoulder. 'Where you're going, things will be a bit tougher, but not dangerous. Make the most of it. Learn. I've got the jeep. If you like I can take you to Haiphong train station.'

Salagnon nodded; the interminable hallway was making him dizzy. The modern building reverberated with echoes, the line of doors stretched out for ever, each one identical but for the number; they opened and closed as men came and went with files, huge piles of dossiers, lock-keepers along the river of paper that sustained the war. War required more paper than it did bombs, a torrent of paper vast enough to drown the enemy. He was grateful that his uncle had offered to take him.

He went to fetch the permit for the Haiphong train, but went to the wrong door. This one was ajar and he pushed it open; he stood on the threshold, since it was dark inside; the shutters were closed and the shadows were pervaded by an acrid smell of piss. A lieutenant in dirty fatigues, his jacket open to the waist, rushed at him. 'You've no fucking business here!' he barked, holding up a blackened hand. He hit him in the chest, pushed him outside, his eyes burning with a spark of madness. He slammed the door. Salagnon stood there, nose pressed to the door. He could hear rhythmic thuds from inside the room, as though someone were beating a stick against a bag filled with water. 'Come on,' said the uncle, 'you got the wrong door.' Salagnon stood rooted to the spot. 'Hey, come away from there.' Salagnon turned to the uncle and said very slowly. 'I thought I saw a naked man in there, hanging upside down by his legs.' 'You thought, you thought... It's hard to see anything in a dark room, especially through a closed door. Now come on.'

He laid a hand on Salagnon's shoulder and pulled him away. Outside, on the bare parade ground, there were lines of tanks, covered trucks, field guns. Officers in a jeep drove along the lines of equipment; they were constantly jumping down from their vehicle before it came to a stop and leaping on again. The base whirled, it thrummed. Nobody walked, because here everyone runs; at war people run. This is one of the precepts of war in Asia, a precept from the West, which invented these machines; speed is another form of strength. Lines of soldiers, sagging under the weight of their kit, raced to board the covered trucks, which immediately started up; parachutists sprinted, their heavy bags slapping against their legs, heading into the distance towards a round-nosed Dakota with its door open, its propellers already turning. Everyone on the base was running; and Salagnon ran too, hot on the heels of his uncle. All this power, he thought, our power: we cannot possibly lose now. In the middle of the vast parade ground, at the top of a tall flagpole, hung a tricolour unstirred by any breeze. At the foot of the flagpole, fenced in with barbed wire, several dozen Annamese were crouched, motionless, waiting. They did not talk among themselves, they simply waited. They were guarded by armed soldiers. While around them the base wheeled frantically, this group of men was the still hub at the centre.

Caught up in a wave of panic, Salagnon could not tear his eyes away. He saw an officer carrying a whip made of reeds come and go several times, gesture for one row of Annamese to get to their feet, then lead them into the building. The others did not move. All the while the guards continued to circle, the bustle all around continued, a reassuring cacophony of engines, voices and the clack of feet marching in step. The door to the barracks closed on the little men in their black pyjamas. They walked with great economy of movement. Salagnon slowed his pace, fascinated by this still hub; his uncle retraced his steps.

'Ignore them. They're Viet Minh, suspects, men we've captured. They're prisoners now.'

'Where are they going?'

'Don't worry about that. Let them be. This base is hopeless. A farcical parody of power. We're the ones out in the jungle, we're the ones fighting. And we fight properly, because we're risking our lives. Risk restores our sense of honour. Come on, never mind what happens here, you're one of us now.'

He clambered into a battered jeep, which he drove recklessly.

'What were they doing in that locked room?'

'I'd rather not answer.'

'I'd like you to answer.'

'They were gathering intelligence. Intelligence is gathered in the dark, like mushrooms or endives.'

'Intelligence about what?'

'Intelligence is what a guy says when he is forced to talk. In Indochine it's worthless. I don't even know if they've got a word for "truth" in that tonal language of theirs. They always say what people want them to say; for them it's a matter of politeness, and in their world propriety is life itself. Intelligence is the grease that oils this war, the dirty grease that stains whatever it touches; but out in the jungle we've no need for grease, just sweat.'

'Trambassac seems decent enough.'

'The only thing decent about Trambassac is his uniform. His battle fatigues are spotless, but well worn. Didn't you wonder how they got like that? He runs them through the washing machine with pumice stone. Otherwise, he travels everywhere by plane, the only things he gets dirty are his shoes. It's his office that sends us out on missions. In this country our lives depend on strange people. The French high command is as much of a danger to us as Uncle Ho and General Giáp. The only person you can count on is yourself. You hold your life in your hands. Be careful with it.'

He was to set off from the port of Haiphong, a soot-blackened city without a speck of grace or beauty; the people there worked like they did in Europe: in the coal mines, on the docks, loading timber and rubber, unloading weapons and spare parts for vehicles and aeroplanes. Everything was shipped by the Tonkin armoured train, which was regularly blown up en route. Sabotaging the train tracks was the simplest act of revolutionary warfare. It was easy to picture the scene as it looked if you lay on the track bed: reeling out the wires, placing the plastic explosive, waiting for the train to arrive. But Salagnon pictured it from above this time, from the train, from the flat wagon ringed with sandbags, from which the bare-chested Senegalese operated huge machine guns. With a slightly forced smile, they aimed the perforated, air-cooled barrels at anything and everything along the track capable of hiding a man; they carried long, heavy ammunition belts that accentuated their muscles. They reassured Salagnon, these bullets as long as his finger that could explode a torso, a head, a limb, these guns capable of firing thousands of rounds a minute. Nothing was blown up.

The train crawled along at a snail's pace and eventually reached Haiphong. He boarded the boat. A Chinese junk operated as a ferry between the islands. Families travelled on deck with live chickens, sacks of rice and baskets of vegetables. They hung up bamboo mats to create shade, and as soon as the boat put out, they lit braziers so they could cook.

Salagnon took off his shoes and let his bare feet dangle over the side; the junk, little more than a floating crate, glided over the clear water. He could make out the seabed through a cerulean veil rumpled by wavelets. Brilliant white clouds floated high above, swirls of cream deposited on blue sheet metal; the wooden boat moved easily through the waters, creaking like a rocking chair. Around them the rocky islets soared steeply out of the bay, fingers pointed at the sky, warning signs between which the large boat weaved without incident. The crossing was calm, the weather magnificent; a sea breeze tempered the sweltering heat. These were the pleasantest hours he spent in his time in Indochine, peaceful hours where he did nothing but stare at the seabed through the crystalline water and watch the succession of precipitous islets on whose sheer slopes grew lopsided trees. Sitting on deck, dangling his legs through the gaps in the guard rail, he felt as if he were on the veranda of a clapboard house, as above, below, all around, the scenery flashed past, while swirling around him, shrouded in the sputtering of hot oil, came the wonderful aromas of their cooking. The families travelling with him did not look at the sea. They crouched in circles and ate; they dozed; they looked at each other, but said little; they tended to the animals they were transporting. Junks are cosy, they are not really like boats; there is no sense of the sea. The Chinese do not really like the sea, they tolerate it; if forced to live at sea, they build floating houses, boats that have beams, partition walls, floors, windows, curtains. If they live close to water – a river, a port, a bay – these boats drop anchor to become extensions of the streets; they live aboard them; they float, but that is all. He crossed Halong Bay in a sweet-scented daydream.

When he reached Ba Cuc, lost in the labyrinthine inlets of the bay, the last village to fly the tricolour, he was greeted by an officer with a less-than-military handshake. The man presented Salagnon with a metal trunk full of cash to pay the partisans' salaries and two others filled with guns and ammunition, gave another quick salute and boarded the junk as it left.

'Is that it?' Salagnon shouted from the landing stage.

'Someone will come to fetch you!' the other shouted, as the boat pulled away.

'How do I go about things?'

'You'll work it out...'

The rest of his words were lost in the distance, drowned by the creaking of the timbers on the landing stage, the fan-like fluttering of the battened sail as it was raised. Salagnon sat on his luggage, while all around him sacks of rice and crates of live hens were unloaded. He was alone on an island, sitting on a trunk; he did not really know where to go.

A click of heels made him start; of the thickly accented greeting, he understood only the word '*lieut'nant*', with no middle 'e' and a hesitant breath after the 't'. An ageing legionnaire was standing to attention next to him; his regulation bearing was impeccable, indeed excessive. Back straight, chin up, his body trembling, his eyes misted over, his lower lip humid with saliva; his stance was the only thing keeping him upright.

'At ease!' he said, but the man remained at attention; he preferred it that way.

'Soldat Goranidzé,' he announced. 'I'm your orderly. I am to drive you while you are on the island.'

'The island?'

'The island you are to command, sir.'

The idea of being in command of an island appealed to him. Goranidzé took him in a motorboat whose engine backfired, making it impossible to talk, and they trailed a black cloud that took some time to dissipate. He pointed to a villa clinging to the cliff of a rocky out-crop. Made of concrete, composed of horizontal lines and expansive windows, it was modern but already crumbling; set into the limestone cliff, it jutted out, hovering high above the water.

'Your house!' he bellowed.

It was reached by a narrow strip of sand, where fishermen were mending nets staked out in the sunshine; they helped to bring the boat ashore and unloaded the trunks brought by Salagnon and his orderly. Together they went up to the villa, taking a path carved into the cliff, some of whose steeper sections had been chiselled into stone steps.

'Like a monastery,' Soldat Goranidzé panted, his face flushed. 'Where I grew up, we had monasteries that jutted from the mountains like shelves from a wall.'

'Where did you grow up?'

'Georgia. The country doesn't exist now. The monasteries were ransacked after the Revolution. The monks were killed or evicted. We used to play in them. The walls in every room were painted with scenes describing the life of Christ.'

Here, too, the walls were covered with huge frescos, in the living room empty of furniture and the bedrooms that overlooked the sea.

'I told you, Lieut'nant, just like a monastery.'

'But I don't think that these are scenes from the life of Christ.'

'I wouldn't know. I've been a legionnaire too long to remember the details.'

They wandered through the rooms. The place smelled of neglect and damp. In the bedrooms, grubby tulle curtains, many of them torn, billowed in front of the unglazed windows, revealing glimpses of the blue sea. In the frescos adorning the walls, larger-than-life women of every race within the Empire were lying naked on lush, green grass, on large blankets woven in warm colours, in the shade of palm trees and flowering shrubs. Their faces were all visible, turned towards the viewer, eyes lowered, smiling.

'Mary Magdalene, sir. Like I said, the life of Christ. One for every region of the Empire: just like it should be.'

They moved into the villa, the summer residence of the colonial governor, who had not used it since the war began.

Salagnon chose a bedroom with one whole wall missing, offering a sweeping view of the sea. He slept in a bed longer than he was tall, as broad as it was long, in which he could lie in any position he chose. The tulle curtain, swelled by the breeze, barely quivered; when he went to bed in this dark room, he could hear the faint roar of the backwash at the foot of the cliff. He lived the life of a kinglet in a fairy tale, dreaming, imagining, his feet never touching the ground.

The walls of his bedroom were painted with women, half-eaten away by the damp. But their smiles were untouched: full, sensual lips gorged with tropical sap; the women of the Empire were recognizable by the splendour of their mouths. On the ceiling was the only man, naked, each arm clasping a woman to him; his graphic state made obvious his desire, but his face alone could not be seen, it was turned away. Sprawled on his back on the huge bed, keeping his eyes open, Salagnon could see him clearly, the lone man painted on the ceiling. He wished that Eurydice could join him. They could have lived as prince and princess in this floating castle. He wrote to her; he painted what he could see through the missing wall: the Chinese landscape of soaring islands, set in a bay of dazzling waters. He sent the letters by motorboat, which once a week made a run to the port where the junk dropped anchor. Goranidzé took care of everything, of the supplies, of the mail, of the meals and the laundry, all without losing that air of irreproachable stiffness; he also dealt with the native dignitaries, announcing them with a stentorian voice whenever they came to the door. But once a week he would come, respectfully announce to Salagnon that this was his day off, and hand him a key. He would get drunk on his own; then sleep it off in the small, windowless room he had chosen for himself, having asked Salagnon to lock the door and to keep the key until the booze had worn off. He feared that otherwise he might fall out of a window or slip on the stairs, either of which would have been fatal. The following morning Salagnon would come and open the door and he would resume his stiff formality, never mentioning what had happened the day before. He would spend these days cleaning the rooms they did not use. The supplies, together with the weapons and the money they had to distribute, provided enough wine for regular drinking binges. But the letters went only one way. Eurydice never responded to his sketches, his ink drawings of diz-zyingly steep islands she would never have believed represented a landscape one might see; he wanted her to be incredulous, so that he could write back and assure her that he had actually seen all the things he drew. He regretted being unable to reaffirm, if only in a letter, the reality of his thoughts. They dematerialized.

Recruiting partisans was an easy task. In these islands peopled by fishermen and swallow-hunters, few had ever seen money, and no one had seen a gun other than the ancient Chinese muskets that no longer worked. Lieutenant Salagnon generously dispensed his riches in exchange for a promise to come and train for a few hours each morning. The young fishermen would arrive in groups, nervous, and one of them would step forwards, shyly, as the others laughed, and sign his enlistment papers: he would scrawl a cross at the bottom of a pink form and the paper, swollen by the damp, would often tear, since he held the pencil clumsily. Then he would take his rifle, which would be passed around, and a thin wad of *piastres*, which he would roll tightly and stow in a tobacco pouch hanging around his neck.

The forms quickly ran out. He had them sign little squares of blank paper, rubbing out the signatures at night, since the act itself was all that mattered, as no one on this island could read or write.

In the morning he organized training exercises on the beach. Many did not show up. He never had an exact count. They never seemed to learn anything. They handled their rifles as poorly as ever, like scooters whose backfire always made them start, made them laugh. When he grew accustomed to their faces and their family relationships, he realized that they attended on a rota basis, one from each family, although not always the same one. Families invariably sent the dull-witted young men, those who were more of a hindrance than a help when it came to fishing. This was a relatively safe way of keeping them busy and it earned them a salary that the family shared.

He went to the village, where he was received in a woven timber longhouse. In the murky darkness smelling of smoke and *nam pla*, an elderly man listened to him gravely without really understanding, although he nodded at the end of each sentence, at every break in the rhythm of this unfamiliar language. The interpreter had only limited French, and when Salagnon talked about the war, the Viet Minh, the recruitment of partisans, he translated with long, complicated phrases, which he repeated several times as if there were no words to communicate what Salagnon was saying. Still the old man nodded, politely, as though he did not understand. Then his eyes lit up; he laughed, turned to face Salagnon, who nodded and ventured a broad smile. He called into the shadows and a young girl with very long black hair appeared; she stood in front of them, her eyes lowered. She was wearing only a *pagne* wrapped around her narrow hips, her small breasts blossoming like buds filled with sap. The old man had her explain that he had finally understood, and that she could go and live with the lieutenant. Salagnon closed his eyes, shook his head. Things were not going well. No one seemed to understand anything.

In the villa clinging to the cliff, he would look at the slowly disintegrating frescos or at the sea beyond the slowly swelling tulle curtains. Things were not going well, yet no one but he seemed to notice this fact. And what difference did it make? How could one not love Indochine? How could one not love these places that, in France, could not be imagined? How could one not love the life here? He fell asleep, lulled by the ebb and flow of the waves, and the following morning he resumed the training exercises. Goranidzé taught the men to fall in, to hold their rifles straight, to march in step, raising their legs high. He had trained as a cadet in one of the tsar's officer schools, briefly, before being catapulted into a long series of untidy wars. He loved nothing better than drilling and discipline; this, at least, was something that would never change. Towards midday the fishermen would return, haul their boats on to the beach and the partisans would break rank, laughing, and talk about how they had spent the morning. Goranidzé would sit in the shade, grilling fish to perfection with chilli and lemon, then he would go up to the villa for a nap. It was futile to think of doing anything else with the day. And so, from his bedroom, Salagnon would stare out at the bay, trying to work out how to paint these precipitous islands that rose abruptly out of the sea. He lived clinging to this cliff like an insect on a tree trunk, motionless for much of the day, waiting for metamorphosis.

By the time they were dispatched to Tonkin, his company was reduced to a quarter of those who had originally enlisted. They immediately hated the countryside. The delta of the Red River is little more than a flat expanse of mud, but the eye could see only as far as the next screen of bamboo encircling a village. There was nothing to see. Here, one had the feeling of being lost in an empty space and yet bounded by a shrunken horizon.

The fishing families of the bay had sent the young, the troubled, the distracted, those the village would not miss, those who might benefit from a little discipline. The one who spoke French acted as an interpreter and he treated his commitment as a journey. With their bush hats pushed down over their eyes, their overstuffed kitbags, their over-large rifles, they looked like children dressing up. They found it difficult to march, keeping their sandals tied to their kitbags, because barefoot they could better feel the path. They travelled on foot, trying to flush out the Viet Minh, who also moved on foot. They marched behind Salagnon in single file, with little space between them and, every fifteen minutes, Salagnon would shout for them to space out and stop talking. And they would move apart and fall silent, only to gradually begin chattering again, steadily closing the gap between them and the officer leading. Accustomed to the sands and the limestone of the bay, they slipped in the mud and fell on their arses in the flooded paddy fields. They would stop, crowd round, laugh and joke as they fished out whoever had fallen, who was now even muddier than his comrades. On manoeuvre they were raucous and unthreatening, incapable of surprising an enemy; on the level horizon they offered the perfect target. They suffered in the heat, since no sea breeze came to temper the hazy sun that beat down on this expanse of mud.

But when they saw the mountain, they did not like it. Triangular hills suddenly sprouted from the alluvial plain, soaring terraced slopes shrouded in mists than merged into the clouds at the summit. This was where the Viet Minh lived, like beasts of the forest that came at night to prey on the villages and devour the unwary.

Posts had been built to seal off the delta, posts set at regular intervals to scan for any sign of movement, tall square observation towers ringed with fences from which it was possible to see a great distance. How many people manned them? Three French soldiers, ten Vietnamese reserves; they guarded a village, monitored a bridge, symbolized French authority in this waterlogged labyrinth of ditches and channels. Back at headquarters, each watchtower was a little flag pinned on a map; it was removed when the post was destroyed during the night.

They had been sent to defend a vulnerable post. They approached it by the track that ran along the ditch, in single file, correctly spaced for once, each man stepping into the footprints of the man marching ahead of him. Salagnon had taught them this, since the trails were littered with traps. The post was protected by several rows of bamboo *chevaux-de-frise*, leaving only a narrow entrance to the stone tower, directly facing a loophole from which projected the perforated barrel of a machine gun. Black slurry trickled down the sharpened bamboo stakes, which had been coated with buffalo dung so that the wounds they caused would quickly become infected. They came to a halt. The door beneath the loophole was closed; it had been set high on the wall, with no flight of steps. A ladder was required to access it, a ladder that was removed at night and stored inside. Beneath it, on poles, were the heads of two Viet Minh, their severed necks smeared with black blood, their closed eyes buzzing with blowflies. It was sweltering on the small patch of ground in front of the tower; a suffocating humidity rose from the rice fields all around. Salagnon could hear nothing but the drone of the flies. A few approached him and flew off again. He shouted up. His voice sounded very faint in this sweeping landscape of flooded fields crushed by the sun. He shouted louder. After he had called out several times, the barrel of the machine gun twitched and a wary, hirsute man appeared at the loophole.

'Who are you?' roared a hoarse voice. A single, bulging eye glittered under a thatch of blond hair.

'Lieutenant Salagnon with a company of native soldiers from the bay, to provide support.'

The machine gun rattled; the bullets blasted a neat line in the mud, splattering them all. The men started, gave little yelps, broke ranks and huddled around Salagnon.

'Put down your weapons.'

When all the rifles had been thrown to the ground, the door opened, the ladder appeared, and a Frenchman hopped down, bearded, bare-chested, wearing only a pair of shorts into which was tucked a revolver. Two Tonkinese in black pyjamas followed, armed with American machine guns. They stood three metres behind him, motionless.

'What the fuck are you doing?' asked Salagnon.

'Me? I'm surviving, my little tin soldier. You, I'm not so sure.'

'Don't you know who I am?'

'Oh, now I see. I know who you are. But I suspect everyone on principle.'

'You suspect me?'

'You, no. No one would suspect you. But a battalion of Viets led by a white man, that can be dangerous. I can't count how many posts have been tricked by the legionnaire ruse. A European deserter, Viet Minh dressed as back-up troops, no one suspects anything, they politely open the door, come down the ladder, and before they know it, their throats have been cut. They realize they've been suckered when they see the blood gush out. Not me.'

'So, happy now?'

'Me? Yes. About you, that's a different matter. Your men aren't Viet Minh, that's for sure. Scattering and squealing at the first burst of gunfire, that makes them strictly amateurs.'

He jerked his thumb at the two Tonkinese behind him, standing stiff, impassive, guns at the ready.

'Now these two, they're Viet Minh who've defected, and that's a whole other deal. Cool under fire, ready to obey at the click of my fingers, utterly without scruples.'

'And you trust them?'

'We're in the same boat now. Well, not a boat, more a dinghy. If they go back to the other side, the political commissar will have them immediately liquidated; if they give up fighting, the villagers will lynch them; they know that. They have no choice. I have no choice. We are a battalion of the damned. We're joined at the hip. Every day we survive is a victory. You want to come up, Lieutenant? I'll buy you a drink. Bring one or two of your men, no more. The others can stay down here, I don't have room.'

It was dark inside the watchtower, the only light came from the door and the loopholes on each wall, all fitted with machine guns. Only gradually did he make out the men, sitting stock-still against the walls: black uniforms, black hair, eyes scarcely open, weapons cradled in their laps. Every one of them was looking at him, watching his every movement. The murky air smelled of aniseed and of an airless barracks. The lieutenant bent over the pile of crates in the middle of the room, picked up something and threw it to Salagnon, who instinctively caught it. He assumed it was a football. It was a head. He retched, almost let it drop by reflex, and by reflex kept hold of it; the open eyes stared up, though not at him, something he found reassuring. He shuddered, then became calm.

'I was going to put it outside before you arrived, change the ones down there, they're starting to stink.'

'Viet Minh?'

'I wouldn't swear to it, but maybe.'

He picked up a cap emblazoned with a yellow star, a flattened piece of shrapnel fashioned by hand.

'Put this on him, that way he's definitely one of them.'

A bodiless head is compact, not particularly heavy, like a football. You can spin it, you can throw it, but when it comes to setting it down, you don't know where to put it. That's where a stake is very practical: you know where to put it, which way to mount the head. The hairy lieutenant handed him a sharpened bamboo stake. Salagnon embedded it in the oesophagus – or maybe the trachea, he was not sure; it made a squeaking noise like rubber pressed too tightly into wood; something small inside the neck snapped. Then he placed the officer's cap on it. The men sitting along the walls watched him in silence.

'This post has already been captured three times. Grenades were lobbed in, there wasn't much left of the soldiers manning it. So now I show them what we're made of. I terrorize them. I've got traps set around the post. I'm a landmine: come too close to me and *boom*! Right, I think you've earned yourself a drink.'

He took the head on the spike and proffered a full glass in exchange that smelled strongly of aniseed. All the men passed round glasses of a milky liquid of an opalescent yellow that managed to gleam in the darkness.

'It's genuine pastis. We make it ourselves. We drink it in our spare time; and round here, all our time is spare. Did you know that star anise – that smell so typical of France – is not actually from Marseille? In fact, it comes from here. Your health! So, what about you? Where are you headed with your gang of clockwork soldiers?'

'Into the jungle.'

'The jungle, sir, no chance. The men don't want to.'

'Don't want to what?'

'To march into the jungle.'

'That's what I enlisted them for.'

'No, no enlist for march in jungle, no change. Enlist for have gun, to have money.'

He had to get angry. That same night, several men absconded. The jungle was not the place for fishermen. It is no place for any man.

When they came under fire for the first time, it was not as hard as they had imagined. Thinking that someone wants you dead, that they are single-minded, determined, is unbearable only if you think about it; but you do not think about it. A black fury blinds men for the duration of the machine-gun burst. There are no thoughts, no feelings; there are only escape routes, criss-crossing trajectories, getaways, stampedes, a mortal but entirely abstract game. There is nothing to do but fire and be fired upon. It takes only a brief respite to think again about how unbearable it is to be fired upon; but it is always possible not to think.

Troubled thoughts can be blocked out, but they return, in sleep, in the silence of the early hours, in unexpected gestures, in the raging sweat that surprises, because you do not know its cause, but that, thankfully, comes later. In the moment, it is possible not to think, to live poised on the boundary that separates one action from the next.

It is strange how thoughts can flame or flicker out, chatter endlessly or shrink to almost nothing, to the clicking of a wind-up toy, a series of cogs that turn, lurch forwards in short jerks, all identical. Thought is a form of calculation, the answers do not always come out right, but it carries on. Nose pressed into the mud, sprawled among the leaves, this is what Salagnon was thinking; it was hardly the time, but he could not move. The first deafening shots rang out almost as one; five, he was counting them; the whistle of shells merged, the mortars fell together, perfectly spaced, the ground beneath his belly shook. A spray of dirt and splintered wood rained down over their backs, their bush hats, their kitbags; pebbles jangled against the metal of their weapons; shell fragments, when they fall, do little damage, but it is important not to touch them, because they burn, they cut. They fire on command, in sequence, five mortars. I didn't realize the Annamese were so organized. But these are Tonkinese; these are no kids, they are veritable machines automatically doing as they are ordered. They are ranged in a line; an officer equipped with binoculars signals his commands with a pennant. Another salvo is fired, falls, closer this time. The next one will hit us. The explosions plough up the earth in a neat furrow. Five metres between salvoes. Twenty seconds between each strike, just time enough for the dust to settle, for the officer to check the results through his binoculars, have them adjust their elevation, and the pennant falls again. The shells fall five metres further. Methodically they creep closer. They wait for the impact before firing another round; they know their targets are lined up on the ground, they intend to hit them precisely, all at once. Three more rounds and we will be dead.

The earth shakes, stones and splinters rain down on them again. 'Next time, we run when we hear the shots, pass it on. We dive into the craters up ahead and hide before they explode.' The shrill shriek splits the sky, crashes into the ground like crates of lead being dropped. They bounded through the rain of earth, passed through the dust, crouched in the freshly dug furrows. Hearts beating fit to burst, mouths champing on debris, they gripped the butts of their rifles, clung to their hats. Another salvo. Five shells passed over their heads and ploughed up the ground where they had been lying a moment earlier, five spades that would have sliced them in half and buried them, earthworms, dead. They didn't notice. How little it takes.

The shelling stopped. At a whistle, the line of soldiers wearing palm-leaf helmets emerged from the jungle, rifles slung across their chests, taking no precautions. They think we have been ripped to shreds. We fire, then we charge. At this point, they start up again. This is what happened, with unbridled ferocity. They fired on the line of soldiers, who went down like ninepins; they bounded forwards, hurled grenades, charged, shattered the skulls, the torsos of men crawling on all fours, men lying, sitting, sprawling on their backs; with a flick of their bayonets they disembowelled those still standing; they reached the mortars ranged along the chalk line in the undergrowth, fired on those fleeing through the trees. The officer fell, clutching his pennant, feet still touching the chalk mark, binoculars resting on his chest. They raged on. At such moments one does not see people, only problematic shapes, sacks into which a blade plunges, hoping it does not snap; sacks to be fired on, they crumple, they fall, they are no longer a problem, we move on. They counted the dead. Several bodies still lay where it had all begun, hit by the mortar shells; they had not moved, they had not understood the order passed from one man to the next, or they had reacted too late. Life, death, depend on unpredictable calculations; this one came out right; as for the next one, we shall see. High up in the jungle they heard long whistle blasts. They ran.

It went on for weeks. Salagnon's fishermen held up as best they could. They came down with diseases they had never encountered on the bay. Their numbers slowly declined. They became hardened. They disappeared one afternoon in a matter of seconds. They marched in single file along the narrow, raised dykes, the sun slanted, their shadows stretched out on the watery expanse of the rice fields; a sultry heat rose from the mud, the air veered orange. They passed a silent village. A machine gun hiding in a clump of bamboo almost did for them all. Salagnon was unscathed. The radio operator, the interpreter and two soldiers, those standing closest to him, survived. After night fell, an air strike razed the village. At dawn, with another section passing along the road, they sifted through the ashes, but found no bodies and no weapons. The devastated company was officially dissolved. Salagnon returned to Hanoi. At night, lying on his back, his eyes wide open, he wondered why the machine-gun burst had been so brief, why it had stopped before it came to him, why they had not started shooting at the head of the line. Surviving made it impossible to sleep.

'The life expectancy of a junior officer just arrived from France is less than a month. Not all of them die, but most. But if you set aside those who die in the first month, then the life expectancy of officers rises exponentially.'

'Tell me, Trambassac, do you really have time to do these macabre calculations?'

'How can you expect to fight a war without using numbers? The conclusion to be drawn from these calculations is that any officer who survives the first month can be trusted. We can give them a command post. They will survive, since they have already survived.'

'That's preposterous. You've just proved that command posts should be awarded to men who manage to stay alive! Who else would they be given to? The dead? We only have the living. So give up on all the calculations and the probability; war isn't probable, it's certain.'

Victorien Salagnon was given a company of Thais from the mountains: forty men who understood nothing of the autocratic egalitarianism of the Viet Minh and, moreover, had for generations despised the lowland Tonkinese. The NCOs spoke some broken French and, in addition to Sous-lieutenant Mariani, fresh out of military academy and newly arrived from France, he was assigned Lieutenant Moreau and Sous-lieutenant Gascard, who had come from God knows where. 'Isn't it a slightly unusual number of officers?' asked Salagnon. They were drinking under the frangipani trees on the eve of heading up the Black River. 'Yep.' This seemed to bring a smile to Moreau's face, a thin-lipped smile like a razor slash beneath a black moustache trimmed to within a millimetre, perhaps less, that glistened with wax. It was impossible to truly know whether he was smiling. Gascard, a red-faced giant of a man, simply nodded his head, drained his glass and ordered another. The sun was setting; a myriad lanterns hanging from the branches gave out a soft glow. Moreau's neatly parted, slicked-back hair gleamed. 'It's a lot, and it's unnecessary. But it's understandable.' His voice was warmer than his sleek, pointy face suggested, thankfully, since otherwise he would have been frightening. He was creepy when he was silent.

'What do you mean it's understandable?'

'You get to be the leader. You get the stripes by sheer fluke, and the kid here, who's just out of school, they're sending him along to learn from you.'

'What about you two?'

'Us? We lose stripes as fast as we earn them. Gaspard, because he's a dipso. Me, because I'm too excitable when it comes to the enemy, and too insubordinate when it comes to my superiors. On the other hand, we're indestructible. We may not look good in dispatches, but we know what we're doing; that's why they're sending us. They're thinking: "Good riddance! We've got ourselves a squad: a survivor, a couple of experienced bushmen, a kid who's bound to learn something, and an unspecified number of local soldiers. Set this lot loose in the jungle and the Viet Minh better watch their arses." In difficult situations, delusion is as good a response as any.'

Salagnon laughed this off. The way he saw it, he was about to head into the mountains with two lieutenants and forty guys, who, since time immemorial, had longed to wage war on the people of the plains; it was as good as a life-insurance policy. They drank quite a lot. Young Mariani seemed to be enjoying Indochine. They stumbled back to their quarters, tipsy, through the unidentifiable, milky scent of the white flowers, passing the huge illuminated windows of the Tonkin Grand Hôtel. Inside, there were civil servants, Annamese of higher caste, women in off-the-shoulder dresses, officers in full dress uniform from all three branches of the military, and Trambassac, wearing fatigues pinned with all his medals. It was glittering. There was music and dancing. Beautiful women with long black hair were waltzing with dainty steps and an aristocratic reserve guaranteed to break the hearts of officers from the French Far East Expeditionary Corps. Moreau, drunk but steady, pushed aside the orderly guarding the door and headed straight for the bar, where generals and colonels, glimmering with gold braid and decorations, stood murmuring gravely, champagne glasses in hand. Salagnon hung back a little, worried, with Gascard and Mariani three paces behind.

'I set off at dawn, Colonel, knowing there is every possibility that I shall be killed. I couldn't touch the food in the mess hall, it was warmed-over slop, and the ration of wine we get is so acidic it could be used to clean our rifles.'

The brass hats turned, but did not dare interrupt this unsettling, scrawny, impeccably coiffed young man, who, though visibly drunk, had perfect diction. The thin-lipped mouth beneath the neat moustache was unsettling. Trambassac smiled.

'I see you're drinking champagne. I trust the foie gras does not melt in this heat.'

Having recovered from the surprise, the generals were about to protest and to deal ruthlessly with the interloper; a few muscular colonels had set down their glasses and stepped forwards. Trambassac stopped them with a paternalistic wave. 'Lieutenant Moreau, please join us as my guest. You, too, Salagnon, and the two men hiding behind you.' He took several champagne flutes from the tray proffered by a manservant and handed them to the astonished young men, keeping one for himself. 'Messieurs,' he said, addressing the company at large, 'you see before you the finest this army has to offer. Here in the city they are gentlemen of unimpeachable honour, but in the jungle they are wolves. They set off tomorrow and I pity General Giáp and his army of rogues. Messieurs, to the airlift, to the Empire, to France; you are her sword of justice. I am proud to drink to your valour.'

He raised his glass and drank. Everyone else did likewise. There was a smattering of applause. Moreau did not know how to respond. He blushed, raised his glass, and drank. The music and the murmur of conversation resumed. No one took any further notice of the four young, undecorated lieutenants. Trambassac set his half-full glass on the tray of a passing waiter, walked over and tapped Moreau on the shoulder. 'You are leaving at dawn, my boy. Stay a little longer, enjoy yourself, but do not get to bed too late. You will need your strength.'

He disappeared into the gilded crowd. They did not stay. Salagnon grabbed Moreau by the arm and they went outside. The warm air did little to sober them up, but it was fragrant with huge flowers. Bats flitted noiselessly around them.

'You see,' said Moreau quietly, 'I always get shafted. It'll take me until tomorrow to get riled up again.'

*   *   *

There is no way of knowing before being there what it is like; for that, you have to go there, and even then words fail. It is clear, yet you talk only about insignificant things; you talk only to those who already understand, those who know, and with them there is no need to explain, it is enough to suggest. What we do not know, we must see and then accept: what we do not know remains for ever remote, for ever beyond reach, despite the best efforts of language, which is designed primarily to evoke what we already know. Salagnon plunged into the jungle with three young officers and forty men whose language he could not speak.

Seen from a plane, the jungle is streaked with fleecy clouds; it looks pleasant. It softens the edges of the Haute-Région, tempers the jagged limestone karsts with a carpet of green wool. It unfurls beneath the plane, dense and compact, and from above it looks like a comfortable place to stretch out. But plunge into it, struggle through the dense, unchanging canopy, and you realize with horror that it is made up of crudely stitched rags and tatters.

No one imagined it was so shoddy, the jungle of Indochine; they knew it was dangerous, that was endurable, but it is a wretched setting in which to die. And this is what most creatures do here: die; the animals that tear each other to pieces with refinements of cruelty, the plants that do not even have time to fall, but are devoured as soon as dead by those that grow around and over them.

In France we have a mistaken idea of virgin forest, since the forests in novels are modelled on the huge houseplants that stand next to windows in overheated living rooms, and films set in the jungle are filmed in botanic gardens. We imagine the dense dark jungle that appears in books to be staggeringly fertile; we imagine hacking our path through it with a machete, with a joyous hunger in our hearts and the strain of conquest in our bellies, coursing with the wholesome sweat of exertion to be washed away in a nearby stream. It is nothing like that. From within, the jungle of Indochine is ugly, sparse, and it is not even green. From a plane it looks soft; from a distance, compact;

but inside, standing at the foot of the trees, it is a shabby mess. It is planted any old how, no two trees side by side are the same; they are all half-choked by vines, propped up by each other, all gnarled, clutching at every branch they can reach, all crudely planted in scrubby ground, in poor soil that is not even carpeted with leaves; things grow every which way at every height, and nothing is green. The grey tree trunks struggle to stand upright, the sickly, yellowish branches twist and twine; it is impossible to tell to which tree they belong; the pockmarked leaves, dusted with grey, struggle towards the light, while liana do their best to strangle everything living, looking more like a rampant disease than harmonious, burgeoning vegetation.

We imagine a forest to be dense; in fact, it's a junkyard. The ground on which you walk is not lush and fecund, but strewn with fallen debris. Your feet get snarled in roots growing halfway up the side of a tree; the trunks are covered with hairs that harden into barbs; the barbs cover the edges of the leaves; the leaves are utterly unlike leaves, being either too waxy, too flabby, too large, too swollen or too spiky; excess is their only rule. The muggy heat liquefies comprehension. Insects buzz about in little swarms, tracking the nearest source of hot blood; or chirrup on the leaves, or crawl along disguised as branches. The soil teems with a phenomenal variety of worms that writhe and cause the earth to move. You are imprisoned in the forests of Indochine, as in a locked kitchen with every hob turned up high, while steaming pans without lids boil away. Sweat starts to trickle the moment you take a step, clothing becomes soaked, gestures dissolve into embarrassment; you skid on the slippery ground. In spite of the hygrothermal energy flowing from everything, gushing from bodies, the jungle gives off an overwhelming impression of unwholesome deficiency.

'Walking in the woods' has a salubrious, joyful sense only in the primeval forests of Europe, where trees grow in serried ranks without crowding out the others; where the supple ground, cool and dry, cracks a little underfoot; where the sky can be glimpsed between the leaves; where it is possible to gaze up while walking without fear of stumbling over some hideous mess. 'Walking in the woods' does not have the same sense here; instead it conjures the idea of stepping into a thick layer of mould growing over huge heaps of rotting vegetation. Here, people do not walk, they do a job of work. For some, this entails tapping rubber trees, for others gathering wild honey, still others discover seams of precious stones or cut down tall teaks that have to be dragged to the river to be transported. People get lost here, they die of disease, they slaughter each other. Salagnon's job of work is to seek out the Viet Minh and get out alive if he can. Escape this mouldering world if he can. If he can, he thinks over and over. Everything here conspires to make life more fragile, more loathsome. He was not sorry to make much of the journey by boat.

The designation LCT – Landing Craft for Tanks – is hardly appropriate for the boats that transport men along the rivers of Indochine. Most people call them barges. They are diesel-powered metal hulks that glide upstream; the roar of their engines is more a series of feeble farts constantly about to stall, a noise that has trouble moving through air that is too viscous, too humid, too hot. Perhaps the noise of the engines does not even reach the banks, and perhaps the children leading enormous buffalo on leashes did not hear them; they saw these machines gliding up the river silently, laboriously, in a slow churn of liquid mud. The LCTs were not designed for this. Built quickly and crudely, they were used during the war to transport heavy artillery to the Pacific Islands and it made little difference if one should sink. When the war was over, there were still hundreds of them. There is little heavy artillery here; things break down, they roll over landmines, they are useless when dealing with a hidden enemy. And so the LCTs were used to transport troops along the rivers, their kitbags and the ammunition were stowed in the large, uncovered cargo bays, flimsy shelters were built on deck to protect them from the sun, and strung wire netting between poles protected them from grenades lobbed from the banks or from a sampan that sailed too close. With the canvas and bamboo shelters, their cargo bays filled with drowsy men, their hulls eaten away by rust, their sides peppered with dents and bullet holes, these American vessels – simple and serviceable as all things American – took on, in Indochine, a tropical, ramshackle air, a tired, makeshift air that accentuated the damp clanking of the diesel engine; it seemed that at any moment it would cut out and everything would come to a standstill.

The ordinary seaman skippering the convoy of LCTs, whom Salagnon called captain, being ignorant of naval ranks, came and leaned next to him on the gunwale and they watched the flowing water. It carried clumps of grass, clusters of water hyacinths, dead branches drifting slowly downstream.

'Over here, the only more-or-less clear route is the river,' he said eventually.

'You call this clear?'

The word amused Salagnon, because the brownish water slipping past the sides of the boat was so thick with mud that the prow and the propellers produced no froth, no foam; the silt-heavy waters roiled a little as they passed and quickly became a still, untroubled expanse.

'I might be a sailor, Lieutenant, but I'm keen to keep my legs. And the only way to do that in this country is not to walk. I don't trust the ground. There are very few roads here and most of those are impassable; they barricade them at night by hacking down trees, dig trenches across them, set off landslides to bury them. Even the landscape here has it in for us. When it rains the road turns to mud and when you step on it, it explodes or it caves in and your foot plunges into a hole with sharpened spikes at the bottom. I don't hang around on what they call terra firma any more, because it's not. I go everywhere by boat, by river. Since they don't have floating mines or torpedoes here, it's clear.'

The three LCTs chugged slowly up the river. The men slept in the hold beneath the tarpaulin shelters; the canvas quivered; you could feel the thick water scraping against the sides of the hull. Along this route with no shade, the sun was crushing; the heat shrouded them in a mist that dazzled in the light. Clay dykes hid the scenery; here and there a clump of trees or a group of thatched roofs emerged. As they passed, small boats tethered to the banks rocked; in them were women bent over their washing, fishermen dressed in rags, naked children who watched them pass, then leapt into the water, laughing. Everything, from earth to sky, was bathed in greenish yellow, the colour of a worn-out military bedsheet, the colour of a threadbare colonial infantry uniform that might fall apart with a single tug. The suffocating clanking of the engines followed them everywhere.

'The problem with these rivers are the banks. In Europe, they're always calm, a bit dreary, but restful. Here, the silence is so complete you're for ever thinking you're about to be shot at. You don't see anything, but you are being watched. And don't ask me by who. I don't know. No one does. No one knows anything in this fucking country. I can't stand their silence, though I can't stand their noise either. As soon as they open their mouths, they're screaming; and when they shut up, the silence is scary. Have you noticed? The cities here are bedlam, but the countryside is a silent nightmare. Sometimes you slap your ears just to make sure they're working. Things happen here that can't be heard. It keeps me awake. I worry I'm deaf. I wake up with a start. The sound of the engine reassures me, but I'm terrified it will stop. I scan the riverbanks, there's never anything. But I know they're there. No way of getting to sleep. The banks would have to be really far away for me to get any sleep. In the middle of the ocean, maybe. There I might finally be able to sleep. Finally. Because I've been storing up missed sleep for years. You can't imagine how much I would sleep if I was on the open sea.'

They heard a dull thud. They saw a human body, face down in the water, arms and legs outstretched, bump gently against the hull; then it slid along the side of the barge, spun slowly and disappeared downstream. Another followed, and another, and still others. Splayed bodies drifted down the river, some floated on their bellies, their faces submerged for so long the watchers felt a rising panic; others floated on their backs, their bloated faces turned towards the sun, their eyes reduced to narrow slits. Whirling slowly, they glided downstream. 'What's that?' 'People.' One of the corpses became stuck against the flat bow of the barge and began to emerge from the water, the body arched, then stopped and headed up the river with them. Another glided past, then became caught in the propeller blades and the water turned a reddish brown, crimson blood mingled with mud, and the severed corpse floated on, hit the next LCT and sank. 'For Christ's sake, move them away! Move them away!' Sailors grabbed boathooks, leaned over the side and pushed the corpses away from the hull, hooked them and thrust them into the current, so they would not touch the barge.

'Move them away, for Christ's sake! Move them away!'

Dozens of corpses were floating down the river, an inexhaustible supply of bodies streamed down the river; the women haloed by their flowing black hair, the children for once not fidgeting, the men identical in the black pyjamas that serve as a uniform for the whole country. 'Move them away, for Christ's sake!' The captain roared the same order over and over, his voice growing shrill. 'Move them away, for Christ's sake!' The fists gripping the rail were white. Salagnon wiped his lips. He had clearly vomited without even noticing; there was an acrid coating in his mouth, a few drops from his knotted stomach. 'Who are they?' 'Villagers. People murdered by looters, bandits, the fucking bastards who hide out in the jungle. People who were going about their business, assaulted, robbed, tossed into the river. I told you, the roads in the country aren't safe. Horrifying things happen every day.'

Bodies continued to drift past the three LCTs and they continued up the river, alone or in dense groups; some seemed to be wearing a brownish uniform, but it was impossible to be certain, since all the clothes here looked alive, and besides everything was wet, bloated, sodden with sallow water; the bodies were too far away and no one went to check. The only sounds were the muted backfire of the diesel engines and the laboured breathing of the sailors wielding boathooks.

'I really need to see the ocean again,' muttered the captain when finally they had passed the gruesome floe. He let go of the gunwale and, through the parched skin of his cheeks, Salagnon could see his jaw muscles pulse like a heart, his tongue frantically rubbing against his teeth. He turned on his heel, locked himself in the cramped cabin next to the engines and Salagnon did not see him again until the end of the journey. Perhaps he was trying to sleep; and perhaps he succeeded.

Farther up the river, they passed a burned-out village. It was still smouldering, but everything had already burned: the thatched roofs, the bamboo stockades, the walls of woven wood. All that remained were upright, blackened beams and smoking piles of ash, ringed by headless palm trees and the bodies of dead pigs.

A four-wheel drive was making its way along the dyke, a black Citroën as in France, but out of place here; it was driving slowly in the same direction as the barges along a track by a bank usually used by buffalos. For a while, they moved in convoy, the Citroën trailing a cloud of dust, then it stopped. Two men in flowery, short-sleeved shirts climbed out, dragging a third man dressed in black, his hands lashed behind his back, a Vietnamese with a thick shock of hair, a heavy fringe falling over his eyes. Hands on his shoulders, they marched him to the river's edge and made him kneel. One of the men in short-sleeved shirts raised his pistol and shot him in the back of the head. The Vietnamese toppled forwards and fell into the river; from the barge, they belatedly heard the muffled sound of the shot. The body floated on its belly, hugging the shore, then found a current and began to drift, moving away from the bank, heading downstream. The man in the floral shirt stuck his pistol in the waistband of his linen trousers and raised his hand to salute the LCTs. The soldiers returned the salute, some of them with laughs and cheers that perhaps he heard. The men climbed back into the Citroën and disappeared.

'The Surêté,' whispered Moreau.

Salagnon could always smell him coming, because every morning Moreau carefully combed his hair into a neat parting and applied a dollop of brilliantine that mantled in the heat. When Moreau approached, it smelled like a barber shop.

'Did you sleep?'

'Dozed a bit against my kitbag between a couple of Thais. They have no problem sleeping, they can kip anywhere; but they sleep like cats. When I got up, as carefully as possible, making not a sound – I was pretty proud of my performance – I noticed that, without even opening their eyes, the Thais had closed their hands around their bayonets. Even when they're asleep, they know what's going on. I've got a way to go to catch up.'

'How did you know those guys were from the Sûreté?'

'The four-wheel drive, the pistols tucked into their belts, the baggy shirts. They're cocky fuckers. They're the hot-shots when it comes to crime. They run this place. They arrest guys, interrogate them, shoot them. They don't even try to be discreet; they're not afraid of anything, until someone shoots them. And then come the reprisals and the whole thing starts up again.'

'What good does it do?'

'They're police. They're looking for information. It's their job. Because if they can criss-cross this country without spotting a Viet Minh when the whole place is crawling with them, they're sorely lacking in information. So they do everything they can to get it. They arrest, interrogate, index the information and liquidate, it's a whole industry. I met one of them in a little village in the delta. He had the same flowery shirt, the same pistol tucked into his shorts. He was wandering around like a lost soul, frantic. He was looking for information, that's his job description, and nothing... He'd interrogated suspects, the friends of the suspects, the relatives of the friends of the suspects, still nothing.'

'He didn't come across any Viet Minh?'

'Oh, that... you can never know. He didn't know. You can interrogate the suspects; they're bound to tell you something, that leads to other suspects. There's no shortage of work and you're guaranteed to get results; it doesn't matter whether the information is useful. But the reason he was desperate, this guy from the Sûreté in the little town on the delta, was because he had liquidated at least a hundred guys and still hadn't had a mention in dispatches or a promotion. Hanoi was acting like he didn't exist. He was bitter. He traipsed up and down the only street, going from café to café, depressed, not knowing what to do, and all the people he passed lowered their eyes, turned tail, stepped off the pavement to let him pass; or they smiled at him, asked after his health with a lot of bowing and scraping, because none of them knew what to do any more, whether or not they should talk to him so he would leave them alone, whether to act naturally or act like him. And he didn't notice. He trudged the streets with his pistol tucked into his shorts, cursing the cumbersome Administration that had failed to acknowledge his hard work. He had never come up with any information, but he was efficient; he had never tracked down the Viet Minh, but he did his job; anyone trying to set up an underground network would have failed for lack of potential revolutionaries that he had pre-emptively liquidated; but no one recognized his true worth. He was mortified.'

Moreau ended with a little laugh, a particular little laugh he had that was not unpleasant, but not funny either, a laugh like his raw-boned face, a laugh like the pencil moustache that accentuated his thin lips; a frank, joyless laugh that chilled the blood for no apparent reason.

'At the end of the day, we can't withstand the weather in the colonies. We rot from the inside. Except you, Salagnon. With you it seems like water off a duck's back.'

'I observe, so I can get used to anything.'

'I adapt to anything, too. I used to be in charge of a group of rowdy little schoolboys. I was a real slave-driver. I made them wear a dunce's cap, slapped them if necessary, made them stand in the corner, kneel on the floor, sometimes on a ruler. No one played up in my class. They learned things off by heart. They didn't make mistakes. They raised their hands before they spoke. They didn't sit down until I gave the word, when everyone was quiet. These were techniques I learned at the École Normale, and from observation. Then the war came along. I took up a new job for a while, but how could I ever go back now? How could I ever stand in front of a group of little boys? How could I put up with the slightest trouble, given what I know? Here, I'm in charge of a whole people. I use the same techniques I learned at the École Normale, and from observation, but since I'm dealing with adults I push them to the limit. I see things on a grand scale. Over here, there are no parents for me to inform about their little brat's behaviour so they can punish him. I have to do everything myself. How could I ever go back to being in charge of a bunch of schoolboys? What would I do to keep order? Would I kill one of them at the first sign of trouble, out of habit, to make an example? Would I conduct ruthless interrogations to find out who fired a spitball? I'm better off staying here. Here, death is not terribly important. They don't seem to suffer. Among the dead, among the soon-to-be dead, we understand each other. I could never stand up in front of a class of kids again; it would be inappropriate. I don't know what do any more. Or rather I do, I know all too well, but I do it on a bigger scale. I'm trapped here. I stay here, hoping that I will never have to go back, for the good of the little boys of France.'

The horizon rose like a folded sheet of paper; triangular hills appeared as though the flat earth had been folded; the river snaked in wide meanders. They sailed deeper into the unremitting jungle. The current grew stronger; the propellers of the LCTs beat the water more forcefully. More than ever there was the worrying prospect that they might fail; a lush green velvet fringed the riverbanks; the hills grew higher and more vertiginous and merged with the low clouds.

'The jungle is no better,' grumbled the captain, emerging from his cabin. 'You think it will be uninhabited, unsullied. You think you'll finally get a bit of peace... The hell you will! The place is teeming. A quick machine-gun burst and you'll kill a dozen. Hey, you back there! Spray the bank!'

The gunner in the stern whirled his machine gun and fired a long burst into the trees lining the bank. The soldiers gave a start, then cheered. The huge bullets exploded against the branches; monkeys howled, the birds took flight. Fragments of leaves and splintered wood fell into the water.

'There you go,' said the captain. 'Not too many today, but the sector has been cleared. I'll be glad when we get there. I'll be glad when this is over.'

He dropped them off at a ruined village on a bank pitted with craters. The crates of ammunition were transported by prisoners with 'PIM' in big letters on their backs, guarded by legionnaires who paid them no heed. Sandbags piled as neatly as bricks encircled the remains of the shacks, cut off the surrounding routes, surrounded the field guns, whose long barrels were trained on the lush, green hills draped with tendrils of mist. The villagers had disappeared, leaving only broken remnants of everyday life: wicker baskets, a sandal, a few broken pots. Legionnaires in helmets stood guard behind parapets of sandbags, while others with shovels dug trenches to further secure the village. They worked in silence, with the implacable seriousness of the Legion. They found the command post in a church whose roof had collapsed. The rubble and the broken pews in the nave had been cleared away and the altar repurposed as a dining table, where the officers were now sitting; the altar was laid out perfectly: white tablecloth, bone china edged with blue; candles set all around cast a flickering glow that was reflected in the gleaming glasses and the cutlery. In dusty uniforms, their white kepis set next to their plates, the officers were being served by an orderly in a morning coat, whose every gesture exuded expertise.

'Trucks? To transport your troops? Are you joking?' muttered a colonel with his mouth full.

Salagnon insisted.

'But I don't have any trucks. All my trucks drive over landmines and explode. You'll have to wait for the infantry convoy. It's bound to get here some day.'

'I need to get to the post.'

'Well then go on foot. It's that way,' he said, jerking his fork towards the gothic window. 'Now leave us to finish. Last night's dinner had to be postponed because of an attack. Thankfully it has survived unscathed. The orderly here worked as a maître d'hôtel in some of the finest establishments in Berlin before Stalin's rocket launchers turned them into piles of rubble. He serves perfectly, even in ruins; bringing him with us was a fine decision. Bring the next course.'

The imperturbable orderly brought meat that smelled wonderfully of meat, something rare in Indochine. So Moreau stepped forwards.

'Colonel, I'm afraid I must insist.'

His fork, having already speared a juicy hunk, hovered halfway between his plate and his mouth; he looked up irritably. But there was something about Moreau, this scrawny, vulgar little man, which ensured that when he asked for something, never raising his thin-lipped voice, people gave it to him as though it were a matter of life and death. The colonel had seen his type before. He did not give a damn about his trucks and he very much wanted to finish his meal.

'Very well. I'll lend you a truck for the munitions, but that's all I have. The men will have to go on foot. The track is more or less safe. But the Colonial Army needs to stop relying on us.'

Moreau turned to Salagnon, who nodded; he was conciliatory by nature, although this was not something he was proud of. Leaving the orderly to serve dinner, they walked out of the church.

'Trambassac wasn't wrong. Out here, it really is the lord, his vassals and their valiant knights; they've all got their gang.'

'Well, this is your gang.'

Mariani and Gascard were sitting on crates, waiting for them; and the forty Thai soldiers were hunkered down, leaning on rifles, which they held like spears. Mariani got up as they approached, smiling when he heard the news; he addressed himself to Moreau.

The trek took three days on foot. They marched in single file, rifles slung over their shoulders. Before long they were streaming with sweat from climbing the steep slopes in the blazing sun. They did not go near the shady edge. This was the jungle and therefore there were an infinite number of traps and hiding places, wires strung between trees connected to mines, patient snipers lurking in the branches. The lush green that flanked the path was dangerous, so they marched down the middle of the track in the blazing sun. Now and then a clearing with scorched edges showed the effects of long-range artillery or air raids; a charred truck lay toppled in the ditch, riddled with bullets, evidence of some skirmish whose witnesses were all dead. Thankfully, the dead were not left to rot, since otherwise the track would have been littered with bodies. Bodies are not left behind, they are recovered, except for those in the river. Except those in the river, thought Salagnon, struggling with his kitbag. What did they signify, the bodies in the river? People are reluctant to touch dead bodies, so sometimes they are left behind, but why throw them in the river? Every step on this steep, rutted track was heavy-going, and with exhaustion came unpleasant thoughts and the despondency that comes from aching muscles. At night they slept in the trees, in rope hammocks, half of them awake, guarding the half that were asleep.

In the morning they set off again on the track through the jungle. He had never imagined it could be so difficult to put one foot in front of the other. His knapsack full of metal objects dragged him backwards; his weapons felt heavier and heavier. His thigh muscles were as taut as the cables of a suspension bridge; he felt them creak with every movement. The sun parched him; water leached from his body; heavy with salt, he was covered in white blotches.

On the evening of the third day they came to a ridge and a rolling landscape of hills suddenly opened below them like a fan. They were surrounded by yellowed grass that glittered with shards of gold in the late afternoon sun, while the trail wound through the tall grass like a dark, gaping trench. From the ridge they could see for miles. The hills stretched out to the horizon. The closest to them were the dewy green of precious stones; beyond them were hills tinged with turquoise, a blueness that gradually faded, diluted by distance, until they became weightless and melted into the white sky. The long line of hunched men, bowed beneath the burden of their knapsacks, stopped to catch their breath, and were infused by this sweeping, strangely weightless landscape, sated with pale blue and green; and with a spring in their step, they set off again for the post perched on the ridge.

A native sergeant opened the door and welcomed them. He was responsible for everything. The infantrymen were crouched in the yard, at the thatched corner towers. Salagnon looked around for a European face.

'Your officers?'

'Adjudant Morcel is buried over there,' he said. 'Sous-lieutenant Rufin is on manoeuvres. He'll be back soon. And Lieutenant Gasquier doesn't leave his room any more. He's expecting you.'

'So you don't have any managerial staff?'

'But we do, Lieutenant. Here, the Franco-Vietnamese forces have become de facto Vietnamese. But isn't it only natural that things should eventually correspond to words?' he said with a smile.

He spoke a fastidious French learned at school with barely the trace of a lilt, the same language Salagnon had learned 10,000 kilometres from here.

The senior officer was sitting at a table waiting for them, his shirt open over his well-padded belly; he seemed to be reading an old newspaper. His red-rimmed eyes flickered this way and that, not focusing on anything in particular, and he did not turn the pages. When Salagnon introduced himself, he did not look up; his eyes remained fixed on the paper, as though he had trouble raising them.

'Have you seen this?' he spluttered. 'Have you see it? Communists! They cut the throats of a whole village again. Because they refused to supply them with rice. And they're trying to cover up their crime, claiming it was the army, the police, the Sûreté, France! But they're confusing us, they're tricking us, they use stolen uniforms. And everyone knows the Sûreté has been infiltrated. Totally. By French communists who take their orders from Moscow. Who kill people on orders from Peking. You, you're new here, Lieutenant, so don't be fooled. Be careful.' Finally he looked up, his eyes rolling in their sockets. 'Isn't that right, Lieutenant? You won't let them fool you?'

His eyes glazed over and he toppled forwards, hitting his head against the table, and stopped moving.

'Give me a hand, Lieutenant,' muttered the native sergeant. They grabbed his legs and shoulders and laid him on the camp bed in the corner of the room. The newspaper had been hiding a bowl of *choum*, and he had a whole bottle under the chair. 'He usually has a sleep around this time of day,' the sergeant said in the whispered tone of someone in a nursery when a baby finally nods off. 'Mostly he sleeps straight through until morning but sometimes he wakes in the night and tries to persuade us to grab our kit and our weapons and set off into the jungle to hunt the Viet Minh by night, when they're least expecting it. It can be tough to calm him down and put him back to bed. The only way is to get him to drink more. Luckily, he's about to head back to Hanoi or to France. Otherwise, he'd get us all killed. You're his replacement. Try to hold out a bit longer.'

The cases of ammunition and the provisions arrived the following day; the truck did hang around, but set off down to the river again, and with it went the sleeping Gasquier and his company of infantrymen. They wedged Gasquier between crates, so that he wouldn't fall off the truck, and the infantrymen followed behind on foot. The dust settled and Salagnon became *chef de poste*, replacing the previous senior officer, who was burnt-out but still alive, saved in spite of himself by the sensible decisions of an indigenous non-commissioned officer.

* * *

Rufin reappeared in the late afternoon, leading a column of men in tatters. They had spent several days marching through the jungle, fording streams, hiding in sticky bushes, sleeping in the mud. Lying in the undergrowth, they had waited; dripping with salt sweat they had marched. They were all utterly filthy; their clothes were stiff with grime, sweat, blood and pus, spattered with mud; morale, too, was in tatters, drained by a mixture of fatigue, abject fear and the fierce courage verging on madness which is the only thing that makes it possible to march, to run, to slaughter in the jungle for days at a time.

'Four days and, more importantly, four nights,' Rufin pointed out as he saluted Salagnon. His beautiful, blond, childlike face was now gaunt, but the fringe that swept over his eyes still shimmered and a smile still hovered on his lips. 'Thank God, years in the scouts prepared me for long marches.'

The stooped men coming back could have collapsed by the side of the track, and in a few hours would have melted and disappeared; it would have been impossible to distinguish them from the humus. But although as filthy and unkempt as tramps, the rifles they carried were pristine. They kept their rifles as good as new, perfectly aligned, well oiled, gleaming; their bodies might be exhausted, their clothes like something from a rag-and-bone shop, but their weapons were indefatigable, chubby and well fed no matter the hour, no matter the effort. The metal fixings glinted like the eyes of a wildcat; they were untarnished by fatigue. In minds dulled by exhaustion there still glimmered a lone, last thought transmitted by the brute matter of their weapons, the thought of murder, cold and cruel. All the rest was flesh, tissue, and had rotted; they had left it by the wayside. Nothing remained of them but their skeleton: the weapon and the will, murder on the alert. Much more than an extension of hand or eye, the rifle is an extension of bone, and bone gives form to the body, which would otherwise be limp. Fastened to the bone is the muscle that makes it possible to exert force. Utter exhaustion has this effect: it strips away flesh and reveals bone. It is a state that can be reached by working to the point of collapse, by marching in the blazing sun, by digging holes with a pick. In each case one will be reduced to what remains, and what remains may be considered what is best in man: and that is obstinacy. War can achieve this, too.

The men went and lay down and fell asleep. After the commotion of their arrival, a great silence descended over the outpost, the sun began to sink.

'The Viets?' said Rufin. 'They're all around. The jungle is crawling with them. They move about at will. They come from the Haute-Région, where we don't go any more. But we can do what they do: hide in the undergrowth so they can't see us.'

He fell asleep on his back, his head tilted slightly, his beautiful, angelic face, so pale, so downy, was that of a child.

In Indochine night is not long in coming. For a few minutes after the sun had set, they were surrounded by a landscape vaporized by porcelain mountains that were utterly weightless, the blue-tinged peaks floated without touching the ground; they ebbed, dissipated, dissolved and it was night. Darkness is the diminution of the visible, the gradual obliteration of distance, a torrent of dark liquid that wells up from the earth. Perched on their ridge, they lost their footing. They hung suspended in the landscape with the floating mountains. Night arrived like a pack of black dogs running up from the valleys, snuffling at the edges of the forest, scrambling up the slopes, covering everything and, finally, devouring the sky itself. Night came from below with a fierce panting, with an urge to bite, with the frenzied restlessness of a pack of baying mastiffs.

When night had come down, they knew they would be alone until daybreak, in a walled room whose doors did not close, encircled by the breath of the black dogs seeking them out, whimpering in the darkness. No one would come to their aid. They closed the door to their little tower, but it was only bamboo. Their flag hung, listless, at the end of a long pole and it quickly disappeared, they could see no stars because the sky was overcast. They were alone in the night.

They fired up the generator, carefully counting the remaining cans of petrol; they fed a high-voltage charge through the network of wires woven through bamboo stakes in the ditches; they switched on the spotlights in corner towers made of tree trunks and packed earth, and the single ceiling light in the blockhouse. Any other light came from paraffin lamps and from oil lamps belonging to the native soldiers huddled in small groups.

What falls at evening is not night – night rises from the teeming valleys that surround the post, from the foot of the steep slopes carpeted with yellow grass – what falls at evening is their faith in themselves, their courage, their hope that they might go one day and live elsewhere. When night comes, they see themselves waiting here for ever; they picture themselves on the last evening, at that last moment heading nowhere, and see themselves dissolve into the acidic soil of the forests of Indochine, their bones carried away by the rains, their flesh transformed into leaves to become food for the monkeys.

Rufin was sleeping. Mariani was tinkering with the radio in the blockhouse, scanning through the static for snatches of French words, checking for the thousandth time that it was working. Sitting next to him, Gascard had begun drinking as soon as day began to wane, casually, without too much attention, as though taking an aperitif on a balmy summer evening; it was impossible to tell when he had drunk too much: he never fell, never stumbled, and the tremulous lamplight concealed his trembling fingers. Moreau and Salagnon, still outside, were leaning on the earthen rampart, staring into the darkness; they could see nothing and they spoke in hushed voices, as though the black dogs encircling the world might hear them, might sense their presence and come.

'You realize we're stuck here?' Moreau whispered. 'We have only two choices: either we hang around here waiting to be attacked, to have our throats cut in our sleep, to be relieved; or we do what they do, we hide in the bushes and we harry them at night.'

He said nothing more. The darkness moved like water, heavy, scented, bottomless. The jungle rang with creaks and cries, producing a steady drone that could be anything, animals, rustling leaves or the shadows of soldiers marching in Paris through the trees. Salagnon reflexively adopted an uneasy silence, a watchful silence that was futile in this dark confusion where it would have been better to speak, to speak French endlessly beneath the lone electric light in the block-house to remind oneself, to remember oneself, to exist, however dimly, to oneself, such was the threat that this sense of self might dissolve in the darkness. Salagnon suspected that in the weeks to come his mental health and his survival might depend on the number of cans of diesel that remained. Here, in the darkness, he would lose himself.

'So, what do you think?'

'I'll leave it to you.'

In daylight the post looked like a fort built for tin soldiers made of packed earth, flat stones and pine needles; they had built such castles on holiday or on a wet Thursday afternoon. Now they lived in one. The little fort was constructed from timber, mud and bamboo, and, using concrete ferried up by truck, they had built the blockhouse, where the French slept: a dungeon no bigger than a room. They lived in their floating castle, four valiant knights with their squires and their menials, on a barren ridge commanding a vast expanse of jungle, lush green seen from above, criss-crossed by the brown meanders of the river. The verb 'command' is used when a fortress geographically dominates the landscape, but in this case it was faintly laughable. Beneath the trees below a whole division could have passed unseen. Salagnon could always fire a few mortars into the forest. He could.

The days passed, they mounted up; the long, unvarying days spent watching the forest. Army life is composed of long periods of empti-ness in which you do nothing but wonder if they will ever end; later the question ceases to matter. Waiting, watching, travelling, it all drags. There is no end in sight. Every day it starts anew. And then time reboots, in the fitful convulsions of an attack, seeming to speed up now, having accumulated reserves. And this, too, drags on: the lack of sleep, the constant vigilance, the hair-trigger reactions; there is no end in sight, except death. Soldiers find it easier returning to civilian life than it is to pass the time, to wait, to sit, to do nothing, motionless, as though floating on their backs while time flows past. They find it easier than others to endure the empty periods. What they miss are the spasms in which the time accrued is abruptly expended, which have no reason to occur after a war.

Every morning they wake up happy, comforted to find that they did not die in the night. They watch the sun emerge from the mists that glide beyond the trees. Salagnon often painted. He had time on his hands. He would sit and try his hand at wash drawing, drawing in ink, landscape; here they all amounted to the same thing, since all the water in the ground and in the air transformed the country into an ink-wash. Sitting in the tall grass or on a rock, he painted the undulating scene, the translucence of the receding hills, the trees thrusting blackly from the clouds. In the late morning the light was harsher; he used less diluted ink. In the courtyard he sketched the Thai soldiers, drawing them from a distance, preserving only their posture. Lying, sitting, crouching, stopping or standing, they could adopt more positions than a European could imagine. A European stands or lies, otherwise he sits; Europeans exhibit a sort of haughty contempt, a disdain for the ground. Thais do not seem to hate the ground they tread, nor fear it; they do not seem to worry; they assume every conceivable position. Sketching them, he learned all the possible positions of a human body. He also tried to sketch the trees, but found none of them pleasing in isolation. Individually most seemed stunted, but taken together they formed a terrifying mass. Like people, like the people here, about whom he knew little. He drew portraits of the four men living with him. He drew rocks.

Moreau was not about to let himself be stifled here, protecting himself from the day by day, from the night by night; so after dark, he would head into the jungle with *his* Thais. He always talked about *his* men – the possessive here is delectable; it would have delighted Trambassac, who scattered mini-despots throughout the Haute-Région. Moreau would strap on his kit and, as soon as the rim of the sun grazed the hills, he would set off through the quivering copper of the tall grasses towards the forest which, in the twilight, glistened a deep bottle-green that was almost black. They trooped out in single file with the clatter that fifteen men make as they march, even when they are silent: the breathing, the rustle of fabric, the click of metal, the soft whisper of rubber soles in the dust. They would march away and the sound would fade; they would step into the jungle and within a few metres would disappear among the branches. Listening carefully, it was still possible to hear them, then that also faded. The sun would drop swiftly behind the hills, the jungle would be swallowed by the darkness; no trace would remain of Moreau and his Thais. They had vanished, nothing more could be heard, all that could be hoped was that they would return.

Gascard, for his part, was happy to be stifled here. Drowning is the gentlest death, rumour has it, so people foolishly say, as though anyone has made the attempt. But then again, why not? Especially if it is possible to drown in pastis. Gascard did his utmost; it was gentle. From dusk to dawn, he stank of aniseed, and the day was not long enough for the fumes to evaporate. Salagnon would bawl him out, order him to cut down on his drinking – but not too much, not completely, since Gascard now was like a fish, if taken out of his life-giving pastis he would drown.

The infantry convoy finally arrived one afternoon. They had been expecting it the day before, but there had been a delay; there were always delays, because the trip never went smoothly, the *route coloniale* is never clear, convoys spend most of their time doing anything other than driving. At first they heard a muffled roar that filed the horizon, then they saw a cloud above the trees, brownish dust, plumes of diesel smoke, moving along the *route coloniale* on the twisting, turning gravel track, then finally, at the last bend before the hill up to the post, they saw the green trucks jolting along.

'What a racket! The Viet Minh can hear us coming a mile away. They know where we are, but we don't.'

The trucks panted as they claimed the hill, if it's possible to say a truck pants, but these GMC cargo trucks, with their peeling paint, their huge, half-bald tyres, their bodywork dented and sometimes riddled with bullet holes, moved so slowly along the rutted track that they seemed to waddle, coughing hoarsely, their engines spluttering and gasping asthmatically. When they pulled up outside the post it was a relief for everyone that they could finally rest. The men who climbed down were shirtless, staggering, mopping their foreheads; their red eyes drooped, they looked as though they were about to lie down and go to sleep.

'Two days, it took us. And we have to go back.'

The trucks alternated with half-tracks full of Moroccans. They too climbed down, but said nothing. They crouched by the edge of the road and waited. Their thin, bronzed faces all told the same tale: immense tiredness, tension and a powerful rage that went unstated. Two days to travel fifty kilometres was not unusual on the *route coloniale*. The Haiphong train goes just as slowly, crawling along the tracks, stopping for repairs and moving off again at walking speed.

Here, machines are a hindrance. A thousand men and women carrying sacks of rice would move faster than twenty trucks in convoy, would cost less, arrive more often and be less vulnerable. The true war machine is man. Communists know this, and Asian communists know it all too well.

'Unload!'

The *capitaine* in charge of the *goumiers*, a colonial soldier hardened by the Moroccan sun and now softened and dampened by the jungles of Indochine, came over to Salagnon, saluted brusquely and stood next to him, hands on his hips, surveying his crippled convoy.

'If you knew how pissed off I am doing this, Lieutenant, leading my lads to be slaughtered just to deliver a couple of crates to the jungle. To outposts that won't survive the first serious attack.' He sighed. 'I'm not talking about you, but still. Come on, get this stuff unloaded so we can head back.'

'Can I offer you a drink, Capitaine?'

The *capitaine* looked at Salagnon, screwing up his eyes, which formed flabby wrinkles, his skin looked like wet cardboard ready to split at the slightest strain.

'Why not?'

A chain formed to unload the crates. Salagnon led the *capitaine* to the blockhouse and poured him a pastis only slightly cooler than the temperature outside. It was the best he could do.

'When I say I'm pissed off, it's because escorting convoys is the least of our job. We spend most of our time swinging picks and shovels, hauling winches. We're glorified navvies, building the road we're travelling on bit by bit. They dig it up to stop us getting through. They dig trenches across the road during the night. You never know where they are. The road goes through the jungle and *bam*! there's a trench. A neat piece of work, perpendicular to the track, sides perfectly straight, bottom perfectly level, because they're conscientious people, they're not savages. So we fill it in. Once it's been filled in, we set off again. A few kilometres later it's trees, neatly sawn and laid across the road. So we get out a winch. We clear them away, we set off again. Then there's another trench. We keep tools in the back of the trucks and we have prisoners to fill the trenches. Captured Viet Minh, dodgy militiamen, suspect peasants from the villages. They all wear the same black pyjamas; they keep their heads down; they never say anything; we take them with us anywhere there's something to be carried or something to be dug; we tell them what to do, and if it's not too complicated, they do it. We had a fresh lot, a Viet Minh column captured by a battalion of paratroopers looking for something they still haven't found. They handed them over to us so we could take them back to the delta. But it's a pain in the arse. You have to keep a close eye on them. Some of them are crafty bastards, political commissars we're too fucking stupid to spot; it can be dangerous. So when we came to the first trench, they filled it, but by the third I sensed things were going to end in disaster. Three trenches so close together. I smelled an ambush, and dealing with an ambush when you've got prisoners to keep an eye on would be very risky. So I had them climb down into the trench, shot them, then we filled it in. The convoy drove straight over it, problem solved.' He drained his glass, slammed it on the table. 'Lighter trucks, fewer hold-ups, and there's no problem with numbers; the paras don't even know how many they gave us, and back at base they've no idea we were even bringing any prisoners. And it's not like we're short of suspects; we don't know where to put them. The whole of Indochine is full of suspects.'

Salagnon poured another glass. He drank half of it in one gulp, stared into the distance distractedly.

'Hey, talking of convoys, did you hear the Viet Minh attacked the BMC?'

'The military brothel?'

'Yeah, the travelling whorehouse. Now you'll say, that's normal. These guys spend months trapped in the jungle with a bunch of Tonkinese officers who aren't exactly sexy. So, obviously, they're bound to crack. Then some guy comes up with the idea: "Hey, boys!"' – he mimicked a Vietnamese accent – '"New target, brothel. Set ambush, get sucky-fucky same time."'

'That would be funny, but that's not how it went down. The BMC is five trucks full of whores – mostly young Annamese and a couple of French girls – that shuttle between the barracks, with a madam as acting colonel. The trucks are kitted out with little beds, little fancy curtains, you go in one side, get your leg over, come out the other; it's a sucky-fucky assembly line. A military escort is provided by four trucks of Senegalese soldiers. It's tough to find guys to escort the BMC. The Moroccans find the whole idea disgusting; they don't want anything to do with sex, except when they're on a raid, but in that case they can slit the girl's throat after or bring her back and marry her. The Annamese are offended, they're romantics at heart; their idea of fun is holding hands and saying nothing. And besides, seeing their countrywomen in that situation hurts their national pride, which has only existed for about five minutes, so it's easily wounded. The Legion isn't interested – they move around in phalanxes, all boys together. Obviously there's the Colonial Army, but they're devious bastards, they harass the prostitutes, they kick up a fuss, they can't really be trusted with providing security. That leaves the Senegalese: they get on well with the whores, give them big smiles, and little Annamese girls aren't really their thing. So they pile everyone into a bunch of trucks and they tour the jungle garrisons. But this time, things turned nasty. A whole regiment of Viet Minh showed up with enough guns to capture Hanoi.'

'What? To raid a brothel?'

'Yep. That was clearly their target. First off, hollow-charge round into the cabs, the drivers were blown to kingdom come; then mortar shells through the slatted sides of the half-tracks riding escort; machine-gun bursts to deal with anyone who jumped down and tried to make a run for it. In a couple of minutes, everyone was dead.'

'Even the prostitutes?'

'Especially the prostitutes. When a rescue party arrived, they found the burned-out trucks in the middle of the road and all the bodies laid out along the verge. Arranged them neatly: the Senegalese, their officers, the whores, the brothel madam. They laid them all out the same way, arms by their sides, spaced ten metres apart. They would have had to measure it out, they're conscientious people, it was absolutely precise. There were a hundred dead, a whole kilometre of corpses. Can you imagine? A kilometre of corpses laid out like they're asleep, it went on for ever. And around the smouldering trucks, a pile of pink wreckage, knick-knacks, pillows, lingerie, knickers, curtains and special cabins.'

'Did they... make the most of it before they left?'

'Sexually, they didn't do a thing. A doctor examined the girls and he was categorical. But they decapitated the Annamese whores and set their heads on their bellies; it was a terrifying sight. Twenty girls with their throat cut, their heads on their stomachs, their make-up, lipstick still perfect, their eyes open. And planted next to them a brand new Vietnamese flag. It was a sign: we don't fuck with the Expeditionary Corps. We wage war on them. A whole regiment just to send a message. When the news got out, it sent a chill through every brothel in Indochine from here to Saigon. A lot of the *con gái* hightailed it back to their villages without even asking for their backpay. The Expeditionary Corps took a hit in the balls.'

They finished their drinks in silence, united by this unbiased observation of the absurdity of the world.

'The revolutionary war is a war of signs,' Salagnon said finally.

'I'm afraid that's too cerebral for me, Lieutenant. All I see is a country of lunatics. Surviving here is a full-time job. We don't have time to think, not like the soldiers with cushy jobs, safe in their blockhouses. I'm out there in a truck filling in trenches. Well, thanks for the drink. Your supplies should be unloaded by now. I'll head off.'

Salagnon watched them drive off down the *route coloniale*. Never had the term 'ramshackle' seemed more appropriate, he thought; they juddered along the stony track in a cacophony of metallic clanks and engine farts. They plodded down the road like a herd of exhausted elephants; and not Hannibal's warlike elephants, more like superannuated circus elephants dragged out of retirement to do a little haulage, and who would one day lie down by the roadside and never get up.

In the courtyard the Thais were stowing crates of munitions, spare weapons, rolls of barbed wire, a searchlight, everything they would need to survive. The posts could exist only because of the convoys supplying them, and the convoys could exist only because of the road on which they travelled. The Expeditionary Corps is not in the blockhouses; it stretches out along hundreds of kilometres of road;

it courses like blood through an infinite number of fragile, slender capillaries, which burst at the slightest injury and bleed out.

The convoy that has just disappeared into the jungle may never reach its destination, or it may arrive, or half of it might make it back. It might be decimated by a volley of mortar shells or bursts of machine-gun fire, whose bullets rip through the cabs like folded paper. The trucks topple and burn, dead drivers slumping over steering wheels; soldiers lying in the road try to fire back, but they can see nothing, then everything stops. When the convoys do arrive, the drivers can barely stand, all they want is to sleep, and yet they drive back all the same.

Each convoy brings with it losses, damage. The Expeditionary Corps slowly grows weaker, losing blood drop by drop. When a road becomes impassable, the posts are relinquished, officially declared abandoned, erased from the High Command map, and those who staffed it are ordered to return. Any way they can. The French zone is shrinking. In Tonkin it is reduced to the delta, and not even the whole of the delta. All around are outposts, regularly spaced watchtowers attempting to secure the roads. There are numerous watchtowers, each manned by a handful of men who rarely step outside. It is like trying to catch water in a sieve: you try to make the holes smaller so as to lose less water, but of course it doesn't work.

They made concrete. The convoy had brought enough materials to build four walls. They repaired the little cement mixer found in every outpost – although it may seem unprepossessing, it is the primary tool for ensuring a French presence in Indochine – and set it turning. Gascard, stripped to the waist, stood in front of it, taking upon himself the laborious task of adding the water, sand, cement, raising a cloud of dust that made you grit your teeth. Bare-chested in the blazing sun, he mixed the ingredients until he was covered in a film of white, white streaked with sweat, but he clenched his teeth and said nothing, just grunted now and then from the exertion; one might even have thought he was enjoying it. The concrete was carried in buckets to the timber moulds. Around one of the corner towers they built a small concrete cube equipped with loopholes. Inside they set a huge American machine gun on a tripod. On top they built a sloping roof, using the tiles brought on the trucks.

'Looks pretty good, doesn't it?' said Mariani. 'This way we can mow them down and still stay dry. Rat-a-tat-tat! We dig trenches and not one of them comes near. They won't take us on now.'

'Given the quality of the concrete, it won't withstand a direct hit,' said Moreau, who had not lifted a single bucket, but simply watched from a distance.

'A direct hit with what? The Viets have no artillery. And if they did have Chinese cannons, d'you think they'd lug them through the jungle? You can't wheel things through the jungle. What do you say, Salagnon?'

'I don't know. But it was a fine idea. Heavy work sobers up Gascard. And we'll be drier inside than we would be in a rammed-earth pillbox.'

'I'm not setting foot inside,' said Moreau.

Everyone looked at him. Submachine gun in hand, his hair neatly parted, in the afternoon heat he smelled of a barbershop.

'Do whatever you like,' said Salagnon.

The rains came after a long preparation. Potbellied storm clouds like war-junks built up over the South China Sea. The clouds slowly rolled their lacquered black hulls, gliding forwards like colossal ships, casting thick shadows on the ground beneath. As they passed, the hills took on the deep emerald colour of thick molten glass. The clouds launched rumbling broadsides, perhaps as they collided or perhaps to cause panic. The roll of huge drums echoed through the valleys, louder, nearer, as a curtain of rain fell suddenly, torrents of lukewarm water splashing against the woven walls, sluicing across the palm-thatch roofs, carving the claggy soil into a thousand red rivulets that raced downhill. Salagnon and Moreau had heard the thunder following them, and the curtain of rain beat down on the trees; they ran along the muddy path, pursued by this roar that was moving faster than they were, the branches strafing, the sky thundering; they ran to the village built on the slope. 'Built' is perhaps the wrong word for the clutch of bamboo huts thatched with dry leaves; better to say 'placed' or better yet 'planted'; like shrubs, like kitchen plants in which one could live. In a forest clearing these vegetable shacks grew indiscriminately from the thin soil littered with dead leaves. Below, the terraced rice fields swept down to a river flanked by large rocks. The *route coloniale* skirted the village; the brown river was three days' walk.

In these mountain villages everything seems precarious, impermanent; here man is merely transitory, the jungle waits, the sky mocks; the villagers are actors from a touring theatre company settled in for the night; they walk stiffly, they are very clean, they say little and their clothes seem curiously opulent in the forest clearing.

Salagnon and Moreau were still racing down the path as the rain inundated the mountains; storm clouds filled the sky, water coursing down faster than they could run, stripping the smooth stones bare, stirring up a seething, reddish mire that surged down the slope; the very road was running with them, overtaking them, a crimson torrent swirling around their legs, beneath their feet. They stumbled, almost slipped, as the rains finally caught up with them. The brims of their bush hats immediately went limp and slapped against their cheeks. They leapt on to the veranda of a big house, the large ornate cabin set in the middle of the shacks. A group of men were waiting for them, sitting in a semicircle watching the rain come down in sheets. They shook themselves, laughing, took off their hats and their shirts, wrung them out and stood there, hatless, shirtless. The village elders watched them in silence. The village chief – they called him this, not knowing how to translate the word that described his function – got to his feet and casually shook their hands. He had seen cities, he spoke French, he knew that in France, where the power was, what he thought of as rudeness was seen as modern and hence the epitome of politeness. And so he adapted, he told everyone what they wanted to hear. He shook hands a little half-heartedly, as he had seen it done in cities, trying to emulate a gesture that was alien to him. He was the chief, he steered the village, and it was as difficult as steering a boat through rapids. At any moment the boat might sink and he would not be saved. The two Frenchmen came and sat with the impassive old men under the eaves; they stared out at the curtain of rain while a cold mist drifted towards them; a hunched old woman came and gave them bowls of a cloudy alcohol that did not smell particularly pleasant, but warmed them considerably. Still the water coursed down the slope, forming a river, a canal, tracing a street through the village. On the far side was a shack with no walls; a simple raised floor with a thatched roof mounted on wooden poles. The materials looked new, the construction solider, all the angles straight. Children were sitting inside, taking lessons from a teacher in a white shirt gesturing to a map of Asia with a bamboo cane. He pointed to places and the children named them, reciting their lesson as one with that birdlike cheeping of a tonal language being spoken by immature voices.

'Our children are learning to read, to count, to understand the world,' said the chief, with a smile. 'I have been to Hanoi. I have seen the world is changing. We live in peace. What is happening in the delta, that is not us, that is far away, many days' walk. It is far from who we are. But I saw that the world was changing. I worked so that the village would build this school and bring a schoolteacher. Now we rely on you to keep peace in the jungle.'

Moreau and Salagnon nodded; their bowls were refilled, they drank, they were drunk.

'We are relying on you,' he said again, 'so that we can go on living in peace. And changing as the world changes, but no faster, at the correct rhythm. We are relying on you.'

Befuddled by drink, girdled by the roar of the rain hammering on the thatch, by the gurgling cataracts tumbling all around, the cascades splashing into the puddles, ploughing up the soil, Moreau and Salagnon nodded again, bobbing their heads to the rhythm of the children's chanting, a Buddhist smile playing on their lips.

When the rain finally stopped, they headed back to the post.

'There are Viet Minh there,' said Moreau.

'How do you know?'

'The school. The teacher, the children, the map of Asia, the elders saying nothing and the chief talking to us; the way he says things.'

'But school is a good thing, surely?'

'In France, yes. But what do you expect them to learn here, if not their right to independence? They'd be better off ignorant.'

'Does ignorance protect people from communism?'

'Yes. By rights we should be suspicious, we should interrogate, even liquidate if necessary.'

'And we're not going to?'

'We'd end up ruling over the dead. And he knows that, the treacherous old bastard. He's risking his neck, too. He's trapped between us and the Viet Minh. He's faced with two ways to die, caught between two rocks that could scuttle his boat. There has to be a route to survival, but it's so narrow that navigating it is almost impossible. Maybe we can help him. That's not what we're here for, but sometimes I get sick and tired of our mission. I'd rather live in peace with these people, instead of having to be constantly on the alert. It's probably the booze talking. I don't know what they put in it. I feel like doing what they do, sitting down and watching the rain.'

All across the world the gathering dark is a time that makes people sad. In their post in the Haute-Région, at night, they have trouble breathing; the darkness weighs on them and they feel a twinge of panic. This is normal. The progressive absence of light is like an absence of oxygen. Little by little, everything was leached of air, their lungs, their movements, their thoughts. Lamps grew dim, they guttered, chests struggled to rise and fall, hearts panicked.

The world existed only through the radio. The High Command issued vague orders. The breach must be closed. The Viet Minh swan around like they own the place. Things have to be made watertight.

They must not be allowed to reach the delta. The mountains must be made inhospitable to the Viets. Seek out contact. Hit squads should be sent out; each post should become a base of operations for a continuous series of raids. The radio crackled in the night beneath the lone electric light in the blockhouse, spluttering advice.

In the evening Moreau would set out with his Thais. Salagnon would man the post; he had trouble sleeping. In the blockhouse, beneath the only bulb, he would paint. The generator purred softly, feeding power into the network of wires in the ditches. He painted in ink. He thought of Eurydice. Without a single word, he told her what he could see in the Haute-Région of Tonkin. He painted the hills, the strange fog, the glaring light when the mists dispersed; he painted the straw huts, the thickets of bamboo, the stiffly formal natives, the wind in the yellow grass around the post. He painted Eurydice's beauty spilling over the landscape, in the faintest glimmer of light, in every shadow, in the dim green glow glimpsed through the leaves. He painted at night, though he could barely see, painted everything shrouded in the beauty of Eurydice; and Moreau would come upon him in the morning sleeping next to a pile of pages warped by the humidity. Half of these he would shred and burn, the rest he would carefully parcel up. These packages he would give to the drivers who brought ammunition and provisions, each addressed to Algiers, although he did not know whether they arrived. Moreau would watch him work, watch him choose, watch him rip up half of his sketches and package the rest. 'You're making progress,' he would say. 'And it keeps your hands busy. It's important to keep your hands busy when you've nothing to do. All I have is my knife.' And while Salagnon was picking through his sketches, Moreau would sharpen the blade, which he kept in an oiled leather sheath.

Things were not going well in this post on borrowed time. The days dragged out. They were aware of their fragility: their fortress overlooked a vast expanse of jungle, clearly visible on the rocky outcrop, where no one could come to their aid. The Thais would squat on their heels and watch the time pass, babble in their trilling voices, smoke lazily, play games of chance that led to long, mysterious arguments from which they would get up and stalk off furiously, to unexpected reconciliations, more games, more long silences as they waited for the sun to set. Moreau would doze in a hammock he had hung in the yard, although he constantly kept watch through eyes that never fully closed; and several times a day he would inspect the guns, the ditches, the door; nothing escaped him. Salagnon sketched in absolute silence; not uttering a word even in his mind. Mariani read little books he had brought with him, re-reading each page so often that he must have known every word better than he knew his own thoughts. Gascard took charge of the heavy work with a squad of Thais; they cut bamboo stakes, sharpened them with a masterly flourish of their machetes and created traps all around the post; when they finished, he would slump in a chair, swig from his bottle and not get up again until evening. Rufin spent his time writing letters using his cache of fine writing paper. He wrote at the table in the blockhouse, hunched over like a schoolboy the better to follow the lines. He wrote to his mother in France in the impersonal tone of a little boy; he told her he had an office job in Saigon dealing with supplies. The office really existed and he had worked there before absconding, slamming the door and running into the dark jungle, but he did not want his mother to know this.

Time did not pass quickly. They knew that the whole Viet Minh army could attack them. They hoped they might pass unnoticed. They would have built another concrete tower, but the convoys had brought no more cement.

Eventually, one evening, Salagnon set out with Moreau. They slipped between the trees, scarcely able to make out the kitbag of the man in front in the inky darkness. Rufin led the way, because he could see in the dark and could recognize the tiny trails of animals that others would easily miss even in broad daylight; Moreau brought up the rear, so that no one strayed; between them Salagnon and the Thais carried the explosives. For a long time they put one foot in front of the other without seeming to make any headway, feeling the distance only through the numbing tiredness. They emerged into an open space a little less dark, whose edges they could not see; they felt a little more ease, a little less oppressiveness now that they had stepped out of the cover of the trees. 'We wait for daybreak,' Rufin whispered in his ear. They all lay down. Salagnon dozed fitfully. He watched darkness dissolve, details appear, a metallic glow suffuse a vast area of tall grass. A path wound through it. Lying on his belly, he peered between the blades of grass as though between tiny tree trunks. The Thais, as usual, did not move. Nor did Moreau or Rufin, who was asleep. Salagnon found it difficult to be comfortable; the grass was itchy, he felt columns of insects march between his legs, under his arms, over his stomach, that just as quickly disappeared; it was probably the sweat that itched, the fear of moving and the simultaneous fear of staying still, the fear of being mistaken for a tree stump by wood-boring insects, the fear of stirring the grass and being spotted; the feel of living plants against the skin is disagreeable, the sharp leaves cut, the flower heads tickle, the roots are uncomfortable, the soil shifts and sucks. Having fought a war, one can come to despise nature. Day was breaking, the heat was becoming oppressive; still his sweat-soaked skin crawled with the urge to scratch.

'There's one. Over there, look. This is a perfect spot. You can identify the enemy easily.'

A young boy appeared on the edge of the jungle, stepped on to the path. He paused, warily glancing to left and right. He clearly did not like the look of this path fringed with tall, swaying grasses. He was Vietnamese, that was obvious even at a distance; his black hair was neatly parted, his eyes were narrowed to a slit that stared, unblinking, making him look like a sentinel bird. He was about seventeen. He was holding something to his chest, cradling it between his hands, clutching it tight. He looked like a schoolboy lost in the woods.

'That thing he's holding, it's a grenade. The pin has been pulled out. If he drops it, it'll explode and bring the whole regiment following down on us.'

The boy came to a decision. He stepped off the path and walked through the grass. He advanced slowly. Without moving, the Thais buried themselves deeper in the ground. They knew Moreau. The young boy kept moving, clearing a path with one hand, while keeping the other pressed against his chest. From time to time he stopped, looked over the tall grass, listened, then walked on. He was heading straight for them. He was a few metres away. Lying on the ground, they watched him come. The thin stalks did little to conceal them. They were hiding behind blades of grass. The boy was wearing a rumpled white shirt stained with green and brown, half hanging out of his shorts. His black hair was neatly trimmed, the parting still visible, he clearly had not been living in the jungle long. Moreau drew his knife, which slipped almost soundlessly from the oiled scabbard with the faint rasp of a reptile's tongue. The young man stopped, he opened his mouth. He had guessed, of course, but wanted to believe it was just some small, slithering animal. His hands came down and slowly parted. Moreau leapt up from the grass, Salagnon followed instinctively, as though wires connected their every limb. Moreau charged at the young boy, swooped down on him; Salagnon caught the grenade in mid-air and held it tightly, keeping the safety catch in place. The knife quickly found the throat, which offered no resistance to the blade; blood pulsed from the severed carotid, gushed with a melodious sibilance; Moreau's hand over the mouth of the boy prevented him from making the slightest moan. Salagnon held the grenade, trembling, not knowing what to do with it, not quite realizing what had happened. He thought he might vomit or laugh or burst into tears, but he did none of these things. Moreau wiped his blade meticulously, so it would not rust, and cautiously, since it cut through flesh more easily than a razor. He held out a small metal ring to Salagnon.

'Put the pin back in. You can't go on holding it like that for the rest of your life. That's all he had, an unpinned grenade. For him it was double or quits. The Viet Minh regiments are surrounded by scouts. If they happen on us, they get killed or they toss the grenade and try to run for it. It's a test for people joining the revolutionary underground or a punishment meted out by the political commissar for those who step out of line. Those who survive get to stay with the group. We should have a few minutes before the others arrive.'

The grenade buried itself for ever in Salagnon's memory; his fingers trembling, he reinserted the pin. The weight of it, the density of the thick metal, the precise shade of green paint, the Chinese character boldly engraved on it, he would remember all these things. The Thais dragged the body out of sight and, under orders from Rufin, who was the expert, set the explosives in alternating lines along the path and spooled out the detonation wire.

'Let's take our places,' said Moreau.

He tapped Salagnon on the shoulder, urging him on. They split up into various groups and positioned themselves in a circle like the teeth of a trap. They dropped to the ground again, set their grenades in a line in front of them and poked the muzzles of the machine guns through the tall grass.

The Viet Minh regiment emerged from the forest: two lines of men, guns slung across their bellies, helmets threaded with palm leaves. They marched in step, soundless, maintaining a uniform distance. In the middle of the path, between the two lines of soldiers, coolies were bent double under the weight of heavy explosives. They reached the mines. Rufin hunkered over his machine gun; Moreau gave the signal and the Thai *sergent* brought the two wires together.

The sky above the jungles of Tonkin is often overcast. The constant seething of vegetation fuels it with fog, with clouds, with mists that mask the blue by day and the stars by night. But one night the whole sky cleared and the stars appeared. Leaning on an earthen rampart, head resting on a sandbag, Salagnon stared up at them. He thought about Eurydice, who probably did not often notice the stars. Because Algiers is always bright. Because in Algiers no one ever looked up. Because in Algiers people talked and went about their business; they did not spend the night alone, staring for hours into the heavens. There was always something to do in Algiers, always something to say, always someone to see. Unlike here. Moreau came and joined him.

'Have you seen the stars?'

'You'd do better to keep an eye on the jungle.'

Moreau pointed to something snaking through the trees. Pinpoints of light were visible through chinks in the forest canopy, but the moonlight made them difficult to see. But if one looked for a long time, for long enough, they made up a single, continuous line.

'What is it?'

'A Viet Minh regiment heading for the delta. They march in silence, with no lights. So as not to lose their way they set lanterns along the path, hidden lanterns that shine down but not up, so the soldiers can see where they are stepping. They pass through our lines, a whole division of them, and we never notice.'

'Do we just let them carry on?'

'Have you seen how many of us there are? The artillery is too far away, planes are completely useless at night. If they intercept a call from us, they'll annihilate us. We're not in a position of strength, so the best thing is to pretend to be asleep. They'll go through the village. The elders won't be happy about it. The chief is risking his neck.'

'So we do nothing.'

'Nothing.'

They fell silent. A luminescent line wound its way across the landscape, visible only to the two of them.

'We're going to die here, my friend, we're going to die. Some day or other.'

By morning a plume of smoke was rising from the village. In the dawn light a line of aeroplanes appeared, coming from the delta. They advanced with a soft purring, round-nosed DC3s scattering a series of parachutes. The canopies drifted down the pink sky like shy daisies and one by one vanished into the valley as though sucked in by shadows. A boom of artillery fire rang out across the slopes; a section of the forest began to burn. The noise subsided and, sometime in mid-afternoon, they had a call, loud and clear, on the radio.

'Are you still there? The mobile unit has recaptured the village. Make contact with them.'

'Recaptured the village? Did we miss something?' grunted Moreau.

They went down to the village. A whole army was stretched along the *route coloniale*. Trucks full of soldiers were chugging slowly up the hill; tanks were parked along the verge, turrets firing at the smouldering hills. The paratroopers stayed off to one side, lying on the grass, swapping cigarettes, staring at the profusion of equipment. The longhouse was burning, the roof of the school gaped, a huge crater in the floor was edged with splintered wood.

In the middle of the village a tent had been set up with tables for maps and field radios; flexible antennas swayed above them. Inside the shelter officers bustled, whispering into machines, addressing their orderlies only in curt phrases, peremptory orders quickly followed by action. Salagnon introduced himself to a colonel wearing a radio headset, who barely listened to him. 'So you're the guys from the post? The whole area is as leaky as a sieve, the village is overrun. What the fuck have you been playing at? Blind man's buff? I hate to be the one to tell you, but the Viets always win at that game.' And he went back to giving firing coordinates over his headset, a list of numbers he was reading from one of the maps. Salagnon shrugged and left the tent. He went and sat next to Moreau; they leaned against a bamboo hut, the Thais crouched in a line next to them, and they watched the trucks file past, the field guns, the tanks that made the ground shake as they passed.

The German appeared in front of them. As elegant as always, although a little thinner, he was wearing a legionnaire's uniform with sergeant's stripes.

'Salagnon? You were the one up at the post? You had a narrow escape. A whole Viet division marched through last night. They must have forgotten you.'

He was followed by two legionnaires as blond as caricatures. They held their machine guns at their hips, straps slung over their shoulders, fingers on the triggers. He spoke to them in German and they took up positions behind him, feet well apart, as though on sentry duty, scanning the surrounding area with chilling attentiveness. Salagnon got to his feet. Had he imagined such an unlikely situation, he would have felt awkward. But to his surprise it was very simple and he had no hesitation in shaking the German's hand.

'Europe is getting bigger, wouldn't you say? Its borders are constantly shifting: yesterday the Volga, today the Black River. We're farther and farther from home.'

'Europe is an idea, not a continent. I guard it, even if people back there do not realize it.'

'Well, I have to admit you certainly do a lot of damage wherever you go,' said Salagnon, nodding to the burning longhouse and the ruined school.

'Oh, the longhouse wasn't us. The Viet division did that last night. When they arrived they rounded up the villagers. They do that when they pass through villages: a big torchlit show trial, the political commissars sitting at a table, the suspects dragged in one by one. They are forced to confess their faults before the people and the Party, counter the slightest suspicion, prove their political purity. They convened a revolutionary tribunal and condemned this guy for collaborating with the French. He was shot and his house was burned. Did you notice anything? You were up the hill at the post. Could you have protected him? As for the school – if you can call it a school – it was hit by a stray shell. Our artillery are twenty kilometres away, so shells sometimes go a little wide of the mark. We were aiming for the revolutionary tribunal, which was set up where our tent is now. The aerial photos pinpointed the spot. By the time we got here, everything was burning, everyone had fled. We spent the whole morning catching them.'

'I'm sorry about the school.'

'Oh, so am I. Schools are a good thing. But over here, nothing is innocent; the teacher was a Viet Minh.'

'You can tell that from aerial photos?'

'Intelligence, my friend. It's a lot more effective than playing hide-and-seek with your mates up in your little castle. Come take a look.'

Salagnon and Moreau followed him, with the Thais several paces behind. They moved between the shacks, where the villagers were crouched, guarded by legionnaires.

'My platoon,' said the German. 'We specialize in search and destroy. We find out what we need to know, track down the enemy and liquidate them. This morning we rounded everyone up. We quickly identified the suspects: those who seem intelligent, those who look like they've got something to hide, those who are scared. It's a technique, something you learn; with a little practice it becomes instinctive and you can get quick results. We haven't tracked down the teacher yet, but it shouldn't take long.'

A kneeling Vietnamese man looked up, his face bruised and swollen. The German stood in front of him, flanked by his blond henchmen, guns at their hips, fingers still on the triggers, patrolling the empty space around him with their glacial stare; it was like a stage, everyone could see what was happening. The German recommenced the interrogation. The Vietnamese bowed their heads, huddled together, crouching together in a quivering mass. The legionnaires standing around did not give a damn. The German bellowed questions, without ever losing control, in a French that was elegantly twisted by his accent. The kneeling Vietnamese man, his face streaming blood, answered in plaintive, monosyllabic French that was almost unintelligible; he did not speak in complete sentences and spat bloody mucus. One of the henchmen lashed out, knocking down the Viet and kicking him repeatedly, his face remaining utterly calm; the thick tread of his boots crushed the face of the man sprawled on the ground, while the other bodyguard glanced around, his weapon cocked and ready. With every kick, the body of the Vietnamese man juddered, blood spurted from his mouth, from his nose. The German went on shouting questions, still calm, this was work. Moreau watched the scene scornfully, but he said nothing. The crouching Thais waited, indifferent, they did not care what happened to the Vietnamese. The women clutched their children, hid their faces, whimpered in a pitch so shrill it was impossible to tell whether they were talking or wailing; the few Vietnamese men did not move, they knew their turn would come. Salagnon listened. The German interrogated in French and the Vietnamese man answered in French. It was not the mother tongue of either man, but in the jungles of Tonkin French was the international language of intensive interrogation. This troubled Salagnon much more than the physical violence to which he was by now inured. He was indifferent to blood and death, but not the use of his mother tongue to express such violence. This too would pass, and the words to express this violence would disappear. He longed for it, that day when words would not be used, when silence would finally come.

The German barked a curt order, pointed to a woman; two soldiers waded into the crowd of Vietnamese and dragged her to her feet. She was sobbing, hiding her face behind her tangled hair. He went back to speaking French: 'Is this your wife? You know what will happen to her?' One of the bodyguards was holding her. The other ripped off her tunic, revealing her small, pointed breasts, two small swellings of pale skin. 'You know what we can do to her? Oh, not kill her, not hurt her, just mess around a little. So...?'

'Under school,' said the other man in a whisper.

The German signalled, two soldiers ran off and quickly returned, dragging the teacher.

'A hiding place, under the school.'

'See? That wasn't so hard.'

The German gave a sweeping backhanded gesture and his bodyguards lifted up the interrogated Vietnamese, supporting him almost gently; they led him away with the schoolteacher towards the edge of the jungle. The German lit a cigarette and walked over to Salagnon.

'What will you do with them?'

'Oh, we'll liquidate them.'

'You're not going to interrogate the teacher?'

'Why? He's already been identified and tracked down. He was the problem. Him and the village chief who was playing both sides against the middle, but the Viets got to him before we could. So there you go, a clean village. *Vietfrei.*'

'You're sure the teacher was the chief Viet Minh?'

'The other guy informed on him, didn't he? And the situation he was in, you don't lie, take my word for it.'

'If you'd liquidated two guys at random it would have had the same effect.'

'It doesn't matter, young Salagnon. Personal guilt doesn't matter. Terror is a broad-brush measure. When properly deployed, implacably, ruthlessly, without a hint of weakness, resistance collapses. You have to make it clear that anything can happen to anyone, that way no one will do anything at all. Take it from one who knows.'

The trucks continued to struggle up the *route coloniale*, to disappear into the jungle with their cargo of soldiers. Others were heading down, taking the paratroopers back to Hanoi and new missions. Two fighter planes came in, flying low, with the shrill buzz of angry mosquitoes. They grazed the treetops, banked in formation and dropped canisters that spiralled down. The planes wheeled and disappeared again, while behind them the jungle flared and quickly burned in a vast circular flame tinged with black.

'They're dumping napalm on the forest to burn out anyone still there,' the German smiled. 'Some of the division that walked right past you last night are probably still hiding out there. The mission isn't over.'

'Come on,' said Morcau.

He took Salagnon by the arm and led him back to the post, followed by the silent Thais.

'You think they really don't give a shit?' asked Salagnon.

'They're Thais, the villagers were Vietnamese, they couldn't give a damn. Besides, Asians see violence differently than we do, they have a higher threshold.'

'You think?'

'Haven't you seen the way they put up with all this?'

'They've got no choice.'

'The problem is our fucking conscience. That guy you were talking to, the German, he has no scruples about what he's doing. We need a little less conscience if we're to do what they do. That's how the Viet Minh work and that's why they're winning. But it's all right, they're only a couple of years ahead of us, maybe only a couple of months. With what we've done today, we'll soon be like the German, like the Viets. And then we'll see.'

'But we didn't do anything.'

'You saw the whole thing, Victorien. When it comes to these things, there's not much difference between seeing and doing. It's just a matter of time. I know about this shit. Everything I've learned, I've learned on the job, by watching. And I can't imagine myself going back to France now.'

In the hazy darkness it was impossible to see much. The attack on the post was brutal. Shadows slipped through the tall grasses, their rubber-tyre sandals made not a sound. A bugle blast woke everyone. The enemy screamed and ran forwards, the first were grilled on the electric wires twined around the sharpened bamboo stakes. The current spluttered, sending out blue sparks; they could be seen screaming, their mouths open, their teeth glittering, their eyes wide. Salagnon had been sleeping in shorts. He pulled on his boots without lacing them, fell out of bed, grabbed the gun under the bed and ran out of the blockhouse. In the ditch the shadows of Viet soldiers were piled on the razor wire. Gascard's traps were working: bodies reduced to black outlines toppled and suddenly fell, shrieking as their feet plunged into craters filled with sharpened spikes. From the corner towers, machine guns raked the base of the walls continuously, the flickering light of the gunfire and the grenades gave a face to those who feel the moment that they died. Salagnon had nothing to say, no order to give, nothing that was said could be heard. Each man, on his own, knew what to do, did everything he could. Later they would see. He joined two Thais on top of the mud rampart. They were leaning against the parapet, their backs to the attackers, hunkered beside a crate of munitions. They were taking grenades, pulling the pins and tossing them over their shoulders without looking, as though shelling sunflower seeds. The grenade would explode at the foot of the wall in a bright glare that shook the rammed-earth walls. Still they kept throwing. Salagnon risked a quick look. A carpet of bodies spilled out of the ditch filled with bamboo spikes. The electric fence had eventually stopped working; the first wave had melted the wires, a second wave attacked, using the bodies of the first as stepping stones. Salagnon heard bullets whistle past his ear. He crouched down next to the Thais in front of the open crate and, like them, began to prime the grenades and toss them over his shoulder, unseeing. A streak of flame ripped the darkness; a hollow-charge shell pierced the concrete cube they had built and exploded inside. The black of charred concrete split and toppled over, the rammed-earth tower half crumbled. Two Thais scrabbled up the ruins carrying a machine gun and lay flat. One of them fired, precise, tenacious, the other kept a hand on his shoulder and pointed out the targets and passed him magazine clips from a huge haversack. The bugle sounded, high and clear, and the shadows retreated, leaving dark stains on the ground. 'Cease fire!' yelled Moreau from somewhere on the wall. In the silence Salagnon felt a pain deep inside his ears. He got to his feet, found Moreau, barefoot, wearing boxer shorts, his face black with gunpowder, his eyes shining. A few Thais here and there did not get up. He did not know their names; he realized that despite spending so much time living alongside them, he did not recognize them. The only way he could know if some were missing was to count.

'They're leaving.'

'They'll be back.'

'They nearly had us.'

'But not quite. So now, they'll talk. It's a commie thing. They analyse the first offensive, they talk it over and then they attack from a better angle, and this time it will work. It's slow but it's effective. We won't hold out, but we have a little time. We run for it.'

'We run for it?'

'We slip into the darkness, into the jungle. We meet up with the mobile unit down by the river.'

'We'll never make it.'

'Right now they're talking. The next attack, we're all dead. No one will come looking for us.'

'Let's try the radio.'

They ran into the blockhouse and called. Through the crackle and static, the radio finally responded. 'The mobile unit is hanging in there. We're focused on the river. Evacuate the post. We're evacuating the region.'

They gathered together. Mariani woke Gascard, who was sleeping off another hangover and had not realized what all the noise was about. A couple of slaps, his head ducked in a bucket of water and an explanation of what was to happen next sobered him up. Making a run for it got his attention. He stood up straight, offered to carry the backpacks of grenades. Rufin combed his hair before they left. The Thais crouched in silence, carrying only their weapons.

'Let's go.'

They ran silently through the jungle, spaced two metres apart. They ran, carrying only a bag, their gun and some ammunition. The Viets were regrouping next to the collapsed tower, but they did not know this; by chance they passed the position the Viets had just left. A small squad was guarding the path. They dispatched them with machetes, silently, left the bloody, gaping bodies by the track, hurtled down the hill and raced soundlessly into the jungle, seeing only the man in front of them, hearing only the man behind them. They ran, carrying only their weapons.

Behind them, they heard the bugle again, and then gunfire, a silence, then a huge explosion and a bright flare in the distance. The arsenal at the post was exploding. Moreau had booby-trapped the blockhouse.

Along the path, at kilometre intervals, they strung grenades along the ground so that they would explode when someone touched the tripwire. When they heard the first grenade, they knew they were being followed. They avoided the village, avoided the main road, zigzagged between the trees, heading for the river. The muffled explosions from behind indicated the Viets were tracking them methodically on their trail; after each explosion, the political commissar reorganized his platoon, appointed a new leader and they set off again.

They fled as fast as they could, running between the trees, hacking at any branches in their way, marking their path, trampling leaves into the mud, plunging down steep hills, sometimes slipping, grabbing at a tree trunk to steady themselves or at someone racing past, bringing both of them crashing down. By dawn they were exhausted and lost. Patches of mist trailed from the branches. Their clothes were stiff with mud, saturated with freezing water, but all the while they dripped with sweat. They went on running, hindered by the untamed plants, some drooping, some prickly, some solid and as fibrous as ropes; hindered by the broken ground that gave way underfoot, hampered by the rucksacks biting into their shoulders, crushing their chests, by the painful pounding in their necks. They stopped. Being spaced out, it took some time for everyone to gather. They sat down, leaning against the trees, against the rocks that jutted from the ground. They ate cold rice balls, not stopping to think. The rain started up again. They could do nothing to protect themselves, so they did nothing. The thick hair of the Thais stuck to their faces like rivulets of tar.

The muted blast of the grenades boomed far away; the echoes rolled around the hills, reaching them from all directions. It was impossible to gauge the distance.

'We need a stopping point,' said Moreau. 'A rearguard to slow them down. One of us and four men.'

'I'll stay,' said Rufin.

'OK.'

Leaning on his backpack, Rufin had had enough. He closed his eyes, he was exhausted. Staying here meant he could stop running. Exhaustion reduces the time horizon to almost nothing. Staying here meant not running. There would be time to think later. They were left with all the grenades, the explosives, the radio. They set up a machine gun behind a rock and a second on the other side, where the Viets would try to shelter when the first gunner fired.

'Let's go.'

They continued to run, taking a path downhill towards the *route coloniale* and the river. The rain stopped, but the trees still dripped at the slightest contact. Behind them, the Viets continued to gain ground, the man in front gritting his teeth until he eventually stumbled on a tripwire and the ground beneath him exploded. The front runner sacrificed himself for Độc Lập, for independence, the only words that Salagnon could read in the slogans daubed on the walls. Sacrifice was a weapon of war; it was wielded by the political commissar, while the sacrificed cut the barbed wire beneath machine guns, hurled themselves against walls, blew themselves up to open doors, used their own flesh to absorb a volley of bullets. Salagnon did not really understand this obedience pushed to the limits; intellectually, he did not understand it; but as he ran through the jungle, hampered by his gun, his arms and legs throbbing with scratches and bruises, exhausted, numb with tiredness, he knew that he would have done whatever he was ordered to do; against others or against himself. This he knew without a shadow of a doubt.

In a single night every outpost in the Haute-Région was wiped out. A breach opened up on the map and General Giáp's troops spilled into the delta. They kept running. When they reached the *route coloniale* they found a burned-out tank, its hatchway open. The carcasses of blackened trucks lay abandoned, the ground was strewn with bits of kit, but no corpses. They hid themselves in the tall grass by the verge, wary, lying on their bellies, utterly still, panicked at the thought that they might fall asleep.

'Shall we go?' whispered Salagnon. 'The Viets are bound to get here soon.'

'Wait.'

Moreau hesitated. A whistle blast split the waterlogged air. Silence descended over the jungle. The animals were quiet. There were no cries, no cracking branches, no rustle of leaves, no chirping birds, no whisper of insects, all those sounds that, over time, you cease to hear but are still there: when they stop, it is terrifying, you expect the worst. On the road a man appeared, pushing a bicycle. Behind him came other men, all of them pushing bicycles. The bicycles looked like Asian ponies, tubby and short-legged. Huge panniers hung from the frames, hiding the wheels. Balanced on the seats were green munitions crates stencilled with Chinese characters. Mortar shells held together with straw rope were strung alongside. The bicycles tilted, each was steered by a man in black pyjamas with the aid of a length of bamboo attached to the handlebars. They moved slowly, silently, flanked by soldiers in brown uniforms and palm-frond helmets with rifles slung across their chests who stared up at the sky. 'Bicycles,' whispered Moreau. He had heard of the intelligence report detailing the transport capabilities of the Viet Minh. They use no trucks, no roads, there are few draught animals, elephants are confined to the jungles of Cambodia; consequently, everything is carried manually. A coolie carries eighteen kilos through the jungle. He must carry his own rations, he can carry no more. The Intelligence Service calculated the range of enemy troops based on indisputable facts. No trucks, no roads, no more than eighteen kilos per man, including his rations. There is nothing to be found in the jungle, nothing more than you bring. As a result, the Viet Minh could not spend more than three or four days there before running out of food. Because they had no trucks, no roads, nothing but scrawny men who carried little weight. The statistics proved that we could hold out longer than they could, thanks to the trucks ferrying endless tins of sardines along jungle tracks. But now they could see that, for the price of a Manufrance bicycle bought in Hanoi or stolen from a warehouse in Haiphong, every man could easily carry 300 kilos into the jungle. The soldiers forming the escort scanned the skies, the road, the verges. 'They're going to spot us.' Still Moreau hesitated. Exhaustion had made him slack. Surviving means making the right decision, with a little luck, and that means being as tense as a length of rope. Without that tension, luck is less favourable. A hum of planes filled the sky. It came from no particular direction. It was no louder than the buzzing of a fly in a room. The leader of the escort brought a whistle dangling around his neck to his lips. The shrill signal slashed the air. The bicycles turned as one and disappeared into the trees. The hum grew louder. The road was completely deserted now. The silence of the animals would not be noticed from the air. The two planes passed, flying low, the special drums fixed to their wings. They flew off. 'Let's go.' Keeping their heads low, they plunged into the jungle again. They ran through the trees, far from the *route coloniale*, towards the river, where perhaps someone was still waiting for them. Behind them they heard another whistle blast, muted by the distance and the foliage. They ran through the forest, heading downhill, sprinting towards the river. As they grew breathless, they slowed to a brisk walk. Marching in single file, they produced a drumming sound, a constant cacophony of panting breaths, the thud of thick soles on damp earth, the rustle of soft leaves, the metallic clatter of rifles. They were streaming with sweat. The flesh of their faces melted into exhaustion. All that was visible were bones, lines of exertion like thick cables, the mouths that would not close, the wide eyes of the straining Europeans and the narrow slits of the Thais scurrying behind. They could hear a continual rumbling, deadened by the distance and the vegetation, by the tangle of trees. Bombs and mortar shells were exploding somewhere farther off, in the direction they were headed.

They stumbled on the Viets by accident, but it was bound to happen. There were so many of them secretly criss-crossing the desolate jungles. The Viet Minh were sitting on the ground, leaning against trees. They had stacked their Chinese rifles in a pile and were talking and laughing; some were smoking, some were drinking from straw-covered flasks, some were shirtless and stretching; they were all very young, they were taking a break, they were chatting. In the middle of the circle a hulking Manufrance bicycle lying on its panniers looked like an injured donkey.

The moment they glimpsed them did not last long, but thought works quickly; and in those few seconds Salagnon was struck by their youth, their gentleness, their elegance, and that joyous air they had when they gathered together informally. These young boys had come here to escape the many burdens – village, feudal, colonial – weighing upon the people of Vietnam. Out in the jungle, when they had set down their weapons, they could feel free, they could smile. These thoughts came to Salagnon as they raced down the hill, rifles in hand; they came to him in a crumpled ball, without unfurling, but they had the power of truth: the young Vietnamese boys at war were younger and more at ease, they took more pleasure in being together than the soldiers of the French Far East Expeditionary Corps, worn down by worry and exhaustion, supporting each other as things fell apart, clinging to each other as the ship sank. But perhaps it was simply the difference between their faces that he was misinterpreting.

A coolie was repairing the back wheel of the bicycle. He was reinflating the tyre with a hand pump, while the others, making no effort to help, made the most of their break, urging him on and laughing. The two groups did not see each other until the last moment. The armed French detachment was running down the hill, staring at their feet; the Vietnamese were watching the coolie as he worked the bicycle pump. They saw each other at the last moment and no one knew what they were doing, everyone acted instinctively. Moreau was wearing a machine gun slung across his shoulder; he had his hand on the grip to stop it from jolting, he fired as he ran and several of the sitting Vietnamese boys crumpled. The others tried to stand up and were killed, tried to grab their guns and were killed, tried to run away and were killed; the stack of rifles toppled, the coolie kneeling in front of the bicycle sat up, still holding the pump attached to the tyre, then he crumpled, his chest pierced by a single bullet. A Viet who had managed to get away, who had unbuckled his belt behind a bush, removed one of the grenades attached to it. He was shot by one of the Thais; he dropped the grenade, which rolled down the slope. Salagnon felt a heavy blow to his thigh, a blow to his hip that cut his legs from under him, he fell. Silence descended. It had happened in a matter of seconds, in the time it took to run down a hill. The act of describing it takes longer. Salagnon tried to get to his feet; his leg felt like a girder attached to his hip. His trousers were hot and damp. He could see nothing but the leaves above him blotting out the sky. Mariani bent over him. 'You've taken a bit of a hit,' he muttered. 'Can you walk?' 'No.' He patched the leg, sliced through the trousers with his knife, bandaged the thigh tightly, helped Salagnon to sit up. Moreau was lying on his belly; around him, the Thais crouched in a circle, motionless. 'Killed instantly,' whispered Mariani. 'Him?' 'A piece of shrapnel, it can cut like a razor. You got one in the leg. You were lucky. He got it in the throat. *Kkkk!*' He drew his thumb across his throat. Moreau's blood had spilled out, forming a ragged circle of dark ground around his neck. They cut long poles, lopped the branches off with their machetes and made stretchers using the shirts of the dead. 'The bicycle,' said Salagnon. 'What about the bicycle?' 'Let's take it.' 'Are you crazy? We don't want to be lugging around a bike!' 'We're taking it. Otherwise no one will believe us if we say we saw bikes in the jungle.' 'That's true, but we don't give a shit, do we?' 'A single guy with a bicycle can carry three hundred kilos in the jungle. We take it. We bring it back. We show them.' 'OK, OK.'

Salagnon was carried by Mariani and Gascard while the Thais transported the body of Moreau. The Vietnamese were left where they had fallen. The Thais saluted the dead, touching their joined hands to their foreheads. They continued down the slope. A little more slowly now. Two men lugged the dismantled bicycle, now stripped of its panniers, one took the wheels, the other the frame. The Thais carrying Moreau moved with the measured tread of men shouldering a bier and the barely jolted corpse did not protest. Meanwhile, Gascard and Mariani held the stretcher like a wheelbarrow, their arms extended, causing it to jerk and judder. The constant shaking caused Salagnon's wound to open and bleed, soaking the canvas and dripping on to the ground. Every footstep reverberated in his bones, which felt as though they were swelling, threatening to pierce his skin, to break out into the open air; he stifled his screams, clamped his lips tight shut as his teeth chattered, his every breath a plaintive whimper.

With their hands occupied, the two porters became clumsy. They stumbled over the debris littering the ground, clipped their shoulders against tree trunks; they faltered as they walked and the jolts to his leg became unbearable. He swore at Mariani, the only one he could see when he managed to lift his head. Hurled vile abuse at him every time he slipped or stumbled, and his insults trailed off in gurgles, in muffled groans as he clenched his jaws so as not to scream too loudly, in deep sighs that emanated from his nose, his throat, from the vibrations of his chest. Mariani panted, gasped, but he stumbled on, hating him as much as any man has ever hated another and longs to kill him on the spot, to strangle him slowly, staring him in the face, out of long-awaited vengeance. Salagnon kept his eyes open; he could see the treetops swaying as though in a heavy wind, although no breeze stirred the hot, heavy air that was stifling them with sweat. He felt a twinge in his leg at every step of the stretcher-bearers, every stone they kicked, every root they stumbled on, every shrivelled leaf they slipped on; all these things quivered through his bones, through his spine, through his skull; this painful journey through Tonkin would be for ever etched on his brain; he would remember every step, remember every detail of the landscape of the Haute-Région. They were fleeing, pursued by an implacable brigade of Viet Minh, who would have trapped them like the rising tide if they paused to catch their breath. They ran on. Eventually, Salagnon blacked out.

The village was a little more ruined, a little better defended. The brick buildings had been reduced to ragged sections of wall. Only the church, solidly built, still stood, with half its roof still intact above the altar. Piles of sandbags concealed the foxholes, the trenches, the emplacements of the mortars, whose barrels were angled low to fire at close range.

Salagnon came to, lying in the church. Stray beams of light passed through the holes in the walls, accentuating the murky darkness where he lay. He had been left on the blood-soaked stretcher. A little sap still trickled from the green branches hacked with machetes to use as poles. His trousers had been neatly cut away; his leg had been cleaned and bandaged; he had not been aware of anything. The pain had faded; his thigh simply throbbed like a heart. Someone had probably given him morphine. Other wounded men were lying next to him in the semi-darkness, breathing regularly. In the undamaged apse he saw there were corpses. Many of them crammed into a small space. In the half-light, he could not make sense of how they were arranged. As his eyes became accustomed to the darkness, he realized that the dead had been stacked like firewood. On the top layer, lying on his back, he recognized Moreau. His throat was black, his thin-lipped mouth finally relaxed, almost smiling. The Thais had obviously combed his hair before handing over the body, because his side parting was neat and his moustache glistening.

'Impressive, isn't it?'

The German was crouching next to him. He had not heard him arrive. He might have been there for some time, watching him sleep. He nodded to the apse. 'That's how we did it at Stalingrad. There were too many dead to bury and we didn't have the strength or the time to hack at the frozen ground, it was hard as glass. But we couldn't just leave them where they fell, at least not in the beginning, so we collected the bodies and stacked them. Just like here. But frozen bodies are easier to deal with. They waited patiently until we finished fighting. This lot are starting to droop a little.'

Salagnon could not count the bodies lying next to him. They gradually merged into each other. Sometimes they emitted little whimpers and sagged a little more. It did not smell good. But the ground did not smell good, or the stretcher, or the air itself, which reeked of gunpowder, burning, rubber and petrol.

'We never did bury them, spring never came, and I don't know what the Russians did with them. But this lot, we'll try to take home,' said the German. 'And you, too. Don't worry, in your case, we'll get you back alive if we can.'

'When?'

'When we can. It's difficult to get out. They don't want to let us go. They launch attacks every day and we stand our ground. If we were to leave, they would shoot us in the back. It would be a massacre. So we stay. They'll attack again today, and tonight, and tomorrow; they don't care about their own losses. They want to prove they're beating us. We want to prove we know how to organize an evacuation. This is Dunkirk, my friend, but a Dunkirk that needs to be seen as a victory. That should ring a bell.'

'I was a bit young.'

'Someone must have told you. Here, in the situation we're in, a well-managed retreat is as good as a victory. The survivors of a rout can be decorated as victors.'

'What about you? What are you doing here?'

'With you? I just came to see how you're getting on. I quite like you, young Salagnon.'

'I mean in Indochine.'

'Fighting, just like you.'

'But you're German.'

'So? You're no more Indo-Chinese than I am, as far as I know. You're fighting a war. I'm fighting a war. What else can you do once you've learned? How could I live in peace now, and with whom? Back in Germany, everyone I know was killed in a single night. What is left of the Germany I knew? Why would I go back? To rebuild, work in manufacturing, in trade? Become an office worker with a briefcase and a little hat? Go to the office every morning, having travelled the four corners of Europe as a victor? That would be a horrible way to end my life. I have no one to tell about what I lived through. So I want to die the way I lived, as a victor.'

'If you die here, you'll be buried in the jungle or left lying on the ground in a place no one knows.'

'So? Who knows me any more, other than the men who are fighting alongside me? All those who might have remembered my name died in a single night, like I told you, they were consumed by the flames of a phosphorus bomb. Nothing human was left of their bodies, nothing but ashes, bones held together by a desiccated casing and pools of fat that were washed away the morning after. Did you know that every man contains fifteen kilos of fat? It's not something you're aware of when you're alive. It's only when it melts, when it liquefies, that you realize. What remains, that desiccated husk floating in a pool of grease, is much smaller, much lighter than the body. It's unrecognizable. You wouldn't even know that it was once human. So I'm staying here.'

'You're hardly going to try and play the victim. The worst atrocities were committed by your side.'

'I'm no victim, Monsieur Salagnon. And that's why I'm here in Indochine, and not working as an accountant in some reconstructed office in Frankfurt. I've come to end my life a victor. Now, get some sleep.'

Salagnon spent a horrifying night trembling with cold. His injured leg seemed to swell until it choked him, then suddenly contracted again, causing him to lose his balance. The pile of corpses gleamed in the half-light, and several times Moreau moved and tried to speak to him. He politely stared at the stack of bodies which, hour by hour, shrank a little more, ready to respond should Moreau ask him a question.

In the morning a large red flag emblazoned with a gold star was hoisted. It fluttered on the edge of the jungle as a bugle sounded. A horde of soldiers wearing palm-frond helmets charged on the rolls of barbed wire, on the foxholes armed with mines, on the spikes, the traps, on the machine guns that went on firing until their muzzles were red. There were so many that they assimilated the shrapnel fired at them; they marched on; they withstood the gunfire. The ground beneath Salagnon's supine body trembled. The trembling was agonizing; it penetrated his leg and travelled all the way to his skull. The effects of the morphine had worn off; no one thought to give him any more.

Many died on the outskirts of the village. The ditches filled with battered, mangled, charred corpses. The Viet Minh army suffered catastrophic losses and still they advanced; the Légion died, man by man, and did not retreat. They were so close, their cannon fell silent. They lobbed grenades by hand. Men found themselves face to face, grabbed each other's shirts, slashed bellies open with their knives.

The amphibious tanks emerged from the river, black, glistening toad-buffalos preceded by flames and belching a trail of smoke. Dripping wet, they clambered up the muddy banks and counter-attacked. Small planes buzzed in swarms above the trees, and behind them the jungle blazed and everyone in it. Armoured barges sailed up the river, their cargo holds empty. The fortified positions were evacuated; all equipment was destroyed, leaving only booby-trapped shells and grenades. 'What about my bike?' asked Salagnon as they carried him out. 'What bike?' 'The bicycle I brought back from the jungle, the one I stole from the Viets.' 'The Viet Minh ride bikes in the jungle?' 'They were using it to transport rice. We need to take it to Hanoi as proof.' 'You think we're going to bother our arses with a bicycle? Do you fancy riding back, Salagnon?' The men calmly boarded the barges, loaded the wounded and the dead. Shells fell at random, some in the water, some on the banks, sending up jets of mud. One of the barges was hit; a shell obliterated the cargo hold and all those inside. A rudderless ball of flame, it drifted with the slow course of the river. Gascard vanished in a vortex of blood-stained water. Lying on the shuddering metal, Salagnon was nothing now but pain.

In the military hospital he woke up in a huge ward where the wounded lay in neat rows of beds. Emaciated men on pristine sheets daydreamed as they stared at the ceiling fans; they sighed and sometimes shifted their position, trying not to rip out the IV drip or press too heavily on their bandaged wounds. A soft light streamed in through the large, open windows screened by white curtains that barely stirred. They cast pale shadows on the wall, on the faded paintings eaten away by the colony's humidity; the serene decay did more to heal their bodies than any medication. Some died the way a flame gutters out.

At the other end of the line of beds, far from the window, a man whose leg had been amputated was having trouble sleeping. He grumbled quietly in German, repeating the same words over and over in a childlike voice. At the other end of the row, a heavyset man threw back his sheet, got to his feet and limped quickly down the line, wincing and leaning on the metal bedframes for support. When he came to the bed of the moaner, he stood stiffly to attention in his pyjamas and bawled him out in German. The other man bowed his head, apologized, addressing him as Obersturmführer, and fell silent. The officer returned to his bed, still wincing with pain, and lay down. The only sounds in the vast ward were restful breathing, the buzz of flies and the creak of the ceiling fan as it turned slowly. Salagnon went back to sleep.

And then? While Victorien Salagnon was recovering from his wounds, the war raged on outside. At all hours of the day and night, armoured columns roared through Hanoi, heading for various parts of the delta. Trucks unloaded their wounded in the hospital courtyard, crudely bandaged cripples were carried in on stretchers by soldiers, and the walking wounded were led by nurses to empty beds. They would slump on to the beds with a sigh, smell the clean sheets, and some would fall asleep immediately, unless they were in too much pain from their scabby wounds; then the doctor would come round, doling out morphine, easing their pains. That strange device that is the helicopter landed on the roof, bringing the seriously wounded, their uniforms unrecognizable, their bodies blackened, their flesh so swollen they had to be transported by air. Aeroplanes flew over Hanoi, fighter planes carrying special drums, processions of purring Dakotas filled with paratroopers. Some came back trailing thick black smoke that rendered them unstable.

Mariani would come to see him. He had come through the evacuation unscathed. He would bring the papers and tell him the news.

'A fierce Franco-Vietnamese counteroffensive,' he read, 'has halted the Viet Minh incursion into the Haute-Région. A line of posts had to be evacuated in order to reinforce the defensive position in the delta. Everything is hunky-dory. I feel reassured. Do you know who they are?'

'Who?'

'The Franco-Vietnamese troops.'

'It could mean us. Hey, Mariani, isn't this getting a bit confusing? Here we are, the French army, waging a guerrilla war against the regular army of a movement waging a guerrilla war against us, who are fighting to protect the Vietnamese people, who are fighting for their independence.'

'When it comes to fighting, we know what we're doing. When it comes to the whys and wherefores, I hope they know back in Paris.'

This made them laugh. There was a pleasure in laughing together.

'Did they find Rufin?'

'They intercepted his last message. I badgered the Signals corps until they gave me a full transcript. He didn't say much. "The Viets are a couple of metres away. Bye, everyone." And after that, nothing, silence, the guy in Signals told me. Well, except for that noise a field radio makes when it's not transmitting, like sand rattling in a metal box.'

'You think he got away?'

'He could do pretty much anything. But if he did get away, he's been wandering in the jungle ever since.'

'That would be just like him. The angel of war leading his own personal guerrilla operation out in the jungle.'

'There's no harm in dreaming.'

They talked about Moreau, who had not had the heroic death he deserved. Then again, when it comes, death is quick; in war, people die furtively. When reported lyrically, it is a white lie. It is to be able to say something, to invent, elaborate, set the scene. In reality, men die secretly, swiftly, silently; and afterwards, too, there is silence.

The uncle came to visit Salagnon, examined the wound himself, asked the opinion of the doctor.

'I need you to come back to us fit and well,' he said before he left. 'I've got big plans for you.'

He rested. He spent his time walking in the tropical hospital, strolling under the trees in the garden, in that sauna on Earth that is colonial Indochine. 'I'm starting to soften,' he would say with a laugh to those who came to see him, 'the way they soften hard tack on ships crossing the ocean, to make it more edible.'

He was starting to soften the better to scar, as wounded soldiers did, although opium did not appeal to him. In order to take it, he had to lie down and it made him sleepy. He preferred to be sitting up; that way he could see and he could paint. For him, using a paintbrush was enough to banish his lethargy, to alleviate his pain, and float. He would go out into the streets of Hanoi, eat soup filled with floating bits at grimy street stalls. He would sit down among the people of the street and stay there for hours, watching. He would sit at tea houses that were little more than two tables and a few stools under trees, where a scrawny man would come by with a dented kettle to pour hot water into the same bowl, on to the same used tea leaves that gradually came to taste of nothing.

He took his time. He was happy to watch, and he sketched the men in the streets and the children who roamed in gangs; he also liked to draw the women. He found they had an extraordinary beauty, and a beauty that befitted sketching. He never got close enough to see them as anything more than a line. They were pure lines of flowing fabric, washing on a line, and their long black hair like an inkspill left by a brush. The women of Indochine moved gracefully, sat gracefully, held their large conical straw hats gracefully. He drew many, but spoke to none. He was teased about his shyness. Eventually he hinted, without providing any details, that he was engaged to a French girl in Algiers. People no longer teased him, but praised his courage with complicit smiles. They made knowing references to the fiery temperament of Mediterranean women, their tragic jealousy, their unrivalled sexual audacity. Asian women continued to pass by in the distance, in a rustle of lace, haughty, elegant, pretending to be out of reach, while discreetly glancing around them to gauge the effect. At first sight they look cold, people would say, but when you get past that first barrier, when you find the trigger, well... That said it all. It suited him to say no more.

The ghost of Eurydice came to him in moments of idleness. He still wrote to her. He was bored. He met only people he did not want to meet. The army was changing. Back in France they were recruiting young men; Salagnon felt old. Blockheads arrived by the boatload, interested only in money, excitement or oblivion; they were enlisting in a career, because they could find no work in France. In the weeks he spent convalescing and walking the streets of Hanoi, he learned the Chinese art of the brush. Although in this art there is nothing to learn: there is only practice. What he learned in Hanoi was the existence of the art of the brush; and that was an education in itself.

Before encountering his master, he had painted to keep his hands busy, to give a purpose to his walks, to better see what was before his eyes. He sent Eurydice jungles, broad rivers, jagged hills wreathed in mists. 'I've drawn you the jungle as a vast velvet carpet, like a deep, plush sofa,' he wrote to her. 'But do not be fooled. My drawing is a lie. It is impersonal. It will appeal to those – fortunate – souls who will never set foot in the jungle. The place itself is not substantial, as deep, as dense; in fact, the vegetation is sparse and chaotic. But if I drew it as it is, no one would believe it was the jungle; they would assume I am suffering from melancholy. They would think my drawing was a lie. And so I have drawn a lie, so that it will seem true.'

Sitting leaning against a tree trunk on the broad avenue lined with frangipani trees, he used a brush to sketch the hints of the magnificent houses visible between the trees. His eyes moved from the foliage to the colonial façades, searching for details; his brush hovered for a moment over the inkwell next to him. His concentration was such that the children crouching around him did not dare speak to him. Through art he achieved the miracle of slowing and silencing a group of Asian children. In their birdlike monosyllables they whispered to each other, singling out some detail in the drawing and pointing to the object in the street, giggling behind their hands to see reality thus transformed.

A man dressed all in white came down the avenue, swinging a cane, and stopped behind Salagnon to peer at his sketch. He was sporting a Panama hat and leaning lightly, more for effect than support, on his polished, bamboo cane.

'You hesitate too often, young man. I can understand your wanting to check whether what you have drawn is faithful, but if your painting is to live, as you live, as those trees you wish to paint live, then it is vital not to interrupt your breathing. You must let yourself be guided by the singular stroke of the brush.'

Salagnon was dumbstruck; his brush suspended in the air, he stared up at the strange, Annamese man who had just addressed him without salutation, without lowering his eyes, with only the faintest trace of an accent, in a French rather more polished than his own. The little boys had scrabbled to their feet, embarrassed, and did not dare move in the presence of this man, who was so aristocratic he could speak to a Frenchman without kowtowing.

'The singular stroke of the brush?'

'Yes, young man.'

'Is that a Chinese thing?'

'It is the art of the brush expressed in its simplest form.'

'Do you paint, monsieur?'

'On occasion.'

'Do you know how to paint those Chinese scenes with the mountains, the clouds and the tiny little people?'

The elegant man smiled benignly, accentuating the network of fine lines and wrinkles over his face. He was clearly very old, although he did not look it.

'Come tomorrow to this address. In the afternoon. I shall show you.'

He gave Salagnon a visiting card printed in Chinese, Vietnamese and French and emblazoned with the red seal that artists there use to sign their work.

Salagnon got to know the man. He visited him regularly. The old man wore his hair tied back, which made him look Argentinean, and he invariably wore pale suits with a freshly cut flower in the buttonhole. His jacket open, his left hand in his pocket, he greeted Salagnon casually, shaking his hand with the grace of a dilettante and an amused detachment from traditional customs. 'Come in, young man, come in.' And with a single gesture he threw open the vast rooms of his house, all bare, whose paintings, eaten away by the frightful weather, took on the pastel tones of tears. He spoke impeccable French, his accent merely a distinctive, barely perceptible phrasing, like a slight affectation that he preserved for its amusement value. He used academic turns of phrase rarely heard outside certain places in Paris, and Chinese words which he always employed in their strictest sense. Salagnon was amazed by the man's extraordinary command of his own mother tongue, a command he himself did not possess. He mentioned this and the old man smiled.

'You know, young man, the most perfect incarnations of French values are to be found in what are called "coloured people". The France that people extol for its grandeur, its lofty humanism, its clarity of thought, its veneration of language, that France is to be found in its purest form in the West Indies, among the Africans, the Arabs and the Indo-Chinese. The white French born in what is narrowly defined as France are always astonished to find that we embody those values they heard tell of in school, which, to them, represent some unattainable utopia and to us are life itself. We perfectly exemplify a France with no superfluity, no excess. We, the cultivated, indigenous people are the crowning glory and the justification of the Empire. We are its triumph, and that will bring about its downfall.'

'Why its downfall?'

'How can one continue to be what is called indigenous, while simultaneously being utterly French? One is forced to choose. It is fire and water contained within a single vessel. One of them must prevail, and swiftly. But come, come see my paintings.'

In the largest room of the old house, where the corners of the ceiling were begrimed with soot and the plaster flaked from the walls, the only furniture was a large rattan chair and a red lacquer cabinet with a circular metal lock plate. From it emerged scrolls wrapped in silk and tied with cord. He had Salagnon sit in the chair, swept the floor with a small brush, and set the rolls at his feet. He untied the cords, slipped off the silk sheaths and, bending gracefully, unrolled them on the floor.

'This is how Chinese paintings are meant to be viewed. It is not fitting to hang them permanently on a wall. They must be unfurled as a path unfurls. In doing so, one can see time appear. The time spent contemplating them merges with the time required to conceive and create them. When no one is looking at them, they should not be left open, but rolled, hidden from view, hidden even from themselves.

They should be unrolled only in the presence of someone who knows how to appreciate their unveiling. This is how they are envisioned, as one might envision a path.'

With slow, measured movements, he unrolled a towering landscape at Salagnon's feet, intent on the emotions flickering over the young man's face. Watching it unfurl, Salagnon felt as though he were slowly raising his head. Vertiginous mountains rose above the clouds; thickets of bamboo soared; from the tangled branches of the trees hung the aerial roots of orchids; water cascaded from background to foreground; a narrow path wound between jagged rocks, scaling the mountain between twisted pines that were rooted, as best they could, more in the mists than in the rock.

'And you use only ink?' murmured Salagnon, filled with wonder.

'Does one need anything else? To paint, to write, to live? Ink meets every need, young man. One needs only a single brush, a single stick of compressed pigment from which to dilute ink, and a hollow stone to hold it. And a little water too. The material for a whole life can fit in one's pocket; or if one has no pockets, in a knapsack. One can move unencumbered with the materials of a Chinese painter: he is a man who paints as he moves. With his feet, his legs, his shoulders, his breath, his whole life in every step. Man is a brush, his life the ink. The traces of his footsteps leave behind paintings.'

He unrolled several more images.

'These are Chinese, very ancient. Those are mine, although these days I hardly paint.'

Salagnon hunkered closer, following the rolls on all fours, feeling he understood nothing. They were not exactly paintings, nor was this the act of seeing or indeed of understanding. A profusion of little symbols, both traditional and figurative, jostled restlessly as far as the eye could see, kindling a thrill in the soul, a delirious yearning for the world, a surge towards life itself. As though he were seeing music.

'You talk about the man who paints, but I see no sign of man here. No forms, no characters. Do you ever paint portraits?'

'No man? You are mistaken, young man, and you surprise me. Everything here is man.'

'Everything? I see only one.'

Salagnon indicated a small figure in a pleated robe, difficult to distinguish, climbing the first part of the path, a figure no bigger than a fingernail, about to disappear behind a hill. The other smiled patiently.

'You exhibit a certain naivety, my young friend. I find it amusing, although hardly surprising. Indeed, it is threefold, the naivety of youth, of the soldier and of the European. You will forgive me if I smile – although at your expense, it is kindly meant – to find you possessed of such innocence: it is a privilege of age. The fact that you can distinguish no human form in no way indicates that the painting does not portray man. Do you need to see the man to infer the presence of man? That would be mundane, don't you agree?

'In this country there is nothing that is not human. The people are everything, Lieutenant Salagnon. Look around you: everything is man, even the landscape; especially the landscape. The people are the reality. If they were not, the country would be nothing but mud; it would have no solidity, no existence; it would be swept away by the Red River, sucked out by the tide, dissolved by the monsoon. All dry land here is the work of man. A moment of inattention, a hiatus in his ceaseless labouring, and all would return to mud and slide into the river. There exists nothing but man: earth, wealth, beauty. The people are everything. It is hardly surprising that communism is so well understood here: to speak of Marxism here, to say that social structures alone are real, is a truism. And so war is waged on man: the battleground is man, the weapon is man, distances and quantities are measured by how far a man can walk, how much a man can carry.'

He rolled up the paintings, slipped them into their sheaths and carefully retied the silken threads.

'Come and see me again, if you wish. I shall teach you the art of the brush, since you seem to be unaware. You have a certain talent, I have seen it at work, but art is a more subtle state than talent. It lies beyond. To be transformed into art, talent must become aware of itself, of its limitations, and must be drawn like a magnet towards a goal which points in an unambiguous direction. Otherwise talent moves aimlessly, it babbles. Come back and see me, I shall be happy to see you. I can show you the path.'

Salagnon spent his long convalescence visiting the old man, who welcomed him with the same elegance, the same fluidity of movement, the same graceful precision in his words. He showed him his scrolls, explained the circumstances of their painting, gave him advice in a way that was at once simple and cryptic. Salagnon believed that they were friends. He talked enthusiastically about the man to his uncle.

'He invites me to his home. He is always pleased to see me. He makes me feel at home. He shows me the paintings he keeps hidden in cabinets and we spend hours talking.'

'Be very careful, Victorien.'

'Why do I need to be careful of an old man who seems happy to show me the greatest achievements of his civilization?'

The emphasis made his uncle laugh.

'You could not be more wrong.'

'About what?'

'About everything. Friendship, civilization, pleasure.'

'He treats me as an equal.'

'He is slumming it. And it amuses him. He's an Annamese aristocrat; and Annamese noblemen are even more arrogant than noblemen in France. Back home, we cut our aristocrats down to size, they keep their noses clean; not here. To the nobles here, the word "equality" is untranslatable; the very idea makes them smile, an example of European vulgarity. Here, noblemen are gods and their peasants are dogs. It amuses them that the French pretend not to see it. They know. If he does you the honour of inviting you in to discuss the hobby of a man of leisure, it's because it amuses him; it is a diversion from more sophisticated acquaintances. He probably thinks of you as a playful little puppy that followed him home. And frequenting a French officer without ceremony allows him to affect a kind of modernity that must serve his purpose in some way or other. I know the guy a little. He's linked to that idiot Bảo Đại, the one they want to make emperor of Indochine, after convincing us to withdraw without actually leaving. To him and his cronies, the nobles of Annam, the French alliance is inconsequential. They count in centuries the way you count in hours. The presence of France here is like the common cold. We'll go. They'll blow their noses. They'll still be here. They make the most of it to learn other languages, read other books, enrich themselves in other ways. Go ahead, learn to paint, but don't set too much store by this man's friendship. Or his conversation. He looks down on you, but he finds you amusing; he has assigned you a role in a play you know nothing about. Make the most of it, learn what you can, but be wary. Just as he is always wary.'

When Salagnon arrived, an elderly manservant – thin, stooped and much older than his master – would open the door and lead him through the empty rooms. The old man would be standing, waiting for him, a faint smile playing on his lips, his pupils often dilated, but his hand steady to greet the Frenchman. Salagnon noticed that he used only his right hand to salute, to paint, to tie up his scrolls, to lift the little bowl of tea to his lips. He never used his left, keeping it in the pocket of his elegant, pale suit, hiding it under the table when sitting, and clamping it between his knees. It trembled.

'Ah, there you are,' he would invariably say. 'I was just thinking about you.' And he would nod to an unopened scroll laid on the long table he had had installed in the largest of his vast rooms. A second rattan chair had been added to the first, with a low table between them, on which were laid out the painting tools. As he set himself to painting, another servant would arrive with a scalding pot of tea, a slender young man who moved like a cat. He never raised his wild face, his lowered eyes flickered furiously to left and right. His master would watch him with an indulgent smile and never commented when he ineptly served the tea, always spilling a little water next to the bowl. The master would thank him in a soft voice and the very young man would turn on his heel, glancing around with brief, angry glares.

After a sigh from the master, a lesson in the art of the brush would begin. They would open the ancient painting and unroll it, each admiring the unfurling landscape. With his right hand the old man would wind up the silk panel at a measured pace, while his trembling left hand pointed out certain strokes without insistence, his ungainly hand fluttering over the unfolding painting, accentuating the soft rhythm of respiration, his trembling movements accompanying the breath of the ink that sprang, living and fresh, from the roll in which it was habitually imprisoned. Sometimes the table was not long enough for the landscape and he would have to work in several stages, furling the base even as the summit continued to appear. They strolled together along a path of ink, he pointing out the details with few words, few gestures, which Salagnon acknowledged with little grunts and nods; he now felt he was beginning to understand the silent music of ink strokes. He was learning.

He made his ink, taking his time, gently grinding the compressed pigment in the hollow stone with a drop of water; and these delicate gestures prepared him for painting. He used highly absorbent paper on which it was possible to make only a single stoke, a single fixed path of no return, a single, definitive mark. 'Each stroke should be precise, young man. But if it is not, what matter? Ensure that the following strokes make it perfect.'

Salagnon held the ineradicable between his fingers. At first it caused him to freeze, then it liberated him. There was no longer any need to go over past traces; once made, there was nothing to be done. But the strokes that followed could heighten their perfection. Time flowed on, and rather than agonize, it was enough to confidently set one's mark on it. As he learned, he explained what he had understood to the old man, who listened with the same patient smile. 'Understand, young man, understand. It is always good to understand. But paint. The singular stroke of the brush is the only path in life. You must set out on it alone. You must live it for yourself.'

It came to an end, one day, at the usual hour, when Salagnon came to the front door and found it was ajar. He rang the bell used to summon the servants, but no one came. He went inside. Alone, he wandered through the empty rooms to the ceremonial room used for painting. The red lacquer cabinet, the rattan chairs, the table rose in the dusty light of afternoon like ruined temples in a jungle. The elderly manservant was sprawled in the doorway. There was a neat hole in his skull, between the eyes, but there was only a thin trickle of blood. His aged, shrivelled body seemed to have had little blood left. His master had been at his table, painting, his forehead rested on an antique scroll now irreversibly tainted. The back of his head was a bloody pulp, his painting tools had been overturned; the ink, mingled with blood on the tabletop, formed a shimmering, dark red pool. It looked solid. Salagnon did not dare touch it.

The young servant was never found.

'It was him,' Salagnon said to his uncle.

'Or maybe not.'

'Why else would he have run away?'

'Here, regardless of what people have done, they run away. Especially a young man whose only support has vanished. If the police had questioned him, he would have been guilty. They know how to do these things. With them, everyone confesses. The colonial police are the finest in the world. They systematically find the guilty party. Everyone they arrest is guilty and eventually confesses. So, even unimportant witnesses run away; and in doing so confirm their guilt. It's inexorable. In Indochine we're spoiled for choice when it comes to finding guilty men. The streets are full of them. You only have to go out and round them up. You could be one of them.'

'Was it my fault that he died?'

'It's possible. But don't overestimate your importance. An Annamese nobleman has many reasons to die. It could be in anyone's interests. Other aristocrats, to set an example, to discourage blatant western-ization; the Viet Minh, to widen the colonial gap and make it seem irreversible; the Chinese merchants, who traffic opium and run the gambling houses with the approval of Bảo Đại, the French authorities and the Viet Minh, since we all get a cut; our intelligence service, to muddy the waters, to throw suspicion on others so they will kill each other. And it could have been the young boy for personal reasons. But even he could have been manipulated by any of the parties I've just mentioned. And they themselves could be manipulated by others, and so on, ad infinitum. You already know that in Indochine death comes quickly, for the haziest of reasons. But if the reasons are vague, death is always clean; in fact, it is the only thing that is clean in this bloody country. In time you come to love it.'

'Indochine?'

'Death.'

Salagnon painted out of doors. The number of children all around was unimaginable. They shouted, they chirped, they leapt into the river, ran barefoot along the dirt road. A line of trucks passed, raising clouds of dust, hawking thick black diesel fumes, escorted by two motorcycles that rumbled like an operatic bass, the riders bolt upright, wearing thick goggles and leather helmets. The boys raced after them; they always moved in gangs and always ran, their small, bare feet slapping against the dirt, jeering at the soldiers sitting in the back of the trucks, the weary soldiers who waved half-heartedly. Then the convoy sped away in a clatter of metal, a roar of engines, leaving a thick cloud of yellow dust, and the boys scattered like so many starlings, then flocked together again and raced off in another direction to plunge into the river. The number of children here is unimaginable, many more than in France. One might think they sprout from the fecund earth, that they grow and multiply like water hyacinths on tranquil lakes. Fortunately, death comes quickly here, otherwise the lake would be overgrown; fortunately, they multiply quickly, because there is so much death that the whole country would be killed off. Just like the jungle, everything grows and comes to nothing, death and life in the same moment, in the same act. Salagnon drew children playing on the water's edge. He painted them with delicate lines, with no shadows, in vibrant strokes, as they constantly scrabbled and scurried above the level line of the water. While in this country he was plunging deeper into death and blood, the sketches he was sending home to Eurydice became increasingly delicate.

When the red sun sank in the west, Hanoi began to bustle. Salagnon went to eat. Tonight he ordered soup again – never in his life had he eaten so much soup. The huge soup bowls were whole worlds floating in a pungent broth, just as Indochine floats on the water of its rivers, in its scents of flesh and flowers. The bowl was set down in front of him and, among the diced vegetables, the translucent noodles and the slivers of meat, was a chicken's foot, claws at the ready. He thanked them for this touch; they knew him. Around him, Tonkinese diners slurped hurriedly; French soldiers ordered more beers, while air force officers, having set their striking caps adorned with gold wings on the table, chatted among themselves, laughing at the stories they took turns telling. They had invited him to join them, seeing that he was an officer, but he had declined, gesturing to his brush and his sketchpad open to a blank page. They had saluted sympathetically and returned to their conversation. Salagnon preferred to eat alone. Outside, the bustle carried on; inside the Tonkinese took it in turns to eat, always hurriedly, while the French lingered at their tables to drink and chatter. A middle-aged woman with a perm served, her eyes daubed with blue eyeshadow, her mouth a vivid red. She spent her time yelling at the young girl in the slit skirt, who served drinks without a word and wriggled like an eel to avoid the soldiers as they laughed and tried to grab her. She tirelessly carried beers to the table and Salagnon could not tell whether the owner was telling her to avoid the soldiers' hands or to allow them to grope her.

The light went out. The creaking fan slowed and stopped. This brought a burst of applause, of laughs and mock-frightened cries, all made by French voices. Outside the sky still twinkled and the paraffin lamps hanging from the street stalls cast a quivering light. Shots rang out. Without a word, all the Tonkinese got up and walked out. The two women vanished, leaving the French officers alone in the restaurant. The conversation trailed off and they began to get to their feet, visible only as silhouettes, their faces reflecting the orange flames from the lamps outside. Salagnon was caught unawares, cupping the bowl in his hands and drinking when the light went out. He did not dare continue drinking for fear of swallowing the chicken claw in the darkness. His eyes adjusted. A crowd swelled through the street. There was a sound of running, shouting, gunfire. A dishevelled Vietnamese youth burst into the restaurant, bathed in red by the flickering lanterns. He waved a pistol and peered into the darkness. He spotted the gold-piped white shirts of the airmen and fired, screaming 'Criminals! Criminals!' in a thick accent. They fell, wounded, or threw themselves to the floor. The boy stood in the doorway, gripping his gun. He turned to where Salagnon was sitting, holding his bowl. He moved forwards, aiming the pistol, yelling something in Vietnamese. This was a stroke of luck: that he shouted rather than fired. Two metres from Salagnon, he stopped, staring intently, his fingers tensed. He raised the gun and aimed it right between the eyes of Salagnon, who was still sitting, cupping the bowl in both hands, not knowing where to look – at the bowl and the floating chicken's foot, the young man's eyes, the ominous hand, the black barrel of the gun – when the Vietnamese boy crumpled in a burst of machine-gun fire. He fell face first on to the table, which splintered. Instinctively, Salagnon jumped to his feet, saving the bowl he was still holding and losing the flask of ink, which fell and shattered. The light came on again and the ceiling fan started up, squeaking intermittently.

In the doorway two paratroopers wheeled slowly, their slim bodies bowed over their machine guns. Their hunter's eyes scanned the room. One of them turned over the dead Vietnamese boy with his foot.

'You're lucky, Lieutenant. A second longer and he would have put a bullet in you.'

'Yeah. Thanks.'

'Luckier than our pilots, in any case. Without their wings, they're helpless.'

One of the airmen got to his feet, his shirt stained with blood, and bent over those still lying on the floor. The paratrooper expertly frisked the Vietnamese boy; he ripped off his pendant, a silver Buddha the size of a fingernail on a leather band. He turned to Salagnon and tossed it to him.

'There you go, Lieutenant. With this, he should have been immortal. But you're the one he brought luck to. Keep it.'

The strap was spattered with blood, although it had already dried. Not knowing where to put it, Salagnon hung it around his neck. He drained his soup, leaving the chicken's foot, claws bared, at the bottom of the bowl. The two women did not reappear. They all left together, taking the dead and the wounded.

Commentaries VI

I saw her around all the time, but I'd never have dared speak to her

'W HAT HAPPENED NEXT?'

'Nothing. Events pursued their sinister course. I survived everything. This was the only event worth reporting. I was protected by something. Everyone around me was dying, I survived. The little Buddha I wore constantly must have absorbed all the available luck and transmitted it to me; all those who came near me died, but not me.

'Look,' he said, 'I've still got it.'

He opened a couple of buttons of his shirt. I leaned forwards. He showed me his emaciated chest, which resembled an arid, windswept plateau where rivers had once flowed. A few sparse grey hairs barely covered it, the flesh had receded, the skin clung loosely to the bones in little folds; it looked like a fossilized network, like the riverbeds of Mars where water no longer flows, except deep below a little blood still flows, perhaps.

Dangling from a leather thong I had never noticed before was a little silver Buddha. He was seated on a lotus, his knees visible beneath the folds of his robe; he held up an open hand and, if you looked closely, you could just make out a smile. His eyes were closed.

'You still wear it?'

'I've never taken it off. It's exactly as it was the day I got it. Look.'

He showed me a crusting of rust in the folds of the little figurine: the neck, the crossed legs.

'I've never cleaned it. Silver doesn't rust, that's the blood of the kid who was wearing it. I keep it with me, a souvenir of the day I died. I shouldn't have survived that moment. All the rest of my life has been a bonus. I wear it next to me. It is a monument to the dead I carry, to the memory of those who were not so lucky and to the health of those who were. If it was a trophy, I might have cleaned it, but it is a testament, so I have left it as it was.'

The leather strap was shiny, oiled by decades of sweat. He clearly had not changed that either; it was probably leather from a water buffalo that had grazed in Indochine in the depths of the last century. Perhaps that had imparted a smell, but I did not get close enough to know. He let it drop against his chest and rebuttoned his shirt.

'He probably serves as my heart, this fat little man with his eyes closed. I've never dared be without it, never set it down for too long. I was afraid something would stop and it would all be over. There is just enough metal in it to cast a bullet, a silver bullet like the ones they use on werewolves, vampires, the evil creatures that cannot be killed by ordinary means. So I picked it up, the bullet that did not kill me, the bullet that had my name on it, and as long as I keep it hidden, as long as I keep it close, it cannot hurt me. No one has seen that Buddha except Eurydice, who's seen me naked, and some of my paratrooper buddies who saw me in my boxers or in the shower, but they're all dead now, and now there's you. In this whole story, the only thing I've kept is this death that was not mine.'

'You didn't bring anything back, didn't keep anything? No exotic curios to remind you?'

'Nothing. Apart from a talisman and a few wounds. Nothing remains of those twenty years of my life, apart from my pictures. I painted so many, so now I'm trying to sell them off. The heat over there cured me of exoticism. That said, Indochine was a weird bazaar, you could buy anything there: American rifles, Japanese military swords, Viet Minh sandals made with Michelin tyres, antique Chinese objects, broken French furniture, everything bought there became exotic. But I never hung on to anything. I gradually lost everything. I left it behind. Some things were stolen or destroyed or confiscated, and what was left, the things you'd expect to find in an old soldier's attic, like a beret or a badge, a medal, maybe a gun, I threw away. I have no souvenirs. Nothing here relates to that part of my life.'

Surrounded as we were by all the pointless objects that decorated the room, which spoke of nothing but their own pointlessness, and visibly confirmed that they were related to nothing other than themselves, I had no trouble believing him.

'All I have is the silver Buddha I've just shown you; and the ink brush I use, which I bought in Hanoi on the advice of the man who was my teacher. And a photograph. Just one.'

'Why that particular one?'

'I don't know. The little Buddha is something I never took off. It hasn't been out of my sight in fifty years. The ink brush is something I still use. But I don't know why I still have the photograph. Perhaps it has only survived by accident, because something always survives. Of the thousands of things I've handled in those twenty years, there are those that disappear, and you find them again one day, and you wonder why.

'I should have torn it up, thrown it away, but I never had the heart. I kept the photo. It has overcome every threat of extinction and it's still here, like one of those insignificant relics that unaccountably survives for hundreds of years when everything else has disappeared, a mark in the sand, a battered sandal, a child's terracotta toy. There is a form of archaeological chance which dictates that, for no particular reason, certain things remain.'

He showed me a small black-and-white photograph, half the size of a postcard, with a white deckle border, the way they were printed back then. In that cramped space a number of people stood grouped around a large vehicle with caterpillar tracks, staring at the camera. It was difficult to see much, because of the size of the figures and the poor contrast. The laboratory assistants would have scrimped on paper and chemicals and those in backwater towns in Indochine were slapdash and churned out pictures too quickly.

'The fact that you can't see much is one of the reasons I kept it. I've always told myself I would work out who was in the picture and find out how many were still alive. I've waited so long that number must be close to zero. I think I'm the only one left. And maybe that machine, a hulking wreck rusting in the jungle. Have you spotted me?'

It was difficult to make out the faces. They were simply a grey blur in which a dark hollow indicated the eyes and a white smudge the smile. I found it hard to recognize the vehicle; the turret was unlike the ones you see on tanks, and the gun barrel looked like a short pipe. In the background there was a mass of hazy foliage.

'The forest of Tonkin. We used to call it the jungle, but people don't say that any more. Have you found me?'

I finally identified him by his height, his leanness and the proud tilt of his head, by the fact that he looked like an ensign planted in the ground.

'Here?'

'Yes. The only picture of me in twenty years and I'm barely recognizable.'

'Where were you?'

'When it was taken? Everywhere. We were the reserve force. We went wherever things were going badly. I was stationed with them after my convalescence. We needed able-bodied men, lucky men, immortals. We never marched, we ran everywhere. We hurled ourselves at the enemy. If someone called, we came.

'I learned to jump out of a plane. We didn't often jump. We went most places on foot, but jumping is an intense experience. We were deathly pale, silent, lined up in the fuselage of a Dakota that was shuddering so hard we couldn't hear anything above the roar of the engine. We would wait next to a door open on to nothing; there was a vicious draught, the whine of the propellers, a flash of different shades of green below. And, one by one, when the signal was given, we jumped on to the enemy below; we jumped on his back, lips curled, teeth bared, claws unsheathed, eyes glowing. We threw ourselves into the terrible fray; we charged the enemy after a brief flight and a fall in which we were little more than naked bodies in the void, our cheeks juddering, our bellies knotted with fear and the urge to kill.

'It was really something, being a paratrooper. We were warriors, hoplites, berserkers. We were expected never to sleep, to jump by night, to march for days on end, to run without ever slackening, to fight, to carry extremely heavy weapons and keep them clean, and always to have a hand steady enough to plunge a knife into someone or to carry a wounded man.

'We would pile into huge, decrepit planes with a pack of folded silk strapped to our backs. We made the flight in silence and when we came to the jungle, the swamp, the vast plains of elephant grass that from above are simply different shades of green, but which are also different worlds, with distinct challenges, particular dangers, different ways of dying, we would jump. We jumped on the enemy hiding in the grass, under the trees, in the mud; we jumped on the enemy's backs to save a friend who was trapped and about to die, in a post under siege, in a column under attack, who had called on us for help. This was all that mattered to us: saving. Get in quick, fight hard, get out alive if we could. We kept ourselves clean, we had a clear conscience. If this seemed like a dirty war, that was just the mud: we were fighting in a humid country. The risks we took cleansed everything. We saved lives, in our way. That was all we did. Save lives; save ourselves and in the meantime, run. We were magnificent machines, catlike, stealthy, we were the light airborne infantry, slim and athletic. We died easily. That way, we remained clean, the beautiful machines of the French army, the most beautiful warriors who ever lived.'

He fell silent.

'You see,' he went on, 'the thing that fascists have, above and beyond that simple thuggishness anyone might have, is the notion of "romantic death" that has them bid goodbye to life while in their prime, a funereal joy that leads them to feel contempt for life, their own and other people's. There is a melancholic will-to-machine aspect to fascists evident in their every gesture, their every word; you can see it in their eyes – they have a metallic glint. That's why we were fascists. Or at least we pretended to be. That's why we learned to jump: to weed out people, to identify the fittest among us, to cull those who would turn tail when things got tough, to keep only those capable of laughing in the face of their own death. Keep only those who could stare it down and keep marching.

'All we did was fight. We were lost soldiers, and losing ourselves was our way of protecting ourselves from evil. Me, I probably saw a little more of what was going on, because of the ink. The ink cloaked me somewhat. It gave me a sense of detachment. Working with ink meant sitting down, saying nothing, observing in silence. The narrowness of our world view gave us incredible solidarity, and it later left us orphans. We were living a boy's adventure story, shoulder to shoulder; in the thick of the fight, as in a phalanx, all we had was our neighbour's shoulder. We would have liked to live that way for ever, for everyone to live that way. In our eyes, bloody comradeship seemed to resolve everything.'

He paused again.

'That machine with the caterpillar treads,' I said. 'Was that parachuted in with you?'

'Sometimes. We parachuted in with heavy weaponry we assembled on the ground to build fortified positions in the jungle to lure the Viet Minh, who would end up impaled on our spikes. We were the bait. The Viets wanted nothing more than to destroy paratrooper bases; we wanted nothing more than to destroy their regular divisions, the only units that were about the same strength. At five to one in their favour, we considered it an equal fight. We played hide-and-seek.

Sometimes we had huge, hulking machines like this dropping from the sky. We would dig them out of the mud, assemble them, and they would break down. In that godforsaken country we were the only things that worked: a naked man with a weapon in his hand.'

'The turret is a strange shape.'

'It's a flame-throwing tank. An American tank left over from the war in the Pacific. It was used in the beach landings. They used it to burn the bunkers made of coconut trunks that the Japanese had constructed all over the islands. They were easy to build – fibrous trunks, sand, solid blocks of coral – they withstood bullets and bombs. To destroy them, you had to blast liquid flame through the loopholes and burn everything inside. Then you could advance.'

'Did you do that too?'

'The Viet Minh didn't have bunkers. Or if they did, they were so well hidden we never found them; either that, or they were in places the tanks didn't go.'

'So what did you use the tank for? You're all posing with it as if it was your favourite elephant.'

'We did ride on its back, and we used it to burn villages, that's all.'

Now it was my turn to fall silent.

A bizarre army had been launched on Indochine, whose only mission was to sort things out for themselves. An ill-assorted army, commanded by aristocrats from days of yore and stray Resistance fighters; an army built from the wreckage of various European countries, comprising a handful of young men who were well-educated romantics, a mob of losers, morons and bastards, and many normal guys who found themselves in a situation so abnormal that they became what otherwise they would never have become. And here they were, all posing for the photographer, grouped around this machine, smiling at the camera. They were the ill-assorted army of Darius, the imperial army. They were capable of thousands of things. But the machine had a single purpose: to burn. And here there was nothing to burn except villages and their huts of wood and straw, and everything within them. This weapon ensured that things could not have turned out differently.

The house burned and everything within it. Since it was made of straw, it burned easily. The thatch of dried palm leaves blazed, flames licking at the wall of woven wood and then at the timber joists and the floor in a thunderous roar that put an end to all cries. These people cried out in their language made up of cries that seemed to mimic the calls of the forest. They shrieked and the roar of the blaze drowned out their cries, and when the fire dwindled and nothing remained but the blackened pillars and the floor, there was nothing but an immense silence, some crackling, a few embers and the sickening stench of burnt fat, charred meat, that hovered over the clearing for days.

'You did that?'

'Yes. We saw so many dead, piles and piles of tangled corpses. We buried them with bulldozers when the business was over – the taking of the village or a skirmish with a Viet Minh regiment. We no longer saw them. We were bothered by the smell of them, so we tried to protect ourselves by burying everything. The dead were simply a part of the problem, killing was simply a process. We had the power and by using it we caused damage. We were trying to survive in a country that was collapsing: we relied for support only on each other. The vegetation was itchy, the ground shifting, the people elusive. They were nothing like us. We knew nothing. In order to survive we devised a jungle code: staying together, being careful where we stepped, clearing the path with machetes, never sleeping, running as soon as we heard a wild animal. That was the price of getting out of the jungle. But what we should have done was never go in.'

'All that blood,' I murmured.

'Yes. That was the problem, the blood. I've had under my nails for days in the jungle blood that was not my own. When I could finally take a shower, the water turned brown, then red. Filthy, bloody water would flow from me. Then the water would run clear. I would be clean.'

'A shower, that's all?'

'A shower was the least of it if you were to go on living. I survived everything and that was not easy. Have you ever noticed that it is the survivors who describe wars? Listening to them, you think you can get out alive, that providence protects you, that you can watch death from the outside, swooping down on others. You end up believing that death is a rare accident. In the places I went it was easy to die. The Indochine I lived in was a museum of ways of dying: you could die from a bullet to the head; a machine-gun burst riddling your body; a leg blown off by a landmine; a gash from a piece of shrapnel that left you to bleed out; a direct hit that reduced you to a bloody pulp; you could be crushed by the wreckage of an overturned vehicle; burned inside the cabin by an armour-piercing shell; spiked by a poisoned trap; or you could die simply – mysteriously – of exhaustion and heat. I survived everything, but it was not easy. In fact, it had little to do with me. I simply avoided everything. I am here. I think that the ink helped me. It hid me.

'But this is the end. Even if I don't really believe it, I will die soon. All these things I'm telling you, I've never told anyone. With those who lived it, there was no need, and those who didn't live it refuse to hear. Eurydice, I told through gestures. I painted for her. I showed her how beautiful it was, nothing more, and I spread a cloak of black ink around her, so she would not suspect.'

'So why me?'

'Because this is the end. And because you, you see through the ink.'

I was not sure I understood what he was saying. I did not dare ask him. He was standing, looking out, his back turned towards me. Through the window he would have seen only the houses of Voracieux-les-Bredins framed by towers, in the grey light of an interminable winter.

'Death,' he said.

And he said it with that French intonation, that timbre of church and palace, the tone I imagine Bishop Bossuet used, a low throb like a bassoon reed inside his nose, which, when as he orates creates a muted yet fearsome note; the note that declares a state of affairs about which nothing can be done, and yet must be proclaimed. Because life must go on.

'Death! It's finally coming! I'm tired of this immortality. I'm beginning to find the solitude weighs heavily. But don't say that to Eurydice. She relies on me.'

I headed back to Lyon on foot, a journey that was never conceived for pedestrians. I kept my fists balled in my coat, wrapped myself around my clenched teeth, and strode on.

Voracieux-les-Bredins had not been planned with walking in mind. No one walks here. The building projects are bordered by a grey area on which you stumble. Beyond that there is no thought. I walked fretfully. It was like a rhythm, the snare drum of my heart, the bass drums of my footsteps, the tom-toms of the vast buildings lining my route. I crossed zones and thoroughfares intended for heavy traffic. I had to step over low walls, walk through patches of waste ground where shoes sink and trousers are dampened by tall, fronded weeds. I had to follow narrow, rubble-strewn paths between badly connected spaces. On a map you can make the journey by car, it is simple, but on a human scale the spaces are cemented by the sweat of footsteps. People pass all the same. They stream along paths not set out on the map. No one ever considered that a person might walk from one place to the other. In Voracieux-les-Bredins nothing is consistent; it was planned that way.

As I followed the dirt tracks through the city, I saw dozens of GAFFES posters plastered over every inch of wall. Rash urban planning throws up countless windowless walls, vast grey canvases blatantly begging to be scrawled on. They are festooned with spray-can paintings and posters that peel off in the rain. The GAFFES posters were blue and had the face of De Gaulle – recognizable by his nose, his kepi, the little moustache he grew during his years in London, the haughty stiffness of the neck. A long quote in dazzling white demanded to be read.

> It is very good that there are yellow French, black French, brown French. They show that France is open to all races and has a universal vocation. But only on condition that they remain a small minority. Otherwise, France would no longer be France. We are still primarily a European people of the white race, Greek and Latin culture, and the Christian religion.

This was all, and it was signed with the GAFFES logo. They stick up posters with these slogans, allowing people to believe that 'The Novelist' himself wrote them. Nothing else is added. The posters are plastered over every wall in Voracieux-les-Bredins. That seems to be enough; they know what they mean. Voracieux is a place where our darkest thoughts ferment. You take a piece of text, superimpose it on a photograph of de Gaulle from his heroic period and that is enough. No reference is given. I know this speech: The Novelist did not write it. He simply said the words. They were published in newspaper accounts. It begins: 'Fine words are not enough.' But they are enough, and he knows that. You can imagine him talking to a reporter who is taking notes, things become heated, he lets rip: 'Let's not kid ourselves! Have you gone to see the Muslims? Have you seen them in their turbans and their djellabas? It's perfectly obvious that they are not French. Anyone who supports integration has the brain of a hummingbird, however educated he might be. Try mixing oil and vinegar. Shake the bottle. After a while they separate again. The Arabs are Arabs, the French are French. Do you really believe the French body politic can absorb ten million Muslims, who will number twenty million by tomorrow and forty by the day after? If we accept integration, if all the Arabs and the Berbers in Algeria were considered French, how could you stop them moving to metropolitan France, where the standard of living is much higher? My village would no longer be called Colombey-les-Deux-Églises, it would be Colombey-les-Deux-Mosquées.'

His voice is clearly audible as he says these words. His voice is clear, because we recognize his nasal whine, his ironic zeal, his witty eloquence that makes use of every linguistic register to castigate, to seduce, to make the listener smile, to muddy the waters in order to get the upper hand. He has a masterful command of rhetorical devices. It is always a pleasure to listen to him. But when the smile has faded, if you have been careful to take notes, you find yourself dumbfounded by the vagueness, the dishonesty, the blind contempt; and by the literary virtuosity. What seems to be a clear vision, built on solid foundations of common sense, is nothing more than bar-room politics, said simply in order to win over whoever is listening, to muddle matters, to hold the floor. When he speaks, The Novelist is a man driven by the most banal motives. No one is a great man in every circumstance, nor every day.

Just read the words! Djellabas, turbans! What is he talking about? Take a look at the people who live in Algiers, in Oran, are they so very different? A hummingbird? Brilliant! You expect a sparrow, but he throws in a little exotic lyricism. You smile and you have already lost the argument. Oil and vinegar? Who is the oil and who the vinegar, and why two liquids that do not mix when, by definition, man is end-lessly mixed? The Arabs and the French? As though it were possible to compare two categories whose definitions are not remotely equivalent, as though the meanings of each were definitively set down by nature. He makes you smile. He is witty, because the brilliance of the French mind lies in wit. What is wit? It is all the advantages of faith with none of the difficulties of credulity. It means acting according to the strict laws of folly, while pretending to be no fool. It is charming, it is often funny, but in a sense this makes it worse than foolishness, because to laugh is to think we are not concerned, but no one here gets out alive. Wit is simply a means of masking ignorance. Forty million, he says, forty million others, as many of them as of us, conceived much faster than we can conceive, a perpetual demographic terrorist attack; is this not simply the age-old fear that the other, the other, the other holds the true power, the only power: sexual?

Fine words are more than enough for The Novelist. He takes the shiniest ones and tosses them in our faces, we gather them up like treasure, but they are fool's gold. People who talk about kinship are always understood, since we think primarily in terms of resemblance. Race is an inconsistent concept grounded in our frantic desire to belong, which aspires to theoretical justifications it will never discover since they do not exist. But that does not matter; what matters is to give the impression... Race is a fart from the body politic, the mute manifestation of a body with digestive problems; race is a means of playing to the gallery, of keeping people busy with the notion of identity, the indefinable thing we struggle to define; we do not succeed, and that keeps us busy. The aim of the GAFFES is not to legally categorize the populace according to pigmentation, the aim of the GAFFES is illegality. What they dream of is the mindless, unbridled use of force, such that eventually the most dignified can lead an unfettered existence. And while the public is applauding their little racist puppet show, behind, below and in the shadows of the wings the real issues are being decided, and the real issues are always social. This is how they unsuspectingly ended up being taken in, those who blindly believed in the colour code of the colonies. The *pieds noirs* were a microcosm of what France is today, all of France, panic-stricken France, whose very language is contaminated by colonial decay. We clearly feel that we are lacking something. French people seek it, the GAFFES pretend to seek it, we search for our lost power; we desperately long to wield it.

I walked, hunched over. I did not really know where I was. I was heading vaguely west. In the distance I could see the Monts du Lyonnais and Mont Pilat. Luckily there are mountains around here, so you know where you are headed. In this sprawling suburb I do not know where I am, I do not know where anyone is. This is the advantage and the disadvantage of living alone, of doing little work, of being entirely, completely self-absorbed. It takes us back to the self, and the self is nothing.

I came to a fenced-off area where a pack of children was swarming all over contraptions intended for swinging and climbing. This meant it must be about five o'clock and the low-rise building with the large doorway had to be a school. Children are subject to regular migrations. I went and sat next to them, on a bench their mothers had left vacant. Sitting with my clenched fists in my pockets, my collar turned up, I had clearly not come here with a child. People kept a watchful eye on me. The children wrapped in puffer jackets climbed up ladders that turned into slides. They chased each other, bounced on seesaws mounted on springs, screaming constantly, and not one of them got hurt. The inexhaustible energy of children protects them from everything. When they fall, they suffer minimal impact. They get to their feet straight away; if I were to fall I would break.

Their scurrying about infuriated me, and the racket they were making all around. I am not like them. They are numberless, constantly in motion, the children of Voracieux-les-Bredins, black and brown beneath their woolly hats, above their scarves, none of whom belongs to me, so pale. They perform dangerous acrobatics, but nothing happens to them; their energy protects them; they resume their initial shape after every fall. They are the cement that proliferates and single-handedly mends the cracked community house. What we most need is a roof, one that will not fall down, to protect us and contain us. The colour of the walls makes no difference to the solidity of the roof. It just needs to stay up.

In what way did they resemble me, these black and brown children playing and shrieking on these seesaws on springs? In what way did they resemble me, these children who are my future, as I sat on a bench in my winter coat? In no *visible* way, but they suckled the same milk of language. We are brothers in language, and what is said in that language we hear together; what is whispered in that language, we all understand, even before we hear it. Even in invective, we understand each other. It is a marvellous expression: we understand each other. It describes an intimate intertwining in which each is part of the other, a figure it is impossible to represent, but which, for the point of view of language, is obvious: we are entwined by an intimate understanding of language. Even confrontation does not destroy that understanding. Try having an argument with a foreigner: it is like banging your head against a rock. It is only among our own that we can really fight, kill each other; among ourselves.

I know nothing about children. I had spent months painting with a man who told me such things that I had to walk home in order to dry out. I needed to take a shower after listening to him. I would have preferred not to hear. But not hearing something does not make it go away: what is there exerts its influence in the silence, like a gravitational field.

I was a child once, too, even if it is difficult for me to remember now. I shrieked for no better reason than my boundless energy. I raced around aimlessly. I amused myself, which is the fundamental verb of childhood, with its strange reflexive form. But sitting as I am now, fists clenched, shoulders hunched, the collar of my winter coat hiding my lowered chin, it is difficult to remember. I am stuck in this moment, sitting on a bench, in this directionless suburb. This is the trouble, this is the tragedy: being stuck in this moment. Being terrified of what has happened, being afraid of what will happen, being irritated by the bustle, yet staying here; and thinking that here is everything.

One little boy who was running – they ran everywhere – stopped in front of me. He peered at me, his tiny nose poking out over his scarf, stray black curls peeking from under his hat, dark eyes shining with infinite gentleness. With his mittened hand he pushed aside his scarf, revealing a little mouth from which came clouds of white mist, a child's breath in the cold air.

'Why are you sad?'

'I'm thinking about death. About all the dead we leave behind.'

He stared at me, nodded his head, his mouth open, wreathed in the vapour of his breath. 'You can't be alive unless you think about death.'

And he raced off again, shrieking and laughing with the children on the seesaws, running in circles on the rubber mat that meant any fall was harmless.

Shit. He can't be more than four years old and he just said that. I'm not sure he meant to. I'm not sure he understands what he is saying, but he said it, said it right in front of me. Children may not talk, but they speak; words pass through a child without them noticing. Through the power of language, we understand each other. Intertwined.

So I got up and I left. My fists were no longer clenched, time had started up again. I walked all the way home, the street lamps lighting the way; the streets here were better planned, the façades better aligned, I was in Lyon, in a city that like my thoughts finally fell into place. I walked calmly towards the centre.

I was a child, too, and like so many children at the time I lived on a shelf. Back then, people were stored in green parkland on huge, grey, concrete shelves, in narrow buildings that were tall and broad. In the orthogonal structure, the apartments were lined up like books, overlooking both sides of the shelf, windows at the front, balconies at the back, like the cells of a honeycomb. On the balconies at the rear everyone displayed whatever they wanted. From the communal gardens, from the vast car park, you could see all the floors, and the balconies that offered a glimpse of something, like the titles visible on the spines of books when they are lined up on the shelf. People could lean over and watch the world go by; leave their laundry hanging out longer than was necessary; shout at each other; complain about each other's children; sit; sit and read; bring out a chair, a tiny little table, and do some work; housework, sorting vegetables, darning socks, sewing for some cottage industry. We lived cheek by jowl, all classes and creeds. Everyone enjoyed watching life played out on the balconies, while

longing to get away. Everyone hoped to make enough money to buy
a house, to have one built, to live alone. Many succeeded. But back
when I was a child, we all still lived together, all classes and creeds, in
the golden age of the *cités*, when tower blocks were built. They were
new, we had more than enough space. Standing by the cypress tree in
the communal gardens where we played, I could see shelves groaning
under the weight of all human life: all ages, every band of wealth –
from the modest to the middle-class – every possible configuration of
the family. From far below, from my child's-eye view, I saw the rungs
of the social ladder. But already everyone was dreaming of building a
little house, of living alone on some remote plot of ground ringed by
leylandii hedges.

We played. The tarmacked spaces between the cars were perfect
for roller-skating. We played urban hockey using ping-pong balls and
sticks made from planks nailed together. We taped pieces of cardboard
to the spokes of our bicycles so they sounded like motorbikes. We
played in the rubble of unfinished building sites, ongoing projects that
always left mountains of excavated dirt, mounds of sand on tarpaulins,
piles of timber crusted with cement, rickety scaffolding we scaled by
shinning up the jute ropes used for hauling buckets, jumping from
long bendy planks that catapulted us into the air. So much building
was going on during those years. Even we were works in progress. It
was all anyone did: build, demolish, rebuild, dig and fill, renovate.
The magnates of the Department of Public Works were masters of
the world, the all-powerful lords of land, of housing and of thought.
If you compare what existed back then with what you can see now,
the whole area is unrecognizable. Back then, buildings were sprouting everywhere to accommodate all those who flocked to live here.
They were quickly thrown up, quickly finished, quickly roofed. These
buildings were designed to have no attics, only cellars. There was no
clear thinking, no memory to be retained, nothing but buried fears.
We would play in the labyrinthine cellars, in the bare stone corridors,
on damp earthen floors as cold and elastic as a dead man's skin, in

corridors lit by bare bulbs in cages whose harsh glare did not travel far but stopped dead, fearful of the shadows, not daring to light the corners, leaving them in darkness. In the cellars we played war games that were not very violent, not very sexual; we were children. We would slink through the shadows and fire at each other with plastic machine guns that made a clacking noise, with pistols of soft polythene whose plosive gunfire we imitated by puffing out our cheeks. I remember being held captive in a cellar, pretending to be tied up, while "they" pretended to interrogate me, torture me, force me to talk – "they" were characters in the game – and the sickening sound of a real slap across my face.

Suddenly, the game stopped and we all flushed red; we were excited, feverish, panting for breath, our foreheads burning. Things had gone too far. My stinging cheek was proof that things had gone too far. We stammered something about the game being over, about having to go home. We all climbed back up into the daylight, heading to our homes, back up on to our shelves.

We were children. We didn't know how to talk about violence or about love. We acted without knowing. We had no words. We acted.

One summer evening we were desperately chalking hearts with arrows through them on the tarmac. We drew them in pink, two hearts interlinked, surrounded by wavy lines, and in the centre we wrote out the names of everyone we could think of; we scribbled furiously, drawing with a fevered excitement that made the chalk break, feeling as though we were writing swear words, but nice ones, and if one of our parents had shown up, we would have scattered, blushing and giggling, our hands covered in chalk dust, incapable of explaining our joy or our embarrassment. We drew these hearts one summer evening underneath one of the first-floor balconies, scarcely a metre off the ground, where a new couple had just moved in. A swarm of kids traced linked hearts under their balcony; the sky slowly shifted from pink to purple; the air was balmy, joyous, and they watched us, their arms around each other, her head on his shoulder; they smiled and said nothing as the blue light of evening slowly thickened.

We did things, we feverishly did things; we shared our elders' passion for public works, and every day we created our own miniature building sites. We worked the soft earth to create flat surfaces on which to play marbles, paths for tin cyclists so we could race our Majorette die-cast cars. We would start out with bulldozers with metal blades found in our toy boxes, but very quickly they proved to be inadequate. We would dig using broken sticks, with toy shovels, with little plastic buckets and spades we brought with us to the seaside or anywhere there was sand to be dug. There we dug up the ground and built our houses, and quickly the small began to spread.

The three tower blocks in the *cité* had been built on a sloping site, which had been levelled in three places in order to construct the tall shelves containing the apartments. The car park was a smooth, steep plane, ideal for skating, and the road out to the street was bordered by a concrete wall that measured two metres high at the street – which was out of bounds – and gradually sloped until, near the tower blocks, it was level with the ground. This smooth concrete wall played a major role in our games. It was an ideal motorway, the smoothest surface in the *cité*, and perfectly adapted to the pocket-sized traffic of Majorettes. Every day scores of little boys raced their cars and trucks along the wall, their pursed lips throbbing, making a roar of engines, coming and going, performing U-turns where the wall merged with the tarmac or where it became too high for them to carry on. The taller boys could go farther before they were forced to turn.

This wall, built on a slope, shored up a bank of bare earth that had not yet been planted; this provided the virgin territory for our building sites. Grass never grew there because of our constant digging, the roads, the garages, the landing strips next to the motorway, which was constantly filled with a traffic of toy cars, except when it was time for meals or for our after-school snack. One tumultuous day, one summer evening when night seemed reluctant to fall, we dug deeper; there were lots of us with shovels, sticks, excitedly digging a hole. The smell was intoxicating. The more we dug, the more it stank. A horde of boys was toiling on the dirt embankment above the wall where our cars were now parked, since no one was interested in pushing them. The bigger boys, the most resourceful, burrowed into the root-tangled soil, making great play of excavating the rubble; some appointed themselves foremen and organized lines of buckets. Most did nothing; they scurried about excitably, wrinkling their noses and giving little disgusted yelps, their limbs quivering. The smell came from the ground itself, like some noxious layer we had accidentally breached and which now spilled out, heavy, viscous, at its most pungent where we were digging. We found teeth. Visibly human teeth, like the ones in our mouths. And then fragments of bone. A grown-up watched us work, amused; another watched from the open window of his kitchen. The rank smell did not reach them, it slithered along the ground. They did not take us seriously, they thought it was just a game, but we were not playing any more. The fetid stench was proof that we had struck reality. It was so overwhelming that we knew we had happened on to something real. The teeth and fragments of bone multiplied. A big boy grabbed them, took them home and came back. 'My father says it's a grave. He said that this used to be a cemetery before. They built on top of it. He said it's disgusting and we should fill in the hole and not go near it again.'

Finally, night fell. The group gradually dispersed. The stench now came up to your knees. We could feel it as we hunkered down. There were only a few of us, hesitating. The smell did not dissolve in the cool of the night. We kicked dirt into the hole. 'Come in and wash your hands, kids. That's disgusting.' The grown-up who had been watching, smiling, had stayed until the end. He came over, crouched down, watching us work without a word, still smiling. He did not speak until we were just about to leave. 'Come on, I live just here, on the ground floor. You need to wash your hands, they're disgusting.' He had a permanent smile and a slightly high-pitched, childlike voice, which made him seem more like us, something we found a little worrying.

He insisted. Three of us followed him. He lived on the ground floor, the first door as you entered the building. All the shutters were closed. Inside it did not smell very nice. He pushed the door, which closed with a metallic clatter. He talked on and on. 'It's a horrible smell. I recognize it. Anyone who has ever smelled it would recognize it. It's the smell of a grave, a grave when it is re-opened. You need to wash your hands. Thoroughly. Right now. And even your faces. It's absolutely disgusting, the putrid dirt, and the fragments, the bones; it can make you seriously ill.'

We tramped through a murky living room filled with objects that were difficult to identify, a glass display case glowed dimly, a rifle hung on one wall, a dagger in its scabbard hanging from a nail beneath a piece of leather preposterously pinned to the wallpaper.

The bathroom was tiny. The three of us squeezed together at the washbasin. The harsh light above the mirrors was frightening. We could see him smiling above our heads, see his lips contort as he spoke, revealing stained teeth we thought were horrible. In the tiny bathroom he brushed against us as he passed the soap, turned on the tap. We were suffocating. We washed quickly, eager to get out of there. 'We need to go now, it's dark,' one of us finally dared to interrupt him. 'Already? Well, if you like...' We headed back through the dark living room, packed together as though beating a retreat. He took the rifle from the wall and held it out to me. 'Want to hold it? It's a real rifle. It was used in a real war.' None of us reached out. We kept our hands pressed against our bodies, trying to make sure nothing stuck out. 'My dad doesn't like me to handle weapons,' one of us said.

'A pity. He's wrong.' He hung up the gun with a sigh. He stroked the square of leather pinned to the wall. He took down the dagger, withdrew it from its sheath, looked at the rusted blade and slid it home again. We headed for the door. He opened the glass display case and removed a dark object and held it out to us. 'Here.' He stepped closer. 'Take it. Feel it in your hands. Tell me what it is.' Without taking it, we could tell it was a bone. A large, broken thighbone, easily recognizable by the bulbous end still crusted with desiccated meat that looked charred. 'Take it, take it.' 'What is it? Something off the barbecue? Did your dog not want it?' His hand hung, suspended. He fell silent, staring at us intently. 'Don't you have a dog?' 'A dog? Oh, yes, I used to have a dog. But they killed him. They slit my dog's throat.' His voice changed and in the dark living room this scared us. The ridiculous piece of leather tacked to the wall reflected a horrid, pinkish glow. We turned on our heels and raced for the door. It was closed, but only latched. 'Goodbye, monsieur! Thanks, monsieur!' It was only a latch. We simply had to turn the knob and we were outside. The air was mauve, the street lamps were lit, the car park was empty and never more than in that moment did I have a sense of vast spaces, of freedom, of fresh air. Without looking at each other, we disbanded, each running back to the building where we lived. I hurtled down the dirt embankment that we had filled in and the ground crumbled beneath my feet, I felt myself sinking. We had dug it over, it was full of bones and teeth. I jumped on to the concrete wall, down on to the tarmac. I ran. I took the stairs three at a time, the most my little legs could manage. I raced home.

Never again did we dig as deeply. We kept to the surface, contented ourselves with minor roadworks alongside the little motorway. Our major excavations were carried out elsewhere, far away. I grew up over a secret graveyard; when you dug up the ground, it stank. It was confirmed to me later: we were living over an abandoned cemetery. Older residents still remembered it. It had been filled in and built over. All that remained was the tall cypress tree in the middle of the grass where we played, oblivious.

I wonder now whether there were murderers lined up on the shelves where we lived. I cannot say for certain, but statistically it seems likely. In the glory years of the radiant *cité*, all the men aged between twenty-five and thirty-five, all my parents friends, had had the opportunity to kill. All of them. The opportunity. Two and a half million former soldiers, two million expatriated Algerians, a million exiled *pieds noirs*, a tenth of the population of what is now France were directly branded with the stain of colonialism, and it is contagious, it can be transmitted by contact and by word. Among the fathers of my friends, among the friends of my parents, there must have been some who were tainted by it, and by the secret powers of language all were sullied. The word 'Algerian' was spoken only after the briefest of hesitations, but one that was audible, since the ear can distinguish the slightest modulation. We did not know what to call them, so we simpered and preferred to say nothing. We did not see them; we saw only 'them'. There was no word that fitted them, so they were nameless; they haunted us, the right word on the tips of our tongues, our tongues searching to find it. Even 'Algerian', which seems neutral, referring as it does to citizens of the republic of Algeria, did not fit, since it referred to others. The French language is a spoil of war according to a writer who wrote in French, and he was absolutely right, but so too is the name 'Algerian', it is a piece of flayed skin, the blood still visible, the dried clots still clinging to the flesh; they inhabit a name as others inhabit the abandoned apartments in the centre of Algiers. We no longer know what to say. The word 'Arab' has been contaminated by those who use it. 'Native' now is a term only in ethnology. 'Muslim' reveals something that should be hidden. We used the whole panoply of insults imported from over there. We invented the term 'grey' to designate those we do not name. We proposed the term 'Maghrébin', which we used without conviction like the Latin names of flowers. Colonial rot was eating away at our language; the deeper we dug, the more it stank.

The windows of the ground-floor apartment remained closed as far as I remember, and I never again saw the man with the childlike voice; and I never discovered what beast he could turn into, since we fled. I left with my parents to go and live in the country, a patch of land surrounded by a hedge; alone. Perched on a hill, behind leafy walls, we could see for miles.

In that horrific military parade that lasted twenty years, twenty years of uninterrupted repetition, the aim of each war was to wipe the slate clean after the war that had preceded it. To clear the table after a banquet of blood everything must be wiped clean, so that the table can be set and we can eat together once again. Over the course of twenty years war followed war; each purged the one that came before, as the murderers from each war disappeared into the next. Because each of those wars made murderers of men who would not have beaten their dog or even dreamed of beating it, delivering bound and naked men into their hands, allowing them to rule over droves of people cheapened by colonialism, a herd of unknown numbers, part of which could be slaughtered in order to save the rest, as cattle are culled to ward off epizootic disease. Those who had got a taste for blood vanished into the next war. The vicious and the mad, those the war had enlisted, and more especially those whom that war created, all those men who would never have thought of hurting anyone and yet had bathed in blood, this huge reserve of fighting men was reallocated like army surplus, like an overstock of weapons, and they found themselves embroiled in grubby little wars, sordid terrorist attacks, fighting alongside thugs. But the rest? What became of the human surplus from the last of our wars?

Given my age, I may have encountered them as a child, in school, in the street, in the stairwells of the tower block. Grown-ups who were parents of my friends, friends of my parents, those wonderful people who had hugged me, lifted me into the air, dandled me on their knees, served me at dinner, might have used those selfsame hands to shoot, to stab, to drown, to activate electrodes that made men howl. Perhaps the ears that listened to our childish prattle had heard that unspeakable howl when a man's scream sends him plummeting down the stages of evolution: the cry of a child, a dog, an ape, a reptile, the groan of a suffocating fish and finally the viscous burst of a trampled worm. Perhaps I lived through a nightmare in which only I was asleep. I lived among ghosts, I could not hear them, each immured in his pain. Where were they, the men who had been taught to do such things? When we finally ceased to fight, what did we do to re-absorb the murderers from the last of all our wars? We vaguely cleaned them up. We shipped them home. Violence is a biological function common to everyone, it is locked inside; but if given free rein, it spreads; if the jack-in-the-box is opened, it may be impossible to close again. What became of all those whose hands were stained with blood? They must have been all around me, silently lined up on the concrete shelves where I spent my childhood. Those marked by violence are a nuisance, because there are so many of them, and there was nowhere they could be absorbed except in embittered nationalist movements.

'Me?' Victorien Salagnon told me. 'I paint, for Eurydice. That's what keeps me from being bitter.'

And he was teaching me to paint. I went to visit him. He was teaching me the art of the brush, an art that had come to him naturally and whose vast potential he had glimpsed when studying with a master. In his little house with its hideous decor, he taught me the subtlest of arts, an art so subtle it scarcely requires a medium, a breath is enough.

I went to Voracieux by metro, by bus. I travelled to the end of the line. It was far. I had all the time in the world. I watched the urban landscape flash past, the *cités* and the tower blocks, the crumbling houses, the tall trees left standing by accident, the saplings planted in rows, the windowless warehouses that are the modern versions of factories, and the out-of-town shopping centres ringed by car parks so vast it is hardly possible to make out people passing on the other side. In silence, face pressed against the window of the bus, I travelled so I could learn to paint. The landscape shifted. The suburbs are continually being rebuilt. Nothing there is preserved except through inadvertence. I daydreamed. I thought about the art of painting. I watched the forms flittering across the windows of the bus. Then I spotted a number of strapping municipal police officers, their belts strung with incapacitating weapons. They moved in groups along the broad avenues, clustered around a rapid response vehicle fitted with a blue stripe and a flashing light. They were on guard duty, arms folded, arms dangling, outside the shopping centres. This shocked me; from this single image I understood: violence spreads, but it preserves the same form. Whether small scale or large scale, it is still the art of war.

There was a time when we entrusted our violence entirely to the State and laughed at municipal police. They were like rural policemen with smaller moustaches and no drums. For a long time the municipal police were men on scooters who would angrily pull up and tell you, no, you cannot park there; then they would zoom off again, helmets perched too high on their heads, belching an oily cloud of the two-stroke fuel mix that powered the scooters. They were also middle-aged women, who tramped the streets in unflattering uniforms hunting out illegally parked cars; in summer they read the riot act to the teenagers who dived into the Seine, warning that they would not be the ones to fish them out, and they bickered with shopkeepers over the cleanliness of pavements, over leaving piles of sweepings or sluicing bucketfuls of water with too much force. Then, like everything else, they were enhanced. A different type of man was drafted in. There were lots of them. They were not issued with guns, but with 'compliance weapons' that they were trained to use. They were heavily built, they looked like soldiers.

After the elections I saw them appear; they moved around Voracieux in groups. They had the same build, the same haircuts as the National Police. On their belts they carried side-handle batons. They were an imposing presence. I saw them from the window of the bus. I had never seen so many. Over and above the state police, I wondered how many municipal officers, prison warders and security guards there were in France, all kitted out in ankle boots, slim-fit trousers and pale blue shirts. The streets were becoming militarized, just as they were over there.

This new type of police officer first appeared in Voracieux because it is our future. City centres are conservation areas; it is in the outlying suburbs that one can see what has happened since. I saw the muscular sergeants through the windows of the bus taking me to my painting lesson. Driving past the tower blocks I saw municipal officers screwing a plaque to a wall. The high-vis plaque was white emblazoned in black with a letter, followed by a dot and a number in smaller type. They were boring into the thick concrete next to the entrance using a large power drill whose whine I could hear despite the distance, despite the window, despite the racket on the overcrowded bus, where, for some reason, the radio was always blaring. I saw other plaques just like it on all the tower blocks in the area, each marked with a different letter, a large black letter visible at a distance. Others had been affixed to the signposts at crossroads or on street corners. I wondered why the municipal police were carrying out public works. But I did not think too much of it.

When I arrived at Salagnon's place, Mariani was there, wearing a hideous green checked shirt and the same semi-transparent glasses that blurred his eyes. He was overexcited, talking nineteen to the dozen and laughing between sentences.

'Listen to this, lad, you're the one interested in things, though you wouldn't dare get your hands dirty. We've taken a step towards resolving our problems. Well, at least we've got someone to listen. The new mayor agreed to meet me and a couple of my lads, the ones with a bit of education. That said, I'm the one who always does the talking and I'm the one people talk to. Anyway, we met him like he promised before he got elected; he didn't want it to get out, because he knows people don't like us. People resent us for speaking the truth, for shouting from the rooftops something they'd rather keep secret, by which I mean our national humiliation. People prefer to keep their heads down, make their money, wait for the problem to go away, or else they fuck off as soon as they've made their fortune. So when we try and force them to lift them up – their heads, I mean – it hurts, because they've been bowed so long they're stuck that way, so they blame us. But the mayor understands where we're coming from. He has to be discreet, because there are people who don't like us; he's discreet, but he understands us.'

'He understands you?'

'That's what he said. He invited us into his office, me and the boys, shook everyone's hand, had us sit down, and we were sitting right opposite him, like it was a work meeting. And that's when he said to us: "I have understood you! I know what has happened here."'

'Really?'

'Really. Word for word. And he went on in the same tone: "I see what you have been trying to achieve. And there are many things I want to change here."'

'I wonder where he comes up with this stuff?' chuckled Salagnon.

'Who knows? He must be a big reader. Or maybe, when he met us, he had a flash of inspiration, he had a vision of his place in history, and the Ancients spoke through him.'

'Or he's taking the piss.'

'No. He's too ambitious; everything is on the level. He asked our advice about how to hold Voracieux, how best to deploy the police to control the population. He appointed me as a security advisor.'

'You?'

'You might not think it, but I've got references. But it's a phantom post. People don't like us. They despise us, even though we're express-ing the dream of lots of people. I'll be advising the municipal police force, and let me tell you my advice won't fall on deaf ears. We'll put our ideas into practice.'

'So you're behind all this, the new cops, the patrols, the plaques on the tower blocks?'

'That's me. Surveillance, control, intelligence, action. We plan to take back the no-go areas and subdue them. Just like we did over there. We have the power.'

His voice quavered a little, with age and with joy, but I had no doubt that people would listen. The History that had stopped would pick up again exactly where we left off. We were inspired by phantoms: we tried to conflate our problems with those of the past, to solve them as we had failed to solve the problems of the past. We are so in thrall to power ever since we lost it. A little more power and we will be saved, we believe, just a little more power than we have now. And we will fail again.

Since we no longer know who we are, we will rid ourselves of those who are not like us. Then we will know who we are, because we will all be surrounded by those like us. We will be we. The 'we' who remains will be those who have cast off those who are unlike them. We will be bound by blood. Blood always binds, it sticks; blood that is spilled unites, blood we have spilled together, the blood of others that we have spilled together; we will congeal into a vast, united clot.

Power and resemblance are two stupid ideas that are incredibly persistent; it is impossible to be rid of them. They are twin beliefs in the physical nature of our world, two ideas of such simplicity that a child can understand them; and when a man who has power is driven by a child's ideas, he can wreak terrible destruction. Resemblance and power are the most elemental ideas imaginable. They are so self-evident that each of us invents them without having to be taught. On these foundations it is possible to build an intellectual monument, an ideological movement, an imposing governmental project, one that *stands or falls on its own merits* (the expression itself is an omen), yet one so absurd and so false that the moment it is raised it begins to crumble, claiming thousands of victims as it collapses. And yet no lessons will be learned, power and resemblance will never evolve. When the project fails, as they count the dead, people will think that if only they had had just a little more power, if only they had more precisely calculated the degrees of resemblance. Stupid ideas are immortal, because we hold them in our hearts. They are childish ideas: children constantly dream of having more power, constantly seek out those who resemble them.

'They're childish ideas,' I finally said aloud.

Mariani stopped. He stopped pacing up and down Salagnon's shabby living room and stared at me. He was holding a beer in one hand and a little foam clung to his moustache, yes, his moustache, he had a grey moustache, the sort of adornment no one had any more, that everyone shaves, I don't know why, but I understand. His tired eyes glared at me through tinted lenses that gave them a crepuscular hue. He glared at me, his mouth open revealing teeth that might have been real or false. His garish jacket clashed wonderfully with the ghastly upholstery.

'We have to show them.'

'But look how often you've tried to "show them", and look how often it has failed.'

'We're not going to let ourselves be gypped; like... like we did over there.'

'Gypped by who?'

'You know perfectly well. You refuse to see the differences. And refusing to see leads to getting fleeced. I mean, you're not stupid, and you're not blind; you're training your eye with Salagnon here and his colouring lessons: you can see the difference.'

'Treating resemblance as a virtue is a childish idea. Resemblance proves nothing, nothing except what you believed before you noticed it. Anyone can look like everyone or no one, it depends on what you're looking for.'

'The difference is there. Open your eyes. Look.'

'All I see is a bunch of different people who can speak with a single voice and say "we".'

'Your boy here is blind, Salagnon. You should stop the painting lessons. Teach him music instead.'

Salagnon was delighted by the conversation, but did not intervene.

'Since you mention music,' he teased, 'and you mentioned my name, have you noticed that, of the three of us – or four, if you include Eurydice, who will be here in a minute – I am the only one with a name whose syllables are a part of classical French? The kid isn't wrong.'

'Don't you start as well! If I'm the only one holding my course, we'll all be fleeced; and when I say fleeced, they can do far worse with a pair of shears or anything with a blade. We won't be able to set foot outside without getting stabbed.'

'But no one carries a knife!' I roared.

No one has a knife. Cutters, maybe, guns, chlorine bombs, but no knives. No one knows how to use them, except to eat, or to flaunt in the street. Yet everyone talks about getting stabbed. They used to carry them, the bad boys long ago, the boys from across the seas, as a sign of their virility. And that is what we are really talking about: an age-old sexual attack. Whoever loses gets his cut off. Someone who strays on to the other's turf gets shafted. We were pretty good at that game. Our soldiers were outstanding.

'It doesn't matter, it's just an image. Images are striking. People remember them, they're useful.'

'So you're going to do what you did over there?'

'And what exactly would you have done over there?'

'I wasn't there.'

'That's no excuse. What if you had been? Have you seen what they could do to you? We were defending people like you. We were keeping the terrorist in check.'

'By spreading terror.'

'Do you know what they did to our boys? To lads like you? To people with faces like yours, with clothes like yours? They slashed open their bellies and filled them with stones. Strangled them with their own intestines. We faced that violence alone. Some people, the people who hid away, who kept themselves safe from the torrent of blood, dare to claim that it was colonialism that created that violence. But whatever the situation, there can be no excuse for such violence, unless you're not human. We were faced with savagery and we were alone.'

'But the people in the colonies *weren't* human, not really, not legally.'

'In my company I had Viets, Arabs and a Malagasy, who wound up there by accident. We were brothers in arms.'

'War is the simplest thing of life. It's easy to get along. But afterwards, when the war is over, things get complicated. It's not surprising some people don't want it to end.'

'So what would you have done, faced with a café terrace littered with victims and debris, with people groaning, kids who've had their leg blown off, covered in their own blood, ripped to pieces by shards of glass? What would you have done, knowing that it would happen all over again? With an axe, a bomb, a pruning knife, a stick. What would you have done with those who were flayed alive simply because of what they looked like? We did what we had to do. The only thing we could do.'

'You sowed terror.'

'Yes. We were ordered to do it. So we did. We spread terror in order to snuff it out. What would you have done in that moment? And when I say "in that moment" I mean when you were wading in blood, your shoes spattered, your soles crunching over broken glass, walking over hunks of still-bleeding flesh, listening to the whimpers of those who had been hacked apart. What would you have done?'

'You failed.'

'That's a detail.'

'It's the most important detail.'

'We almost succeeded. We didn't get the support we needed at the end. A decision taken for ridiculous reasons botched up years of work.'

I looked at Salagnon and saw that he did not agree; he did not agree with any of this, not with Mariani and not with me. He got up, tidied away the beers, walked over to the window and came back, dragging his leg; he had problems rotating his hip, something that affected him when nothing was going right. I could see that all was not well, it was written on his face. I could see he was distressed; I wanted to ask why, but I was caught up in a squabble where we both needed to have the last word, needed the other to stop talking. Because every word of the one who stopped talking first would be contemptible.

'Wars are straightforward when you describe them,' Salagnon sighed. 'Except for the wars you have fought yourself. Those are so confused that every man tries to cope by telling a sad little story, but everyone tells it differently. If wars are to be used to forge identity, then we truly have failed. The wars that we fought wiped out the pleasure we had in being together, and retelling them now simply speeds up that disintegration. We cannot comprehend them. There is nothing about them that we can be proud of; we miss that. And saying nothing makes it impossible to love.'

'What would you have done?' Mariani yelled. 'Would you have gone into hiding so you didn't have to deal with it? Would you have run away? Would you have pretended to be sick so you didn't have to act? Would you have holed up somewhere? Where? Under your bed? How can someone who hides be right? How can someone who wasn't there be right?'

Mariani had a point, in spite of his provocative tone. Our only distinction was being absent. To participate, in whatever way, constituted tacit support; even living itself was a form of support. And so we forced ourselves to live a little less, to be almost invisible, as though we had a sick note.

I am not sure where we should have been in those moments we were absent. How to go about things is something we learn, something we test through movies. Cinema is a window on to adulthood, one we look through while sitting in a comfy chair. Through it we learn how to drive during a car chase, how to brandish a gun, how to kiss a beautiful woman without being awkward; all these things that we will never do, but which matter to us. This is why we love fictions: they offer solutions to situations that in life are labyrinthine; but distinguishing the good solutions from the bad makes it possible to live. Cinema gives us the opportunity to live multiple lives. Through this inaccessible window, we see those we should reject and those that should serve as an example. Fiction puts forward a means of going about things, and the movies everyone has seen present the most common solutions. When you take your seat in a cinema, you fall silent and you watch what has been, what might have been, together. In the Great French Films, we learn how to survive not being there. None of the solutions really work, of course, because there can be no solution to absence; all of the solutions are shocking, but all have been used, all offer us an alibi we can believe in; these are our sick notes.

Long before I saw it, I had heard of *Les Visiteurs du Soir*. The film is a part of our national heritage, a film considered to have certain aesthetic qualities, moral virtues, a historical sense. It was filmed in 1942. The story is set in the Middle Ages. As I sat in the cinema, I instinctively wondered what connections I might find between 1942 and a medieval tale. It is the academic reflex of the film buff to think there must be some connection between a film and the period in which it was made. Not this time! I thought, as I sank into my seat. But the film portrayed the dregs of our society in 1942. The devil appears. He wants the lives of a pair of lovers. He wants their souls. He longs to destroy them. And, to his fury, they turn to stone in front of him: he can no longer rip out their souls. Their bodies no longer move, but their hearts continue to beat, they wait for things to pass. Oh yes, I thought when I finally watched *Les Visiteurs du Soir*, this is the classic French solution to the problem of evil: we do nothing, keep our opinions to ourself, turn to stone so that evil can do nothing. And nor can we.

It is easiest to say nothing specific about the delicate moments of our history; we were not there. We have our reasons. Where were we? De Gaulle tells us in his memoirs: we were in London, we were everywhere. He single-handedly satisfies our taste for heroism.

It is also possible to claim to have acted, but alone. We have our reasons. Here is the most pernicious film of our cinema, and as such one voted a favourite. The plot is a meticulous account of vigilantism with a concocted justification. The main character in *Le Vieux Fusil* is utterly in love with his beautiful wife and wants nothing more from life. He cares nothing about history. He owns a ruined château. He is French. When the occupying Germans first arrive, his relationship with them is distant but polite. They kill his wife in the most grotesque fashion, the camera lingers on the scene. And he decides to kill them, one by one, in the most brutal manner. The camera does not miss a single ingenious detail of the sadistic murders. The film is a piece of blackmail: because the pretty wife is murdered, a beautiful woman who has nothing to do with the events and is simply peacefully living her life in a country château, because we witness her being burned alive, the viewer is allowed to see the excruciating details of the deaths that follow, is permitted to wallow in them, is forced to wallow in them. The viewer cannot condemn the later deaths without being complicit in the first murder. Eyes wide in the darkened cinema, the audience is compelled to violence; they are made complicit in the violence meted out to the guilty men by the violence done to the wife, which the film so lovingly showed. Violence binds people. By the time they left the cinema, the audience was complicit. In its day, this film was considered the favourite film of French audiences. It makes me sick. At the end, when all the bad guys are dead, when the main character is alone in his cleansed château, a group of *résistants* with their Cross of Lorraine, their Citroën traction, their berets, arrives. They ask what happened, whether he needs help. He tells them he does not need anything. Nothing has happened. The *résistants* drive on. We stay behind with this man who had his reasons. We are steeped in blood.

I don't know what to do. There is no shower that can wash off that kind of blood. There is no way to be clean except by pretending one was not there. I cannot pretend that it did not happen: the humiliation, the death, the redemption through carnage and the silence that followed in the years when I was growing up, a silence heavy with condemnation of the use of force. It was better not to talk about it; to scorn it in silence. To refuse to support the military, to relish the constant failures of our armies, to think of these close-cropped heads as the embodiment of brutish stupidity. Violence was there, right there, outside us. It was not us. We feared power like the plague; we dreamed of it in shameful reveries.

In the mental ruins that strewed the ground after twenty years of war, all that remained were victims who could see nothing but their own pain. These victims searched among the rubble for some clue to their torturer, since such suffering could not have happened without a torturer. This violence had to be perpetrated by someone, someone who was utterly evil, someone who is still evil, since such atrocities cannot be expiated: they are in the blood. Society fragmented into an infinite number of victims' associations, each designating its own torturer, each having suffered; everyone went through it in all innocence, and the others fell on him.

There is too much violence. There are too many victims, too many torturers. The whole thing is a muddle. History does not make sense. The nation is a ruin. If a nation is defined by will and pride, then ours has been broken by humiliation. If a nation is defined by shared memories, ours has splintered into shards of memory. If a nation is the will to live as a community, ours is crumbling as the *cités* and the housing estates are built, as the subgroups who refuse to integrate increase. We are dying slowly of no longer wanting to live together.

'Everyone is innocent, everyone is a victim after these wars, like the village of Porquigny,' said Salagnon. 'I went back to visit Porquigny just once. People remember the massacre; in fact, they remember nothing else. People show up in coaches and there are signs indicating what there is to see. There is a little museum you can visit. There are German rifles there, shorts worn by the Chantiers de Jeunesse, pieces of shrapnel, even a model of the armoured train which they call the Train from Hell. You can see the bloodstained summer dress of the young woman I saw lying dead. In the village itself they have preserved a stretch of wall pockmarked with bullet holes; it is protected by a sheet of glass, so it doesn't disintegrate. If they'd been able to preserve the blood and the blowflies, they would have. The streets in the villages are called the rue des Martyres, the rue des Innocents-Assassinés. In front of the town hall there is a limestone plaque with the names of all the victims in letters twenty centimetres high. The last line is highlighted in gold leaf. It reads: *You Who Pass By, Remember*. Like there was a chance anyone could forget in that village; as though they might forget the duty of memory. In France we've always been very big on duty, we treat it like homework.

'Next to the plaque they've erected a bronze memorial that features several raw-boned innocents who are visibly victims, but no killer is depicted. They are wild-eyed; they don't know what is happening to them. So no one forgets, the square outside the town hall is called the place du 20-août-1944. Also known as Day-of-the-Massacre or the Day-of-Our-Death Square. But this is not the only thing that ever happened in Porquigny! Why not call the square something else? Why choose tragedy and death for all eternity? Why not name the square Liberty or Dignity-Restored Square or the Square-of-the-Timely-Arrival-of-the-Zouaves, The-120-German-Soldiers-We-Killed or even The-Final-Destruction-of-the-Armoured-Train?

'In Sencey, on the other hand, there is no trace. There is a place de la Mairie, a place de la République, a memorial commemorating the First World War. On the plinth, where there was a little space, they have screwed a plaque with the names of the seven people who died in 1944. But they died fighting, while those in Porquigny were bound and sacrificed, lined up against a wall and slaughtered. We prefer to remember innocent victims. It allows us to think of war as a depravity: France was raped. It was not her fault. France does not understand, she still does not understand; and so we are authorized to use violence. France whimpers and threatens, and when it holds its head high, it's to beat its dog. Do your homework, your duty of memory; they give you the right to legitimate force.'

'Salagnon,' Mariani sighed, 'you talk too much, you dig deeper and deeper, but where are you going with this? You should be on our side.'

'Eurydice will be here any time now.'

'Are you scared of her?' I asked, amused. 'Oh, they're tough, the Light Airborne Infantry!'

'If the problem could be resolved by fisticuffs, I wouldn't hesitate, but Eurydice wouldn't go for that. When she sees me, she turns her head. When I'm in her house, she stomps around, grinds her teeth, sulks, slams the doors, and eventually explodes.'

'She yells at you?'

'I don't think it's personal, but I'm the one that gets it in the neck. She hates everyone.'

'Everyone who was ever involved gets dragged through the mud,' added Salagnon. 'And Eurydice has a fine pair of lungs on her! A pair of lungs fashioned by centuries of Mediterranean tragedy, by centuries of grief: Greek, Jewish, Arabic. She knows what she's doing, her words hit home.'

'Personally, I prefer not to hang around. They upset me, the things she says, and deep down I think she's right.'

'What has she got against you?'

'We should have protected her. We didn't.'

Mariani broke off. He looked tired and old behind the crepuscular glasses that dulled his eyes. He turned to Salagnon, who picked up.

'We sowed terror and we reaped worse; everything she knew, everything she loved, dissolved into flames and slaughter. Everything is gone. She suffers like the princesses of Troy, scattered with no descendants in palaces that are not their own, their former lives obliterated by fire and the sword. And she is not allowed the memory. She is not allowed to complain, she is not allowed to understand, and so she wails like mourners at the graves of murder victims, she calls down vengeance.

'When she sees me, I remind her of the death of a significant part of herself, and the silence that cloaks her and her loved ones. They are an irritant. All her bitterness and her grief have been sealed in a thermos flask, my being here opens the flask and it all pours out again. You can't imagine how much it reeks, that rancorous bile. I want to tell her that I understand, that I share her pain, but she won't let me. She wants to rub my face in it, make me eat it. And I eat it. The *pieds noirs* are our guilty conscience; they are the living evidence of our failure. We wish they would disappear, but they're still here. We can still hear their howls and their outrage. The accent is dying out, but we hear it still, like the cackling of ghosts.'

'But that's all done with, isn't it? They were repatriated.'

'There's a word that makes me smile. Because we were all repatri-ated. The repatriation exceeded all expectations. Everything we ever shipped over there, we brought back. Applied to people, the word was absurd, although it was used again and again: how can you repatriate people who have never even seen France? As though being French was in their nature; in fact, this just proves that it wasn't. It was not people we repatriated, it was the frontier spirit we had sent over there, the spirit of aggression and conquest, the illegalism of the pioneers, the use of force among one's own. All that we brought back.'

Now I can see them, the ships in 1962. I can see them floating on a noonday sea like hot blue sheet metal, the white haze above it twisting up into the cloudless sky, distorting the outline of the ships as they move slowly, scarcely visible unless you squint your eyes and stare at the sea, that searing, cruel sea. I can see them appear in the darkness strewn with lights, the ships of 1962, making their tireless rotations, trembling with rage and tears, crammed with people packed on to the decks, in steerage and the cabins, soldiers, refugees, murderers, innocents, conscripts coming home and immigrants leaving theirs; and between the people thronging the boats of 1962 are the ghosts that came with them, phantoms bounded by the spaces between them, by a particular use of language. In between the passengers as they sat or sprawled or curled into a ball, those who leaned on the gunwales or paced the decks, those who clung to their suitcases and those who had nothing but rage and tears, between the people hurriedly shipped home on the boats of 1962, the ghosts were wide awake. All through the crossing, they kept watch, they were clear-headed and single-minded and, as soon as they reached the shores of the shrivelled rump that France was now reduced to, as soon as they landed at the quays at Marseille, teeming with lost souls, they flourished.

Ghosts are fashioned from words, from words and nothing else. We imagine them shrouded in sheets, but that is a metaphor for the text or the screen on which it is projected; these ghosts were made of figures of speech whose origins we have forgotten; they were woven from certain words, certain implications, the unseen connotations of certain pronouns, of a certain way of thinking about the law, a certain approach to the use of force. Repatriation succeeded beyond all expectation. The ghosts repatriated on the ships of 1962 made themselves at home; they melted into the crowd that was France; we adopted them; after that, it was impossible to get rid of them. They are our guilty conscience. These ghosts that haunt us here as they did over there.

'I'd better get going,' said Mariani.

'You see, it is possible to talk to the kid.'

'Yeah, but it's exhausting.'

'Does she shout at you too?' I asked Salagnon.

'Me? No. But I never look back. I paint for her, only for her. I spit ink, it forms a cloud that cloaks me. We live here, we don't draw attention to ourselves, and if Mariani didn't come round we would be long gone. But I won't stop him from coming. I won't stop seeing him. Hence the jungle with its presences, its absences. I try to make sure their paths don't cross.'

'I'm off,' said Mariani.

The two of us stood there, Salagnon and I. In silence. Perhaps the moment had come to ask him what was troubling him, but I did not ask.

'You want to paint?' he asked after a moment.

I hurriedly accepted. We sat down at the broad, fake walnut table on which he had laid out the painting tools, the paper that inexorably absorbs, the Chinese brushes hanging on a little stand, the hollow stones each with a drop of water, the sticks of compressed ink to be diluted with careful gestures. I sat down, as to a banquet; my hands were slick with sweat, lubricating my fingers as though they were so many tongues. I was hungry.

'What are we going to paint?' I asked, glancing around and seeing nothing worth the ink or the brushstroke to capture it. This made him smile. He found my quizzical look, my expectancy, my pupil's expression amusing.

'Nothing,' he said. 'Paint.'

In his small, horribly furnished home, he taught me that there was no need for a subject; that one need simply paint. I was grateful to learn from him that anything was as good as anything else. Before he taught me this, I constantly wondered what to paint; having no answer, I searched in vain for a subject that suited me, the burden of the search for a subject became overwhelming. I stopped painting. I told him this, he smiled; it was of no importance. 'Paint trees, paint rocks,' he said, 'real or imagined. There are an infinite number; all of them the same, all of them different. You simply need to choose one and paint, and immediately the boundless world of painting will open up. Anything can serve as a subject. The Chinese have spent centuries painting the same non-existent rocks, the same falling water that is not water, the same four plants that are merely symbols, the same clouds that are really just the vanishing of ink; the life of a painting is not its subject, but the trace lived by the brush.'

I am grateful to him for teaching me this; it is something he said in passing. Shortly afterwards we made the ink and we left traces of beautiful trails of perfect black that represented trees. The lessons calm me: there is only ink and breath; there is only the life flowing through my hands, leaving behind traces. He taught me that; it does not linger when you say it, but it takes a long time to understand; he taught me something more important than all the secrets of the artist's studio, more fundamental than technical skills, which will fail you and betray you: it is futile to choose a subject, only paint. Oh, how that soothed me. The subject is unimportant.

'Paint. Only paint. Anything. Paint true,' he would say. 'Place yourself in front of the tree, imagine it, paint its life. Take a pebble, paint its soul. Consider a man; paint his presence. Only that, his simple presence. Even a desert plain is filled with pebbles, it can be painted. It is enough to look around you to begin.'

The infinite possibilities reassured me: it is enough to be present, and to act. He taught me to see the river of blood without trembling, and to paint it, to feel the river of ink within me without trembling, to allow it to flow through me. I could see, understand, paint. Only paint.

I went to places where there were lots of people. I went to the train station and painted anyone. I sat in the plastic shells that serve as seats and I watched the vortex moving through the pipes. The Gare de Lyon Part-Dieu is a multimodal setting, an assemblage of huge pipes through which people pass. People are constantly arriving. I would sit there to sketch passers-by, to draw anyone. I did not choose. I would never see them again. The Gare de Lyon Part-Dieu is the perfect place to paint what comes next.

It took me a long time to understand what the man sitting next to me was doing. Like me, he watched the people passing, ticking off boxes on a form on a clipboard in his lap. I did not know what he was ticking. I could not read the headings. I could not work out what he was counting. I saw his eyes follow the police officers patrolling the station. These muscular young men moved through the crowd. There were several groups, truncheons beating against their thighs, clips on their belts, the cracked visors of their helmets indicating the direction they were looking. From time to time, they stopped someone. They had them set down their luggage, verified their ticket, had them put out their arms and checked their pockets. They asked for their papers, mumbled into walkie-talkies, arrested no one. At this point the man next to me would tick a box.

'What are you counting?'

'The police checks. To know who they're stopping.'

'Because?'

'They don't just stop anyone. Ethnic affiliation is the differentiating factor.'

'How can you judge?'

'By eye, the same way they do.'

'Not very precise.'

'But real. Ethnic affiliation is indefinable, but real: it cannot be quantified, but it can trigger actions that are measurable. Arabs are eight times more likely to be stopped by the police, black men four times more likely. No one is arrested. It's just about control.'

Treatment is not equal or to claim it is equal is to claim that there are eight times more of 'them'. Like 'over there'. Over there has come back again. They have no name, but they're instantly recognizable. They are here, all around, so many of them. The suppressed memories from over there haunt even the numbers here.

And then I saw her, walking through the station, pulling a suitcase on wheels, walking with that lithe sway of her hips I liked so much, that I could feel in my hips, in my hands, when I saw her walking. I got up, said goodbye to the sociologist, who went on ticking boxes. I followed her. I did not get far. She took a taxi and disappeared. I have to meet her eventually, I thought, I have to meet her. I have to speak to her.

How is it possible to imagine, given a social situation as dysfunctional as mine, that I could still have a love life? How is it possible to understand why women still allow me to take them in my arms? I don't know. We are still Scythian horsemen. We owe our women to the prowess of our horses, the strength of our Scythian bows, the swiftness of our feet. Anyone who doubts it should take more interest in statistics. Statistics appear to say nothing, but they unwittingly describe how we behave. Social disintegration leads to isolation. Social integration promotes bonding. How is it possible, given my degraded social status, that some women are still prepared to kiss me? I don't know. They are the oxygen, I am the flame. I gaze at women. I think of nothing else, as if my life depended on them: without them I would snuff out. I talk to them about themselves, at breakneck speed, and they are the story that I tell them. It keeps them warm, it gives me air. That's right, that's absolutely right, they say to me as I reflect on what they have just told me. The flame flares. And then they gutter out. They have used up all their air. I leave them panting, I am almost extinguished.

But this woman, for some reason, made me burn hotter. I was no longer a candle flame but a furnace capable of melting anything, needing only more oxygen in order to leap before her, a blazing inferno.

I often saw her, but only in the street. I constantly spotted her in the distance. It seemed to me some sensitive part of my being, the eye, the retina, that part of the brain that sees, everything receptive in me seemed to sense her presence wherever she was, and in the midst of the stream of cars, the trails of fumes, the scooters, the bicycles, the huge buses that blocked my view, the pedestrians randomly coming and going, in the midst of all this, I would immediately spot her. Her form was already traced upon my eager retina; I needed only the slightest clue and, among a thousand milling pedestrians, among hundreds of cars moving in contradictory orbits, I would see her. I saw only her. I was capable of extracting her presence with the sensitivity of a photon trap. I saw her often. She must have lived near me. I knew nothing about her, apart from the way she moved, the way she looked.

She walked quickly in the street, using that particularity of walking that is the bounce. I saw her often. She crossed streets where I shuffled along with the elasticity of a bouncing ball, all elegant curves, never losing her energy, an energy contained within her, which rebounded on contact with the ground and propelled her ever forwards. In the congested, noisy street I could detect her presence from the slightest clue. I would notice her swaying gait as she moved through a crowd, seeing in the throng only her movement. And I would notice her hair from a distance. Her hair was completely grey, except for a few stray hairs that were utterly white. And this lent her apparition a strange clarity. Her hair whirled about her neck with the same exuberance as her gait; there was nothing drab about her hair, it was alive, billowing, dazzling despite being grey streaked with white. It framed her face like a halo of feathers, of silvery down, a tremulous cloud positioned as precisely as snow settling on the bare branch of a tree, with perfection, poise, certainty. Her pretty, finely delineated mouth with its full lips, she painted red. I did not know her age. She was ageless; she was my age, which I also did not know, unless, from time to time, I made the tally. I found these contradictory signs perplexed me vaguely. Intensely. But this ignorance of age, mine, hers, is not a dearth but a duration, the gentle current of individual time. She was every age combined, as real people are: the past she wore, the present she dances, the future about which she does not fret.

I knew her as I knew my own soul, without ever having spoken to her. City life meant that we ran into each other several times a year, but the feelings it inspired made me feel as if it were every day. The first time I saw her lasted only a few brief seconds. The time it might take for a car at moderate speed to pass a shop window. I still had a car back then, which I spent a great deal of time parking, inching from one traffic light to the next, joining the queue of other cars, crawling through the streets little faster than those on foot. I saw her for only a few seconds, but this first image was imprinted on my eye like a rambler's foot on soft clay. It lasts no longer than a single footstep, but the slightest details of his foot are imprinted there; if it should dry, it will be there for a long time. If it is fired, for ever.

I still had a wife at the time. We were driving home through the dark streets and I saw her suddenly in the illumined window of a patisserie I knew. She was standing in the white fluorescent glare. I remember her colours: the violet of her eyes edged with black, the red of her lips, her skin ocellated with tiny freckles, the gleaming brown of her well-worn leather jacket, and, framing her face, the mixture of grey and white, the glistening snow that settled perfectly over her gestures, her beauty, over the fullness of her features. Those few seconds quite took my breath away. A whole life was presented to me, folded and refolded like a little note, a message tightly packed into a few short seconds. Those few seconds passing the window lit by fluorescent strips had a phenomenal density, a weight that would bow my thoughts the whole evening, and the night that followed and the next morning.

I should, I thought, have stopped the car in the middle of the street and left it there, doors wide open, raced into the patisserie and thrown myself at her feet, even if she were to laugh. I would have offered her an eclair oozing Chantilly cream, so white. And while I gazed at her, mute, groping for words, while she tasted the delicate cream with the tip of her tongue, my car idling, doors open, in the middle of the street would have brought the traffic to a standstill. Other cars would have piled up behind it, blocking the street, then the neighbouring streets, the whole *quartier* and half of Lyon. Lined up on the bridges and the quays with no hope of moving forwards, they would have sounded their horns angrily, endlessly, no one able to do anything but moan loudly, while I searched for my words, accompanying the timorousness of my first declaration with a colossal chorus of massed horns.

I did not do it. I did not think of it at the time; the shock was such that my mind was completely paralysed. My body carried on driving by itself; it parked the car and made it home; unaided, my body undressed itself, put itself to bed and slept, closing my flesh-and-blood eyelids out of habit, but even in their sheltering darkness my mind did not sleep, it carried on searching for words.

I saw her without her knowing with a frequency that allowed me to believe that I was almost living with her. I knew her wardrobe. I recognized her umbrella in the distance. I noticed when she had a new handbag. I merely oriented myself towards her. I did not do anything, did not speak to her. I never followed her. With the efficiency of a censor, I redacted from my memory the faces of the men who were sometimes with her. They changed, I think, though I never knew what connection they might have to her. When I moved back to Lyon after changing my life, I ran into her again. She moved through the same streets where I had seen her so often, as enduring as the spirit of place.

There are people who believe that what is bound to happen, happens; I have no opinion. But opportunity had knocked so often and with such insistence, such constancy, and I had never answered, never opened, that I finally decided to speak to her. I was sitting in a large, empty café and there she was, a few tables away. I was not even surprised. A man was talking to her; she was listening with amused detachment. He left hurriedly, wounded, offended, and still she had the same faint smile that made her so radiant, and aware of that radiance, and amused by what was emanating from her. I felt relieved as I watched the man walk away. We were alone in this café, empty but for the two of us, sitting on distant benches, our backs to the mirrors, grateful for the silence that had finally descended. We both watched the man leave, gesturing angrily, and when he had stepped through the door, we looked at each other across the empty room, multiplied by the reflections in the mirrors, and we smiled at each other. The café could hold fifty people, there were only two of us. Outside it was dark. We could see nothing but the orange glow of the street lamps and rushing shadows; I got up and went over and sat opposite her. The beautiful smile still played on her full lips. She waited for me to speak.

'You know,' I said, although I did not know yet. 'You know, I have been involved with you for years.'

'And I haven't noticed?'

'But I remember everything. Would you like me to tell you the story of our life together?'

'Go ahead. I'll tell you afterwards whether I like it, this life I have no part in.'

'You have a part in it.'

'Without my knowledge.'

'Does anyone really know their whole life? What we know are only a few trees in a clearing in a dark forest. Our lives are always more vast.'

'So, tell me.'

'I don't know where to begin. I've never approached someone like this. Nor have I ever lived so long alongside someone without their knowing. I've always waited for something beyond my control to connect me to the woman I desire, for something that was already there, outside me, to empower me to take the hand of a woman that I want to be with. But I know nothing about you. We run into each other by accident, something I find infinitely reassuring. That recurring coincidence creates a story. How many meetings does it take for a story to begin? I have to tell you.'

I told her about them, these encounters. I began with the first, when I was dazzled by her colour. She listened to me. She told me her name. She agreed to see me again. She kissed me on the cheek with a smile that made me melt. I went home. I longed to write to her.

I all but ran home. I hurtled up the staircase, which seemed to me too long. I struggled with the lock, which resisted. I dropped my keys. I was trembling with frustration. Eventually, I managed to open the door. I slammed it behind me, ripped of my jacket, my shoes. I sat down at the wooden table I used for everything and which I had always known would one day serve as a writing desk. Finally, I began to write to her. I knew that talking to her would not be enough to hold her. Only sheets of paper saturated with verbs might keep her for a time. I wrote the words. I wrote to her. I wrote letters pages and pages long that weighed down the envelopes. These were not passionate letters. I told her a story, my story, her story. I recounted my every step in Lyon. I described her presence, which glowed like phosphorescence on the things I encountered in the streets. I described Lyon with her, me walking, her presence all around me like an incandescent gas. I wrote in a sort of fever, in an irrational exaltation, but what I wrote had the gentleness of a portrait, a smiling portrait with a sweeping landscape as a backdrop. The portrait depicted what I saw of her; she was looking at me; the landscape in the background was the city where we lived together, painted entirely in her colours. She was eager to see me again. She had read my letters; she had enjoyed reading them. I felt relieved. 'All this for me?' she smiled softly. 'This is just the beginning,' I told her. 'This is the least of it.' She heaved a sigh and this air she fed me, this oxygen, turned my flame into a roaring blaze.

But mostly I wanted to paint her, since it would be an easier way to show her to herself. I marvelled at her appearance, the flowing movement she constantly radiated. I marvelled at her body, which inscribed itself in the figure of an almond, in the shape I saw when I laid both hands flat on the table, palms open, fingers touching.

I believe I could have traced her silhouette with a single brushstroke. Contemplating her filled my soul. Out of politeness, one should prefer the individual to the form, but the individual cannot be seen except through form. Her body delighted my soul through anagoge and I ardently longed to paint her, since this would show her, name her, assert her presence and thereby bring us together.

I loved the curve one had to trace to circumscribe her body, from the feet scarcely touching the ground, to the silvered cloud of feathers that wreathed her face. I loved the curve of her shoulder, which welcomed the curve of my arm. Above all I loved her face, the vivid line of her nose, the peremptory line that shaped the beauty of her features. The nose is the marvel of the human face; it is the idea that, with a single stroke, brings together the disparate details, the eyes, the eyebrows, the lips, even the delicate ears. There are feeble ideas and vulgar ideas, ridiculous ideas and insipid ideas; there are amusing ideas, ideas that are quickly sapped and those that are essential and endure for ever. The Mediterranean contribution to the universal beauty of women is the arrogance of the nose, unapologetically traced, the gesture of a matador; something that should be translatable into all the languages that ring this sea that was once ours.

I marvelled at her, marvelled at her appearance, and more than anything I longed to inscribe that body in almond shape formed by a pair of hands laid flat, fingers touching. And this I did.

Novel VI

Trifid, hexagonal, dodecahedral war; self-consuming monster

Ɪᴛ ɪs ɪᴍᴘᴏssɪʙʟᴇ ᴛᴏ ʟᴇᴀᴠᴇ ᴀʟɢɪᴇʀs just like that. The sea cannot be crossed so easily. You cannot do it alone: you must find a space. It is impossible to leave Algiers independently, on foot, walking through the countryside, slipping between the bushes. No. It is impossible. There are no bushes, there is no countryside, there is only the water, the impassable sea; to leave Algiers means finding a space on a boat or a plane. From the railings above the port you can look out at the sea and the horizon. But to get beyond requires a ship, a ticket, an exit visa.

Victorien Salagnon spent several days waiting for his ship to leave. When he stared out at the sea he felt the whole weight of the country behind weighing down on him. The bloody, shrieking mass of Algiers behind him rumbled, sliding like a glacier into the water, while he focused on the sea, on the flat horizon he longed to cross; he wanted to leave.

In the grey early hours of the previous summer a number of colonial paratroopers in a jeep turned on to the avenue de la République, overlooking the port. The boulevard has only one side; the other is the sea. They pulled to a stop and clambered down, stretching, strolled over to the stone balustrade and leaned over. They watched the grey sea turn pink.

When a jeep full of men in combat fatigues pulls up on the pavement, people make themselves scarce. The soldiers jump down, they run, they dash into a building, take stairs four at a time, kick down doors and re-emerge with men, dragging men, who struggle to keep up. But this morning, in the grey dawn light of their last summer there, they casually stepped down from the jeep and stretched themselves. Each of the five paratroopers in battledress moved slowly, unhurriedly, his sleeves rolled up, hands in his pockets, as if he were alone; they did not say a word, but walked with a weary nonchalance. They came to the balustrade overlooking the quayside and, spaced several metres apart, they rested their elbows on the rail. Heavy smoke hung in the streets. From time to time an explosion shook the air, glass fell tinkling to the ground. Flames roared from the shattered windows of the buildings. They gazed out at the sea as it flushed red.

Propped against the railing, they stayed for a moment, revelling in the coolness that came only with morning, staring vaguely into the distance, dreaming of being beyond the horizon as soon as possible, silent, feeling an exhaustion in the very depths of their being, as though, after a long sleepless night, several sleepless nights, several years of sleepless nights, suffering, while suffering the mother of all hangovers in a devastated Algiers.

All of it had been for nothing. All the blood had been for nothing. It had been spilled in vain and now it was impossible to staunch the flow; blood coursed down the steep streets of Algiers, rivers of it flowed into the sea, spreading over the water in a putrid slick. In the morning, as the sun rose, the sea turned red. The paratroopers leaning on the balustrade above the port watched it redden and darken to become a pool of blood. Behind them, fires roared through the broken windows of all the buildings destroyed in the course of the night; black smoke crept through the streets; from everywhere came screams, the sound of brutish passions, hatred, anger, fear, pain, and sirens wailed through the city, the miraculous sirens of the last remaining emergency services still functioning for no apparent reason. Then, finally, the sun broke free of the horizon, the sea turned blue, the heat began to rise; the paratroopers walked back to the jeep parked on the pavement that passers-by fearfully avoided. It had all been for nothing.

Eventually, they left in a huge ship. They had packed, stuffing everything into the cylindrical kitbags that were impractical but easy to carry. They were driven through the city in covered trucks from which they could see nothing much. They did not want to see anything. Algiers was in flames; its walls were crumbling under the impact of bullets; pools of blood coagulated on the pavements. Cars with their doors wide open lay abandoned in the middle of the street; shop windows gaped on to shards of broken glass, but there was no looting. They marched up the gangway of the ship in strict formation, something they had often done, although it felt that they were doing so for the last time. They felt that this had all been for nothing, that they had served for nothing, that they would not serve again.

When they left and the ship pulled away from the quay, many of them holed up below deck so they could see nothing, could allow themselves to be deafened by the roar of the engines and sleep at long last; others remained on deck and watched as Algiers receded, the port, the jetty, the Casbah like a melting icecap that poured forth blood, the bustle on the quays and the crowds lining the waterfront. Algiers was receding, but still they could hear the screams of *harkis* having their throats cut. This is what they thought, *harkis* having their throats cut, but this was simply to maintain a certain propriety, a certain tact. But they knew all too well, having lived in this country of blood, they knew that the screams rising from the milling crowds were those of *harkis* being dismembered, being castrated, being burned alive as they watched through a mist of bloody tears, their own tears, their own blood, the ships sail away. Those leaving told themselves that the screams they could hear were those of *harkis* whose throats were being cut; they did so to reassure themselves, so as not to conjure other images, grisly images that would keep them awake for ever. But they knew. From a distance, such things do not matter. Man is merely a certain capacity for screaming: once reached, it does not matter whether his throat is being cut or his skin is being hacked off piece by piece with carpentry tools. The colonial paratroopers on the deck of the ship, watching Algiers recede, preferred, out of politeness, to think their throats were being cut, these men they could hear screaming; that it might be over quickly, for the *harkis*, and for them, too.

In the middle of the Mediterranean, as the ship chugged towards France to the muffled pounding of the engines, Victorien Salagnon sat on deck, in the middle of the night, and wept for the first and last time in his life; he emptied himself of all the tears he had been accumulating for too long. He wept for his humanity as it drained away, for the masculinity he had never quite mastered and had been unable to save. When finally the dawn broke, he saw a sunlit Marseille. He was exhausted and his eyes were dry.

And yet things had started out so well. They had arrived in Algiers in mid-winter, the cruel Mediterranean winter, when the sun slinks behind a wind as grey and sharp as a steel blade. They had marched through the streets of the European quarter, led by Josselin de Trambassac, who was magnificently stiff, magnificently precise in every gesture, magnificently strong. Victorien Salagnon marched through the streets at the head of his men, through the streets of a European quarter that looked like Lyon, like Marseille, inhabited by French people who cheered them on. They marched slowly, the whole division of colonial paratroopers, their battledress immaculate, their sleeves rolled up, their jaws clenched in smiles like statues, their bodies lithe and athletic, all marching in step. They would win this time. They were entering the city. They could do anything they wanted in order to win. They could do anything they wanted as long as they won.

On a January day of wintry sunlight they had entered Algiers. They had marched together through the streets to great cheers from European crowds, agile, limber and invincible, free from all misgivings, hardened by the most terrible war imaginable. They had survived.

They survived everything. They would win. Together they were a war machine devoid of scruples, and Salagnon was one of the pilots of that machine, pack leader, centurion, a guide of young men who placed their trust in him; and, as they marched through the streets, the French inhabitants of Algiers cheered them. The French inhabitants. Were there any others? There were none to be seen.

Bombs went off in Algiers. Constantly. Anything could explode: a bar stool, an abandoned rucksack, a bus stop. When people heard a bomb in the distance, they flinched, but for a few minutes they felt relieved. They sighed. Then their hearts began to hammer again, another might explode right here; and they carried on down the street as though a chasm might open up, as though at any moment the ground might disappear. People avoided an Arab man carrying a bag; shunned a woman wearing a white veil that might hide something; they wished they would stop moving, wanted to slaughter them all, perhaps, wanted nothing to change. Anyone who could not be judged at a glance by their physical features and their dress elicited a shudder of unease. People crossed the street for no better reason that a person's appearance. Resemblance, it seemed, could save lives. No one knew what to do; this was why they had been called in. They would know, the lean wolves freshly returned from Indochine; they had survived; people trusted their strength.

They set up camp in a distinguished Moorish villa above Algiers. It included a vast basement, tiny rooms with barred windows, an attic that had been converted into soundproof cells, a large ceremonial hall that had once been a ballroom to which Josselin de Trambassac summoned his officers, who listened to him, hands clasped behind their backs, standing 'at ease' in military parlance, which should not be confused with at ease. A bomb exploded in the distance.

'You are paratroopers, messieurs, you are soldiers. I know that you are worthy. But war is changing. It is no longer a matter of leaping from a plane or running through the jungle, it is about knowledge. In the days of Agincourt, to use a bow, to kill at a distance, was incompatible with chivalric honour. The knights of France were slaughtered by thugs armed with longbows. You are the new knights of France. You can refuse to use the weapons of modern warfare, but if you do, you will be slaughtered.

'We have the power. We have been entrusted with a mission to win. We could, like American pilots, annihilate those areas of Algiers sheltering the enemy. But that would be pointless. They would rise from the rubble. They would wait for a period of calm and, in increased numbers, they would attack again. Those whom we are fighting do not hide, but we do not know who they are. If we pass them in the street, they may salute. If we talk to them they may not seem hostile, but they are waiting. They hide behind their faces, inside their bodies. We must flush out the enemy behind those faces. You will find them. You will subject the guilty to intense interrogation using recognized methods we all find distasteful. But you will win. Are you aware of who you are? Then we cannot lose.'

He concluded his short speech with a little laugh. A smile flickered on the faces of these lean, angular men. They all saluted, clicked their heels, and went back to makeshift offices furnished with school tables scattered all over the Moorish villa. In the ceremonial hall Josselin de Trambassac had an organizational chart in which empty boxes were linked to each other by arrows to form a pyramid.

'This is the enemy camp, its battle array,' he announced. 'You will need to put a name in each box and arrest every one of them. That is all. When all the boxes have been filled, the unmasked army will disappear.'

This appealed to Mariani. He no longer read much. The vast knowledge he had acquired from books he devoted to filling in the chart. He treated men like words. He wrote down names, rubbed them out, working with a pencil and a rubber. And in the real world, like a bloody simulacrum of the synoptic world of the whiteboard, they seized bodies, manipulated them, extracted names and then discarded them.

How to find people? Man is a *zoon politikon*, he does not live in isolation; someone is always known to others. They would be harpoon-fishing in murky waters, plunging the weapon in at random to see what floated to the surface. Each catch would lead to others. Capitaine Salagnon and two armed men presented themselves at the police headquarters. They demanded the surveillance records on the Arab population. The official in shirtsleeves did not want to hand them over. 'These are confidential documents, they belong to the police.' 'You either give them to me or I take them,' said Salagnon. His pistol was in the holster hanging from his belt; he was standing with his hands behind his back. The two men flanking him held their sub-machine guns at their hips. The man in the shirtsleeves gestured to a shelf and they left with wooden boxes filled with files.

In them they found the names and addresses of all those who had come to police attention. There were crooks, agitators, union members; there were men who, at some point, had indicated nationalist sympathies, a willingness to act, a rebellious spirit. All of the files were written in the conditional tense. Since there was a shortage of informers, a shortage of police officers, they relied on hearsay. All of the ferment in Algiers was contained within these boxes.

They brought the individuals named in the files to the Moorish villa to ask them why the bombs were exploding. Who was setting them? If they did not know, they were asked the name of someone who did know; he was then brought to the villa and the process started over. The paratroopers' mission was to know, and they applied themselves to it. They were relentless in their interrogations. In the jungle of the body, they hunted, they set ambushes, they tracked the enemy. When a man resisted, they destroyed him. Some of those who gave up information were never seen again.

Day and night, jeeps hummed around the villa. Men were brought in, dressed in pyjamas, stupefied, terrified, handcuffed, sometimes bloodied or bruised, goaded on by the paratroopers, who ran everywhere. Everything moved quickly. When a name was given up in the basement of the Moorish villa, a jeep would set off at top speed carrying four paratroopers dressed in fatigues; it would careen down the winding roads and stop outside a building; the officers would jump down before the jeep came to a halt, rush inside, dash up the stairs and re-emerge, dragging one or two men, who were bundled into the jeep, its engine still idling. They would drive back to the Moorish villa sitting in the same seats, although crouching at their feet now were one or two men whose backs alone were visible. Back at the villa, they tried to find out why the bombs were exploding. They ruthlessly interrogated and then another jeep carrying four paratroopers in fatigues would set off in a squeal of tyres and come back within the hour, bringing more men, from whom they tried to drag more information, at any price. And so on. Once a name was given, the man was brought back by jeep within an hour by four men in fatigues and he, in turn, was interrogated in the same basement where his name had been given up. Language acted on matter; only French was spoken. In the morning, officers would come up from the basement with a pencil and a crumpled, sometimes stained notepad. They would go into the ceremonial hall, where the rising sun streamed through the tall windows, illuminating the huge organizational chart. They would stop in the doorway of the great hall, then approach the chart and fill in certain boxes, copying from the pages of their notebooks. Salagnon watched as each day, box by box, the chart filled up with the regularity of a printing process. When it was full, this would all be over.

Josselin de Trambassac followed the progress of his chart with the same obsessiveness as a *maréchal d'Empire* might a map studded with pins. He arrived in the morning to see it being filled in, but first and foremost he asked all the men emerging from the basement to show him their hands. Those whose hands were still stained from the night's work were summarily dismissed and sent to the washbasins in the office, where they were to carefully wash and dry them. Only clean hands could touch the organogram and contribute to its progress.

Josselin de Trambassac could not allow it to be sullied. If it were, it would have to be completely recopied.

The villa was surrounded by dusty gardens planted with palm trees. Any shadows were sketchy and shifting. No one spent time there; no one collected the dead palm fronds that littered the pathways. The openwork shutters were permanently half-closed, like the eyes of a cat. Eyes that saw little of Algiers, beyond the glare outside, stray shafts of sunlight and the swaying of the palms. They never opened. Inside, the villa stank in a variety of ways. It reeked of sweat, cigarettes and third-rate cooking, of latrines and of something else besides. Sometimes a faint breeze came off the sea far below. They could hear cicadas chitter, but without the scent of pine. They were in the city; they were working.

It was Mariani who first came up with the idea of putting on music, of playing the huge record player at full volume, while they were work-ing in the basement. Beyond the walls of the villa gardens was a road; people passed by and could hear work going on in the basement. It was a constant nuisance. Music was played at certain times, the volume cranked up as if it were a party. People passing the villa would hear songs, a whole record by some hip girl singer. At full volume. But scarcely perceptible sounds, when combined with music, can create discords that are barely audible, although they register because of the inexplicable dissonance they cause. Anyone passing the Moorish villa found that the Franco-Mediterranean easy-listening music they could hear triggered a strange unease.

When Capitaine Mariani steps into his office with his gold-rimmed aviator sunglasses, the suspect in the chair instinctively presses his legs together.

A smiling Mariani perches one buttock on a desk that has not a scrap of paper, not a single pencil. The work carried out here is man-to-man. Around him are his goons, his bloodhounds, who obey his every command. On a chair in front of him a young Arab in torn clothes is strapped down by his wrists. The bruises on his face give him a faintly ridiculous expression.

'What have you been up to?'

'I did not do anything, monsieur l'officier.'

'Don't give me that shit. What have you been up to?'

'I am a medical student. I did not do anything.'

'A medical student? You're happy to take advantage of France, but you won't help her.'

'I did not do anything, monsieur l'officier.'

'Your brother has disappeared.'

'I know this.'

'You know where he is.'

'I do not know.'

'You're all brothers, aren't you?'

'No, I have only one brother.'

'So, where is he?'

'I do not know.'

'You brother has run off to the bush, to the *maquis*.'

'I do not know. He disappear one night. I know nothing. They come and take him.'

'How can I trust a man whose brother is with the *maquis*?'

'I am not my brother.'

'Oh, but you are your brother. You look like him. There is some of him in you, and he is with the *maquis*. So how can I trust you? We need you to tell us where he is. Who contacted him? We need to know how people get to the *maquis*.'

'I know nothing about these things. I am a medical student.'

'You should tell us where your brother is. You look just like him. It is written in your face. It would be easy to superimpose your brother's face on yours. How can you not know?'

The man shook his head. He was weeping from helplessness, rather than from pain and fear.

'I know nothing. I am a medical student. I know only my studies.'

'Yes, but you are your brother's brother. And he is with the *maquis*. You know a little, the part of him in you knows where he is. And you refuse to tell us. You should tell us.'

Mariani sits down, spreads his hands and gestures to his dogs. They grab the man under the arms and drag him away. Mariani remains sitting at the table, poker-faced; he never takes off the gold-rimmed sunglasses. The louvered shutters cast bars of light across the empty desk. He waits for them to come back, waits for the next one, and all the others that come through his office. They will tell what they know. They will tell everything. This is work.

Salagnon would always hold his breath while going downstairs, then, at the bottom, take a breath, feel his stomach lurch, and become accustomed. Bad smells never last long, a few breaths at most; we cease to smell anything that lingers. Confused noises came from the closed doors, echoing around the vaults, merging to become the vast cacophony of a railway station compressed into the space of a cellar. Wine had been stored here. They had emptied out what remained, installed electric cables, hung bare bulbs from the vaulted ceiling, lugged metal tables and bathtubs down the narrow staircase. The uniforms of the paratroopers working down here were filthy, their jackets open to the waist, their sleeves and trouser legs were soaked. They moved through the corridor, always careful to close the door behind them, faces haggard, eyes bulging from their sockets, their dilated pupils like bottomless wells. Trambassac could not bear to see them like this. He insisted his men were spotless, clean-shaven and full of energy; one pack of detergent per uniform, he recommended. In his presence their words were clearly enunciated, their movements economical; they knew precisely what to do at every moment. Before the press, he paraded impeccably dressed men who were lithe, dangerous, their all-seeing eyes capable of peering through the walls of Algiers, of flushing out the enemy behind the faces, of tracking them through the catacombs of the body. But some men spent days wandering around the *carceri* beneath the Moorish villa. They terrified everyone, even the parachute officers who stayed on the surface, who managed the fleet of jeeps, picking up suspects, filling in the vast, synoptic chart. These were men that Trambassac never saw; nor did he ever ask to see them.

Some of the men in handcuffs pushed or dragged here by armed paratroopers turned to jelly as soon as they smelled the dank stench of the basement, as soon as they saw themselves reflected in the lemur eyes of those they passed in the corridor, covered with oily sweat, their khaki shirts open to the waist and soaked down the front. Others held their heads high and the door was carefully closed behind them. They would find themselves in a tiny cell with a number of men. A bare bulb, an officer with a notepad asking questions – very few questions – and two or three others, filthy and close-mouthed, who looked like tired car mechanics. The clamour of the basement, broken now and then by screams, trickled down the walls. In the centre of the cell were the tools: a basin, cables and electrodes, and a full bathtub, which some found surprising. What filled the bath was no longer water but a viscous liquid that glistened darkly in the glare of the bare bulb hanging from the vault. The process began. Questions were asked. All this took place in French. Those brought back upstairs sometimes had to be carried. They were not sent home.

When Salagnon came upstairs with the pad on which names were noted, he was vaguely thinking that if they worked quickly enough to arrest those making the bombs, those planting them, they might prevent a bomb going off on a bus. All the paratroopers thought much the same thing, except for the lemurs in the basement, and there was no one now who knew what they were thinking, as they repeated the same questions endlessly to the drowning, who could not answer for spewing water, to the electrocuted, whose clenched jaws blocked off all sound. Trambassac was very clear in his statements to the press. 'We must act, quickly and without scruple. When a man is brought to us having just set twenty bombs that might explode at any moment and will not talk, when he refuses to tell us where they are and when they are set to explode, exceptional measures are required to compel him to do so. If we capture a terrorist we know has planted a bomb and we interrogate him quickly, we avoid further victims. We need to get such information rapidly. By any means necessary. It is the person who rejects those means who is the criminal; his hands are stained with the blood of dozens of victims whose deaths could be avoided.'

Put like this, it was above reproach. The argument was flawless, it should be said. Arguments are always flawless – except in the hands of the inept – because they are designed to be so. It is true that if a terrorist is captured who is known to have planted bombs, he should be bombarded with questions. Bombarded, barraged, blitzed, shelled, it does not matter. It has to happen quickly. Put this way, it is unanswerable. Except that they never arrested anyone that they knew had planted twenty bombs. They arrested 24,000 men without knowing what a single one of them had done. What they had done was determined by the interrogation.

Trambassac told anyone who would listen that they arrested the guilty and interrogated them, not to establish their guilt, but to limit the damage caused by their crimes. In fact, they did not arrest guilty men: they created them by the process of arrest and interrogation. Some, by sheer chance, may have been guilty already, others were not. Many disappeared, guilty or otherwise. They cast wide nets and brought in all the fish. There was no need to establish guilt in order to act. All that was needed was a name; they took care of the rest.

On that particular day Trambassac was brilliant. What he told the reporters asking him questions, the justification he gave for what was happening in the Moorish villa, would be repeated in more or less the same words for half a century; the mark of great literary creations is that they imprint themselves on the mind; they are regularly quoted, in a slightly distorted form, without anyone knowing who first penned them – in this case, Josselin de Trambassac.

*   *   *

They saw Teitgen going down into the basement with another civilian who was General Secretary of the Algiers Police, the city police force that had been stripped of its powers. They were carrying sheaves of military arrest warrants, administrative papers and various forms to be signed. They were also carrying a photo album. They showed it to everyone they encountered. They showed it to Trambassac. It contained photographs of hideously mutilated bodies taken in the German camps.

'This is something that we personally experienced, and now we see it again here.'

'I lived through it too, Teitgen. But let me show you what is happening here.'

He waved the front page of *L'Écho d'Alger*, a full-page photograph, mercifully in black and white, showing the wreckage of the bar L'Otomatic, the patrons lying amid the rubble and shattered glass.

'These are the men we're looking for: the ones who did this. We will do anything to find them, to stop them. Anything.'

'You cannot do anything.'

'We have to win. If we do not win, you're right, all this will have been useless carnage. If we bring peace, it will simply be the price that had to be paid.'

'We have already lost something.'

'What are you thinking of? Law and order? Don't you find such concepts a little preposterous in times like these? They are not designed for wartime, they are intended to regulate the humdrum routine of everyday life. But I am more than happy to sign every one of your slips of paper.'

'Whether or not what we are doing is illegal is unimportant, Trambassac, on that point I agree with you. But we have gone beyond that. We have resorted to acting anonymously and without responsibility, which can only lead to war crimes. On every one of my "slips of paper", as you call them, I want the name of a man and a legible signature.'

'Leave me to my work, Teitgen. Among my men, those who don't want to do that work, don't have to. But those who do not offload their burden on to others carry it themselves.'

'Even those who don't do that "work" will be sullied. All of us will be tainted. Even in France.'

'Leave me alone, Teitgen, I've got work to do.'

They were constantly moving, through the stairwells, through the hallways, into the bedrooms. They smashed down doors, blasted locks, laid traps in corridors, blocked doorways, windows, roofs, court-yards. They worked day and night. The cellars of the Moorish villa were always full. They rarely saw daylight. The temperature scarcely varied, hot and muggy beneath a bare bulb. Salagnon was dead on his feet. He slept fitfully. When he came upstairs he was surprised by the shifting sunlight in the ceremonial hall. They had to work quickly, to discover names, places, collar suspects before they made a run for it. They scrawled names on the walls, crossed out those arrested in red, pinned up photographs of the leaders still in hiding; they saw them every day, lived with them, knew their faces; had they passed them in the street they would have recognized them. They could spot them hiding in a crowd. They were hiding. The enemy hid behind false ceilings, behind false walls, the enemy holed up in apartments, melted into crowds, hid behind faces. The enemy had to be torn out. The false walls demolished. The body searched. The sheltering faces destroyed. Night and day they worked. Outside the bombs went off. People they had spoken to had their throats cut. They had to work faster still. The fleet of jeeps brought a continuous stream of ter-rified men to the cellars of the Moorish villa. Teitgen insisted they be counted, that their names be taken on arrival. This they did. He insisted, he persisted, this little toad-like man with his thick glasses sweating in his tropical suits, a little fat, a little balding, the only civilian present, so different from the lean wolves who wrested names, who snatched men after a brief chase in a stairwell. But Teitgen was stubbornly determined. His papers had to be signed. He came every day and 24,000 slips were signed. And when a man was released, he checked. He cross-referenced lists. Some were missing. He queried. He was told they had disappeared.

'We can't send them back like that,' Mariani would say, nodding at those who were too badly mutilated. 'They're fucked one way or another.' Salagnon drove a covered truck filled with those who would never be released. He drove at night, heading out past Zeralda. He pulled up next to a pit in a glare of spotlights. Mariani's dogs were there. They unloaded the cargo. Their arms dangled by their sides, some holding pistols, others knives. Salagnon heard gunfire and, afterwards, the gentle sound of something soft falling on to something soft, like a sack falling on a pile of sacks. Sometimes the sound of the fall was preceded by nothing, no gunshot, just a liquid gurgle that did not even make him flinch – and that was worse, the fact that he did not feel a faint shudder.

He asked Trambassac whether he could be relieved of having to do this, having to drive the truck to Zeralda or to the port or to the helicopter that took off in the middle of the night to make brief flights over the sea.

'OK, Salagnon. If you don't want to do it, don't do it. Someone else will do it.' He was silent for a moment. 'But there is something I would like you to do.'

'What's that, sir?'

'Paint my men.'

'Is this really the time to paint them?'

'It's now or never. Take a little time now and then. Paint portraits of my lads, of your comrades. You paint quickly, as I understand it; they don't need to pose. They need to see themselves. To see themselves as more handsome than they are right now. Because otherwise, with what we're doing here, we will lose them. Give them back a little humanity. You can do that, can't you?'

Salagnon obeyed. He did this strange thing that was painting the portraits of the paratroopers, who worked day and night until they collapsed, drunk with exhaustion, who thought as little as possible, who avoided mirrors. He painted heroic portraits of men who no longer thought beyond the plan to apprehend the next suspect.

When the feverish excitement abated around some guy covered in blood, in spittle and vomit, in the tearful silence that followed great moments of tension, they could clearly see what was before them: an excremental body whose stench pervaded them all. 'We can't put this one back into circulation,' Mariani would say. And he disposed of everything. They were among comrades. It did not matter who did this or that, who did more or less, who had acted and who had watched. They were the same; the man who had done no more than listen and watch was like the others. They contemptuously scorned those who affected to know nothing, those who pretended not to be involved. They would have liked to plunge these men into a bucket of blood, or send them back to France. They were not keen on Salagnon painting them; they preferred to be in a group or utterly alone. When they went to bed, they rolled themselves in their sheet and turned their faces to the wall. They lay beneath the sheet, unmoving, whether or not they were asleep. When together, they liked to laugh raucously, to bawl, to tell crude jokes, and to drink as much as they could until they collapsed and threw up. Salagnon asked them to remain stock still and silent in front of him. They did not like the idea, but Salagnon was one of them so, one by one, they agreed. He painted huge ink-wash portraits of them as lean, strong, taut, the consciousness of life flickering within them, the consciousness of death all around them, but holding strong, their eyes open. Though they did not tell him, they loved this dark romanticism. They agreed to pose in silence for Salagnon, who did not speak to them but simply painted them. Trambassac hung several of the portraits in his office. He met with colonels, generals, senior civil servants, representatives of the Governor-General beneath the dark gaze of his painted paratroopers. And he always mentioned them. He would gesture to them, point to them as he spoke. 'These are the men I am talking about. The men who are defending you. Take a good look at them.' The portraits, which radiated a dark, crazed magnetism, were part of the blackmail of heroism that took place almost every day in his office. In Algiers in 1957 the Grim Reaper was a mechanical harvester, and Salagnon's portraits were a part of it, like the painted, metal bodywork holding it all together. It held together. 'All of them are guilty, but they are guilty for you. So they stick together, they remain united. It doesn't matter what they do. They do it together. That is what matters. If someone should leave? Let him go. We will not blame him, let him disappear.'

Civilians now only reluctantly came into his office to get figures. Trambassac would be standing waiting for them in pristine battle-dress and, behind him, the imperturbable heroes would look down on the newcomer; he would set out his figures, magnificent, impressive figures: the number of terrorists eliminated, the list of bombs recovered. He would flourish marvellously clear organizational charts. Teitgen held him to account, he brought his sheaves of arrest warrants. Behind his thick glasses he did not tremble; he made his calculations and showed the results to Trambassac. 'If my calculations are accurate, Colonel, there are two hundred and twenty men missing from your figures. What has become of them?'

'Well, they've disappeared, these men of yours.'

'Where?'

'If anyone asks you, you can tell them that Trambassac takes full responsibility.'

Teitgen did not tremble, not from fear, nor from disgust; he never lost heart. From behind his thick glasses he looked the world straight in the eye, the colonel in front of him, the hecatomb of ink inscribed on the walls, the figures that were traces of the dead. He was alone in keeping count of people. Eventually, he resigned and publicly gave his reasons. It was easy to think him ridiculous, with his manner and his forms to be filled in. He looked like a frog demanding answers from a pack of wolves, but he was a frog gifted with superhuman strength, whose words were not his own but an expression of what should be. Throughout the Battle of Algiers he held the post of frog-god before the Gates of Hell: he weighed the souls and noted everything in the Book of the Dead. It is easy to mock him, this little man who suffered from the heat, who peered through his thick spectacles, who worried about forms being filled, while others were in blood up to their elbows, but it is possible to marvel at him as at the animal gods of Egypt and to worship him discreetly.

'Mariani is out of sorts. Have a word with him. I'm putting him on enforced leave for three days. You too. Go and find him. I don't know where the hell he is. When you go too far, there's no knowing where it will end.'

The streets of Algiers are more agreeable than those of Saigon; the heat here is dry; it is possible to shelter from the sun; cafés line the streets like shady grottos full of life and chatter; from a table on the pavement one can watch the passers-by. Mariani and Salagnon sat down at a table; in uniform, they risked being gunned down, but they showed themselves. Mariani took off the sunglasses he always wore. His eyes were red and glazed, stupefied by insomnia.

'You don't look so good.'

'I'm tired.'

They watched the evening crowd stroll along the rue de la Lyre.

'I can't stand all these fucking ragheads. They hate us. When we pass them in the street, their only expression is servility; but murderers are hiding behind those faces. And you, Salagnon, you've abandoned us. You spend all your time doing the schoolkid stuff, that girl's stuff. You were always doodling in Indochine, too, but at least you could do other things.'

'I don't like the work, Mariani.'

'So what? I liked it better in the mountains, too, but the enemy is here. We've nearly done it. We've got them on the run. Are you with us or not?'

'I've got no problem hunting men down, but it bothers me, them being in pyjamas. And as for what we do to them back at the villa, I can't hack it any more.'

'I don't know who you are any more, Salagnon.'

'Neither do I, Mariani.'

They fell silent. They watched people passing, sipped their anisette, then picked up again. Salagnon could not identify the thoughts flitting across Mariani's face as it quivered like laundry in the wind. All of a sudden he was composed again.

'I've been told to exterminate rats, so I'm just executing orders; well, actually, I'm executing *others*,' he snickered. His face was confident now, callous. He was not looking at anyone, not even Salagnon. 'I'm happy here,' he went on. 'I don't want to have to leave. This is home.'

'We'll have to go back sooner or later. And we've changed. What will become of us back in France?'

'France will have to change.'

He had come to Algiers because a decision had been taken in Paris that he and his kind should be sent here. It had been decided to use brute force, and no force was more brutish than the lean wolves who had trained in the jungle. They had come here on a slow boat; they crossed the pale blue January sea, had watched Algiers grow larger on the horizon. He had stepped on to the quay, being careful not to think about Eurydice. Working day and night he no longer had time to write to her, but, overwhelmed by exhaustion and horror, steeped in other men's blood, silently, almost unbeknown to himself, he continued to think about her.

He did not look for her. It was Salomon who found him. They ran into each other on the threshold of the Moorish villa. The sun had barely risen. Salomon Kaloyannis was coming up the steps strewn with dead palm fronds and sand that no one thought to sweep away. He was wearing a black trilby and carrying a doctor's bag. Salagnon was running out, machine gun slung over his shoulder, the jeep waiting for him idling at the foot of the steps. Both men stopped, surprised to see the other here, in this place that everyone believed they alone knew, where everyone believed they were absolutely alone, that everyone believed they had to roam alone, regardless of their purpose.

The jeep's engine growled. The other three paratroopers were already installed, feet on the dashboard, legs dangling out of the windows, hanging on to the slatted sides, sub-machine guns slung over their shoulders. Salagnon had scrawled addresses and names in his chest pocket.

'Come and see me, Victorien. Come and see Eurydice. She would like that.'

'Is she married?' Salagnon asked. It was the first thought that occurred to him. It was the only thing he could think to say, there on the steps of the Moorish villa, something he had not thought about before.

'Yes. To a guy who used to make her laugh, but now just bores her. I think she misses you.'

'Me?'

'Yes. He came back during the time of the swashbucklers. Though I'm not sure that ever ended. Come and see me some day when you've got time.'

He stepped into the Moorish villa, lugging his bag. Salagnon leapt into the jeep, which instantly roared off. They hurtled down the hill towards Algiers, almost throwing themselves clear at every hairpin bend. 'Faster! Faster!' muttered Capitaine Salagnon, hanging on to the windshield, savouring the bright sun as it rose, lighting up Algiers harbour below, the white buildings and the ships moored on the quays.

The past twelve years had marked Salomon Kaloyannis, these twelve years particularly.

'Every year is like a heavy stone in my pack,' he explained, 'and every year the stone is bigger. The years weigh me down. I'm stooped over. The stones I gather drag me down. I'm not even able to stand up straight. Look at my lips, the way they droop at the corners, and even when I do manage to lift them it looks less and less like a smile. I am no longer funny, Victorien, and I no longer find anything around me funny. I feel as if I'm being corroded by rust, like a light flickering out. I'm aware of it. I try to turn myself on again, but there's nothing I can do.

'What I do up at the villa? I quantify pain. I tell the men in the cellars whether they need to stop for a while or whether they can carry on. Distinguish between a loss of consciousness and certain death. This is war, Victorien. I was a medical doctor. I was with the army in Germany. I can read the signs. I know when someone is dying. Why me? Why should a little doctor from Bab el Oued be coming to the villa with my little doctor's bag? Why should I help you do things that you will never dare tell your children? I fear their violence, Victorien. I have seen them cut off noses, ears, cut out tongues. I have seen them slash throats, eviscerate, disembowel. This is not a figure of speech, a rhetorical expression. I have watched young men I knew by sight become murderers and justify their acts. Their fury terrifies me. All the more so because I know the supply of cut-throats is inexhaustible, because of the flagrant injustices in the colony. It was only fear that stopped them from killing us. They killed each other. But now they have no fear. We are the ones who are afraid. I was afraid, Victorien. And now they are setting off bombs everywhere. They can explode everywhere. They can destroy what I hold most dear. I know that we need more justice, but the bombs make it impossible to change, the bombs leave us frozen in terror. My daughter's life is much dearer to me than any idea of justice, Victorien. I have come to shelter behind your strength. You have become the finest soldiers in the world. You will make this stop. If you cannot, no one can.'

He fell silent. He raised his glass. Salagnon did likewise and they sipped their anisette. They nibbled at some pickled carrots and lupin beans. Crowds passed in both directions, coming up from the place des Trois Horloges and heading on to Bouzaréah.

'But even so, I think you're making too much of this,' he said gently.

Salagnon saw her. Though the streets of Bab el Oued are seething with people, teeming with beautiful, dark-haired women in flowery dresses so light they float around the hips, flutter up at every step as they move like a breeze through tall grass, trailing a wake of perfume and shy glances, he saw her, a tiny figure walking towards them, growing very slowly in his eye, close to the innermost part of his being. He knew it was her. There was no proof. He had simply known the moment the distant figure appeared in the crowd, and that barely visible silhouette, that and that alone, he followed with his eyes. My memory is marvellous and she is coming, he thought quickly, his words confused, his thoughts muddled. I remember a beauty that dazzled me, that dazzled me so much I could scarcely see it, my eyes burned, my face burned, my body was on fire, and she is come, she will be here in front of me and I will realize that she is just a woman with a face marked by twelve more years, twelve years in which I have not seen her; a drab woman, a woman with sagging flesh, a woman whose face I will find harmonious but older, her every wrinkle, every fold attesting to the faintly repulsive weight of real flesh. He saw her hips move towards him, saw the glow of her face, saw her lips part in a radiant smile meant only for him and she kissed him. He was dazzled. He could see nothing but this smile meant only for him, a smile that floated in a halo of light. A miracle was taking place. He found her beauty perfect, with no surplus, no shortfall.

'You've hardly changed, Victorien. A little more broad, a little more handsome. Just the way I dared to hope you might be.'

He solemnly got to his feet, pulled out a chair and had her sit next to him. Their legs nestled together, as though they had never been apart, and each contained within itself the form of the other. She fits me perfectly, like a coat I've worn for years, he thought, still confused. Her face dazzles me. It radiates beauty and I cannot seem to see her as flesh and blood. She moves me, that is all. She is just as she is in my soul. And when she looks at me with that smile of hers, it makes me sigh with relief. I am home. She takes up the precise same space as my soul; or perhaps my soul is a dress and I fit her perfectly. The beauty I could make out from a distance was like a portent. Eurydice, my soul, here I am before you once more.

Eurydice found a place in the perfect space that was Victorien's heart. Everything about her, her eyes, her voice, her face, her whole body radiated the same glow that had suffused him twelve years ago and throughout the twelve years since. 'How she dazzles me,' he murmured, a half-articulated mumble only Salomon heard. Everything was moving so fast, everything. He felt himself choke. The words would not come. He could not say anything. Thankfully, Salomon kept the conversation going, beaming, recovering his volubility.

He talked of everything and nothing, lectured, laughed, greeted passers-by, teased his daughter, who did not respond, but stared hungrily at the handsome Victorien, studying his face, older now, sanded by time. Kaloyannis could see this and he left her to her contemplation, while he questioned Capitaine Salagnon about his travels, his adventures, his achievements, and Victorien responded clumsily, confusedly, talking about jungles, ravines, the night-time escape through the waterlogged forest. He unspooled his memories, showing them off as he might send a series of postcards. He could do nothing but show off his collection, since his mind was entirely focused on studying Eurydice's face, brushing against her legs beneath the table, legs whose skin, whose curve, whose heft he remembered better than if they had been his own.

Eurydice's husband arrived, warmly greeted everyone, sat down and immediately joined the conversation. He was brilliant, the perfect foil for Salomon. A dramatically handsome man with dark, curly hair, his bright white shirt open to reveal his tanned chest, he rivalled Salomon's virtuosity, effortlessly coming out with a torrent of words that were intelligent and droll, but deafened more than they convinced, stated or even charmed. The best thing to do, when listening to him, was to respond with exaggerated gestures and to laugh a lot. It was a sport at which Salomon excelled, quickly outdistancing Salagnon, who rapidly became breathless and simply watched.

He was very handsome, the dark-haired man who fed on the sun, who employed language like a musical instrument. But the first moment Victorien set eyes on him, at the moment he stopped at their table and bent down to greet them, proffering his hand, flashing a luminous smile, he wondered what Eurydice was doing with him. What he was doing with her, Victorien readily understood. Eurydice was the cherished treasure of Salomon Kaloyannis, a wonder that one could not but desire; but he was not her equal. This was precisely what Victorien was thinking as he shook the man's hand and gave him the fine, confident smile of a parachute officer. Privately, he dismissed him. He is out of place, he thought simply. He is out of place in this place that belongs to me. But in the long conversation that followed, punctuated by jokes, shouts, greetings to passers-by and laughter, in this *pataouète* piece of theatre being performed al fresco near the place de Trois Horloges, Salagnon said little. He did not have the time. He was not quick enough. He did not know how to slip in a witty remark just when the others were catching their breath. He did not know how to embellish trivial nothings with sound and fury. While the father and the husband were performing, he was watching Eurydice, and Eurydice gradually felt herself blush.

She remembered the letters, the sketches, the long, one-sided conversation he had kept up for twelve years, and the soft hairs of his ink brush caressed her soul, made her skin prickle. In this strange Algiers where language was street theatre, painting was not visual at all; it was silent, slow and tactile.

When they went their separate ways, the husband vigorously shook Victorien's hand and invited him to come and visit; Eurydice nodded, embarrassed. They walked off together, a handsome couple. Victorien heard him say – his voice carried and Salagnon's keen ear had been honed in the jungle, or perhaps the husband intended him to hear – 'They're poseurs, those fellows, that's the word for them, poseurs, with their swords and their uniforms. They strut around in their ridiculous helmets and tight trousers, but when you sit down with them, face to face, they haven't got a thing to say.'

He slipped his arm around Eurydice's shoulders as silently as a stone and they melted into the crowds of Bab el Oued. Victorien watched until he could see nothing, hear nothing. He went on sitting, unmoving, his eyes still fixed on the point where they vanished into the human jungle of Algiers.

'Beautiful woman, my daughter, huh?' Salomon said, slapping his thigh with an enthusiasm so charming it brought a smile from Salagnon.

His uncle was waiting for him outside the villa in a jeep parked on the driveway. He was smoking and staring into space, half sprawled across the seat, one arm hanging out of the window. Finally, Salagnon appeared, kissed him on the cheek and slid into the passenger seat. The uncle flicked the cigarette over his shoulder and turned the key in the ignition, without a word. He drove him to a little café in the hills that overlooked the bay of Algiers. Pine trees shaded the terrace; outcrops of limestone sprouted between the trees, even in winter; this was the Mediterranean coast. The café owner, a pot-bellied *pied noir* with a patter so typical it was clearly rehearsed, would offer a round of anisette on the house to paratroopers who regularly frequented his establishment. With an apron hugging his ample paunch, he would come out from behind the bar and personally serve, loudly dispensing advice and encouragement, rapping the flat of his hand on the table to underscore his point. 'We need to show those fucking *bougnoules*. Violence is the only language they understand. Let your guard down, they'll smack you. Turn the other cheek and they'll slit your throat.

Turn your back on them and they'll put a knife in it, and you'll never see it coming. But look them in the eye and they don't move. They stand stock still, like tree trunks. They can stand like that all day and not move a muscle. I often wonder what's in their blood. Something cold and viscous, probably. Like lizards.'

He would set the aperitifs down on the table, with some olives or some lupini beans, depending on the hour. 'Your good health, messieurs.' Then he would go back to his bar to wash glasses and listen to the radio softly playing endless sentimental songs.

Salagnon and his uncle sat in silence, gazing down at the bay stretched out before their feet. The sea in winter was an unbroken expanse of pale blue, the whitewashed buildings clustered along calm shores.

'That's what they all say,' the uncle muttered after a moment. 'They say they understand them, because they went to school together. That's why it's so terrible. That's precisely why.'

'Why?'

'The *pieds noirs* don't understand the violence being done to them. "We were all getting along so well", that's what they think. But, strangely, the Arabs have no trouble understanding the violence being done to them. So either they're a completely different species or they live in completely different worlds. Going to the same school and ending up in different worlds is dangerous. You can't go teaching the concepts of liberty, equality, fraternity to the very people you deny them to.'

They drank, stared out at the perfectly flat horizon; the winter sun warmed their faces and the part of their forearms that protruded from the permanently rolled-up sleeves of the uniform jackets.

'What are you doing?' Salagnon asked at length.

'Much the same as you, I imagine. Only somewhere else.'

He said no more. His uncle's face looked drawn. His complexion was sickly and pale; the corners of his mouth drooped, sinking into his cheeks, gradually twisting his lips.

'If we manage to achieve nothing. If we are forced to leave some day, then what we have done will simply be a crime,' he whispered, his voice barely audible. 'We will be despised.'

Silence returned. It weighed on Salagnon. He glanced around, looking for some way to change the subject, to set it on a new course. The pines swayed gently, the glassy waters of the Mediterranean stretched out to the horizon; below them, the large white buildings, like blocks of plaster, huddled together to form shady alleys.

'Are you still learning the *Odyssey*?' he asked.

The uncle's face relaxed; he even smiled.

'I'm getting there. You know, I read something very strange. Odysseus visits the House of Death to ask the prophet Tiresias how it will end. He offers a sacrifice to the dead and Tiresias comes, eager to drink.

> *Stand back from the trench – put up your sharp sword so I can*
> *drink the blood and tell you all the truth.*

'Then he tells Odysseus how it will end: ten years of war; ten years of violent ventures to get home in which, one by one, his friends will die without glory, and finally a massacre. Twenty years of carnage that Odysseus alone will survive. Tiresias, the voice of the dead, who had drunk the blood of the sacrifice to tell the truth, also tells him how he can endure, how he can live after the war.

> *go forth once more, you must...*
> *carry your well-planed oar until you come*
> *to a race of people who know nothing of the sea, [...]*
> *When another traveller falls in with you and calls*
> *that weight across your shoulder a fan to winnow grain, then*
> *plant your bladed, balanced oar in the earth*
> *and sacrifice fine beasts to the lord god of the sea,*
> *Poseidon – a ram, a bull and a ramping wild boar –*

then journey home and render noble offerings up
to the deathless gods who rule the vaulting skies,
to all the gods in order.
And at last your own death will steal upon you...
a gentle, painless death, far from the sea it comes
to take you down, borne down with the years in ripe old age with
all your people there in blessed peace around you.

'When people no longer recognize the instruments of war, it will be over.'

Far below, on the glassy mirror of the sky, a white ship sailed towards Algiers. Very slowly it grew in size, glittering in the winter sun, trailing behind a wake that quickly closed up again, scarcely rippling an impassive, oil-blue sea. It probably carried passengers, people coming home, French officials and recruits, countless recruits coming here to do things they never imagined themselves capable of. Some would not go home, others would go back steeped in blood, all would be marked.

'Do you think it will end some day?'

'It took Odysseus twenty years to make it home. Twenty years is the usual span to repay a debt. We haven't quite finished yet.'

They carried on. They squeezed Algiers to extract the last drop of rebellion. As they did so, they discarded the dry skins left in their hands. They daubed numbers on the houses in black tar. They knew each one; every house was a file on which they wrote down names. They interrogated the bricklayers, since they could build secret caches; they interrogated the builders' suppliers, since they could supply materials that would explode; they interrogated the clockmakers, since they could create detonators; they interrogated those who went out at odd hours; they interrogated those who were not at home when, as good fathers, they should have been at home; and those who visited other people's homes with no pressing family reason. The slightest deviation from routine required clarification. Four paratroopers in a jeep would fetch the person who could offer an explanation. He would be interrogated in the cellars of a Moorish villa.

They searched behind the faces. They tracked through the jungles of the body. They hunted the enemy in the other, strapped to a chair in front of them. Medieval questioning with the aid of implements was the only tool in this internal war, this war of treachery, this war that could not be seen, since it was inside each man. They used what evidence they had to hand. They categorized the faces. They believed in the truth of pain. They squeezed using questions. They squeezed until there was nothing left, nothing but dried husks of skin that they discarded. Unable to win, they devastated; in this war of interiors, there was scarcely room to fight. The battle they waged was a phenomenon that was simultaneously cognitive, ethical and military. It spawned many incredible techniques, new policing methods, original ways of flouting human rights, the elevation of common sense to new levels, and it was an astonishing success; one that paved the way for abject failure.

It ended when no more bombs went off in Algiers. There was no longer any noise from the cellars of the Moorish villa, just a fetid smell that stagnated like a heavy gas unable to escape. All the agitators had been eliminated or they had fled. All those capable of voicing opposition had been reduced to silence. All that remained was a voiceless, mutual hatred, beating like a muffled heart in the peaceful streets. You could hear it as you walked through the Arabic quarter, but no one walked there now. Then the paratroopers were sent out into the *bled* to track down outlaws living in groups in the mountains. The task of the paratroopers was to destroy the *maquis*. In Algiers, the water had been drained, the fish were dead.

He was assigned young men fresh from France, little more than children, who had just left school, just left their families, who stepped off the boat shouldering big green kitbags; they climbed into trucks behind tight-lipped paratroopers in tight-fitting uniforms with rolled-up sleeves, and they crammed into the back, their cumbersome green kitbags wedged between their knees, and were driven through Algiers. Most of them had never seen a city like this, bustling, coastal, squalid, a teeming city, the streets filled with people in strange garb, who passed each other without seeing, and soldiers, soldiers everywhere, in assorted uniforms, carrying guns, on patrol, standing sentry, passing by, on foot, in jeeps, in armoured cars, in dusty trucks. If they arrived on a fine day when the sun blazed on the whitewashed façades, it had a certain style, and the unhealthy tension that fell from the sky of sheet metal, blistering and blue, electrified them. The trucks drove through the garrisoned gates of the barracks, fortified with sandbags and *chevaux-de-fris*, and pulled to a halt on the parade ground. Next to the flagpole from which fluttered the tricolour, lean and stiff, stood Capitaine Salagnon in battledress, feet apart, hands clasped behind his back, his red beret tilted at an angle; and those in the truck did not yet know what the colours of the berets meant. It was something they would learn, together with many other things. But curiously, the colour of the berets and colours of the uniforms would be one of the most important things they would learn here; they would learn not to confuse the blues, the greens, the reds, the blacks, not to have the same feelings for those who wore this colour or that. They clambered down and immediately orders were barked; they fell into line, stood to attention, the kitbags at their feet. Chins up, they waited, looking at Capitaine Salagnon planted in front of the flag.

The young men came from France and had never been so far away; they were all volunteers. On their smooth faces it was hardly possible to tell what they were. They had trained in France, had learned to present arms, to shoot, to jump – this last simply to see whether they were capable, since they would not get to jump; the greatest height they would jump was from the door of a helicopter as it landed, its rotor still whirring. In their bright eyes, where an innocence and a toughness both born of childhood vied with each other, they fanned that little flame that tried to give the impression they were raring to fight. When, finally, they were still, Salagnon addressed them in a loud, clear voice. Everyone spoke to them like this: loudly, so they would hear; clearly, so they would understand. 'Gentlemen, I intend to make paratroopers of you. It is something that is hard, something that is earned. You will be soldiers and you will command respect; you will suffer more than you have ever suffered. You will be admired and you will be despised. But those who follow me will never be left behind. That is the only thing I can promise you.'

And in this he kept his word. They expected no more; this was why they had come.

The first time they met was in a little hotel on the rue de la Lyre. Salagnon had arrived early; lying on the bed, he waited for her. He did not like the place, the drab wallpaper, the dark, old-fashioned furniture, the mirror that returned a warped reflection of half his body, the dreary curtains, the constant noise from the street. She would not like it either. He considered getting up, asking for another room, but at that moment she knocked, came in and joined him on the bed before he even had time to sit up. They slotted together. She pressed herself against him, buried her face in his neck, nuzzled his ear, whispered his name and something else he did not understand. She sat up and gazed at him intently.

'I've waited so long for this moment, Victorien. The worse things got, the more I dreamed they would send you here. That they would send little Victorien, now that he is battle-hardened, send him to save us, to save me especially, and you would come and save us from all this, from this terrible violence, from the senselessness, the treachery, the endless grief.'

'You never told me.'

'I didn't really realize myself. I've realized it now, as I'm saying this, but I always felt it. When I read in the paper that they were sending the paratroopers here, my heart leapt. My unspoken wish had been granted. All this, all this war, all this violence and all these horrors have led to this moment, to us, here, now. We were so far apart, we were born so far apart that it has taken two wars to bring us together. I secretly hoped that things would get worse, that you would come soon. The others don't know why they're fighting. I'm the only one who knows: they are fighting for us, so that we can be together.'

She kissed him. He was no longer thinking about the room. It no longer truly existed. They spent the whole day there, and the night, but parted the next day. At 6 a.m. Capitaine Salagnon climbed into the lead vehicle and, followed by a column of trucks filled with soldiers, they set off on their mission.

He wrote a brief letter on which, with a single brushstroke, he traced the curve of her hip as he remembered it; he gave her the address where he would be stationed, so that she could reply. Eurydice borrowed her father's Peugeot 2CV and came to visit. She had draped a white *haik* over her clothes, keeping it fastened by holding the ends between her teeth. Behind her she left a trail of confusion and amusement. It is rare for a woman wearing a *haik* to drive across the country at breakneck speed. She did not go unnoticed: someone is trying to disguise herself, to hide, people thought as she passed. We don't know who she is, they thought, but we know she is hiding something, because she is clearly not who she pretends to be. Spectral and feverish, she arrived at the paratroopers' camp. She asked the dumbfounded orderly if she could speak to Capitaine Salagnon. She shrugged off her *haik* as she spoke, pushed open the door and fell into the arms of a startled Victorien, who told her she was crazy, reckless, anything could have happened to her on the road.

'I came in disguise,' she laughed. 'No one can see me.'

'This is a war, Eurydice, not a game.'

'I'm here.'

'And your husband?'

'He doesn't exist.'

He found this answer satisfactory.

*　　*　　*

A brief cloudburst had scoured the air clean. It quickly dried, cleansing the distance, the sky, the horizon, of the tawny dust that floated here and shrouded everything. The landscape unfurled in every direction, as dazzling as a freshly laundered sheet, beneath a clear blue sky. They left in Salomon's 2CV, taking the rocky path to the mountain pass of Om Saada. There they would find trees, shade, a scant expanse of grass on which they could lie down. He had shown Eurydice the sketchpad he was bringing with him and, without telling her, slipped a revolver into the holster beneath the passenger seat. They drove slowly, chatting and laughing about everything. The flaps of the windows were open to let in the whipping breeze that smelled of hot stone, scorched grass and pine trunks oozing resin. The winding road played havoc with the weak suspension of the 2CV, which jolted along like a carriage on springs. They jostled and bumped against each other, laughing, steadying themselves on a thigh, an arm; from time to time they tried to kiss, but risked banging their heads together, and the absurd risk made them laugh all the harder. Eurydice was behind the wheel. He was happy to let himself be driven, gazing out at everything, the landscape, the clear air. He watched her as she drove with touching concentration, forgetting the gun stowed under his seat. At the Om Saada gap they took a narrow trail that led to the edge of a forest of twisted pines. They were greeted by a grassy meadow. In spring, plants believe they can triumph over the scree, and cushions of vivid green, short-stemmed flowers, patches of grass, had set off to conquer the world. Things would be different come summer, but today, the season's life force was victorious. They left the car and sat in the shade of the pines, whose lowest branches, as fat as a human thigh, snaked along the ground. She brought the *haik* and spread it on the ground like a white sheet they could lie on. Far below, like the floor of their bedroom, a carpet of hills rippled as far as the horizon, gold and green, beneath a sky of unbroken blue; they could see no road, no villages, nothing more than stone on stone, infrequent and infinitesimal – from here no man-made structures were visible. The warm air stirred, their lungs quivered like set sails and swelled with the landscape. An auspicious Algeria lay spread out before them.

They spent the whole day there: chattering happily, kissing until their tongues were sore, making love bare-arsed in the sunshine, consuming the basket of food they had brought, sketching a little, dozing in each other's arms, twitching briskly to shake off a lone, persistent fly that buzzed around them. They could not believe that twelve years had come between them. Twelve years is a long tunnel; by rights the memories at the far end should have faded into the distant haze; by rights they should have changed. But no. These twelve years had simply been a page: it takes time to read a page, time to turn the page and read the next if one follows the lines; but the previous page is still right there, on the other side of the thin sheet of paper; elsewhere, but close enough to touch.

The afternoon was passionate, a fat sun painted everything the colour of copper. Pressed together, their skin melted into one. Victorien's cock never tired, though he began to ache a little. He could have carried on for ever, going in and out, plunging into Eurydice as into cool, refreshing water, and it made him laugh, the way someone in a swimming pool might laugh, their warm skin warm, sprayed with cool water, revelling in a limitless freedom.

'We have to stop and head back,' he whispered into her ear.

'Is the *capitaine* sounding the curfew?'

'In this part of the country, the *capitaine* knows what he's doing. Come.'

The car would not start. Teetering on the edge of the road, covered in dust, it gave only a wheezing cough when Salagnon keyed the ignition. He pored over the engine, checked the wires, nothing happened. The sun had vanished, the air was turning blue.

'We're stuck.'

'We'll go back on foot. It's not far.'

He shook his head.

'Being on the road at night is dangerous for people like us.'

'Like us?'

'Two Europeans, one of them an officer. This area isn't safe.'

'Did you know that before you were sent here?'

He didn't answer. He took the gun from beneath the seat and tucked it into his belt. He picked up the *haik* and the remains of the food.

'What are we going to do?'

'Hide somewhere, sleep a little. Then at dawn we'll set out to meet the search party looking for us.'

'Will they find us?'

'Yes,' he smiled. 'Safe and sound, with a little luck, or dead and maimed if we run into the Big Bad Wolf.'

They lay down on a patch of grass between two boulders that cast deep shadows. They stared up into an ink-black sky strewn with more stars than they had ever seen, except perhaps for one night they had spent together in France. They could see big stars, smaller ones and an infinite dusting of tiny stars that made the shadows shimmer. The air smelled of pine.

'Back to where we started,' said Eurydice, squeezing his hand.

'A new start,' said Victorien, pulling her to him.

He was trained not to sleep. He knew how to doze lightly, reduce his physical and mental activity to a minimum, as though hibernating, while remaining alert to sudden noises, voices, the crunch of gravel, the crack of branches. Eurydice slept with her head on his shoulder. His left arm cradled her, keeping his right hand on the gun, half out of its holster, the metal warm.

Between two sighs, he heard the sound of whispering voices. The murmurs came and went on the shifting night breezes, faded and returned. He thought he could make out Arabic, several voices in conversation. He did not know whether they were rebel *djounnouds* or mythical *djinns*. His hand moved over the warm steel, his index finger found the trigger. Still Eurydice slept, a wisp of hair over one eye, her body pressed against his. He watched her. She was breathing evenly, breathing into his neck, smiling. He felt himself harden. This is not the time, he thought, but at least it doesn't make any noise. The whispering faded away.

Very gradually, the darkness brightened. He was woken by the Alouette, the bubble-cockpit helicopter flying high to avoid gunfire. The distant hum of the rotors stirred the pure morning air; the rosy sun glimmered on the transparent cockpit. On the ground they were still in shadow. Salagnon climbed up on one of the huge boulders and waved frantically. The Alouette responded by turning in small circles, then flew off. Victorien climbed back down and crouched next to Eurydice, who was wrapped in the rumpled *haik*, now stained with mud and grass. She looked at him with those penetrating eyes, which immediately transformed him into a furiously beating heart.

'Good news. They're going to find us alive.'

She opened the *haik*. She looked as she had in sleep, tender and slightly rumpled, smiling at him, and that smile meant for him alone hovered in the air, showing him with dazzling arrows of light that blinded him to everything but this: this floating smile meant for him alone.

'Come over to me. Just until they arrive.'

They heard the sound of engines in the distance. Juddering along the track came a jeep, a half-track mounted with a machine gun, and two trucks. They waited for them next to the 2CV, having smoothed their hair and their clothes as best they could. Salagnon had tucked his gun back into his belt.

'All this just for us?' he said to the relieved lieutenant as he jumped down from the jeep and saluted.

'The area is not secure, sir.'

'I know. I'm the one who pins the little flags on the map.'

'Let me say that again: it is not safe to travel alone, Capitaine, sir.'

'But I'm not alone.'

The lieutenant said nothing and stared at Eurydice. She returned his stare, the *haik* wrapped around her like a shawl.

'You're Capitaine Salagnon, you survive everything,' he sighed. 'But you'll see one day that immortality will weigh heavy.'

He went to supervise the 2CV being towed.

That guy is ten years younger then me, thought Salagnon, and he knows what he's doing. We're educating a generation of specialists in war. What will they do afterwards?

'As we were heading to the post…'

'The *burj*, sir, the *burj*,' interrupted Chambol. 'I insist on this word. In Arabic it means "tower". It is a very powerful word in their language. It is a noble word that describes a sign in the desert.'

'All right, fine, as we were heading to the… *burj*, we saw dead donkeys along the side of the road. Several of them in varying stages of decomposition.'

'That's the no-go area, sir.'

'A no-go area for donkeys?'

'The whole population has been moved out, no one is allowed through. We keep a careful watch to make sure there are no traffickers bringing supplies to the outlaws. Let them starve, let them come out of the woods and fight us. The rules are simple, Capitaine, they are what makes it possible to hold the region: it is a forbidden zone, therefore anyone found there is automatically classed as an outlaw.'

'But donkeys?'

'Donkeys are a means of transport in Algeria, therefore in the forbidden zone they are classed as enemy convoy.'

Salagnon bemusedly looked at Colonel Chambol, who was in deadly earnest.

'During various skirmishes we've killed a number of donkeys that were carrying olives or wheat. You might think it's a mistake, but it's no mistake: we're starving out the rebels.'

'Have you ever seen these rebels?'

'The rebels? Never. They're probably not hungry enough to come out of the forest yet. But we're waiting for them. Victory will go to those who have the patience to wait.'

'Or maybe they're not there.'

'I'm sorry, I have to stop you there. We intercepted a donkey carrying weapons. The women leading it were wearing men's shoes – that immediately aroused our suspicions. We killed them on the spot. When we examined the bodies we discovered they were actually men, and in the donkey's panniers, under the sacks of couscous, there were two rifles. That dead donkey justifies all the others, Capitaine. We're on the right track.'

'I suppose you're still tracking donkeys.'

'We will go on tracking them. We will never give in. True grit is the greatest quality in a man. It is much more important than intelligence.'

'I can see that. The truth is a long path strewn with dead donkeys.'

'What do you mean, sir?'

'Nothing, Colonel. I'm trying to make sense of everything.'

'And are you succeeding?'

'No. The bodies will keep piling up, I think,' he smiled.

Chambol looked at him. He did not understand. He did not smile.

'Why exactly are you here, Capitaine Salagnon?' he asked eventually.

'To intercept a *katiba* transporting real weapons.'

'And you think we're not capable of stopping them?'

'A *katiba* is a unit of one hundred and twenty highly trained men, Colonel, armed to the teeth and extremely wary. At the very least, we'll come in handy.'

'Have it your way. But you could have spared yourselves the journey.'

Salagnon did not take the trouble to answer. The paratroopers moved into Chambol's office, cleared a space, installed a field radio and a blackboard, unrolled maps. They clustered around Salagnon, who stood there, issuing no orders, simply waiting for everything to be set up. Chambol, his arms folded, stood fuming in the corner; visibly, very visibly, he disapproved.

'Vignier, Herboteau?'

'Yes, sir.'

'If you were the rebels, which route would you take?'

The two young lieutenants pored over the map. They studied it intently, their concentration obvious from their posture, one massaging the bridge of his nose, the other tugging his bottom lip between thumb and forefinger. They each took turns running fingers along the contour lines of the map, first here, then there, murmuring to each other as though undecided; they were showing that they were thinking; they were showing that they intended to respond to the question with a carefully considered answer. Alone, they would not have carried on so long, but they were thinking, while Salagnon watched.

Their uniforms aside, they looked nothing like each other. Two men could hardly be less alike than Vignier and Herboteau: one was tubby, the other scrawny; one garrulous and funny, the other pasty and withdrawn; one the son of a factory worker from Denain, the other the son of a bourgeois from Bordeaux; one earning, the other inheriting; yet by some miracle they got along famously, understood each other perfectly, went everywhere together. The only thing they had in common was that both were paratroop lieutenants. They were twin reflections in a fairground mirror, they joked with each other; they had the same tics; one was small and fat, the other tall and lean.

Salagnon was fond of the two lads, who greeted each of his questions with deadly earnest. He had trained them. He liked to think he had taught them the hide-and-seek of war.

'There, sir,' said Vignier, running his finger along a narrow valley.

'Or maybe there, sir,' said Herboteau, tracing a different valley.

'Two is two too many, You have to choose.'

'How can you possibly know what these people think?' grunted Chambol.

He had given up his office, but he could not bear for the paratroopers to behave as though he were not even present. The maps were spread out over the big desk. They had cleared it with no consideration. They were studying pairs of aerial photographs of the region using stereoscopic glasses. As though they could know the terrain without ever having climbed it. When all they had to do was ask. After all he, Chambol, was the focal point of all the posts in the region, and here they were pretending he did not exist, these men in their clownish combat uniforms, who refused out of bravado to wear steel helmets, so they could show off the ridiculous little caps perched on their bony skulls.

'They can disappear at will. We never spot them.'

'Despite all your posts?'

'That just proves that they can disappear.'

'Or that your posts are blind and useless.'

'We control the sector.'

'With all due respect, Colonel, you control fuck all. That's why we're here.'

'They know the terrain. They melt into it like butter into hot bread. You won't find anything.'

The simile fell flat. Salagnon stared at him in silence. The two lieutenants looked up and waited. The orderlies operating the radio slowed their movements; those next to the blackboard stiffened, standing almost to attention, in the hope of becoming invisible.

'It's bullshit, this thing about "knowing the terrain", Colonel. People keep mentioning it, but it's meaningless.'

'This is their country. They know the terrain. They disappear at will before our very eyes.'

'You're talking about a hundred and twenty men transporting crates of arms and munitions. A convoy of donkeys, Colonel. They can't hide behind a rock. Wherever it goes, it can be seen.'

'I'm telling you, they know the terrain.'

'Not one of these men comes from around here, most were born in the city like you and me; the others are from various regions. People only know the area they live in, and even then only if they walk around a lot. We're not tracking shepherds but an army of men who are competent and cautious and who are trained to move about unnoticed. You guys up in the lookout posts, they never walk around, and worse, they sleep at night. They know nothing about the area where they're based, they're just waiting to be relieved.'

'We're talking about Arabs, and this is Algeria.'

'Arabs aren't genetically predisposed to having an intimate knowledge of Algeria, Colonel! Any Arab living in Algeria learns about it gradually, just like everyone else.'

Chambol rolled his eyes, exasperated.

'You don't know what you're talking about, Salagnon. You don't know this country or its people.'

'But I do know what it takes for an armed unit to cross a sector. Because I'm part of an armed unit. The world is the same for everyone, Colonel.' He turned to his lieutenants. 'Gentlemen?'

'There!' they said in concert, placing their fingers on one of the valleys.

'This is preposterous,' said Chambol. 'That route would mean crossing the main road and passing close to one of our lookout posts.'

'Yes, but it's the shortest route, and they would be hidden by the forest for most of the time.'

'But what about the road? The post?'

'There are a hundred and twenty of them. They're heavily armed. They can take it by force. But I suspect they're betting that the lookout post won't be a problem.'

'Why would they think that?'

'You said it yourself: your lookouts never spot them. They turn a blind eye. They look the other way. They're not protecting the sector, they're protecting themselves. Lookout posts simply serve to immobilize men, scattering them over a large terrain and, in doing so, turning them into targets. Their main job is surviving.'

'Ridiculous.'

'I couldn't have said it better myself. So, lieutenants, where do we position ourselves?'

They drew a diagram on the blackboard, holding positions, drop zones, pick-up zones, under the mocking eye of Chambol.

'Happy trapping, messieurs. We'll expect you for dinner when you get bored of waiting.'

The paratroopers are lying against large boulders. They have taken cover along the crest of the ridge of limestone blocks that burn if you touch the side facing the sun. They dominate the wadi, where, in winter – is there a winter here? when summer comes it is quickly forgotten – a powerful river flows that is now no more than a rivulet. The banks are pockmarked with dark soil flourishing with rose-laurels, wild grasses whose dried flowers flicker in the sun, and trees; the trees along the riverbanks form a small forest, a dense thicket of gnarled branches, glossy leaves that run the length of the valley, forming a covert ideal for hiding. Far below, a gravel road winds down into the valley and fords the river by what may be a Roman bridge that is too wide for the stream trickling through, but is designed to cope with the flash floods and the rainstorms; then the road snakes up the far slope until it reaches the opposite ridge. There is a second unit there, hiding amid the confusion of boulders and grey shrubs that cast a tracery of fractured shadows. It is impossible to see them, even with binoculars. Their dusty combat fatigues blend into the scree that covers everything, the slope down, the opposite slope and, beyond that, the arid hills that stretch out for ever. Their camouflage hides them. The colours are washed out, the pleats worn and crumpled, the fabric threadbare and tattered in places; their green canvas straps are ripped. They are wearing work clothes. Even their guns are scratched and dented, just like tools that the hand uses most often. The limestone boulders they are lying on protect them from being seen, but not from the heat. Like lizards on a wall, they are motionless, their eyes narrowed to slits. They watch and wait. They doze from time to time. They have been here all night. They have felt the sun on their backs all day as it rose. They watched the sky flush purple, then pink, the clear blue of a French summer, and finally white, which it remains for the rest of the day, all the colours of sheet metal slowly heated until it is white-hot. Lying as still as they can, they are sweating.

If I could be truly still, thinks Salagnon during these long hours, perhaps I might not sweat at all, or at least I wouldn't feel it. The body may not adapt, but it is possible to decide not to care. Heat has followed me around. I have spent my whole adult life sweating. But here, at least, I'm stewing in my own juice. In Indochine the very atmosphere was poisonous. The muggy air was oppressive. I felt myself fester as I was slowly steamed alive in the rancid sweat of all the people packed together. Here at least I am festering in my own sweat. And that is better.

They watched the edges of the dark forest, this rustling covert of dusty leaves. They were expecting a column of 120 armed men to emerge, then cross the road in broad daylight. They were waiting. One hundred and twenty men: given the scale of this war, it represented a whole army. Most of the time, there is nothing to be seen. You scour the countryside and find nothing; you know they are hiding. A jeep was ambushed on a deserted road as though the very rocks and scrubland had attacked it; the bodies of the passengers were found hacked to pieces by the roadside. This was what passed for a battle. The best they could do was overrun the village closest to the attack and interrogate everyone they managed to capture. The suspects did not understand the questions and they did not understand the answers. This was what passed for a counter-offensive. So they were relieved to be expecting 120 armed men. It is better to fight than to live in constant fear of being taken by surprise. The young men lying between the rocks tried not to pass out from sunstroke, to control the beating of their hearts, to keep a flame burning in every muscle like a pilot light, ready to flare up when the column of 120 armed men finally broke cover.

Salagnon had set up the field radio under a scrawny mimosa tree; the antenna blended with the branches, nothing could be seen; any piece of metal that might gleam had been daubed with green paint and sprinkled with sand. Thirty kilometres away, two helicopters were waiting; the pilots were ready, sitting in the shade, ready to drop a section wherever it was needed, and to set off again to replace men here and there. Trambassac used helicopters in every operation now. He carefully planted tiny flags on his map, pinning them at higher altitudes represented by contour lines. He was informed by radio when they arrived. He created networks of little pins, played draughts on his map, boxing in the enemy, cutting off his route, waiting around a corner, surrounding him with pins. Meanwhile, out here, between the hot rocks, midpoint on the ringed horizon, men crawled over stones to fight. Trambassac jabbed a finger and men were transported to the point on the map where his finger landed.

Two Siko H34s could set down a unit anywhere. Thirty men is not a lot, but with enough punch, enough precision and equipped with automatic weapons, they could deal the fatal blow. The fifteen men carried in each helicopter knew that they could count on each other. A battalion made up of young men who know and respect each other is invincible, since none of them will dare back down in front of his friends, none of them will abandon the men he has fought with, the men he lives with, to do so would be to abandon himself.

Eyes half closed beneath his beret, Salagnon was waiting for something to move. On the white pages of the little pad he kept in his pocket, he drew the valley, sketched out the terrain in pencil, shaded, filled in the details, then turned the page and drew the same thing again. He sketched the valley so often he knew every hollow, every tree; he did not miss a single one of the shrubs that had been growing here for centuries. He thought that by working quickly, moving from one drawing to the next, he would notice anything that moved, he would see them coming. The radio operator next to him was half-asleep, cap pulled down over his eyes, leaning against the mimosa.

Slipping between the stones without disturbing a single one, Vignier suddenly appeared before him. Salagnon started, but the young man reassured him, touching a finger to his forearm, then bringing it to his lips.

'Look, Capitaine,' he whispered. 'Along the river, near the bridge.'

Instinctively, Salagnon reached for his binoculars.

'No,' Vignier hissed. 'They might see a reflection. They're there.'

Salagnon set down the binoculars and squinted into the light. Wary figures were stepping out of the dense thicket. The shade beneath the trees concealed them until the last moment. They were moving in single file. Donkeys weighed down with crates moved with them. The sound of distant engines reached them from somewhere along the road. A plume of dust moved slowly towards them, making the distinctive thick growl of army trucks. At this point Salagnon, forgetting caution, grabbed the binoculars and jumped to his feet. A jeep leading a convoy of trucks filled with men was moving up the valley, heading straight for the bridge.

'Shit! That fucking idiot Chambol!'

The first mortar shell, fired from the riverbed, hit the road in front of the jeep. It skidded and came to a halt on the verge. A second shell hit one of the trucks, which burst into flame. The men jumped down, scattered, diving for cover as bullets raked the gravel.

'The fucking idiots! The fucking idiots!' screamed Salagnon. 'Let's go!'

The trap, which had taken hours to prepare, had been tripped at the wrong moment. Shells exploded on the riverbed; the machine guns hidden between the rocks started to strafe the ground; the air was filled with gunfire and explosions. Hidden by the rocks, Salagnon's men crawled forwards, and when the men of the *katiba* began to retreat, they leapt to their feet and attacked. Several donkeys collapsed with a squeal like a siren; the muleteers hesitated, then left them lying on the crates and ran for the shelter of the trees. Shots came from the forest, bursts of rifle fire, and the paras threw themselves to the ground; it was impossible to distinguish between unconscious reflex and the impact of the bullets.

'This is bullshit!' growled Salagnon. 'Complete fucking bullshit!'

He radioed Trambassac and ordered that the valley be cordoned off at both ends to close the trap, the sections to be set down by helicopter at the prearranged points. The paratroopers kept moving from one boulder to the next until they reached the riverbed. For those on the road, things had improved. Warily, they got to their feet. Gunshots rang out in the distance, carefully measured, as though this were a shooting drill. The *katiba* retreated along the valley and ran into the bases stationed along the ridge. Two helicopters thundered across the sky.

'It seems to be working, more or less, but what a fucking waste.'

The dry riverbed was littered with bodies of men in the threadbare uniforms of the ALN, which attempted to be a regular army, but did not quite succeed. The wounded lay still, making no sudden movements, staring silently at the armed paratroopers moving between the bodies. Among the men were the donkeys that had collapsed under the weight of the munitions crates; some raised their heads and from their gaping mouths came that distinctive braying wail. All of them had suffered from the terrible injuries inflicted by hollowpoint bullets and fragments of shrapnel, their guts spilled out, their coats were matted with blood. A sergeant moved from one animal to the next with his handgun, crouching down gently, carefully pressing the muzzle to their forehead and firing a single shot, then getting up and moving on when the animal had stopped braying and its limbs had ceased to spasm. One by one he killed the donkeys until eventually silence descended. At every gunshot, the wounded men flinched. The rebels were wearing uniforms and carrying weapons of war. They were rounded up. Those who did not look much like soldiers were taken to one side. They would not come back. Those who had clearly fought with the French army would be considered deserters. Those who were spared were handcuffed and ordered to sit next to paratroopers holding their weapons at their hips. On one of the rebel officers they found maps, papers, forms.

Vignier was lying on the slope. The bullet had hit him in the forehead, just where skin creases when you frown. He had probably died instantly, struck in mid-air and dead before he hit the ground. Herboteau stood for a moment and stared at him in silence. Then he took a handkerchief from his pocket, moistened it with his tongue and cleaned the blood around the perfectly round hole in his skull.

'It's better like that. This way he died clean.'

He got to his feet again and carefully put away his handkerchief. He picked up his gun, asked for authorization to follow the *katiba*, then set off, followed by his men. Upriver, the fighting carried on in the dense woodland.

Chambol had sprained his ankle when he fell from his jeep. He arrived, hopping and limping. The men from the trucks hobbled back to their vehicles and stood around aimlessly. They were young, with the soft, smooth faces of boys, their baggy, ill-fitting infantry uniforms looked as though they had been stolen from a dressing-up box. They were new recruits, freshly arrived. They had been very scared. Salagnon could not decide whether to clout them or comfort them. They held their weapons awkwardly. On their heads, the steel helmets looked lopsided and too large. The paratroopers dressed in order to fight. It may not seem like much, but it changes everything. When they had all assembled, Salagnon realized that they had scarcely anyone to tell them what to do, save for two sergeants. One of them reeked of alcohol and the other looked exhausted; he had probably been worn down by this country for decades. They were better off hiding in their lookout posts, rather than coming out to be fired on. He caught sight of Chambol, wincing with pain as he put his foot on the ground.

'What the fuck were you doing here?'

'We were going to reinforce one of our posts.'

'Just like that? Some random post in your stupid network?'

'An informant told us that the post was about to be attacked. We were going to lie in wait. That way they would have been met with men who had been forewarned. We thought we could steal a march on them.'

'You believe your informers?'

'He's an ex-soldier, completely trustworthy.'

'Look around you, look at the bodies of the men we just killed. There are ex-soldiers among them. You can trust no one here. Except my men. You're a fucking idiot, Chambol.'

'I'll have you demoted, Salagnon.'

'And if I'm not here to save your skin, what will you do? Hole up in your fucking posts? How long would it take someone to come and get you? Go ahead, have insubordinate paras demoted and the *fellagas* will cut your balls off in your bed. And your sentries won't even notice. And from the looks of these no-hopers here – to say nothing of their half-witted officers – they won't even notice their own balls being cut off until they feel the cold steel.'

'I forbid you...'

'You forbid me nothing, Colonel. And now you can make your own way back. I've got better things to do.'

That night they brought him Ahmed Ben Tobbal. He recognized him by the huge black moustache that had so impressed him before he had started shaving. He still had it, bushy and unruly, on a face that was haggard but more intense. In the gathering darkness there were no more sounds of battle and a little cool air spilled from the sky. Everything smelled of pine resin, of those succulent plants that find relief in exhaling heady perfumes, of hot stones that smelled of flint. The paratroopers began to trudge back, leading prisoners whose hands were bound, guiding the donkeys carrying the crates of munitions and two of their own dead. When the prisoner was brought before the *capitaine* in his camouflage uniform, a Roman ensign planted in the ground among the dead, his face drawn from thirty-six hours without sleep, Salagnon recognized him and smiled.

'If you'd fallen into my hands, young Victorien, I would not have been kind to you,' said Ben Tobbal.

'We wouldn't fall into your hands, Ahmed, not us.'

'These things can happen, Capitaine, they can happen.'

'But it didn't happen.'

'No. Which means this is the end for me. And pretty quickly, I assume,' he said and gave a smile that softened all his features as though heaving a sigh of relief, as though he were about to stretch himself and lie down to sleep after a long march, a smile that was intended for no one and one for which he could feel a flicker of comradeship.

'I won't let him do it.'

He shrugged.

'It's out of your hands, Capitaine. The only reason your boys didn't put a bullet in my head is because I was leading the convoy. So they brought me back. I know who you will hand me over to. And even if you let me go, I would be liquidated by the other side. For having lost the *katiba*, for allowing myself to be captured. That has left me tainted and, for us, there is only one way to be clean again. Haven't you noticed that in this country the past is cleansed with blood? It is all blood under the bridge, the way you might say water under the bridge. Because water is scarce here, but there is no shortage of blood.' He laughed at this, then crouched down, a wave of relief surging through him, like a giddiness. 'So I can see my future clearly. It is short, although I appreciate your kindness in listening to me, young Victorien. Doctor Kaloyannis was very fond of you. He wanted you to marry his daughter. But things changed, I don't know why. The good doctor became a fearful man; the beautiful Eurydice married a man unworthy of her; I went from being a nurse to being a cut-throat; and you, young Victorien, who used to paint so beautifully, here you are, a proud soldier a few hours, a few days, before my execution. Everything went wrong, and everything will continue to go wrong until everyone has killed everyone. I am not sorry it is the end. Years I have spent criss-crossing the country, slipping through your fingers, meeting people only to kill them, you cannot imagine how tiring it is. I'm not sorry that this is the end.'

'Ben Tobbal, you're only a prisoner.'

This made him smile again; crouching on the ground, he looked up at the *capitaine* bending over him solicitously.

'You remember your friend back in France? He was the only one who ever asked me my surname. For everyone else, a first name was enough to label an Arab. And they address me as *tu*, not *vous*, because they say that my language has no formal form of address, although none of those who said so spoke my language; they know a lot about us, *les Françaouis*. They don't know a word of Arabic, but they would recognize an Arab anywhere.'

Herboteau, tight-lipped, stared down at Ben Tobbal, his fingers twitching nervously, as if holding himself back.

'What do we do with him, sir?' he asked, not taking his eyes off the man.

'We evacuate him. We interrogate him. He's a prisoner.'

Herboteau sighed.

'That's the way it is, Lieutenant,' Salagnon insisted. 'Having finally fought a battle rather that slitting each other's throats in dark corners, we are going to follow the laws of war.'

'What laws?' grumbled Herboteau.

'The laws.'

He opened his canteen and passed it to the crouching prisoner. Ahmed drank with a long sigh, then wiped his moustache.

'Thank you.'

'They will come and fetch you.'

The helicopter set down for a few minutes to collect the wounded, the bodies of the dead, and this one prisoner. Mariani, still wearing sunglasses, although it was dark, stooped under the whirring blades and took the battered leather briefcase, the little accountant's briefcase that contained all the FLN documents, the forms, the lists, the maps.

'That should be enough,' he said, watching Ben Tobbal walk towards the helicopter.

With his hands bound, he found it difficult to climb aboard. He gave Salagnon a little shrug, like a wink, a sign of helplessness, then disappeared inside.

'Take good care,' said Salagnon.

'No problem,' said Mariani, patting the briefcase, then he climbed into the helicopter, which took off with a roar.

A cool breeze came from the hills; the indigo sky darkened. The helicopter rose until it captured a glint of pink, one last ray of sunlight that hovered at that altitude; it banked and headed towards Algiers. The sun continued to sink and, against a sky the colour of violets, they saw a figure fall from the helicopter, wheel in the air to be swallowed by the shadowy hills. The helicopter continued on its appointed route and disappeared into the dark air. The engine faded and was silent.

'Did you know that was going to happen?' asked Herboteau.

'With Mariani, it was more than likely. Let's go back.'

The trucks had come to fetch them, headlights glaring, lighting the rocky desert road. Herboteau's fingers had ceased to twitch. Cramped in the back of the truck, he could not sleep, even though the others, exhausted, had somehow managed to nod off on the wooden benches. He felt drowsy, but a roiling nausea prevented him from closing his eyes. The truck juddered and jolted and, in the end, he vomited out of the window, while the driver yelled at him, but did not even think to stop.

'Are you sick, Herboteau?' Salagnon asked when they arrived.

'Yes, sir. But it's nothing I can't deal with.'

'Will you be all right?'

'Yes.'

'Good, now get some sleep.'

They went to sleep. They were worn out from the watching, the marching, the waiting, from the sudden flare of battle that had sparked them into life, making them capable of extraordinary feats that left them panting, dreaming of beaches, cold beer and soft beds. The strain was getting to them. Lit by the dim glow of low-watt bulbs, the corridor in the barracks seemed interminable; they could not see the other end. They dragged their feet, their dusty rubber soles scuffing the thin linoleum, trudging mechanically towards sleep. The returning troops were far from smart: eyes red, uniforms stiff with mud, skin sticky with musky sweat, they trooped towards their barrack room, towards the iron bedsteads where they could curl up in a blanket and not move. And this time most of them had come back alive; they did not have to drag the weight of many dead – only three – while they, their bodies exhausted, their souls washed in too much blood, glittered in the darkness. Things had gone well, overall. They had managed to surprise. They had not been surprised. Most of them had come back alive. Overall. The dim lighting in the barracks made it impossible to tell them apart, it accentuated the ridges of their skulls, painted their faces with deep shadows, traced a rictus around their thin lips; their eyes, sunk in their sockets, reflected nothing, saw nothing. They were tired. They did not like themselves. They held it together by sticking together, by leaning, shoulder to shoulder. They want to sleep, thought Salagnon, only to sleep. I can see them moving through the yellow light aflutter with insects. I can see them dragging their feet, thinking of sleep in the grim barracks corridor, these soldiers who feel strong. They look like the living dead and I am their leader. It is night, the day about to break. We return to the cave and I roll the stone closed behind them. Here we will spend the day. I carry on living when I should not, that is the source of the potent sweat that shrouds me like the mists of the tomb. I was killed in Indochine, shot at point-blank range while eating a chicken's foot. I should not be here. And yet I go on. We all go on. We should not be here. What we are living, what we are doing, is something no one can rise above, something no one can survive unscathed; and still we go on, a zombie army spreading across the world, sowing destruction. Our thirst assuaged, we return to the grave to spend the day; tomorrow night, scenting blood, we will set out again. How long can this go on? Until we crumble to dust, like the desiccated corpses we find in the desert, which, if we try to move them, become no more than a fistful of sand. The water had to be emptied out, all the water, so we were ordered. The ground had to be dry, so that no fish could survive; all that remains is dust. We did as we were ordered: and at the end of the night we come back to our cave to spend the hours of daylight.

'Bulletproof,' he said. 'I've tested it. Maybe not at ten metres, but I'm sure we'll find out. What I have checked is that it can stop a burst of machine-gun fire at fifty metres. A bullet might get through, but it gives me a chance.' The driver tapped the piece of sheet metal he had screwed to the car door, and the second piece, like a visor, which covered half the windscreen. 'I'd like to have bulletproof windows,' he went on, 'but I'm not a head of state. You can't buy bulletproof glass from ordinary glaziers.'

He had come to fetch Salagnon and his men after two days of ambushes. Salagnon sat in the passenger seat, letting the cool evening breeze pour through the open window. He was caked in sand and dried sweat, which formed white crystals on his face and his faded combat fatigues.

'I'm a coppersmith and I'm very meticulous,' the driver said, not taking his eyes off the road. He needed to keep an eye out for potholes. The truck jolted. What was called a road around here was a track of crudely compacted stones and gravel that is washed away by the summer storms, collapses without warning, and slithers down into the ravine during the long autumn rains.

'And does it help?' Salagnon asked distractedly, staring out at the landscape.

'You see, the driver's seat is a lot more dangerous than the one you're sitting in.'

'You think so?'

'Statistics, Capitaine. More drivers die than parachute officers. The difference is we die in our seats, slumped over a steering wheel in a burning truck. You die out there, your arms flung wide, a bullet in the forehead, staring at the sky.'

'If we're lucky,' Salagnon smiled.

'It's just an image. But in an ambush, they always aim for the driver – that stops the truck and the whole convoy behind; that way they can casually spray the whole lot with a machine gun. But the one who gets the first bullet is me, the guy behind the wheel. Sometimes, when I'm driving, I can feel my head burning because I'm so exposed.'

'Hence the armour-plating?'

'I would have put more on, but I need to be able to see the road. But to hit me now they'll need a high-quality rifle and a sniper with good aim. I'm not such an easy target. I'm not a sitting duck. They'll try and shoot the driver of some other truck. On paper, I survive.'

'You're very meticulous.'

'And a coppersmith. Take a look, it's all hand-made. Ten-gauge galvanized steel fitted together like paper cut-outs. It's a fine piece of work, Capitaine.'

They passed Chambol, standing on the bonnet of his parked jeep. He was holding on to the windscreen, gazing at the village down the hill. The slanted afternoon light sculpted his face, carving it into a mask like a military statue. He stood stock-still.

'What the hell is that idiot doing there?'

Salagnon gave a curt, two-finger salute and the colonel responded with an imperceptible chin jut. Two half-tracks blocked the road and the entrance to the village. A few young soldiers stood around, steel helmets lopsided, holding their rifles like brooms, childlike in their overlarge uniforms. The sun grazed the horizon; the dust that hung in the air caught coppery reflections; the youthful faces of the soldiers radiated confusion. They stood where they were planted; they didn't know what to do. Salagnon climbed down from the truck. The viscid evening air warmed by a low sun made him blink; he heard flies. They droned in the thick amber in which they were all stuck;

the soldiers clumsily clutching their rifles, standing rigid and silent. The gunners on the half-tracks had their fingers on the stocks of the machine guns; they were staring straight ahead of them and did not move. He heard a scream; a scream in a French that stretched the vocal cords to braking point. He could not make out the words. Several bodies lay on the scree between the houses. It was from here the drone of flies was coming. The mud wall above them was peppered with random holes; the machine-gun bullets passed straight through with no problem, gouging out lumps of mud. A sergeant was screaming at an Arab lying on the ground, an old man paralysed with fear, mumbling through his toothless gums. Several soldiers stood, watching the scene, like spectators; some had their hands in their pockets; not one said a word or dared to make a move. The sergeant kicked wildly at the old man, shrieking louder than his vocal cords could manage. Eventually, Salagnon understood what he was saying.

'Where is he? Where is he?'

'*Sergent*, are you looking for something?'

The sergeant stood up, his eyes glittering, the corners of his mouth flecked with foam from screaming without stopping to catch his breath.

'I'm looking for the bastard who gave us the false information. I lost four of my men in that ambush, four kids, and I want to find that bastard.'

'Does he know anything?'

'They all know. But they won't say. They shield each other. But I'll find him. He'll tell me. That bastard will pay. If I have to burn down the whole village to make him pay, I'll do it. They have to be taught. We can't let anything slide.'

'Leave the old man. He doesn't know anything. He doesn't even understand your questions.'

'He doesn't know anything? In that case, you're right, let's stop this right now.'

He took his regulation-issue pistol from its holster and, with a single movement, aimed it at the old man and fired. Blood from his shattered skull spattered the shoes of the soldier standing closest, who recoiled, eyes wide, and the fingers gripping his rifle tightened; a gunshot rang out, the bullet boring into the dirt, raising a cloud of dust, rattling him, and he blushed as though caught out and muttered an apology. Salagnon took a step forwards. The sergeant watched him approach. He reeked of alcohol. Salagnon punched him under the chin. The sergeant crumpled to the ground and stopped moving.

'Clear the road. Roll these gun trucks on to the verge.'

The half-tracks complied in a haze of diesel smoke. The soldiers stepped aside. Salagnon climbed back into his truck. They drove slowly through the village, avoiding the potholes and the large stones scattered across the road. The constant whine of the flies joined the whine of their engines. The sergeant was still lying on the ground. The bewildered rookies stood, frozen, rifles pointing at the earth, blinking into the late afternoon sun. The corpses sank into the shadows.

'Just a bit of tidying up to do,' muttered Salagnon. 'They'll be fine without us.'

'They don't seem too smart,' said the driver.

'They're asked to do appalling things. They're trained by arseholes, led by a colonel from a third-rate comedy, and all for nothing in particular. They'll hate us for this. They'll hate us for a long time.'

In 1958 The Novelist once again became head of state. He was an *écrivain militaire*, of the sort that might have existed during the Empire or the *Grand Siècle*; the sort to scrawl great battle lines in red pencil on a map, to juggle mistresses in every barracks town, to get to know his army on campaign as he might a pack of hounds; the sort who is ostensibly obedient to his prince, yet in the field heeds no opinion but his own; the sort who writes brilliant letters on the eve of battle and heavy tomes of memoirs late in life. But the man who returned as head of state never presided over a war, never flaunted a mistress and never found a prince he could obey.

In 1958 the army placed The Novelist at the apex of the state, where there is room for only one man. It is strange to think that in a position designed for a prince, they placed a soldier. It is strange that they were devoted to a soldier who did not fight, whose only extravagance was verbal, who relentlessly created himself through an extraordinary literary brilliance. His towering oeuvre is not entirely contained within his books; it is most marked in his orations, like so many dramatic monologues; in speeches like prophecies and in epigrams cited in a welter of anecdotes, most of them apocryphal, since he would not have had time to say them all, but which nonetheless form part of the oeuvre. He had spirit, this great general with no troops who marshalled only words; he had a romantic spirit, one he breathed into his books and into the minds of those who read them. The spirit of the French people was The Novelist's masterpiece: he rewrote them; the French people were his great novel. It is still read to this day. He had spirit, which is the French manner of using language, with him, and against him.

The military men, ill at ease with the pen, made him head of state; he was entrusted with writing History. He had already written the first volume: he was asked to write the sequel. In this novel featuring fifty million characters he was to be the omniscient narrator. Reality would be entirely composed of what he said; what he left unsaid would not exist; what he slyly hinted at would come to pass. People ascribed to him the omnipotence of the creating Word. With him they had the little-known relationship that the characters in a novel have with their author. Most of the time they are silent, they are merely the words of the other, they have no autonomy. The narrator alone is entrusted with the word. He tells the truth. He dictates the criteria for truth. He gives the impression of truth and everything else, everything that resides outside the categories of his narration is nothing but noises, moans, eructations and rumblings destined to go unheard. The characters are haunted with pain at amounting to so little that they die noisily, torn apart.

From the helicopter they could see the Commandos de Chasse scouring the countryside. He watched them march in long lines through the wastes of the forbidden zone. Atop the pale rocks he saw the dotted line of dark figures, weighed down by heavy kitbags, canteens of water, guns slung over their shoulders. They criss-crossed the zone, letting nothing through, tracking the remnants of the beaten *katibas*, searching out and killing small groups of starving men with Czech rifles who marched through the night and spent their days in caves. The Commandos de Chasse marched a lot and much of the time they found nothing, but their muscles became thick cables, their skin became bronzed, their souls became impervious to blood, their minds could identity the enemy by his face, his name, the timbre of his voice. Salagnon flew over the area in a helicopter. He set down at just the right point when a sledgehammer blow was needed to break down the barriers. With his men of noble presence they formed a mighty force. They stormed caves and intercepted a powerful unit led by officers trained in Eastern Europe. 'We're the shock troops,' Trambassac would say to the other officers, whom he treated like old fogeys. 'We take the fight to them. We take it to them and we win.' They moved out in fleets of helicopters. They were victorious, always victorious; they came back in trucks. And nothing changed. They decimated the countryside; a good part of the population was rounded up into camps; after every operation they publicly displayed the corpses of the slaughtered rebels; they kept a count, and nothing changed. In Algiers, a general hostility sapped the strength of French Algeria. Tactical terror spread fear as a fine powder that blanched everything, a lingering smell it was impossible to escape, like industrial waste, like pollution, like the oily smoke belched by factories, so pervasive it impregnated the sky, the earth, the bodies. Salagnon and his men continued to strike hard, here and there. Nothing changed. Fear pervaded the very stones they walked on, the air they breathed, leaving a dusty film over skin and soul, thickening the blood, obstructing the heart. They died of congestion, of hypercoagulation, of general circulatory failure.

'There is no way for this to end. There are no Arabs left for me to interrogate,' he would say. 'They're dead, on the run, or they say nothing and disapprove and they look at me with fear. They don't answer when I speak. They shun me. Walking down the street, I feel like a stone in the middle of a river. The water avoids me, washes around me, it scarcely dampens me, it goes on flowing without me, and the stone that I am is dying for want of being saturated, dying because it is impermeable, because it can see the water flowing all around, paying it no heed. I'm nothing but a stone, Victorien, I am as wretched as a stone.'

'He says he knows you,' said Mariani.

He recognized Brioude, despite the black eye, his swollen face, the dishevelled clothes that were stained down the front, the ripped collar with one button dangling from a thread about to fall; he recognized him, Brioude, sitting on the ground, leaning against the wall, a little slumped, his hands tied behind his back. A young Arab next to him, in exactly the same state, curiously had a small silver cross pinned to the lapel of his frayed jacket.

'Father Brioude,' Mariani went on, 'a Catholic priest, that much is definite, and a war veteran, or so he claims. The other guy calls himself Sébastien Bouali and says he's a seminarian.'

'Lebanese?'

'Algerian Muslim. Converted. It's a bit too pat.'

When Mariani sent for him, Salagnon went down to the 'fridge', the stark cellar in the basement of the Moorish villa where prisoners were kept waiting. Sometimes a few hours in the 'fridge' was all it took, since they could hear the screams through the walls, could smell the stagnant, musty stench; they could see the heavyset men stride past, their shirts unbuttoned, but could never manage to catch their eyes, sunken deeply in their sockets like wells in the dim light. Putting them in the fridge was sometimes enough to reduce them to a terrified jelly; and sometimes not. In which case they were taken to one of the other cellars in the basement of the Moorish villa, one where they would be bombarded with questions until they talked or until they died.

'What the hell are you doing here?'

'Helping, my friend, I'm helping.'

'Do you even know who you're helping, Father?' asked Mariani curtly.

'Of course, my son,' he said, a sardonic smile tugging at his thin lips.

'You're helping cut-throats, terrorists who set bombs off in the street to kill at random. You know who the FLN are?'

'I know.'

'So how can a Frenchman like you support them? And even sympathize with them? If you were a Communist, I might understand, but a priest!'

'I know who they are. A monstrous hotchpotch that we ourselves created. But whoever they are, the Algerians are right to want to throw us out of their country.'

'The Algerians are French, and this is part of France.'

Salagnon straightened up.

'What did he do?'

'I don't know yet. He's suspected of being a liaison officer for the FLN.'

'Let it go.'

'Are you joking? We've got him. We're not going to let him go. He can give us a lot of information.'

'Forget it. Send him and whatever he knows back to France, unharmed. I'm sure it's not much. He's been rattled enough as it is. He fought with me during the war. Let's not tear each other apart.'

Brioude was helped to his feet, the handcuffs were removed and he rubbed his swollen wrists.

'What about him?'

The three men standing glanced at the young Arab leaning against the wall, who looked up at them in silence.

'The Christian name and the little crucifix, is it a front?'

'He is genuinely Catholic. He was baptized. He chose this name when he was christened, because he was originally named after the Prophet and wanted to keep Him out of this. He converted in order to become a priest. He wants to know God and he found Islamic studies mindless. Forty boys sitting around reciting the Koran without understanding a word, in front of some fanatic who whacks them with a stick at the slightest mistake; it only leads to submission, but submission to the stick, not to God. He decided that Love and Incarnation were closer to what he felt. He is not a Muslim any more, he is a Catholic. I'll vouch for him. You can untie him and send him back to France with me.'

'He'll stay here with us.'

'He doesn't know anything.'

'We'll find that out for ourselves.'

'I've told you, he's not Muslim! There's nothing now standing in the way of him being a Frenchman like you and me.'

'You don't really understand Algeria, Father. He will always be a Muslim, and a French subject, not a citizen. Arab, native, if you prefer.'

'He has converted.'

'You do not stop being a Muslim by converting. Let him be Catholic if he wants, that's his business, but he's still a Muslim. It's not an adjective. People cannot change their nature.'

'Religion is not a "nature"!'

'It is in Algeria. And nature confers rights and reserves them.'

The young man hunkered against the wall did not move, did not protest. He followed the conversation with a sad, dejected air. Terror would come later.

'Come on, Father, they know what they're doing. What they say may be absurd, but in this case, they're right.'

*　　*　　*

'This is a war of *capitaines*,' the uncle whispered to him.

The brushwood tossed on to the fire quickly blazed, illuminating them all. He no longer even noticed the uniform; his life was spent with people in uniform. He saw only the faces and the hands of his companions, the faces bare and shorn of hair, the hands and the fore-arms bare, since they all rolled up their sleeves. The tall flames from the brushwood cast dancing shadows on the faces of the young men around him. He thought about ink. The flames died down. The thick branches and solid roots they had piled up underneath produced a measured, enduring blaze. He could see the stars once more. Wisps of distant breeze brought the scents of aromatic plants and cooling rocks. The air smelled of wide open spaces; they were spending the night in the mountains.

'These are our men. They follow us. We go where we please. We are the *capitaines*. We are the masters of our lives, our deaths. Isn't that what you wanted?'

'Yes.'

The circle of embers warmed their faces. Small blue flames danced over the black branches. The thick wood burned slowly, producing a heat that radiated into the darkness.

'Are you with us, Victorien?'

'With you in what sense?'

'Seizing power, killing de Gaulle if necessary, keeping those French territories we have now, preserving what we have fought for. Winning.'

'It's too late. There have been so many deaths. All those we could have questioned are dead.'

'The FLN is not the people. They exist only through terror. We cannot let anything pass. We have to draw them out slowly.'

'I'm tired of all the deaths, and all those still to come.'

'You can't stop now. Not now.'

'They're not wrong to want rid of us.'

'Why should we have to leave? We made Algiers what it is.'

'Yes. But in doing so we created an open wound within ourselves. The colonies are a worm eating away at the République. The work is eating us on this side of the sea and when we go back, when all those who have seen what happened here go back, the colonial rot will cross the sea with us. It needs to be amputated. De Gaulle wants to amputate.'

'To go now, to leave everyone to fend for themselves would be cowardice, Victorien. De Gaulle is nothing more than a living pun. He is France only in the sense of a play on words, an example of French wit. He has decided to break us just when we were about to recover ourselves. Come with us, Victorien, in the name of everything you wanted to be.'

'I don't think this is what I wanted.'

'Do it for Eurydice. If we leave, she will be nothing.'

'I will protect her. By myself.'

The uncle sighed and for a long time he said nothing. 'Have it your way, Victorien.' One by one the men settled down in their military sleeping bags around the glowing embers and fell asleep. Lying on the rocks above, sentries watched over them.

Operations continued for several weeks, then they returned to Algiers. They kept a careful count of the passing days, so as not to become confused, a precise count of the weeks of sunshine like a scalding liquid, scree that smelled of lime kilns, gun battles in the dust, ambushes in the scrubland, restless nights beneath a pitch-black sky with the cold stars all present and correct, gulps of tepid water that tasted of metal and sardines eaten straight from the tin. They went back to Algiers by truck. The men dozed in the back, crammed on to wooden benches. Salagnon sat in the passenger seat, his head lolling against the window. Not all of them were going back; they knew precisely how many of them were missing. They knew how many kilometres they had covered on foot and how many by helicopter; they knew the number of bullets they had fired, the supply corps kept a detailed record. They did not know the precise number of outlaws they had killed. They had killed a lot of men, but they did not quite know who. Rebels, rebel sympathizers, protesters who dared not take up arms and innocent passers-by, they all looked alike. They were all dead. But could those who believed themselves innocent truly be innocent, when they were all alike? If colonialism breeds violence, then they are all colonials by blood. They did not know who they had killed: combatants, certainly, villagers from time to time, shepherds on the roads; they had counted the number of bodies left behind on the scree, in the scrubland, in the villages; to this figure they added the numbers of those they had seen fall, those who had disappeared or been taken away, and that gave the total that they noted down.

Every dead body was an outlaw. All of the dead had something to be ashamed of. Punishment was the mark of guilt.

They headed back to Algiers by truck, taking their time, the drivers for once respecting the speed limit, yielding right of way, trying not to jolt too much, to avoid the potholes, since they were transporting a cargo of men being sent back to rest. They drove slowly through the streets of Algiers, stopping at junctions and traffic lights. The girls of Algiers gave little waves, the kind of girl who has dark hair and deep, dusky eyes; the sort who has vivid red lips, who smiles a lot and chatters, who wears flower-print dresses that sway with her body, revealing her legs at every step. The other girls did not matter. Algiers has a population of one million, only half of whom can speak. The other half learn from childhood to be silent. They cannot speak, because they have not mastered the language that expresses thought, power, force. When they do succeed in learning it, determined to master the language of force at any cost, they are congratulated. And everything they say is scrutinized for the slightest inflection, the tiniest mistake, the smallest impropriety. And it will be found, since, to find fault, one has only to look; it might be simply an unusual modulation. And we smile. We praise them for their command of the language, but still they do not get to have a voice. They still fall short, that much is clear.

The scrutiny is intensified; some fault will be found. In their bodies, in their souls, in their faces, in the timbre of their voices. We commend them on their fluency, but still they will not truly have a voice. It is never-ending. We need something we can be proud of having done together, Salagnon was thinking. Something good. These are childish words, but we only really respond to childish words.

We can be proud of refusing to bend. This is what we will tell, the reflex that allowed us to save face. Over everything else we will draw a veil. And that veil, the shroud thrown over the dead, through which we can still make out the mutilated bodies, will suffocate us. But right now the girls of Algiers, the ones who walk around with flowing hair, coppery legs and brazen eyes, are waving at us; at us, the soldiers in the truck coming back from the mountains, as lean and tanned as shepherds, covered in crystallizing sweat, stained with black blood, unshaven, giving off the smell of hunted animals, of fear endured and overcome, of powder, gun grease and diesel; they give us little waves to which we hardly respond. The others don't count. The paratroopers doze on benches in the back of the truck, their heads lolling on their neighbour's shoulders, their legs spread, their well-oiled weapons lying at their feet. They did not all come back. They are what they appear to be: boys of nineteen crowded together. One of them is driving. Salagnon, who has long since passed that age, is in the cab, giving directions. He tells them where to go. They blindly follow.

The big GMC trucks could not negotiate the narrow, stepped streets of the Casbah. If they could, they would have driven through the Arab quarter, engines roaring, spewing diesel fumes, since nowhere should be a no-go area: in this war such things had to be shown, these people had to be shown. But the wide-wheeled trucks could not drive through these steep streets, so they circumnavigated this neighbourhood of whitewashed houses teeming with men, swarming like an anthill, taking the rue Randon and the rue Marengo through Bab El Oued, before turning uphill.

The trucks slowed. Pedestrians were walking down the middle of the street. There were so many. It's them! Salagnon said to himself. Snapping awake, he sat up in the passenger seat. Them! The idiocy of this exclamation appealed to him: it was that simple. The men in the back sat up, too, suddenly alert, like hounds scenting a trail. *Them*. The trucks slowed to a crawl in the crowded street, brushing against passers-by, who did not look at them, their eyes being level with the huge, dusty wheels of the GMCs, but scrabbled to make sure their feet were not run over. Them. There are so many, he thought. They are a river and we are the impermeable stones. They are so many they will engulf us.

Shattered after weeks of operations in the mountains, lulled for hours by the gently rumble of the convoy, as they came into Algiers Salagnon suffered an attack of demographic phobia. Brought on by the crowd, perhaps, the narrowness of the streets, by intoxication from the black fumes of the GMCs in such a confined space, perhaps. Demographic phobia manifested itself by a sudden revulsion at the numerical reality of fertility. To be repulsed by a number is a form of madness, but when it comes to race, everything is madness. Measurement is madness.

The Arabs did not look up, did not look away, did not look at them; they are rejecting us, thought Salagnon. They are simply waiting for us to leave. And we will have to leave or break them all, and that is something we cannot do. Eight to one, and so many children. A vast river in which we are a few large rocks. Water always gets its way. One day or another we will leave, because of their patience, their endurance.

Them and us; seeing us without looking. Them down there, us up here in the big trucks, never face to face, all of us looking at something else, and yet constantly in close contact. We are all the more *us*, all the more determinedly us, because they are them; and they are all the more *them*, because they reject *us*. I have not known a single one of them in the time I've been here, thought Salagnon. Not one have I spoken to without expecting the answer I wanted to hear; not one has spoken to me without trembling at what I might do. I have never spoken to one of them, and it is not an issue of language. I have used French to silence them. I ask the questions; their answers are constrained. Between us, language was barbed wire and, for dozens of years to come, when the words used then are said again, their very sound will be electrocuting. Uttering the words will send the jaw into a galvanic spasm; it will be impossible to speak.

But Salagnon saw their faces as they brushed past the truck, moving at a snail's pace; having painted so many, he knew how to read faces. They are rejecting us, he thought, I can see it, they are waiting for us to leave. They are proud to be rejecting us, together, resolutely. We will leave one day, because of what they suffer together and are proud to endure. We pretend not to understand what is happening. Were we to admit that we are like them, we would understand immediately. We share the same desires, even the values of the FLN are French and are expressed in French. The orders, the accounts, the reports, all the blood-soaked documents taken from dead officers are written in French. The Mediterranean gleaming in the sun is a mirror. On one side and the other, we are flickering reflections of each other, and separation is unbearably painful and bloody; like close-knit brothers, we kill one another over trivial squabbles. The most extreme violence is a reflexive action when faced with slightly distorted mirrors.

The truck at the head of the convoy stopped, the crowd was clotting in the street below the Arab quarter; it stopped moving. The engine growled; the deep powerful note of the horn rang out and slowly people stepped aside, slowly because they were shoulder to shoulder. They are so many they will engulf us, thought Salagnon, eight to one and so many children. The French government does not want to give them the right to vote, because it would mean a hundred *députés* being sent from here to the Assemblée Nationale. The Europeans here do not favour equality, because they would be overwhelmed. Eight against, and so many children.

We have the power. Give us a lever and a fulcrum and we will move the Earth. The fulcrum, in this case, is one little word: 'them'. With 'them' we can use that force. Each in this looking-glass war, this war in a hall of mirrors; everyone is leaning on everyone else. 'Us' is defined by 'them'; without them, we do not exist. 'They' are defined by us; without us, they would not exist. Everyone has a vested interest in our having nothing in common. They are different. Different how? In language, in religion? Language? The natural state of humanity is to speak at least two. Religion? Is it so important? For them, yes; according to us. The other is always irrational; a fanatics exists, it is always *him*.

Islam separates us. But who believes in it? Who believes in religion? It is like borders in the jungle that were set down on a map at some point and everyone agrees not to change, and eventually we come to think of them as natural boundaries. France considers Islam to be a species barrier, a natural barrier that divides citizens from subjects. There is nothing in the République that justifies citizens and subjects living in the same territory. Religion supplies the justification, as though it were an innate, infectious characteristic of certain individuals, which for ever renders them unfit for democratic citizenship.

The FLN considers Islam as an almost physical, hereditary characteristic, which renders France and the Colonial Subject incompatible, leaving only one possible future: the full independence of a new nation which is Islamic and speaks only Arabic.

What are we afraid of? Of the power of the other, of loss of control, of the battle of fecundities. We apply leverage to the little word 'them', one we cling to above all others. Islam occupies the whole landscape of a common accord. People who could not care less are compelled to think of nothing else; those who do not wish to think about it are eliminated. Everyone is told to choose a place on one side of the line, a line drawn on paper, which we now accept as a natural boundary. All one would need to do is take away the stone on which the lever is balanced, take away *them* and replace it with a larger *us*. As long as it is a question of *us* and *them*, they are right to want us to leave. For us to stay would mean trampling principles, which we invented and which are fundamental to who we are. It is in us that the tensions are greatest. It is we who are overwhelmed by contradictions. They are tearing us apart inside and we will leave before the pain we are inflicting on them forces them to let go. We will leave, because we carry on using this little word: *them*.

How long will this carry on?

A radiant Eurydice had rented a tiny apartment, a single, sixth-floor room with a balcony overlooking the street. Leaning on the black, wrought-iron railing, she was watching the bustle from above, from far above, a joyful smile playing on her lips. Victorien had just arrived; he was racing up the six flights of stairs and clasping her in his arms. Their pulsing hearts beat in time. He was panting for breath and this made him laugh, a laugh punctuated with wheezing breaths, despite the fact that he was accustomed to running, to marching through the mountains, despite his tireless legs and his stamina. When he had caught his breath sufficiently, so that his mouth was relieved of the task of breathing, they kissed for a long time. She was working as a nurse in Hussein-Dey, working shifts during the day and sometimes at night, when she would come home in the morning and fall asleep to the clamour from the street that crept up the sides of the buildings, slipped over the balcony, through the half-open shutters and lulled her in her bed. Without waking her, he would slip in beside her; as his arms enfolded her, she would open her eyes.

She spent long hours of her erratic schedule staring out the window or gazing at the ceiling above her bed, and finding in this unoccupied time the makings of a boundless happiness. She read Victorien's letters, studied the sketches he sent her, searching in the lines, in the brushstrokes, in all the ink effects the slightest vestige of his slightest gesture. Now she wrote back. He visited irregularly when his armed gang came back to rest, to nurse their wounds, to fill in the gaps, a short spell in the city like a period in dry dock, when they could think of something else before being sent out again. They did not all come back. Salagnon would run up the stairs, sometimes in his neatly pressed leave uniform, clean, freshly shaved, and sometimes still steeped in sweat and dust, his jeep abandoned on the pavement, getting in the way, blocking the whole street, but his appearance and his well-worn uniform meant that, in Algiers, he could do whatever he liked. Sometimes people would even salute as they stepped off the pavement and walked around his jeep. He would have a shower and slip into bed next to her, his dick permanently hard.

'What about your husband?'

'He doesn't care. He spends all his time with his friends. They meet up a lot. He had a screaming match with my father, because he thinks he's spineless. I don't think he even noticed me moving out. He and his friends talk big and play with guns. They garrisoned our apartment. There's no place for me there any more. They want to turn Bab El Oued into a fortress, an impregnable Budapest no one can ever drive them out of. They want to kill the Arabs. As long as I'm not seen in public with you, he doesn't care what I do; and if anyone taunts him, he'll kill them.'

She said this with a strange smile and kissed him.

'He doesn't beat about the bush.'

'Algeria is dying, Victorien. There are too many guns. Everyone wants one. Things people used to think only to themselves or say only in a whisper, they do these things now. You can't imagine how happy I am at the hospital when I have to deal with a ruptured appendix or someone who's fallen off a bicycle and broken their arm, the sort of things other hospitals get to deal with. Because day and night at our hospital we get people with bullet wounds, stab wounds, people suffering burns from explosions. There are armed police in the corridors, army units outside the wards to make sure that no one comes to finish the job, to shoot or kidnap or cut the throats of the patients. I dream of an ordinary epidemic, an outbreak of flu. I dream of being a nurse in peacetime, so I can heal children's cuts and scrapes, comfort old people who are losing their marbles. Take me in your arms, Victorien. Kiss me. Come inside me.'

They clung together for a long time, breathless, drenched in sweat, their eyes closed. From time to time a breath of wind came from the sea, bringing with it the scent of flowers and of grilling meat. Through the half-open shutter they could hear the clamour of the street and sometimes an explosion stirred the muggy air. It did not make them flinch.

His uncle came to fetch him.

'The time has come to decide what you want, Victorien. And what I want is to keep what we have won. We have saved our honour. We must defend it.'

They went to see Trambassac. Groups of armed men prowled the corridors wearing berets of different colours, and when two groups met, they stared hard at each other, not knowing quite what to do. They considered each other's berets, weighed up the stripes and the badges and went on their way, casting suspicious looks over their shoulders, slipping their fingers into the trigger guard of their weapon. It was a generalized coup d'état; everyone was an independent putschist. Trambassac went on sitting behind his desk. He had filed away his reports, cleared out his belonging; all that remained were a few paintings on the walls; otherwise he was ready to move. He was waiting.

'What are you going to do, Colonel?'

'Obey the Government, messieurs.'

'Which one?'

'Whichever it may be. Change the Government and I will continue to comply with orders. But do not count on me to change it. I obey. I was asked to recapture territory for certain reasons; I recaptured. Now I have been asked to relinquish it for other reasons, or perhaps the same reasons, so I relinquish. Command and countermand, march and retreat, that's military routine.'

'We're being asked to give up, Colonel, to give up everything we've won.'

'The military mind does not dwell on details. We are men of action; we act. Undoing is a form of doing. Forward, march! Sound the retreat! I obey. My role is to protect all this.' With a sweeping gesture he took in his uniform, his office and Salagnon's framed portraits on the walls. 'It doesn't matter what I do. I must protect.'

The ink-wash paratroopers stared down like an imperturbable guard of honour; each had a name, several were dead; Trambassac carefully preserved them. 'I protect all this. I'm proud of my men. I obey. Do as you must, messieurs.'

The uncle brusquely got to his feet and stormed out.

'What about you? Victorien?'

'I don't want power.'

'Neither do I. Just respect for what we have achieved. We will prevail. We must prevail. I will prevail. Otherwise I'll never get over this humiliation, which has been going on now for twenty years. And all the dead I carry with me will have died for nothing.'

'I carry my dead, too. Sometimes I think that simply knowing me is fatal. It has gone too far. I have to stop. I should have stopped long ago.'

'To stop now would mean losing everything. Losing everything that came before.'

'It's already lost.'

'Are you with us?'

'Count me out.'

Painting saved his life and his soul. He spent several days doing nothing else. Painting makes it possible to reach that glorious state where language disappears. In the silence of gestures, he was nothing more than what was there. He painted Eurydice. He painted Algiers. He slept in his quarters, so that everyone would know where he was. In the turmoil that followed the coup d'état, he was arrested. Four men in civilian clothes burst into his room, formed a circle around him, so as not to hinder each other and to cover all lines of fire, leaving no blind spots; in a calm but slightly worried voice, they told him to follow them. He got to his feet, making no sudden movements, ensuring his hands were clearly visible; he cleaned his brushes and went with them. His uncle had disappeared, to Spain, he had fled to Spain, he discovered. The men in civvies interrogated him at length, but did not touch him. He was put in solitary confinement. He was allowed to keep a sketchpad and a pencil. He could remain there for a long time, reduced to a blank page the size of a hand.

He was released. Not everyone had been arrested. If they had been, who would guard the prison? He rejoined his battalion, now restructured and given a different name.

The opposing armies swelled. Soldiers like him were no longer the only ones to have guns. Young conscripts who had only just left their families had guns. Uniformed police officers had guns. The various police services had guns. Men in civilian clothes arriving from France had guns. The Europeans of Algiers, baffled and bellicose, had guns. The Arabs, radical and disciplined, had guns. There were sporadic bursts of gunfire every hour. Muffled explosions rattled shop windows. Ambulances careened through the streets of Algiers, taking the wounded to Hussein-Dey. People killed each other in their bedrooms. All operations were suspended. There were no more raids. The important thing was to stay alive. Others fought, set ambushes in cafés, blew up villas, tossed mangled corpses into the sea. Trambassac fretted in his office, his useful tool now useless.

They were sent home. They crossed the sea by boat. Salagnon was posted to Germany. He was back where he had started, he smiled, but what a detour! He was stationed at a base he shared with a tank regiment. The helicopters lined up on the pristine concrete never flew. The huge, brand new houses in Germany served only as places to live in; everything was functional; there was no life in the streets. The permanently overcast sky looked like a canopy of grey canvas swollen with an unbelievable quantity of water, constantly seeping, ready to spill.

When the war ended 'over there', he resigned his commission. There would not be another for a long time and he could not imagine blindly manoeuvring tanks against other tanks. He contacted Mariani. He had resigned his commission and did not know what to do. In July they took a flight to Algiers.

Since they looked like each other – the build, the close-cropped hair, the clear-cut gestures, the wary eyes, the garish shirts worn over their trousers – they looked like secret agents on a secret mission dressed up as secret agents on a secret mission.

On the plane, theirs were the only occupied seats. The stewardess came and chatted with them for a moment, then took off her shoes and lay down on a row of empty seats. No one went to Algiers any more, but the return flight would be jam-packed, people would fight to get aboard. From a distance, high above the sea, they saw the columns of black smoke. As the aeroplane banked to line up with the runway, through the window they watched smoke from the fires rising from the whitewashed streets they knew so well. They each had a small carry-on bag and, under their garish shirts, a pistol tucked into their belts. No one checked their passports; no one checked anything any more; since they looked like twins, with their build and their military bearing, and their rather suspicious little flight bags, everything seemed normal. They were ushered through; people stepped aside as they passed; some saluted – the soldiers, the police officers armed to the teeth, the civilian officers. The air terminals were crowded with families slumped over piles of suitcases. Small children, old men, everyone was there, everyone had too much luggage; the men paced up and down, sweating through white shirts that were stained at the armpits; a lot of the women were sobbing quietly. They were all Europeans. Arab staff moved through the crowd, cleaning, servicing, carrying luggage, doing their best not to bump into anyone, careful to watch where they stepped, constantly followed by hateful stares. The Europeans of Algiers were waiting for planes. The planes arrived empty and left almost immediately, ferrying them to France by the hundreds. No one was selling tickets any more. To board a plane required nerve, bribery and threats.

All over the city the walls were marked by gunfire, single bullet holes and huge clusters. The burned-out cafés were boarded up. Most of the shops had rolled down their metal shutters, but some of these had been ripped, twisted and pried open with crowbars. The streets were littered with objects of every kind. Piles of furniture – beds, tables, dressers – were blazing. They saw a man open the door of his car, set a canister of petrol on the front seat and torch it. He watched it burn, although bewildered passers-by, avoiding the debris from the houses, scarcely gave it a glance. A bed tumbled from a window and crashed on to the ground. Almost every scrap of bare wall was daubed with dribbling graffiti: OAS was everywhere. A woman dashed across the street pulling her *haik* tightly around her. A scooter carrying two young men came zigzagging down the road, swerving to avoid the broken glass and the bullet-riddled cars. It came up behind the woman, who, in her haste, was not looking around her; the pillion passenger took out a pistol and shot her twice in the head; she crumpled, her *haik* now soaked in blood, and the two boys carried on weaving down the street on their scooter. People stepped over the dead woman as though she were a piece of rubbish. They saw two other women in the same street, lying in their own blood. A whole family appeared from a building, weighed down with luggage; the short, overweight husband was dragging two suitcases; his wife had bags slung over her shoulders; the four children and the grandmother were carrying as much as they could. The sweating man yelled at them; they stumbled about fifty metres, only to be stopped by young men in white shirts, who gestured for them to go back. There followed an argument, voices were raised, there was much waving of hands; eventually the man picked up his suitcases again and took a step forwards. One of the young men whipped a gun from his belt and killed the little man with a single bullet. 'No one is leaving!' they shouted to any open windows and to the people leaning over balconies, as they walked away. 'Everyone is staying!' And everyone in the street nodded vaguely, bowed their heads and stepped away from the dead man. Mariani and Salagnon did not stop for anything. They drove to Bab El Oued to fetch Eurydice. Her little apartment was empty. They found her at her father's house.

Salomon, utterly frantic, no longer left his house. He had closed the shutters and now lived in semi-darkness; he had screwed metal plates to cover the bottom half of each window. Victorien tapped one with his finger, it rang hollowly.

'Where did you get this, Salomon?'

'They're plates from the gas cooker.'

'You think they'll protect you?'

'Victorien, they're firing guns in the street. They're shooting at people. You can get killed just walking past a window. They don't even know who they're killing. They fire based on what you look like, and round here we all look pretty much alike. I'm protecting myself. I don't want to die by accident.'

'Salomon, a bullet would go through a piece of metal like that and not even notice. You're not protecting yourself, and you can't see a damn thing. All you're doing is putting nails in your own coffin. You have to leave. We're taking you with us.'

As soon as the two men stepped into this murky apartment, which was beginning to smell like a cellar, with their broad shoulders, their precise movements, their wary eyes, a relieved Eurydice slipped into Salagnon's arms.

'I've come to get you,' he whispered in her ear, suddenly overwhelmed by the scent of her hair.

He felt her chin dig into his shoulder as she nodded, but she said nothing: had she opened her mouth to speak, she would have sobbed. A bomb exploded close by, rattling the window panes. Eurydice flinched, but did not open her eyes. Salomon cowered a little more. He was standing in the middle of his home, his eyes closed, frozen.

'Come on, Kaloyannis, let's go,' said Mariani.

'Go where?'

'To France.'

'What do you expect me to do in France?'

'It's the name of the country on your passport. Given that you have to barricade your windows with sheets of metal here, I think it's not your home any more.'

'Let's go, Papa,' said Eurydice.

She went and fetched the suitcases she had already packed. There was a knock at the door. Mariani went to answer it. An excitable man burst into the living room, his white, unbuttoned shirt gleamed in the half-light. He stopped dead in front of Eurydice.

'What are you doing with those suitcases?'

'I'm leaving'

'Who is this guy?' said Mariani.

'Her husband.'

'So you're the one taking her away, Salagnon?' he roared.

He took a gun from his belt, waving it around as he spoke, his finger on the trigger.

'There's no way you're leaving. You – you can go. Go back to France. You weren't capable of killing the *crouilles*, so go home, let us deal with it. Eurydice is my wife. She's staying here. Doctor Kaloyannis might be half-Yid and half-Greek, but this is his country. If he moves, I'll put a bullet in him.'

He was very handsome, Eurydice's husband. He spoke passionately, his thick black hair falling over his forehead, spittle frothing at the corners of his beautiful lips. He aimed his gun as he spoke. 'Kaloyannis, touch that suitcase and I'll shoot you. And you, Salagnon, you pitiful excuse for a paratrooper, you're a traitor, a coward, so you can fuck off, you and the little queer in the flowery shirt, before I get angry. Let us handle this.'

The gun was pointing at Salagnon's head, his finger quivered on the trigger. Mariani raised his hand as though this were target practice and shot him in the back of the skull. Blood sprayed over the steel plate screwed to the window frame and the man crumpled, lifeless.

'You're an idiot, Mariani. The slightest twitch and he would have put a bullet in me.'

'You can't have everything... but all's well that ends well.'

Eurydice bit her lip and followed them. They took Salomon by the shoulder and he came meekly. A bomb shook the air; a plume of white dust rose from the far end of the street. Debris littered the pavement; a shop was ablaze; broken furniture lay waiting to be burned. Several cars, their doors open, their windscreens spidered with cracks, had been overturned; in one of them, the blood-spattered driver was slumped over the steering wheel. An elegantly dressed Arab man was inspecting the Citroën 2CV parked at the kerb.

'Doctor Kaloyannis, so nice to see you.'

He straightened up. The butt of a revolver poked out of his belt. He smiled genially.

'Just the man I've been looking for. I've just bought Ramirez's shop. I didn't pay much, but it was more than they would have got if it had been seized. I was also planning to buy your car.'

They put the suitcases in the boot.

'I want to keep it.'

'He's not selling,' growled Mariani.

'I could simply take it, but I'm offering to pay,' he smiled again.

The gunshots rang out quickly, but in the chaos of the street no one noticed. Mariani had aimed for the chest. The man staggered and fell, the hand emerging from his pocket clutching a few crumpled banknotes.

'Mariani, you can't go round killing everyone.'

'I don't give a shit. I've seen too many dead. Anyone who gets in my way had better get out of it, fast. Now let's go.'

They drove through the crumbling ruins of Algiers, Salagnon at the wheel, Mariani with his elbow jutting out of the window, tapping the grip of his gun. In the back seat Eurydice was holding her father's hand. On the road to the airport they had to stop at a barrier manned by Garde Mobile militiamen. The men's hands never left the butts of the sub-machine guns slung across their chests; they were sweating under their black helmets. Off to one side, a group of Arabs in new uniforms were waiting, sitting on the bonnet of a jeep.

'Who are they?'

'The army of the FLN. We're leaving tonight. They're taking over, and after that no one gets to leave. Actually no one really knows anything. No one cares. Let them sort it out themselves.'

Salomon opened the car door and got out.

'Where are you going, Papa?' Eurydice's voice died in her throat.

'France is too far,' he muttered. 'I want to stay here. I want to live in my own home. I'm going to talk to them.'

He walked over to the FLN officers, said something to them. They struck up a conversation. Salomon became animated. The Arabs grinned broadly. They laid a hand on his shoulder and had him get into the back seat of the jeep; one of them sat next to him. They went on talking, but from the 2CV it was impossible to make out what was said. Salomon looked worried. The Arabs went on smiling, keeping a hand on his shoulder.

'Are you going?' the officer of the Garde Mobile said irritably.

'Eurydice?' Salagnon said, his hands on the steering wheel. He did not turn. He did not look at her. He simply asked, preparing himself for anything.

'Do what you like, Victorien.'

Without looking at her face in the rear-view mirror, trusting to the calmness of her voice, he started the car and drove through the barrier. Cars of all sorts lay abandoned by the side of the road.

The airport was heaving with crowds still pressing to get inside. A line of soldiers cordoned off access to the runway. The two men flanking Eurydice pushed their way through the crowd. People jostled, shouted, waved tickets. The soldiers stood, shoulder to shoulder, blocking their path. Planes took off, one after another. Victorien talked to the officer, whispered a few words in his ear. After a few minutes a jeep appeared. Trambassac got out. They walked through the cordon.

'Not very nice, your last mission, Colonel.'

'I do what I'm ordered, but I can't imagine you painting it.'

'No.'

Space was found for them in a small government aeroplane transporting senior civil servants from the Governor General's office, who had left their office carrying briefcases bulging with documents; they were going home; they had no interest in the new arrivals.

The plane took off, banked over Algiers and headed north. She did not sob, the tears trickled silently down Eurydice's face, as if draining out of her, so Victorien gathered her in his arms. They both closed their eyes and did not open them until they landed.

Mariani could not tear himself away from the window. He stared out at the ruins and the pall of black smoke for as long as he could, cursing the waste. When he could no longer see anything, when they were over the sea, a seething rage prevented him from closing his eyes; and, hovering always in front of him, he could see his fratricidal anger rebuking him. He did not know how to answer.

Commentaries VII

We watched, uncomprehending, the Paseo *of the dead*

Writing is not my forte. I would have liked to show, to paint if necessary, and for that to be enough. But my mediocre artistic talents mean that I ended up a narrator. This will be of no interest to anyone, this account of trifling events, but I stubbornly insisted on retracing in French something of the life of those who speak it. I persisted in recounting the story of a community of people who can speak to one another because they share the same language, but who fail to speak to each other because they stumble over dead words. There are words that are no longer spoken, yet they remain, and we speak with gobbets of blood in our mouths that hinder the movement of our tongues; we feel we might choke and, in the end, we say nothing.

This is one of the banal consequences of violent periods of history: certain common words explode from within, gorged with curdled blood, victims of a thrombosis of meaning. These words that die from their use can no longer be uttered without staining our hands. But since they still exist, we avoid them, we go around them, pretend they aren't there, but it's obvious we're avoiding them; we use circumlocutions and one day we stumble, because we forgot we could not say them. We use these words engorged with blood and they spurt out, spattering everything with the clots they contain, staining the shirts of those listening to us; they shout, they recoil, they protest, we apologize.

We fail to understand each other. We have inadvertently used a dead word that was lying around. We could have avoided using it, but we said it. We want to use it, but we can no longer do so; it is burdened by history and history is blood. It lies there, this word, sick with clotting, sick with the perishing of that which moved within it; still it remains, dangerous, like the threat of a conversational thrombosis.

Writing is not my forte, but I write for him who can tell nothing to anyone, so that he can teach me to paint; and I write for her, too, to tell her what she is, and that what I am writing opens her arms to me.

Writing is not my forte, but, by virtue of necessity and a lack of other means, I force myself to do it when all I want is to paint, to silently point the finger and for that to be enough. It is not enough. I want to go on listening to people talk. I dread that my language will gutter out. I want to hear it. I want to restore my mutilated tongue. I want to find it whole among all those who live through it and make it live, for it is the only country.

Words are lost with the gradual unravelling of empire, and this amounts to losing some of the territories in which we live; it amounts to diminishing the extent of 'us'. There is a decaying part in our language, a diseased tissue of necrotic words whose meaning has clotted. Language, like an apple, rots where it has been bruised. It dates back to the time when French, the language of empire, the language of the Mediterranean, the language of teeming cities, of deserts and jungles, the time when French, from one end of the world to the other, was the international language of interrogation.

I am trying to tell those things about him that he never said. I am trying to tell those things about her that she has never dared imagine. I would have preferred to show; I would have preferred to paint; but we are dealing with language, which courses through us, flows between us and threatens to coagulate, and language cannot be seen. So I narrate, to avoid the calamity that would leave us clotted, paralyzed, quickly putrefied, all of us, both of us, me.

*   *   *

I write for you, my heart. I write so that you will continue to fight me, so that the blood will go on gliding beneath your skin, beneath my skin, in the pliant vessels sheathed in silk. I write to you, my heart, so that nothing will stop, so there will be no lull of breath. In order to write to you, to keep you alive, to keep you supple, warm, flowing, my heart, I must use all the resources of language, all the tremulous, almost hazy verbs, the sum total of nouns like a casket of precious stones, like a huge trunk, each gleaming through every facet worn smooth by use. I need everything in order to write to you, my heart, to create a mirror of words in which you see your reflection, a shifting mirror that I hold between my clasped hands, in which you gaze upon yourself and do not fade away.

I reflect, I fashion a mirror, all that I do is reflection. I examine each detail of your appearance, every epiphanic detail of your body, all of which echo in the reality of the blood beating within you, my heart, of the rhythmic pulse of blood through your vessels encased in silk, resonating in the crimson cave I enter, oh! velvet cave! where I stay, in a swoon.

And most of all I love in you the blending of time, that state of presence which is a perpetual gift to me, these marks which shape you and which are parts of your life, some past, others present, still others yet to come; I love this energy at work like the flow of blood that is the promise that nothing will cease, that later will come, like now, like a perpetual present created for me.

More than anything I love the rough edges of your appearance; they demonstrate that life has been for ever passing and will pass for ever and that in its flow, in its very movement, it is possible. Oh, my heart! You pulse within me like the rhythm of time itself. I love the flesh of those lips that smile when I speak to you, that give and receive those caresses that hands cannot; I love the quivering down of your hair, grey, white, a cloud of swan feathers framing your features. I love the heft of your breasts, which swell slowly like soft clay taking the form of that which contains it; I love the flare of your hips, which gives you the pure, curved almond shape, the curve of two hands pressed together, thumb to thumb, forefinger to forefinger, the precise form of timeworn femininity, the shape of fertility. You are fertile; the Word flourishes all around you; I hear time gliding through you, my heart, time which has no beginning and no end, like blood, like the river, like the word that runs through us all.

That you are my age, my heart, exactly my age, is part of what I love in you. Men of my age strive to dream of something that does not exist, they dream of a still point in the flow of time, of a stone placed in the river, a stone that emerges from the water, one that will never be wet, one that will endure, unmoving, for ever. Men of my age dream of coagulation and death, of everything finally coming to a standstill; they dream of women so young they bear no marks of time and have all eternity before them. But eternity does not move.

You cannot imagine what I have in you. Those fine wrinkles at the corners of your eyes, which you sometimes lament, that you think of hiding and I immediately kiss, offer me the whole span of time. This I owe to Salagnon. I am grateful to him for giving back to me the whole of time, for having taught me – perhaps he did not know it, but he showed me – how to seize it, how to slip into it without creating ripples, how to float peacefully on its irrevocable surface; following the same rhythm, precisely the same rhythm. The mystery, I whisper in your ear. The mystery, I murmur softly, lying next to you. The mystery is that I did not have to fight to attain it. Treasures are guarded, yet I found you without having to fight. 'Because I was waiting for you,' you whispered. And that answer explained everything; it was enough.

I would take her to the cinema; I love the cinema. Of all the ways of telling a story, it is the one that shows the most, the one that is most accessible, since all you need to do is look; the one most common to us all. We see the same films; we see them together; the stories told by cinema are shared between us.

I would take her to the cinema, holding her hand. We would sit in the huge, red plush seats and together we would look up towards those vast, luminous faces that spoke for us. In a cinema we are silent. Cinema recounts invented stories that are played out in bright light, while we sit, barely moving, dark forms in neat rows, open-mouthed before these huge, dazzling faces that speak.

The stories are captivating, but there are too many, and gradually we forget them. It serves no purpose to collect more. We might wonder why we press inside, why we come to see, again and again, these fabricated stories. But on the other hand, cinema is a process of recording.

The camera, the little chamber, captures and preserves the image played out before it. In twentieth-century films, sets had to be built and actors found to play out these scenes. What was filmed, misrepresented as fiction, had actually existed. And so, in the cinema, our eyes wide, gazing up in hushed silence, we watched, enlarged, in dazzling light, the dead in their eternal youth, places long since vanished reappear, cities now destroyed rise up again and faces whisper their love to other faces that now are dust.

Cinema will change. It will become a minor subdivision of comics. It will require no real locations, no living faces. Film-makers will paint directly on the screen. The story itself will be played out on the screen, but when that comes it will no longer concern us. I am passionately interested in the beginnings of the technology, this story machine that was a contemporary of the steam train, the internal combustion engine, telephones, this physical machine that made it necessary for people to play out scenes in actual locations; and what we were seeing on the luminous screen, the only light in the darkness apart from our rows of shining eyes, apart from the green box indicating the emergency exit, what we were watching had actually taken place. The screen we stared at in silence was a window on to a vanished past, an open window in the wall of time that closes as soon as the houselights come up. Peering through this window, forbidden to go outside, sitting in rows in the darkness, we watched, uncomprehending, the *paseo* of the dead.

I would take her, she trusted me to choose. I had lived so long with the magic lantern that I knew what would give us the most pleasure. And so I went with her to see Gillo Pontecorvo's *The Battle of Algiers*.

The film was legendary, because nobody had seen it. It had been banned; people talked about it in hushed whispers; it was a left-wing legend. 'A magnificent film,' it was said. 'Magnificent because of the people, the actors, some of whom were real protagonists... There is almost no restaging... You have a real feeling of being there... It is a great film that has long been banned... in France, of course,' so it was said.

When it was finally possible to see the film, I wanted to take her. I explained it to her. 'This old guy I'm seeing, he's teaching me to paint. In exchange, he talked to me about the war.' 'Which war?' 'The one that lasted twenty years. He was there from start to finish, so I'd like to see this movie everyone is talking about; I want to see what they filmed, so I can understand what he's been telling me.'

We finally saw this left-wing legend, this film that had been banned for so long, written by the military chief of the Autonomous Zone of Algiers, who played himself. I saw the film. I was surprised that anyone had ever felt the need to ban it. Everyone knows about the violence. Everyone knows that when Faulques and Graziani said that they got information with a couple of slaps, it was a lie. Everyone knows that 'a couple of slaps' is a piece of metonymy, the visible part one can admit of the dark mass of cruelty and torture that is passed over in silence. We know all this. The film evokes it, but does not linger on it. Torture is a long and demanding technique that is ill-suited to the demands of cinema. The paratroopers interrogating suspects are doing their jobs. They are hunting information in the body where it is hiding, without sadism, without racism; the film shows no excesses. They track down the members of the FLN, find them and arrest or kill them. These military operatives feel no hatred. Their professionalism may be frightening, but they are waging a war and trying to win it; in the end, they lose.

The Algerians, for their part, have the nobility of a Soviet people; each one of them on the film is a Marxist exemplum, filmed by the director as he might a sculpture. He shows close-ups of the people in the street scenes, nameless individuals in the midst of a crowd of their fellow men, joyous when necessary, angry when appropriate, always dignified, and each of these portraits hints at how we should feel when they appear.

The film has an admirable clarity. The Algerian heroes die, but the anonymous people will replace them; the unrest on the streets is irrepressible; the technicians of war are powerless against the direction of history. The film will be shown to all Algerian children; they will learn about their heroic struggle; they will be proud to belong to this tenacious people; they will wish to be like the handsome portraits of people in the crowd, in the grainy black and white of left-wing fictions that try to pass for documentaries. Colonel Mathieu – it is obvious who he is meant to be – is remarkably intelligent. Without a trace of hatred, he conceives and carries out the perfect plan. Yacef Saadi is the epitome of swaggering heroism. Ali La Pointe, the killer, has the romanticism of the lumpenproletariat, and he dies in the end, because no one knows what to do with him – he is provisional. Everything is neatly tied up, everything is clear, nothing is unresolved. I had no trouble understanding this film. No one is bad, but there is a sense of history that cannot be defied. I could not understand why anyone thought it should be banned. The reality was much more sordid.

It was much more sordid than the film dared to show. The FLN cut off noses, lips and balls with secateurs; the paratroopers electrocuted men fouled with their own shit, their feet drenched in their piss. Everyone was fair game: the guilty, the suspect, the innocent. But there were no innocents, there were only actions. The meat-grinder ground people up without asking their names. People killed mechanically; they died by accident. Race, the rough-and-ready attribution to a group, as read in people's faces, brought death. People betrayed, they liquidated, they did not really know who belonged to what, they were murdered on the strength of physical resemblance; duplicity was the indefatigable engine that powered the war, a combustion engine, an electrical engine, wedded to a violence we strive not to depict.

But let us forget that. Now is the peace of the brave. Trinquier the paranoiac and Saadi the ham actor can chat together on television. The people united will never be defeated. Everything is clear in Gillo Pontecorvo's *The Battle of Algiers*. But I found it strange, this simple film. Something intangible in the locations left me with an uneasy feeling I did not understand. I knew that it had been filmed in Algiers itself, using the people who lived there, those who are now call Algerians. The locations seemed empty to me. The Europeans stood on the balconies like puppets in a toy castle. The stadium we see during one of the terrorist attacks is filmed in a tight medium shot, like scenes in historical films, where the cameraman is trying to avoid electric wire and passing aeroplanes. A jeep filled with soldiers marches down an empty street, its doors closed, its shops closed, with a handful of Europeans planted on balconies like geraniums, a scant few, standing stiffly. The setting for this simple screenplay caused a nagging disquiet of which I was barely conscious. I did not really think about it; then finally I saw the tanks.

I say 'tanks', but there was only one, surrounded by officers from the Garde Mobile at the hairpin bend above Climat de France. It alone represented *the tanks*, which in left-wing mythology represent the forces of law and order, the subjugation of the people. In the final scenes of Gillo Pontecorvo's *The Battle of Algiers*, we see the repressive engine of the proto-fascist French state trying to bring the Algerian people to heel – I have avoided adding 'progressive' to 'people', it would be redundant – and failing, despite its immense technical resources. The vitality of the people triumphs over the repressive machinery of state. Beneath the walls of Climat de France, between the black-clad officers of the Garde Mobile, a tank appears. I burst out laughing.

I was the only one to laugh and, sitting next to me, she was shocked, but I squeezed her hand with so much love that she smiled in turn and snuggled closer to me.

I recognized the tank that had just appeared at the bend in the road above Climat de France. As a child I read the *Encyclopédie Larousse*, the illustrated version with colour plates, and my favourite parts were the 'Uniforms' page, the 'Aeroplanes' page and the one on 'Armoured Vehicles'. The tank on the screen was not French, but Russian. It was an ISU-122, a heavy-armoured vehicle, a tank-hunter. It's recognizable by the low gun barrel set into a fixed turret with a hull that looked like a pair of hunched shoulders, and the canisters at the back used for storing I don't know what – maybe nothing. I know about armoured vehicles. I used to doodle them in the margins of my copybooks at school; and I had drawn this one, with its low canon and its rear tanks. Pontecorvo had filmed on location in Algiers, with the people who lived there. In the left-wing legend, this was proof of authenticity. But shooting a movie set in 1956 in Algiers in 1965 is a lie. By 1965 the city of 1956 no longer existed. Where would you find Europeans in Algiers in 1965? They would have had to be shipped back from God knows where and positioned on the balconies like so many potted plants; and the stadium shot would have to be carefully framed, because it would be impossible to fill. The only way to film in the European quarter in 1965 was to evict its current inhabitants, to close the shops that had been abandoned in 1962 and hope no one would notice; to blockade the streets so that the crowds of new inhabitants would not be seen. Where could you find paratroopers and Garde Civile officers in 1965, except by dressing up Algerian soldiers and policemen? How could you find a French tank in Algiers in 1965, except by using one of the ALN tanks supplied by the Soviet Union and hope no one would recognize it? There were lots of those tanks in the streets of Algiers in 1965 after the ALN seized power. The army was there with its troops and its tanks, all that was needed was to dress them up to shoot the film.

Pontecorvo was in Algiers in 1965, the official film-maker of the coup d'état. He was a vile human being, film-makers understood this. Several years before he had used a tracking shot in a different film that became a moral issue. He had set up the tracking shot to begin at the moment when a young girl in a concentration camp commits suicide, throwing herself on to the barbed-wire fence, and at the moment of the electric shock, at the moment of her fictional death on the fictional electrified barbed wire, he used a travelling shot to reframe it as a tableau of suffering. Leaving aside the fact that the act was improbable, according to inmates of the camps, there are moral rules in film-making. The man who decides at this moment to make a forward tracking shot to reframe the dead body, this man is worthy of the most profound contempt.

At the moment the coup d'état took place, Pontecorvo was packaging history and handing the military republic of Algeria the basis for its myth. *The Battle of Algiers* is the official film of the Évian Accords: the treaty between the two politico-military systems, the one leaving and the one replacing it. Saadi, the murderer of passers-by, and Trinquier, the electrocuter general, signed the peace of the brave. In a confused free-for-all in which so many adversaries were battling it out – three, six, twelve – these two alone had the last word. They divided up the spoils and made the others disappear. This was the unease I felt, I finally realized: the European quarter of Algiers was deserted, too deserted for a Mediterranean city. It had just been emptied. Those who lived there had just been obliterated.

Trinquier and Saadi can chat like old comrades; they have a tacit agreement to speak only of a single Algerian people, a united people, radiant in their new-found identity, a people that does not exist; they came to an agreement to say nothing about the *pieds noirs* evacuated in the space of a few weeks. They were an embarrassment; their very existence was uncomfortable; they were denied the right to History. When empires are transformed into nations it is important to erase those for whom there is no sense of belonging.

These, then, are the only bad guys in the film, the people we never see in close-up, those we see only from a distance, who are loudmouths, racists, lynchers of children, lynchers of old men, yelping, cowardly mutts who no longer have the right to exist. They are wrong simply to exist, the film maintains, history has left them by the wayside, abandoned corpses already beginning to rot. The tank that climbs the hill at Climat de France concludes the history, and the fact it is camouflaged shows what is happening. The fake French tank which is a real Soviet tank surrounded by extras dressed as French soldiers, who are actually Algerian soldiers oppressing genuine Algerians playing Algerians. But they are the true oppressed. Parked in the surrounding streets are the tanks of the ALN; they control the capital; they have seized power. This image, the tank at the bend in the road above Climat de France, could be used as a still and blown up into a poster bearing the slogan: *The Tomb for the whole of the Algerian People*. The Algerian people who had been either slaughtered or subjugated, twice in the same image. The Armée des frontières was seizing power; Gillo Pontecorvo was filming *The Battle of Algiers* in the deserted city; they were writing history. In this war which went so far as to divide individuals in their inmost self, in which betrayal was the driving force, two parties spoke clearly on behalf of all: one for France, the other for Algeria. And that is lying.

Cinema is a fiction; it is also a means of recording. The tanks had been there, the deserted streets had been there, the crowd of costumed extras had been there: reality was fixed on to the light-sensitive film and there it remained. When the screen went dark and the murmuring cinema was once again bright, when the lights were inverted, I jumped to my feet, rigid and furious; and she was worried by my anger, since she did not understand the cause. I would have liked to explain why a single image had riled me so, but I didn't know how to say it in a few words. I would have had to start by explaining about the illustrated Grand Larousse, how I knew so much about tanks because of my hobbies as a kid, and then tell her Salagnon's life story as he had told it to me and as I had understood it, and explain what has been going on in this country for the past forty years. People were leaving the cinema looking excited. They felt they had just seen a banned film, one that must be telling the truth since people had tried to suppress it. It's likely that no one there saw the lie on the screen, because no one there knew anything about tanks.

She walked beside me, silent and self-confident. We left the cinema and stepped out into the mid-afternoon roar and the heat of the pedestrianized street, where the crowds flowed in both directions. 'I'm taking you to Voracieux,' I said to her. 'You'll get to meet the man who's teaching me to paint.' We took the metro to the end of the line, then the bus. She was sitting next to me, her head on my shoulder; she was curious, but asked no questions. 'He's teaching me to try and paint. I'm not very good, but there's nothing I want more.' She kissed me gently. I thought of the terrible image at the end of the film that caused it to suddenly tip into falsehood, when every detail had been true, that image of the tank at Climat de France, like a slip of the tongue where we try to say what we think is the truth and end up telling the real truth, because of a single stubborn detail it's impossible to hide.

Sitting in his ugly living room, I explained the situation to Salagnon. He laughed.

'Of course I know what you're talking about. I've been living with a *pied noir* for a long time.'

And he softly stroked the cheek of Eurydice, who was sitting next to him, and she gave a smile so gentle that all the wrinkles that marked her skin of crumpled silk vanished. Leaving only her beautiful, dazzling face. She was no older than that smile: a few seconds.

'There's nothing here, nothing that explains what you lived through. There's not a single trace.'

With a sweeping gesture I took in the oppressive, impersonal decor all around us.

'The absence of traces is the trace.'

'Stop it with the Chinese aphorisms. It's just bullshit to make things seem profound. Be honest.'

'There should be traces, but there are none. I brought back Eurydice. If I want her to stay with me, we can never go back there; never. Otherwise she would be swallowed up by the well of bitterness left by the *pieds noirs* when they came here. I cannot go back, only rescue her from Hell and be with her, and never speak of what went before.'

'What have you done since? Since you've been together?'

'Nothing. Have you never wondered what happens to a man and a woman who meet in an action movie? They do nothing. The film ends, the lights go off, you go home. I made the little garden that you've seen where nothing much grows.'

'You never had children?'

'Not one. When you have lived through such a thing, either you have lots of children or you have none and you think only of yourself. We love each other enough, I think, to think only of ourselves.'

The two of them fell silent; they fell silent together and this was even more intimate than when they spoke together. I did not interrupt.

Through the open door I could see a hallway and, at the far end, a knife hung on the wall, swaying slightly, moved by some breeze, although I could feel nothing and the windows were closed. The battered leather sheath gave off a dark red glow, the colour of raw, undyed leather, the colour of the night that was just drawing in, the colour of a blade eaten away by rust, the colour of crusted blood covering the whole blade. It was impossible to see the blade sheathed in leather, sheathed in rust, sheathed in dried blood, all that was visible was a reddish emanation that swayed at the end of a piece of string hanging from a nail. Blood moves of itself, tirelessly, it gives off a dark glow, a gentle heat that keeps us alive.

'Painting helped me,' he said at length. 'It helped me not to go back. Painting requires me to be here, nothing else; thanks to painting, my life can be content with a sheet of paper. I can teach you the art of the brush if you come to see me again. It is a humble art, adapted to what can be achieved with a human hand, a dense tuft of hair, a drop of water. The art of the brush, if you practise it faithfully, allows you to live without pride. It simply allows you to assure yourself that everything is there, in front of you, and that you have seen correctly. The world exists, and that is enough, even if it is crueller than you could possibly have imagined, and more indifferent.'

He fell silent again. I did not interrupt him. I could hear only our breathing, mine, hers, and the breathing of the two old people sitting facing us, this tall thin man and this woman with her finely furrowed skin, their slightly sibilant, slightly curdled breath, fitful from passing through their battered bronchial tubes, worn thin by years of breath. Sitting beside me, my heart did not say a word. She had been looking at Salagnon, hanging on his every word, staring at the old man who was teaching me something about which I knew nothing and who, in exchange, was teaching me an art I wanted to use with her. The light of evening streamed through the window veiled with muslin. Her bushy hair flecked with white haloed her like a swan's feathers. Her firm lips glistened a deep red; her eyes gave off a glow that to my eyes looked violet; three blood-coloured stigmata at the heart of a cloud of feathers. I do not know what you were thinking just then, my heart; but had you known what I was thinking at that moment, as we all sat motionless, had you known what I was incessantly thinking about you, you would have nestled into my arms and stayed there for ever. I was convinced that through the open door, at the far end of the hallway, the knife in the scabbard hanging from a nail was moving.

Salagnon shifted his position with a grimace. He stretched his leg.

'My hip,' he muttered. 'I get a pain in my hip sometimes. I don't feel a thing for years on end and suddenly it comes back.'

I wanted to ask him what exactly pained him. Perhaps if I asked this man to tell me what torments him, I could heal his wounds. My heart beating, I shifted forwards in the drab, uncomfortable, shabby, velvet armchair. My heart was looming at me; she could sense that I was going to say something to him; she encouraged me with her eyes, her lips, with the three deep red glimmers haloed by swan's feathers. I shifted forwards, but I lowered my eyes, and instinctively I picked up a small, heavy object that was lying on the coffee table. I had seen it there before, in the same little bowl, which was hardly surprising in Salagnon's apartment, where everything was carefully placed with the precision one only sees in catalogues or in a television series. This dense object had always been there. I had never wondered what it was, because we never notice things that are always there. I had shifted forwards, falteringly, to the edge of my chair; it was in front of me, just within reach. I picked it up. It was heavy and compact, a couple of steel plates set into a Bakelite handle. I had never known what it was. That evening, I dared to ask him:

'What is this thing that's always here? A Swiss army knife? A souvenir? I thought you didn't keep anything?'

'Open it up.'

With a little difficulty I opened out the metal sections: a short, sharp, ordinary blade and a weighty awl about the length of a finger extended from the rusty handle.

'It is a Swiss army knife. Only there's no tin opener, no screwdriver, no serrated blade. What do you use it for? Collecting mushrooms?'

He smiled happily.

'You don't know what it is?'

'No.'

'You've never seen anything like it before?'

'Never.'

'It's a break-neck blade, used to kill someone silently, you push the tip of the awl into the small hollow in the nape of the neck, at the base of the skull. A firm shove and it goes in easily. You use your other hand to cover the guy's mouth; he dies instantly, and no one is any the wiser. It was designed for that very purpose; it's the only thing it's good for, killing guards without them crying out. I learned to use it. I taught others to use it. We carried them in our pockets when we were in the jungle. That one's mine.'

He set the object back on the table, careful not to knock it, daring not to close it.

'I'm glad you didn't recognize it.'

'I didn't even know such things existed.'

'We had tools for fighting wars. I come from a world no one understands any more. We killed each other with knives, splattering ourselves with the blood of others, wiping it away without thinking. These days, if someone bleeds, it's you; soldiers have no contact with anyone else's blood. They don't get close to each other, they kill at a distance, they use machines. The days are long gone when we could smell the other, feel the warmth, sense the fear of the other mingle with our own fear as we killed him. These days, I see TV commercials for the army. You can sign up, make a career for yourself; it's a profession aimed at protecting people, saving lives, excelling yourself. The only lives we ever saved were our own; we protected when we could, but mostly we just tried to outrun death. I can finally die if you don't recognize the tools of war. You can't imagine how happy your ignorance makes me.'

I contemplated the object lying open on the table; now I recognized its simple purpose, it was clear from its form.

'My ignorance makes you happy?'

'Yes, it reassures me. It's as though my uncle's prophecy has finally come to pass: we will finally be able to end this. The last time I saw him was in prison. It only lasted a few minutes. I was ushered into his cell; the military guards couldn't bring themselves to look me in the eye as they turned the keys, pushed the doors open. He had been sentenced to death. He was in solitary confinement, but there was the law and there was loyalty. They let me in, so I could see him one last time; they told me to be quick and to never mention the visit to anyone. He missed having his copy of the *Odyssey*. He knew the poem by heart now; he had finally finished learning it, but he would have liked to have it within reach, where it had always been for the past twenty years. There, in the prison, we didn't have much to say to each other about events; a shrug of the shoulders was enough to convey the utter collapse of everything; the only other solution would have required a whole lifetime of recriminations; so he talked to me about the *Odyssey*, about how it ends. The end finds Odysseus and Penelope "Rejoicing in each other, they returned to their bed, the old familiar place they loved so well." And when they have exhausted the pleasure of love, they give themselves over to the pleasure of conversation. But it does not end there. Odysseus must leave again, "must carry a well-planed oar until I come to a people who know nothing of the sea". When finally he comes to a place where the people ask why he is carrying on his shoulder a fan to winnow grain, when he has gone so far that no one recognizes what an oar might be, he can stop, plant the oar in the earth like a tree; only then can he journey home to have a gentle, painless death steal upon him.

'My uncle was sad that he, too, could not live to this end of ease and forgetfulness, when no one recognized the tools of war. At the time, everyone was still killing everyone else. Everyone had learned to kill and waited to be killed. Guns circulated freely in Algiers, everyone had them, everyone used them. Algiers was havoc, a bloody labyrinth; men killed each other in the streets, in the apartments, tortured each other in cellars, dumped bodies into the sea, buried them in gardens. And all those who fled to France had weapons stuffed into their suitcases, bringing home the terrified memory of all the guns they had ever seen. All their lives they would recognize them, they would forget nothing, and it would be a narrow cage around their heart, preventing it from beating. We will find peace only when everyone has forgotten this twenty-year war in which men were taught to trap, to murder, to inflict pain like so many craft skills. My uncle knew he would not see that peace, that he did not have the time. He had finally managed to learn his book by heart, and he knew that this was the end. We said goodbye and I left the cell.

'The following morning my uncle was shot by firing squad for high treason, plotting against the République and the attempted assassination of a head of state. Attempted, the charge specified, because they botched it; they botched everything. I'm still surprised that men who had been so effective in other circumstances could have been so sloppy. In that final uprising, all they managed to do was kill people indiscriminately. They simply aggravated the atmosphere of terror, decided who was guilty more or less at random and gunned them down; they interfered in the politics and their only achievement was the most simplistic, the stupidest political act, the most ridiculous display of strength: kicking a dog, putting a bullet in the first head they saw. In their desperation at the end, people killed passers-by. In return they ensured ignominy, waste, their own death and that of others. The river of time cannot be diverted or even slowed by throwing stones into it; they didn't understand anything.'

He sat up a little, winced, brought a hand to his hip. Eurydice gently ran her slender, liver-spotted hand over his thigh. I had to ask him now. He had taught me to paint, he had told me his story; I knew every modulation of his pain, every timbre of his voice. I had to ask him what it was, this torment that followed him everywhere, this pain that had been boring into his hip for so many years, this nagging wound that no one wants to know about any more in this world in which he was barely alive, in which I would live on.

'Monsieur Salagnon,' I asked finally, 'did you torture?'

She looked at me, my heart, as she sat next to me. She held her breath. At the far end of the hallway, the knife hanging from the nail swayed, glowing a reddish crimson glow that might have been the leather, the dying light or dried blood. Salagnon smiled at me. For him to smile at that moment was the worst possible thing he could do. You were quivering next to me, my heart, your eyes, your lips, three bloodstains in a halo of swan feathers.

'That's not the worst thing we did.'

'What could be worse?' I yelped, my voice sounding shrill.

He shrugged. He spoke to me gently. He was patient.

'Now the war is ended, the war that lasted twenty years and con-sumed my entire life, all people talk about is the torture. They try to find out whether it really happened or they deny it did; they want to know whether reports of it were exaggerated or not; they point the finger at those who carried it out. It's all anyone thinks about. But it's not the issue. It was never the issue.'

'I'm talking to you about torture and you're telling me it's just a detail?'

'I didn't say a detail. I said it was not the worst thing we did.'

'What, then? What was worse?'

'We failed humanity. We carved it into groups when there was no reason to. We created a world in which, judging simply by someone's face, by the way they pronounced a name or spoke the language that was common to us, they could be classed as subject or citizen. Everyone was pigeonholed, a pigeonhole passed down from father to son, one that could be read in a man's face. This was the world we had agreed to defend; there was no atrocity we would not have committed to preserve it. From the moment we accepted the untold violence of colonialism, whether we did this or that was just a matter of scruples. We should never have come; but I came. We all behaved like butchers, every one of us, all twelve antagonists in that terrible war. Everyone was meat to be battered by everyone else. We slashed, we hit out with whatever was to hand until we had reduced the others to a bloody pulp. Sometimes we tried to be chivalrous, but it was never more than a fleeting thought. The fact that the other was evil proved that we were justified; our survival depended on our separateness, on their debasement. And so we distinguished between accents, we laughed at names, we sorted human faces into categories, each assigned with a clear-cut action: arrest, suspicion, elimination. Generally, we made things simple: them and us.'

Salagnon squirmed. He could not bring himself to stop, because he was expressing the realization that had come to him, year on year, one he had never had anyone to whom he could tell it. Not because nobody talks about it – on the contrary, everybody talks about that war, but it just results in a garbled cacophony of bitterness and hatred. The roles of victim and executioner are constantly shifting among the twelve protagonists in that terrible war, and in the social milieu I grew up in, it was accepted without question that Salagnon and his like had been the bad guys. The so-called silence surrounding the twenty-year war was a deafening row, a vicious circle where everyone joined in that went round and round, endlessly avoiding the crux of the problem. If over there was also France, then who were the people living over there? And if they are living here, who are they now? And who are we?

Victorien and Eurydice, between them more than a century old, sat huddled together, frail and wrinkled, two relics of the twentieth century whose breathing we could hear, she and I, she sitting next to me, their slight sibilant breath, like a light wind fluttering paper.

'Colonial rot was eating away at us. We all behaved inhumanly, because the situation was impossible. Only within our armed gangs did we behave with even a shred of the respect that all men owe each other if they are to remain men. We stuck together. There was no humanity, there were only comrades and enemy meat. In taking power, this was what we wanted: to organize France like a Boy Scout camp, one modelled on the bloodthirsty units that roamed the countryside following their *capitaine*. We imagined a republic of comrades who would be feudal and fraternal, who would follow the lead of the most worthy. We considered it egalitarian, logical, thrilling, like those times we spent together in the mountains cleaning our guns by the light of the campfire. We were naive and strong. We mistook a whole coun-try for a gang of boys in their own little world. We were the honour of France at a time when honour was measured by one's capacity to murder, and I don't quite know where it all went.

'We were eagles, but no one knew because we wore camouflage and scrabbled on all fours through scrubland or crouched behind rocks. And our enemies were not equal to us. Not because they lacked courage, but because of their appearance. If they had beaten us, we would have been impressed that these poor little men could beat us; if we defeated them, we would joke about our kill rate and grumble that they were easy prey, these pathetic, poorly armed men in ragtag uniforms lined up in front of us in our battledress. We were eagles, but we were not fortunate enough to be struck like the German eagle, the eagle of the Reich Chancellery, toppled by bombs and shattered on the ground. We were eagles, but we were ensnared, like those gulls whose feathers become matted with oil, and as the black slick spreads over the water, they shrivel and die an ignominious death, where asphyxia vies with absurdity. The spilled blood has clotted over us, giving us a gruesome aspect.

'And yet our honour was saved. We picked ourselves up again, we regained the power we had lost; but afterwards we applied it to causes that were confused and ultimately contemptible. We had the power, we lost it, and we never quite knew where. The country bears us a grudge. In that twenty-year war there were only losers who spitefully snipe at each other. We don't know who we are any more.'

'You're exaggerating, Victorien,' said Eurydice in a tiny voice. 'Life over there was not so bad. There weren't very many wealthy *pieds noirs*, most of us were ordinary folk. We didn't have much to do with the Arabs, but we got along well enough. We lived among ourselves and they lived among us.'

'Eurydice,' I interrupted her, 'do you hear what you're saying?'

'That's not what I meant to say.' She blushed.

'But it is. We always say what we mean to say.'

'Sometimes we make mistakes. Words just come out.'

'The thing is, they were there, like the stone under the sand that makes the car swerve and sends you off the road. You told it like it was, Eurydice: you among yourselves and them among you, constantly, day and night; them, who obsessed you, destroyed you, ruined your lives simply by their presence, because you ruined their lives by your presence, and they had nowhere they could go.'

'You're exaggerating. We got along well.'

'I know. I've heard all the *pieds noirs* say that they got on well with their cleaning lady. I understand what Victorien is saying now, the tragedy of Algeria was not torture, it was "getting along well with your cleaning lady".'

'That's not how I would have put it,' Victorien said, amused, 'but it is what I believe.'

'We could go on talking about colonialism,' I said. 'We could talk about it for years. People pick sides, they bandy words like "abuse" and "injustice". We balance public works against a detailed history of violence. Everyone draws their own conclusion, one that confirms what they thought in the first place: a noble cause that tragically failed or an original sin and an ongoing disgrace. To anyone who challenges their right to exist, those who lived in the colony always say "we all got along well". That's the best they can do: the best that colonialism can achieve is getting on well with the cleaning lady, calling her by her first name – something she would never dare do without prefixing it with "madame". At its best, colonialism allows people to be human, respect-ful, full of finer feelings, to be benevolent to an inferior, coloured people with whom they do not mix. At best, colonialism allows for an entrenched, affectionate paternalism established by the simplest criterion: hereditary resemblance. When people talk about it, they tell us how well they got on with the cleaning woman, how the children adored her, but they always called her by her first name.

'How could it be possible to have three French *départements* with *préfectures* and police stations and schools, three *départements* with war memorials and café terraces with people sipping aperitifs, and shady streets of plane trees with men playing *boules*; how could any expect these three *départements* to function with eight million invisible people trying to keep quiet, so as not to disturb anyone? Eight million shepherds, shoeshine boys and cleaning ladies without a name, a place; eight million pharmacists and lawyers and students with nowhere else to go, who will be the first to encounter violence when the time comes to separate *us* from *them*. Camus, who knew a lot about the subject, offers the perfect image of the Arab: always in the background, never saying anything. He is there wherever you go, and in time he becomes a burden; he haunts you like the spots of light dancing before your eyes, he clouds your vision; in the end, you shoot. In the end, we are condemned because we don't regret what we did; we brushed away the spots with a wave of the hand, but the general contempt is a relief. We did what everyone else longed to do, and now we have to pay, but at least it was done. The violence of colonialism is such that it requires regular human sacrifices to ease the tension that would otherwise destroy us all.'

'I was right to tell you what I did,' said Salagnon.

Eurydice looked at me, her lips trembling. She wanted to answer, but did not quite know what to say. This could be seen as another attack on her right to exist.

'Don't misunderstand me, Eurydice. I hardly know you, but I'm glad that you exist. You are here, and everyone has a right to exist. I think it's tragic that French Algeria disappeared. I don't say "unfair" or "a pity", but "tragic". It existed, it was created, this thing where we lived was created and nothing of it remains. The fact that it was founded on violence, on the injustice of the segregation of races, on a terrible human price paid every day in no way diminishes it, because existence is not a moral category. French Algeria existed; it no longer exists. It is tragic for one million people who were erased from history without being given the right to speak of their grief. It is tragic for the seventy-four *députés* who got up and walked out of the Assemblée never to return, because they no longer have constituencies to represent. It is tragic for the one million Algerians who were living in France – who we referred to as Muslims to distinguish them from real 'Algerians', who were the French living over there – who had their citizenship revoked because another country had been created somewhere else. The names were utterly confusing. We changed the names. Everything became clear. But we never quite knew what we were talking about. Now the young people over here who look like the people over there, to whom we don't grant full citizenship because of their confused heritage, want us to call them Muslims, as we used to over there, to accord them a dignity to replace the one that we deny them. It is utter confusion. War is close. It will relieve us. War reassures, because it is simple.'

'A simplicity I no longer want,' murmured Salagnon.

'So history has to be rewritten, to be willingly rewritten, before it scrawls itself. We could ramble on about de Gaulle, argue over his talents as a writer, express surprise at his ability to use the truthful-lie when he misrepresents things that are problematic or passes over in silence those that might be disturbing; we can smile when he compromises with history in the name of higher values, in the name of novelistic values, in the name of creating characters – first and foremost, himself – we could; but he wrote. His imagination made it possible to live. We could be proud to be among his characters, this was how he created us, to be proud to have been part of what he wrote, even if we suspected that, beyond the pages he allotted us, there existed another world. We need to rewrite now, we need to expand the past. What is the use of brooding over a few seasons in the 1940s? What purpose is served by this idea of a national Catholic identity, by the image of rural villages on a Sunday morning? None, not any more, it has all vanished; we need to expand.

'We were broken by refusing to recognize the humanity of those who were a part of us. We laughed at the fact that we did not dare call what happened in Algeria a "war", but only *"les événements"*. We thought that by finally calling it a "war" we would put an end to the hypocrisy. But to use the word "war" implies we fought a foreign country, when in fact the violence was *between us*. We knew each other so well. It is only possible to kill so efficiently among one's own kind.

'The violence committed in the Empire broke us; the obsessive controls of the nation's borders continue to break us today. We invented the *universal nation*, a rather absurd notion, but marvellous in its absurdity, since people born on the far side of the world could be a part of it. What does it mean to be French? The desire to be French, and the recounting of that desire in French, a tale that hides nothing of what happened, neither the horror nor the life that emerged in spite of it.'

'The desire?' said Salagnon. 'Is that enough?'

'It was enough for you. It's the only thing that connects. And all the black veils that hide it are hateful.'

She looked at me as I was speaking, my heart. I knew she was looking at me all the time that I was speaking, and so, when I had finished, I turned to her slowly and I saw the three bright radiances in a cloud of swan feathers. I saw her eyes shining in the twilight and her full lips smiling at me. I laid my hand on hers as it came to find me, and our two hands, so perfectly matched, clasped each other and did not let go.

At length we got up and said our goodbyes to Victorien and Eurydice, who had welcomed us into their home, and we left. They walked us to the door. They stood at the top of the three steps, beneath the glass canopy flushed red in the evening light. As we crossed their barren garden where nothing grew, they watched us and they smiled, his arm around her shoulder, her head nestling against him. When we came to open the gate, I turned to wave and I saw Eurydice, pressed against his shoulder, smiling and weeping over what had been said.

We went home. We caught a bus heading west. We rode through Voracieux-les-Bredins again, but heading in the right direction, in the urban direction, towards the city centre. In its last moments, the sun dipped at the far end of the avenue, directly in line with this concrete trench lined with cars, lorries and buses, chugging slowly, all stinking, all rumbling, all belching fumes, spewing a vast, coppery cloud that was dirty and hot. Lyon is not very big, but there are a lot of us living here, squeezed into the simmering cauldron of the city in which human currents move like lava flows, spreading through the streets, clustering around the entrances to metro stations, which suck them in in slow, infinitely flexible eddies. We are lucky to have a huge urban melting pot into which everything can blend. People got on and got off the bus, they took *our* mode of transport – a possessive I feel I can use only because we had boarded it a few stops earlier. There are so many of them, so many people, even though Lyon is not very big.

We are so tightly packed in the bus, juddering down the avenue of tarnished copper. We share the same clattering floor, we breath the same warm air, shoulder to shoulder, and in each one of us, in this metal box transporting us, moving at a snail's pace down the avenue towards the sunset, slowly cleaving the dazzling copper cloud, in each of us is a silent tongue that quivers according to the distinctive tones of French. I can understand each one. I grasp the meaning of what they say before identifying the words. We are packed together and I understand them all.

It was hot in the bus heading west, shrouded in clouds of fumes tinted reddish copper by the dying rays of the sun; we were able to sit, my heart, because we had boarded before the others, simmering as we sat in this copper pot, while others got on, got off, taking the same means of transport, all of us in this urban melting pot set on the banks of the Rhône and the Saône; we are lucky that it is positioned here, since from it comes the richness, the infinite richness of the magic cauldron, a cauldron that is never empty and from which we get much more than we put in; in it everything is mingled, everything is remade, we are blended in the precious soup, simmering and changing, ever varied, ever intense, and the spoon that stirs it is the male member. Sex brings us together. It unites us. The veils that we hang to hide this particular truth are hateful.

That should be enough.

I did not take my eyes off you on the journey back; I never tired of the beauty of your face, of the harmonious curves of your body. You were perfectly aware that I was watching you, and you let me, pretending to watch the city flashing past the window, a faint smile playing on your tremulous red lips, constantly about to speak to me, and that smile while I was watching you, in the field of signs, was the equivalent of kissing me endlessly.

When we entered the metro tunnel, the windows looking out on to nothing became mirrors, and I saw myself looking at you in the black mirror that reflected your perfect face framed by white swan feathers, and your eyes, which to me seem violent, and that red mouth that is a source of pleasure, and the splendid arrogance of your nose that is the Mediterranean's gift to the universal beauty of women.

When we were back at her place, she made me tea, green tea that smelled of mint, strong, sweet, as thick as petrol, that instantly boiled through my veins. I wanted to be still closer to her. I wanted to undress her, to paint her, to come with her, and to show, to tell these things. Together. Lying on the cushions she had arranged on a low sofa, we drank this tea that inflamed me. We talked for a long time, but our hearts were beating too loudly for us to really hear what we were saying. She told me that in families that move here from elsewhere, the traces of that elsewhere fade gradually, in stages. The yearning to go back dissolves, then the gestures and the postures that had a sense elsewhere, then language, not so much the words – words linger awhile like stones scattered on the ground, like the rubble of some magnificent building whose blueprints have been lost – not so much the words, but the deep understanding of the language. In the end, among the children and the grandchildren of those who settled here, all that remains is a whiff of vanished scents, a fondness for a certain music, because they heard it before they learned to speak, certain names that could be from here or from elsewhere, according to how they are pronounced, and culinary preferences, certain drinks at certain times of day or a ceremonial dish that is rarely cooked but often mentioned. As I listened to her, I drank the tea she had made for me, which smelled of mint, which she had sweetened, this tea that I drank like burning petrol, a viscous oil rolling over my tongue, whose surface dances with flames, and tongues of fire trickled all the way to my heart, consumed my soul, blazed in my mind, shimmered on my skin, while she, warming to her theme, shone too. We both shimmered, because we were bathed in a light sweat, a fragrant sweat that enticed us, that would facilitate our movements, allowing us to glide against each other, smoothly, tirelessly, indefinitely.

I placed my hand on her thigh and left it there, to feel the liquid warmth coursing beneath her skin. Beneath the skin of my fingertips it sparked a tingling of longing for her, and a longing for ink. I don't know whether it had something to do with her skin. I don't know whether it had something to do with my fingers. I don't even know if it was a tingling, although I know it was about ink. But I was stirred by a physical ache. And when, deep inside me, I imagined taking her in my arms, or when I imagined taking the ink-laden brush between my fingers, it soothed the ache. Gazing at her unsettled me; thinking of taking her in my arms or painting her calmed me. As though in her presence I was suffocating from the intensity, from too much life; as though in her presence my flame guttered for lack of air; and when, in my mind, I began to paint her, the air returned, I could breathe again, I could burn brighter. It might seem strange that ink should mingle with desire; but that, surely, is what painting means, only that? Desire, matter and vision melded in the body of the painter and in the body of the viewer?

Painting with ink produces a particular feeling. The diluted ink is too fluid, the slightest gesture affects it, a breath ripples it; like the breath of someone drinking ripples the surface in his bowl. I learned. I use the rage I could never manage to express and which made my life a long series of accidents. I paint awkwardly, but powerfully. What I paint is not figurative. With my meagre ability, using black liquid spread by a brush, my painting would have trouble representing what I see. But ink-wash painting does not represent, it is. In each stroke you see the shadow of the object painted and the trace of the furious brush that painted it. In speech, too, what is said merges with the vibrating air it produces. What we hear has nothing, absolutely nothing in common with what we want to say, but no sooner is it said than it is revealed. Such a miracle cannot be explained. We spend the first years of our lives mastering it, and still it remains a miracle. Like speech, ink painting is the Word incarnate, revealed as it is set down, in the quivering cadences of mental images appearing. Ink-wash painting appears in the beam of consciousness, and it illustrates, in sync with the constant beating of our hearts.

The Chinese, who have an explanation for everything, must surely have a myth about the invention of painting. It would involve a master calligrapher going into the mountains one morning; followed by his apprentice, who carries his tools, asks foolish questions and memorizes the answers. He would settle on a pleasant spot propitious to noble thoughts. Behind him the soaring mountain, at his feet a roaring torrent. Pines would cling to rocky outcrops, a cherry tree would be a sign of spring, vivid orchids would tumble from branches, thickets of bamboo would sway and rustle. The servant would set up a silk screen around his master. It would be morning, the day still hesitant, and in the chill air each of the master's words would be accompanied by whorls of mist. With his brush the master would improvise poems about the wind, about the movements of the air, the rippling of the grasses, the shifting shapes of water. He would recite them aloud as he set them down in ink, and the mist modulated by his words would drift back to be absorbed into the silk of the screen protecting him. When evening came, he would set down his brush and get to his feet. His servant would pack everything away, the teapot, the meditating cushion, the writing paper covered with poems, the ink stone in which he ground black pigment with pine resin. In his haste, being a simple man, he would stumble and spill the contents of the ink stone, spattering the panels of the screen. The precious fabric would greedily consume the ink; but in the place where his vaporous words had impregnated the silk, the ink would not stay. The embarrassed servant, not knowing what to do, would contemplate the ruined screen, waiting to be rebuked. But the master would see. The trails of ink brushed on to the silk panel would balance subtle whites, where he had been speaking, between great splashes of black, where he had been silent. He would be seized by an emotion so powerful it would leave him reeling. A whole day of lofty thoughts would be there, intact, faithfully noted down, more perfectly preserved than anything possible through calligraphy. And so he would tear up all the poems that he had written and toss the scraps of paper into the rushing torrent. Why write, when the smallest thought was here, captured in all its precision, and did not need to be read? He would head home, serene, with his barely reassured servant trotting behind him, carrying everything he needed to carry.

Ink painting tends to be the penultimate trace of breath, the slight stirring of air that accompanies a murmur before it fades completely. This is what I want: to preserve the movement of language before it stops, to conserve the trace of breath and the moment that it vanishes. Ink becomes me.

I felt you quivering next to me, my heart; more than anything I longed to paint you; more than anything I yearned to approach you, to hear within you, to resonate within myself, the constant pulse of presence.

You left me in the morning, my heart, and you murmured as you kissed me that you would come back soon, very soon, and so I stayed in your apartment and waited. All alone in your apartment, without bothering even to get dressed. I wandered from room to room. It was not very big. There was the room where we had slept and a room whose window overlooked the Saône. I moved from one to the other, impregnating myself with you, although you were absent. I waited for you with the infinite patience of one who knows you will return. I spent time at the window. I looked at the bridge spanning the river in three arches, and when the smooth, glassy waters of the Saône reached the stone pillars its surface rumpled lazily, like the sheets of a bed with someone sleeping under them. I watched the gulls float-ing on the river, trying to rest on the water, which required them to perform slow loops if they were not to disappear into the distance, which demonstrates the impossibility of stopping while time con-tinues to flow. They settle on the water, fold up their wings, and the current carries them along. Having been carried a few hundred metres downstream by the sluggish current of the Saône, whirling like plastic ducks, they shake their feathers, take to the wing, fly a few hundred metres upstream and land, and allow the current to carry them downstream again. Perhaps they manage to sleep between these brief flights to make up the time. They never float twice on the same water, yet always sleep in the same place. I leaned on the windowsill, taking the morning sun, watching the gulls and the people in the street. You cannot imagine what I have with you. Time restored; the stream flowing once more.

I saw a woman veiled in black coming into the building. I could see nothing of her but a moving shadow. A few moments later she left and disappeared around the corner. She came back carrying a full shopping basket, although I had not noticed a basket when she left. She went out again, but without the basket. She was carrying a bag. Instinctively, I looked at her shoes. She disappeared around the same corner only to reappear almost immediately, but without the bag. She came into the building. I leaned further out of the window the better to see her come in.

'A lot of coming and going, huh?'

To my right, a middle-aged man in a vest was leaning on the wrought-iron railing of his window. Like me, he was watching the gulls on the Saône and the people in the street.

'Absolutely. She never stops.'

'*They* never stop. Plural, young man, plural. There are several of them. That woman you've been watching rushing around for a while is actually several women. They live in the big first-floor apartment.'

'Together?'

He gave me a pitying look. He leaned further over the rusted iron railing, so he could whisper.

'The guy on the first floor, the one with the beard, he lives with them all. He's a polygamist.'

'Officially? But you can't marry multiple times, unless I've missed something...'

'Well, he might as well. He lives with them all. I don't even know how many there are. He's a polygamist.'

'They could be his sisters, his mother, his cousins...'

'You're blessed with a naivety that borders on stupidity. Or fascination. They're his wives, I'm telling you. They're married according to their own laws. They don't respect our laws. They all pretend they're the only wife so they can receive benefits, allowances they're not entitled to. We signed petitions, made formal complaints to have them thrown out.'

'Thrown out?'

'Of the building – and out of France, while we're at it. It's intolerable, what they get away with.'

The polygamist came round the corner, bearded, smiling, wearing a crocheted *kufi* and a white *gandoura*; one step behind him floated a black shadow.

'There he goes,' said the neighbour.

Before coming into the building, he looked up and saw us. He smiled a strange, sardonic smile. He held open the door for the formless shadow accompanying him and let her go through, looked up again with the same mocking smile, then stepped inside. The neighbour at the next window, leaning on the railing like me, choked and muttered, 'Fuck off back to where you came from,' making a gurgling sound, since he was frothing with rage.

'You see the nerve of the fucker? When the GAFFES are in power, he'll be laughing on the other side of his face. There won't be any sarcastic smirks. They'll all be sent back where they came from.'

'You'd like to see the GAFFES in power?'

'Absolutely. As soon as possible. The guys who belong to GAFFES see things the way they really are and aren't afraid to say so.'

'Guys like Mariani? You think Mariani sees things the way they are?'

'You know Mariani?'

'Yeah, a little. But when it comes to seeing things and saying things, I think he's all over the shop.'

'I don't give a toss. All I know is he bangs his fist on the table and we need men like that. To show them we're not joking.'

'Well, as far as that goes, he's certainly not joking. Which is a pity, really.'

'We have to show them. It's the only language they understand. We can't keep putting up with this.'

'This?'

'This.'

The first-floor neighbour re-emerged, followed by two floating shadows of the same height, impossible to tell apart. He walked stiffly, dressed all in white, and they followed behind. After a few steps he raised his head and shot us a mocking glance; his smile widened. He stopped and deliberately stuck out his tongue.

'You see that! What did I tell you? A polygamist, right here under our roof, and he's thumbing his nose at us.'

'Makes you envious, doesn't it?'

He stared at me, his eyes boring into my skull. He spluttered and slammed his window shut. I stood there alone, staring at the Saône, naked in the morning light. I was waiting for you in your apartment, my heart.

Salagnon had told me: with 'them' it always turns to rivalry, to who cuts who, who electrocutes who, who will fuck who. We desire each other too much to separate; we resemble each other too much to drift apart. If the GAFFES were in power, who would we throw out? Those who look a bit funny? And who would get to be the 'we' who throws them out? Those who feel united by blood? But what blood? Spilled blood? But whose blood?

Over there, Salagnon used to say to me, we tried to enforce a shameful boundary. We were determined. We got everyone involved, so that everyone would be implicated. Over there we were given free rein; we had carte blanche and we jeopardized everyone; we ensured that everyone took a pound of flesh from the victim. We. I've started to talk like Salagnon. I'm slipping into the style of Salagnon's story. But what else can I do? We implicated everyone. We. I can't say who 'we' were in the beginning, but it became everyone. Everyone is elbow-deep in blood. Everyone has their head in the bath of blood until they can't drink any more, until they can't breathe, until they throw up. We ducked each other's heads in the bath of blood. And when it was all over, we acted like schoolboys caught in the act. We sauntered around, whistling innocently, hands behind our backs, looking around aimlessly. We behaved as though nothing had happened, as though *they* were the ones who started it. Everyone pretended to go home, because no one really knew who they were any more, no one really knew where 'home' was. We squeezed into the narrow confines of metropolitan France, packed tightly together, saying nothing, doing our best not to look to see who was there; and who was no longer here. France was leaving history. We decided to no longer be responsible for anything.

When the GAFFES appeared and began to monopolize the conversation, we – the mild-mannered, middle-class idiots – mistook them for a fascist group. We could replay the founding myths, we could 'join the resistance', something The Novelist used to write pages and pages about. We organized demonstrations. We decided they were the enemy, when in fact they were simply a flatulent sideshow to distract attention. They played on the notion of race, but race is little more than a fart, a flatus, a burp brought on by poor digestion, an unintelligible babble that masks something we do not want to see, because it's so terrible, because it concerns us all, all the mild-mannered, middle-class idiots. We wanted to think of the GAFFES as a racist group, when in fact they are something much worse: an illegalist party, a party favouring self-segregation and the use of force, for whom colonialism is utopia on Earth. The reality of life in the colonies – the fake bonhomie and real beatings, the gentlemen's agreements and the illegalism applied to all – is the true policy of the GAFFES, a ghost party that came back on the ships in 1962.

*   *   *

But who, then, are we? It is a question that is never asked. Identity is believed, it is invented. It can even be lamented, but it is not spoken. Open your mouth to define it and what comes out is gibberish; there is not a word to be said on the subject that is not nonsensical; keep talking and it becomes a madness. The separation of the races, utterly irrational, completely illegal, has no criteria that can be stated, but everyone practises it. It is tragic: we can feel it, but we cannot express it. A fart is meaningless. It is simply a fiction to describe identity, and it is a lie. We think about it and we think in vain, because identity in itself tends towards idiocy; it is idiotic, invariably, because it wants to be, itself, by virtue of itself; it wants to exist of and by itself. It leads nowhere.

If you listen to what people say, you might think that identity around here is Berrichon: an identity based on claggy soil and damp forest, an identity based on autumns and rains, of callow youths and felt hats, of manure heaps behind the farm and slate steeples that threaten to pierce the sky. You might think that the Mediterranean has nothing to do with identity around here. Surely it is incredibly false and stupid to be defined by the kingdom of Bourges? Because the Mediterranean is right there! The Mediterranean in all its forms, the distant Mediterranean, the Mediterranean right at our feet, the northern view of the Mediterranean, the southern view and even the side-view of the Mediterranean, *la Méditerranée* seen from everywhere and expressed in French. Our Sea. Rumour would confine us to the kingdom of Bourges, but I hear voices speaking in French, with different phrasings and strange accents, but in French I understand everything spontaneously. Identity is pure make-believe. Identity is simply self-identification. To believe it is inborn, in the flesh or in the earth; it is to stray into the lunacies that would have you believe in the external existence of something that animates the soul.

We feel the troubles. We do not know who exactly, but someone is stirring them. We are packed tightly in the narrow confines of France, not knowing exactly who, not daring to look, not saying a word.

Following the wise precepts of The Novelist, we had set ourselves outside history. Nothing should happen – and yet. We try to identify who among us, trapped in narrow France, could be stirring up trouble. We talk around the subject of race without ever naming it. We have come to think of differences in religion as differences in nature. Race is a fart. The air here in cramped, confined France has become unbreathable; still the troubles continue. The origin of the violence is much more basic, much more French, but we are loath to see this naked truth. We prefer to be entertained by professional farters, to be part of an audience where supporters and opponents of farts rip each other to shreds. Our taste for literary squabbles is turning into a brawl.

The origin of the trouble, here and over there, is not simply a lack of respect and the fact that the unequal distribution of wealth is not shocking. This reason is utterly French, and the war over there was French from beginning to end. They were too much like us to go on living in the place we had assigned them. The coming riot will also be fought in the name of the République, values now somewhat watered down, eroded, as they have been by the understanding of lineage, by the illegal illegality, but values still cherished by those who, more than anything, want to live here. Here, because over there a war is waged between us, who are so alike, and we furiously seek out something that might distinguish us. The classification of faces is a military operation; the concealment of bodies is an act of war, an explicit refusal of any peace that does not entail the elimination of the other. The battlefield in civil wars is the image of the body, and any art of war consists of its abuse.

I saw Mariani on the front page of *Le Progrès*, but I may have been the only one, since the intent of the photo was not to show him. *Le Progrès* is the newspaper of Lyon. As it claims to anyone who might wish to read it, on posters, in small letters on the masthead, in huge letters on the sides of buses: 'If it's true, it's in *Le Progrès*.' Mariani was in *Le Progrès*. He was on the front page, in the corner of a large photo showing the police in Voracieux-les-Bredins. They were posing, proud and athletic in their militarized uniforms, hips girded with gun belts, trousers cinched at the ankles by parachute boots. Hands on their hips, they made a show of strength. The article quoted liberally from speeches which were panegyrics to power regained. 'A new police force to counter delinquency and incivility. Return blow for blow. Take back the no-go areas surrounding the tower blocks, where the police do not venture, where by night the rule of law does not apply, retake the alleys and the car parks, the stairwells, the doorways and the halls, the public squares and the benches, which at night, and even during the day, have become the territory of menacing shadows moving through a constant haze of hashish fumes. Drug dealing. Brutality. Urban violence. The ancestral law of the *caïds* in the shadows of the towers. We must strike hard, assert the power of public authorities. Reassure genuine citizens.'

The photo was not of Mariani. It was a full-page photograph of the new police force in Voracieux-les-Bredins, the municipal force forged by willpower, equipped for shock and awe; but Mariani was there. In the crowd clustered around the boys in blue, around the musclemen of law and order posing in a show of force, I recognized him. He was present at the introduction of the first local anti-gang brigade. His face was not visible, no one knew who he was, but I knew, and I knew the role he played. In the crowd of faces I recognized the tinted glasses, the antiquated moustache, the hideous checked jacket; he was laughing. He understood his role. He was laughing silently in the crowd gathered around the police.

I bought a copy of the paper. I took it with me. I showed it to Salagnon, who immediately spotted Mariani in the crowd thronging around the musclemen, the sort of men France seems to turn out in large quantities and unthinkingly launches into the fray. How many private, municipal, national, militarized police forces are there? How many uniformed men trained in shock tactics? How many strongmen in France, whose strength is primed and misdirected?

The image of the policeman with his truncheon, his pot belly, his uniform cape wrapped around his arm to parry blows, is a part of a past we barely understand these days: how did we manage to maintain law and order without non-lethal weapons, without offensive weapons, with chubby men who could not run and barely knew how to fight? We find it difficult to believe. The Republic's security companies, over-equipped, over-trained, over-efficient, take care of everything – sundry infractions, riots, abuse – they criss-cross France in armoured minibuses, stamping out trouble before it starts like stamping out small fires, sparking as many fires as they extinguish, only to be called in again and getting there too late, arriving like the cavalry to save the day, when they were partly responsible for the chaos. Oh, they are good at what they do! Three by three, behind their polycarbonate riot shields, one takes the force of the blow, the second props him up, the third has the truncheon ready to launch a counter-attack, seize the malefactor and drag him to the back. They know how to fight better than anyone; they know how to operate; they are called in: they come, they see, they effortlessly conquer. They move around France like Roman legions. They douse fires, but fire breaks out again as soon as they leave. They are the elite, the shock troops; there are not enough of them. If they group together, they lose ground; if they spread out, they lose their strength. So they need to do further training, so they can move faster, strike harder.

'They are as handsome as we once were,' Salagnon sighed. 'They have as much power as we once had, and it will be just as useless. They are as few as we once were, and those they hunt will always escape, into the jungles, into the stairwells and the basements, because their numbers are inexhaustible; they create as many as they catch. They will experience the same failure we once did, the same bitter, hopeless failure, because we had the power.'

There were violent clashes. At first it was minor, a hold-up at a casino, a robbery at the sort of business that anticipates such things and takes effective countermeasures, not a bakery. Some guy decided to turn gangster, to take money from a place where there were piles of it, rather than working for a living and being drip-fed. This can easily be explained in terms of free-market theory without becoming heated, without moralizing: it is simply an appraisal by a rational economic actor of the potential gains and losses. Things took a nasty turn. Following a chase and a series of gunshots, the thief was dead. That might have been the end of it, but his ancestry was mentioned; by common agreement, on all sides, his ancestry was discussed. It was enough to mention his name and his surname; that would indicate his bloodline. With this dead thief, sprawled in a housing estate with a bullet in his body, they did one of the above: they took a problem which essentially relates to microeconomics and turned it into a critical moment in history. On this, we were all agreed. This is what we thought: they come here, they come here armed with guns to try and take back the wealth accumulated in the city centre.

Because the distribution of wealth in the world we live in is far from clear: there is obviously no correlation to the efforts expended. So it is possible to imagine that what we have earned we have in fact stolen; and that we are entitled to take what we have not earned. And when the poor are identified by their facial features, by the sound of their names, it is possible to believe that one racial group wants to take back what another has taken from it. It is possible to believe that certain facial features, taken to express a common ancestry, will choose to demand reparations. Such things tend to be settled with guns, but they could be settled through sex. Within three generations, sex would muddle facial features and confuse ancestries, leaving only language intact; but we prefer guns. We cover women with black tarpaulins. We keep them at home. We hide them and we brandish guns. Weapons offer immediate gratification. The effects of sex are a long time coming.

There were violent incidents. It began with something minor. A hold-up in a place where a man can flaunt the fact that his wealth is worth that of a thousand others or a hundred thousand others; in a world in which money is flourished like a taunt, in which one does not have to go far to help oneself, in which guns can be bought cheaply. A heist is a simple solution, a rational, feasible strategy; there are movies about it. But in our world there is another factor: ancestry can be read in faces. This means that every social problem is coupled with an ethnic problem, which is further aggravated by historical unrest. Violence flares, it only takes a spark. A riot is brewing; a riot is fun, a riot is coming.

It started with something trivial: a hold-up. A man turned gang-ster. He wanted to help himself. He was killed. If this had simply been about money, there would be nothing more to say. But his ancestry was highlighted. The hold-up, followed by the chase, triggered a state of siege. There were violent incidents: several nights of unrest and insomnia, the glow of fire reflected on the high ramparts of towers, dustbins set ablaze, cars burning and exploding when the flames licked at the petrol tank; there were several nights of stones being thrown at firefighters who came to douse the fires, of catapult bolts raining down on the police officers who came to protect the firefighters, to restore order, to dissolve the thrombosis threatening to choke the city; the hail of objects crackled in the night that glowed with petrol fires, on the riot shields and the helmets, a dangerous shower of steel hailstones; there were gunshots, several of them in the darkness, fired with sin-gular ineptness; gunshots that killed no one, that scarcely wounded; less than a steel nut fired from a slingshot, which might fracture a skull, break a hand, but a gunshot is a different matter. They had not come for this, the young men who arrive in the armoured column; they had not come to be the target; they were athletic and efficient, they were trained, but they were civilians. They seized, they searched, they frisked without the slightest consideration; they threw people to the ground, slapped on the plastic handcuffs, dragged them up by their armpits and shoved them into wagons with barred windows. This they could do flawlessly – these young men had just completed their training; most of the men in the anti-gang brigades sent into these cities are very young; they are just starting out; they understand the tools, the procedures, the techniques, but they know little about people. They arrive in armoured columns to the roar of fires and the hail of stones; they take prisoners, they wreak havoc and they leave again. They are peacemakers. We have the power. Our national reflexes are like mantraps.

In the days that followed, six young men were arrested, based on tip-offs; all were released for lack of evidence the following day. There was no proof, no case, the tip-offs were anonymous. The riot swelled; riots are fun. Militarized police leapt from their armoured minibuses in full riot gear, shielded themselves from the hail of stones and bolts, arrested anyone who could not run fast enough. The riot carried on. It is useless to be so powerful. The use of force is absurd, because the nature of the world is liquid; the harder you hit, the harder the surface, the greater the force exerted, the greater the resistance, and if you go on hitting you crush yourself. It is our force that actually produces the resistance. Of course it is possible to dream of destroying everything. It is the dream outcome of force.

Hoarding money creates thieves, gunning down a thief starts a riot, quashing the riot strikes the country so forcefully that is seems like two, two countries occupying the same space, fighting to the death to extricate themselves. We are so entwined that we scrabble for anything to disentangle us. A curfew was imposed. A law from over there was exhumed; using it was like pouring petrol on the fire. Foreign gang-members were accused of instigating the riot, but those caught in the nightly round-ups were neither foreign nor gang members, they were simply disappointed. They had been promised they would be treated the same; the law guaranteed they were the same, and yet they are not. You only had to look at them so see the difference. On the basis of their facial features, young men were arrested who were ordinary, educated, eager to be a part of France, yet found themselves pushed to the sidelines for illogical reasons we cannot seem to overcome. We don't even know what to call them. We don't know who we are. This is something that someone needs to write.

When they invited me to go fishing, I was momentarily taken aback. This made them laugh.

'What's so surprising about us go fishing? I mean, we're old fogeys, so it's hardly strange that we have old fogey hobbies. We wade into the middle of the river and wait there, without moving, for the fish to come. It relieves the passing time, consoles us for the times gone by; as for the time to come, we don't care: it's so slow in coming when we're at home that it might as well not bother. Come with us.'

Mariani had two of his lads take his Zodiac dinghy down to the river, across a shingle beach where it was possible to get the four-by-four and trailer close to the greenish water. We climbed aboard the rubber dinghy, loaded the plastic boxes, the fishing lines, enough food and drink for the day and a little more. We sat on the inflatable tube. All the equipment was military green. A cool, clear sun rose. We took off our waterproof parkas. The soft light warmed everything it touched. Mariani started the outboard motor and we left the two lads on the bank with the four-by-four and the trailer. They watched us move off, hands in their pockets, kicking at the shingle.

'Are they going to stay there?'

'They'll wait for us. They know that war is mostly about waiting, the way we used to in the foxholes in the jungle or crouching behind hot stones. They're training.'

We headed down the Rhône, flanked by gallery forests; the clean lines of the white buildings rose above the treetops. Beneath the overhanging branches were stretches of shingle. Men came and stood there. They took off their coats, opened their shirts, some stripped to the waist. Their eyes half-closed, they let themselves be painted pink and gold by the mellow sun. They formed a curious collection of silent, half-naked beach attendants. Mariani suddenly accelerated. We clung to the rubber dinghy. The Zodiac reared up and skimmed across the water, leaving behind a wake like a trench carved in the water. He headed towards the shore, turned hard and a huge wave splashed the men standing there, who scattered. 'Chicken-shit landlubbers!' he roared, turning back to them, and this made them laugh.

'Stop it, Mariani,' said Salagnon.

'I can't stand them,' he grumbled.

'It's illegal.'

'Don't give a fuck if it's illegal.'

He came back to the middle and headed straight downriver, the motor whining as he skimmed the current, the Zodiac bouncing off the hard surface of the water.

'Who exactly are you talking about?'

'If you don't know, you don't need to know – much like a lot of things.'

They both laughed. We crossed Lyon at water lever. Mariani steered, keeping a steady hand on the rudder, his feet firmly wedged against the bottom of the boat. The engine thundered, pushed to the maxi-mum. We sped along smoothly, we cleaved space with no resistance, we were strong and free, we would pounce upon our prey, the fish, as deftly as kingfishers. We passed the confluence and sailed several kilometres upriver on the calmer waters of the Saône. We stopped on the glassy river between two lines of trees. Huge mansions of golden sandstone looked down on us with their antique, unruffled air; large, middle-class houses lay languidly at the far end of manicured lawns. We fished. For a long time, in silence, each with our own line. We baited the hooks. Salagnon plonked – I don't know the technical term, but he beat the water with a hollow tube that made a hollow, plonking sound that resonated through the water. This attracted the fish, those that were half-asleep and slithering through the mud. They woke up, came to the surface and took the bait without thinking. Each of us fished, chatting lazily about nothing much. A satisfied sigh said all there was to say. They got along well. They always seemed to understand each other. They could laugh at a single word pronounced a certain way.

Their conversation was cryptic, allusive, and I couldn't understand it, because the roots of my language did not extend so deeply in time. So I asked questions, explicit questions, about what had happened. They answered me, then we carried on fishing. The soft sunshine kept us warm without ever burning us. The size of our catch was ludicrous. But we drained all the bottles we had brought.

'And the German, what became of him?'

'He died over there, with all the rest. The equipment, the people, it was all second hand, it didn't last; it quickly gave up the ghost. We fought a second-hand war with the surplus from other adventures, with American weapons, soldiers that had deserted from other armies, patched-up English uniforms, with resistance fighters with nothing better to do and blue-blooded officers who dreamed of glory: all second-hand equipment of no use anywhere else. He died in his own shit, where his fate took him. He was in Diên Biên Phu. He was manning a trench with his Teutonic legionnaires. He withstood the shelling and the assaults. He was captured with the others when the position fell. He was taken into the jungle and died of dysentery in one of the Viet camps. People died quickly in those makeshift, poorly guarded camps; they died of exhaustion, of malnutrition, of neglect. They caught tropical diseases; they ate rice and leaves, sometimes with a little dried fish.'

'Were you ever prisoners?'

'Mariani was, I wasn't. He was also captured in Diên Biên Phu, but he survived. The kid he was when I first knew him was battle-hardened by then. He had become a madman. That helps you not to go under. I was there when he came back, when the prisoners were exchanged, not many of them, all skin and bone: he marched behind Bigeard and Langlais, as thin as a rake, his eyes wild, but his beret firmly crammed on his head, properly tilted, as if he were on parade; and they all marched in step, even though they were about to collapse, barefoot on the dirt track, in front of the inscrutable Viet Minh officers. He wanted to show them.'

'I was in good shape when I was captured. The German was, too, but he had spent too long living in a kind of no-man's-land. He had had enough, I think. He just gave up. The guys who stood around waiting, who had nothing to cling to, they died quickly. I was fuelled by rage.'

'What about you, Salagnon?'

'Me? I was nearly one of them. I'd volunteered to go with them. A certain number of us had volunteered to rejoin the fighting just before the end. With magnificent thoughtlessness, our requests were granted. I was scheduled to be in the last flight. I was standing on the airstrip, parachute on my back, helmet on my head. Most of us had never jumped in our lives. We were getting into the plane when the engine stalled. Kaput. We all had to get out again. By the time it was fixed, Diên Biên Phu had fallen. I regretted it for a long time.'

'Regretted not being a prisoner, not being killed?'

'You know, of all the suicidal, bullshit things we got up to, that was the worst. But it was the only thing we didn't have to be ashamed of. We knew the last positions were about to fall, air support could do nothing, the rescue party would never arrive, and still dozens of us volunteered to go there, so as not to let them down. The high command, intoxicated by the smell of bravura, authorized this final, foolish stunt, supplied the parachutes and aircraft, and came and stood to attention to see us off. We didn't have much left after all the years of war, we had lost most of our human qualities; all we had left was intelligence and compassion; all we had left was the *furia francese*. Senior officers, with their gold-braided kepis and their decorations, lined up in silence and saluted the planes as they took off, carrying guys with a one-way ticket to a camp in the jungle. We wanted to die together, that would have wiped out everything. But, unfortunately, we survived. We came back changed, our minds furrowed with ugly creases we would never get out. The Viets just dragged us into the jungle, fed us very little; they scarcely bothered guarding us and we watched each other melt away and die. We learned that even the strongest mind can self-destruct when left to fret and languish.'

He fell silent for a minute, because there was a tug on his line. He pulled it up too quickly and a bare hook appeared. The fish had eaten the bait and gone back to sleep in the mud, without us noticing. He sighed, re-baited the hook and carried on.

'Obviously we were walking into the lion's den, but only to kill it. It had to end: we resorted to shock tactics; we were trying to provoke it. It worked and we lost. It all depended on a bluff, a single strike that would decide everything. We went up into the mountains, far from Hanoi, to serve as bait. We had to seem weak to lure them in, but to be strong enough to destroy them when they came. But we were not as strong as we thought and they were much stronger than we anticipated. They had bicycles they pushed through the jungle. I saw them myself, but no one would ever believe me, everyone just left when I talked about the bikes. While our planes, hampered by the mist and the cloud, had trouble transporting supplies, their bicycles could negotiate the jungle trails, bringing the rice and the munitions that meant they were invincible. We had limited power. We were an army of second-hand goods merchants. We didn't have the means. We didn't have enough machines, so we sent the best of what we had: ourselves, beautiful human machines, the light airborne infantry; we dropped from the skies into muddy trenches, just like in Verdun, to be buried alive to the last man. We were captured, we gave up, we left. We were good losers, though. But I wasn't there. I survived. It would have been better if we'd lost everything; what came after would never have happened. We would have remained clean, purified by our deaths. That's what I regret. It's absurd.'

The light became thicker, piercing the golden, sandstone mansions sculpted from translucent honey, dusk was drawing in.

'And your father?'

'I never saw my father again after 1944. I was in the Haute-Région when I got the news of his death in a letter from my mother that had taken months to arrive; the paper was buckled, the edges frayed from so much handling; there were whole sentences where the ink was washed out, as though she had been crying when she wrote it, but I knew it was just the humid weather in the jungle. Something sudden; his heart, I think. It didn't really affect me, his death. I saw my mother after I came back from Algeria; she was tiny and so thin, and she hardly remembered anything. She lived for a few months in a hospice, where she just sat, silent, expressionless, her eyes vacant and bulging slightly; her atrophied brain couldn't store anything. She died without even realizing. I had never tried to see them after I got back. I was afraid.'

'Afraid? You?'

'Never wanted to turn around, never wanted to look back. Why would I? To see the people whose deaths are on my conscience? I was doing fine. But the father, unfortunately, is unavoidable; the man whose blood we carry has already ploughed the furrow which we will drain away. We follow it without realizing; we believe we are simply going a little way only to find we cannot get out without undertaking expensive excavation works. I look like him, our faces are identical; I was afraid that in seeing him I would see my own end. The circus of his life disgusted me, the constant playing with rules, playing with words, the constant self-justification, all the things I didn't want to learn. It took me three wars to get away from that furrow, and I don't know whether I've gone far enough. I think painting saved me. Without it, like Mariani, I would have retreated to a small world where I had control, where the windows were closed, ruled by dreams and power.'

'Your world isn't exactly big,' grunted Mariani. 'A blank piece of paper. I wouldn't want it.'

'I had no desire to be where other people wanted me to be.'

'And that's why you lived a life full of adventures? A life you could be proud of?'

'I'm proud of nothing, except maybe being alive. I did what I did and nothing can undo it. I don't really know what my life is. There are things you cannot decide for yourself.'

'Salagnon is no adventurer,' Mariani interrupted. 'He's just a guy with an itchy arse.'

'What?'

'When he's been sitting down too long, he needs to stretch his legs. In a different age, sport and a bit of travelling would have done the business. He might have been a mountaineer or an ethnologist, but he grew up during that brief period when you could handle weapons without meaning any harm. Before that, it was considered pathetic; afterwards, it was shameful, in France at least. If he had been born earlier or later, his whole life would have been different. He might have been a painter, a real painter, and I wouldn't have taken the piss. I would have admired his delicate sensibilities.'

'What about you?'

'Oh, me... At some point I felt a burning need to fight. Maybe when we were running through the jungle with the Viets on our arse. Ever since then I've been angry.'

Salagnon patted his arm gently.

'It makes you a dumb fuck, that anger of yours, but it saved your life.'

'That's why I don't get it seen to.'

We went back to our fishing. We were slowly drifting downstream on the Saône. Night was falling. The riot erupted. There were sirens, fires blazed and were reflected in the still waters. Mariani ignored the outboard motor and let us drift; we moved with the sluggish current. I was floating down the reddening river with two old fishermen. We could hear the muffled thud of grenades being launched and the clear crack of their impact.

'You remember that sound, Mariani? The *pff* when a grenade was launched. We'd duck our heads, hold on to our helmets and wait for it to land.'

'You see, it finally happened. I'm proud I can say I was right. It's reassuring. The riots have started.'

'It won't lead anywhere. A couple of burned-out cars, that's all; a problem for insurance companies.'

'You know what would be good? If we capsized and died tonight. That way we could disappear without having to argue. Without one of us having to be right and the other wrong. It would be better that way. It's a good night for making peace with each other.'

'Don't talk shit, Mariani. We've got the kid with us.'

'I'm sure he knows how to swim.'

'We haven't told him all this stuff for him to go and die.'

'We'll set him down on the bank.'

I had a date with her in any case. They dropped me at the jetty and the Zodiac set off again slowly, drifted on the crimson current, and disappeared behind a bridge. She lived on the Saône, the windows of her bedroom overlooked the river. The horizon glowed red.

I came back to you, my heart, you were waiting for me. The glistening water of the Saône quivered in the darkness, folding in on itself to pass the bridges, only to unfurl again, a black mirror; the current, so powerful and so slow, carried it south. Ever since I have known you, my heart, I am that river, and over its black, viscous surface, over its impenetrable surface glided the red glow of the fires, glided the sound of the sirens, glided the flickers of the riot, all gliding over without passing through.

I undressed to be closer to you, but I wanted to paint you. You were lying on the bed, on the floor, arms folded behind your head, your glittering eyes haloed by swan feathers, and you watched as I approached you. You showed your curves. We did not turn on a lamp; the light from outside was enough. I poured the ink into a bowl, a bowl made for the purpose, crusted with dried ink like so many layers of lacquer, like so many skins, like so many sloughs. I hold the ink in my hand when I paint, because painting is like drinking and this way I can see how much the brush imbibes, I can see my brush taking ink from the bowl, drinking it. I control how much it drinks and I paint. The ink in the bowl evaporates, it thickens; you have to paint quickly. The first strokes have the fluidity of damp breath, an approaching kiss, but afterwards the weight of the ink increases, it becomes stickier, it clogs the hairs of the brush, it is heavy, you can feel it in your fingers, in your arm, in your shoulder; the strokes become weightier and the ink as viscous as mineral oil, a slick of tar coating the bottom of the bowl; it gives the final stroke the terrifying weight of water from a well. Knowing this, I started by painting you with a feathery grace, then gained in gravity. I painted your curved lines. I painted your face in clear strokes; the arrogant flick of your nose, the rounded mass of your breasts, balanced like a pair of dunes; I painted your resting hands, your outstretched legs, your navel like a water drop against the curve of your belly. The reflections of the Saône trembled on the ceiling, on the walls, glimmered in your eyes, watching me paint you; the red reflections from the riot that howled outside trembled on the glossy surface of my ink, just on the surface, nothing passed through. My ink grew thicker. I painted you, you who were watching me, with an ink that gradually became heavier. My brush plunged into the bowl and soaked up nothing but red glows that glided over the surface of the ink and left no trace on the paper, just the line of your beautiful form. I finished. I had painted your extraordinary hair without touching anything. I had left the paper intact. I rinsed the brush, so it would not dry out, so I could use it again, again and again, so that I could paint you for ever.

I came to you. I was naked. I had painted naked, my penis did not hinder me; it rested against my thigh and I felt it throb. And when I lay down next to you, it lengthened and hardened. The contrast between the grey and white of your hair, swan's feathers, and your vivid mouth and your full body moved me beyond measure. I went to you, I took you in my arms, you welcomed me, I entered you.

Outside the riot raged on. We heard screams, desperate pursuits, crashes, sirens and explosions. The red reflections from the Saône quivered on the ceiling. The viscous river, never stopping, continued on its course. A dark river, flushed red with fire, gently flowed through the city. This disinterested, unremitting flow saved me. I liked the fact that the Saône looked like blood. I was grateful to Victorien Salagnon for teaching me to see it and not to fear it. The whole of me swelled, my penis, too. I was full and I was coming inside you. Finally, I was happy.